LAST FRIENDS

Jane Gardam

LAST FRIENDS

Europa
editions

Europa Editions
214 West 29th Street
New York, N.Y. 10001
www.europaeditions.com
info@europaeditions.com

Library of Congress Cataloging in Publication Data is available
ISBN 978-1-60945-093-9

Gardam, Jane
Last Friends

Book design and cover illustration by Emanuele Ragnisco
www.mekkanografici.com

Prepress by Grafica Punto Print – Rome

Printed in the USA

CONTENTS

LAST FRIENDS

PART ONE

Dorset

Chapter 1

The Titans were gone. They had clashed their last. Sir Edward Feathers, affectionately known as Old Filth (Failed in London, Try Hong Kong) and Sir Terence Veneering, the two greatest exponents of English and International Law in the engineering and construction industry and the current experts upon the Ethics of Pollution, were dead. Their well-worn armour had fallen from them with barely a clatter and the quiet Dorset village to which they had retired within a very few years of each other (accidentally, for they had hated each other for over fifty years) mourned their passing and wondered who would be distinguished enough to buy their houses.

How they had hated! For over half a century they had been fetching up all over the world eye-ball to eye-ball, Hector and Achilles, usually on battlefields far from home, championing or rubbishing, depending on the client, great broken bridges, mouldering reservoirs, wild crumbling new roads across mountain ranges, sewage-works, wind farms, ocean barrages and the leaking swimming pools of moguls. That they had in old age finished up by buying houses next door to each other in a village where there was absolutely nothing to do must have been the result of something the lolling gods had set up one drab day on Olympus to give the legal world a laugh.

And the laugh had been uneasy because it had been said for years—well, everyone knew—that Edward Feathers' dead wife, Betty, had been the lover of Sir Terry. Or maybe not exactly the lover. But something. There had been something between them. Well, there had been love.

Elizabeth—Betty—Feathers had died some years before the arrival of Sir Terry next-door.

Her husband, Old Filth, Sir Edward, the great crag of a man seated above her on the patio pretending to shoot rooks with his walking-stick, a gin and tonic at his elbow, had, quite simply, broken his heart.

Birds and beasts were important to Old Filth. Donkeys' years ago his prep-school headmaster had taught him about birds. It was birds and the language of the natural world and the headmaster whose name was briefly 'Sir', who had cured him of his awful child-hood stammer and enabled him to become an advocate.

His house, Dexters, lay in a long narrow dell off the village hill, bird-haunted and surrounded by trees. Beyond his gate, up the same turn-off and out of sight, Veneering's house stood at the top of the view. His taller, darker trees hung over the lane but the rooks ignored them. 'Rooks,' thought Old Filth, 'choose their friends. They will only abandon a friend if they have fore-knowledge of disaster.' Each night before sleep and each morning Filth lay in his bed straight as a sentry, striped Chilprufe pyjamas neatly buttoned, handkerchief in breast pocket carefully folded, and listened to the vigorous clamour of the rooks and was comforted. So long as he could hear their passionate disputations he would never miss his life at the Commercial Bar.

He did rather wish they had been cleaner birds. Their nests were old and huge. Ramshackle and filthy. Filth himself was ostentatiously clean. His finger nails and toe nails were pearly (chiropodist to the house every sixth week: twenty-five pounds a time) his hair still not grey but curly, autumnal bronze. His complexion shone and was scarcely lined. He smelled of

Wrights coal-tar soap—rather excitingly—a commodity beginning to be rare in many parts of the country. 'He must have had something to hide,' said young barristers. 'Something nasty in his wood-shed.' 'What, Old Filth!' they cried, 'Impossible!' They were of course wrong. Eddie Feathers Q.C. had as much to hide as everybody else.

But whatever it was it would have nothing to do with money. He never mentioned the stuff. He was a gentleman to the end. There must have been buckets of it somewhere. Bucket upon bucket upon bucket, thanks to the long, long international practice. And he spent nothing, or nothing much. Maybe a bit more than the mysterious Veneering next door. He was not a vain man. He strode about the lanes in expensive tweeds, but they were very old. Not much fun, but never pompous. If he ever brooded upon his well-organised millions, managed by impeccable brokers, he didn't think about them much. He joked about them occasionally. 'Oh yes, I have "held the gorgeous East in fee,"' he would say, 'Ha-ha,' and quoting Sir, his headmaster. He himself never went to the theatre or read poetry, for he wept too easily.

After a time a lethargy had fallen upon Feathers. He lost the energy even to think about moving house. And maybe the old enemy up the slope had begun to feel the same. They never met. If occasionally they found themselves passing one another at a distance during an afternoon walk in the lanes, each looked away.

Then, after a year or so, something must have happened. It was never discussed even in the village shop but there were some astonishing sightings, sounds of old-English accents, staccato in the blue-bell woods. It happened over a snow-bound Christmas. Before long it was reported that the two old buffers were playing chess together on Thursdays. And when Terry Veneering died during a ridiculous jaunt—foot in a hole

on a cliff-top on the island of Malta and then thrombosis—
Edward Feathers said, 'Silly old fool. Far too old for that sort
of thing. I told him so,' but was surprised how much he missed
him.

Yet he refused to attend Veneering's memorial service at
Temple Church in London. There would have been comment
and Betty's name bandied about. For all his Olympian manner
Old Filth was not histrionic. Never. He stayed alone at home
that day making notes on the new edition of *Hudson on
Building Contracts* that he had been (flatteringly considering
his age) asked to re-edit some years before. He had a whisky
and a slice of ham for his supper and listened to the News.
When he heard the returning cars of the village mourners passing the end of his lane from Tisbury station he sensed disapproval at his absence like a wet cloth across his face; and
turned a page.

Nobody came to see him that evening, not even sexy old
Chloe who was never off his doorstep with shepherd's pies: not
his gardener or his cleaning lady who had travelled to the
memorial service to London and back together in the gardener's pick-up. Not Dulcie who lived nearby on Privilege Hill
and was just about his oldest friend, the widow of an endearing old Hong Kong judge dead years ago and much lamented.
Dulcie was a tiny, rather stupid woman, and grande dame of
the village. 'Let them think what they like,' said Old Filth into
his double malt. 'I am past all these frivolities.'

But the next frivolity was to be his own, for the following
Christmas he took himself off alone to the place of his birth,
which he still called The Malay States, and died as he stepped
off the plane.

A nd so, on a cold morning in March the Dorset village of St. Ague was off to its second memorial service within a few months, first for Veneering, second for Filth, off to Temple Church again, waiting for the London train on Tisbury station. In prime positions were a group of three and a group of four all sombrely and correctly dressed but standing at different ends of the platform because although they were neighbours they were not yet exactly friends.

The group of four had recently bought Veneering's house, invisible from the road but known for its brashness and flamboyance and ugliness like its old owner and, like its old owner, keeping out of sight. They were father, mother, son and daughter, most *ordinary* people it was said, though it was vaguely thought that the father was some sort of intellectual.

Waiting at the front end of the train was the elder of the village: Old Dulcie the widow, with her daughter Susan and her twelve year old grandson Herman, an American child, serious and very free with his opinions. Dulcie was half his size, a tiny woman in grey moleskin and a hat made of what could have been the feathers of the village rooks. It was a hat bought forty years ago in Bond Street for the Queen's birthday in Dar-es-Salaam where Dulcie's husband had been an easy-going and contented judge even at a hanging.

Susan, Dulcie's stocky daughter, was a glum person, married to an invisible husband who seldom stirred from Boston,

Massachusetts. Granny, mother and son were about to travel first-class in reserved seats.

The group of four, who had never reserved a seat for anything in their lives, were stamping noisily about waiting to fight their way into the last carriage, quite ready to stand all the way to Waterloo among the people who'd been down to Weymouth for the bank holiday and would be drunk or drugged or singing and drinking smoothies, some of the tattooed young men wearing dresses. These old Dulcie would somehow be spared. She had a heart-murmur.

The group of three settled themselves in first-class. Susan began to demolish the *Daily Telegraph* crossword, flung it from her completed within minutes and said 'I don't know why we're going. We're hardly over Veneering's.'

'Oh, *I* am,' said Dulcie, 'I quite enjoyed it.'

'It's not good for you, Ma. All this death. At your age.'

'Oh, I don't know,' said Dulcie, 'It keeps people in touch.'

'I'm not keen on touching people.'

'I know dear,' said Dulcie looking at her grandson and wondering how ever he had come into the world.

'I don't suppose there'll be anyone there we'll even remember, you know. Filth was much older than you. You married from the school-room.'

'Did I? Good gracious,' said Dulcie.

'Ma,' said Susan and amazingly touched her mother's hand, 'You mustn't be upset if there's nobody much there. At his age. Veneering was younger.'

* * *

But surprisingly the church was full. There were young people there—whoever were they?—and people who didn't look at all like lawyers. Groups seemed to be arranging themselves in tribes, nodding and smiling at each other. Some stared with

polite surprise—some with distaste. There was a dwarf. Well—
of course. He'd been Filth's instructing solicitor for decades—
but surely he was dead? Here he was, legs stuck out in front of
him, face creased like an old nut, vast brown felt hat on his
knee and sitting in one of the lateral seats reserved for Benches
only: and refusing to move. The intellectual family man whispered to his wife that the dwarf was a celebrity, to tell the children to look at him. 'Must be a hundred. They will tell their
grandchildren. Said to have been dead ten times over. Had
some sort of power over Filth.' The two children looked unim-
pressed and the little girl asked if the Queen would be coming.

There was a pew full of generations of a family with the
queer pigmentation of expats. Britons—a pale cheese-colour,
like Wensleydale. There was a row of Straits Chinese and some
Japanese who were being reprimanded about their mobile
phones. There was a huge sad man rambling about at the back
of the church near the medieval knights who lay with broken
swords and noses. 'Barristers?' asked the children but the
intellectual man wasn't sure. The old man was silently refusing
to be moved to a more distinguished seat, it having been discovered that he'd once been a Vice Chancellor.

There was Old Filth's gardener and cleaning lady, who had
parked the pick-up in the Temple this time round and had just
finished a slap-up lunch at the Cheshire Cheese in The Strand.
And there was a very, very old, tall woman, just arriving, sliding in among the Orientals, in a long silk coat—pale rose-
pink—as the choir and organ set-to on the opening hymn.

'I'll bet that was his mistress,' said the intellectual.

'More likely it's a ghost,' said his wife.

And then they all began to sing, 'I vow to thee my country'
which, for Old Filth, born on the Black River in the jungles of
Malaysia, wrapped in the arms of a childish ayah, rocked by the
night sounds of water and trees and invisible creatures and
watched over by different gods, had never been England anyway.

CHAPTER 3

After the service old Dulcie found that she didn't want to stay long at the gathering in the Parliament Chamber across Temple yard. Talk had broken into chorus as they all streamed out. Conversation swelled. The dwarf was being waved off in a splendid car, tossing his hat to the crowd like a hero. Streams of guests were passing up the steps of Inner Temple hall and towards the champagne. Dulcie clutched Susan's arm, then, inside the Chamber, watched people looking uncertainly at each other before plunging. She watched them watching each other furtively from a distance. She examined—and recognised—the degrees of enthusiasm as they asked a name. She saw all the things that had made her worried lately. So much going on that she seemed to be seeing for the first time, or analysing for the first time though she knew that it was everyday, as habitual as looking at the clock or holding out a hand. Yet whatever did it mean?

She was sure that she knew any number of the looming, talkative, exclaiming faces if she could only brush away the threads and lines that now veiled them. And the curious papery, dried-out skin! 'I'm afraid it was all the *cigarettes*,' she said to someone passing by in pale pink silk. The woman immediately melted off-stage. Over in a corner rowdy people seemed to be passing around the dwarf's hat and a cheer went up. 'It is like a saloon,' she said. She moved towards the lovely long windows, hearing everywhere half-familiar voices. And names of old friends lamented for being long-gone.

But they were not long gone to her. Oh, never! Since school-days, and just like her mother, Dulcie had kept all her address books and birthday books and a tattered pre-war autograph book. Some of the names, of course, were hazy on the page. Some were firmly crossed out by Susan. ('But there were *always* Vansittarts at Wingfield. Susan, do *not* cross that out. I'll be sending a Christmas card.') *I must learn this e-mail*, she thought, *tomorrow*. 'Susan—could we go home?'

Susan fetched her mother's coat. Naturally Dulcie had kept her hat on. It made for a pleasant, feathery shadow but she had a wish that she were of this generation who would have left a hat in the cloakroom and shown that she wasn't going thin on top like most of them; but she didn't quite dare. Her fur coat was expensive and light as wool and smelled of evening-in-Paris, setting the odd old nostril quivering, as she passed.

A taxi had been called for Waterloo Station and the train home and Herman was being hunted down. Large and grave, the boy stood looking towards the Thames across the Temple gardens, 'Where,' he told his grandmother, 'as I guess you know they organised the Wars of the Roses.'

'Such lovely lime-juice,' said Dulcie, 'and *how* we missed it in the War.'

Herman glowered, saying that clearly only Americans were historians now.

'They have so little of it to learn,' said Dulcie.

'Romantic vista?' asked the ex-Vice Chancellor, plodding by. 'Hullo Dulcie. I am Cumberledge. Eddie and I were lads together in Wales.'

'Magnificent,' said Dulcie. 'They call it Cumbria now. So affected. Herman darling, I do think it's time to go.'

'The Thames once stank so much they had to move out of The House of Commons,' said Herman.

'Quite a stink there sometimes now,' said a new Queen's Counsel going by with tipping wine glass.

'I think you should qualify that,' said Herman, but the Silk had faded away. 'Granny, nobody's talking to me.'

'Why should they?'

'And there's no music.'

'Well, I don't think Old Filth was—big—on music, darling.'

'Veneering was. I liked Mr. Veneering better anyway.'

'So you always say,' said his mother. 'I don't know how you knew anything about him. And he was Sir Terence. Terry Veneering.'

'Gran, I was nine. He was at your house. His hair was like threads and queer yellow. He played The Blues on your piano. Gran, you *must* remember. There was an awful man there, too, called Winston Smith or something. Like *1984*. I hope the Winston Smith one's dead like most of these here. Why's Mr. Veneering dead? He noticed me. I'll bet he was an American. They never forget you, Americans. Mr. Feathers' ('Sir Edward,' said Dulcie) 'never had a clue who I was.'

'Taxi now, Herman. Stop talking.'

A little old man seemed to be accompanying them as they left the party.

They had seen him in the church with a second-class railway ticket sticking up from his breast pocket.

When they climbed in to their waiting taxi he climbed in with them. 'Dulcie,' he said, 'I am Fiscal-Smith.'

The name, the face had been at the rim of Dulcie's perception all day, like the faint trail of light from a dead planet. Fiscal-Smith!

'But,' she said. 'You told me you were never coming to London again after Veneering's party. I mean Memorial. Don't you live somewhere quite north?'

'Good early train. Darlington,' he said. 'My ghillie drove me down from The Hall. Two hours King's Cross. Excellent.'

'What's a ghillie?' asked Herman.

'You know, Dulcie, that I never miss a memorial service. I wouldn't come down for anything else. Well, perhaps for an Investiture—. And you'll remember, I think, that I *was* Old Filth's best man. In Hong Kong. You were there. With Willie.'

'Yes,' said Dulcie—in time—her eyes glazing, remembering with terrible clarity that Veneering of course was not present. Not in the flesh.

Fiscal-Smith was never exactly one of us, she thought. No-one knows a thing about him now. Jumped up from nowhere. Like Veneering. On the make all his life. In a minute he's going to ask to come back to Dorset with us for a free bed-and-breakfast. He'll be asking me to marry him next.

'I'm nearly eighty-three,' she said, confusing him.

He took his cheap-day second-class rail ticket from his pocket and read it through. 'I was just thinking,' he said, 'I might come back with you to Dorset? Stay a few nights? Old Times? Talk about Willy? Maybe a week? Or two? Possiblity?'

In the train he sat down at once in Herman's reserved seat. 'That,' said Herman, 'is not legal.'

'Justice,' said Fiscal-Smith, 'has nothing to do with Law.'

'Well you'll have to help me to get Mother out,' said Susan. 'Tisbury has a big drop.'

'I wouldn't mind a big drop now,' said Fiscal-Smith, 'or even a small one. Will there be a trolley?'

* * *

There was not. The journey was slow. Fiscal-Smith had trouble with the ticket inspector, who was slow to admit that you have a right to a first-class seat with only the return half of a Basic, Fun-day Special to another part of the country. Fiscal-Smith won the case, as he had been known to do before, through relentless wearing down of the defence, who went shakily off through the rattletrap doors. 'Ridiculous man. Quite untrained,' said Fiscal-Smith.

The train stopped at last at Tisbury, waiting in the wings for the down-line train to hurtle by. 'Excellent management,' said Fiscal-Smith as they drew up on the platform and the usual Titanic-style evacuation took place from its eccentric height, passengers leaping into the air and hoping to be caught. 'Very dangerous,' said Fiscal-Smith. 'Very well-known hazard this line. "Every man for himself",' and then completely disappeared.

Dulcie and Susan were rescued by the intellectual family man who came running up the platform to take Dulcie in his arms and lift her down.

'How well you can run,' she said to him. 'Your legs are as long as dear Edward's. An English gentleman could always be identified by his long legs you know, once. Though in old age they all became rather floppy in the shanks.' Seeing suddenly Old Filth's rotting remains in the English cemetery in Dacca and nobody to put flowers on them, her pale eyes filled with tears. Everyone gone now, she thought. Nobody left.

'Come on back with us,' said the family man, 'It's a foul night. I'll drop you at home. We have a car rug,' but she said, 'No, we'd better stay together. But you can have Fiscal-Smith,' she added, which he seemed not to hear. Fiscal-Smith had already found Susan's old Morris Traveller in the car park and was fussing round it.

'Well, keep our lights in view,' called the family man, who was at once invisible through the murk and lashing rain.

As Susan drove carefully along behind, they all fell silent as they passed Old Filth's empty house, in its hollow. Dulcie didn't peer down at it, thinking of all his happy years, his steady friendship and noble soul. What Fiscal-Smith was thinking it was hard to say. The car swished through lakes of rain in the road, the deluge and the dark. All looked straight ahead.

* * *

They began to speak again only as they reached Privilege House where in minutes lights blazed, central heating and hot water were turned up higher, soup, bread and cheese appeared and the telly was switched on for the News. The smell of fat, navy-blue hyacinths in bowls set heads spinning and the polished blackness of the windows before the curtains were drawn across showed that the wet and starless world had passed into infinite space. Dulcie thought again about the last scene of the last act.

'Why were all the lights on in his house?' asked Herman.

'Whose house? Filth's?' said Susan. 'They weren't. 'It's been locked up since Christmas. Chains on the gates.'

'Didn't notice the gates,' said Herman, 'but the lights were on all over it. In every room. Shining like always. But there seemed to be more than usual. Every window blazing.'

'I expect it has caught fire,' said Fiscal-Smith, searching out Dulcie's drinks cupboard, as old friends are permitted to do.

CHAPTER 4

The next morning Dulcie awoke in her comfortable foam-lined bed with a sense of unrest. Her window was open in the English tradition, two inches at the top for the circulation of refreshing night air (how they had dreamed of it in all their years in Hong Kong) long before the European central-heating. In their native English bedrooms Dulcie and Willy had always eschewed central-heating as working-class.

Outside was country silence except for the clatter of an occasional wooden-looking leaf from the Magnolia Grandiflora hitting the stone terrace. Her watch said 5 A.M. Excellent! She was in time for Prayer for the Day on faithful BBC four, which she still called the Home Service.

Where was she? Was it today they had to go to London to dear Eddie's thing? No, no. They'd done that. *Flames*, she thought, *Flames. Ashes to ashes—*, and drifted off to sleep again.

* * *

Quite soon she woke once more, the flames retreating. She trotted downstairs in slippers and her old dressing-gown of lilac silk, feeling a sort of twitch in a back molar. Oh dear. Time for a check-up. So expensive. Own teeth every one of them. Thanks to Nannie. A full five minutes brushing morning and night. More than the teeth at yesterday's party—. Oh, the awful rictus grins! And the *bridges*! You could *see* them. Queen Elizabeth the first who never smiled. The old Queen

Mother who never stopped, and should have done. Early-morning tea.

Willy had always made the early-morning tea. Not in Hong Kong, of course. There had always been a slender maid with a tray, smiling. They thought, the Chinese and the Americans, that it was disgusting. Called it 'bed-tea'. Oh Willy! She tried not to think of Willy in case once again she found that she had forgotten what he had looked like. Ah—all well. Here he came on the stairs, his fastidious feet, balancing tea-cups and deeply thinking. 'Oh, *Willy*! So many years! I haven't really forgotten what you looked like. "Pastry Willy"—but you grew quite weather beaten after we came home. It's just, sometimes lately that you've grown hazy. Doesn't matter. Changes nothing. I wish we could have a good *talk* Willy, about money. There doesn't seem to be much of it. I always put the Bank letters in your desk. Very silly of me. I don't open many of them.'

He was watching her up by the kitchen ceiling, very kindly, but noncommittally. No need ever to discuss the big things. He knew she was—well—superficial. Hopeless at school. Men love that, Nannie had said. But shrewd, she thought. *Oh*, yes. I'm shrewd. An unshakable belief in the Church of England and God's mercy, and *Duty* and 'routine'. Early tea. Clocks all over the house (fewer now I've sold the carriage clocks) wound up each Sunday evening after Evensong. Jesus had probably never seen a clock. *Were* there any? She tried to imagine the Son of Man with a wrist watch, all the time putting from her hazy early-morning mind the fact that she couldn't remember Willy at all. 'I can't see your *face*,' she called.

Come on. Hospitality, said his voice from behind the kitchen curtains. Tags and watch-words, she thought. That's what all the love and passion comes down to. We never really talked.

And imagine, sex! Extraordinary! I suppose we did it? Susan was a lovely baby.

She made tea from the loose Darjeeling in the black and

gold tin and carried up a pretty tray with sugar basin and milk jug—. What am I doing all this *for*, Willy? It's no wonder Susan just thumps down a mug. Our bloody parents. Highest standards. But what of, Willy? Standards of what? Oh! He had vanished again.

Good. He couldn't answer her.

'Now then, Fiscal-Smith. Rockingham china for Fiscal-Smith. I bet he lives off pots and shards in Yorkshire. Mugs there, certainly. And I'm still trying to show him the rules.' She tottered up to the guest room and found it empty.

'Hullo?'

'Fiscal-Smith,' she called. (What *is* his first name? Nobody ever knew.)

'Hullo?'

(That must be sad for him. Nobody ever asking.)

'Hullo?'

Silence. The bed in his room was tidily turned back—his pale pink and white winceyette pyjamas folded on the pillow, his dressing-gown and slippers side by side by an upright chair. (So he'd brought his night-things. He'd intended to stay from the start. The old chancer!)

Except that he was absent.

She sat down on his bed and thought, he says he comes in honour of Filth and yet all he wants is to be looked after here. That's all he's after. Being *looked* after. You were so different, Willy. And now all I want is someone to deal with those letters (My slippers. Time for new slippers) and peace and quiet. And—absolute silence.

There was a most unholy crash from below stairs.

As she shrieked, she remembered that she was not alone. There were others in the house. Left over from yesterday. She couldn't actually remember the end of yesterday. Any yesterday. The evening before had usually slipped away now by morning. King Lear, poor man—.

But last night hadn't there been something rather sensational? Rather terrible? Oh dear, yes. Poor Old Filth's empty house had burned to the ground. Or something of the sort.

She looked at her feet. Yes, it was time for new slippers. Then through the window she saw Fiscal-Smith tramping up the hill towards her, from the direction of Filth's house, still in yesterday's funeral suit and he was looking jaunty. Eighty plus. And plus. 5.30 A.M. Beginning to rain. He saw her and called out, 'All well. It's still there.'

'What?'

'Filth's nice old place. The boy was wrong. No sign of fire. I've a feeling that boy is a *stirrer*. He was a stirrer years ago at that lunch you gave. A little monkey!'

'Do you never forget anything, Fiscal-Smith? What lunch? A life-time of lunches. And with'—for a wobbly second she forgot her grandson's name. 'When? Where?'

'Two fat sisters. And a priest. And Veneering, of course. Oh, I forget nothing. Mind never falters. It is rather a burden to me, Dulcie.'

'You *are* arrogant, Fiscal-Smith.'

'I simply put my case,' he said.

He was with her in the kitchen now. She said, 'Your case is in your bedroom. Do you want help with packing?'—and shocked herself.

There fell a silence as he stepped out upon the terrace with his cup of tea.

* * *

At the same moment, down in Old Filth's house in the dell, Isobel Ingoldby, wrapped now in his Harrods dressing gown instead of her own pink silk coat, was turning off the lights which she had left burning all night. Foolish, she was saying, I'm the one paying for the electricity now. Until I sell. Why did

I light the whole place up through the dark? Some primitive thing about the spirit finding its way home? But he won't be searching. His spirit is free. It's back in his birth-place. It maybe never quite left it.

She boiled a kettle for tea but forgot to make any. She wandered about. Betty's favourite chair stood packed up in the hall. His present for Fiscal-Smith. Nobody gave Fiscal-Smith presents.

This house—the house she had inherited—watched her as she went about. So tidy. So austere. So dead. Betty's photograph on a mantelpiece, fallen over sideways.

Isobel had slept in his bed last night. Someone had removed the sheets and she had lain on the bare mattress with rugs over her. She thought of the first time she'd seen him in bed. He was about fourteen years old. He was terrified. We both knew then. I was only his school-friend's older cousin, but we recognised each other. All our lives.

* * *

Fiscal-Smith still stood on Dulcie's terrace half an hour later, still examined the view over the Roman road towards Salisbury, the wintery sun trying to enliven the grey fields through the rain.

Dulcie came walking past him towards the wrought-iron gates, fully dressed now in tweed skirt and cardigan, remarkably high heels and some sort of casual coat, not warm, from the cupboard under the stairs. She carried a prayer-book. Fiscal-Smith shouted, 'Where are you going? Filth's house is perfectly all right.'

'I am going to church.'

'Dulcie, it's six o'clock in the morning. It is clouding over. It's beginning to rain. That coat you had in Hong Kong. And it isn't Sunday.' He came up close to her.

'I need to say my prayers.'

'It will be locked.'

'I doubt it. The great Chloe is supposed to open it but she usually forgets to shut and lock it the night before.'

'The mad woman who runs about with cakes?'

'Yes. Well-meaning, but the mind's going. Sometimes she locks in the morning and un-locks at night. We shall have to tell the church-warden soon. Actually I think she may *be* the church-warden. There's nothing much going on in the church. Not even anybody sleeping rough. It's too damp—.'

He was padding along behind her.

'There you are,' she said. 'Unlocked. Unlocked all night.'

* * *

Inside, the church scowled at them and blew a blast of damp breath. Hassocks looked ready to sprout moss and there was the hymn-book smell. Notices curled on green baize gone ragged, and the stained-glass windows appeared to bulge inwards from the flanking walls. Two sinister ropes dangled in the belfry tower. It was bitterly cold.

'Stay there,' Dulcie ordered him, making for a chancel prayer desk up near the organ. 'I can't pray with anyone watching.'

'The Muslims can,' he said, trying to bring the blood back to his knobbed hands. 'This is a refrigerator, not a church.'

'*Muslims,*' she said, 'can crowd together on mats and swing about and keep their circulation going and you don't see what the women do but I don't think they pray with men, in a huddle. Anyway, I need what I know,' and she vanished, eastwards.

'Five minutes,' he shouted after her as her high heels tapped out of sight. 'Utter madness,' he said to the stained glass windows. 'Hopeless woman. Hopeless village.' His voice echoed hopelessly around the rood-screen and its sad saints. Rows of regimental flags hung drooping down the side-aisle like shredding dish cloths, still as sleeping bats. 'They're all off their heads here,' he called out. There was the sound of a heavy key being turned in the lock of the south door, just behind him. The one by which they had entered.

He sprang towards it, flung himself first through the wire, then the baize door, the south door they had just pushed heavily through. He tugged and shouted.

But the door was now firmly and determinedly locked from the outside. Chloe, on her bike, had been thinking that it was evening again.

* * *

Up in the chancel there was no sign of Dulcie but at length he saw the top of her head and her praying hands. She was like a—what was it called? A little Dutch thing. Little painting on wood. 'Praying hands,' he thought. 'They have them on Christmas cards. Dürer. The Germans were perfectly all right then.' Her head was bowed ('She still has thick, curly hair'). 'Five minutes,' he called, like a tout, or an invigilator.

* * *

Soon he began to hum a tune from his seat in front of the choir-stall and after a minute she opened angry eyes.

'We are locked in,' he said.

'Nonsense,' she said.

'I heard the key thrust in and turned. It was Chloe.'

Dulcie went pattering back down the central aisle, tried the oak door first with one hand, then the other, then both hands together. She regarded the broad and ancient lock. 'You heard her? Chloe?'

'Yes.'

'Why didn't you shout?'

'I think I did. Now, leave all this to me, Dulcie, I banged and rattled and yelled. I will do it again.'

'Yes. She *is* getting deaf.'

They stood in icy shadow and he called again, 'Hullo?'

'It's no good shouting, Fiscal-Smith. Nobody in the village is up yet except Chloe.' But he roared out, '*Hullo* there?'

'There may be someone walking a dog?'

'Nobody walks a dog as early as this in winter. We are all old here.'

'I'm tired of this "old",' said Fiscal-Smith. 'We don't have it in the north. Won't Susan be coming by on the horse? And where's that boy?'

'Sleeping. And Susan won't be out for at least two hours. She may notice we are missing, but I don't think so.'

'I *suppose*,' he said, 'you don't carry such a thing as a mobile telephone?'

'Good heavens, no. Do you?'

'Never.'

'We could try shouting louder.'

And so they did for a time—treble and bass—but there was no response.

'Of course, there are the bells,' said Dulcie. She was shaking now with cold. 'It might warm us up.'

Fiscal-Smith released the tufted, woolly bell-ropes from their loops in the tower and handed one to her, icy to the touch. She closed her eyes and dragged at it with childish fists. It did not stir.

'I'll have a go,' he said, and after a time, sulkily, on the edge of outrage, the damp and matted bell-pull began to move stiffly up and down: but Fiscal-Smith looked exhausted.

'Go on, go on,' cried Dulcie. 'You got it up I think,' and thought, I believe I said something rather risqué just then, and giggled.

'This is quite serious, Dulcie. Don't laugh. Go over there and pull the blue one.'

And so they toiled, and after what seemed to be hours they both heard the sad boom of a bell.

'I think it was only the church clock striking seven,' she said.

'We must go on trying.'

But she couldn't and made for the chancel again and possible candles on the altar for heat. He followed, but the candles looked like greasy ice and all the little night-lights people light for memorials to the dead were brownish and dry and there were no matches. Dulcie's lips were turning blue now. 'This,' she said, not crossly, 'will be the death of me. We have no warm clothing and between us we are nearly two hundred years old. My mother stayed in bed all the time after eighty. There was nothing wrong with her but everyone cherished her.'

Through a door they found a vestry and a wall full of modern pine cupboards, 'Bequeathed,' said a plaque, 'by Elizabeth Feathers'. 'I wish she'd bequeathed an electric fire,' said Dulcie.

Inside, the cupboards were crammed full of choirboys' black woollen cassocks, and Fiscal-Smith and Dulcie somehow scrambled into one each. Dulcie said they were damp. But then, over in the priests' vestry nearby, there was treasure. Albs, cottas, chasubles and a great golden embroidered cope beneath a linen cover.

'Wrap it round you,' ordered Fiscal-Smith.

'It's reserved for Easter only,' said Dulcie. 'It's for the Bishop and it's too big. It could go round us both.'

So they both stood inside it, their faces looking out from it side-by-side. 'My neck is still very cold,' said Dulcie. 'Look, there is the ceremonial mitre and the St. Ague stoll. This church! This church you know was once High. And very well-endowed.'

'I can't remember what High is. I'm a Roman Catholic,' said Fiscal-Smith, 'but I'm in favour if High turns up the heat.

Remember Hong Kong. No copes there. Too hot. This is very curious head-gear, Dulcie. We are becoming ridiculous.'

'I wish this was a monastery,' she said. 'There'd be a supply of hoods.'

'That was because of the tonsures.'

'I'm not surprised. I had terrible tonsils as a girl. Before penicillin and I wasn't a monk. Wonderful penicillin.'

'I'm lost,' said Fiscal-Smith.

'It was God's reward for us winning the war, penicillin.' ('She's bats.') 'Willy used to say that every nation that has ever achieved a great empire blazes up for a moment in its dying fire. Penicillin. I wouldn't have missed our Finest Hour, would you, Fiscal-Smith?'

'I bloody would,' he said. Then after a silence, 'Look here, Dulcie. Where do they keep the Communion wine?'

* * *

It was later that there came a loud knocking on the vestry door into the churchyard. 'Are you in there? An answer please. Are you there? Who are you?'

'Yes, we are locked into the church. Accidentally. Dulcie is not well. It is very cold. This is Sir Frederick Fiscal-Smith speaking.'

'Have you tried to open the door?'

'Of course we've tried the bloody door.'

'I mean this door. The vestry door. It is beside you. There is an inside bolt.'

Fiscal-Smith leaned from his princely garment, considered the unobtrusive little modern door, slid open a silken brass bolt and revealed the misty morning. There, in running shorts among the graves, stood the family man.

Out through the doorway, laced across with trails of young ivy, a door which, like Christ's in Holman-Hunt's *Light of the*

World in St. Paul's Cathedral, only opened from within, stepped a pair of ancient Siamese twins in cloth of gold, one of them wearing a papal headdress and both of them blue to the gills.

Away down past the churchyard at the foot of the steep stepped path sped old Chloe on her bicycle bearing on the handlebars a jam sponge and in her other hand the ancient church key. She called a greeting and waved.

'Just wondered if I'd remembered to unlock. So glad I had,' and pressed on.

In the village shop, she said, 'There's something going on in the church. I think it's a pageant.'

CHAPTER 5

Dulcie had been put to bed by Susan.
Fiscal-Smith, with his overnight case beside him on the terrace, was awaiting transport.

'You might call me a taxi.'

Susan said, 'There are no taxis. I'll drive you to the station. Do you want to say goodbye to Dulcie?'

'Oh, no thank you.'

'She will not be pleased.'

'Whatever I say or do makes not the least difference to her. I make no difference to anyone.'

'Oh, I'm sure——.'

'All the years we have all known each other, do you know, Susan, I've never actually been invited anywhere. And I was present when Betty saw Veneering for the first time. Party. Filth was like Hyperion. Betty looked like the captain of the school hockey team. Gorgeous Betjeman girl. Stalwart but not joyful.'

'You don't have to tell me this——.'

'As she came in to the party she saw Veneering across the room. Hell-raising, blond-yellow hair falling over his face, already half drunk (and with a case starting against Eddie next morning) and I saw him get hold of a pillar. White and gold. Fluted. His face became very still and serious. Yes. I saw the beginning of it. The disgraceful love affair.'

'We have five minutes to get to the station. You may catch it but you know, you're very welcome——.'

'No I am not.'

* * *

In the train he stood inside the doors on the high step and looked down on Susan. 'No. I am not welcome. But thank you for the lift. Edward and Betty never invited me to stay either. At that lunch at Dulcie's I had to walk in from Salisbury. Seven miles.'

'Oh, Fiscal-Smith,' she said, 'until yesterday you were one of the last friends. Her last and best.'

'I wonder if she remembers,' he said. 'That I was Edward's best man?'

The doors clashed together, clapping their hands a couple of times. There were some fizzing and knocking sounds and then a long sigh. Then the train clattered off, and Susan stood staring at its disappearing rump, wondering why the ridiculous man cared so much about these people who were dead and hadn't liked him anyway. He'd said in the car that Veneering was the best of them. That Veneering *could* have invited him down here. That he'd known him from boyhood.

'But couldn't you have invited them to *you* anyway? To stay with you up in the North?'

'Not possible,' he had said. 'Anyway, I am the only one who knows Veneering's secrets.'

'Did you never have a wife, Fiscal-Smith?'

'Certainly not,' he had said.

God, thought Susan, these old fruits are boring.

CHAPTER 6

Anna, the young wife of the poet from the house that had been Veneering's, had been at the village shop that morning at the same time as Chloe, buying bread and milk for breakfast, and she had heard the words 'pageant' and 'church'.

She was interested in the church, and the unlikely Saint Ague, and had been allowed to do something about the vestry. She loved robes and the clergy. She came from a vicarage family and wasn't usual. She was the reason why the brass plates in memory of Betty Feathers shone so bright. What a homely name! Some old villager! Then someone else corrected her and told her about wonderful dead Betty, very distinguished woman, and she thought, Oh Lord, another old dear. And it was Anna now, the family woman who put the Cope in clean sacking and starched the choir boys' surplices so that they looked like preening swans. Sadly there were only three choir boys now and seldom visible. Or audible.

Soon, the old guard predicted this woman (Anna) would be in Charge of Altar Frontals, then Communion Silver and Candle-sticks (already rumoured to be in her attic). Not, of course, Flowers. Only Betty Feathers had dared take Flowers unasked. Betty Feathers had not had much to do with churches except in Hong Kong but she was unbeatable on flowers. During her mature years at St. Ague with her perfect husband Sir Edward (Filth) Feathers, vicars of the parish had been grateful for such a conventional and pleasant woman and nothing churchy about her. You would never guess she might take over. And here most exceptionally, for most of St. Ague was fashionably atheist now, was another. This Anna. 'Labourers,' said the village elders, 'do still seem to keep the vineyard going even late in the day. And for no pay.' Anna had been a god-send at the last harvest festival and for the first time in years there had been more than tins of baked beans round the lectern.

There had been a bit of a fuss about Anna surrounding the Easter pulpit with bramble bushes. Not only had she taken them up by the roots (she put them back down her drive-way, where they thrived) but they had damaged several small children who had come with chocolate eggs and rabbits.

Mothers—one or two—enquired if she was interested in the *cleaning* rota and she said, 'I don't want to push in but if you like we've got a power hose and we could cover the Saxon frieze of The Wounds of St. Ague in bubble-wrap.' 'Or Elastoplast,' said her husband, the poet, the family man.

In the end they let Anna fix up only the vestry. Just for the present.

'I do not care for "fixing up",' said one of the ex-flower committee, now confined, like her twin sister, to a wheel chair. They lived with a Carer up the lane and went to church on separate weeks, as the Carer could take only one at a time.

The Vicar tearing past to the next of his string of churches each Sunday, gave thanks for Anna (whoever she was), prayed for new hassocks and fungicides and matches.

'It will take a hundred grand to deal with the vestry. Half a million to save the church,' said Anna. 'We'll have a go with the power hose.'

St. Ague's became Anna's secret passion, her plan for life to supersede (or kill) Chloe. Her heart had gone cold with dread when Chloe, that morning, had said the word 'pageant'.

* * *

'Oh yes,' Chloe had said. 'Scarlet and gold. Robes. Pushing out through that little narrow door. Very queer. Something double-headed. Like black magic. We're wondering if it was art? Your husband seemed to be in charge, Anna. Is he a film director?'

'In *charge*!' she cried. 'I left him in bed.'

'Well he was in running shorts. And he was either on his mobile or directing, like in a play. His arms going up and down.'

Anna said that she had better get home, but instead launched off her car with the breakfast in it towards Privilege House which seemed to be empty except for Herman who was standing in the kitchen eating fish-fingers on his own. He was staring out at the now heavily falling rain. 'Can I come round to you, Anna? To play? I mean music. We're going back to America tomorrow.'

'Where's your grandmother?'

Anna turned to ice when she saw the gold and crimson vestments gleaming around the Aga, a mitre contracting on one hot plate, and Dulcie's yesterday's funeral hat on the other.

'They put her back in bed I think.'

'And you didn't even go up to *see*,' said Anna. 'You are rubbish, Herman.'

* * *

Dulcie was sitting up in bed, her hair fallen into extraordinary Napoleonic cork-screws, her eyes immense, and downing a double Famous Grouse. 'He's gone,' she said. 'He didn't say goodbye.' She wept.

'Who?' Anna took her in her arms and rocked her.

'No need for that,' said Dulcie. 'Fiscal-Smith of course. I've known him over 60 years. My oldest living friend. I can't believe it. I am *mortified*.'

'But Dulcie, you didn't want him. You didn't invite him. He drives you mad. And to be truthful you deserve better. Dulcie?'

'Yes. Well, no. You see, he's never been *known* to leave anywhere early unless, of course, he's been kicked out. I'm afraid that *does* happen. He was never exactly one of us. Not important to us. We didn't know much about him. Though I believe that somehow Veneering did. Somewhere long ago, I was never close to him, he was so boring. But you see, this morning I was locked in the church with him. We had to wrap ourselves up together in the golden Cope.'

'Oh, Dulcie! He'll get over it. He's used to being ignored.'

'Oh, the vestments!'

'Dulcie, I'll see to them. Now get up, I'll find you some clothes and you can come over to us. I've sent Herman over already. I'll make the kids cook the lunch. Where's your daughter?'

'Susan's driving him to the station.' Dulcie began to cry. 'He's so ashamed. He was always frightened of being shamed. It is the Yorkshire accent. And—he never said goodbye.'

'Come on. Get this jersey on.'

'He won't come back. He's a terrible bore. I don't like him, but Willy said he was a very good lawyer. Incorruptible.'

'Like Veneering then?'

'No,' she said, her mind at last at work. 'No. Not like Veneering. Simpler than Veneering. But he's the last link. The last friend.'

'Coat,' said Anna, 'Gloves. Head-scarf, it's still raining. Put your feet in these boots.'

As Anna's car, Dulcie in the head-scarf beside her, hardly up to her shoulder, passed Old Filth's house in the dell Anna looked down at its front door and saw a window slightly open. The five-barred gate was padlocked but something very queer and large had appeared behind it wrapped in a tarpaulin.

There came a sudden insolent puff of smoke from Old Filth's medieval chimney.

Better say nothing, thought Anna. Enough for one day. And it's only nine in the morning.

CHAPTER 7

Susan, clamp-jawed, had not looked towards Old Filth's house as she took Fiscal-Smith to the station, nor did she alone, on the way back. She was taken up with thoughts about her mother, who was obviously going down-hill fast.

Not fit to be left alone. These new people are a god-send, but you can't expect—. And Herman and I go back to America tomorrow. I wonder when I ought to tell her that I'm not married anymore? Herman hasn't told her. Well I *can't* tell her. It would be all over the village.

And as to what she's done *now*! Not so much this senile episode in the church. It's what she's done to poor little Fiscal-Smith. She's bloody hurt him. She *can* hurt. She does. She used to hurt poor old Dad but she doesn't remember. He had to find new books to read all the time and work for the Thomas Hardy Society, which got him only as far as Dorchester. He asked me to look after her but she's so silly. He knew she was silly. I don't think he ever spotted that she's also rather *nasty*. Got me off from Hong Kong soon as I was out of the pram to a boarding school in England—her old school of course. I hated Hong Kong. I hate all that last lot who came home, with their permed hair, thinking they're like the Last Debutantes curtseying in the court of heaven. Hate, hate, hate—.

'My mother,' she told the passing trees along the lanes towards St. Ague, 'let everyone call me Sulky Sue from the beginning. I guess she was the one who invented it. She's hard, my mother. She's not altogether the fool she makes herself out to be: the fool who is very sweet. She's neither foolish nor sweet, really. She's manipulative, cunning and works at seeming thick as a brick. And *nasty*.'

Through tears, on Privilege Hill Susan braked as a woman passed in front of the car. It was the tall old woman who was at the do in London yesterday. In pink. Silk. Long coat. She's still in it! It's Isobel. She's got Betty Feathers' pink umbrella. Lovely-looking person. Wish she was my mother.

At least there's plenty of money. She's not a burden to me. But we must think about death-duties one day soon. She won't like it, but we must.

And Fiscal-Smith. Ancient little Fiscal-Smith. Ma's really hurt him this time. Deep—twisted in the knife. Whatever has she said to him? Oh God—I wish I had a mother I could love. I wonder if she's beginning to like him, or something.

I must go and see these new people to say goodbye.

PART TWO

Teesside

Florrie Benson—that's to say she was Florrie Benson before she married the man from Odessa in Herringfleet, Teesside, England ten years back in 1927 and became Florrie Venetski or Venski or some such name—Florrie Benson walked every day of the school term with her son to see him on to the school train. The son was ten, the place the cold east coast, the time 7.30 in the morning and the year 1937.

The boy, Terence, did not walk beside her. He never had, from being five. He disappeared ahead of her the minute they were over the front doorstep.

It was not that he was in any way ashamed at being seen with his mother. He never had been. It was just that life was an urgent affair of haste and action and nothing in it should be missed.

He was a big, blond, good-looking, lanky, athletic sort of child, in top-gear from the start, his mother plodding behind him. By the time she had caught up with him on the station platform he had disappeared into the raucous mob of local children, his flash of white blond hair running among them like a light.

Florrie never even turned her head to look for him. Never had. She arranged herself against the low rails by the ticket-office her kind, big hands hanging down over it, her smiling brown eyes gazing at the cluster of girls—always girls—who rushed to her like chickens expecting grain. All she seemed to do was smile. What the girls talked to her about goodness knows, but they never stopped until the train came.

Florrie was not particularly clean, or, rather, her clothes were rusty and gave her skin a dark tint. Sometimes the schoolgirls, daughters of steel-workers and not very clean either, stroked her arms and hands and offered her sweets which sometimes she accepted.

Florrie didn't fit in. Her essence seemed to be far away somewhere, way beyond her stocky figure. She suggested another life, a secret civilisation. She looked a solitary. For her ever to have shouted out towards the boy, Terence, to remind him of something would have been almost an insult to both, but an invisible string seemed to pass between them.

Terence—Terry—the spark running in the wheat—never looked at his mother as he ran in the crowd, never waved goodbye when the train came in. When the children had been subsumed into it and it had steamed away on its six-mile journey along the coast Florrie would heave herself off the railings, nod towards the ticket-office ('Now then, Florrie? 'Ow are yer?') and make for home. Her daily ritual was as much a part of local life—quite unexplained—as the train itself, its steam and flames, the fireman shovelling in the coal with the face and muscles of Vulcan. She never seemed to watch him but he was not unaware of her. He sweated in the red glow and wiped his face with a rag.

No other mother came to the station. When the children were smaller the other mothers used to shout ''ere Florrie. Can you look to him? Or her?' Very occasionally at the beginning Florrie would find herself near one or other licking a handkerchief and scrubbing at faces, straightening the slippery scrap of a tiny green and yellow rayon tie. Never Terry's.

Every morning then, for five years, Florrie would heave herself off the railing and back down the road again to No. 9 Muriel Street, so close she could have waved him off at the front door. And from the very start he'd got home again from the station alone. He had crossed over the iron footbridge out of the alley and into some bushes. Everyone, including Florrie, seemed vague about the home train's time of arrival and as he got older he began to make small differentials to his front door, preferring the back door in the paved grey alley where there were sheds and a cart house and black stains of blood. The blood was ingrained into the dip around the central soak-away where for years the butcher had slaughtered a beast every Thursday morning. The back street stank of salt. Then he ran round home and in at the front.

When he grew to be eight or nine he told them at home that his day at school was longer now and he would be late, then he began to take off regularly down Station Road, past the chip shop and the corn-store to the band-stand on the promenade looking towards the sea. He clambered about on the flaky iron lace-work and the peeling iron pillars that supported its dainty roof. He stayed there maybe half an hour doing somersaults on the railings, or dancing about or just staring at the grey sea. Herringfleet had once had a brass band that played airs from *The Merry Widow* or Gilbert and Sullivan to people in hats and gloves who sat out on deck chairs on the promenade but Terry knew nothing about that. He didn't know the meaning of 'band-stand'. He'd slide away home through the back streets again and come in at the front door as if he'd just got off the train.

Inside the tiny house the scene was unchanging and he scarcely registered it. His father lay on the high bed facing the street door, beside him a commode covered with a clean cloth. An iron kettle hung from a chain over the fire, puffing and clattering its lid and the window over the sink was misted over with steam. Occasionally, on good days, his father might be in a chair, but usually, summer and winter, the long, tense figure lay on its back, coughing and coughing and sometimes swearing in Russian 'or whatever they speak in Odessa,' as Nurse Watkins down the street said. She would have left a minute or so before Terry got home from school, and a tray put out on the kitchen table with big, white tea-cups with a gold trefoil on the side and a broad gold rim. There'd be a plate of bread and butter with another plate on top of it. Nurse Watkins came in every day and was paid half-a-crown now and then because the families were in some way connected. She would wash out the Odessan's long flannels in Lux flakes and put him in clean ones, rub his joints, shake the bit of sheep-skin someone had once brought down from Long Hall on the moors, which still smelled of sheep-dip. It prevented bed-sores.

Nurse Watkins didn't seem to have had any training any-where but there was nothing she didn't know. She was midwife to the town and she laid everyone out at death and told lascivious corpse-stories. She had Gypsy eyes and earrings and had been briefly at school with Florrie but had left at twelve. Over the years she had looked long at the Odessan whilst he had looked only at the ceiling. She stroked back his bright hair on the pillow and shaved him with a cut-throat razor when he would allow it. Florrie did the toe-nails but not well.

'Train late again then?' his father said to Terry. 'Gets later.' He spoke in Russian.

'Yes. Late,' said Terry, in Russian. 'She'll be late in, too. Winter coming. Getting dark.'

Terry made tea in the brown pot and let it stand on the hob until it was brewed.

'Are there no biscuits, Dad,' and then in English 'Why's there never a biscuit, then?' and his father roared back in Russian about his grammar.

'Dist wan' a biscuit then, Dad?'

'*Do you want*,' said his father.

'Or there's bread.'

Sometimes his father lifted up a hand, which meant yes.

Then Florrie would be back with them, telling Terry in broad Teesside patois where to find biscuits (in her bag to stop

Nurse Watkins). She would refill the kettle and swing it back over the fire for the next brew. All three knew how tired she was.

* * *

All that day she had been unrecognisable, black as a Negro, a man's thick tweed cap pulled over her hair, back to front. A man's thick coat, made thicker by years of grime, had been tied with rope round her middle. All day she'd been perched up high on a bench across the coal-cart that she kept in the alley alongside the shed of the scrawny little horse and the coal store. The butcher's men often gave her a hand, if they were there.

Three days a week she clopped round the town on the cart through all the back streets, shouting 'COAL' in a resounding voice. The lungs of a diva. 'Coal today,' she shouted and from the better houses of the iron-masters' in Kirkleatham Street the maids ran out in white cap and apron, twittering like starlings. 'Three bags now Florrie,' 'Four bags,' and watched her heave herself down off the dray, turn her back, claw down one sack after another with black gloves stiff as wood. She balanced them along into coal-houses or holes in stable yards showering out coals and coal-dust. She took the money and dropped it inside a flat leather pouch on the rope belt around her stomach. She adored her work.

'Cuppa tea, Florrie?'

'No time, no time.'

A long slow sexy laugh, then back on the dray. Street after street. The horse knew where to stop. Trade was steady. Her call was tuneful, rather like the rag-and-bone man but richer. Almost a song. Fifty years on, Sir Terence Veneering QC, sitting in the Colonial Club, happened to mention to someone in the Sultanate that he had been born in Herringfleet, was told that there had been a northern woman, larger than life, who had delivered coals. Or so it was said. In the poverty-stricken North-East—in the middle of the Thirties.

Once home Florrie drove the dray round to the back. She took the horse to the shed and fed it, rubbed it down and if there was no-one about to help her she dragged the dray into the cart-house. There was a communal bath-house for Muriel Street and she paid a penny to have it to herself on coal days. She poured hot water from the brick tub all over herself with a tin can. She washed her hair and feet and hands and then her body with a block of transparent green Fairy Soap. Then she dried herself on a brown towel, rough as heather.

* * *

Above the crooked, unpainted doors of the cart-house hung a hand-painted, wooden sign in green and gold saying Vanetski Coal Merchant and the exotic flourish to it was the register, the signature, the stamp of proof of Florrie's past happiness.

The sign-painter was the foreign acrobat and dancer who had arrived in the town over ten years ago with a circus troupe who put up a Big Top on the waste ground by the gasworks for 'One Week Only'. The tent had sprung up overnight like a gigantic mushroom, with none of the glitter and coat-tails of Bertram Mills but an old, threadbare thing, grey and rather frightening, an image from the plains of Ilium. And how it stank!

'They're called Cossacks,' said the cognoscenti of Her-ringfleet. 'They can dance and kick right down to their ankles with their bottoms on the floor. They shout out and yell and make bazooka music, like the Old Testament Jericho Russian.'

'What they doing 'ere?'

'It's since they murdered the Tsar. They want the world to

see them. It's a sort of mix of animal and angel. Russia's not a rational country.'

He doesn't go in much for angels—the man selling tickets. Long, miserable face. They killed the Tsar years ago!

But young Florrie Benson saw an angel that night. She had taken money from her mother's purse to buy a ticket for the show and was at once translated. She heard a new music, a new fierce rapture. She watched the superhuman contortions of the exciting male bodies. Her skin prickled all over at their wild cries. In a way she recognised them.

There was one dancer she couldn't take her eyes off. Her friend next to her was sniggering into a handkerchief ('For men it's right daft') and the next day she stole more money and went to the Cossacks alone. She went every night that week and the final night she was up beside him on the platform when he fell from a rope. She was ordering a doctor, roaring out in her lion's voice. People seemed to think she must be his woman. She never left his side.

* * *

The rest of the Cossacks melted away and they and their tent were gone by morning in their shabby truck. Florrie, the English schoolgirl, stayed with him at the hospital and wouldn't be shifted. Doctors examined him and said his back was probably not broken but time would tell. Someone said, 'He's a foreigner. Speaks nowt but heathen stuff! He'll have to be reported.'

Yet nobody seemed to know where. Or seemed interested. The local clergyman who was on the Town Council went to see him, and then the Roman Catholic priest who tried Latin and the Cossack's lips moved. Each thought the other had reported him to the authorities, without quite knowing what these were.

'They'll no doubt be in touch any day from Russia to get him back.' They waited.

'There was a couple of Russians died of food-poisoning last year off a ship anchored in Newcastle. Meat pies. The Russians was in touch right away for body-parts. Suspected sabotage.'

But nobody seemed to want the body-parts of the Cossack who lay in the cottage-hospital with his eyes shut. He talked to himself in his own language and spat out all the hospital food. And only the school-girl beside him.

'Back's gone,' they told her. 'Snapped through. He'll never walk again.'

The following week he was found standing straight at the window, six-foot-four and looking eastward toward the dawn and the Transporter Bridge at Middlesbrough, an engineering triumph. It seemed to interest him. When the nurses screamed at him he screamed back at them and began to throw the beds about and they couldn't get near to him with a needle. Someone called the police and somebody else ran round to find Florence.

She was taken out of school and to the hospital in a police car, no explanations; and when she was let into his isolation ward she looked every bit woman and shouted, 'You. You come 'ome wi' me. *Away*!' '*Away*' is a word up there that can mean anything but is chiefly a command.

She left her address at the hospital and commanded an ambulance. The ward sister was drinking tea with her feet up so Florrie got him from the ambulance herself, half on her back. She had a bed made ready. The aged parents, never bright, shook their heads and drowsed on. 'Eh, Florence! Eh, Florrie Benson—whatever next?'

The dancer stayed. He lay, staring above him now. Nobody came. Florrie went to the public library in Middlesbrough to find out about Cossacks. She came back and stood looking at his curious eyes. She imagined they were seeing great plains of snow spread out before him. Multitudinous mountains. The endless

Steppe. She got out some library books and tried to show him the photographs but they didn't seem to mean anything to him.

She gave up school. She was sixteen, anyway. Her old parents went whimpering about the house, faded and both were dead within the year.

Florence was pregnant, and even so, nobody was interested in the Cossack. Neighbours came round but she was daunting. If she had been a boy it would all have been different. Serious enquiries. But, even pregnant, nothing was done for Florence.

After a time the man began to walk again, just to the window or the door on the street. Or into the ghastly back alley.

One day Florrie came home from buying fish to find him gone.

It was for her the empty tomb. The terror and the disbelief were a revelation. She ran every-where to look for him, and, in the end, it was she—out of half the parish—who found him, on the sand-dunes staring out over what was still being called the German Ocean. The North Sea.

She brought him limping and swearing home and, at last, being well-acquainted now with the Christian Cross that lay in the warm golden hair on his chest, she went to the Catholic priest, leaving Nurse Watkins in charge for two shillings and four pence. There were very few half-crowns left now.

The priest lived in a shuttered little brick house beside his ugly church beside the breakwater. Nobody went there except the Irish navvies in the steel-works. 'Russian?' asked Father Griesepert. 'Communist you say?'

'No. He's definitely Catholic.'

'How do you know?'

'He doesn't believe in taking precautions.'

Father Griesepert said that he would call. He said that, actually, he had already been thinking about it.

'Name?' Father Griesepert shouted.

Nobody had actually asked the Cossack's name. The Catholic priest bullied the sick man in a loud voice. He tried a bit of German (on account of his own strange name which was one of the reasons for his isolation here).

'Address? Home address?'

The man looked scornful.

'Name of circus?'

Silence. Then 'Piccadilly' and a great laugh.

Suddenly, in good English, the Cossack said, 'My name is Anton' ('Anton,' whispered Florence, listening to it).

'Very unlikely he's a Cossack. I'd guess he comes from Odessa,' said the priest. He rubbed his hands over his face as if he were washing it. 'This woman,' he said in loud English to the man, 'Is with child.'

Anton understood.

'You must be married before the birth.'

Anton looked at Florence as if he had never seen her before.

Florence went to get the priest his whisky.

They all said prayers together then, and Griesepert named the wedding date. 'We must, of course, inform the authorities.' He was met by two pairs of staring eyes.

'You are a Catholic, Florrie Benson.' She seemed uncertain. 'Your parents were lapsed. But I remember baptising you as a child. That child has now to have her own child and it must be brought up as a Catholic. It must go to a Catholic school. You must bring it to the church. And your marriage must be preceded by a purification.'

'A *purification*, Father?'

'Have you no concept of your faith?'

'You never gave me any.'

She stretched out her rough hand in a gesture which was— for her—hesitant, towards the Cossack's hand and together they both glared at the priest. Then, between them in assorted words, from God knows where, they made a stab at the Catechism, Anton's face rigid with contempt.

Florrie's face was alight with joy. The baby in the womb stirred.

* * *

Anton tried. When Florrie was in the ninth month and couldn't walk far he began to limp about the town looking for work.

There was almost no money left by now from the wills of Florrie's parents and so he became a caretaker at a private school at the end of the town. When they found that he spoke several languages he began to teach classes there. His English improved so quickly that it almost seemed that it had always been there, beneath the other languages. He began to meet educated people in the good houses across the Park towards Linthorpe. The new great families, the iron-masters. Some of them German Jews. In these houses he behaved with a grave, alien formality: but with a seductive gleam in his eye. It seemed that he was a gentleman. It was confusing.

Soon he was being invited to dinner—always, of course, without Florrie—by the headmaster of a local private school and his artistic wife while, in Muriel Street, Florence suckled the child over the kitchen range. She sang to it, made clothes for it, wished her mother were alive to see it. Wished she had been kinder to her mother.

Her husband, seated at the headmaster Harold Fondle's great mahogany dining table with its lace mats and good crystal, spoke in improving English and fluent French of Plato and Descartes. His English was without accent, he looked distinguished and he appreciated the wine. When anybody broached the question of his past life or his future, or his allegiances he would raise his glass and say, 'To England'.

He grew strong again, and after the child was weaned decided to go into business as a coal merchant. He carved and then painted the gold and green sign in the slaughter-house alley. The butcher thought little of it ('You don't start a business by mekkin a painting of it'). When Anton's back gave out for the second time, Florrie found him twisted, lying in the alley under a sack of coal, the thin horse munching into its nose-bag.

She hauled him somehow back indoors where Nurse Watkins came and they got him up at last on the bed. The baby—the alert and golden, happy baby—lay watching from his cot, which was a clothes drawer. The doctor came.

Both parents that night wept.

* * *

The next day was the day of the week when Griesepert came to them with the Sacrament. He never missed. He rolled in like a walrus, snorting down his nose. He stretched out his legs towards the fender.

Today Florrie ignored the Sacrament and sat out in the yard letting them talk. There was whisky, and firelight in the room and the knowing-looking baby wondered whether the grim man on the bed or the fat man over the fire mattered more. The word 'father' kept recurring. The baby seemed to listen for it. As to his mother, she was milk and warmth and safe arms but he didn't pat and stroke her like other babies do. He seldom cried. Occasionally he gave a great crow of laughter. Nurse Watkins with her brass earrings and heavy moustache called him a cold child.

Out of earshot of others Father Griesepert told Florrie she must sleep with the Cossack again or she would lose him (What do you know? she thought). 'He needs a woman. It is Russian,' (And him never gone a step beyond Scarborough!

she thought. And not knowing the state of his back). Anton had, occasionally, visitors, Russian-speaking, who came and went like shadows. She and the baby sometimes slept on a mattress out by the back door. She lay often listening to the Cossack shouting at invisible companions somewhere she would never know. In the end she told the priest who thought it came from some terrible prison in his past and he was talking to the dead. 'We know *nothing* here, nothing of what goes on in these places. One day we might if we live through this next war.'

'Never another war!' she said. 'Not again.'

She tried to imagine Anton's country. She knew nothing about it but snow and golden onion-topped churches and jewels and stirring cold music and peasants starving and all so blessedly far away. She did not allow herself to imagine Anton's life before he came to her. She would never ask. At night sometimes, to stop his swearing in his sleep, in words she could only guess, she'd pull out a drawer from the press where she kept her clothes and tuck down the baby among them and a chair on either end to keep the cat off and then climb on to the high bed with Anton and wrap herself round him. Sometimes he opened his eyes. They were unseeing and cold. There were no endearments. The sex was ferocious, impersonal, fast. There was no sweetness in it. She didn't conceive again.

Her silent faith in the little boy never lessened. Her trust and love for him was complete. As he grew up she asked no questions as he arrived home later and later off the school train. When he was eleven she stopped taking him to the station.

* * *

For by now Terry was wandering far beyond the chip shop and the band-stand. He was roaming over the sand-dunes down over the miles of white sands towards the estuary and the light-house on the South Gare. On the horizon sometimes celestially, mockingly blue, shining between blue water and blue sky stood the lines of foreign ships waiting for the tide to take them in to Middlesbrough docks. Spasmodically along the sand-dunes the landward sky would blaze with the flaring of the steel-works' furnaces. They blazed and died and blazed again, hung steady, faded slowly. The boy watched.

He was not a rapturous child. The crane-gantry of the Blast Furnaces turned delirious blue at dusk but he was not to be a painter. He noted and considered the paint-brush flicker of flame on the top of each chimney leaning this way and then that but he sat on his pale beach noting them and no more.

He had no idea why he was drawn to the place, the luminous but unfriendly arcs of lacy water running over the sand, the waxy, crunchy black deposits of sea-wrack, slippery and thick, dotted for miles like the droppings of some amphibian, the derelict grey dunes rose up behind him empty except for knives of grey grasses.

There would usually be a few bait-diggers at the water's edge, their feet rhythmically washed by the waves. A lost dog might be somewhere rhythmically barking out of sight.

Sometimes one or two battered home-made sand-yachts skimmed by; only one or two people watching. No children. This was not sand-castle country. No children in this hard place were brought to play by the sea.

But there was a single recurrent figure on the beaches. It was there mostly in winter as it began to get dark: an insect figure stopping and starting, pulling a little cart, bending, stopping, pacing, sometimes shovelling something up, always alone.

After weeks Terry decided it was a man and it was pushing not a cart but a baby's pram. For months he watched without much interest but then he began to look out for the man and wonder who it was.

* * *

One cold afternoon he did his usual rat-run of railway bridge to the back of Muriel Street—he now passed through the room with the bed in it—and found his father's fist stuck out of the blanket towards him grasping a ten shilling note. The wireless crackled on about Czechoslovakia and his father's lips were trying to say something. Terry pocketed the note and said in Russian, 'D'you want tea?'

'Whisky,' said his father.

'It's for the Holy Father. How are you?'

'I'm well.'

'You have a good Russian accent. Are you happy?'

Terry had never been asked this, and did not know.

'I'm going down the beach now, Pa.'

'Why?'

'Don't know.'

The wireless blared out and then faded. They had been first in Muriel Street for a wireless. It stood with a flask of blue spirit beside it. Where had the money come from?

'I'm glad I know Russian,' Terry said.

'How old are you son?'

'Going on twelve.'

Tears trickled out over the Cossack's bony face running diagonally from the eyes to the hollows of the neck and Terry knew that, watching, there was something he should be feeling but didn't know what. He took the money and went to the shop. Let them get on with their lives. He was getting his own.

* * *

He sat down in the dunes facing the sea and soon began to be aware that he was being watched from somewhere behind his left shoulder. Before him the white sands were empty. The sea was creeping forward. He watched the trivial, collapsing waves. The steel-works' candle-chimneys were not yet putting on their evening performance against tonight's anaemic sunset.

There was a cough above him on the high dune.

Turning round, Terry saw the insect-man in an old suit and a bowler hat. The pram hung in front of him, two wheels deep in fine sand that flowed in spreading avalanches down the slope.

'Good afternoon,' said the man. 'Parable-Apse.'

Terry stared.

'And Apse,' he said. 'Parable, Apse and Apse; Solicitors and Commissioners for Oaths.'

Terry stared on.

'My name is Peter Parable, senior partner, and you I believe to be Florrie Benson's boy? I was briefly at school with your mother. I am being obliged to ask for your help.'

Terry's Russian eyes watched on.

'I am a man of principle,' said the creature. 'I am not in the least interested in children. I am not of a perverted disposition. I am able to survive without entanglements and I ask only your immediate assistance in conducting the pram down to the harder level below this dune. Today I have attempted a different route home. It has not been a success.'

The pram was up to its axles in sand.

'When I lean with all my might,' said the tiny man, 'you may assist by tugging at the back wheels, those nearest you. And then if you could sharply—*sharply*—spring to the side I think the vehicle might achieve the beach in an upright position and of its own volition.'

Terry sat a minute considering this new language and then plodded up the dune. He kicked the rear of the pram facing him with a nonchalance close to insolence. Close to hatred. Bloody man.

He soon stopped kicking. He tried to heave the pram

upwards in his arms. He said, 'It's not going to shift. Is't full o' lead? What you got in't?'

'Black gold,' said Parable-Apse. 'Black diamonds. Tiny black—and white—pearls. Now then—again!'

After at least seven heaves Terry yelled and fell to the ground, rolled sideways and watched the pram lumbering and slithering down the slope to tip over on its side upon the beach. A heap of gravelly dirt spilled over the silken sand. Using a shovel as a walking stick Mr. Parable (or Apse) toddled after it, legs far apart, and Terry sat up.

'We have, I fear, a weakened axle,' said the insect-man.

'You'll have to leave it 'ere,' said Terry.

'Oh, it hasn't come to that. Perhaps we should empty it completely, scatter the load with simple sand and, later, return.'

Terry regarded the heap of dirt.

'And if, boy, you would carry the broken wheel and we were to push the rest of it home, then you could take tea with me.'

Terry thought, Here we go and said, 'Is't far?'

'Not at all.' The man was busy covering up the mound of black gold, scratching the last of the dirt from the pram. He snapped off the damaged wheel, handed it to the boy and fell flat on his face.

'Oh, God,' said Terry, hauling him up. ''ere. Gis 'ere. Give over. Tek't wheel. Where we goin'?'

They paraded over the sandy path behind the dunes, across the golf-links, somehow got themselves over a wooden stile watched by a lonely yellow house with empty windows. They followed a track that put them out into a street of squat one-storey houses Terry had not seen before, the long, low street of the old fishing village built before the industries came, before the ironstone chimney and the foreign workers and the chemicals and the flames. The sandstone dwellings had midget doors and windows like houses for elves. Mr. Parable-Apse,

Commissioner for Oaths, let them both in to one of these houses, leaving the pram outside, and inside they walked down a long, low tunnel of a rabbit-warren-like passage-way into a kitchen scrubbed clean. Some of Mr. Parable-Apse's under-clothing hung airing from a contraption of ropes and wooden bars overhead. He lit a hazy, beautiful gas-light on a bracket, crossed to the coal fire, flourished a poker and flung a shovel-ful of glittering, hard dirt, like jet, into the flames. The coal fire in the grate blazed up, hot and brilliant.

'What is't?' asked Terry.

'Sea-coal. *Washed*, of course. I wash it in a bath in my yard several times a week. Out of office hours of course, and never on the Lord's Day. In my back yard I have a pump with clear, unbounded water that cleanses like the mercy of God. The sea-coal's what washes off the ships, you know. In the estuary. Sea-coal is a bonus. Clean and beautiful, sweet-smelling, effective and *free*. Your mother should market it.'

'She has enough to do,' said Terry.

'So I hear. But you haven't yet, my boy. I expect you are meant to leave school shortly and slave at The Works? Oh, my dear boy! Sweeping a road 'til the end of your life.'

'They need the money.'

'You could begin now, working casually for me. While you are waiting. I make money. I have never had any difficulty there. We could expand across this world. Apse and Benson. In the name of the Lord, of course.'

Apse, Benson and God, thought Terry. He said, 'But I'll have to go full time to The Works. For the money.'

Apse—or Parable—was washing his hands at the shallow stone sink, drying carefully between his fingers.

'How old did you say? Ah yes. I remember the visit of the Cossacks to the Gas Works though, of course, I was unable to attend. A circus is one of the devil's plays. There is a rumour abroad—tell me, what is your name?—that you are particularly clever. Your intelligence is above these parts. You might bring your intelligence to us. Come in with me as a lawyer. It could be arranged. It is called 'Doing your articles'—a ridiculous and medieval concept—but a solicitor's work is the top of the world.'

('This man's a loony!')

'And even now,' said Parable-Apse, 'Think of Christian commerce. Sea-coal. It is your family business.'

'You shut up,' said Terry. 'Stop looking down on my mother.'

'Oh never! Never! Known her since she was born. Since her mother put her in long drawers. I loved her.'

'My Dad loves her and nowt to do wi' frills. They don't speak now, me Dad and Mam, but it's only because of his shame. Shame at being crippled and nobody caring. And being lost.'

'He talks to you?'

'Nay—never! We's beyond talk. We talk his language together less and less. He grabs me wrist as I pass the bed. Like a torturer but it's himself 'e's torturing.'

'Why does he do that?'

'There's always money under his fingers. Tight up in the palm. He needs whisky. The Mam don't know. Nurse Watkins does. She's foreign, too. He pushes the bottle under his mattress. When it's empty. I've seen it going home in her leather bag with the washing. The money must come from the Holy Father. How do I know? He's beginning to need more and more.'

He was dizzy with revelation. Revelation even to himself. None of this had emerged as words before. Not even thoughts.

'A man comes,' said Terry. 'Mam don't know. A foreign man. Talking Russian—or summat like it. When nobody's in.' He burst into tears. 'Maybe I dream it.'

Parable-Apse, having dried his coal-dusted hands on a clean tea-towel, sat down by the sea-coal fire and speared a tea-cake on the end of a brass toasting fork. The medallion on the toasting fork was some sort of jack-ass or demon, or sunburst god. 'How wonderful the world is,' said Parable-Apse.

The fire blazed bright and the tea-cake toasted.

'We must get him vodka,' said Parable-Apse. 'It does not taint the breath. Goodbye. It is more than time you went home. Take the tea-cake with you. I will butter it. I shall expect you to relish it.'

On the doorstep Terry heard him bolting the door on the inside. They sounded like the bolts of a strong-room. 'Loopy,' he thought. 'Silly old stick.'

* * *

He didn't go again to the beach that week. He wandered to the nasty little shops in the new town and the new Palace Cinema. He had a bit of pocket money and went in and asked for vodka at the Lobster Inn. He was thrown out. He wanted a girl to tell this to. It surprised him. The girls at his school sniggered and didn't wash much. They hung about outside the cinema. One or two had painted their mouths bright red. You could get a tube of it at Woolworths for sixpence. They shouted to him to come join them, but he didn't stop. He dawdled home.

CHAPTER 9

The headmaster of Terry's school did not live on the premises or go in daily on the train. He lived several miles inland on the moors. He was a healthy man and often pedalled in to Herringfleet on a bicycle with a basket on the front stuffed full of exercise books corrected the night before, for he was a teacher as well as a headmaster.

He and the bike made for the Herringfleet beaches—he always checked the tide-tables—and, dependent on the condition of the sand—he walked or rode the six miles to school, thinking deeply. He always wore a stiff white riding mac with a broad belt and a brown felt homburg hat. Sometimes he had to walk beside his bike when the sands were soft, sometimes push it hard, but he was always very upright and to his chagrin rather overweight. There were little air-holes of brass let in to the mac under the arms for ventilation. Despite his healthy, exhausting regime he was a putty-faced man who never smiled. It was rumoured that there was a wife somewhere and he had a son at the school who got himself there on the train like most of them and home again by his wits. A clever, little younger boy. Fred. Terry liked him.

On the morning beaches the headmaster (a Mr. Smith) often came upon Peter Parable doing an early sea-coal stint before going to his solicitor's office. They nodded at each other, Parable's gaze on the black ripples in the sand left by the tide. Smith would briskly nod and pass by, growing smaller and smaller until he was a dot disappearing up the path that led to

his school assembly and the toil of the term. Smith and Parable
had been at the school together as boys but hadn't cared much
for each other. They had only their cleverness in common.
Now they never talked.

That summer Parable began to watch Smith's straight back
diminishing away from him. He noted the little eyelet holes of
the mac and the plumpness and the rather desperate marching
rhythm. Even if he was on the bike Mr. Smith always looked
tired. Better hurry up, thought Parable. Smith, who knew that
he was being watched, also knew that at some point he was
going to be asked for something.

One beautiful, still morning Parable shouted out, 'Smith!'

Smith stopped the bike and placed both feet on the sand
but didn't turn his head. 'What is it, man? Hurry up. I'll be
late.'

'There's something you have to do. At once.'

'Indeed?' (What does Parable do at once or even slowly?
Plays on the beach.)

'You have a boy at school who in my professional opinion—
and Opinions are my stock-in-trade as a lawyer—is remarkable. They're going to put him in The Works when he leaves
you next year and you have to stop it. He must go to the university. He already verges on the phenomenal. I've begun to
play chess with him. We debate. He has an interesting foreign
father. Rather broken up.'

'You mean Florrie Benson's boy?'

'And—?'

'They need his wages. Sooner the better. It's a bad business
there. She can't go on.'

'She'll try. We both know her.'

'How could they afford a school until he's university age?'

'There are scholarships. We each got one.'

'We had better parents.'

'I won't have that,' shouted Parable after him across the sand, 'You have a boy yourself who's clever. I bet he'll be spared The Works.'

An hour later at the end of School Assembly and prayers Smith paused for a long minute before clanging the hand-bell that sent the rabble of Teesside to their class-rooms and announced that he wanted Terry Benson in his study.

'Terry Njinsky? Venetski? Benson? A letter for you to take home.'

Terry, in some dream-scape, was kicked awake by his neigh- bours and looked about him. ('What you done, Terry?' 'Only tried getting vodka for me Dad.' 'What—nickin'?' 'Nah— cash.') A new respect for the already-respected Terry ran down the line.

Smith surveyed the crowd of spotty children, all thin. Grey faces. Poor. All underfed. Terry whatsname—Benson's white- gold hair and healthy face shone amongst them (It's said she gets them tripe). We'll get that hair cut, Smith thought. Start at the top. I'll write to the father.

'Take a letter down now, Miss Thompson,' he said back in his office.

'I'm not sure Florrie Benson can read,' said the secretary. 'Me Mam said she was useless at school. And the father's a cripple and only talks Russian. He's a retired Russian spy.'

* * *

The letter was typed, nevertheless, that day and sat waiting for Terry to collect and take home. At the end of the afternoon the headmaster, Smith, came in and pointed at it and said, 'Letter, Miss Thompson?'

'Oh,' she said, 'He never came. I'll tek it. I know where he lives, down Herringfleet. On my way home.'

'No,' said Smith, 'I'll drop it in. I can take the bike that way. Say nothing to the boy. He's probably been trying all day to forget it. I'll bike along the sand.'

'You tired, Sir?'

'Certainly not,' he said, pulling on the ventilated mackintosh that made him paler still. 'Certainly not! Box on.'

By tea-time, Florrie cooking brains and hearts on a skillet, the letter was lying across the room on the door-mat. The Odessan was having a better day and was in a chair. His back was to the door, but he sensed the letter. He said, 'We have a letter. I heard a bicycle and a man cough. Pick it up, will you, Florrie?'

'No,' said Florrie adding dripping, peeling potatoes.

'Then I'll wait for Terry to do it. Where is he?'

'It may not be for you,' she said. 'The last one was to me. And what came o'*that*?'

* * *

Years before there had come a letter on the mat that she remembered now like excrement brought in on a shoe. It was a letter in a thick cream envelope written in an operatic hand in purple ink.

In those days the situation at No. 9 Muriel Street was still an interesting mystery in Herringfleet. Most people kept themselves at a distance. People crammed together in mean streets are not always in and out of each other's houses.

The letter had been sent without a stamp and delivered 'By Hand'. It said so in the top, left-hand corner. The letter-paper inside was the colour of pale baked-custard and thick as cloth.

Dear Mrs. Vet(scrawl)y, it had said, 'I would be so delighted if you would bring your little boy to a fireworks party—with supper, of course—on November 5th for Guy Fawkes'

Celebrations at The Towers. A number of local children will be coming and we hope to give them a lasting and happy experience. Five o' Clock P.M. until 8 P.M. Warm coats and mittens. Sincerely yours. Veronica Fondle.'

'She has asked me to a party,' Florrie said. 'Me and Terry.' Anton watched her blush and smile and thought how young she was. How beautiful. 'With Terence,' she said. 'Our Terence. For Guy Fawkes.' She gazed at the letter. 'It's to be a supper—unless she means we take our supper?—and at *night*!'

'What,' he asked, 'is Guy Forks?'

'We burn a model of him every year. For hundreds of years. Because he once tried to burn down the Parliament in London.'

The Odessan considered this.

'But we can't go. I haven't any clothes.'

He said, 'It just says a warm coat and mittens. You have your better coat and we can get mittens.'

'I think that means only the children. The mothers will be in furs.'

'Here, in Herringfleet?' said Anton and at once wrote the acceptance in fine copperplate on a card they found in an old prayer book. Nurse Watkins brought an envelope and took it round to the local private school, The Towers, where Veronica Fondle was the headmaster's wife.

On the party day Terence, then not yet four, was scrubbed, polished and groomed but then became recalcitrant and unenthusiastic. He lay on his face on the floor and drummed his feet. When his mother walked in from the bath-house where she had been dressing, he roared and hid under his father's bed, for this was a woman unknown. The lace on her hat (Nurse Watkins' cousin's) stood up around her head with black velvet ribbons enmeshed. Her cloth coat Nurse Watkins had enriched with a nest of red fox tail bundles round her throat. Beneath the chin, the vixen's face clasped the tails in its yellow teeth. Poppies swayed about round the black straw hat brim. Her shoes were Nurse Watkins' mother's brogues worn on honeymoon in Whitby before the First World War, and real leather.

'You're meant to wear the veil tight against the face, like Greta Garbo, and tied round the back with the black ribbon, Florrie,' said Nurse Watkins, shushing Terry on her knee.

'I'll never get it off.'

'You're not meant to get it off.'

'Then how do I drink tea?'

Even Nurse Watkins didn't know this.

The veil was left to float around the poppies. Anton said suddenly, 'How beautiful you are,' and Florrie disappeared out the back.

She came back saying that Nurse Watkins was to go instead of her and Terry kicked out at the table leg while Anton picked up the book on Kant he'd been reading which Florrie had ordered for him from the Public Library. All he said was, 'Go!'

So outside over the railway bridge from Muriel Street the gas lights inside their glass lanterns were beginning to show blue as mother and son set off hand in hand.

There was no driveway up to The Towers just three wide, shallow steps, a big oak door with circles of wrought-iron leaves and a polished brass plate alongside saying The Towers, Headmaster, HAROLD FONDLE M.A. OXON. A chain hung down. Florrie picked up Terry and held him tight. Terry was in the full school uniform of Nurse Watkins' nephew who went to a paying Kindergarten. He had had his first hair-cut. As Florrie stood miserably beside the chain the child shouted, 'Me, me!' and she let him drag it down. Far inside the house came a tinny clinking.

Florrie knew that something was now about to go wrong.

Terry on her shoulder—rather heavy—seemed to be transfixed with terror by both the sound of the bell and the poppies in the hat. She set him down and clutched his hand. When the door opened she thought she might faint. The colours and heat within, the noise and laughter, the smell of rich food and spiced fruit and sweet drinks, the rasping whiff of gunpowder, the snap of crackers, the squealing of children running madly, waving sparkling, spitting lighted things into each other's faces. The girls were all in heavy jerseys and gaiters with button boots, the boys in corduroy and mufflers. Several wore the tartan kilt. Across the entrance hall, propped against a carved fireplace, leaned a huge stuffed man with a grinning mask for a face and straw tufts coming out of his ears. He was waiting to be burned.

The maid who had answered the door however was only Bessy Bell, the Gypsy girl who'd known Florrie since school. 'Eh, Florrie!' she said. ''Ere. I'll tek Terry in.'

'I'll tek 'im in meself, Bessie.'

'No, it's just to be 'im,' said Bessie, 'She said.'

'*Marvellous*,' cried a large woman, wearing a musquash coat, square shouldered, bearing down on them in the porch. 'You found your way then Mrs. Van—Van Erskine? *Splendid*. We are short of *boys*.'

Behind the woman a door stood open upon a glittering dining room, a gleam of white cloth and shiny glasses. Silver cakestands. Three-tiered, laden plates.

Then Florrie was out again on the steps alone.

* * *

She wondered if she was meant to sit there until it was eight o' clock. Three hours. It was getting quite dark already. And cold.

She wasn't going home, though. *Oh*, no! Nurse Watkins

must never know. But there was nobody she knew round here to call in on. Especially dressed like this. There was the refreshment room over the station but the sandwiches were all curled up under glass and anyway she'd no money. And it might be closed. Father Griesepert? His church down by the beach would be locked up. It was a creepy place anyway. In the Presbytery he'd be drowsing now all by himself, alone with his whisky and his thoughts about purity. She'd never gone to him—nor he to her—even when her parents were dying.

The mist was thickening outside the ironwork porch of The Towers and she longed suddenly for her parents. Her father had once been a powerful, forceful, political man. Oh, she wanted a man. A man who stood straight and strong, who'd have brought the child here instead of her and looked round to see if the place was good enough. She folded herself down on the top step and began to disentangle the veil from the vixen's teeth.

She wondered what Terry was doing.

If he needed the you-know-what, would he ask?

He still had to be helped with buttons. He'd not long finished with the chamber-pot. She often went with him down the privy in the yard especially in the dark. All those other children! Shouting and dancing about with the flaming wires. They were all so much older. Why ever had Terry been invited?

He wouldn't be crying though. Terry never cried.

But, well, he might just be. He might be crying now. Would they notice him? Would they, any of them have the gump to think he might never before have been out in the dark? Would they look after him around the bonfire? Would he scream when he saw the man burning? Would they care?

That daft Bessie. No help there. Fourpence in the shilling. And she'd seen other people. All their proud horse-faced nannies in that hall. Eyebrows raised. She'd known Anton was wrong about the kids all being in uniform. Maybe in his country. Not here. Except if it was a sailor-suit and where would she get a sailor-suit? He's not Princess Margaret Rose in London.

They might be being unkind and laughing at him. At this moment he might be screaming with fear. She'd seen his face as they grabbed him and carried him away. They all said he was advanced. Very, very, very clever—. But she'd seen his solemn face—.

He thinks I have left him and he won't see me again. Fear blazed to inferno and she scrambled from the step through a laurel border and round to the back of the house to its rows of lighted windows and doors and the waiting bonfire. She stepped into a flower-bed and looked into a long room full of children sitting round a banquet.

It was a Christmas card of pink and gold and scattered with glitter. There were cart-wheels of cakes, pyramids of sweets and fruit. Nannies in dark blue dresses stood behind almost every child's chair talking to each other out of the sides of their mouths but never taking their eyes off their charges. Iron-masters' children. The other side of the tracks. She couldn't see Terry.

One Nannie was pressing a rather torpid child into a high chair facing Florence. All the children were being firmly controlled. They'll not forget the rules, these ones, she thought. There'll be no fight left in them. She knew that this stuff wasn't for Terry. Where was he?

She sensed an event. A few children were being restrained from banging spoons on the table-cloth and a tall iced cake was being carried in by a heavy smiling man who gripped a pipe between his teeth. Mr. HAROLD FONDLE, OXON! A maid came and began to cut the cake. Where, where was Terry?

Then she saw him. He was so close to her that she could have stretched to touch him but for the glass in the long window. He had his back to her. With his newly cut hair he looked like a tiny man. In both hands he held a glass of orange juice.

He was drinking from it. He was lifting it up in the air. He was bending backwards. Then he slid off his chair and turned towards the window and she stepped back. And, oh, he was beginning to cry!

And there was blood on his face and there was a jagged arc in the glass and on his hand and he was spitting out blood. He had swallowed glass!

She began to beat her fists against the window as first one person and then another noticed that there was a crisis. Shouting and consternation surged among the nannies. One gave Terry a savage shake and glass shot across the room. Terry stopped crying and grinned and Mrs. Veronica Fondle came swanning up like a barge at sunset.

Through the window Florrie heard her pea-hen cry that the child was probably only used to mugs, All well. All well.

But Florrie was by now at the front door again hanging on the bell chain, dragging it up and down and when Bessie answered she was across the hall and into the dining room to see Terry composedly eating porridge which some plumed assistant was spooning in to him. Mrs. Fondle in her furs stood nearby, en route to the garden where the bonfire was being lit. Smoke and one crackling flame. 'Oh! Aha! Oh—Mrs. *Verminsky*!' (She was laughing) 'He took a *bite* from a *glass*! But *please* don't worry. Nannie has counted all the bits and we have most of them. Boys tend to do this more than girls. We give them *porridge* just in case. Wonderful in the intestines—.'

Florrie seized the child in her arms as his mouth opened for more porridge. He looked at his mother and began to cry again.

'There are worse things we have to face than glass.' Mr. Harold Fondle strode by, his arms spiky with rockets, towards the bonfire.

'Well, he's coming home with me now,' said Florrie. 'I've had enough.'

* * *

'But however did she *know*?' Veronica Fondle called across to her husband that night in their avant-garde twin-bedded room. Outside, the bonfire was dowsed and ashy, the straw man a few fragments of rags and dust. 'She must have been watching through the window. Crept into the garden. Peeping in at us!'

'Perhaps we should have invited her in to the party,' said Fondle. 'He's very young.'

'Oh, I think not. There are limits.'

'I have my reasons you know for keeping an eye on that boy. He could become one of my stars.'

'So you say. Look, he's perfectly all right. He'd eaten an enormous tea before that orange juice. He wasn't worried when his mother came barging in.'

'Well, his mother was. Very worried.'

They laughed as they turned off their individual bedside lights, like people in a dance routine. Click, then click.

'Oh, and darling,' she said in the dark. 'The *hat*!'

'Do you know,' he said from the other bed, 'I thought the hat was rather fine.'

PART THREE

Last Friends

When Fiscal-Smith's train reached Waterloo after the dreadful morning in Dorset he found himself reluctant for some reason to continue his journey to King's Cross and then on to the North.

He was, for one thing, not exactly expected at home. He had intimated that he had been invited to stay for some time with old friends. And, also, he was now feeling distinctly unwell.

Already it had been a long morning for a man of his advanced years: up at 5 A.M. in the Dorset rain to examine a building half a mile away, said to be burnt out and which had turned out to be in perfect condition. Then that idiocy with Dulcie, locked alone with her inside the parish church and having to ring the bells for rescue. And so on.

And then Dulcie herself. Distinctly unwelcoming. And the awful daughter. And the glaring grandson. Sometimes, he thought, one should take a long, hard look at old friends. Like old clothes in a cupboard, there comes the moment to examine for moth. Perhaps throw them out and forget them. Yes.

But he had been able to make his mark with the delightful, new village family who had bought Veneering's pile, his frightful Gormenghast on the hill. Fiscal-Smith would rather like to keep his oar in there. He would be pleased to have an open invitation to sleep in Veneering's old house, tell these new people about their predecessor. Though maybe not everything about him.

Not that Veneering himself had ever once invited him there.

Not even after that ridiculous lunch of Dulcie's years ago, where all the guests were senile except himself and that boy and that desolate Carer. Like lunch in a care-home. Turned out in the rain. Had had to walk to the station on that occasion. Walk! Couldn't do it now. Taxi would have cost three pounds even then. God knows how much now.

But there wouldn't be much chance of making his mark with the new people either. Very casual manners these days. And Dulcie had taken against him. She'd always been a funny fish. Probably never see her again. Probably never see any of them again. Oh, well. End of it all.

At Waterloo he burrowed for his old man's bus-pass and stood for a bus that crossed the bridge and turned towards the Temple. Taxi fares prohibitive and the drivers not pleasant any more. Mostly Polish immigrants. Very haughty. One had told him lately how the Poles had saved us in the War and then added, 'Now we're saving you for the second time. We *work*.' He had not replied. For the second day running Fiscal-Smith made for the Strand and the Inns of Court.

Only twenty-four hours since the bell was tolling for Old Filth.

Different scene now. Earlier in the day.

Streams of black gowns pouring about, papers flapping, lap-tops gleaming, wigs on rakish, neck-bands flopping in the breeze. Home, he thought, I am home and young again. Bugger Dorset and the living dead.

And it was lunch time. I'll go to lunch at the Inn. They'll remember me. It can't be more than ten years. Say fifteen. And it's free. I am a life member, A Bencher—of this Inn.

Inner Temple Hall was roaring as he used his old key to let himself in (watch-chain). Then up the stairs. He pushed at the swing doors to the Hall. Hundreds of them inside, hundreds! Yelling! How much bigger they all are than we were. No rationing now. What a size some of them—. Sitting down to plates of what looks like excellent hot food. Stacks of it. Fiscal-Smith had not been offered breakfast. Only that watery tea.

Fiscal-Smith set down his substantial over-night valise and went to pee. No gentleman now, he thought, ever makes use of the facilities on British Rail. So sad. There were once towels even in third class. The W.Cs. now look like oil-drums. They can trap you inside them. Enough of that for one day.

Fiscal-Smith tidied himself up and made for the dining-hall, and was stopped on the threshold. 'Yes, sir? May we help?'

'Fiscal-Smith.'

'Are you a member of this Inn, sir?'

He tried a withering look.

'Bencher. For more than half a century. I am from the North. I am seldom here.'

'We may have to ask you to pay, sir.'

As he turned the colour of damson jam someone called to him from the High Table where senior Silks and judges were leaning about like a da Vinci frieze. Sharks, whales, porpoises above the ocean floor. Scarcely registering the shoals of minnows in the waters below but not near them.

'Fiscal-Smith! Good God! Over here, over here. Excellent!' and he felt at once much better.

'Been staying with old Pastry Willy's widow in Dorset. Invited me back after Filth's do yesterday. Very old friends of course.'

Nobody seemed to have heard of Pastry Willy.

'Good do, I thought,' said the oldest of the great fish. Touching. Very well-attended, considering his age. Weren't you a particular friend?'

Fiscal-Smith sat down, comforted. Roast pork, vegetables with nuts in, gravy and apple sauce were put before him and he was asked if he would like a glass of wine.

'Extraordinary,' he told a childish-looking Silk beside him. 'When I was starting out and we came to lunch here it was bread and cheese and soup and beer. And free. We were thinner, too. And more awake perhaps in the court in the afternoons.'

'During the War?'

'Afterwards. Just after. Place here all dust you know. Direct hit. First made me think there might be a future in Building Contracts. Early in the War I don't think there was any lunch at all. But I was still at school then.'

'Really? Were you? Where were you?'

'Oh, in the north. I'm Catholic you know. Roman Catholic.'

'Not much in the way of work in those days, I hear?'

'No. Not for years after the War,' said Fiscal-Smith. 'Fighting was passé. We'd lost the taste for it. So poor we washed our shirts and bands ourselves. Fourpence at the laundry. We bought this new stuff—detergent. 'Dreft' it was called. And a Dolly Blue. Starched them too. Too poor for wives. Tramped the streets in our de-mob suits looking for Chambers.'

'It's said that even Filth and Veneering couldn't get Chambers. Did they hate each other from the start? Did you know them then?'

'I knew Veneering from being eight years old.'

'Yet nobody ever *really* knew him—we understand?'

Fiscal-Smith kept a conceited silence.

At length he said, 'I was Veneering's oldest friend on earth.'

Then he added, seeing a suggestion of Veneering's sour old man's face somewhere up in the repaired rafters of the Great Hall, 'He was much cleverer than I was of course. So was Old Feathers—they called him Old Filth. Both wonderful brains.'

'So,' someone eating apple-crumble and custard, called from down the table, 'So we understand. One wonders why they stuck so long with the Construction Law. Charismatic, well-educated, intellectuals. Double Firsts. A life-time writing building contracts and a twilight of editing Hudson. No politics. No crime. No international high-lights.

'I can tell you why.'

Fiscal-Smith stretched his short—very old—legs under the table, legs that earlier that day had been disguised under a choir-boy's cassock. 'I was present. They made a joint decision. It occurred in the Brighton County Court. I was Veneering's unpaid pupil and I'd gone down with him there to observe. It was a gross indecency case.'

'Yes,' said the apple-crumble eater, 'Can't see Old Filth distinguishing himself there. Veneering—possibly. More worldly man. And merrier. Bit of a clown.'

'None of us was merry that day,' said Fiscal-Smith. 'All of us fairly depressed. We went to Brighton of course by train—none of us had a car. Train called The Brighton Belle. Beautiful train. Ran every hour on the hour. Pink linen table-cloths and table lamps even in the Second Class which I think was still called Third. What the first class was like—. Maybe solid silver and bits of parsley on the sandwiches—I don't know. Veneering and I sat at one table and aristocratic Filth sat as far away as possible from both of us at another, with his back to us, fountain-pen poised. Small glass of dry sherry. Filth and Veneering hadn't then exactly quarrelled. It was long before the infidelity. Long before Filth marrying Betty. Or perhaps that is all forgotten now? It was just something brewing. Inexplicable. Witch's brew. Or simple distaste.'

'Ah, it happens,' said the apple-crumble eater.

'Well, the train was late. Stood still God knows how long. Fizzing steam. Could hear people cough. No information of course. No tannoys then. We stuck on the line for an hour, took two taxis to the Brighton County Court from the station, arrived after mid-day. Furious judge. Sent us to the back of the queue. Didn't get on till after three o' clock. Filth prosecuting, Veneering for the defence.'

'Gross indecency?'

'Yes. Ridiculous. Occurred in a circus.'

'What, with animals? Bestiality?'

'No. Lion-tamer's apprentice.'

'You're not making this up, Fiscal-Smith?'

'No. Lump of a lad. Retarded. Maybe Down's Syndrome. Employed most of his time shovelling dung. Dirty-looking child. He'd been going round during the performances under the tiers of seats in the Big Top, and tickling the private parts of women in the audience with a long straw. Up through the slats.'

'You are making this up!'

'No. Tickle-tickle. They would all start wriggling and scratching. All round the tiers like a Mexican wave. In those days, you know, ladies' tights hadn't been invented (Yes thank you. I will. The claret is still excellent) and there were all these pale pink arcs of skin between the stocking-tops and the knickers. Schoolgirls, I believe, used to call the gaps 'smiles' or 'sights'.

'Well, the lion-tamer's boy went along beneath the rows tickling all the smiles and you should have heard the pristine Filth going on about him. "Obscene", "Depraved" etc. and the judge nodding his head. Veneering and I wriggling about, at first trying not to laugh. Shaking the papers about. "Perverted." Then Veneering just slammed down the Brief and walked out.'

'What! Out of Court? He walked out of *Court*!'

'Yes. Slam, bang up the aisle, through the swing doors and out. Filth had risen to his feet, turned and watched him go. Closed his eyes as if the King had died. And nobody said a word.'

'So, I thought I'd better go and find him. I asked for permission and ran out. Judge said nothing. Looked struck by lightning. "Unheard of." "Unbelievable." "Taken ill?" etc. whispered around. I bowed, and then ran and found Veneering dragging on a cigarette in the corridor. I said—and by the way Filth's solicitor, the dwarf, had appeared from somewhere—

'Yes. The Albert Ross. Dodgy—.'

'Veneering was shouting, "Bloody, pompous, fucking toffs."

Never been in the world—I happened to know that Veneering had a penchant for circuses—and he thundered back into court—no excuses—and put up a great performance about what fools we were making of ourselves. Wastage of court's time. Harmless prank. Bleak life in the circus. Boy orphaned. Neglected. Confused. Unloved. Half-starved.

But that boy got three months. *Three months*! Filth standing there, Holy Moses. Very pleased with himself. And we all paraded out except for the lion-tamer's boy who was taken to the Black Maria in hand-cuffs.'

'Unbelievable! When was this?'

'Well—look it up. It's in the statute book. Just after the War.'

'I suppose a century before it would have been a hanging.'

'A century before,' Fiscal-Smith said, 'it would not have come to court at all. Audience would have dealt with it on site.'

'Thrown him to the lions,' said the apple-crumble Lord.

'Well, anyway—this is an excellent cheese—on the way home Veneering said to me—we'd treated ourselves to a small gin and orange—"That's settled it, Fiscal-Smith. I don't think I've much of a future in Crime. I'm going for the Commercial Bar." I told him that he'd probably find Old Filth there too. Filth may have won but he was way out of his depth with circuses. And easily shocked. Veneering said, "Well, I suppose that will have to be endured."

After the coffee, Fiscal-Smith made for the London Underground feeling greatly restored. Yet as the tube rattled along to King's Cross, everybody sitting blank and dreary staring at their thoughts, his good-humour ebbed. It was now mid-afternoon.

In the Flying Scotsman, heading North—not the old patrician Flying Scotsman but a flashy lowlander calling itself so—the seats, his being one of the last free, were lumpy and small.

The train was cold. In two other seats at the small table for four there were two lap-tops plugged in and hard at work. In the fourth seat was an unwashed young man rhythmically nodding his head, an intrusive metallic hissing emanating from the machinery in his ears. The journey was to take three hours, the corridor packed solid towards the Buffet and a cup of tea. No drinks' trolley. Where had he put his over-night case? The luggage rack was too narrow for anything but a brief-case or a coat. He was wishing for a coat. A coat on his back. He was really cold now. Actually, he was shivering.

Nobody spoke. Nobody smiled. Many coughed. Above the perpetual restless shuffling noises of the lap-tops, raucous, overhead messages about where the train was going and where it would stop and which would be the next station-stop quacked out every few minutes. Ding-dong signals shouted into mobile phones up and down the coach had one loud universal message: that their owner was expecting to be met by a car at his destination.

Met. Fiscal-Smith had made no arrangements to be met at Darlington. He was slipping. Why ever had he wasted all that time telling those old bores on the Bench about the lion-tamer's apprentice of over sixty years ago? Shouldn't drink at lunch-time. Broken the life-time rule of his profession. Long day. Those church vestments! That time with Susan on Tisbury station telling her about Veneering. Sulky Sue. Feeling hot now. And cold. Not so young as I was. Ninety in a few years. Ye gods!

At York many alighted but many more struggled aboard. 'You OK, chum?' asked a Jamaican who was replacing the man with the electronic ears. Still strange to see a Jamaican up north. Like Jamaicans. Good case there once. Six months sunlight. Veneering's junior. Old Mona Hotel outside Kingston. Sunsets. Lizards. Rum and pineapple. Case about a gigantic drain. Old Princess Royal there. Could she drink gin! Wouldn't go to bed. All her ladies-in-waiting asleep on their feet. Queen Mother? Blue eyes. Blue as Lady Mountbatten's. Now, *there* was a—. Should have told those babes in arms at the Inner Temple how the Queen Mother once came to dinner in Lincoln's Inn and beamed round and said, 'What a lot of Darkies.'

I really do feel rather ill.

At Darlington he clambered out, the Jamaican helping with his bag, coming along the platform with him, trying to find someone to give the old guy a hand.

No-one. Dark night.

He tramped the long platform, down the steps and through the tunnel of white glazed brick. Contemptuously—no *contemporary*—with Stevenson probably. Graffiti. Strange faces in the shadows. Urine-smells. On the empty taxi-rank he waited, feeling his forehead. It was on fire.

'*Where?*' asked the taxi driver twenty minutes later. 'Yarm? It's ten miles!'

'The Judges Hotel.'

'I doubt it's going to be open this time of night. It's dark.'

'I can't get to my own house tonight, it's up on the moor. On my grouse moor, actually.'

'They'll have to fly you in then. I'm not risking that road up. Come on then, mister, hop in. We'll try the Hanging Judges. I'll give them a bell.'

'I was ringing church bells this morning at half-past five,' Fiscal-Smith told him, and thought, I'm wandering. This day is a feverish dream. Not good. Lived too long.

But through the oak door of what had once been the very comfortable Assize-Court lodging for itinerant judges, a woman in disarray was coming running, shouting and waving a torch.

'Whatever time o' night d'you call this, Fred? Why din't yer book in? Yes, there's a bed and yes you can have the downstairs Sir Edward had with the gold-fish and the bears. Quick, you're

not well. Top and tail wash while I find you a hot-water bottle.
I'll bring you a tray to bed. At your age! Should be ashamed.
A man with a good brain—except for living in that daft place
up the hill. Hot milk and aspirins. No—no whisky. You're
shaking. It'll be the bird flu and stress. Doctor first thing
tomorrow. I looked down the *Telegraph* list of folk at Sir
Edward's memorial service and first thing I thought, Now
then, did he tek his coat? I meant you.'

Deep in good wool blankets—none of your duvets—roast-
ing with two hot-water bottles, fore and aft—and a tray across
his stomach (ham sandwiches which he did not want) Fiscal-
Smith sank into fitful sleep. Old Filth had slept in this bed.
What's left of him now in Malayan swamp? Gold-fish bubbling. Terrible teddy bears. Queer massage machine for feet.
Chamber pot! *Chamber-pot!* Like the Cossack and Muriel
Street. 'Please do not feed the fish.' 'Click here for music'. No,
no. Silence in court.

Someone was switching things off. Covering him with an
extra blanket. Talking about him, but just to herself. Didn't
have to answer. North is a better country.

* * *

Did I really tell them about that case? The ladies' parted
legs? The 'smiles'? Personally never seen such things.
Wouldn't want to. Dulcie. Very long day. Poor Veneering dead
on Malta! Never thought ahead. None of us.

I shall probably die now. Bugger the Temple, The Knights
Templar.

What's left of them will have to come up here to mine. Do
them good.

CHAPTER 11

About ten years after the Guy Fawkes Party, London blazing and bombardment of cities all over the country, Terry Venetski, safe from the Works, and now one of Mr. Fondle's elite, came home from school at The Towers one day to No. 9 Muriel Street carrying a third letter to his parents, formally addressed and sealed.

He was taller now than either of them, broader and stronger. His hair was still extraordinary, wild and long, and white gold, and he had the same alert charm as the baby born nearly fourteen years ago after the Russian circus came to town. The letter said:

"In view of hostilities in the south of the country and the attacks on our ports and industrial centres I and the Governors of my School, The Towers, are asking for parents' views on its evacuation to Canada in September.

A magnificent newly-built cruise-liner recently completed in India, *The City of Benares*, has generously been put at our disposal by the government, mostly for London children rendered homeless by the Blitz. There are berths for two hundred children, all of whom will travel free. There are also private passengers, trained voluntary foster-parents for the journey, excellent fostering promised for the time in Canada, however long this may be.

The ship is luxuriously appointed with excellent food, entertainments and comforts. The stewards are highly-trained, and love children. They almost all come from the city of Benares in

India. All are ready for torpedo attacks and the ship will of course be escorted by corvettes of the Royal Navy. Mrs. Fondle will be accompanying us and we plan to remain in Canada for the duration of the war.

Nothing can be agreed upon unless all parents support the evacuation. *We ask for an immediate reply*. Signed HAROLD FONDLE, M.A. OXON."

Terry tossed the letter upon the bed as he came in, then went out again and down to the Palace Cinema where he met up with a waiting girl and they went into the back row, supposedly to watch Deanna Durbin in *A Hundred Men and a Girl*.

The Cossack lay on his bed. He held the letter unopened in his hand for an hour.

Later Peter Parable came in. He and the Odessan read the letter.

The Odessan said, 'This will be the end of Florrie.'

'Send her with him. I have money,' said Parable.

'She'd not leave me. And no-one will take me to Canada.'

Before long Florrie arrived, warm and clean from the sand-stone bath-house and drying her soft hair. She stopped and looked at them.

'What's this then?'

She took the letter and after reading it slowly put it down again on the bed. She filled the kettle and set it to boil. She said, 'I'm glad we somehow got that wireless in. It's terrible you know in London.'

'They'll be up here next,' said the Odessan. 'You must move in with us, Peter Parable. They'll not let you live on by the shore.'

'Aye,' said Florrie, 'You can have his room. He'd best go, Anton.'

All three, all thinking that she never spoke Anton's name in public, began to pass the letter between them.

'Fondle's running,' said Parable. 'Calls it "escorting". In luxury. He's running away.'

'Saving himself,' said Florrie, 'and her with him.'

'If he saves his boys—? His star boys—?'

Florrie was pouring tea carefully into the trefoil cups. 'He'd best go,' she said. 'Canada's very English. A great clean amiable country and a good long way off from trouble.'

CHAPTER 12

The night before the departure to Canada of Mr. Fondle's unanimously evacuating school, Terry Vanetski slid out of Muriel Street and down to the rabbit-hole houses by the sand dunes to say goodbye to Mr. Parable.

He was at home. The flames from the sea-coal fire could be seen far down the passage behind him, glittering and painting the walls a rosy orange.

Parable opened the door wider and said, 'Yes? I have been waiting.'

'I couldn't come before. There's big activity. Piles of clothes. I don't know where she finds them. I told her I'd leave her all me coupons. I shan't need them in Canada.'

'Who knows?'

'She doesn't. Dad's come up with things, too. Things we never knew. There's a crucifix and a Missile.'

'It will be a Missal. A prayer book. Come in. I'd have thought that would have been for the Holy Father to give you.'

'He's given me a bobbly thing. A rosary.'

'You know my feelings about the Roman Catholic Church. Well I suppose you've come to see what I am going to give you?'

'It never entered my head, Mr. Apse.'

'Just as well. I am giving you nothing. Nothing for the moment, that's to say, except naturally my prayers. Nothing extra for now, but there will be something in the years to come. It will be handled by my head office—you may have heard that I have branches in other parts of the country? I am speaking of my Will.'

'Thank you very much, Mr. Parable.'

'Apse—Peter Parable-Apse—it will not be a fortune. You must make your own: as I had to do in London on—.'

'Yes, Mr. Apse. On ten shillings a week.'

'Did me no harm. But all this is for after the War. When you are back home again. You will come back. We shall win the war. But I think you should not come back up here. Go to London where I have significant connections, which will quietly endure. You will not want.'

'I'll write, Mr. Apse. From Canada.'

'Remember your Bible, boy. And I shall need to know your address before I die.'

'But, if you die, Mr. Apse—?'

'—in order for my executors to send you your inheritance. I don't mind telling you that, chiefly on account of my esteem for your dear mother and my admiration for your father's courage, I intend to leave you twenty-five pounds.'

'Will that be per annum, Mr. Para—Mr. Apse?'

'No, it will be net, boy. Your capital.'

'Why are you doing this, Mr. Apse?'

'Don't grin, boy. Do not mock. I do this wholly for your mother, fool though she was not to marry me.'

* * *

'Did you nearly marry Mr. Parable, Ma?'

'Peter Parable? I did not.'

There was a roar from the bed.

'More fool me,' she said, stirring the pot.

'No,' said Terry and from the bed came a more acquiescent rumble. 'It wouldn't have done, Ma.'

'Well, I suppose I might have had silk stockings and a fur coat by now if I had.'

'More like,' said Terry, 'you'd have been singing hymns on the sands in a bonnet,' and the three of them laughed.

'And you'd not have had me,' said the child.

'Well, that could have been a relief.' She ladled out dumplings and rabbit stew. Then there was apple tart and custard.

'You'll miss this good stuff in Canada,' she said. 'It'll be plain stuff there.'

* * *

'Bed then, aye? Sleep well,' she said later.

His bag for tomorrow by the door. His papers in a satchel nearby. 'Up early now,' she said. They did not kiss. The Odessan took Terry's hand as he passed the bed. He put money in the hand and spoke to him in Russian. Then the Odessan roared out a spate of some other language in a new horrible, terrifying voice and his eyes looked blind. Florrie ran out to the yard. Terry stood like an object. He said nothing. The Odessan said, 'You have Russian blood, say something, for the love of Christ. I have nothing to give you. Nothing.'

'Yes. A chess set. Make me a chess set, my Da.'

'You will write or cable? Every day, my boy?'

'Of course.'

'We cannot speak directly of the love of God,' said the Odessan. 'But, I can bless you.'

'Thanks, Da.'

The next morning there was the Holy Father in the house. There was bustle. Sleeplessness had ceased with dawn and now they were all bemused by late heavy slumber. 'Come on. We go,' said the Canon and Terry found himself out on Muriel Street where Florrie said, 'Goodbye then. I'll not come to the train. Did years of that. I'll go get your father his breakfast.' He walked with the priest to the end of the road and turned to wave, but she had gone.

On the station all Mr. Fondle's evacuees were gathered just as if it were an ordinary school day of years ago. Today however they were going the opposite way.

There did not seem to be very many evacuees. The parents—quite a small group—stood together in a clump talking to each other rather than to their children. Most parents were being very bright. Most children seemed very young. They coursed about the platform being aeroplanes, bright and smiling, noisy and wild. Some swung their gas-masks round their heads. The gas-masks were on long shoulder-strings and in square cardboard boxes. Even Mrs. Fondle carried a gas-mask but it was boxed in black satin and on a ribbon.

'You can throw them all in the sea the minute we're out of sight of land,' Mr. Fondle called, and Mrs. Fondle marched about, smiling.

* * *

The officials in the ticket-office crammed up against the glass partition some with handkerchiefs against their faces. A few of the better-dressed parents gathered closely around the headmaster and his wife and the tall handsome boy (is it Terry? They can't be sending *Terry!*) so much older than the rest.

'Is he your son?' a woman asked Griespert. Two tiny girls in smocking dresses and Start-Rite London sandals stood silently beside her. 'He's surely too old to be an evacuee?'

'I am a Catholic priest. He is not mine.'

'Oh—the poor boy must be an orphan.' The woman waggled a finger at Terry. 'And *so* good-looking. You'll be an American Hollywood star one day.'

'We're going to Canada,' said Terry. 'Do your children know?'

'Oh, it's about the same thing,' she said.

'This boy's parents are both living. He means everything to them.'

Terry was examining the chocolate slot-machine, empty since sweet-rationing, with its metal drawer hanging out. The priest watched, hoping that Terry had heard.

Terry was still dazed and unnerved by Florrie's absence.

She'd stood at the door steady and confident as a sergeant-major. Hand on latch had said, 'Well now. Got everything then? Got the cake? Stamps? You'll need one when you write home tonight from Liverpool.'

She—and Terry—knew that he would never say 'Aren't you coming as far as the train?' That she would never kiss him in front of anybody. He had moved his feet on the step, looking to each side of her, marking time. The shadow of his father crawling back to the bed, skirting the chamber-pot, moved behind her. In a minute his father's pointed knees rose like Alps inside the snowy counterpane.

'You've got one of your socks going to sleep inside one of them shoes,' said Florrie. 'That won't suit Canada. It's a good fault though, too big. No doubt they'll wash them in too-hot water. It's good to see you in long trousers. I'll send a second pair. Now, you'll remember to write *tonight*. And watch your manners.'

That was when she had gone in and shut the door behind her.

When the train steamed in, it gathered the children in to itself, the parents' flustering, faces against windows. Few children cried. Some looked unconcerned, and remote, blank as the dead. Some of the parents on the platform tried to wave little paper flags.

Inside their carriage the Fondles were talkative and encouraging as with their entourage they set off across the world to safety.

Terry had a corner seat in the Fondle's first-class carriage but as the train gathered speed he stood up, opened the window by its leather strap and leaned forward to push his head out into the blowy day. At one blast he was caught into the slide and clatter of the train, the sudden, knowing hoot from the funnel. He watched the strings of coarse red council houses, the gaunt chimneys of the iron-works above them. At his back were the Cleveland Hills where Mr. Smith lived with his sick wife and little Fred. Behind the chimneys, in front of Terry and invisible, rolled in the sea towards the mine-fields of the sand-dunes and the barbed wire and Mr. Parable. All his life's landscape was passing out of sight. Here was the long fence at the end of the grounds of Mr. Fondle's school. There was a For Sale notice up, facing the train, beside the open Fives Court.

Pressed up against this fence, arms outstretched before her towards the running train, mouth gaping, face yearning, eyes blank and terrible and blind, stood his mother.

Then the train had swished and trundled by and Terry stood at the window until Veronica Fondle twitched at his coat and told him to close it, and sit down.

He never knew if his mother had seen him passionately waving.

CHAPTER 13

A mile or two inland and over sixty years later, old Fred
Fiscal-Smith was deep in some gleaming, bubbling
ocean. Seaweed trailed in it and there were soft, gulping bubbles, tropical ripples and gentle waves. Java, perhaps?
Wonderful case there in the seventies. Faulty refrigeration
plant, junior to Veneering. And to Filth.

But Fiscal-Smith's forehead seemed to be resting now on a
smooth glass, globular surface, and he was a baby again. More
alarmingly he was gazing into a wide mouth with bright lips
turned inside out like a glove, opening and shutting, moving
tirelessly, eyes staring with disbelief. Ye gods, it was a gold-fish
and he was slipping off the edge of the bed!

Where'd she gone? The Madame?

A bang and a rushing figure, and she was back. It was
morning in the best bedroom of The Judges' Hotel and the
curtains were being drawn back. Her voice rattled on. And on.

'Now then, Fred. Thermometer. Straighten yourself out
before we're gathering up the gold-fish off the floor. They're
meant to soothe the guests, not frighten them. My own idea.
Copied from dentists. It's raining and right cold this morning—almost afternoon. You've slept twelve hours, Fred. You'll
be right in a day or two and you'd best stay here till you are.'

'No, no. I must get home.'

'I've told him, your so-called "ghillie", I call him Bertie as I
call you Fred, Fred, when we're alone. Since Herringfleet
school—'

'Tell Bertie—'

'I've told him. Returned from one of his memorial services, I said, with the flu. Staying here. Told him to bring down any post, except that, knowing him, he won't. Bone idle. Here's the paper. More about the Service. What a mob of double-barrels!'

'Do go away. I'm not awake. Home—.'

'Now don't tell me Lone Hall's ever been home, Fred. Just as Fiscal-Smith's not the name you were baptised. You and I hailed from Ada Street first, just as his high-and-mighty hailed from Muriel Street. It was your Dad fancied the Hall up here long since and now you can't get rid of it. Smith was your name.'

'I'd never try. I'm denying nothing about Ada Street. I've come back up here. In the North. Might never have left Hong Kong. I'm faithful.'

'Breakfast. Here. Eat it. They've done you eggs and bacon.'

He munched, his back against the pillows. Beside him on the table the gold-fish hung in their blob of ocean, then shrugged and shimmered away into some ornamental pebbles and ferns.

'You're kind, Margaret. You'd never order me out. I'll stay a day or so for old time's sake. I can't really afford—.'

'You're worth millions, Fred. Shut up. What happened down there? Something's upset you.'

'Oh—didn't know many people. Didn't feel very welcome as a matter of fact. Old friends change. Or die. Or both. Thinking of Hong Kong—I was Sir Edward Feathers' best man there you know—and, well, rather aware that nobody has ever, exactly, wanted me. And the obituaries were full of mistakes. Terry Veneering's "childhood in Russia". Old Filth's "uneventful life"! Ha!'

'Come on, get your own life, Fred.'

'Bit late now, Margaret. Everything's getting right dim, now.'

'You said that like a local, Fred. Go back to sleep.'

'Aye. And put a cloth over them bloody fish,' he said in a voice that would have been unrecognisable in The Temple. As he fell asleep he said, 'Remember Florrie Benson? Terrible business that. Terrible world.'

CHAPTER 14

The huge four-decker cruise ship stood like a city in Liverpool Dock and the faces looking down from the upper decks were dots. Gang planks stood robust and heavy. Rows of lifeboats, all tested and passed, hung like fruits.

There had been a last-minute delay and now the date of embarkation would be tomorrow, Friday the thirteenth. Normally no big ship would have risked such a date, but there was a waiting group of convoy ships and Liverpool was being heavily bombed and more bombardment expected. There was a sense of urgency.

The ship was carrying around a hundred children mostly the East End of London poor, homeless, and some orphaned already in the Blitz. National newspapers had been carrying photographs of dead children laid out in rows. Churchill had not yet vetoed these evacuations by sea but, there was serious lobbying about patriotism for one's country being the noblest place to die; and also suggestions, since the sinking of a similar ship carrying children less than a month earlier, of nervousness.

Most of the London children had said goodbye to their parents at Euston Station and continued by train to Liverpool where the delay had meant a stay of two nights in rat-infested hostels. Some had cried, a few fallen ill—there was a case of chicken-pox (this boy was taken home)—but most of the rest were noisy and excited and looking forward to the six days of crossing the Atlantic to a new life. None of them mentioned the partings from home. They had transformed themselves into a new, intimate community consisting only of each other.

'When are we *going*?' they lamented. Not only the German bombs at night but the huge barrage of Liverpool gun-fire thundered all around them, hour after hour all night. 'Soon,' they were told, 'Soon.' Two of the children had been on board the earlier evacuee ship a fortnight ago which had been torpedoed, but everyone saved. These two seemed stolidly unconcerned.

There were also the paying passengers, 'business-men, diplomats and professors and people of pre-war opulence,' as was later reported in the press. Among these were Mr. and Mrs. Fondle and their party from North Yorkshire, expecting to board the *S.S. City of Benares* at once.

But the train had been slow and they had been obliged to sit with their elite group of children in one of the sheds on the quay. And, later, their supper was the same as the children's. Veronica Fondle picked at the slices of National Wholemeal bread—pale grey—a little grey pie, some wet grey cabbage and a dollop of 'instant potato' called Pom.

The Fondles did not seem to be hungry. They leaned back from the communal bench and smoked black cigarettes with gold tips. Mrs. Fondle patted the seat next to her and said, 'Not long now, Terence.' The poorer children raced about and screamed and shouted like a flock of autumn starlings suddenly wheeling, like smoke, out of sight of the dormitory sheds. Terry said, 'There's not one of them older than ten.'

'Oh, I wouldn't say that, Terry. Terry you must stop saying "*Wan*". You are travelling with us.'

He could think of no answer. He could not bear her face or her voice. After a time he took a last bite into the so-called tart (Apricot, but it was marrow jam) and said, "*One*" and she said, '*Much* better.'

'Can I get a message home? I've got the priest's number. It's only one and twopence.'

'Oh, I don't think we want to unsettle them.'

'Well, I'll write, then, Mrs. Fondle. I promised. She give me the stamp for it.'

'*Gave*,' said Mrs. Fondle. She and Harold Fondle then disappeared.

Terry wrote his letter and went to find a post-box, with no success. It was bed-time apparently now and they were sent to a place full of bunks. Two big, plain, confident girls—twins—were to sleep below him. They looked to be eleven at most, but large and commanding. 'You an escort?' one asked. 'You're no evacuee. Not *your* age.'

'I'm not quite fourteen.'

'D'you not want to stay and fight then?'

'I don't know about that. Do you?'

'We're girls,' they said 'It would just to be in Munitions. I don't want to make bombs for anyone. There must be kids like us, over there.'

In the night he heard one of the girls crying and her sister's head rose up like a vision beside his face on the bunk above. 'Our dad and mam's dead in the raid. Faery's weak. I'm her twin sister.'

He rose early next morning, both sisters humps in grey blankets below. He dressed and put on the hooded coat his mother had made him. He was so tall he might have been anybody.

He climbed aboard, up a steep gangway unnoticed. He walked about on deck. He slipped amidships and soon came to a graceful staircase like Hollywood. Like *A Hundred Men and a Girl*. And high above him on the stair he saw the toes of shiny golden curled slippers jutting over the top step. He found that these feet were attached to the graceful Aladdin-trousers of a golden man in a golden coat and purple turban. This smiling man beckoned and bowed.

'Come little sir. Welcome to the East. Welcome to the *City of Benares*. See what is now before you.'

What was before him was *The Arabian Nights*. The palms. The languid loungers, the gleaming restaurants, the clean cabins for them all—not only for the paying passengers. The white linen hand-towels, the ballroom, and everywhere a glorious smell of spices and food he seemed somewhere to have known. An orchestra was tuning up upon a white marble dais.

There was a play-room for the little ones, full of toys. A rocking-horse stood there against a wall, its nostrils flaring. It was a strong rocking-horse with basket-work seats fastened one to each side of the saddle, all wicker-work but very firm and beautiful. Then away went the steward, about the ship. Coloured streamers, big white teeth smiling, princes bowing to him. It must be a film!

Terry felt very much afraid. He was being mocked. He needed to speak, not to his father but to his mother. There were no women on board this ship. They were all princes, all bowing at him and all false. He had never seen anything like this in the Palace Cinema in Herringfleet.

'I don't think I am meant to be here,' he said. 'Who are you?'

'I am a steward on this glorious ship. It is only one year old. It is known as The Garden of the East. You, all you children, are going to be in heaven. You will be Royalty, even the smallest, away from all harm of war. You will eat chicken and salmon and eastern fruit, rich meats, wines, sherbets, bananas and ice-cream—.'

He was terrified. 'I have to go back. I am not meant to be here. It's a dream.'

'Perhaps the whole world is a dream.'

He ran back on deck. Children were beginning to climb the gangways now, some hand in hand, some solemn, some excited, none looking back, none crying. All so little.

On the quay a few flags were being waved. Someone began to sing half-heartedly 'Wish Me Luck as You Wave Me Goodbye' and from across the harbour on one of the escort ships which were to come with them to keep them safe, the song was taken up and sailors on her deck began to sing and to wave and cheer. The two stolid twins, big and heavy in what looked like their mother's winter clothes, passed Terry by without noticing him. From the inside of the ship came cries of amazed delight, the Pied Piper's children passing inside the mountain.

He asked someone about the Fondles, and was told that they would already have boarded by a different gangway for the paying passengers.

He said 'I'll go back to the quay then, and find it.'

'No need,' said another golden Indian man in white. 'Come this way.' He had gold tabs on his shoulders.

'I have to go down. I've left my bag.'

'Someone can escort you.'

'I can manage.'

'Hurry then, little master.'

He began to push against the stream of passengers coming up the gangway. He pushed harder, knocking them out of the way, and he was free.

Across the quay, in and then out of last night's dark lodging—his luggage was still there.

'Get *aboard*!' A Liverpool voice. ''Ere—you! You's a passenger—I seed yer. I remember the hair.'

'Just going.'

He pulled up the hood of the coat and half an hour later he was far away, running like mad from the port, wandering in battered, broken Liverpool, looking for a phone-box.

* * *

He had the right money and he telephoned Father

Griesepert. There was no answer, so he rang Mr. Smith's number, up in the house on the moor—no phones yet in Muriel Street—and after a long time and the telephonist twice asking if she should disconnect him, little Fred Smith's voice answered.

'It's Terry. Is yer Dad there?'

'Yer'll 'ave ter 'old on. They're not awake yet after last night.'

'Get him, Fred.'

* * *

'Hullo? Terry? Terry!'

'Yes. Sorry, Mr. Smith. I'm comin' home.'

'You can't. It is utterly impossible.'

'Well, I'm coming. I have the money from Da.'

'You can't. There's no trains. Middlesbrough station was destroyed last night. The lines are broken everywhere.'

'Yes. Well. I'm still coming. Somehow. The ship's awash with bairns and little kids and them Fondles is after me. I don't know why, I don't trust them. They think I'm theirs. I'm not theirs. I'm me Mam's. And me Dad's. I'se jumped ship. The ship's about to sail. I'm somewhere in Liverpool. They'll never find me.'

The operator said, 'Your three minutes is up. Do you want to pay for more time?'

He pushed some shillings and then pennies into the slot and after they had clattered down there was silence again.

But then, at last, Mr. Smith's voice saying, 'D'you think you can find The Adelphi Hotel? Terry? Very big. Dark. Ask anyone.'

'Yes. I think it's right near. I think I'm beside it. I must have gone in a circle.'

'Go in there. I'll phone them and say you're coming. Right.

Now, sit in the main Bar there if they'll let you. Out of sight if you can. Say someone's coming for you. Say you've had bad news from home that means you are unable to leave the country just now. Give anyone this number. Terry—if this is panic it may not be too late—.'

There was a boom like the Last Judgement across the City of Liverpool and *The City of Benares*, its funnels calling out like organ pipes, began its graceful journey towards the Atlantic Ocean.

'It's not panic, Mr. Smith. And it *is* too late. I know I'm doing right, Mr. Smith. I'm sorry.'

'You've been listening to the slaughterer, Mr. Churchill, forbidding us to run away.'

'No. Look. Will you tell Mam and Da? I'm coming home.'

'You've had your three shillings' worth and more,' said the operator. 'I couldn't help listening. I'm not sure of Churchill neither. Always was a war-monger. Death and glory. I'd go home meself if I was you lad.'

'Thanks. I know what I'm doing,' said Terry. 'Thanks, Mr. Smith. I'm fine.' But his hand shook so much that it took him three attempts to get the heavy black hand-piece back on its hook. Behind it he saw his face in the small spotted mirror. It looked set and certain. Totally certain. I look like me Da, he thought. So that's O.K.

CHAPTER 15

S till there?'
    The barman at the Adelphi's shadowy and vast main bar was, towards evening, still polishing glasses. Terry was almost out of sight as he had been for hours around the side of the bar on a black-painted step near the floor, his case beside him, waiting for the telephone to ring.

'You's sure now that he's coming? It's after tea now.'

'If Mr. Smith said so——.'

'Well, he said there'd be someone coming to get you, not him. Someone nearer, but not that near. Fromt Lake District. Not nobody, not God, could get over from Teesside today. News travels. It's not int papers or ont wireless yet. Bombed and flattened the steel-works. First bad 'un they've had there. We's all but used to it 'ere. You's well away—there'll be more. Aren't you the daft 'un not on that luxury liner with the toffs?'

Terry sat on. 'Can I have a drink? A bar drink.'

'I'll give you one small beer.'

'No. I want Vodka. I'm partly Russian.'

'I've been noticing the hair.'

'I've been collecting round my school for the Red Cross Penny-a-Week fund for Russia.'

'Why?'

'I'm a Communist.'

'Oh God,' said the barman. 'Switch off. You've got ground to cover yet. Never mind your father. Hullo? Oh, good evening? Yes. Along here. Someone is coming.'

It was a false hope. Terry sat on. He said, 'We never met anyone from the Lake District. Where's the Lake District? I thought it was Canada—like Erie and Michigan and that.'

'By God, you're ignorant. Where you been all your life, Lenin? Herringfleet? Cod's-head folk.'

'That's right. Can you get me a sandwich?'

'There's none here to get it for you and nowt to put in it if there was! Mebbe in the police-station if none turns up here for you.'

'Bit longer,' said Terry, 'Mr. Smith won't forget. What's that?'

Far away in the main foyer of the hotel there was, drawing nearer, a clear, rhythmic, distinctive mechanical sort of voice. '—let that be understood. From the beginning. Thank you, yes.' A small man was walking towards them from the far end of the long shadowed passage, talking as if addressing an audience. 'And this is my passenger, I dare say?'

'If you've come from a Mr. Smith,' said the barman.

'I have. Good afternoon. Stand up, boy. Shake hands with me. A straight back and a direct look. Good. Good. My name is Sir. Just Sir. I am the headmaster of a school in the Lake District where Mr. Smith was once my deputy. All my deputies are called Mr. Smith but this Mr. Smith is authentically Smith. A fine man. My school is called a Preparatory School, or Prep School. My Outfit. I'm afraid you are rather too old for my Outfit but we shall see what can be done.'

('He's a Communist,' said the barman. 'We must discuss the matter,' said Sir.)

'It is a pity that you are so old for I believe there is much I can do for you. *Hair-wise* (look up hair in Latin. Roman customs and barbering) and now what *exactly* is your name? I gather that it is uncertain.'

'Yes. It has always been a sort of uncertainty.'

'It must be settled at once. It is most important. If I can do nothing else I can do that. Venitski? Vanetski? Varenski? Are you all illiterate in Herringfleet?'

'Dad never really discussed it. He came from Odessa.'

('It's Ivan-Skavinski-Skavar,' said the barman and began to sing the tune.)

'Enough!' shouted Sir. 'This is a very serious matter. Your name henceforth shall be Veneering. Yes. Delightful. Polished. In Dickens, Veneering (look up *Our Mutual Friend*) is an unpleasant character and you will have to redeem him. Veneering has a positive and memorable ring. Rather jolly. You do not look *un*-Dickensian, but you look far from jolly.'

'*So*—let us leave at once. Tonight you will be staying in the Lake District mountains in my Outfit. Mr. Smith is coming to remove you tomorrow.'

'Does he know that you will have given me a new name?'

'He won't be surprised. A most sensible man. Has a son of his own. Maybe I'll get him. Such a pity Mr. Smith had to leave me to get married. I have no married teachers in my Outfit. Marriage brings distractions. In my Outfit we are too busy for distractions.'

Handing the barman a five pound note the small loquacious man turned and left the Adelphi Hotel and Terry followed dragging all his worldly possessions in the suitcase.

'The Adelphi Hotel is haunted,' said Sir. 'It is the hotel where doomed passengers of ship-wrecks have always gathered before embarkation. Filled with shadows. Such rubbish. In the back, now. The dickey-seat. I don't ever drive with a boy along-side me for there is always talk in a Prep School. Mine is a clean school. Was yours?'

'I don't know what you mean, Sir. Mine was run by a man called Fondle.'

'That,' said Sir, 'is a bad start.'

They roared away north-north-east towards the Cumbrian fells, Sir occasionally blasting off into the empty night, upon the car's bulbous horn, at resting rabbits. After a time the light around them began to fade into a gentle sunset. Sir stopped the car.

'Bladder relief.'

'Now,' he said, 'another day is done. By what I hear it has been a day you are unlikely to forget. Time will tell us if you were directed by some spiritual force of nature, by instinct or by selfish whim. I heartily advise you to beware, if it is because of "whim" (look the word up. Old English sudden fancy or caprice OED), never to do such a thing again. Is that understood? I dare say?'

'Yes.'

'Yes, Sir.'

'Yes, Sir.'

'Now, look at the dark hyacinth-blue of the umbrageous mountains (look up 'umbrageous': and 'hyacinth' too, they both have a splendid classical root). Tell me, do you care for birds?'

'Well, I think we only have sea-gulls at Herringfleet.'

'A pity. And most unlikely. Birds can be a great solace. They never love you and you can never own them. Dogs often—and even cats sometimes—can cause pain by their enduring love. Sycophancy (look that up) is never to be encouraged.'

(Who is he? A madman? I like him.)

'And although I wish I could have the privilege of teaching you, you are, as I say, a little old. We stop at twelve or thereabouts. Where are you bound for next, I wonder?'

For the first time it occurred to Terry that he had not the faintest idea.

'I should like to come to your school, Sir, but I don't think there is any money. I stand to inherit £25, but not until my benefactor is dead.'

'Is that per annum, boy?'

'No. It will be net.'

'Ah.'

'I could make an exception,' said Sir, 'but I will not. We might grow fond of each other, I fear that we are unlikely to meet again.'

'I'm very sorry, Sir.'

'Yes. I have to admit that I am often very sad, when a boy leaves my school (though not always). There was one excellent boy called Feathers came to me. Left a year or so ago. Had a cruel stammer. We cured it in a term. He'll be a barrister. You'll see. Rather your sort of calibre. Feathers will have a charmed life and he deserves it for he had a terrible start. He was unloved from birth. Whereas you—boy—I understand have had a loving home and interesting parents. This will get you through everything. Almost. Because you were loved you'll know how to love. And you will recognise real love for you. Here we are.'

The school was on a hill up from a lake that gleamed through black fir trees. Boys erupted through its front door and took charge of a large package, the size of a double-bedded bolster, which Sir took from somewhere beneath his feet. 'Warm it up at once. Fish and chips. Hake. Irish sea. Made me late at Liverpool. Hake a wonderful fish, not common. Good for the brain (look up "hake". Is it Viking?). God bless our fishing boats. No car here yet? No Mr. Smith to take you home? Boys, this is Terry Veneering. Yes.'

The boys were all disappearing into the school with the bolster. 'Veneering, you'll have to stay the night,' said Sir and Terry felt suddenly that it had been a long day.

* * *

He stayed for three nights with Sir and there was no message from Herringfleet. He slept in an attic and listened to the birds. He was hauled in to help with football and was a success. In the gymnasium it was even better. 'You may start them on Russian,' said Sir, passing by on the third day. 'We may all be needing it soon. I forbid German, however.'

'I think there's a car, Sir.'

'Where?'

'Standing in the drive. It might be Mr. Smith.'

'Excellent. Start now. First Steps in Russian with Class 1. Call them "First Steppes" and see if they get—. I will send for you. You are right. It is Mr. Smith. They are approaching slowly: There seems to be a priest with him.'

An hour later Terry was summoned to the Parents' Waiting Room where a tray of tea and Marie biscuits, off the ration, had been laid out and Mr. Smith and Father Griesepert told him that both his parents had been killed in the air-raid on Herringfleet the night he left home. Muriel Street was gone, as were the old rabbit-hole houses in the dunes. Mr. Parable-Apse was dead, along with the people in the ticket-office, and nobody had seen Nurse Watkins.

* * *

Terry was to leave that same evening in Mr. Smith's car. Father Griesepert was a governor and an old boy of a famous Catholic boarding school where it was hoped Terry would remain for the next few years. He went to see Sir again by himself and found him seated at a desk which looked far too big for him, staring ahead.

But he was talking before Terry was through the door. 'Remember,' he said, 'You will not only survive but you will shine. Remember the boy, Feathers. You will outshine him. I know, I am never wrong.

'But remember—I am only a walk-on part in your life. This is merely a guest-appearance. You will have to get down to your own future now.'

Pompous, Terry thought. Totally self-absorbed. Stand-up comedian. Needs adulation. Probably homosexual. Twerp.

'And so, goodbye, Veneering.'

'Goodbye, Sir. And thank you.'

'Hurry up. I have work to do. Mr. Smith is waiting.'

Veneering turned at the door to shut it behind him and saw Sir staring ahead, his eyes immense, wet beneath his glasses. Unseeing.

On her Memory-Dream mattress sixty years later Dulcie was now listening to the Dorset rain. A sopping Spring. At last she heard the swish of Susan's car returning from the station, the front door opening and closing. Some kitchen sounds. The radio—.

(She's taking her time to come up.)

'Susan? Susan? Is that you? Are you back?'

'You know it's me, I'm getting your lunch. Here. Sit up. Soup and cheese. I seem to have been bringing people food all day. Oh, don't *snivel*, Ma. I suppose you've forgotten that I'm going home tomorrow?'

'No, I haven't. Is Herman going too?'

'Where else d'you think he'll live?'

'And I'm not snivelling. It's a cold. I must have caught it in the church.'

'The less said about that the better. Ma—tell me something. Did Fiscal-Smith have some sort of a *thing* about Veneering? I always thought it was Old Filth he was mad about.'

'Thing?'

'Is he gay?'

'Oh my dear! Good heavens, no. He's 80 plus.'

'He's not related to Veneering, is he? Told me at the station he'd known him since they were eight.'

'Well, they're both from the North somewhere. Nobody knows. The North is big I suppose. I must say they've both dealt pretty well with the accent. They're both Roman Catholics. Expensive schools and Oxford.'

'How weird. It's just that Fiscal-Smith, poor little scrap, flipped a bit as the train came in. Made a speech at me about Veneering. *At* me. Eyes glittering. Very odd. He kept pressing that lighted button on the carriage door and all the doors kept opening and closing.'

'Once,' said Dulcie, looking away, 'you were fined twenty-five pounds for that. Pulling the cord for fun. We did it once at school and then we all jumped out and ran across the fields and my foster family nearly killed me. I wrote to my father in Shanghai to come and rescue me and he wrote back saying he would never write to me again and nor would my mother until I'd written letters of shame to everyone, including the railway company. It was the dear old LMS.'

'Whatever that was. Here, Ma. Eat your rhubarb.'

'I hate the way people call it rhubarb now. It should be rhu-BUB. Only the Queen and I pronounce it properly.'

'When did you discuss rhubarb with the Queen? The last thing—when the doors did close—Fiscal-Smith was saying was that Veneering once had a different name and he was some sort of a hero. Very brave. Huge admiration. Did you know?'

'Perhaps he was Veneering's best-man, too.'

'Oh now! Veneering was married frightfully young. When he was doing his national service in the Navy after the War. His ship was showing the flag around the Far East. He met and married Elsie ten years before he met the rest of us. Before he met Betty.'

'Yes. We know all that. Everyone knew his wife drank. People always do.'

'Elsie was Chinese of course. Never saw anyone so beautiful. But she drank.'

'We knew all that, too.'

'She was rather after the style of that pink-coat woman at the funeral, Isobel.'

'Isobel does *not* drink!'

'That will do, Susan! Do you know Isobel?'

'O.K.—keep your hair on. I did once. It can't be the same one.'

'*Actually*,' said Dulcie, spooning rhubarb, 'there *was* some link between little Fred Fiscal-Smith and Edward. Something awful. Orphans, of some sort. Well, you don't ask, do you? Not done.'

'*I* was a Raj Orphan,' said Susan.

'Yes. You made a great fuss. I can't think why. It is such a character-forming thing to be separated from one's parents. I never saw mine for years. I didn't miss them at all. Couldn't remember what they looked like after about a week. But then, I've never been very interesting and I'm sure they weren't.'

'I missed mine,' said Susan.

'Your father, I suppose.'

'No. I missed you. Dreadfully.'

'Susan! How lovely! I had no idea! How *kind* of you to tell me. I did write you thousands of letters—. But—. I think I'll get up now and write to Fiscal-Smith. I think I was a little hard on him for bringing that overnight-case. He'll be nearly home by now. I hope there was a dining car on the train. He remembers—and so do I—when railway cups and saucers—.'

'"Had rosebuds on them". Yes, we know. And for godsake, Ma, don't get up until I've done down-stairs. The kitchen's full of damp church vestments.'

'And after this,' she said in the kitchen, 'thank God, we must start packing for America.'

Dulcie, not waiting to dress got out of bed, found some writing paper and sat at her dressing table.

My dear Fiscal-Smith,

I am sorry that we did not say a proper goodbye after

our little adventure this morning. I had not expected you to leave immediately and I am *very* sorry if we seemed to be hurrying you away, Sincerely, your oldest friend, Dulcie.

PS: I don't seem to be able to get *not* Old Filth—Eddie—out of my mind, but *Veneering*. Am I right in thinking that you knew him better than anyone else did? That there are things you never told us? Just a hazy thought. I've so often wondered how he got where he did. So flashy and brash (if I dare say so) so brilliant in court, so good at languages, so passionate and so—whatever they say about him with women—so common. But oh so honourable! Don't forget, I knew Betty very well. But I am saying too much—too much unless it is to a dear last friend which I know it is.

DW.

* * *

And now I am completely restored, she thought the next day, waving Susan and her grandson off in the hired car for the airport, back to Boston, Mass.

Susan had kissed her goodbye. Even Herman had hugged her, if inexpertly. This visit had been a success! Susan talked of returning soon. Even of sending Herman to boarding school here with the boy his own age over in Veneering's old house, the poet's son. Well, well! I wish she'd say what's happened to her husband. An electric fence around her there.

* * *

Today and probably for the next few days Dulcie decided she would do nothing. It was time for her to be quiet and reflect. So idiotic at my age, but I must reflect upon the future.

'Reflect', perhaps the wrong word. It has a valedictory conno-
tation. But I am not too old to consider matters of moral behaviour. There is Janice coming to clean on Wednesday and Susan's
already done the sheets. I will *not* go over to Veneering's house
to see that new family. I mustn't get dependent on them. I
mustn't become a bore. I shall—. Well I shall read. Go through
old letters. Plenty to do. Prayers. Wait for Fiscal-Smith's reply.

But when this had not arrived by Friday Dulcie began to
think again how much he irritated her. She knew she had hurt
him by sending him home, but, after all, she had not invited
him. It was that supply of clean shirts she'd seen in the case
that she couldn't forget. The image brought others: his ease the
night before with her drinks cupboard, his arrogance in the
church. How he had criticised the vicar. He knew that the
Church of England had to regard their priests as wandering
planets now, the current one arrived on a scooter dressed as a
hoodie and vanished after the service without a word to anybody; but Fiscal-Smith need not have looked so RC and smug.
And disdainful of St. Ague's.

Of course she knew the village was dead. Dorset was dead.
It was gone. Submerged beneath the rich week-enders, who
never passed the time of day. Came looking for *The
Woodlanders* of Thomas Hardy and then cut down the trees.
The only life-timer in The Donheads was the ancient man in
the lanes with the scythe. Willy used to call him the grim
reaper. Lived somewhere in a ditch—never talked. Some said
he was still here.

There was no-one to talk to. The village Shop, as Fiscal-
Smith had said, was dying on its feet. He didn't have to tell her.
She scrapped another letter to him, written this time on an
expensive quatre-folded writing paper, thick and creamy, from
Smythson's of Bond Street—which Fiscal-Smith would never
have heard of—and set out on foot to the village shop herself.

It was pure patriotism and she hoped that there were some faces behind the beautiful polished windows and luxury blinds of the weekenders in the lanes to see her. She didn't need anything. Susan had stocked up for her as if for a siege, in the Shaftesbury Co-op. She bought at the little shop a tin of baked beans and listened to Chloe discussing whether Scotts Oats were better than Quaker when making flap-jack. There rose up a vision of golden heaps of sea-wrack, squid, banana fritters, marigolds and the smell of every kind of spice. A tired, dreamy Chinese chef spinning pasta from a lump of dough for the tourists; a stall piled high with cat-fish. Mangoes. Loquats.

On the way home she decided to get eggs from the farm. There was a wooden box hung on a field-gate. It had been there fifty years. You took out the eggs and left the money. Beautiful brown eggs covered in hen-shit to show how fresh they were. Today she opened the flap of the box and there were no eggs and no money but a dirty-looking note saying, 'Ever Been Had?'

She was all at once desolate. The whole world was corrupt. She was friendless and alone. Like Fiscal-Smith she had outstayed her welcome in the place she felt was home. There was absolutely nothing for her to do now but walk back to empty Privilege Hall.

No she would not! There must be someone. Yes. She would go and call on the two old twins up the lane. The people in the shop had said that there was a new Carer there. Well, there nearly always was a new Carer there. (Oh! When was the last time there was anybody happy? It's not that I'm really already missing Susan. I wonder if I'd have loved Susan more if she'd been a boy? With a nice wife who would sit and talk and play Bridge?)

She tottered up to the cottage of the two old high-powered (Civil Service) twins and was greeted by a dry young woman with a grey face, smoking a cigarette.

'Yes?'

'I am a friend—.'

'They're having their rest.'

'But it's lunch-time.'

'They rest early.'

'I am a very *old* friend. May I please come in?'

She walked through the nice cottage that seemed to be awash with rubbish awaiting the bin men, and saw Olga and Faery playing a slowish card-game at a table. They raised their eyes sadly.

'Thank you.' Dulcie turned to the Carer. 'That will be all for now. You may take a break. I'm sure you need one. Please take your cigarette into your car.'

The twins looked frightened. 'She's from a very expensive agency. They said she *did* smoke but not in the house. But she does.'

'It's so strange that we mind,' said Faery. 'We all smoked once.'

'And I suppose we are a horrible job,' said Olga. 'Even though she gets double. She goes on and on about how wonderful her last job was. "Lovely people". She calls them by their first names, Elizabeth and Philip. Do you think it was with the Royal Family?'

'I don't. And if it was, Down with the Royal Family.'

'Oh, don't start, Dulcie. We're wiser now.'

'I want to kill her. Oh, for some *men*.'

'Don't be a fool, Dulcie, we're all over eighty and we're feminists.'

They sat. The room was cold with no sign of a fire. Faery's legs were wrapped in loose bandages.

'Marriage must be a help in old age,' said Olga, 'but since the husband usually goes first it doesn't rate much now. No penniless spinster daughters at home to look after us either. Must say, I'd like one.'

'Well, my Susan would be hopeless as a Daughter at Home.'

'But she comes and takes charge often,' said Faery. 'You don't know how lucky you are Dulcie. You never did.'

'But she makes me feel such a fool all the time. She's married and clever and well-off and has a son and yet she's never happy. Never was.'

'She has her girl-friends,' said Olga and there was a long pause. The Carer was hard at work across the front hall, complaining on her phone at high speed in an unknown tongue.

'Did you know? Well of course you'll know.'

Faery said, 'Hugely rich, we hear. And no girl. Woman almost your age.'

'Oh yes, of course,' said Dulcie.

The Carer returned and said that she must start to get the girls to bed. Dulcie saw her lighting up another cigarette as she held open the front door.

In the sitting room the two women stared at their playing-cards and listened to the Carer texting messages (plink, plink) in the kitchen.

'My special subject at Oxford was Tolstoy,' said Faery.

'You don't have to tell me,' said Olga.

'Perhaps fiction was a mistake, it has rather fizzled out.' said Faery. 'We should have pioneered Women's Rights.'

'Rubbish,' said Olga. 'It was the wrong moment. Fiction got us through. Fiction and surviving the ship-wreck at 15 years old.'

'Yes. And just look at us now.'

'It's nothing to do with us being born women that we're wearing nappies and in the charge of a drug-addict,' said Olga. 'Men get just the same. No family backing, that's the trouble. Poor old Dulcie's an example. Hardly went to school you know. Married in the cradle. Daft as a brush. Like a schoolgirl. Silly women haven't a brain to lose.'

'Yes. I wouldn't have wanted to share a cradle with Pastry Willy! He never liked us, you know.'

'No. I suppose we shouldn't have told her about Susan and her old girl? Nasty of us. Poor Dulcie.'

'Lesbians are always looking for their mothers.'

'It must be hard for them.'

The two old trolls sat over their cards thinking occasionally of Tolstoy.

* * *

Dulcie, having left the aged twins, began to walk home through the lanes, past the infertile egg-box, the village shop. When Janice, her cleaning lady, drove by in her new Volvo Dulcie stared at her as at a stranger.

Susan loving someone who is a woman and not her mother! Such an insult to me. I suppose it's been going on for ages and I am the last to know. It was that boarding-school at eight, in England, when we were in Shanghai or somewhere—I forget. I've done everything wrong. I wrote her *hundreds* of letters at school. I did try. She hardly answered them.

But she was so *happy* here in England. All her friends were here, everyone's parents over-seas. All seemed so *jolly*. Everyone did it. I can't bear it. I can't bear it. *Lesbian!* I wonder if they all were? I'm sure I didn't know the meaning of the word. Well, anyway, we'd never have talked about it. Men get turned on by divine discontent, and challenged when a woman's mind is always somewhere else, dreaming. I wonder if Betty—no. I heard once that there had been something between Old Filth and that Isobel, but of course I won't believe *that*. Edward would have had an apocalyptic fit if he'd thought that Betty had ever embraced a woman. Whatever would my mother have thought? Well—I suppose there was Miss Cleaves—.

I'm not sure that the word is apocalyptic?

I wonder who's got Filth's house? And fortune! A

woman—that pale pink woman? Isobel. The femme fatale. No not Isobel. No—there was only ever Betty for Filth. Nobody else. Not ever. Surely? Do you know, Willy (Willy, where are you?) I think I've been left behind.

Oh, is nobody ever virtuous any more—as our mothers were? Well, I *think* mine was. I didn't see her very often—Pastry—please tell me. *Whatever* would you make of this?

I suppose Pastry, you never—? No. No. Had a—?

You would say, my faithful man (though I was never happy about that old Vera) you would say, 'Dost thou think, because thou art virtuous, there shall be no more cakes and ale?' Pastry? Listen to me.

The point is that, as a lonely widow in a big empty house and few friends left (I've forgotten a handkerchief) there is nobody to discuss anything with any more. That is the sharpness of loss. The feelings don't go, even when the brain has begun to wither and stray. I know some very nice widowed people who manage so well. There's poor Patsy, laying up dinner-places for all her dead relations. Seems perfectly happy. She's got that funny middle-aged son who goes round clearing everything away again. Those with latter-day brains are the lucky ones.

I can hardly discuss anything with Olga and Faery. You would have told me to keep clear of them. They smell of decay. They can never forget that they went to the university and think I am beneath them. They're senile, though. Serves them right for being so patronising at school. And *they* only got upper-seconds someone said, or was it actually *lower*-seconds? I bet they both remember that. And I will not leave them comfortless even if they are church-going atheists. I will always be their old friend. I suppose. For what I'm worth. Oh. Oh, dear. I must not crack up.

In the drive of Privilege House stood her rickety car and finding the key in the lock Dulcie climbed in and drove away. She reversed, ground the tyres into the cattle-grid, and swept down the hill and up the un-metalled driveway jointly shared by Old Filth's ghost and Veneering's ghost, dividing, one down, one up, and leading nowhere now, she thought. Even those awful rooks don't seem to be there anymore.

She accelerated noisily towards Veneering's yews and here, head-on towards her, came a huge crucifix with a pretty woman marching behind it and smiling. Anna.

* * *

Anna saw Dulcie's cigarette-lined, little monkey face peeping behind the wheel and her expression of panic and she flung the crucifix aside (it was a home-made sign-post), pounced on Dulcie's car and opened its doors.

'I'm just fixing up a bigger B and B sign, Dulcie. *Whatever's* the matter!'

'Nothing. The car looked as if it needed a little run. We used to say "a spin". So I'm spinning.'

'You're crying! Come on. I'm getting in with you. Can you drive on up? I'll get you something to eat with us.'

'Oh, but I must get back.'

'Nonsense. Go on. Re-start the engine. Don't look down Filth's ridiculous precipice. Stupid place to build that lovely house, down in a hole. I'll bet he had a bad chest.'

* * *

She bundled Dulcie into the chaos of her own—once Veneering's—abode above, where children's clothes, toys, a thousand books and a thousand attic relics were scattered about the hall and her husband, Henry, was painting the walls bright yellow.

'Hi, Dulcie,' said he. 'Did you know van Gogh called yellow "God's colour"? Everything here was the colour of mud.

Bitter chocolate. Well, they were farmers before Veneering. Fifty years. Well, you must have known them? Wanted the colour of the good earth inside as well as out. Hate farmers. Holes in the floor, no heating except a few rusty radiators that gurgled all night, electric fires just one red glow, worn light-fittings that blow up. And that's *after* the farmers left. That was Veneering's taste too, and he'd come direct from a sky-scraper in Hong Kong. Wasn't a SOP—Spoiled Old Colonial—anyway, whatever he was. What was he, Dulcie? They say he was an ugly little old man bent over. With dyed hair. Dulcie, kiss me!'

'He was my greatest friend,' lied Dulcie, stern and angry. 'To the end' (another lie!) 'he was one of the finest-looking men in the Colony' (true). 'Amazing white-gold, floppy hair' (Henry's was looking like mattress-stuffing tied back with string). 'It wasn't dyed. He could have been a Norwegian or one of those eastern-European people. Odessans? Slavs? He was a glorious man once. He was said to have had a mysterious father. But not *dour*—you know. No, no, never. He was noisy and funny and sweet to women, and he could read your thoughts. *Could read your thoughts*! And a constant friend. And—do you know—we none of us had a notion of how he got to England. Or about his past.'

'Herman says he could play the drums. And the Blues. Wonderfully. We're finding revelations in the attics. What do you think—*five* rocking horses! Come and see. Take anything Dulcie.'

'And take a glass of sherry with you?' said Anna. 'There's dozens of photographs up there. A lovely boy at Eton and The Guards. Film-star looks. Very fetching. A somewhat over-the-top boy I'd say.'

Dulcie said, 'That was the son, Harry. Killed in Northern Ireland. Doing something very mad and brave. It broke—.' (But why tell them? All this is mine. And Betty's.) 'It broke his father's heart.'

'Yes, I thought there was something. This is a broken-hearted house,' said the husband. 'We'll change it. No fears. I wish you would tell us what to do with all his jig-saws.'

'Nobody could really get near Terry Veneering,' said Dulcie. 'Nobody but Betty—Elizabeth—Old Filth's wife.'

'Yes. We have heard about that,' they said. 'Just a little.'

* * *

After lunch Dulcie was put back in her car on the drive and, looking up at the house behind her, she saw that already it was losing Veneering. There was the same hideousness of shiny scarlet brick-work, the same chrome-yellow gravel and the view at the top of the drive over the miles of meadow was the same shimmering water-colour dream. But Veneering's house was coming to life. Filth's great stern, phallic chimney still broke the dream apart but from the inside of Veneering's house—doors wide—now came the sound of hearty singing and the family man (Henry) with his pig-tail, exploded across the doorstep in overalls covered with paint and kicking the cat.

'Get out!'

The cat vanished into a thicket.

'Goodbye Dulcie. Come back soon. Come for B and B. We're going to make our fortunes when I've finished painting this place. Cat in the paint tins. Paws no doubt permanently damaged. Colour "Forsythia" like the bush. Horrible colour. Like urine, I always think, but the staircase seems happy with it. We are all going to be, like it tells us in the prayer Book, "in perpetual light". I'm never sure about wanting that, are you? Tiring. "Perpetual light".'

'Goodbye,' said Dulcie. (They are very self-confident, these people, for new-comers to the village.) 'And thank you very much.' (But you can discuss things with them and they're not senile.) 'By the way, I may not see you for a while. I am think-ing of going on a cruise.' (What? Am I?)

Through the driving mirror as she went off towards the road to her own Privilege Hall she saw them standing side by side, non-plussed. She waved a hand at them out of the car window and laughed. With her back to them, they could not see the imprisoned girl in her.

Oh, this is not such a bad little place, she thought. Donhead St. Ague. It hasn't always been boring like now. It's the cooling of the blood.

The cat rushed out from somewhere and under the car and into the scrub behind the bed-and-breakfast crucifix, and then dashed across the lane. As Dulcie turned towards home she saw it watching her, haughty and yellow-pawed in the bushes.

* * *

But it's true, she thought, nobody really knows a thing about another's past. Why should we? Different worlds we all inhabit from the womb.

CHAPTER 17

Old Filth, Terry Veneering, Fred Fiscal-Smith. Two accounted for, life completed.

And in the shadows, like a little enigmatic scarecrow, Fiscal-Smith, born to be a background figure.

Fred Smith, has lived his life-time in the same lonely Yorkshire landscape—what happened to him? Each day, he saw to his mother, who was an invalid and almost always in bed, getting himself to and from school from a bus-stop down in Yarm. His father (its headmaster) left the house at six A.M. often to walk with his bike to the school along the shore. A splendid headmaster but a cold father.

But Fred? After his success at secondary school and evening classes, and the deaths of both parents, silence.

Fred Fiscal-Smith is a qualified lawyer living alone.

* * *

Scene I: Lone Hall, Yarm, North Yorkshire.

Set: A room, upper floor of large tumbledown, scarcely furnished house where, at a window overlooking the sea a young man FRED sits upright at a desk, back to audience, writing a letter. The wide window he faces shows huge extent of racing sky.

Hour: just before sunset.

Month: October.

Year: Say, 1955

*

Stretching below are the great Chemical Works of the North East, a thousand narrow chimneys each one crowned with an individual flame. They stretch from the estuary of the busy river Tees and include the remains of the old fishing village of Herringfleet.

Pan to a dreary jerry-built town built over bomb damage of twenty years before. Trees that once marched along the ridge of the Cleveland Hills are limp and dying and stand out black and tattered, reminders of an ancient domain. Only the sea survives un-changed. It frames the shore of the flat and sorrowful land-scape. It swings out. Swings in. For the letter-writer it is silent, and distant.

Figure at desk (Fred Fiscal-Smith) is writing a letter with a fountain pen (ink, Swan. Blue-Black). As he writes light is slowly fading from the sky which by the end of the scene has left darkness outside and the windows a splash of black light. Lights have begun to show across the estuary. A little flat, waltzing blue flame tops each of the forest of chimneys.

The smell of the chemicals rolls across the land and more dis-gustingly as night falls. Letter-writer holds handkerchief to his face. (Handkerchief white cotton. Large and clean. Marks & Spencer.)

Letter   Lone Hall
                          To Terence Veneering M.A. Oxon. Herringfleet
                                                                    Yarm
                                                        North Yorkshire

My dear Terry,

This is a letter of congratulation on the news I see in today's *Times*: that you have passed out top in the Bar Finals Examinations and are henceforth to be revered as the best-qualified lawyer in England and life member of the Inner Temple.

But perhaps you don't remember me? We haven't met since our early school days. Nor have I heard of you since 1941 September 15th as I recall, 2 days after the air-raid when my father and Canon Greisepert came to collect you from some-where in the Lake District and took you to your new school, Ampleforth College: the day after you had so cleverly, providentially, jumped ship, *The City of Benares*, as she set sail to drown, or rather cause a German U-Boat to torpedo and drown, over a hundred people, most of them children in Mid-Atlantic and including your headmaster and his wife, the Fondles.

I did not come with my father and Griesepert to find you, but stayed with mother who was ill. We lived inland from the bombing of the coast and here I still reside. I breed a few Highlanders.

I have never set foot in Ampleforth College although it is nearby. I went to Middlesbrough Grammar School and then to Middlesbrough Tech a few miles from home. I too have become a Barrister, but on the despised Northern Circuit. It serves me well.

My parents are dead. I still live (alone) in the old house that looks across to Herringfleet and the sea, and its only disadvantage is that it is far from the railway. I am less prosperous than you people in the South but I am still in touch with those at the Bar, and I go to stay with them as often as possible. I very much hope that you and I might meet again? Trains from York are frequent and I can get to York with the aid of a series of buses.

It has taken me a little time to realise that Terence Veneering MA (Oxon) is the Terry Venetski (or Varenski? How insular we were!) of my school days. You made a wise move, to my mind. There are some very dubiously-named members of the Bar at present, many of them dusky.

You would not recognise Herringfleet. Nothing is left of what we knew. No slum terraces, no cooking on the firebacks. Muriel Street? Ada Street? Who were they? Muriel and Ada? No weekly animal-sacrifice for the Sunday joint takes place in the slippery back alleys. You may well remember, just before the War, some of us coming with bowls to buy the blood? A salt-black—a black salt smell?

There followed after the war the smell of the chemical works. It was very toxic, but we sat it out. It rolled down the coast and up here into the hills. I wish some artist might paint the chemical chimneys. There will be no record left soon. The poisons here are now quite muted, though still released at night.

Some sort of phantom of the smell rolls yet along the coast and up here into the hills at nightfall when they hope we are asleep. And all the trees along the Cleveland ridge—Captain Cook's statue you will remember?—are dying.

If you do think of returning for a visit however, there is an excellent hotel in Yarm. It was once the Judges' Lodging, where they all stayed on Circuit—maybe for Assizes—I don't know. Sometimes, even now, you can come upon nostalgic members of the Judiciary drowsing there on vacation and hoping for some decent conversation. Rather terrible vermilion and ermine, portraits grace the staircase. It is a place where, if you visited, I should be delighted to come if you thought of inviting me to dinner?

But, first of course, it would be pleasant to come and stay with you in London in your hour of glory.

Sincerely yours, Fred Smith

PS: You will see from the Law Lists that I am now

known as Fiscal-Smith. Fiscal is my own invention, as (perhaps) Veneering is yours?

* * *

Scene II	Fade to a dark place under the rafters of a brothel and a dodgy dentist on Piccadilly Circus, London.
	The room is unfurnished except for books and a canvas bed with a metal frame. Coloured lights swing past its dirty window all night long; a released rainbow after years of war-time blackout. Noise of traffic and shouting continuous. The noise of post-war, but still threadbare, London trying hard for joy.
Figure	(Terry Veneering) is lying on bed fully clothed. It has long blond hair. It is very drunk. The room is carpetless. The wash basin is blocked.
	A bashing on the door. The figure on the bed, Terence Veneering, top of the lists of the International Bar Examinations of Great Britain and the Commonwealth, puts a cardboard box over his head and shouts that he is not in.
Girl's voice:	It's not the rent. I've got a letter for you.
Terry	
Veneering:	Money in it?
Girl:	How should I know? Come on, I'll cook you a dinner.

Silence falls. At last footsteps retreat. Outside, the crowds are screaming in Piccadilly Circus, the ugliest piazza in Europe, for the return of the statue of Eros the god of love, removed for safety during the Blitz. The lights revolve upwards and in the rafters it is like a light-house. Round and round.

Slowly light fades away and noise of crowds, too. From this tall and narrow old house behind the hoardings you hear only the odd occasional street-fight, tarts shouting, students singing. Lights, lights, lights, after the years of darkness still seem a daring extravagance. The blond man on the canvas bed groans.

The letter from Fiscal-Smith has been pushed under the door. Terry Veneering has no shilling for the meter and it is cold. He staggers about. Finds a cigarette. Takes letter to window in case they've cut off the electrics. Reads the letter.

It is from a lonelier man than he is. This shows in the reader's face, which softens slightly. (Voice-over of letter here perhaps?)

Then he moves, finds paper to reply. There is only a defunct and grubby Brief long-settled out of court.

* * *

Dear old Fred,

Well I never! Thanks old chum for the congrats. Often wondered what became of you. I went up to Oxford for five minutes before the War. After school—R.C. Ampleforth College, fees paid in full by the school itself, thanks to old Greasepaint (remember?). Then Oxford again. Followed by National Service, showing the flag around the Med. In white and gold and proud salutes. Nothing nearer heaven than then! The girls at all the ports, all waving us in! Malta—oh Malta! The priests shook holy water over us. And the processions and the flowers! Mind you, the mothers made the girls get home by nine o' clock for Mass next morning. Every morning! Hard to leave behind, Fred. Hard to leave. I'll go back one day. Place to die in. (I'm a bit drunk.)

I waved goodbye to the ship off Point and waited for

passage home, when, bugger me, Royal Navy sends me off again to parade ourselves around the Far East to show that England is England Yet (pah!). Married there. Yes. Chinese girl—very rich. Boy born rather soon. Harry. I am not of The Orient and I guess a weird son-in-law.

My wife Elsie (yes!) is said to be the most beautiful woman in Hong Kong. She has a bracelet round her wrist of transparent jade. There since birth and will be all her life. It was the transparency of the seamless jade did it for me. God, I am drunk, Fred Smith!

By the way—look again. I was not top of the Bar Finals. I share the silly honour with one Edward Feathers. I expect you've heard of him? Or know of him? We were at Oxford together on return visit—cramming—after the War. We hardly spoke. He was the Olde Worlde star of the Oxford Union and I was never called upon to open my mouth there in debate because I am *louche*, Fred, *louche*. Feathers is one of those born to the Establishment. Cut in bronze, unfading. *Big* connections I've no doubt. He dominated his Year. Hates the Arts. Does not drink or wench. Bloody clever. We hate each other—God knows why—we pass each other now in the Inns of Court without a word. He of course has got Chambers already. I am still cap in hand—wig in hand—but I can't afford a wig. Nor a cap, come to that.

I can think of nobody I would have preferred NOT to share an honour with than Eddie Feathers. Remember Harold Fondle? No—he's not as bad as that: but he has the fatal APLOMB.

Feathers is Prometheus. He is thoroughly, wonderfully good. The idea of sharing an honour with him is almost as terrible as that of sharing a woman with him. I cannot however think that this could ever, possibly, happen.

Also—how I run on!—he was ahead of me at the Prep

School I would have given almost anything to go to. Where your father taught once, Fred. Man in charge called 'Sir'. Met him when your Dad came and rescued me when I ran away from being an evacuee (and a corpse) on *The City of Benares*. Feathers was Sir's star student. Sir clearly in love with him. Well, well, 'this little Orb'. In-it amazing?

Why am I so full of hate for this man Feathers? 'He hath a certain beauty in his life/That makes mine ugly'. We'll go to a Shakespeare together shall we Fred? When you do come down to London? If I can afford a ticket. There's Olivier being something or other in St. Martin's Lane. Sorry. I'm drunk. Did I say that before?

Oh yes—don't expect to stay with me. I'm sleeping on the floor at present. There's no respectable accommodation to be had in London unless you have Oxford 'connections'. No doubt Les Plumes of this ghastly world have. By the way, how interesting that you are 'breeding Highlanders'. Do they wear the kilt? Do you know Bobbie Grampian?

London's a bomb-site Fred-boy. Stay among your stinking chimneys.

Love from

Terry

* * *

Curtain to some solemn music.

Chapter 18

O*ne week later*
Terry sat in the Law Library of the Inns of Court looking at the envelope addressed to Fred Smith he had found in his pocket. It had been there for some days. Letter to the dreaded Fred of yester-year, the meanest boy in the school. He wondered about putting a penny or a penny-halfpenny stamp on it. Penny would do. He had few enough. F. Fiscal-Smith, Lone Hall, Near Yarm, North Yorkshire. A really merry-sounding address.

Think of swatty little Fred turning up! Well, well. And a lawyer. Post it when I go out. On the way to the interview. Why ever did I write so much to him? Terrible bore when he was eight. Will be worse now. Lawyer. Of *course* a lawyer! Well, he can't come and land down here with me. I'm on the pavement.

Tonight would be the first Terry Veneering had no bed to go to. The landlady, so called, in Piccadilly Circus had said as he left the house that morning, 'Oh, yes. There'll be another man here tonight. I told him I thought you wouldn't mind sharing'.

'Well, you were wrong,' he'd said, slamming upstairs, picking up his case, crashing out of the front door after leaving four shillings on the hall-stand.

Where to go? Think about it in the Law Library. He'd already been the rounds of the few people he knew in London. Might try MacPherson. Lived in Kensington somewhere with his mother. Thoroughly nice man. No side to him.

'Hullo? Oh, *hullo*! So glad you're in, Robert. It's Terence.

Yes, Veneering. Yes. Oh, thanks. Well of course I'm only joint top with Feathers. No—I haven't actually met up with him lately. Listen Bobby, you once said if I was ever stuck for a bed in London—could I possible stay tonight? I've an interview for a place in Chambers around five o' clock in Lincoln's Inn and nowhere to sleep. I'd be gone by breakfast.'

Silence. Then 'Tomorrow night is that, Terence? Tomorrow night?'

'Well, actually tonight. My landlady told me this morning that she thought I wouldn't mind sharing—with a stranger. So I . . .'

'Good God. That's terrible. Of course you're welcome. Delighted. I'll just check with mother. We're having a bit of a party here tonight. Scottish dancing. We've a piper coming. I don't suppose you have the kilt in your luggage? No? Well, never mind. Can lend.'

'Actually, I haven't much luggage at all. Toothbrush sort of thing.'

'We have some splendid people coming. Do you reel?'

'Well, no.'

'Never mind. I seem to remember that you play?'

'No! Well, saxophone. Bit of Blues. Piano.'

'Oh, well. Shame. Just come. Not too early or late. Mother has very early dinner and goes to bed at nine.'

'Actually, could I come another time? I can't be sure of times tonight—I mean this evening—you see. Depends on how long this interview's going to last. I'm looking for a seat in Chambers—anywhere, of course will do.'

'Where's the interview?'

'Oh, just general. Libel and slander. Nothing distinguished. Not sure where. It's on a bit of paper. Tutor at Christ Church set it up.'

'Be careful. Libel's a vile life. Come some other time won't you, Terence?'

'Thanks.'

'Oh—and do you sing? Madrigals! Next week . . . ?'

'Not very well, Bobby.'

'Oh, pity. I live at home here you know. Shan't bother with Chambers just yet. Bit nostalgic for the old days after three years in the German nick. Picking up the old life . . . '

* * *

Where would he sleep tonight?

Veneering crossed the Strand, the letter to little Fred in his pocket. He dropped it into a letter-box on the corner of Chancery Lane and thought of it being opened in the despoiled—and by him never re-visited—Cleveland Hills. It was late afternoon now and the fog had come down. He thought of Malta gleaming at dawn. Thought of Elsie's jade bracelet, her creamy skin, the startlingly beautiful little boy, Harry. Veneering was wearing his only suit, his demob suit which was already getting shiny. Hideous. Cold. He was hungry.

Why in the name of God did he want a job as a working court-room lawyer? In a set of Chambers nobody had ever heard about? Because there were ten applicants and more for every vacancy and often war heroes and/or rich. Had to try everything that was offered. Otherwise—No Room at the Inn. Ha-ha.

He found the Chambers and walked in.

* * *

The Clerk—a very famous Clerk he had been told: Augustus, the king-maker—looked him up and down and said, 'Oh yes. I remember. All right, I'll see if he can see you. He's very busy,' and vanished, pretending to yawn.

Then, 'Follow me.'

'Mr. Veneering, sir, of Christ Church College, Oxford and new member of the Inner Temple, starred First, top of Bar Finals, introduced by old tutor, an old friend of these Chambers.'

The tall, dapper Head of Chambers, very scarlet about the face, shiny-lipped, found his way from among the crowd of young men, all drinking wine and shouting with laughter. 'Mr. *Who*? Oh, yes, yes, yes. Mr. Veneering. Your tutor—he was mine, too, you know—I'm younger than I seem. How unbelievably young you all look now despite the recent conflict. I hear that you have travelled about the Globe? Showing the Flag? What a joy. All our troubles ended by the dropping of the splendid atomic bomb. Your—our—tutor never thought much of me you know, yet here I am at last proving myself useful to him. Soaking up the latent talent of our great College. He says you're Russian? I don't think—I'd better say at once— that these are *quite* the Chambers for a Russian. Have you tried one of the more *un-noticeable* professions? Perhaps the Civil Service?'

Veneering said that he was a lawyer.

'Well exactly. *Exactly.* But we are exclusively Libel Chambers here. We are, I'll admit, on the verge of being fashionable—even Royalty hovers—but all is very slow and fragile. So *very* few decadent duchesses. *Huge* sums to be made of course eventually, but, dear boy, not yet. Tell me, why did you become a lawyer?'

'Someone said I'd make a good one. He left me all his money. He wasn't born rich. He qualified down here in London living on ten shillings a week. He set up offices in various parts of the country for worthy chaps like me. He was a sort of saint.'

'Oh, I'm afraid he would never have been in the swim.'

'No, he wasn't. As a matter of fact I'm living on about ten shillings a week myself.'

'He was a member of the *Bar*, this benefactor?'

'No. Just a solicitor. In the north-east. He was killed in an air-raid. His name was Parable . . . '

'I can't believe it! It is *pure* John Bunyan! He can't, if you don't mind my saying so, have left you very much money if you have to live on ten shillings a week?'

'It turns out that my inheritance has gone missing. His house and office both took direct hits in the north in 1941. I only received twenty-five pounds in notes which had been in a friend's keeping and a letter saying all his other assets were to be mine when I'd taken Bar Finals. I have my Royal Navy pension of two hundred a year.'

'Oh, my dear chap—yes, thank you Hamish, just up to the top—and, he impressed you?'

'Of course. He made sure I left home and didn't get killed myself in the same air-raid. I was en route to Canada as an evacuee . . . '

'Oh, my God! What dramatic lives we have all led. Thank your stars you weren't torpedoed aboard *The City of Somewhere*. All the little babies floating upside down in the water like dead fish. Depth-charged. Wonderful accounts of the few survivors plucked from the debris. Upturned boats, basket chairs—even a rocking-horse! *Not* very sporting. Now—just a minute, Toby,'—and the red-lipped man walked Terry out of the room, a manicured hand around his shoulder. 'Dear boy, I would *dearly* like to have you. Have you tried other Chambers? You have? Ah well, you know, the chance will come. Give it time. There's no work anywhere at present. Nobody sane is going to Law. The price of victory is lethargy and poverty. We must bide our time and use our private money. I'm sure you'll find Mr. Parable's treasure somewhere. But as you can see . . . As you can hear . . . '

The noise and the odours of bibulous men, the cigarette smoke, the good white burgundy followed Veneering out and back in to the stately planting of Lincoln's Inn Fields.

'I have simply no room for another pupil,' said the Head of Chambers, shaking hands. 'Dear Fellow, how I've packed them in already! I've got them swinging from the Chandeliers!'

* * *

'So!' said Veneering. 'Ha!' and he walked across the grass and up to the stagnant static-water tanks set in place years ago to deal with the coming fire-bombs on the Inn. 'It has come to this. A decadent country, threadbare, idle, frivolous, cynical, hidden money.'

He longed all at once for Herringfleet. For his shadowy brave father, for Peter Parable. High-mindedness. The coal-cart. He kicked his feet in the tired grass.

'So much for the Law. The Law is still a ass, as the great man had said over a hundred years ago. Dickens. Lived near here. Must have had a splendid view of the Law in action when you think about it. Five or ten minutes' walk from his house in Doughty Street. I'll go and see it. I'll go now. I'll pay homage. I'll prostrate myself on his study floor and I'll say, "Dickens, you did what you could (And why didn't you get a knighthood? Queen Victoria liked you. Was it the infidelity?) and you did a lot. And you changed it all without a Law degree. You did it on your own with a pen and a bottle of ink."

'I am not going near the Law now. I'm going to be a journalist. A left-wing journalist. *The New Statesman* offices are up at the end here, up the alley. I'll walk in now. I'll demand a job.

'And I'll be given one. I feel it in the wind.'

* * *

Back in the Libel Chambers the clerk, Augustus, was pushing his way through the throng of the party. Finding his Head of Chambers he said, 'Sir? Where is he?'

'*Who*? Augustus, have a drink.'

'Him. The foreign fellow. Looking for pupillage?'

'Oh, *him*. Goldilocks. No good, Augustus. Useless. Too odd. Too foreign.'

'You never sent 'im away, Sir?'

'Oh, he wasn't desperate.'

'But *we* are desperate, you fool, Sir. That one's a winner.'

'Now then, Gussee, how d'you know?'

'I'm a Clerk. I know what I can sell. He's young and fit and he misses nothing. Brilliant. Better qualified than anyone in this room. You've lost us all a fortune you bloody fool, Sir.'

'Oh, don't say that! Get him back then, Gus. We'll take him on. I'll write to his tutor.'

'He won't come back. Not that one. It's love me or leave me with that one. You'll hear of him again all-right, but he'll always be on the other side. That one's a life-time type. Not that he'll want much truck with libel and slander now. It'll be the Commercial Bar for him, he's poor. You've lost him his beliefs, about helpless widows and orphans. That one's for Lord Chancellor. He'll be on the Woolsack if he wants to be. I feel like going with him. You dolt, Sir.'

'Oh dear! Augustus—Augustus, have a pint with me later in the Wig and Pen Club.'

* * *

Veneering walked away from the static-water tanks on Lincoln's Inn Fields and towards the offices of *The New Statesman and Nation* where he would, of course, be taken on immediately. Then a short walk to Dickens' house in Doughty Street, a hand-shake with his ghost, then cadge a lift somehow back to Oxford to recover his books, lecture-notes and dissertation, then burn the lot.

After which . . . ! Back East, and into the iron grip of Elsie's family business.

Oh!

Towards the north end of Lincoln's Inn the crowds, en route to their buses and trains home to north London, were tramping beside and behind him. Crowds tramping south towards the river and Waterloo Bridge and station were advancing towards him in similar numbers. Nobody spoke or smiled or paused.

But Terry Veneering stopped dead.

He stopped dead.

The crowds washed round him, one or two people looking up at his pale face and glaring eyes and platinum hair. (About to faint? Hungry? Gormless? Mad?) Some grumbled, 'What the hell' and stumbled and some said, 'Bloody hell! You had me nearly over.'

Terry turned round and began to walk slowly back with the south-bound throng, retracing the last twenty or so yards. Then, he stopped again, turned again and looked, fearfully, at the building to his right. There was a little patch of old garden, its railings taken away years before to make Spitfires, a scuffed stone archway with a scuffed stone staircase twisting upwards. Up the first two steps of the staircase, on the wall of the old building was a faded wooden panel with its traditional list of the Lawyers' names who worked within. The list was far from new, but painted in immemorial legal copperplate. He read the words 'Parable, Apse & Apse, Solicitors.'

* * *

The door was not locked. He walked straight in expecting a derelict abandoned store-room, fire-buckets, stirrup pumps, tin hats abandoned since the Blitz. Just inside he saw instead a row of iron coat-hooks where someone had hung a bowler hat and folded a pair of clean kid gloves on top of it.

Terry opened an inner door without knocking and facing him sat a young man at a desk, a sandwich suspended in time en route to his mouth. Beside him on a smaller and more splintery desk stood a gigantic Remington type-writer on which was arranged a pocket mirror, a paper napkin, paper plate and similar sandwich. A middle-aged woman wearing a seal-skin coat sat behind it.

Four jaws ceased to move. Four eyes stared. Terry said, 'I believe that you are a firm of solicitors?'

'Ah,' said the young man, putting the sandwich down on a clean handkerchief on his desk. 'Not exactly! Not for a few years. We are in a state of flux. But may we help you?'

'You must know—have known Mr. Parable? Mr. Parable-Apse?'

'No, sir. I'm afraid all the old partners in the firm are dead. We keep the names on the door in the old tradition. It is rather like the memorial friezes on the walls of the tombs of the Pharaohs. I am a very, *very* distant Apse. Thomas.'

'And so this is—a set of Chambers?'

'Well no. For years it seems to have been a solicitor's office. One of a string of almost charitable centres for the poor—an early Legal Aid—set up by the founding Apse, a northerner. A lonely philanthropist who made a considerable amount of money.'

'And he . . . ?'

'Was killed in the war. We are in the process of being dis-possessed by the Inn. Desperate for space. Work here is rather slow and no-one is really in charge. All the first Mr. Apse's fortune was left to someone quite outside the family with a strange name, and he is dead.'

Very carefully Terry sat down on an upright chair with one leg missing and propped up by books. He said, 'I should like to negotiate for these Chambers.'

'I'm afraid it is quite impossible,' said the woman in the seal-skin coat. She delicately tore the sandwich apart with her pink finger nails.

'My name is Veneering.'

'Oh, yes?'

'I was born Varenski.'

'That has a *ring*,' she said.

'It seems that I am the one who inherited Mr. Parable-Apse's estate. Though he promised me only twenty-five pounds.'

After he had finished his sandwich the young man repeated, 'I am Tom Apse, a very distant relation just keeping the premises open. And this is my secretary, Mrs. Flagg.'

She nodded and picked up her knitting. She said, 'I'm afraid that buying these premises will be impossible, Mr. Varenski. We will of course inform the Inn of your offer, as we do everyone else who comes in. Our only safeguard up to now has been that Mr. Apse is an *Apse*, like on the door. To keep them off . . . '

'And,' said Tom Apse, 'Upkeep for *any* tenant will be astronomical. And I have my Egyptology to consider, and Mrs. Flagg, well, she has Mr. Flagg. There is money though. I'm sorry sir, in spite of your interesting name—I'm sure we've heard it before somewhere—I'm afraid you won't be able to make a case for yourself. Old Mr. Parable's Slavonic heir was drowned at sea in 1941 on the evacuee liner *The City of Benares*.'

Terry stood up.

'I am that evacuee,' he said. 'Except that I wasn't. I had a premonition and good friends.' (The world is singing! The light of heaven fills the sky! Dear God! Dear Sir. Dear Father Griesepert.) 'I changed my name.'

Tom Apse and Mrs. Flagg also rose to their feet and the three shook hands.

'At present I am without money,' said Terry.

'Then how do you think you can buy this?'

'Borrow,' said Terry. 'There must be Security somewhere. And a proper search. There doesn't seem, if I may say so, to be much paper-work about the office.'

'We get few clients,' said Tom Apse. 'We pass them on. The Apse archive is very daunting.'

'You must consider us *Caretakers*,' said Mrs. Flagg, 'as the desultory fight drags on. The cupboards and the cellar are full of paper, though some of it is still dampish after the Blitz.'

She arranged her coat around her shoulders and on high heels rocked towards the wall where she opened a cupboard and watched several shelves of documents, tied up with tape that had once been red, vomit all over the floor.

'Work to be done! We'll start tomorrow,' said Veneering. Now, the three of us are going to The Wig and Pen Club. Right NOW!'

'Sir,' said Tom Apse. 'I'm sorry—but identification? We only have your word. How do we know who you are?'

'You don't,' said Veneering. 'Put your coat on fully Mrs.— I can't call you "Mrs. Flagg". What's your—Daisy. Oh, pretty. Come on Tom.'

'But *money*, sir?'

'Mr. Parable lived on ten shillings a week. I haven't broken into next week's yet and I'll be sleeping here free tonight if we can find a hammock.'

* * *

In The Wig and Pen Club in the Strand sat the red-lipped Libel Silk with friends. He rose at once and came across.

'So delighted to see you again, Mr.—er—I have been sending out search-parties. I find that I have a place for you in my Chambers after all. My Clerk, The Great Augustus, is very cross with me for not making myself clear.'

'Too late!' Terry shouted, signalling a barman. 'I'm fixed up. I'm off to discuss matters with the Treasurer of the Inn tomorrow morning. I seem to have inherited a sleeping set of Chambers of my own.'

'You are fixed up? Already? You'll find it a very lengthy business on your own. Take years. Ask anyone about the Parable-Apse fiasco for instance. A disgrace. Dragging on. Dickensian.'

'Well, I have an inheritance looming. Fallen, by the grace of God, into my lucky lap. Meet my secretary Mrs. Flagg—and my—junior clerk—Mr. Tom Apse. I have a good senior clerk already in mind.'

'I'm afraid Mr.—er—, you have simply no idea! It will take a life-time.'

'Yes. But I'm young. I have wide connections, you know, especially in the Far East. And thanks for the interview. And thank Augustus. Tell him I shan't forget him.'

'I don't forget anything,' he added.

'And now Mrs. Flagg and I are off to find a bed.'

Dizzily on the pavement Daisy Flagg burst into joyous tears. 'Oh, come *on*,' said Terry, spinning her around, 'Beautiful coat. Is it real?'

'It's only coypu,' she wailed, happily. 'It's only a superior kind of rat.'

'When I come into my Kingdom,' said Terence Veneering of Parable Chambers, Inns of Court, 'You shall have sables.'

And so Terry Veneering was established in his own Chambers as if by angelic intervention. And so began the long, slow, interminable legal process of disinterring his Parable inheritance.

He was never one to reflect on the meaning of life. Or the shape of his own life. He knew that from childhood he presented the figure of one certain to succeed, charm, delight and conquer. Not for him the grave, moral pace of the gentlemanly Edward Feathers.

But had he ever considered doing anything as dull as writing an autobiography he would certainly not have chosen as a pivotal point. He would have chosen the day some six months later when he had had to scrape the bottom of the judicial barrel down at the Brighton County Court alongside the beginner, little Fred Fiscal-Smith, and against—needless to say— Edward Feathers: the case of the over-sexed lion-tamer's apprentice. For this was the day he realised that he had no stomach for Crime, even if it had not been so badly paid.

Stepping out of Victoria station at the end of that dreadful day his heart sunk even further, for in London there was fog. London fogs were getting worse again. During the War coal had been rationed. Now coal was back and so were the fogs that swirled about the East and West End. They nuzzled and licked and enwrapped everyone in yellowish limp fleece. They stained your clothes, your hair, got up your nose and down your ears. Your chest wheezed. When you sneezed, your handkerchief was dark ochre. You muffled your mouth. You coughed and coughed.

It was only when they stepped out of the Brighton Belle on Platform One that the three lawyers realised that, during their day in breezy, wholesome Brighton, the fog in London that had hung about for days had reached Dickensian proportions. It had turned into 'The Great Fog'. It might last for days. It was also getting dark and there was no transport of any kind to get them home.

Old Filth was all right, he lived just round the corner in his spartan, curtainless apartment where there were two small electric radiators, and Fiscal-Smith suggested that he might stay the night there as well. In case—though he knew he was probably safe—Feathers asked him to stay too, Veneering announced that he would go to The Goring Hotel near Buckingham Palace and not more than two minutes from the station and he set off holding his arms out in front of him, his brief-case between them. He immediately vanished thinking vaguely that somewhere there would be a taxi. Any hotel was way above his means, let alone The Goring. So, as a matter of fact, was a taxi. The brief fee for the lion-tamer's boy had been seven guineas—the shillings to go to Tom Apse as Clerk—and anyway it hadn't yet been paid.

London had fallen into the silence of death and all its lights were gone. Abandoned cars stood in the middle of the road. Occasionally a shadow trudged past him emerging from and disappearing into the mist like the ghost of Hamlet's father. London had lost its voice.

Taking twenty minutes to cross into what he hoped was Grosvenor Street he collided with an elephantine shape standing lightless and empty. It seemed to be a bus. He turned from it, thinking that this was going to be slow, and stepped in front of a car whose lights were smudges. He thought that the nearest Underground station would be the only hope and can-

noned into a lone newspaper boy shouting a cracked refrain—
Star, News, Standard—to nobody.

'Goin far, Guv?'

'Inns of Court.'

'You'll not be there by morning.'

'How are you getting home then?'

'I'll doss down the back of the statue.'

'What, Marshall Foch?'

'Don't mind which Marshall. Any Marshall. Marshall and
Snelgrove. Cheers, Guv.'

It was three hours later that Veneering reached Fetter Lane.
There were a few flares burning here and there and along the
Strand in front of the empty shops and restaurants. He went
almost hand over hand towards Lincoln's Inn—what he hoped
was Lincoln's Inn—decided that it couldn't be, clutched at
some masonry beside him and toppled upon the steps of
Parable-Apse.

He fell inside. He found a light. He slammed his front door
upon the murk. There came a flash of memory of a blue sea—
his sunburst of life in the post-war Navy. His—hum, yes,
well—his wife and lanky little boy.

In the office the fire was not lit but a sack of coals stood
beside the shabby old grate. There was nobody now to tumble
the coals down to the cellar via the coal hole in the road and
nobody to drag it up to the grate from the cellar if they did.
Coal, he thought.

He kept his in the sack, covering it with a blanket on the
few occasions when anyone called. But too late—too tired—to
light a fire tonight. He found a bottle of whisky in the cupboard and some cream crackers and swigged down the whisky.
The greatest joy he had ever known!

He thought of the threat that the government were to ban
coal fires in London and he thought of his mother. He
informed her and asked what she thought, but received no

answer. The fog had entered the house with him. It was wreathed above his head. It smeared the window. How it stank.

'Mam—I'm packing this in. The Law. I've an interview with a paper. Foreign correspondent.'

'Your collar's filthy,' she said.

'It's the fog.'

'Steep it and wash it. You've got an iron?'

'You lived by coal.'

'I'd no option. You have.'

'I need sleep.'

'There's time to sleep and there's time to waken.'

Veneering crawled across the floor towards the bedroom stair. 'I'm drunk, Mam. I want to go to bed.'

'You'll do it. Remember your father.'

'He had you.'

'Well, you have me, too.'

He was in his bed. He drew a cover over him. He slept. The horrible city sprawled outside in thick unanswering silence. Veneering was ready to leave it for ever. And so, to the horrible, still-yellowish morning.

* * *

The knocking upon the front door had the desperate, dogged quality of a long assault. On it went, on and on.

At last, 'Message,' said a youth Veneering had not seen before as he peered blearily round the door.

'What?'

'Message for Mr. Veneering. Urgent. Reply essential. Shall I step in?'

'No,' said Veneering, taking the note and shutting the door on the boy, feeling about in the dark vestibule, finding the door to his office, groaning and grunting. He read:

'*Mr. Veneering.* Appointment this morning, April 30th, ten o' clock at No. 21, St. Yyes Court, Gray's Inn. Respectable dress essential. Clear head. Mr. William Willy will see you for interview for possible place in new Chambers at present being established. Anticipating overseas connections. Reply to boy. Signed Augustus.'

'Nobody could be called Mr. William Willy,' said Terry Veneering. 'On the other hand the Great Augustus—I'll put my head on the block to it—has never made a joke.'

'Oh, well then. Shame. After yesterday's fiasco in the world of the eternal circus, he's too bloody late, Augustus. I go a hundred miles to defend a poor little gormless insect who tickles ladies' private parts as they're sitting enjoying the lions and tigers and he gets three months! *Three months* for a bit of harmless fun. Clearly I'm not cut out for Crime. First and only time most of them ever got tickled. Most of them never even noticed. Great Grandee Edward Feathers has palpitations of shock-horror. He's never tickled anybody's legs. Never will. *Gross* indecency—etc. Is this what we got our First Class honours for? "Pom, pom, pom" honks Feathers, County Court moron judge nodding in support, all his chins wagging like blancmange. Little lad gets three months in gaol. Fuck the English Bar, I'm off to *The New Statesman.* Journalism for Veneering. Get the words about the world, not into the fly-spotted Law Reports. Sorry, Augustus, Willy is too late. I'm dressed for a different play. I am about to approach the political rostrum. You—laddikins—take a note back saying I'm busy.'

'I can't do that, sir.'

'And for-why?'

'Because Augustus has you in mind. You can't *not* reply to Augustus, Mr. Veneering.'

'It is, I know, very early in the morning but could you just try to realise, BOY, that even you are not the slave of this

Olympian monster? Whoever he is—you are not in his THRALL. There are many barristers in thrall to their clerks. There are *Judges* in thrall to their clerks. Some clerks on the other hand have been murdered by—I am my own man, Boy, I make my own choices. Thank Augustus and say I have a previous engagement.'

He shut the outer door and listened to the boy marking time on the stones on the other side of it. After a while the boy rang the bell for a second time

'YES?' Veneering immediately flung it open. 'YES?'

'I think you better come, sir. Nothing to lose. Much to gain. And Augustus—well, you don't want 'im for your enemy, now, do you?'

'Oh, well then. O.K.' said Veneering, 'O.K. Say I'll come. Soon. Better shave. I've a very important interview this morning already, at *The New Statesman and Nation*. Tell Augustus. And tell him that to be summoned before someone called Mr. Willy sounds an unusual command.'

'Yes, sir. Shall I wait and take you round?'

'Whatever,' said Veneering, slamming the door, stamping up his stone spiral stair and surveying himself in his fur-lined waistcoat, pink open-neck shirt, tight black trousers, brown boots, long platinum new-look hair. He stared at the mirror for some minutes.

The boy had disappeared when he eventually emerged into Lincoln's Inn and its water tanks. Ah well. Got the message. *New Statesman* first priority. The literary Editor there a woman. Sounded daunting. Not young. Apparently somebody. Chat her up. Who's afraid? Not I who knew Mrs. Veronica Fondle—and I drowned her. This one had said on the phone that she promised nothing except a sandwich together in Lincoln's Inn Fields sitting on the grass to talk about his future. 'You sound so very young, Mr. Veneering. Did you not think of staying at Oxford—life as an academic?' (She ain't seen me yet!)

No, Mrs. Beetle-Bags, I did not. I don't want to interpret the world, I want to put it straight. To spread the globe out flat like pastry on a slab like Ma made. Pick it up, slap it down, turn it over like a Tarte Tatin in Le Trou Normand in Hong Kong. Oh hell, that was wonderful! I don't want a careful bloody life. Why am I turning to the right? This place in St. Yves Court— St. Yves, the Breton lawyer. And saint. (Might write a book on him?) Augustus's chambers—

Where there is nothing but a gaping door and windows and a heap of rubble on the pavement with a rope round it and a red lamp you light with a match. And it's eight years on. 1953— Christ! However did we win the War? No-one will ever know. I'll tell my grandchildren.

Or will I? Will I reminisce? Will they give a fuck for historic Britain? Little ragged-edged, off-shore island and not my country anyway. Go to Russia soon, let's hope. Everywhere fighting their neighbours to the death. Death doesn't bring life—ever.

He saw his house-master at his Roman Catholic school saying, 'Sharpen up, Veneering. The Resurrection?' Oh, fuck.

He took his eyes off the heap of rubble and looked up steps to a tall row of early-Victorian houses where doors and window frames gaped empty. In front of each house was a heap of rubble similar to that at his feet: beams and floorboards and shelving and corner-cupboards and lead fire-backs. Nearby there was a little marble chimney-piece. It had a small deep-carved circle at the top of each pillar. Around 1740, he thought. He lusted after it. A man was loading all the rubble into a lorry.

'Can I have that?'

'What—that broke fireplace?'

'Yes, how much?'

'Take it for free. How you goin' to get it home?'

'I will. Leave it aside.'

He stood looking at the silken marble skin under the grime. Smooth as jade. He saw the translucence and perfection of the surface under the dirt of the war. He thought there must always have been people who stared at such things. He imagined his wife's terrifying family at her birth, fastening the tiny jade rings around her baby wrists. Her shackles. He thought of his mother, pushing tripe about in the black frying pan on the coal fire. Her worn hands. He thought of all that his mother had had no knowledge of. Her tiny world where she, among all her family and friends, had alone pondered and sought helplessly for explanations.

Augustus was standing on the top steps of one of the unrestored houses. At the bottom of the steps near him, a girl's bike was propped on one pedal, its basket on the handlebars full of flowers. A girl pushed past Augustus and came running down the steps towards the bike. She passed Veneering by like a whip-lash, but he had the impression of happiness, good temper, laughter, excitement. She leapt on the bike, balanced, kicked the pedal and hurtled away out of sight. She was bare-legged, sandaled, in a crazy new-look skirt that did not suit her (legs a bit short—though good). She had not seen him.

Augustus called from above, 'Please come in, Mr. Veneering. I *hope* you are in time.' A dreadful look was cast upon the fur-lined sleeveless jacket.

'Mr. Willy can see you now. I hope.'

But there seemed to be nobody there.

The room was large but far from ready. The windows were newly glazed but still with builders' finger-marks. There was no carpet. Bookshelves were not yet filled. There was a big plain desk with little on it except an enormous concoction of cellophane-wrapping with a bunch of spring flowers in the midst, and a book.

A voice said, 'My god-daughter left them. The girl you were watching getting on to her bicycle.'

The man was small with a pasty face and sitting rather out of the light in an alcove beside a roundabout book-case. He had a sweet smile.

'I'm so sorry. I didn't see you.' Veneering found that he was tugging down the waist-coat. Pushing back his hair.

'Veneering?'

'Yes, er—you sent for me.'

Mr. William Willy said, 'I have been asked to establish a new set of Chambers for specialising in engineering and construction Law. There is to be a great deal of building work—'sky-scrapers,' bridges, roads—which we hope will continue to be in the hands of British lawyers. English engineers are still very much the best, except for the Italians, and in Hong Kong and Singapore for instance, there are some huge contracts brewing for what we call "The Far East" and the Americans call "The Orient", which shows a certain romanticism in them I suppose. I am Shanghai-born, Mr. Veneering. I am not a romantic. I understand you speak Mandarin? And you are a travelling man?'

'Well, only post-war Navy. Round the China Sea. Showing the flag. Yes, I do speak Mandarin. I find languages easy.'

'So you will travel?'

'Yes. I have few allegiances.'

'But you have a wife and small son in Hong Kong, Mr. Veneering.'

After a thoughtful space Veneering said, 'This isn't generally known. But yes.'

'Would you stoop to practice in the Construction Industry? They often call it "Sewers and Drains". High fees, international experience but you would be doomed to personal obscurity. No honours.'

'I haven't really thought . . . '

'About whether or not you care about obscurity?'

The pale-faced man walked to the window behind his desk and turned his back on Veneering and looked across London.

162 · JANE GARDAM

'You haven't really started thinking yet. You and Feathers.'

'If you are inviting Feathers,' said Veneering, 'then I'm not interested.'

'And nor, I'd guess, is he. He has connections of his own. You of course could become an academic. Or you would make a very good journalist. Maybe at *The New Statesman*? I expect you are left wing? But you—I have made enquiries—like big money. And power. The power in the East of your father-in-law's family?'

'This is like the night I arrived at Ampleforth and the monks grilled me,' said Veneering.

'Ah, yes. That was the night *The City of Benares* went down. You were very lucky to escape. Have you second-sight, Mr. Veneering? That is always useful. You might be very useful all round.'

'I don't talk about it. No—I jumped ship because—I wanted to go home. But I thought nobody had been told about that business.'

Augustus came in and took the god-daughter's flowers away to put them in water, leaving the book.

'Your name is not really Veneering, is it?'

'However do you know that . . . ?'

'Because I know my Dickens. You can't use a good name twice. It is a joke. Veneering was a *nasty* man . . . '

'I haven't actually read . . . '

'But you are *not* a nasty man. I knew your father. His name was Venitsky. Was it not?'

Silence.

'Your father, whatever his name, was I think from Odessa? A blond Odessan—very unusual. He had been a hero. He was left totally alone for years, at great risk, abandoned, crippled, fearless to the end. They got him of course. Not that I am suggesting that the whole purpose of the German air-raids in the north-east was to eliminate one defunct—shall we say specialist er—thinker? Political activist? Your father was a great man.'

Veneering said, 'Are you telling me my father was a spy?'

'I'm telling you, my dear fellow, to work for me in . . . the Construction Industry.'

* * *

'And have this.' He handed the book that the god-daughter had brought across the desk. 'I have any number of copies. *Life's Little Ironies*. Thomas Hardy was a builder and architect by trade you know. In the construction industry.'

Out on the street—a very thin Brief in his jacket—Veneering flagged down a taxi and persuaded the driver to heave in the fireplace. Then he opened the book and read on the fly-leaf, 'To my darling god-father Uncle Willy from Elizabeth Macintosh'.

During that last year in The Donheads, Feathers and Veneering, as we have said, drew slowly together step by hesitant step as they had walked the lanes around their village. First they had pointedly ignored each other from a distance. Later they had nodded and looked away. Then came the famous Christmas meeting when Feathers had shut himself out of his house as, cut off from the rest of the world by a snowfall and the Dorset earth beneath his feet beginning to freeze, feeling death clutch at his wheezy throat, seep into his ancient bones, at last, hand over hand, up Veneering's drive he went, from one branch of Veneering's dreary over-hanging yew trees to the next, until he had dragged himself, ancient, decrepit orphan of many storms, to Veneering's peeling front door.

Nobody locally—nor anywhere else—ever discovered what went on during the rest of that Christmas day, but afterwards the two old men met regularly in Feathers' (much warmer) sitting room in his house down their joint driveway, for chess. Chess and a drink. Or two. But never more (though we don't know what Veneering did back home up the slope, later in his lonely night).

Feathers never offered food. Nor did Terry Veneering ever suggest a return visit up the slope.

Their chess improved, their concentration deepened. The photograph of old Feathers' dead wife Elizabeth (Betty), with whom Veneering had been in love since he first set eyes on her on a bike outside Pastry Willy's office—and beyond her death, for he was still in love with her—surveyed the two old men from the mantel-piece.

It was a flattering photograph taken on a picnic on Malta where she and Feathers were completing their honeymoon half a century ago.

That day for the young couple (he had bought her a fat crimson and gold chair in a back street in Dacca during the honeymoon) had been a day of blue and gold on the cliff tips, the sea, far, far below—St. Paul's Bay, where he slew the serpent—running bright green.

There has always been on Malta the belief that there is a crack in the cliff top where a fresh-water stream runs silver. It trickles down the slope, falls, sprays out into the dark below. Far, far below a spout of spittle shining like light above the ocean. Betty, the bride had said, 'There! You see! There is a fresh-water spring dropping down to the shore.'

And the girl had stretched herself out and looked down through the crack, her legs out behind her. Her legs were not her best feature. They were Penelope's legs, not Calypso's—but they were brown and sleek and strong and her pretty Calypso feet kicked up and down and she lay, watching the clear water turn to mist. She shifted slightly and the water shifted slightly like a net. It revealed a very small glimpse of the creeping emerald tide below.

Sixty years on, comfortable in his winter sitting room, fire blazing, whisky coming along any minute and—(ha-ha!)—he'd taken Veneering's queen—a sweet peace fell upon Edward Feathers and for the first time since he'd acknowledged his wife's infidelity with this jumped-up good-looking cad he knew that his jealousy was over and that he could now look back over his life—and at his beloved wife with pleasure and pride.

Well, perhaps not. Perhaps love shall always be divorced from time.

What a delicious, young and merry face looked at him from the mantel-piece. The trophy of his successful life.

And only a photograph.

She was not necessary to him anymore.

She had never been a siren. There had been one or two of those, and he smiled kindly at his young self—oh almost possessed by that other one. Isobel. She must be gone by now. She never told her love. They say she only loved women. Rubbish. Did I re-write my will? I expect she's gone by now. All shadows.

But potent shadows. We strengthened ourselves, Betty and I. Isobel weakened me.

Sometimes I mix them all up.

On the whole, he said, addressing an audience of some great court, I managed well. Better than Veneering and his idiot adolescent marriage. How lonely that shrill Elsie must have been. She left him of course and the boy didn't love her. If we are honest, it was Madame Butterfly who left Pinkerton (I say, that's rather an original thought) and Veneering knew his weakness. He knew from the beginning he was not the man he might have been.

'Veneering,' he said. 'Check-mate, I think? Yes? Whisky now—you ready?'

Silence. Then Veneering saying, 'Yes. Good idea' and continuing to stare at the board.

'Tell me,' said Filth, 'that's to say if you have no objection—how did you get yourself entangled with Elsie?'

There was such a long silence that Filth looked down into his glass, then up at the ceiling, then winked at Betty's photograph and wondered if he had gone too far.

Or maybe Veneering—God he was ugly now, too—was becoming deaf. He had rather wondered. Didn't appear to be listening. He looked keenly now at Veneering's ears to see if there were any of those disgusting pink lumps stuck in them like half-masticated chewing gum. Thank God no need of that himself.

No sign. What's the matter with the man? Sulking? Thinks I'm prying. Not answering.

'Sorry, Veneering. Shouldn't have asked. Never even asked you about that ship-wreck incident you were in. *City of Benares*? They tell me you were in a life boat for twelve days and only a child. Amazingly brave.'

Still silence. A coal dropped in the grate. Then Veneering moved a pawn with a smart crack as he put it down. 'Check-mate to me, I think?' He picked up his glass and drained it at a gulp.

* * *

'Elsie?' he said. 'Do you really want to know about Elsie, Filth? More dignified if you'd never asked. Rather surprised at you. And I wasn't a hero of the *Benares*. I ran away before she sailed. Not brave at all.'

'Good God, it's not what we all believe.'

'Ran off across Liverpool till I heard her hooter sounding off goodbye. Three days later she was torpedoed. Well, I probably wouldn't have drowned. Some didn't. Two in this village didn't. Those fat twins. Never speak. I was sent away afterwards to a Catholic boarding school—I'm Catholic—because my family had copped it the same night in an air-raid. Then I started at Oxford and got called up for National Service postwar.

'I missed that,' said Filth. 'Done the army. Older than you.'

'Then off to the Med in the RNVR. Six months paradise. Every port. Showing the flag. God, the girls! Standing screaming for us on every quay. No reason not to spring into their arms. No Penelopes sitting sewing blankets back home and wishing we were there to take the dog out. Heaven. Then, just about to sail for Portsmouth—floods of tears and gifts and promises of eternal love—and they sent us *on*! *On*—out East to the Empire of the Sun. Hong Kong. Singapore. Unbelievable pleasure. Sun. No chores. Splendid naval rations, enough money, Tiger beer and all of us like gods, bronzed and fit and victorious, dressed in white and gold. Parties at governors' residences. Parties, parties. I never read a book. I never thought beyond the day. I had no home to hurry back to. I met Elsie.'

'I remember her.'

'Oh, yes. Singapore. She was—well, you saw her.'

'Not until about ten years later. She was so beautiful. To me she was beyond desire,' said Filth.

'D'you remember,' said Veneering, 'how when anyone saw her for the first time, the room fell silent?'

'Yes.'

'Chinese. Ageless. Paris thrown in. Perfect French. Poise.'

'We all wanted poise in women after the war. The women who'd been in the war were all so ugly and battered. The rest were schoolgirls and they slopped over us. We thought nothing of them. We were looking for our mothers I think, sometimes. Beautiful mothers.'

'Elsie was like your mother?'

'No. My mother was a figure from—beyond the Ural mountains.'

'She gave you your blond hair?'

'No. Not exactly. She could have organised the Ural mountains.'

'Elsie—?'

'Just stood there at some meaningless party. Tiny pea-green silk cheongsam. Made in Paris. They were rich. Her father hovered. Seldom spoke. Watched me. Had heard I had a future. Knew I had a bit of a past but could speak languages. Bit of a reputation at Oxford—. Knew I had no money. I needed, *wanted* money. Women—well, enthusiastic. He invited me with the family group—I didn't know that—to a dinner to eat crabs in black sauce on the old North Road. This is Hong Kong now. I think. Everyone shouting and clacking Chinese. I was already good at it. Showed off. Unfortunately got drunk—but so did they. So did Elsie. She wore these little jade bracelets on her wrists, fastened onto rich girl-babies. Tight, sexy. Just sat there. You know what it's like. Round table. Non-stop talk. Suddenly all over and everyone stands up. Shouting. Laughing. Family—well, you know, unbelievably rich and—well—cunning. I found myself taking her home. It was considered an honour.'

'You needed a friend, Veneering, to get you out of that one.'

'I know. D'you know, I remember thinking that it would be good if Fred—little Fiscal-Smith—had been there.'

'Well, I had to go back and marry her.'

'Couldn't old Pastry Willy and his Dulcie have helped?'

'Not then. Well, they might have done. I don't think they wanted to know me. I had swum through life after the war as I'd never have done on board *The City of Benares*. (Yes, thanks. A small one.) We were pushed into it in those days by—well by the Church. There is a Catholic church in Singapore. It survived. It is thronged. It was home. Somehow you keep with it. And so amazing that Elsie was Catholic. Or so they said. And we had a son.'

'I remember your son. Who didn't? Harry.'

'Yes. He was a wild one. He had my language thing. I sent him to the same English prep school as the Prince of Wales. Elsie's family flew him back and forth. He was—. He was, such a *confrère*. Such a brilliant boy—.'

'I remember.'

'Then they thought he was dying. Cancer in the femur.'

'I heard something—.'

'Betty—your Elizabeth—well, you must know. Looked

after him. It wasn't cancer. Back in England. Tiny, wonderful little hospital in Putney. I couldn't be there in time.'

'And his mother—?'

'Elsie was in Paris. A hair appointment.'

'And after that, you still stayed with Elsie?'

'Yes. Well. I stayed with my boy.'

* * *

'I'll walk you home,' said Filth.

'Elsie died,' said Veneering. 'An alcoholic.'

'I am so sorry. We did hear—. But you had the boy.'

'Oh, yes. I had the boy.'

'I had no child,' said Filth. 'Come on. Bedtime.'

'Your supper smells good,' said Veneering. 'My mother could cook.'

'I never knew mine,' said Filth. 'Now are you all set for your visit to Malta? Strange place. I envy you,' and he waited to see if Veneering would say, 'You should come with me.' But Veneering did not.

'Actually,' said Veneering, 'Elsie got very fat.'

'She needed your love,' said Filth.

* * *

But late that night, after his orderly, reflective bath-time, the evening lullaby of the rooks harsh and uncaring, Filth thought, He needed more than Elsie could give. He needed Betty. And Betty was mine.

* * *

The next morning Veneering's hired car for the airport swished along his drive at six o'clock and he didn't even look down at Old Filth's great chimney as they sped by. It was raining hard and still not really light.

Interesting evening, though. Never talked to the old fossil before. Maybe never known him. Or each other. Maybe once could have talked about women with him before the Betty-Elsie days. I might have helped him there. The ones who could never have talked to each other were Betty and Elsie. Perhaps the seeds of hatred had always been in them?

And this black and wintry morning in the cold rain Filth was realising that, at last, he was seeing Betty from a little distance. As a man, not even loving her particularly. Seeing her away from this eerie village, thick with history, hung with memories like those ghastly churches in Italy hung with rags. Rags and bandages and abandoned crutches, abandoned because prayer had been answered, wounds all healed, new life achieved. Betty Feathers lay dead in Donhead St. Ague churchyard. The monumental husband was, at what must be the end of his life, turning out to have a persona apart from his wife. Level-headed, a comrade, all passion spent. Urbane enough to play chess with his life-long sexual rival, and forget.

What idiot years they had passed in thrall—whatever thrall is—to this not exceptional woman. Not a beauty. Not brilliant. Stocky. What is 'falling in love' *about*? And her attitude to life—it was antique.

She could love of course, thought Veneering. My God I'll never forget the night she was with me. And she said so little. When I think of Elsie! All we hear about the silent, inscrutable Chinese! Elsie screamed and screeched and spat. She flung herself up and down the stairs in front of the servants. Hecuba! All for Hecuba! Didn't care who heard her. Put off little Fiscal-Smith for life. White, as he watched her. Bottles flying. Jewels flung out of windows. How flaccid she became. Rolls of fat. She had the bracelets cut away. Her wrists above began to bulge and crease. She couldn't understand English—

not the words. Her 'English' was faultless. But what it meant! In Chinese there is no innuendo, irony, sarcasm. Bitch-talk she could do. She asked Betty, who was in her twenties, if she was a grandmother and Betty said, 'Oh, yes I have seventeen grandchildren and I'm only twenty-seven' and Elsie had no idea what she was talking about. The most hateful thing about Elsie was her fragile hands. She would pose with them, cupping them round a flower, and sigh, 'Ah! *Beautiful*' and wait for a camera to click. Life was a performance. A slow pavane.

For Betty it was a tremendous march. A brave and glorious and well, comical sometimes, endurance. All governed by love. Passion—well she'd forgone passion when she married. Her own choice. She'd taken her ration with me. She wouldn't forget that night. Hello—Heathrow? Still raining. Why the hell am I going to Malta for Christmas?

* * *

Veneering was staying in what had been the Governor's residence, or rather in the hotel wing of his ancient palace. Throughout the network of the cobbled streets of Valetta the rain poured down, turning them to swirling rivers. There was thunder in the winter rain. No-one to be seen. Cold. Foreign. Post-Empire. Oh, Hong Kong!

The hotel, or palace, stood blackly in a court-yard that was being bombarded by the rain and the huge doors were shut. Veneering sat in the taxi and waited while the driver with a waterproof sheet on his head had pounded at them and then hung upon a bell-rope. At last, after the flurry of getting him in, tipping the genial driver well—but not receiving quite the same excessive gratitude as long ago—Veneering stood in a pool of rain on the stones of a reception hall that rose high above him and disappeared into galleries of stony darkness. He was then led for miles down icy corridors with here and there a vast stone coffin-like chest for furnishing, the odd, frail tapestry.

The dining room reminded him of the English House of Commons, and he was the only guest. The menu was not adventurous. There was a very thick soup, followed by Malta's speciality, the pasta pie, the pie-crust substantial, and then a custard tart. A harsh draught of Maltese red wine. There was no lift to take him back to his room which was huge and high, the long windows shuttered, the bed a room in itself with high brocaded curtains that did not draw around it. In one of them a hole had been cut for the on-off switch of a reading-lamp that stood on a bedside table that was a bridge too far. The sheets were clean but very cold. Rain like artillery crashed about the island. There was thunder in it. He lay for a long time, thinking.

But in the morning someone was grinding open the shutters and the new day shone with glory. Palm trees brown and dry but beautiful rattled against a blue sky and racing clouds. At breakfast, with English marmalade and bacon—and bread of iron—there was a pot of decent tea strong enough for an old English builder. A man on the other side of the breakfast room with another pot of it lay spread out like a table cloth over a rambling, curly settee. His feet reached far into the room. He said, 'Hullo, Veneering. It *is* Veneering isn't it? I'm Bobbie Grampian.'

'Good Lord! Yes, I am Veneering. I'm said to be unrecognisable.'

'Not at all. We're all said to be unrecognisable. It's just that there's no one much left to recognise us. Staying long? I'm here with Darlington.'

'I used to live near there.'

'No, no. Chap. Darlington. Always been here. He wants to be a barrister's clerk. Viscount or something. He'll be delighted—.'

'Hasn't he left it a bit late? I've been retired about twenty years.'

'Eccentric chap. Lives in the past.'

'Are you still dancing? I mean reeling, Bobbie?'

'O, God, yes. Never without the pipes. Mother's gone I'm afraid.'

'Well yes. Are you in the same house?'

'Where you came that night? Kensington. Splendid evening—or was it the Trossachs?'

'Actually I never quite got there.'

'Remember you doing the reels—. But you inherited those marvellous Chambers! People pay to visit them now. Listed. Apparently once belonged to John Donne.'

'John Donne? The poet?'

'Wasn't he the King of Austria?'

'No, I don't think so.'

'Yes, "John Donne of Austria is marching to the War". Dear old G. K. Chesterton. He was a Catholic.'

'I think that was Don John.'

'Yes? I'm very badly educated. Very sexy man John Donne. Sexy poetry.'

'He was Dean of St. Paul's.'

'Extraordinary. To think you inherited a royal dwelling. Sold it I suppose? Get rich quick. What d'you think of this hostelry? Bit like after the war. What a funny new-old world we've lived through.'

'Well,' said Veneering, 'it's large and cold. I came here for Christmas cheer. A break from Dorset winter.'

'Alone? Oh, most unwise. We must get together. There's a Caledonian Club I'm sure, and I have the pipes. Ah—and here's the man. Here's the man!'

Unchanged since Betty and Edward Feathers' honeymoon, a shambling person shuffled towards them demanding porridge. 'Hullo?' he said. 'Know you, don't I? Golf? Are you on your own?'

'It's Veneering,' said the Scot.

'Oh.'

'Veneering. The retired judge. Friend, no, contemporary, of The Great Filth. Come here for a Christmas break.'

'Ye gods! Very few of us left. Splendid. Anything special you want to see? Some wonderful ancient tombs, and so on. And the skeletons of pygmy elephants. No?'

'Well I would rather like to see the cliffs again. There was a fresh-water spring.'

'Place we used to go to for picnics. Very *British* place. Take you there now if you want. You'll be able to see to the horizon and down to the depths. Heaven and hell, ha-ha. You coming with us, Grampian?'

'No thanks.'

'Ready then, Veneering? Porridge good here isn't it? Actually Veneering, I have something to ask you.'

'Yes?'

'I've always had a hankering to be a Barrister's clerk. Don't know why. I can organise, and I like the Ambiance.'

(He must be eighty!)

'You may have heard of me. Always around.'

'What was—is—your profession?'

'Never had one. It wasn't a thing all the expats wanted after the war you know. Bit knocked about. Prison-camps and so on.'

'You were in one of the camps?'

'Not actually. A good many friends. Pretty upsetting—. I ought to write my memoirs. Trouble is I haven't many of them. Getting on a bit! "Riff-raff of Europe" they used to call the English in Malta after the war, but actually I think we were harmless. Just rather *poor*—. Not unhappy.'

'And you must know everybody?' said Veneering.

'I know the villagers of my village. And a good many ghosts. Could be worse.'

The exile from Darlington laughed heartily, not knowing

what else to do. Stopped his ancient Rover on a hair-pin bend at the top of a steep slope and began to lead Veneering across a rough terrain of scrub.

'A bit slippery,' said Veneering. He looked about him. There was nothing but underbrush. Up above there was a circle of unfinished housing, ugly and raw, little stone gardens, scarcely a tree. Standing by itself, at the very edge of the cliffs was a small rose-pink palace with stone-work of white lace. 'Eighteenth-century,' said the would-be clerk. 'For Sale. Dirt cheap. I could arrange something if you were tempted. Here we are. Stretch yourself out on your belly and you might see the silver stream. Runs under-ground most of the way. Then it falls towards the sea. Noise like choir-boys singing.'

'Mind you I haven't lain out flat on my belly for a long time. No-one to appreciate it—ha-ha. Not sure I'd know what to do now with a woman even if she was all laid out like lamb and salad as we used to say. We're all impotent here you know. Don't know what's become of us all. If you ask me what we need is another good war.'

Veneering moved further off. The stones beneath his unsuitable shoes became sharper. Twice he stumbled into what might be a fissure in the cliff but saw and heard no running water. He decided to crawl about and dropped slowly and painfully to his knees. He put his ear to the rock.

'You're a game old bird,' said his companion. 'You know, the last time I was here was over half a century ago. Picnics up here were special. Planned months ahead. Time of "the six-penny settlers". More money than ever before. Each other's houses, or sailing. Lots to drink. Fornicating. We came up here once though for a sort of honeymoon party. That arrogant old bugger Eddie Feathers (Old Filth they call him now, and I wouldn't disagree) had his bride Betty with him. Should have seen his face when I asked him to arrange a clerkship for me.

'As for her! Never forgot her. I was sitting cross-legged with my wine glass and she was standing right beside me, and she dropped on her knees and looked down the crack. She was like a kid. And she splayed herself out and I patted her bottom and she was up like a kangaroo, and she *hit* me! Yes, hit me. Don't think he saw.—On their honeymoon it was. She said, "I'm going to get out of this. I'm going down the cliff to the sea" and she went off and him after her. Old Filth. Mind you, *she* was the one who I'd have thought not exactly pure as a lily. Some very nasty stories about her going off with men into the New Territories in Hong Kong. Even though she looked like a school girl. *Oh*, yes. She stepped on me! Small of my back, and made off down the cliff, him after her. Expect he knew she wasn't all she might have been, even on the honeymoon. Hey, what's the matter? Stop that. What have I done?'

Veneering's pale fist had clenched and cracked into the monster's jaw. Both men fell sideways and began to shout and yell.

Away over at the rose-pink palace some Germans were being shown round by an estate agent. They called out. One of the Germans looked through his enormous binoculars and said 'It seems to be two old men fighting. It looks like a fight to the death.'

Across the seaside tundra there came a snapping sound and the thin old man with streaks in what had once been golden hair was lying still, one leg apparently missing. It had invaded the terrifying opening in the cliff from which the fresh water poured into the ocean.

'Locally it is called the water of life,' said the estate agent, but when they reached the two combatants this did not seem apt. Veneering's ankle was broken, his foot hung limp and he had passed out. He came round only briefly when mobile phones had summoned help and he was being carried off on a stretcher towards the hospital. Before he died, after a thrombosis had set in, he told the would-be barrister's clerk that he wasn't having one word said, ever, against Elizabeth.

* * *

When Old Filth heard the news he said, 'Silly old fool. Off on a jaunt like that at his age. I'd not have gone with him even if he'd asked me.'

Then Filth sat out the long day and the evening in Donhead St. Ague, listening to the rain, not looking up behind him at Veneering's darkened house, not bothering with whisky or the television news or the supper left out for him in the kitchen. He sat on and on in the mid-winter dark.

When a post-card from Veneering arrived—written his first evening in the tomb-like hotel—Filth read how happy he was now with no desire to come home.

'So he did get to heaven, then,' said Old Filth to his wife's photograph on the mantelpiece and Betty's young face smiled back at him from another world.

CHAPTER 21

In Donhead St. Ague half-a-century on the family man and poet, hard at work clearing Veneering's attic, his wife Anna cooking and laundering for her burgeoning bed-and-breakfast business, their children at school, their cat with activity of its own. A raw cold day and nothing in the village stirring. The family man appeared in the doorway of the ironing-place holding a battered photograph.

It is of a lipsticky young woman with bouffant hair. The photograph has been stuck long ago on cardboard and its margins covered with kisses.

'Veneering again,' he says. 'I wonder which this one was? I'd guess it isn't Betty Feathers.' She takes it and turns it over. She reads, 'From Daisy Flagg with love and gratitude.'

'Isn't she lovely?' says Henry, the family man (and poet). 'Like a juicy fruit.'

'But she's not his floozy,' says Anna. 'My head on the block, she's not. I wonder what he did for her. That's a fine fur coat. I'd guess a secretary of some sort. Adoration in the eyes. I'll take it round to Dulcie. I expect she'll know.'

But they forgot, and the photograph was put aside on a window-sill and then upon a pile of books and then tossed in the rubbish collection. A week later Anna yells at Henry to take the rubbish to the gate before he leaves for a Poetry Festival next day and he sees the photograph again and stands in contemplation. He says, 'Anna—all this stuff in the attic and there's not a sign of Betty Feathers anywhere. Not a letter. Not a post-card.'

'Men are like that,' she says. 'I don't expect her husband kept anything of hers either. It's women who press flowers in books. Keep letters.'

'Do you? Will you?'

'No. Because I've got you.'

'Don't be so sure. I might run off with Dulcie.'

* * *

Then he left the photograph on the kitchen table and went off to the tip. When he came back he said, 'We haven't actually seen Dulcie lately. Go and show her this while I'm away.'

'Isn't she on a cruise?'

'Oh, we'd have heard. Janice would have told us.'

'Janice is on holiday. Two—no three—weeks. D'you know, I don't think we've seen Dulcie since that day the cat went mad. I'd better go round. She'll be on her own. The dismal daughter is back in America with the eccentric yoof.'

'Go tomorrow after I've left. The sole of my shoe's hanging off. You're better at sticking it back on. And I've not finished my lecture.'

'Sorry,' said Anna, 'There's glue somewhere in a box. I'm going to Dulcie *now*.'

* * *

And she knocked and rang, although both the kitchen door and the front door of Privilege House stood open. She walked in, stood in the quiet hall and called, 'Dulcie.'

Deep silence. Her neck prickled. The house felt cold, unoccupied. In the kitchen, a slowly-dripping tap. Everywhere empty of life.

In Dulcie's bedroom her bed was un-made and the floor strewn with old clothes, probably sorted for a charity. Looking again Anna saw the crumpled expensive wool suit and the black funeral hat. There were some tiny antique corsets. White cotton stockings like Victorian fashion plates. However old *is* she? Are these menstrual rags? Virginia Woolf used menstrual rags. She only died in 1941. Dulcie must have been planning a fire like the cremations on the ghats of the Ganges.

And she is gone.

Then through the open door at the end of the landing she saw Dulcie's child-like back, very upright at a writing-desk that faced the fields and empty sky. She appeared to be writing letters. Thick yellow paper around her feet was crumpled into balls.

'Dulcie! Good heavens!'

She waited for the little figure to keel over sideways from the current of air disturbed by her voice; to slide to the floor. Dead for weeks.

'Yes?'

'Dulcie! You're freezing up here. *What* are you doing? We thought you'd gone on a cruise.'

Dulcie shivered and tore up another letter but kept it tight in her fist, staring ahead.

'You are—Dulcie, you are not *still* writing to Fiscal-Smith!'

'Trying to. He hasn't answered *any* of them the past weeks. He doesn't seem to be on the phone or have this e-mail thing. Neither do I. Nearly a month and no thank-you letter. It's unheard of. And this great pink chair has come for him. Wrapped in tarpaulin. It's not that I want to see him, it's just so out-of-character. When a friend of sixty years begins to act out-of-character you begin to wonder if you might never . . . There's nobody up there—it's called Lone Hall—to contact. I don't think it's anywhere near a police-station . . . '

'Oh, I'm sure we can find it.'

'Anna, I was very cruel to him. I let him know that we had always thought him mean and grasping. All his life he's been longing for company and nobody has wanted him because he's, well, so awful, really. So disgracefully conceited. Clever of course. Efficient. But withdrawn and obscure. But—oh Anna!—he's always been *there*. He has no charm and he knows it. Can't connect. Can't hear people thinking. Can't *help* being what he is. He knows that nobody ever liked him. Haven't I a *duty* to him, Anna?'

'Certainly not!'

'But I *do*. He's broken the pattern. The cracks will spread. They'll spread across all our crumbling lives, the few of us who are left.'

'Oh, come on, Dulcie.'

'He's disappeared, Anna. It isn't senility, Anna, and it isn't spite or resentment because we've laughed at him all these years. It's simple, determined rejection of us, of the very, very few last friends. Where *is* he, Anna?'

'Come home with me. We'll find out. Get your things—not the ones on the floor—and stay the night. I'm not leaving you here alone. You've got no tights on. No shoes. Your feet are navy blue.'

'Oh, but I don't do that sort of thing. Stay with people, if it's not in the diary.'

'You're coming.'

* * *

'Hi, Dulcie,' said Henry holding cellotape and a shoe. 'All well?'

'It's not,' said Anna, and gave a resume.

'Well, O.K. then,' he said, 'I'm off up North tomorrow, Dulcie. I'm lecturing on the Cavalier Poets at Teesside University tomorrow night. It's about ten miles from Yarm. I'll fix up the famous Judges' Hotel, Execution Court, or whatever, for you to stay the night. I'm staying with the Dean at

Acklam and a few Cavaliers, but you'll be well-looked after at the Judges' by all accounts. Then, next morning, before I bring you home, we'll visit the Mandarin's marble hall on the blasted heath and thunder on his door. Then we'll come home. That very evening. I'll—Anna will—ring the hotel now.'

'Oh, but I couldn't possibly! I don't travel any more you know. I haven't had my hair done. And—Anna—I'm afraid I have to get up in the night now you know. I'd never find my way back to my room in an hotel.'

'They have things called "en suite" now, Dulcie.'

'Oh, but I try not to eat them.'

'RIGHT,' shouted Henry returning to his pizza and Pesto at the supper table, children munching and doing homework unperturbed, 'All fixed. Hotel's got a room. Sounds rather an odd one but apparently The Great Old Filth once slept there. Probably Judge Jeffries, too. It's en suite and much in demand. I said I'd take you up to the Fiscalry first and then see you in and make sure you'll get a good dinner and then I'll pick you up the following morning and bring you home. All right?'

Anna said, 'I'll go up to Privilege House now and get anything you're going to need. Pills? Shoes? No. Be quiet. You're going.'

'But, it's hundreds of miles and . . . '

'Hong Kong's a few thouands . . . '

'Oh, but I *know* Hong Kong. And actually, Anna, I'm afraid I'm not very reliable on the motorway.'

'You won't be driving.'

'No my dear, I mean the facilities. I would have to stop at least twice.'

'Me, too,' said Henry. 'Always did. Don't boast. We'll be on the road by eight o' clock. Could you manage that?'

'I wake at four,' said Dulcie, proudly.

'And you go upstairs and finish that lecture *now*,' said Anna.

'And there are other things,' said Dulcie. 'I have to check on Filth's house.'

'There've been lights on,' said Anna. 'Someone's taking care of it.'

* * *

Isobel heard the hired car arrive at the garden gate above. She put on her long silk coat, noticed that it was raining, noticed Filth's old mac hanging on the back of the kitchen door. But no, she'd take nothing. She had everything she wanted (the house she would leave to the boy—Dulcie's grandson) for Filth had given her everything, not only his worldly possessions, but his living spirit.

She pressed her face briefly against the old waterproof mac on the door and left the house.

On quick feet, without a stick, she climbed up the slope of the garden to the waiting taxi.

* * *

By eight-fifteen the poet's car was heading North, Dulcie crouched like a marmoset in the back, defying whip-lash, her eyes pools of fear. By the motorway, however, she had settled and started the *Telegraph* crossword. After a stop at a service-station, cross country towards Nottingham she began to take notice. By lunch-time, when they stopped at a country house hotel Henry had known from literary Festivals before, she had a light in her eyes and was talking about the landscape of D. H. Lawrence and the Mitford sisters and Chatsworth. Soon she appeared to have blood in her veins again and was chatting up the austere black waiter over the cheese, telling him of arbitrations in Africa where he had never been.

'Now—*I* am paying for this,' Dulcie said and blinked when

she saw the bill, holding it up first one way and then the other. A deep breath—then, '*Oh* yes. I am, and I am leaving the tip.' She put down a pound coin. 'Henry, this is wonderful. We must do this again and I will pay the petrol. Are you doing the Edinburgh Festival in August?'

It was already dark by the time they reached Yarm. Henry's lecture was at eight o' clock. 'I'll ring the hotel and say you'll be late and to keep dinner for you and we'll go up to Fiscal-Smith's for a quick look now. I'll make sure your room will be ready when I drop you back. Here we are, here's The Fiscal turning. *Hup* we go to Wuthering Heights. God! There's nothing!'

The steep lane ran on and up, up and on, white with moonlight, black with wintry heather and, lying to either side of it and occasionally on it, the green lamp-eyes of sheep. A few ('Oh, *look*,' she cried) new lambs with bewildered faces. Henry honked and tooted and the sheep ambled aside. 'I have never . . . ,' she said.

Down they went again into a village with a noisy stream, a small stone bridge, arched high. Up they went again, twist and twirl, and the stars were coming out.

'Such stars!' she said. 'And I thought The Donheads were the country!'

'You can see the Milky Way,' he said. 'They say it's disappeared now over London. We've blotted it out.'

'I don't remember stars in Hong Kong,' she said. 'It's such a competitive place.'

'Aha!' he said.

A gate across a track.

'Henry—turn! You're going to be late. It's seven o' clock. We can come back tomorrow on the way home.'

'Won't be beaten,' he shouted, getting out, opening the gate, dragging it wide for the return journey, jumping back in, splashing the car through another rattling torrent. Over a narrow bridge came a sharp bend upwards, a one-in-three corkscrew, and a shriek from Dulcie. The car made it with only a foot to spare along the edge of a dark brackeny precipice.

'The man's a mad-man,' said Henry. 'Living here. Oh—hullo?'

Mist had been gathering but now, up here, moonlight broke through and in front of them stood another barred gate. A man stood behind it in silhouette carrying what looked like a pitch-fork or perhaps a rifle. To either side of his head behind the gate swayed the great horns of two wild beasts. Henry stopped the car once more and waited to see if it would roll back.

'So what's this then?' asked the man.

'Visitors.'

'Visitors! This time of night. It's past six o' clock. Are you daft? Mek an appointment.'

'*Visitors.* To Sir Frederick Fiscal-Smith.'

'Fred's out. I'm his ghillie. And these are two of his Highlanders.'

'*Out?*'

'Aye. An' 'e's not comin' back. Hall's for sale. He's gone to Hong Kong.'

Dulcie stepped carefully out of the car and went over to the gate. She held out her hand to the ghillie. The two wild beasts disappeared into the mist. 'I am so sorry,' she said, 'to descend upon you in the dark, and we must go at once—there is a very important engagement. A poetry lecture in Middlesbrough. On *The Cavalier Poets.* But I just wanted to look in on my very old friend. I *quite* understand. We hadn't realised that Sir— Fred's house was so remote. Might I come and take another look tomorrow? Could I just have a look in the letter-box? I have been trying to contact him.'

'*Letter-box?* No letter-boxes. The letters get dropped down the bottom under a stone. I've been posting on yeller envelopes but I send them by the batch. Not straight off. You can't catch the postman. You know, our Fred was always a mystery.'

* * *

'I'll have to abandon you,' said Henry at The Judges' Lodging Hotel. 'I'll be back to take you home after breakfast. I'll have to step on it now. Here's someone.'

An amiable-looking man in porter's uniform was hanging about. He disappeared with Dulcie's case and in a moment came a strong-looking woman down the hotel steps. She had the look of someone who had seen too many hotel guests from the south lately.

When she spoke, however, all was well. 'Hot water, hot-water bottles and your dinner's ready in half an hour and you can have the same room as the others had. We seem to get more judges than we ever did when they were on Circuit. Poor old Feathers crying into his coffee after his wife died. Fiscal-Smith up the hill, he nearly died in the room you're having not six weeks ago. Pneumonia. Well, second memorial service in a few months. He can't resist a train-ride to London . . . '

Henry said, 'He's in Hong Kong now.'

'Doesn't surprise me. Now, you get off to your poetry and we'll get this one installed.'

Lying in the lights from the bed-side lamp Dulcie was put early to bed. She watched the gold-fish as they flicked and turned.

* * *

And at breakfast next morning she sat in the dining room looking up into the frowning hills and she was smiling. Susan—not any one of them knew where she was. There was no-one who would be screeching at her on a telephone to say that this journey had been foolish.

'Sheer bravado!' 'Showing off.' 'At your age,' and so on.

Such an interesting visit up to the moors last night. *Such* a good hotel! Black-pudding for breakfast. Delicious. Here came the manageress. 'Oh, yes, *perfectly* thank you. I slept perfectly. I wish I could stay here for a proper holiday.'

'Well, it's possible,' said the lady—more coffee was being hustled to the table, unasked. 'In fact I am afraid it is inevitable. There has been a message . . . '

'Yes?' (Oh God! Oh God, it's Susan!)

'From the University, I'm afraid your friend—that poet— he's in the Great North Eastern hospital with a broken ankle.'

'He is *what*?'

'He slipped as he came off the stage last night after his lecture. Shoe fell to pieces. Got caught up in the audio wires. Foot left hanging like a leaf. They're hoping to operate this morning.'

'I must go there at once. *At once*!'

'Have some more coffee. They've informed his wife and she's on the train. We'll go to Darlington to meet her. She'll drive you back home tomorrow but—something about arrangements for the school-run. I said that we'd see to you.'

'Oh, but I must go to poor Henry!'

'He won't be round from his anaesthetic yet. They may not even operate today. He has high blood-pressure.'

'That doesn't surprise me. Could you get me a car? I haven't got my actual driver's licence with me. I haven't driven for quite some time, except around the village. But someone might lend me a map. I do thoroughly enjoy driving. I could drive Anna home—or just go by myself.'

'Michael will drive you to the hospital whenever you need to go.'

'Is he the ghillie? I'm not sure . . . '

'No. He's over there. The front-of-house receptionist standing by the portrait of Lord Justice MacPherson, drinking milk.'

Michael gave a little wave.

'The milk,' she said, 'is one of his harmless peculiarities but I suppose it's a good fault in a driver. Yes, it's hard to get insurance when you're over eighty. I hope I don't speak out of turn?'

'Oh, I can easily take a taxi just to the hospital.'

'I don't think they're going to want you at the hospital my lady. You're not next of kin. But where would you like Michael to take you? Is there someone you can visit?'

'Oh no. I don't know a living soul. Oh—oh yes, I must ring my daughter Susan. In America. But perhaps, well—no. She is rather easily annoyed. Though a *wonderful* person. Quite wonderful. Do you think—would it be possible to visit Lone Hall again?'

'There is a call for you.'

'Yes—oh Anna! Anna, *yes*, I'm very well.'

'Dulcie. I'm on the train. The silly great fool.'

'Who?'

'Henry.'

'Now don't worry about me, Anna. I'm perfectly all right. I was often stuck in Ethiopia, you know (that road across the Blue Mountains), I do just wonder if I left the iron on. But we must think of Henry first.'

'I'm coming. See you later. I'll have to get Henry home. I'll bring you back with him. I'm afraid he may be in rather a dreadful mood.'

'All will be perfectly well Anna, and could you possibly ring Susan in Massachusetts in case she worries? You have the number. I'm going to drive about today with a splendid young man and we'll leave some flowers for Henry though it's still very wintry up here—bring a big coat—and there's nothing but black heather. Oh, yes. Fiscal-Smith? I'd forgotten him. He's not here. He's gone to Hong Kong. I was mistaken ever to have worried about him.'

* * *

'And now,' she said, 'young man, come along. They say you'll get me to the hospital.'

'I'll get you there,' he said, 'but I can't say what we'll do next. It's like a city. They made it out of the old chemical works. They were the steel works before that and the iron works before that and before that they were the Big Wilderness. Kept thousands working for a hundred years. Always work. Dirt and clatter. All gone now. Most folks have no jobs. They just stay in bed most days unless they have a profession like me.'

'But this hospital's enormous! There must be plenty of jobs here?'

'Oh, aye. Mind, how many *does* any work in it?' D'you want a bit of Cadbury's fruit and nut?'

'So very different from Dorset. And from Hong Kong. We'll never find poor Henry here,' she said.

But a car-park appeared and someone to take them to the right ward where the family man-poet lay with eyes closed and mind elsewhere. She felt affection for him and stroked his face.

'He didn't speak,' she said when she came back. 'I left him a packet of smarties.'

'Hey ho,' said Michael. 'So where now?'

'Well. I suppose back to the hotel.'

'No—come on. I'll show you Herringfleet. First we'll go to Whitby for its fish and chips and I can get blue-top. Then there's the museum with the preserved mermaid, mind she's not that well preserved, being dead. We'll take the old trunk road through the skeletal chimneys. They're not that old,' he said. 'Younger than me! Mind not much. Can't think of the place without them now.'

'You were born here then, Michael?'

'Oh, aye. Michael Watkins. Me great auntie was Nurse Watkins. Lived to be a hundred. Gypsy stock. Black eyes. Delivered us all here and laid us all out. She delivered your great man, Judge Vanetski or whatever . . . '

'I'm afraid I don't know . . . ?'

'Changed his name and went south. Something you could spell more easier. Me Auntie Watkins knew 'em all. His mother worked the coal-cart round the streets. His dad were a Russian spy. Common knowledge.'

'You *can't*,' she said, 'mean Judge Veneering?'

'It could be,' said Michael, 'they're all dead now. Here then—Whitby. Home of Dracula and a load a' saints. And, see them choppers ont' cliff-top? Visiting whale. Made *Jaws* look like a minner. And here's a human hand of some lass hanged somewhere. Stick a candle in it and you'll never be frightened of ghosts.'

'There's nothing like this in Hong Kong,' she said. 'Though I wouldn't answer for Java. In Java they keep the bodies of the dead for years. They take them food.'

'Well there you are then,' said Michael, 'It's a funny old world. What you think of this? Look up, now.'

Hanging on wires from the museum's roof glimmered a painted wooden banner, pale green and gold. Trailing squirls and tendrils of delicate foreign flowers surrounded lettering she couldn't decipher.

'It's wonderful. What is it? What does it say?'

'Nobody can make out. But it's not that old.'

'It looks almost Classical.'

'No. It was something from Muriel Street. The street was flattened with a bomb and this thing somehow survived.'

'It looks as old as The Odyssey.'

'Aye, it's odd all right. Kind of sadness in it too. Horrible back-alley it hung in. They used to slaughter cattle there on a Thursday.'

She looked at him. 'I'm not a complete *ingénue*, Michael.'

'The guy painted that,' said Michael, 'wasn't no jane-you

neither. He was like a god. But he was broken up. He was that Vanetski's dad. The Russian spy.'

'I'm out of my depth, Michael.' She took his arm.

'Who isn't?' said Michael.

* * *

'And,' she said back in the car, 'you've lived here all your life? How very interesting.'

'I've had some foreign holidays. Now, before we set off back, tek a look down there. Look around.'

'Sea?' she said. 'It's rather pale—if you saw the Caribbean, Michael . . . '

'Look along the coast-line. Right? All ripped off in the war. The big raid took the heart out of it. See that yellow house with the black holes for windows? Never re-built. Streets of little dwellings down the old high street. All gone. I never seed 'em. Ripped away like the flounce on a skirt, me auntie says. Bessie. She's still alive. D'you want to meet her?'

'Well, I think we should get back.'

'You've to see Grangetown. Ugliest place, it's said, in Europe. Covered in red dust off the old ironstone works. It crosses the sea on the wind. They say Denmark's covered in it too. It's on a level with Ayres Rock Australia. D'you know, they used these beaches for filming D-Day? In that film. Nowhere in France poor enough. No. 326 Palm Tree Road, here's auntie's. She's near a hundred, too. I'll get her.'

Dulcie sat alone in the car. The long, long street of red houses was by no means derelict or poor but it was lifeless. Re-built since the war, dozen after dozen, all alike. Well-kept, anonymous, identical. Curtains were pasted against the windows. No-one to be seen. Concrete and weeds in the long, long vista of tiny front gardens. Silence. No people. Then a boy with small eyes came up beside the car and spat at it.

After a while a shuffling old man with a dog appeared, stopping and looking, looking and stopping. He put his face near hers at the passenger window and said through the glass, 'Is it Lilian?'

'No, I'm Dulcie.'

'I'm looking out for our Lilian. She's seldom coming by.'

'I'm sorry.'

'I'd say the Germans have her.'

'That was a *very* long time ago.'

'Behind that Iron Curtain.'

'That was a long time ago, too.'

'No, it were yesterday. Not even the blacks come here, you know. Too dismal for 'em. Our Lilian was a grand girl.'

Michael came down his aunt's concrete path, ignored the old man and said Dulcie was to come in. 'And you get on with your walk,' he said to the man.

'Michael, this old man is crying. For his sister.'

'Oh aye. Lilian. Half a century on. Killed in Middlesbrough. Shut up now, George. There was worse going on than Lilian. What about the Concentration Camps?'

'It's all stood still,' said the old man.

'Aye, and that's the trouble,' said Michael.

As Dulcie pulled on her little mohair gloves as she walked up the path the old man shouted, 'It was wireless won us t'war. If it had been only bloody television we'd have lost it and mebbe got some soul back in us. It went out, did soul, with Churchill. We was all listening to him when the Dorniers come that night.'

A woman was watching them from the door-step.

'Are you comin' in then?'

* * *

She didn't look a hundred, she looked fifty and very alert. 'Friends o' Terry's? Terry Vanetski? Cup o' tea?'

'I'm afraid Terry is gone,' said Dulcie, drawing off her gloves, Bessie watching, stretching over and taking one and stroking it. 'I went to his memorial service. He died in Malta.'

'What in heck was he doing there? He was that restless. Is't true he married a Chinese?'

'Yes. Elsie. I hardly knew her . . .'

'Now then tell us. One thing we can still do here is talk. I wonder if she was like his mother, Florrie. Now she was a fine woman, like a man. With a back-to-front man's cap. Here's your tea and a fancy. It's only shop.'

'They—didn't exactly get on. Terry and Elsie.'

'Then there'd be someone else. Terry was born to love women. Serviette? You can't see where he lived. Nowt left. Nowt much left of Florrie neither nor the Russian. Eighty-seven killed that night. Terry was out of it you know because they'd put him on some getaway-train that afternoon. He left without a tear. I helped get his mother home where she'd been waving at the train from the fence. Oh, she was a fine woman. She never knew if he'd seen her waving.'

'And you've never moved away?'

'Well, bus-trips with Michael, in a club, to foreign parts but I can't recommend them. Up here's better, even with the drugs and the knives—even in *Turner* Street! Turner Street where the doctors used to live and the manager of the Co-op. Even now it's better than the Costa del Sol where you can't understand a word they say. All those fat English women, they're a disgrace. I was maid at a posh school here once you know. That was a nasty place, but interesting and you never saw anything like that Mrs. Fondle in her purples and satins. She fancied young Terry. Yes she did. Just as well she got drowned. There was tensions all right, what with Mrs. Fondle and circus performers and spies and coal-carts—bit of Dundee? I mek me own Dundee.'

'It must have been a very—vivid—time,' said Dulcie. 'I was

in Shanghai about then. It was really my country. I don't know why we were all so mad on this one we'd never seen.'

'I'd not think Shanghai would have been all water-lilies and flowers-behind-the-ear neither. But, like wherever you go, there's great compensations. Great people.'

'Oh—yes.'

'Like Mr. Parable in Herringfleet. Now *he* was mad. He was what's called a religious maniac but he was one of the nicest men you could hope to meet. I wonder where his money went?'

'And then,' she said, 'there was that Mr. Smith. He had a son, too. Tight-up little chap. Never very taking. Father took no note of him but they say he did well, mebbe better than Terry. But yet, with little Fred, nobody ever seemed to take to him.'

'Yes. I see. It's another world to me you know. You make me feel very *narrow* Mrs.—'

'Miss,' she said. 'Thank God.'

There was a silence, Dulcie thinking of all the countries she had lived in where nobody now cared for her one jot, Bessie thinking of the children of this grey place who had shone here once. 'Did you say our Terry's *gone*?' she asked and Dulcie said again she had been to his memorial service. 'We don't go in for that round here,' said Bessie, 'whoever you are. It's York Minster if you're someone, but otherwise it's Mr. Davison at Herringfleet church digging a hole. And we don't go for these basket-work caskets neither. Remind you of the old laundry down Cargo Fleet. I suppose little Fred's gone too.'

* * *

'Thank you,' Dulcie said to the milk-drinking Michael on the way back from the sea to the Cleveland Hills.

'Pretty great, in't she?'

'What a memory.'

'Aye, but Dulcie—what a terrible life.'

'Michael, I don't think so. Oh good! Look,' for here was the Donhead car in the forecourt of the hotel. 'Oh thank God! She's back from the hospital. Now we can go home.'

B ut the next morning they were both still at the hotel. Henry was being kept in hospital for another day and arrangements had to be made for an ambulance.

'We'll drive in convoy,' said Anna, 'you and I in the car. It'll be rather slow. But more restful than the journey up. Today, I'll go to the hospital and see the surgeon and arrange about physio. But what will you do?'

'I'll go to Lone Hall again.'

'But you said it was grim.'

'Yes. But I can't stop thinking about him all alone in it.'

'I hope you're not thinking of joining him in it?'

'Don't be ridiculous Anna. I shouldn't tell you this, but I can't really afford Privilege House anymore and it's in very good condition. This one needs a million pounds spending on it. Dear Anna—it's idle curiosity that's all. Could they get me a lift up there and back d'you think? The hotel?'

They could. She did. The ghillie was on his way up there now. He was meeting a possible buyer.

'But would he let me in?' she said. 'I want to go round it alone.'

'Dulcie?'

'I tell you, Fiscal-Smith's not there. He's gone to Hong Kong.'

'Look—it has nothing to do with you where Fiscal-Smith lives. He's only there because he can't shake off his childhood. That's why he's such a *bore*, Dulcie. You deserve better. Or just memories of Willy. Fiscal-Smith clings to his miserable past like a limpet to a rock.'

'I don't think anyone has ever loved him,' she said.

'I'm not surprised.'

'Anna, you are being unpleasant. Fiscal-Smith is pathetic because he doesn't know how to love. But there's a For Sale notice up and this time—he never tells you anything—something must have happened. I believe, Anna, that he's a virgin.'

'I hope you're not thinking of doing something about that.'

'That will do, Anna. We don't talk like that. And I'd be glad if you tell *nobody* that I'm short of money.'

'Oh—ah! Well, well—Fiscal-Smith's worth millions, just like the other two. Now I understand.'

'I hope we are not about to quarrel, Anna.'

* * *

The ghillie dropped her off and she was allowed to go alone into the gaunt, wind-blown house on the moor. 'I'm glad you trust me,' she said as he handed her a key the size of a rolling pin. 'I can tell a good woman,' he said. 'Ye'll not pilfer. And it suits me because I have to wait outside for the estate agents. They're bringing in a possible buyer. Some lunatic. I'll look him over. Off ye go now and mind ye take care on the boards.'

'Is it clean?' she said.

'Och, aye, it's clean.'

Inside Fiscal-Smith's Lone Hall, the smell of wood fires and heather. No carpets, no curtains and very little furniture. A kitchen range like a James Watt steam engine, rusted and ice-cold, a midget micro-wave beside it, an electric toaster, almost antique. Taps high above a yellow stone sink, and an empty larder. An empty bread-crock, a calendar of years ago marked with crosses indicating absences abroad. All colourless, clean, scrubbed. Eighteenth-centry windows, light flowing in from moor and sky.

Where did he sleep? Where did he eat? Where did he read—whatever did he *do here*? Room after room: empty. Not a painting, not a clock, not a photograph.

On her way out she opened a door on the ground floor behind a shabby baize curtain. The room within was cold—another tall window, unshuttered, the walls covered with shelves and upon them row upon row of boxes all neatly labelled. There was a man's bike with a flowing leather saddle and a round silver bell. It stood upside down. A very old basket was strapped to the handlebars. On a hook nearby hung a dingy white riding-mackintosh with brass eyelet holes under the arms. It hung stiff as wood. There was a black, tinny filing-cabinet labelled 'Examination Papers'. There was no sign anywhere of a woman's presence, or touch.

There was a complete set of the English Law Reports in leather, worth several thousands of pounds—Dulcie knew this because she had recently had to sell Willy's. There was an iron bed, like the campaign bed of the Duke of Wellington. Beside the bed, a missal, its pages loose with wear. Then she saw, on the wall behind her, a photograph of familiar faces: Willy waving. Herself in a rose-scattered hat—my! Wasn't I gorgeous! Those tiresome missionaries in Iran. Eddie Feathers, magnificent in full-bottomed wig, Veneering cracking up with laughter, holding golf-clubs, hair flying. Drunk. Row after row of them and no girl-friends, no children, no-one who could have been Fred's invisible, ailing mother. In the dead centre of the collage was a wedding group outside St. James's church, Hong Kong. Eddie Feathers, so young and almost ridiculously good-looking in his old-fashioned morning suit and bridegroom's camellia; the bride Elizabeth—darling Betty—in frothy lace, with a face looking out like a baby at its christening.

And there, beside her, astonishingly in a tee-shirt and what must have been the first pair of jeans in the Colony, was Fiscal-Smith the super-careful conformist, never wrongly-dressed.

200 - JANE GARDAM

Asked to be best-man at the last minute, his face was shining like the Holy Ghost. The best day of his life.

No sign of Veneering in this photograph. No sign at all. Nor of Isobel Ingoldby, the femme fatale.

Willy was there. Oh, look at us, look at us! Still damp from our cocoons!

* * *

But it was the huge floor of the room in Lone Hall that held Dulcie now. It was slung from end to end with swathes of tiny metal 'Hornby' rolling-stock: points, buffers, level-crossings, signals, water-pumps, platforms, sheds, long seats, lacy wooden canopies, slot-machines; luggage trolleys like floats with unbending metal handles long as cart-shafts. Portmanteaux, trunks, Gladstone bags, sacks red and grey and all set up for midgets. And calm, good midgets stood in dark-blue uniforms blowing pin-head whistles, punching pin-holes in tiny tickets. Branch-lines swung far and wide, under the Duke of Wellington's bed, and were criss-crossed by bridges, paralleled by streams where tiny men in floppy hats sat fishing. And the station platforms, up and down the room, were decorated with tiny tubs of geraniums. Time had stopped.

In the green-painted fields around lived happy sheep and lambs and cardboard figures carrying ladders over their shoulders and pots of paint. They went smiling to their daily bread. And the engines! And the goods-wagons! And the carriages up-holstered in blue and red and green velvets. And the happy pin-sized families untouched by care, all loving each other.

There was someone else in the house. The ghillie was at the door. He was furious. 'This room is not on view. You are here without permission,' and he locked the door behind her as she scurried out.

Another car, a Mercedes, was on the drive now, with the

estate agent kow-towing and she heard someone say 'Very sad. Hong Kong business-man. Made his pile. No, no—a local. Not in residence at present but lived here for years. Matter of fact we've just heard he has recently died—back in Hong Kong.'

'Good afternoon,' said Dulcie as she passed.

'So sorry about your wasted journey,' called the man with the shooting-stick. 'I've bought it already. Fixtures and fittings. Splendid shooting lodge. I'd better not tell you how cheap it was.'

And he stood aside, laughing, and watched her climb into the ghillie's car.

* * *

The next day she was driving south with Anna to The Donheads, the ambulance somewhere behind them, cautiously bouncing and now and then sounding its siren.

'They wanted to keep him in longer, Dulcie, oh, I wish they had! He's going to be hell downstairs at home. Physios coming in three times a day—on the good old NHS of course—and, pray God, they're pretty. Oh—and he'll be surrounded by the yellow staircase! Oh help me Dulcie.'

'I suppose—did you hear anything about the lecture?'

'Brilliant, of course. The wilder the preliminaries the better he always seems to be.'

'It's not like that in law-suits.'

In time:

'Dulcie? You're very quiet. You did want to come back home I hope?'

'Yes. I did. I do. All is settled now.'

'I'm so sorry. We messed it all up for you. It was meant to be a treat. We're so dis-organised.'

'Anna, stop. You have taken the leathery old scales from my eyes and I love you both.'

'Why?'

'Well, I've rather gone in for romantic secrets in other people's lives. "Romantic" is not quite right. It's a dirty word now, meaning sexy and silly. But, for me, it has always meant imaginative and beautiful and private. By the way, did I tell you that poor Fiscal-Smith is dead?'

The car swerved and swung in an arc from the fast lane to the central to the slow and stopped with a screech of brakes on the verge. Traffic swore at them.

'Dulcie! *What*—?'

'Yes. Fiscal-Smith is dead. I heard up at the house. A rather awful man has bought it. He shouted it at me.'

'Oh, Dulcie! It *can't* be true. He was perfectly all right at Old Filth's party—I mean memorial service. Who the *hell* are these morbid northern lunatics? I'll e-mail Hong Kong. Where's he staying? The Peninsula, of course,'

'Not if he was paying the bill himself. No, Anna. It would have been the Y.M.C.A. He liked it there. Maybe I should go out there. At once.'

'You do not *stir*, Dulcie. Not till we have the facts.'

'I think I may. I think you've given me the urge to travel again, Anna. Oh, I do hope that at least some of my letters got there in time. I'm afraid I was very outspoken though. I apologised rather pathetically—I don't really know why. I said too much. But actually—I don't think one *can* say too much at my time of life, do you? Or ever. About love.'

'I'm sorry, Dulcie. I just don't believe he's dead,' and they drove on for many miles.

'Life,' said Dulcie, south of Birmingham, 'is really ridiculous. Why were we thought worth creating if we are such bloody fools? What's happiness? I wish I could talk to Susan like this.'

'Well, you can't. The idea that mothers and daughters can say everything to each other is a myth. But I know she loves you. In her way.'

'That makes me feel better. But, Anna—why does it *have* to be "in her way"?'

* * *

They turned off at last into the unlikely lane off the A30 towards the Donheads and Dulcie felt herself pointing out to dear, dead Betty Feathers the tree in the hedge that looked like a huge hen on a nest. And the funny man—look he *is* still there!—who wanders about with a scythe. ('He won't go into Care you know. I can't say I blame him. I'm going to stick on as long as I can at Privilege House, even if I have to sell the spoons.')

'Here we are Dulcie. I'm going to stop here and wait for the ambulance. It's not far behind. Here it comes. Marvellous!'

'And I'm getting out here,' said Dulcie, 'if you'll get my pull-along out of the back. Yes—yes I mean it. You must go with Henry. I'll walk to my front gate—you can see it from here, look. Don't go on until I turn and wave.'

'I'll ring up in half an hour,' said Anna. 'And I'll watch you in. We'll bring you some supper. Soon. *Now don't forget*, turn and wave at the gate.'

Dulcie trailed her case on wheels to the wrought-iron gate, which she was surprised to see open, and turned and waved.

Then she turned back towards the courtyard where Fiscal-Smith was standing surrounded by an enormous amount of luggage.

CHAPTER 23

It was Easter Day. St. Ague's bells were clanking out and the
steep church-path was at its most slippery and dangerous.
Filth's magnificent legacy was still being discussed. And
discussed. What first? Heating, roof, floor, walls, glass, pews,
path? In the meantime, in spring, the clumps of primroses
would go on growing like bridesmaids' bouquets in the nooks
and crannies of the old railway-sleeper steps. Dulcie and Fred
were proceeding cautiously towards the Easter Eucharist and
on every side around them tulips, and daffodils and pansies
graced the graves for Easter, in pots and jars and florists'
wreathes.

'It's like a fruit-salad,' said Fiscal-Smith, 'I don't care for it.
Never did. Pagan.'

'Oh, "live and let—",' said Dulcie. 'But no. That's not very
apt.'

'I want these railway-sleepers out,' said Fiscal-Smith.
'They're black and full of slugs. We can get good money for the
Church for them. Install proper steps! There's a church I've
heard of in south Dorset where they've put in a lift and an esca-
lator. I'll have to get on with it.'

'You're a Roman Catholic, Fiscal-Smith. St. Ague's is nothing to do with you.'

'Wait til I'm on the parish council,' he said. 'Dulcie! Stand
clear. Here's that Chloe.'

'On, on,' he said. 'End in sight. Doors wide open. Or we
could construct a sort of poly-tunnel.'

A gold haze hung inside the church door. Lilies. Tall candles, a glinting Cope. 'Don't fuss—they can't start without us,' he said and Dulcie said 'What rubbish.'

They had to pause again. Up in the porch they could see the gleam of one of the twins' walking-frames and the Carer skulking round the back of a tomb-stone having a quick drag on a gauloise.

'The gravestones are a disgrace too,' said Fiscal-Smith. 'Tipping about. I can see to that. The most useful thing I've learned in my long career at the construction-industry Bar is the importance of a reliable builder.'

'I like them tipping about,' she said.

'I knew a man *killed* by a gravestone tipping about,' said Fiscal-Smith.

'I expect it was trying to tell him something. Just listen to Old Filth's rooks! They're back again.'

'Were they ever away?' he said.

'Fred—the organ! It's *roaring*. The Procession's gathering up for "The fight is o'er, the Battle done"—. Come *on*. Wonderful! Hurry!'

'Reminds me of old Eddie's wedding day in Hong Kong,' he said. 'I don't know if you remember, Dulcie, but he chose me to be his best man.'

'Were there no *girls* in your life, Fred?'

Arm in arm, they tottered.

'Just you, Dulcie. Otherwise I'm afraid it was only trains.'

Singing mingled with the flooding thunder of the organ. 'Calm, my dear,' said Fiscal-Smith. 'Calm.'

And so they made their way towards the Resurrection.

* * *

The End

ABOUT THE AUTHOR

Jane Gardam is the only writer to have been twice awarded the Whitbread Prize for Best Novel of the Year (for *The Queen of the Tambourine* and *The Hollow Land*). She also holds a Heywood Hill Literary Prize for a lifetime's contribution to the enjoyment of literature.

She has published four volumes of acclaimed stories: *Black Faces, White Faces* (David Higham Prize and the Royal Society for Literature's Winifred Holtby Prize); *The Pangs of Love* (Katherine Mansfield Prize); *Going into a Dark House* (Silver Pen Award from PEN); and most recently, *Missing the Midnight*.

Her novels include *The Man in the Wooden Hat*, *God on the Rocks* (shortlisted for the Booker Prize), *Faith Fox*, *The Flight of the Maidens* and *Old Filth*, a *New York Times* Notable Book of the Year.

Jane Gardam lives in England.

THE MAN
IN THE WOODEN HAT

Jane Gardam

THE MAN
IN THE WOODEN HAT

Europa
editions

Europa Editions
214 West 29th Street
New York, N.Y. 10001
www.europaeditions.com
info@europaeditions.com

Library of Congress Cataloging in Publication Data is available
ISBN 978-1-933372-89-1

Gardam, Jane
The Man in the Wooden Hat

Book design by Emanuele Ragnisco
www.mekkanografici.com

Prepress by Plan.ed - Rome

Printed in USA

CONTENTS

for David

"Old, forgotten far-off things
and battles long ago."

PART ONE

Marriage

CHAPTER ONE

There is a glorious part of England known as the Donheads. The Donheads are a tangle of villages loosely interlinked by winding lanes and identified by the names of saints. There is Donhead St. Mary, Donhead St. Andrew, Donhead St. James and, among yet others, Donhead St. Ague.

This communion of saints sometimes surprises newcomers if they are not religious and do not attach them to the names of village churches. Some do, for the old families here have a strong Roman Catholic tinge. It was Cavalier country. Outsiders, however, call the Donheads "Thomas Hardy country" and it is so described by the estate agents who sell the old cottages of the poor to the rich.

And not entirely truthfully, for Hardy lived rather more to the south-west. The only poet celebrated for visiting a Donhead seems to be Samuel Taylor Coleridge, who came to see a local bookish bigwig but stayed for only one night. Perhaps it was the damp. The Donhead known as Ague seems connected to no saint and is thought to be a localised Bronze Age joke. Even so, it is the most desirable of all the villages, the most beautiful and certainly the most secluded, deep in miles of luxuriant woodland, its lanes thick with flowers. The small farms have all gone and so have the busy village communities. The lanes are too narrow for the modern-day agricultural machinery that thunders through more open country. At weekends the rich come rolling down from London in huge cars full of provisions bought in metropolitan farmers' markets. These people make few friends in their second homes, unless they have connections to the great houses that still stand silent in their parks, still have a butler and are now owned by usually absent celebrities. There is a lack of any knockabout young.

Which makes the place attractive to the retired professional classes who had the wit to snap up a property years ago. Their children try not to show their anxiety that the agues of years will cause the old things to be taken into care homes and their houses to be pounced upon by the Inland Revenue.

In Donhead St. Ague there is a rough earth slope, too countrified to be called a driveway, to the left of the village hill. Almost at once it divides into separate branches, one left, one right, one down, one up. At the end of the left-hand, down-sloping driveway stands the excellently modernised old farmhouse of Sir Edward Feathers QC (retired), who has lived there in peace for years. His wife Elisabeth—Betty—died while she was planting tulips against an old red wall. The house lies low, turned away from the village, towards the chalk line of the horizon and an ancient circle of trees on a hilltop. The right-hand driveway turns steeply upwards in the other direction to be lost in pine trees. Round the corner, high above it, is a patch of yellow gravel and a house of ox-blood brick; apart from one impediment, it shares the same splendid view as Eddie Feathers's house below. The impediment is Feathers's great stone chimney that looks older than the house and has a star among the listed glories of the area. Maybe the house was once a bakery. The people in the ugly house above have to peep round the chimney to see the sunset.

There have been the same old local people in the ox-blood house, however, for years and they are even-tempered. The house has become a sort of dower house for elderly members of a farming family who don't mix and, anyway, farmers seldom look at a view. They have never complained.

One day, however, they are gone. Vans and cars and "family

members" whisk them all away and leave Eddie Feathers to enjoy the view all by himself. He is rather huffed that none of them called to say goodbye, though for over twenty years he has never more than nodded to them in a chance encounter by the road. He wonders who will be his new neighbours. But not much.

The village wonders, too. Someone has seen the hideous house advertised for sale in *Country Life* at an astounding price, the photograph making it look like a fairy palace, with turrets. And no chimney in sight.

But nobody comes to visit it for some time. Down by the road a London firm of estate agents puts up a smart notice which Edward Feathers fumes about, not only because of the vulgarity of having to *advertise* a house in the Donheads, especially in St. Ague, but because someone might just possibly think that it referred to his.

Weeks and months passed. The right-hand driveway became overgrown with weeds. Somebody said they had seen something peculiar going on there one early morning. A dwarf standing in the lane. But nothing of any newcomer.

"A dwarf?"

"Well, that's what the paper boy said. Dropping in Sir Edward's paper down that bit of drainpipe. Seven in the morning. Mind, he's not what he was." (The paper boy was seventy.)

"There are no dwarfs now. They've found a way of stopping it."

"Well, it was a dwarf," said the post boy. "In a big hat."

CHAPTER TWO

Rather more than half a century earlier when cows still came swinging up the Donhead lanes and chickens sat roosting in the middle of their roads, and there were blacksmiths, and the village shop was the centre of the universe, and most people had not been beyond Shaftesbury unless they'd been in the armed forces in the war, a young English girl was standing in the bedroom of a second-class Hong Kong hotel holding a letter against her face. "Oh," she was saying. "Yes."

"Oh, yes," she told the letter. "Oh, yes, I think so!" Her face was a great smile.

And at about the same moment, though of course it was yesterday for the Orient, an unusual pair was sitting in the glossy new airport for London (now called Heathrow) in England (now being called mysteriously the UK) waiting for a Hong Kong flight. One of the men, pretty near his prime, that's to say just over thirty, was English and very tall, and wore a slightly dated hand-made suit and shoes bought in Piccadilly (St. James's Street). He was a man of unconscious distinction and if he'd been wearing a hat you might think you were seeing a ghost. As it was you felt he had been born to an earlier England.

His companion was a Chinese dwarf.

That at any rate was how he was described by the lawyers at the English Bar. The tall man was a barrister; a junior member of the Inner Temple and already spoken of with respect. The dwarf was a solicitor with an international reputation, only notionally Chinese. He preferred to be known as a Hakkar, the ancient red-brown tribe of Oriental Gypsies. He was treated with even greater respect than the barrister—who was, of course, Edward Feathers, soon to be known as "Old Filth" (Filth an acronym for Failed in London Try Hong Kong)—for he held a gold mine of litigation at his disposal all over the world wherever English Law obtained. The dwarf could spot winners.

His name was Albert Loss. It was really Albert Ross, but the R was difficult for him to pronounce in his otherwise flawless English. This annoyed him, "I am Loss" being not encouraging to clients. He claimed to have been at Eton but even to Feathers his origins were hazy. He worked the name Ross as near as possible to the Scottish nobility and hinted at Glamys and deer-stalking in the glens. Sometimes he was jovially called "Albatross," hence "Coleridge" or "Ancient Mariner," to which he responded with an inclination of the head. He was impossibly vain. To Eddie Feathers he had been, since the age of sixteen, a wonderful, if stern, friend.

Below the waist, hidden now by the table in the airport's first-class lounge at which he was playing a game of Patience, Ross's sturdy torso dwindled down into poor little legs and block feet in Dr Scholl's orthopaedic sandals. The legs suggested an unfortunate birth and a rickety childhood. No one ever found out if this was true.

Like a king or a prince he wore no watch. Eddie Feathers had, in wartime, as bombs were falling about them on a quayside in Ceylon and Ross had decided to make a run for it, presented Ross with a watch, his most precious possession. It had been Eddie's father's. The watch, of course, had long disappeared, bartered probably for food, but it was not forgotten and never replaced.

On Ross's head today and every day was a size 10 brown trilby hat, also from St. James's Street. Around the feet of the two men stood two leather briefcases stamped in gold with Eddie Feathers's initials. It was the class of luggage that would grow old along with the owner as he became Queen's Counsel, Judge, High Court Judge, perhaps Lord of Appeal in Ordinary, even Queen's Remembrancer, and possibly God.

Feathers would deserve his success. He was a thoroughly good, nice man, diligent and clever. He had grown up lonely, loved only by servants in Malaya. He had become an orphan of the Raj, fostered (disastrously) in Wales. He had been moved to a boarding school, had lost friends in the Battle of Britain, one of whom meant more to him than any family and whom he never spoke about. Sent back to the East as an evacuee, he had met Ross on board a leaky boat and lost him again. Eddie returned to England penniless and sick and, after a dismal time learning Law at Oxford, had been sitting underemployed in a back corridor of ice-cold Dickensian Chambers in Lincoln's Inn (the Temple having been bombed to rubble) when he was suddenly swept to glory by the reappearance of Ross, now a solicitor carrying with him oriental briefs galore, a sack of faery gold.

Directed by Ross, Eddie began to specialise in Bomb Damage Claims, then in General Building Disputes. Almost at once Ross had him in good suits flying about the world on the way to becoming Czar (as the saying is now) of the Construction Industry. In the Far East, there began the skyscraper boom.

And now, during the lean Attlee years post-war, Eddie was being discussed over Dinners in the Inns of Court by his peers munching their whale-meat steaks. Most of them had little else to occupy them. Litigation in the early 1950s was as rare as wartime suicide.

But there was no great jealousy. The Construction Industry is not glamorous like Slander and Libel or Crime. It is supposed to be easy, unlike Shipping or Chancery. Indeed, it comes dangerously close to Engineering, ever despised in England. It is often referred to as Sewers and Drains. Hence Filth? No—not hence Filth. Filth was an entirely affectionate pseudonym. Eddie, or Filth, who always looked as if he'd stepped out of a five-star-hotel shower, was immaculate in body and soul. Well, almost. People got on with him, always at a distance, of course, in the English way. Having no jealousy he inspired none. Women . . .

Ah, women. Well, women were intrigued by him. There was nothing effete about him. He was not unattractive sexually. His eye could gleam. But no one made any headway. He had no present entanglements, and there was no one to hear him talk in his sleep in the passionate Malay of his childhood.

His memory was as mysterious and private as anybody's. He knew only that his competence and his happiness were at their greatest in Far Eastern sunlight and the crash and rattle of monsoon rain, the suck and grind and roar of hot seas on white shores. It was in the East that he won most of his cases.

His only threat was another English lawyer, slightly younger and utterly different: a man who spoke no language other than English, had a degree in Engineering and some sort of diploma in Law from a Middlesbrough technical college often called a "night school," and was bold, ugly and unstoppable, irrepressibly merry in a way a great many women and many men found irresistible. His name was Terry Veneering.

Terry Veneering was to be on the other side in the Case Edward Feathers was about to fight in Hong Kong. He was, however, on a different plane, or perhaps staying in Hong Kong already, for he had a Chinese wife. Eddie was becoming expert in forgetting about his detested rival, and was concentrating now in the airport lounge on his solicitor, Ross, who was splattering a pack of playing cards from hand to hand, cutting, dealing, now and then flinging them into the air in an arc and catching them sweetly on their way down. Ross was raising a breeze.

"I wish you wouldn't do that," said Filth. "People are becoming irritated."

"It's because hardly any of them are able to," said Ross. "It is a gift."

"You were messing with cards the first time I met you. Why can't you take up knitting?"

"No call for woollens in Hong Kong. Find the Lady."

"I don't want to find the bloody Lady. Where's this bloody plane? Has something gone wrong with it? They tell you nothing."

"It shouldn't. It's the latest thing. Big square windows."

"Excellent. Except it doesn't seem to work. The old ones were better last year. Trundling along. Screws loose. Men with oilcans taking up the carpets. And we always got there."

"We're being called," said Ross. He snapped the cards into a wad, the wad into a pouch, and with some Gypsy sleight of hand picked up both briefcases and thumped off towards the lifts. From above he looked like a walking hat.

Filth strode behind carrying his walking stick and the *Daily Telegraph*. At the steps up to the plane Ross, as was proper, stood back for his Counsel to pass him and Filth was bowed aboard and automatically directed to turn left to the first class. Ross, hobbling behind in the Dr Scholl's, was asked to set down the hand luggage and show his seat number.

But it was Ross who saw the cases safely stowed, changed their seats for ones that could accommodate Filth's long legs, the plane being as usual half empty, and Ross who commanded Filth's jacket to be put on a hanger in a cupboard, declined to take off his hat and who demanded an immediate refill of the complimentary champagne.

They both sat back and watched England gallop backwards, then the delicious lurch upwards through the grey sky to the sunlit blue above.

"This champagne is second-rate," said Ross. "I've had better in Puerto Rico."

"There'll be a good dinner," said Filth. "And excellent wine. What about your hat?"

Ross removed it with both hands and laid it on his table.

A steward hovered. "Shall I take that from you, sir?"

"No. I keep it with me." After a time he put it at his feet.

The dinner trolley, with its glistening saddle of lamb, was being wheeled to the centre of the cabin. Silver cutlery—real silver, Ross noted, turning the forks to confirm the hallmark—was laid on starched tray cloths. A carving knife flashed amidships. Côtes du Rhône appeared.

"Remember the *Breath o'Dunoon*, Albatross?" said Filth. "Remember the duff you made full of black beetles for currants?"

Ross brooded. "I remember the first mate. He said he'd kill me at Crib. He *wanted* to kill me. I beat him."

"It's a wonder we weren't torpedoed."

"I thought we *were* torpedoed. But then, I have been so often torpedoed—"

"Thank you, thank you," roared out Filth in the direction of the roast lamb. He was apt to roar when emotionally disturbed: it was the last vestige of the terrible stammer of his Welsh childhood. "Don't start about torpedoes."

"For example," said Ross, "in the Timor Sea. I was wrecked off . . ."

But vegetables had arrived and redcurrant jelly and they munched, meditating on this and that, Ross's heavy chin a few inches above his plate. "You ate thirty-six bananas," he said. "On Freetown beach. You were disgusting."

"They were small bananas. This lamb is splendid."

"And there'll be better to come when we've changed planes at Delhi. Back to chopsticks and the true cuisine."

After the tray cloths were drawn and they had finished with their coffee cups they drowsed.

Filth said that he'd have to get down to his papers. "No— I'll fish them out for myself. You look after your hat. What do you keep in it? Opium?"

Ross ignored him.

Hot towels were brought, the pink tape round the sets of papers undone, the transcripts spread and Ross slept.

How he snores, thought Filth. I remember that on the old *Dunoon*. And he got to work with his fountain pen and a block of folio, and was soon deaf, blind and oblivious to all else. The sky that enwrapped them now blackened the windows. Below, invisible mountain ranges were speckled with pinpricks of lights like the stars all around and above them. Before long, seats were being converted into beds—not Filth's; he worked on—and blankets and warm socks were distributed. Night already.

"Brandy, sir? Nightcap?"

"Why not," said Filth, pulling the papers together, taking off his cashmere pullover and putting on a Marks & Spencer's. A steward came to ease off his shoes.

I have seldom felt so happy, he thought, sipping the brandy, closing his eyes, awaiting sleep. I wonder if I should tell the Albatross why? No. Better wait till after Delhi.

But then: Why not? I owe him so much. Best person, just about, I've ever met. Most loyal. My salvation. I've had other salvations but this one looks like lasting.

He watched the strange sleeping face of the dwarf, and Ross opened his eyes.

"Coleridge?"

Albert Ross looked startled.

"Coleridge, I have something to tell you."

At once the playing cards were flying. Ross began to shuffle and deal them.

"Will you put those bloody things away?"

"Do I understand," said Ross, setting them carefully down, "that there is to be some sort of revelation?"

"Yes."

"Much better find the Lady," said Ross, beginning to deal again.

"I *have* found the lady, Coleridge. I have found her."

There was silence; only the purr of the plane.

The silence lasted until Delhi and all through the stopover, the pacing in the marble first-class lounge, the buying of trinkets in the shops—Ross bought a case of blue butterflies—the resettling into Air India. Along swam the smiling painted girls in their cheongsams. The final take-off for Hong Kong.

"So," said Ross. "You are about to be married. It is a revelation all right, but immaterial to your profession. Wait until you've done it as often as I have."

Filth looked uneasy. "You never told me any of that, Albert."

"I consider that they are my private affairs. Who is she?"

"She'll be in Hong Kong when we get there. Waiting. Today."

"She's Chinese?"

"No. No, a Scottish woman. But born in Tiensin. I met her—well, I've been meeting her off and on for a year or so. Whenever we come out East. The first case you got for me. In Singapore."

"So that I'm to blame?"

"Yes. Of course. I'm very glad to say. You will, I hope, be best man at my wedding. Without that hat."

"Her name?"

"She's called Elisabeth Macintosh. Betty. She's a good sort. Very attractive."

"A *good sort*!" The cards again were flying. "A *good sort*?" He was wagging his weird Johnsonian head from side to side.

"She hasn't actually accepted me yet," said Filth. "I've only just asked her. In a letter from Chambers sent to her hotel and marked 'To await arrival.' She's just passing through with a friend. They've been in Australia—or somewhere. She has had some sort of work—I'm not sure. Rather hush-hush. She's a natural traveller but not at all well off. She's at the Old Colony Hotel."

"Never heard of it." Without apparent volition the cards rose like liquid into a circle, and subsided.

"Look, Albert, on the whole perhaps not mention it yet. I think she *may* accept me. Seems quite fond of me. She hasn't actually said—"

"I'm glad that she seems fond of you. It is the usual thing."

"And I'm really very fond of her. What's the matter?"

"You haven't slept with her then?"

A steward looked away but went on listening.

"No," cried Filth, loud and unaware. "No, of course not. She's a lady. And I want to marry her."

"How young?"

"I've never asked. She's a young girl. Well, she can't techni-cally be a girl. She grew up in the war. Japanese internment camp in Shanghai. Lost both parents. Doesn't speak about it."

"Have you ever asked her about it?"

"One doesn't intrude."

"Edward, what does she know about *you*? That you ought to tell her? What have you talked about? Will she stay with you?"

"She's good at birds and plants. So am I. My prep school. She's very lively. Infectiously happy. Very bright eyes. Strong. Rather—muscular. I feel safe with her." Filth looked at the throbbing structure of the plane. "As a matter of fact," he said, "I would die for her."

"Yes, I will," the girl was saying in the shabby hotel in the back street, and street music playing against the racket of the mah-jong players on every open stone balcony. The overhead fan was limp and fly-spotted. On the beds were 1920s scarlet satin counterpanes with ugly yellow flowers done in stem stitch. They must have survived the war. Old wooden shutters clattered. There was the smell of the rotting lilies heaped in a yard below. Betty was alone, her friend Lizzie out somewhere, thank goodness. Betty would have hated not to be alone when she read Edward's letter. What lovely handwriting. Rather a shame he'd used his Chambers writing paper. She wondered how many rough drafts he'd made first. Transcripts. He was wedded to transcripts. This was meant to be kept.

And she would. She'd keep it for ever. Their grandchildren would leave it to a museum as a memento of the jolly old dead.

Eddie Feathers? Crikey! He does sound a bit quaint. (*Would you consider our being married, Elisabeth?*) Not exactly Romeo. More like Mr. Knightley, though Mr. Knightley had a question mark about him. Forty-ish and always off to London alone. Don't tell me that Emma was his first. I'm wandering. I do rather wish Eddie wasn't so perfect. But of course I'll marry him. I can't think of a reason not to.

She kissed the letter and put it down her shirt.

Over the South China Sea Albert Ross was saying, "Do you know anything about this girl? Do you think she knows a bloody thing about you?"

"I'd say I was pretty straightforward."

"Would you! *Would* you?"

The plane lurched sideways and down. Then again sideways and down. It tilted its wings like a bird that had suddenly lost concentration and fallen asleep in the dark. Though, thought Filth, the prep-school-trained ornithologist, they never do.

"Elisabeth," he said, "makes me think of a kingfisher. She glitters and shines. Or a glass of water."

"Oh?"

"A glass of clear water in a Scottish burn rushing through heather."

"Good God."

"Yes."

"Has she ever *seen* heather? Born in Tiensin? Is she beautiful?"

Filth looked shocked. "No, no! My goodness, no. Not at all. Not *glamorous*."

"I see."

"Her—presence—is beautiful." (It must be the glass of champagne that had been served with breakfast.) "Her soul is right."

Ross picked up the cards. "You are not a great connoisseur of women, Edward."

"How do you know, Coleridge? We didn't talk about women on the *Breath o'Dunoon*."

"So what about the Belfast tart?"

"I never told you that!"

"The shilling on the mantelpiece. You talked of nothing else when you were delirious with poisoned bananas."

Filth in his magnificence pondered.

"You'd better tell Miss Macintosh the outcome."

"How did you hear the outcome?"

"Oh, I know people."

"Look here, I'm cured. I have a certificate. 'VD' they called it. Peccadilloes up there on the frontier. Old as soldiers. Old as man. Mostly curable."

"You weren't on the frontier. You went to bed with an Irish slag in a boarding house in Belfast."

"I was sixteen."

"Yes. Well. You were curiously unperturbed. I'm worried about your . . ."

"What?"

"Fertility."

"For the love of God, Ross! I'm not sure I can go on know-ing you."

"*Think*, Eddie. Nobody knows you like I do."

Below them the sun was rising from the rim of the globe. Mile-high columns of mist stood about in the air. Curtains of a giant stage. Stewardesses were clicking up the blinds letting in one bar of sunlight after another. The canned music began. Chinese music now. Ting-tang. Sleeping bodies began to stir and stretch and yawn, and Edward Feathers smiled. Looking out, so near to landing and yet so high, he waited for the first sight of the three hundred and twenty-five islands that are called Hong Kong.

On one of them Betty Macintosh would be reading his let-ter. He saw her smiling and skipping about. Sweet child. So young and dear and good.

What would she have made of him on the *Breath o'Dunoon*? Young, ravaged, demented, shipwrecked? She'd have been a child then. He'd been a gaunt, sick boy, just left school. With an Adam's apple. Though women had never been scarce, from the start.

Isobel.

Nowadays women looked at him as if he were a cliff face. I'm not attractive, he thought, but they've been told there's a seam of gold about. Called money, I suppose.

"We're here," said Ross and Kai Tak airport was waiting below.

They swung round the harbour: the familiar landing pad that stuck out over the water like a diving board. During the war a plane a week had been lost there. Since then only one had tipped over into the harbour. But passengers on beginning to land always fell quiet for a moment.

"And so, Edward," said the bright-eyed girl that night, as the red sun dropped back into the sea, "Eddie, I will," and she took his hand. "I will. Yes. Thank you. I will and I will and I will."

Somewhere in the archipelago her friend Lizzie would be drinking in a bar.

All morning she had been saying, "Betty—you can't. It'd be a dreadful mistake."

Finally, she had said, "All right. I'll tell you something. I *know* him."

"You never said! How? You know Edward?"

"See this pinhead? It's the world. The middle classes. The Empire club. It'll all be gone in a few years and I suppose we should be glad."

"You know Eddie?"

"Yes. In the biblical sense, too. I was wild for him. Wild. He had this quality. I don't know what it was. Probably still is. But you can't forget Teddy Feathers. He doesn't understand anyone, Bets, certainly not women. Something awful in his childhood. He's inarticulate when he's not in Court and then you hear another voice. As you do when he's asleep—I know. He speaks Malay. D'you know he once had a horrible stammer? He's a blank to everyone except that dwarf lawyer person, and *there's* a mystery. Bets, you will be perfect for him as he becomes more and more boring. Pompous. Set in stone. Titled, no doubt. Rich as Croesus. But there's something missing. Mind, he's not sexless. He's very enjoyable. It was before I was the other way—"

"Did you ever tell him about that?"

"Good God, no! He'd be disgusted. He leaves you feeling guilty as it is, he's so pure. But there's something missing. Maybe it's his nanny—oh, Betty, *don't*."

She said, "Lizzie-Izz, you're jealous!"

"Probably. A bit."

*

All day Betty had walked about, crossing and recrossing the city, changing twice from Hong Kong to Kowloon-side. It was Sunday and she went into St. John's Cathedral and took Communion. She got a shock when the Chinese priest changed from Cantonese to English when he administered the Bread to her. She always forgot that she was not Chinese. She walked afterwards towards Kai Tak. Planes were landing and taking off from the airport all the time. She had no idea when Eddie's would arrive. The planes shrieked over the paper houses of the poor. The people there were said to be deaf.

Not noticing the noise, she wandered on among the filthy streets and came to a blistered building four storeys high with rubbish on every cement stair. She climbed up and up, noise bursting from each doorway and gallery, like feeding time at the zoo. The dear, remembered childhood chorus, the knock-out smells of food and scraps. She clambered over boxes and bundles of rags and birdcages and parcels guarded by immobile individuals glaring at nothing. Rice bubbled thick on little stoves. On the third floor some Buddhist monks were chanting, and there was the smell of lamp oil, spices and smoke. On the top floor there was an antique English pram, inscribed Silver Cross, nearly blocking the apartment door, which her friend Amy opened when Betty knocked, a blond and rosy child on her hip and another child imminent. She had a Bible in one hand and was holding the place in it with her thumb. School-friends, they hadn't met since Amy became a missionary several years ago. She had been a dancer then.

Amy said, "Oh. Hullo, Betty Macintosh. Come on in. There's a prayer group but there'll be some food. Can you stay the night?" Behind her the corridor was packed with noisy people.

Inside the apartment there appeared to be no furniture except a piano where a very old Englishwoman was going hell for leather at Moody and Sankey hymns, as children of several nationalities were being fed, cross-legged on the floor. The old lady began to sing to her own accompaniment. "She's a missionary, too," said Amy. "But she's got Depression. We have her round here every day in case she jumps into the harbour. She lives towards the New Territories behind barbed wire and guard dogs—she has some antiques—and does it stink!"

A chair was found. Betty sat on it and was given the baby to hold while Amy went off to dollop out rice from a black pot. The old lady stopped playing and singing and began to cry, and a different surge of wailing Buddhist chant rose from the floor below. From a sort of cupboard burst a young Englishman who ran out of the apartment, leaned over the Harrods pram on the landing and began to shout down to the monks that they could damn well give over. He was trying to work. If they wanted food, here it was, but they could stop chanting and let God have an alternative for half an hour. His Cantonese was very good. In a moment several monks in orange robes had negotiated the pram. They came into the apartment where they stood about, smiling in a row, awaiting rice.

Amy, ladle in hand, took the baby from Betty's knee and dumped it on the knee of the Depressive. It immediately began to cry, which made the Depressive stop, and Amy, holding two dishes of rice, squeezed herself down on the floor near Betty, and said, "So?"

"Hello, Amy."

"So, when did you get home?"

"Home? I've not had a home for years."

"Oh, get on," said Amy.

"I'm on holiday. Passing through. I'm drifting."

"Alone?"

"With a girlfriend. Lizzie Ingoldby. D'you remember? Older than us, at school. Where's Nick?"

"That was Nick, yelling at the Buddhists. He's trying to write a sermon on Submission to God. He's upset. They all fall in love with him out here and he hates to disappoint a woman. By the way, we're having another."

"I can see."

"It will make four. And we're broke. Have you any spare money?"

"Not a bean. I'm coming into money when I'm thirty. My parents thought I might be flighty. Instead, I'm hungry."

"Well, don't become a missionary. We're not hungry but we'd like a sideline. We're not allowed a sideline. A rich one who puts his arms round me would be nice."

The old lady, a Mrs. Baxter, had now silenced the baby with *Hymns Ancient & Modern*, and called out, "Oh, I do agree! I am not a nun." And began to dab her eyes. Amy passed her a very small cup of rice wine.

"We're just about all she's got," said Amy. "She hasn't the fare to England and there's nobody she knows there now if she even got there. So what sort of sideline have you got, clever old Elisabeth of the Enigma Variations and always top of the form, star of St. Paul's and St. Anne's?"

"I think—well, I think—I'm going in for a husband."

"Oh? Really? Oh, very, *very* good. Who is it?"

"You don't know him. Well, I don't think you do. I don't know him very well, either. I came to ask you if I should do it. He's flying in tonight. I'll have to make up my mind. I'm sick of fretting on about it. By tomorrow. Maybe tonight."

"What is he? English or Chinese? Is he Christian or ghastly agnostic? Your eyes have tears in them."

"He's English. Christian. Not Christian like you are, full time. More like I am. Doesn't talk about it. Oh, yes, and he's already pretty rich. He'll get *very* rich. He's got the touch. He's an advocate. He'll be a judge."

"Oh, he's in his nineties. Does he dribble?"

"No. He's quite young. He's brilliant. And he's so good-looking he finds he's embarrassed walking down the street.

Thinks they belong—his looks—to a different man. He's very, very nice, Amy. And he needs me."

"So?"

"I don't know."

"Have you slept with him?"

"He's not the sort. I don't even know . . ."

"He's a virgin?"

"Oh, no. Not that. I've heard. In the war he was close to Queen Mary."

"He had an affair with Queen Mary?"

They stared at each other and began to howl and laugh and roll about, as at school.

"He must be very grand," said Amy.

"No. Oh, no. He never knows who anyone is. Social stuff doesn't interest him."

"And you? You, you, you? D'you love him?"

"I don't know. I think so. I suppose I should but you see I'm retarded. I want the moon, like a teenager."

"You *should* want the moon. Don't do it, Bets. Don't go for a forty-watt light bulb because it looks pretty. You'll get stuck with it when it goes out. You are so loyal, and you'll have to soldier on in the dark for ever afterwards."

Mrs. Baxter announced that Jesus was the Light of the World.

"That's right," said Amy. "Have some more wine."

"And Him only shalt thou serve," said Mrs. Baxter.

"Amy, I must go. He may already be here. At any minute."

"But come back. You will come back, won't you? Bring him."

Betty tried to see Edward standing in the pools of rice in his polished shoes, the Buddhists chanting, Mrs. Baxter weeping.

"I'd love your life, Amy."

"So you say," said Amy.

CHAPTER THREE

And so, a few hours later, into the sea dropped the great red yo-yo sun and darkness painted out the waters of a bay. Then lights began to show, first the pricking lights under the ramparts they stood on, then more nebulous lights from boats knocking together where the fishermen lived in houses on stilts, then the lights of moving boats fanning white on black across the bay, and then across faraway bays and coastlines of the archipelago; lights of ferries, coloured lights of invisible villages and way over to the south dim lights staining the darkness of Hong Kong itself.

Edward Feathers and Elisabeth Macintosh stood side by side, looking out, and a drum began to beat. Voices rose in a screech, like a sunset chorus of raucous birds: Cantonese and half a dozen dialects; the crashing of pots and pans, clattering pandemonium. Blue smoke rose up from the boats to the terrace of the hotel and there was a blasting smell of hot fish. Behind the couple standing looking out, waiters were beginning to spread tablecloths and napkins, setting down saucers decorated with floating lights and flowers. The last suggestion of a sun departed and the sky was speckled with a hundred million stars.

"Edward? Eddie—yes. Thank you. Yes. I will and I will and I will, but could you say something?"

Some of the older waiters would respond to Elisabeth's voice in the slow English of before the war. It was beginning to sound Old World. Proud, unflinching, Colonial. Yet the girl did not conform to it. She was bare-legged, in open-toed sandals with clean but unpainted toenails. She was wearing a cotton dress she had had for years and hadn't thought about changing to meet her future husband. The time in the Shanghai detention centre had arrested her body rather than matured her and she would still have been recognised by her school first-eleven hockey team.

Edward looked down at the top of her curly head, rather the colour of his own. "Chestnut," they call it. Conker-colour. Red. Our children are bound to have red hair. Red hair frightens the Chinese. Our children'll have to go Home to England, if we settle here. If we have any children . . .

She said, "*Edward*? Please?"

At last then he embraced her.

"We must get back," he said and on the ferry again across the harbour they sat close together, but not touching, on a slatted seat. Nearby sat a pasty young Englishman who was being stroked and sighed over by a Chinese girl with a yearning face. She was plump and pale, gazing up at him, whispering to him, kissing him all the time below the ear. He flicked at the ear now and then as if there were a fly about, but he was smiling. The ferry chugged and splashed. The Englishman looked proud and content. "She's a great cook, too," he called in their direction. "She can do a great mashed potato. It's not all that rice."

At Kowloon-side Edward and Elisabeth walked a foot or so apart to his hotel, climbed the marble steps and passed through the flashing glass doors. Inside among the marble columns and the lilies and the fountains Edward lifted a finger towards the reception desk and his room key was brought to him.

"There's a party now."

"When? Whose?"

"Now. Here. It's tomorrow's Judge. It's going to be a long Case and he's a benevolent old stick. He likes to kick off with a party. Both sides invited. Leaders, juniors, wives, girlfriends, fiancées. And courtesans for flavour."

"Must we go?"

"Yes. I don't much want to, but you don't refuse."

When he looked down at her she saw how happy he was.

"Have I time to change?"

"No. It will have begun. We'll just show our faces. Your clothes are fine. I have something for you to wear, as it happens. I'll go up and change my jacket and I'll bring it down."

"Shall I come up to the room with you?"

The new, easy, happy Edward faltered. "No. I don't think they care for that here. I'll be back in ten minutes. I'll order you some tea."

"It's a strange betrothal," Betty told the lily-leaf-shaped tray, the shallow cup, the tiny piece of Battenburg cake and the cress sandwich so small that a breeze from the fountains might blow it away. A trio behind her was playing Mozart. Two Chinese, one Japanese, very expert and scornful. She remembered how people in England used to say that no Oriental would ever be able to play Mozart. Just like they used to say that there would never be Japanese pilots because the Japanese are all half blind behind dark glasses. She was all at once overcome by the idiotic nature of mankind and began to laugh. God must feel like me, she thought. Oh, I love Hong Kong. Could we live here? Could Edward?

Here he came now, washed and shaved in a clean shirt and linen jacket, loping over from the lift, smiling like a boy (I'm going to be with this person all my life!) and he dropped a little cloth bag into her lap and she took out from it the most magnificent string of pearls.

"Yours," he said. "They're old. Someone gave them to me.

When I was sixteen. In the war. Just in time. She died a few minutes later. She was lying next to me under a lifeboat on deck. We were limping Home up the Irish Sea—everybody sick and dying. She was very old. Raj spinster. Whiskery. Brave. Type that's gone. She said, 'One day you can give them to your sweetheart.'"

She thought: He's not cold at all. Then, Oh, OH!! The pearls are wonderful. But they're not what matters.

"There's a condition, Elisabeth."

"About the pearls?"

"Certainly not. They are yours for ever. You are my sweetheart. But this marriage, our marriage . . ."

"Hush," she said. "People are listening. Later."

"No—NOW," he roared out in the way he did; and several heads turned. "This marriage is a big thing. I don't believe in divorce."

"You're talking about divorce before you've proposed."

Mozart behind them sang out, *Aha! Bravo! Goodbye!* And the trio stood up and bowed.

"Elisabeth, you must never leave me. That's the condition. I've been left all my life. From being a baby, I've been taken away from people. Raj orphan and so on. Not that I'm unusual there. And it's supposed to have given us all backbone."

"Well, I know all that. I am an orphan, too. My parents suffered."

"All our parents suffered for an ideology. They believed it was good for us to be sent Home, while they went on with ruling the Empire. We were all damaged even though we became endurers."

("May I take your tray, madam?")

"It did not destroy me but it made me bloody unsure."

"I will never leave you, Edward."

"I'll never mention any of this again." His words began to

stumble. "Been sent away all my life. Albert Ross saved me. So sorry. Came through. Bad at sharing feelings."

"Which, dear Eddie, if I may say so, must be why you haven't yet proposed to me."

"I thought I had—"

"No. Your Chambers stationery has. Not you. I want to hear it from you. In your words. From your lips." (She was happy, though.)

"Marry me, Elisabeth. Never leave me. I'll never ask again. But *never* leave me."

"I'll never leave you, Edward."

A waiter swam by and scooped up her tray though she called out, "Oh, no!"

Bugger, she thought, I've had nothing all day but that rice at Amy's. Then: I shouldn't be thinking of cake.

In the lift on the way up to the Judge's party, her bare toes inside the sandals crunching the sand of the distant sunset harbour, she thought: Well, now I know. It won't be romantic but who wants that? It won't be passion, but better without, probably. And there will be children. And he's remarkable and I'll grow to love him very much. There's nothing about him that's unlovable.

They stood together now at the far end of the corridor where the Judge had his suite. They could see the open doors, gold and white. The noise of the party inside rose in a subdued roar.

Edward said, "Unclutch those pearls. I want to put them round your neck." He took them, heavy and creamy, into both hands and held them to his face. "They still smell of the sea."

She said, "Oh, ridiculous," and laughed, and he at last kissed her very gravely in full view of the waiters round the distant door. She saw that his eyes brimmed with tears.

Why, the dear old thing, she thought.

CHAPTER FOUR

T he Judge was standing just inside the doors of his suite to welcome his guests and ostentatiously waving about a glass of Indian tonic water to make clear to everyone that tomorrow morning he would be in Court. He was a clever, abstracted little man with a complexion pale and freckled like cold porridge. He had been born in the East and his skin still didn't seem to know what to make of it. His wife, Dulcie, much younger and here with him on a visit, was vague and dumpy in paisley-patterned silk. The arrival of the up-and-coming Edward and the unconventional-looking young woman appeared to mean little to either of them. The Judge was looking everywhere around.

"Aha, yes. Eddie Feathers," said the Judge (he was known as Pastry Willy). "Well done. Arrived safely. Good flight? Well, don't let me monopolise you. We'll be head-on for months. Sick of the sight of each other. I've said exactly the same to the other side for the same reason. They're all over there."

Gales of laughter were arising from across the room and there was the impression of someone bigger than the rest buffooning about. He had a flap of flaxen hair.

"I can't remember how well you know Veneering?"

"Quite well."

Pastry Willy quickly looked away. Something about a mutual and inexplicable loathing.

"May I introduce Elisabeth Macintosh?" said Edward. "She is about to become my wife."

"Delighted, delightful," said the Judge, and his wife Dulcie blinked at the gingham dress and pearls.

Elisabeth leaned forward and kissed Pastry Willy on the cheek. "Hello, Uncle Willy. I'm Betty Macintosh." She kissed him again on the other cheek.

"Oh, my goodness! Little Betty! Joseph's girl!"

"Father died," she said and disappeared into the crowd.

"But this is splendid! Splendid, Feathers! I used to read fairy tales to her on my knee." Edward was hurrying after her. "In Tiensin!"

"Elisabeth!" He caught up with her. "You kissed Willy?"

"Well, I knew him when I was seven," she said.

In the heart of the throng Edward, looking joyous, began to declare to left and right, "Hello, my—my fiancée."

The room became more crowded still, the talk all London Inns of Court and how the Colony was awash this month with English lawyers. A drift of excited wives just off the plane surged by in new silk dresses they'd already had time to buy, their hair and lipstick all in place and shiny. A lovely Chinese woman in pale yellow with chandelier earrings was reclining on a chaise longue. She had a face of perpetual ennui. From the corner of the room where the noise was wildest the flaxen-headed man separated himself from his friends, roaring with laughter. He was wearing khaki shorts and a khaki shirt, which made him seem not eccentric but ahead of fashion and in the sartorial know. "No, not that way," Edward commanded Elisabeth, and the man with the bright hair cried out, "Oh, God! It's Old Filth!" Then he saw Elisabeth in the pearls and gingham and stood perfectly still.

"I'm Veneering," he said to her, "Terry Veneering." His eyes were bright light blue.

Elisabeth thought: And it is just one hour too late.

"Come and meet—" Edward was steering her away. "You

must meet my clerk and—I don't see Ross anywhere yet. I hope you're going to like him. I'll tell you—oh, hello! Hello! Tony, Desmond. Safe here, all of us. This is—"

But Elisabeth had slid away. Through some glass doors on to an airy balcony she had spotted a glitter of dishes. Her holiday money she'd used up in Australia, and for the past week she and Lizzie had been eating nothing much except noodles and deep-fried prawns off the market stalls. At the end of this frugal day of celebration (when she'd thought there'd be a feast, looking out over the sunset harbour), she was ravenous and—with a percipience she would keep and be thankful for throughout her coming life—she'd noticed that Edward hadn't mentioned dinner. And she knew that after the party he would find urgent work to do for the next day.

Belshazzar's feast was laid out on white cloths on the balcony, a row of robotic waiters standing behind.

"I'm your first customer," she said, and with faint disapproval one of them handed her a plate and she passed down the buffet alone, helping herself hugely to crab and lobster mayonnaise. Oh, glory!

She sat down alone at an empty side table with a long white cloth to the floor, stretched her sandy feet beneath it and touched something that squeaked.

Putting her chopsticks neatly down, she lifted a corner of the tablecloth and saw a boy cross-legged on the marble, crunching a lobster. He had black Chinese hair that stood up spikily in an un-Oriental way. His eyes were blue.

"Good evening," said Elisabeth. "Do you usually eat underneath tables?"

"Sometimes they let me in ahead of time. I get hungry at my father's parties, too."

"Oh, I'm always hungry," she said. "But I'll stay in the open tonight. Who are you? I'm Betty Macintosh."

"Like a raincoat?" He licked each finger thoroughly before holding out his hand. "I'm Harry Veneering. I'm an only child. My father is a very famous barrister. He works out here a lot of the time but I'm at school in England. I'm flying back to school tonight."

"Is the lobster then altogether wise? Do you think?"

"Oh, yes, thanks. I'm never sick. I can eat anything. I'm like my father. My mother eats just about nothing, ever."

"Where are you at school in England?"

"Near London. It's a prep school. For Eton, of course. My father being who he is."

"Is he the one in the shorts?"

"Yes. He says if you are anybody you can wear what you like anywhere. Some lord or duke told him. Or maybe it was a prime minister. He's a terrible, terrible inside-out snob, my dad, and he's very, very funny."

"Ought you to discuss your father with a stranger?"

"Oh, yes. He's fun. He's just a joke. And very, very brilliant."

"I've seen him. Yellow hair?"

"Yes. It's gross. But it's not dyed. I've got my mother's hair. She's the one with the long earrings."

"You have your father's eyes."

"Yes." He looked at her from across the small table where he was now attacking the crabmeat. "He's a hypnotist. That's why he wins absolutely every one of his Cases."

"*Oh*, no," she said, "*Oh*, no. I am about to be married to another barrister and he wins Cases too and some of them against your father. And he *never* boasts. And he wasn't at Eton. And he's not a snob of any kind, ever. How old are you and why are you arguing about matters beyond your under-standing?"

"I'm nine. I'm small, but I expect to grow. My dad says boys grow to their feet and my feet—look at them—they're vast. I suppose you're going to marry Mr. Feathers. Did you know he's called Old Filth? It's because he's so clean and so clever. Well, of course he is *fairly* clever."

"You don't need to tell me about my future husband. It's pert. Now then, come over here and bring that big table napkin with you. I'll clean you up. And remember you are talking to the new Mrs. Edward Feathers."

"'Mrs. Feathers' sounds like a hen." And the child came over and shut his eyes, presenting his silky Chinese face to her as she dipped the dinner napkin in cold water and mopped up the mayonnaise from round his mouth. He opened his blue eyes and said, "I know, I absolutely know I've seen you before. I didn't mean to be rude. I love hens."

"No," she said. "I don't believe we've met before."

"If you're ever back in England," he said, "would you like to come to my school sports days? I'm very good. I win everything and there's never anybody to see me because my parents are always somewhere else. Such as out here."

"I should have to ask their permission."

"Oh, it'll be all right. The school won't mind. I could say you're my nanny."

She looked at him.

"What's the matter? You'd look exactly right. My mother's supposed to be the most beautiful woman in Hong Kong, you know."

"That must be very difficult for her," said Elisabeth.

The languid Chinese woman of the chaise longue was all at once standing behind them, holding a champagne glass round its rim in the tips of her fingers. The fingers of her other hand balanced her against the wall.

People were now crowding in for the buffet and the waiters were coming to life. Behind Elsie Veneering stood Veneering. Veneering was looking at Elisabeth's unlined face, his wife at Elisabeth's unpainted sandy toenails.

"Harry," said Elsie. "It's time to go. Introduce me to your friend."

"She's Miss Macintosh, she belongs to Mr. Feathers. She's going to marry him. This is my mother."

"*Marrying?*" Elsie's eyes were black and still. "What secrets! We all rather suspected . . . How kind of you to talk to Harry. Have you children already? Grandchildren?"

"Oh yes," said Elisabeth. "I have twenty-seven grandchildren and I'm only twenty-eight years old."

Elsie looked out of her depth but Harry laughed and fell on Elisabeth like a puppy. "You will come, won't you? Come to my school? On sports day?"

"Only if your mother and father will let me."

"There'll be no sports days at all if you don't tuck your shirt in your shorts and get smartened up. We've not finished your packing yet and the plane goes at midnight. Your mother needs a rest." Veneering's voice was all right. O.K. Just a trace of elocution lessons, maybe?

"Aren't you taking me? Dad? You always take me to the airport." The boy who had looked as if he could outface a battalion crumpled into a baby and began to cry.

"Can't this time," said Veneering, "Work to be done for tomorrow. Sorry, guv'nor."

"Why didn't you do the bloody work instead of coming to this awful party?" And biffing everyone out of his way, the child kicked out at his yellow-headed father and ran from the Judge's apartment.

Veneering stood looking at Elisabeth and Elsie drifted away.

"He must learn to travel alone," said Veneering. "Hundreds of them still do. Hardens them up. It's in the British genes."

"What rubbish you talk," said Elisabeth.

"They travel first class. Well looked-after. Met at the other end. We take a lot of trouble. Not like in your old man's time."

"It's a fourteen-hour flight. And there's a change of plane in India."

"He's a self-reliant little beast. He's done it before."

"If you ever need anyone to meet him we'll probably be living in London at first. I should like to. Please."

"I hear you're marrying Old Filth. It's the sensation of the party. "Who is she, my dear?" No—he'd never let you have anything to do with a son of mine. We don't get on. He thinks I'm common. So when did he get rid of his stammer and manage to ask you?"

"About three hours ago."

"Is he weighing up your acceptance? Considering your sentence? I can see that you are."

She stood up. "You are as vulgar as they say you are." She handed him her empty plate, crumpling his son's dinner napkin on top of it as if he were a waiter, and walked away.

S he had been right about dinner. A junior in his team had asked Edward for a consultation after the party. It might make a vital difference to the Case. Edward would of course walk her back to her hotel first.

"Will we meet later?"

"I never know how long—"

"Edward, we've not been engaged for a day yet. Can't you even stop for some dinner? I didn't see you eating anything. We've said so little—"

"Not hungry. My clock's not settled yet, it's the middle of the night, I think." He took her arm above the elbow and said, "Anyway, I'm too excited."

"Oh! Oh, well. Eddie, come to my room afterwards. At the Old C. It's number 182. I'll be alone. Lizzie's out."

"Rather not promise. The end of the week will be ours for two full days. Then we have all the years we're going to live."

He dropped her outside her hotel, which was pulsing with lights and screeching music.

"Well, goodnight, my future husband who doesn't ever kiss me."

"Well, certainly not here. You know I love you. I always will. Thank you. Please live for ever. Stop me from being a bloody bore. I can't help working. It's been a safety valve since school. Device for not thinking. But I'll be all right now. Always. We'll have a long, long honeymoon when this Case is out of the way."

He kissed her like a brother.

Her room was unlocked and she had to turn out four uni-
formed room-boys who were lying on the floor and on the
beds watching her tiny flickering black-and-white television.
Lizzie must have turned the *Room Free* label the wrong way
round instead of to *Do Not Disturb*. Lizzie's reading of Cantonese was getting hazy. There was a musky smell in the room
and Elisabeth opened the window, turned off the television
and the lights and the air-conditioning. Warm harbour smells
floated in. The water pipes along the walls clanked to the
rhythm of somebody's shower above. She took off the pearls
and put them on a chair. She picked up the yellowing finger-
marked breakfast menu and then thought, no, she'd order in
the morning. She only needed sleep.

About midnight she woke in panic. The sky above was
throbbing with planes. The boy Harry would be at the airport
now. No, he'd already be in the air, sitting in his first-class seat.
"Flying out at midnight." To be hoped that the mother . . . The
mother had looked drunk. You'd think the father would have
cancelled that Con. An only child. Will Edward cancel a Consultation for a child? She decided, no. But there will be me.

Our children will always have me.

Where's Lizzie? Secret life. Always had. All these secrets.
She thought of the codes at Bletchley Park in the mild English
countryside. We took it so lightly. Secrets. Elisabeth slept now
against the madhouse clamour of Kowloon. Blank. Jet lag. Still
partly in Sydney. Hole in the air, *c'est moi*. Ought to be better
at all this. Calmer. I am getting married. I'm twenty-eight.

In a dream she was informing her long-dead and always
shadowy parents not to worry. She was back on the blistered
floor of the Camp. The dust. Her father's voice suddenly
boomed out at her, "There'll be money when you're thirty.
Do nothing hasty." His ribcage had stuck out. His nose sharp
in the skull. "I'm quite safe," she shouted. "I'm doing all right."

In the morning she woke to Lizzie's radio playing beside the other bed and sat up bleary and tousled blinking across to where Lizzie lay prone. The radio rattled on in Cantonese.

"Lizzie-Izz! You're back! Where were you? I've something . . ."

"Shut up a minute. There's terrible news."

"Oh. What news?"

"Plane crash. Early this morning. Over the Indian Ocean. It broke in two."

Elisabeth was out of bed and dressing, "Which?"

"Which what?"

"Plane. Airline. Going where?"

"British Airways, to Heathrow. The new design. A lot of children flying home to boarding school. What *are* you doing?"

Elisabeth was in her clothes. She did not do her hair or wash or look in the glass. She felt for her sandals by the bed, ran into the bathroom, ran out again, pulling up her knickers. She left the rope of pearls lying on the chair. She did not look for her purse. She ran from the room.

"I think actually they said it happened after it had left Rome," Lizzie called, but Elisabeth was out of hearing.

Elisabeth ran into the street, on to the quay, ran across the roads in the drumming relentless Monday morning crowds that marched to work in their thousands, not looking at her, not speaking, not touching, not stumbling, and nor did she. She ran up the marble steps of the Peninsular Hotel and the bellhop boys in their white uniforms and pillbox hats pulled back the glass doors and blinked as she passed by.

Beside the fountain she stopped. The white piano on the dais was covered with a cloth and the gold music stands were folded up. She ran to the lifts and eyes turned from her in embarrassment, two immaculate men at the reception desk looking pointedly away. Somewhere above her in the hotel

Edward would be getting up, thinking of the coming day in Court. It never occurred to her to ask for him.

She didn't know the number of the Veneerings' rooms and asked the lift boy who said "Suite Number One" but looked uncertain about taking her there. "It's urgent," she said. "It's about a legal Case in the Courts." He looked at her wild hair and crumpled dress.

But the lift rolled up, the gates slid open and she was running towards the double doors of Suite Number One and ringing the bell. She rang and rang.

The door at last was opened by a maid—no, by a nanny. One of the old amahs in black and white, her face gaunt. Behind stood Terry Veneering. And beside him stood Harry.

"We missed the plane," the boy shouted. "I'm still here. Mum passed out and we missed it. And one just like it crashed in the Med." He flung himself on Elisabeth.

The amah vanished and Veneering said, "Harry—quick. Go and tell them, Miss Macintosh needs some coffee. Go on. Go on."

Then he stepped forward and took her hands and led her inside.

"No, no, I won't come in," she said. "It's all right now. I don't need to come in."

His clownish face of the night before looked thin and white, his blue eyes exhausted. His hands holding hers shook. "I thought so, too," he said. "But it wasn't his."

"Must go back," she said. "Find Edward. Tell friend. Isobel. All right now. I'm all right now."

"Stop crying."

"I must be mad," she said.

"I'll send a car for you tonight. Your hotel the Old C? I'll send a car at six-thirty. Look. Stop. He's all right. It wasn't his flight. Sing *Te Deum* and *Laudamus*. Elisabeth, *it was a different plane.*"

"Yes. Yes, I will sing—I'll sing for ever."

"You met him—shut up or I'll shake you—you met him for about half an hour. He's mine, you know, not yours. Soon you'll have your own."

"Yes. I can't understand. It must be hysteria. I'm never, never—Oh, but thank God. Thank God, Terry!"

"Six-thirty," he said, shutting the door on her.

CHAPTER SIX

She went out. She did not telephone Edward or wait for him to ring her, or explain anything to Lizzie who had again vanished. She went to a small, expensive shop and with the end of her money, labelled "emergencies," she bought a dress.

The girl selling was shivering with cold because of the new, Western-style air conditioning. She looked ill and resentful. Elisabeth moved the ready-made silk dresses along the rails and found her fingertips covered with oil. She showed them to the sneezing girl, who at first looked away in denial. Then, when Elisabeth said in Cantonese, "Please take a cloth to the rails at once!" went to get one and at the same moment Elisabeth saw a sea-green silk, the dress of a lifetime. She held her black oily fingers out to let the girl clean her hands and when the girl had finished said, "I would like that one." The girl shrugged and moved her hands in a disenchanted gesture that Elisabeth might want to try it on and Elisabeth said, "No, thank you. It will be perfect. Have you shoes to match?" She paid for it (a price) and walked back towards the hotel room. It was still empty of Lizzie and there was no message light on the bedside telephone. She stood the stiff paper bag on her bed and went to find a hairdresser.

The hairdresser preened above her head.

"Is it for an occasion?"

"I don't know. Well, yes, I'm going out tonight."

The hairdresser smiled and smiled, dead-eyed. Elisabeth had the notion that somewhere there was dislike.

"Would you like colour?"

"I don't know."

"Would you like to be more *seriously* red?"

"No. No, not at all." (Am I making sense?) "Just wash my hair, please. Take the aeroplane out of it."

"*Aeroplane* out of it." Silly giggle.

High on the wall above the line of basins, probably unnoticed for years, was a studio photograph, from before the war, of an English woman of a certain age, her hair sculpted into marcel waves, her ageing manicured hand all rings. And she was resting her cheek against it. Her mouth was dark and sharp with lipstick, her fingernails dark with varnish. Her smile was benevolent but genuine and sweet, and she had signed her name across the corner with I *shall remember you all*. She was so like Elisabeth's mother's Bridge-playing friends in old Tiensin that for a moment Elisabeth smelled the dust of her early childhood that had settled on everything without and within, covered her mother's dressing-table mirrors, the long parchment scrolls on the walls, the tea tray with cups and silver spoons, the little grey butterfly cakes, the cigarette cases and cigar lighters and dried grasses in china vases. Memory released an instant image, and sound too, for she heard her mother's laugh as the amah carried her into the room to sit quietly at her mother's feet for half an hour as the four ladies gazed at their cards and smoked their cigarettes. Her mother would look at her sometimes to check that she was tidy, and she would smile back, at her mother in the silk tea gown, silk stockings, the boat-shaped silk shoes, a diamond ring (where had it gone?) glinting through the dust in the shaft of sunlight through the blinds.

"Who is that woman?"

The hairdresser looked up at the photograph. "Oh, it will be a client from before the war. Long ago."

"Can you read her name?"

A long giggle. "No, no! We must take it down. It is old. The frame is very old-fashioned. The salon will be modernised soon."

"She must have liked you all. The frame is expensive. Was she the Governor's wife?"

All the girls laughed. The embarrassed, tinkling laughter.

"There are fly spots on it. We must take it down."

"I think she gave it to you before she left for Home. Maybe when the war began. Before the Japanese." They laughed again, watching her. She saw that one girl was Japanese. Elisabeth's hair was being dried by a new-fangled hand-held blower, like a gun. The woman would have sat for over half an hour under a metal helmet that roared in her reddening ears while she wrote letters on her knee or drifted among copies of *Country Life* or *The Royal Geographical Magazine* or *John o'London's*— happy, loving her warm unhurried life, sure of the future, certain that she and her country were admired. She would always have left a tip, but unostentatiously, and at Christmas—but not at the Chinese New Year—she'd arrive with little presents for everyone wrapped in paper printed with mistletoe and holly, which none of the girls had ever seen. Little Christmas puddings and mince pies that would all be thrown away. How do I know all this?

"She is like my mother."

"We must take it down."

The hairdresser brought her some tea.

Back at the Old Colony there was still no message from Edward so the Case must by now be groaning into life: a Case about land reclamation. Edward was for the architects, Veneering for the contractors. The villagers living on the doomed land were for neither, and nobody represented them except the legendary monsters and serpents that lurked in the depths below the site which was at present a marsh where they had always wallowed in the imagination, seeking whom they might devour. The projected dam would produce water for the new Hong Kong which would arrive years and years later, after the handover. The villagers came out after dark to appease the monsters with offerings and saucers of milk. In the morning the Western engineers removed the untouched offerings. Nothing was getting done.

Elisabeth, in her frowsty bedroom, the beds still not made, sent for a room-service lunch and when it came did not want it. She slept, and woke at six o'clock. No phone messages, no word from Edward or Lizzie. She combed her new shiny hair and thought of the photograph of the virtuous woman who looked like her mother. Then she took the sea-green dress and slid it on. There was a small, matching, sea-green purse on a string. She slipped it over her shoulder. Then she put on her evening shoes. Pale, silk, high-heeled sandals. Then she looked out of the window.

("I'll send a car. Six-thirty.")

It had been a time so early in the morning, half in dream, half in nightmare. Perhaps it had all been imagined.

Only hours ago she had been all set to become the next reincarnation of a virtuous woman, like the one in the benevolent photograph. She had stood beside her man—and how her parents would have approved of Edward Feathers—watching the stars in the heavens, thinking that she would tell her children about how she had said "I will" and had meant it. She saw her mother's face, imprisoned in the emptiness of Empire and diplomacy.

A cab was standing by itself without lights across the road from the Old Colony. She turned the notice in Chinese characters on her door to *Do Not Disturb*. She left no message. She took the lift down. She carried only the little green purse. It had her passport in it and her final travellers' cheque ticket strip, but not her return ticket to England.

As she walked over to the dark cab, the driver got out and opened the passenger door. He said, "Veneering?" and she said, "Yes."

They turned quickly away from the lights and quays, then inland. As they climbed, the traffic and people thinned and they drove towards the New Territories among cities of unfinished blocks of workers' flats, all in darkness, waiting for the New Age. The road curved and climbed, flattened and then climbed again. It climbed into trees, through trees and then into thick woods.

Woods?

She had not known about the woods of Hong Kong. Woods were for lush landscapes. She had believed that outside the city all would be sandy and bare. The cab plunged now deep into a black forest. The sky was gone and the road levelled and began to drop down again. The cab turned on to an unmade-up track. Small dancing lights began to appear, around them, like a huge entourage, the moving shadows of hundreds of people carrying the lights in their hands.

The shadows did not rest. Sometimes they came up close to the cab. They were moving, sometimes quite close to the cab's closed windows. They were in twos and threes, not speaking. Not one head turned. They even seemed unaware of the cab which was moving through them now quite fast, but still silent, the driver never once flashing his lights or sounding his horn. Nobody moved out of their way. Nobody turned his head. There seemed to be a white mist near the ground and the cab became very hot.

The strangeness of the crowded forest was its silence.

To left and right in the trees, a little off the road, a bright light would now and then shine out, then vanish, masked by trees and trees. There must be big houses up there, she thought, rich men's second homes. She had seen the sort of thing long ago in Penang, most of the year empty, shadowy palaces locked inside metal armour lattice and on the gates the warning with a zigzag sign saying *Danger of Death*, blazing out in English and Chinese and Malay.

The hosts of the shadows paid no attention to the houses hidden in the trees. The shadows swam altogether around the cab in a shoal. They concentrated on the dark. They became like smoke around her in the forest and she began to be afraid.

I want Edward. He has no idea where I am. Nor have I.

The driver's little Chinese head did not turn and he did not speak when she leaned forward and tapped his shoulder and shouted at him in Cantonese, "Will it be much longer? Please tell me where I am. In God's name."

Instead, he swung suddenly off the road, obliterating the moving shadows, and up a steeper track. After a time, a glow appeared from, apparently, the top of some tree. In front of the light the cab swung round full circle and stopped.

The light was glowing in a small wooden house that seemed to be on stilts with tree branches growing close all round it. There was some sort of ladder and a gate at the bottom bore the electric charge logo and *Danger of Death. All Admittance Forbidden.*

She looked up at the top of the ladder and saw that a wooden cabin seemed held in a goblet of branches. Its doors stood open and light now flowed down the ladder. Veneering was beside the cab. He opened the door and took her hand. He stood aside for her at the ladder's foot and at the top she looked down at him and saw that behind him in the clearing the cab was gone.

So was the silent, shadowy multitude and so were all the dotted lights of houses among the trees. This house seemed less a house then an organic growth in the forest, sweet smelling, held in the arms of branches. Veneering shut the door behind them and began to take off her green dress.

CHAPTER SEVEN

T he next morning *Do Not Disturb* was still hanging from the door handle of room 182, the beds still unmade, unslept in. There was the untouched chaos of scattered clothes and belongings, the smell of yesterday's scent. Nobody there. And no light flashing from the bedside telephone. No messages pushed under the door.

Perhaps no time had passed since yesterday morning. The hairdresser, the green dress, the taxi standing waiting, the strange journey, the glorious night, the dawn return with the black cab again standing waiting in the trees, perhaps all fantasy? A dream of years can take a second.

But I'm not a virgin any more. I know that all right. *And* it's about time. Oh, Edward! Saint Edward, where were you? Why wasn't it you? Pulling off the dress, she stuffed it in the waste-paper basket. She made the dribbling shower work and stood under it until it had soaked away the hours of the sweltering, wonderful night, until her hair lay flat and brown and coarse. It's like a donkey's hair. I am not beautiful. Yet he thought so. Who was it? Oh! It *must* have been Edward! I'm marrying him. He hates—she couldn't say the name. I've been bewitched. Then, thinking of the night, she moaned with pleasure. No, it was you. Not Eddie. Eddie was preparing the Case. He had no time. Yet you had time. The same Case.

And it's always going to be like this. She watched, through the window behind the shower, white smoke puffing up from the air conditioning into the blue sky. His work will always come first. He'll sign and underline and ring for it to be collected by the typists, before he comes home to me. And where is he? And Lizzie? I'm alone here now. I can't stand here all day, naked. My new, used, happy body. I suppose I should sleep now. I must need sleep, but I've never felt so awake. I'll ring Amy.

"Yes?"

In the background to Amy's voice was a hornet's nest of howling and shouting.

"I must see you, Amy. I have to see you. *Please!*"

"I'll come now. I'll do the school run and then I'll drive in. What's wrong?"

"I'll tell you. Well, not *wrong*. Well, yes—wrong."

Amy's tin-can car appeared in less than half an hour outside the Old Colony, stopping where last night's cab had stopped. And this morning's. Elisabeth saw it, put on some cotton trousers and a shirt, and ran out. The alternative had been the crumpled cotton check or the green silk in the trash basket. She fell into the clattering car and, as they drove away, said, "Oh, Amy! Thank God!" Amy had less than an inch of space between herself and the steering wheel. The coming child inside her was kicking. You could see it kicking if you knew about such things. Betty, who didn't know, sat staring ahead.

"Where are we going, Amy? This isn't your way home."

"No, it's my day for health visiting. New babies. Home births. I'll say you're my assistant. You can carry a clipboard. Now then, what's the matter?"

"I can't actually tell you. Not yet. I've just got in. I was out all night."

"Sleeping with Eddie Feathers? Well, about time. That I will say."

"No. No. He won't do it. He thinks if it's serious, you don't do it before marrying."

"He said this?"

"Not actually. But he sort of indicates."

"Well," she said. "It's a point of view. Mine, as a matter of fact. And Nick's. But we couldn't stick to it. So who were you with on the night you became engaged? You'd better tell me. Oh, we're here. Get out and I'll tell you how to behave. Then tell me what's going on."

They were on a cemented forecourt of what looked like an overhead parking block ten storeys high. "Take the clipboard. Walk behind me with authority. O.K.? We are weighing and measuring babies born at home. Every family will greet us with a glass of tea. If there is no tea it will be a glass of water. If there is no water then it will be an empty glass. Whichever is handed to you, you greet it as if it were champagne. O.K.?"

Inside the rough building among the shadowy wooden joists Elisabeth was reminded of the unseen people of the wood. At doorways they were bowed to, and tightly wrapped babies were presented, unwrapped and hung up by Amy from a hook above a little leather hammock. Like meat, thought Elisabeth. The baby was examined, peered at with a torch, tapped and patted, then measured and returned. The mother or grandmother—it could have been either—bowed and offered the glass. The babies' eyes shone black and narrow, and looked across at Elisabeth with the knowledge of Methuselah. She caught one proud young mother's glance and smiled in congratulation. "Beautiful," she said and the mother made a proud disclaimer.

"That last one will die," said Amy as they walked back to the car. "We'll go home and I'll get you some breakfast. Let me hear your earth-shattering experiences with your substitute future husband."

"He wasn't. I told you."

"Then who was it?"

"Someone else. I'd just met him."

"Ye gods! Here, help me." She was unloading the back of the car of the paraphernalia of the maternity run. "Met him here? In Hong Kong?"

"Yes. I think it was hypnosis."

Weights, measures, bottles were heaped in Elisabeth's arms.

"Rubbish, it was lust. It was natural desire. Or maybe it was only resentment," said Amy.

"How do you know?"

"I know because you told me, yesterday, that your marriage frightened you, because it meant you would never know passion. You did it to have something to remember and to have known desire."

"No, it was love. I'm not excusing myself. Edward will never know. It is love."

"Elisabeth, what *are* you doing?"

"Is it so wrong to want a glorious memory?"

"It's sentimental and obscene. You won't like yourself for it in the end. You don't like yourself now."

"I never thought you were a puritan, Amy."

"Well, you've learned something. I am."

"After the way you went on at school."

"That was ten years ago."

"So you have been purified by Nick?"

Amy was rolling from side to side up the dirty stairwell, trying to support the unborn baby as it kicked to get clear of her ribcage and slide into the world. From above came the wailing of apparently inconsolable children and the voice of a roaring man.

A saffron monk stuck his head out of his doorway as they passed, his hairless shining face determinedly blissful. He asked if he could eat with them. "No," said Amy. "There's too much going on," and the monk blissfully retired.

"Where in *hell*—" shouted Nick at their open door. "You've been hours. We're going mad."

Mrs. Baxter, in a rocking chair, held an unhappy bundle. "I'm afraid she's wet again." An untouched bottle of formula stood near, untouched, that is, except by flies. "It's time to get Emily back from school."

"Well, here's the car keys," said Amy, picking the baby out of Mrs. Baxter's bony lap, dropping the nursing gear, scooping another child out of Nick's struggling arms. "Oh, and can you give Bets a lift back to the Old Col?"

"Bets?" Nick took a hold, looked at her and switched on the polite. "So sorry. Don't think we've met. Are you new here?"

"I'm passing through."

"We were at school," said Amy.

"Oh. *Excellent.* Sorry about the scenes of married bliss. Didn't see you there, ha-ha. You'll want to be off."

"No. I don't want to go." She looked at Nick in his plastic dog collar. "Amy, I don't know what to do."

"Pray you're not pregnant," said Amy, also behaving as if the two of them were alone. "Try prayers. Go ahead with earlier plans."

"Someone will tell him. You know they will. You know Hong Kong."

"Oh, probably. If so, I suppose that'll be it. But I wonder? He doesn't sound the ordinary old blimp, your future husband."

"What is all this?"

"It is something, Nick," said Mrs. Baxter, "that I don't think we should be listening to. You are making us eavesdroppers, Amy."

"I've more to do than stand here dropping eaves," said Nick. "I'm teaching a Moral Sciences seminar in twenty minutes."

Amy and Elisabeth continued to stand in silence and it was (surprisingly) Amy who began to cry.

"You're—oh, if you knew how I envy you, Bets! You're so *innocent*. You're going to be so *ghastly* soon. All this will be an uneasy memory when you're opening bazaars around the Temple church in the Strand, and organising book groups for barristers' wives. You'll metamorphose into a perfect specimen of twentieth-century uxorial devotion. You'll have this one guilty secret and you'll never forgive me for knowing."

"I don't know what the hell's going on," said Nick.

"You and I, Bets, will be the last generation to take seriously the concept of matrimonial fidelity. Wait until this lot gets cracking with sex and sin in the—what?—in the sixties."

"How do you know?" said Elisabeth.

"I know."

"Are you *happy* about it, Amy?"

"I am bloody, bloody *unhappy* about it. Have a child at your peril, Bets. It will hurt you to hell."

One of the children then began to cry for its dinner and slap, bang went Amy with the rice pot.

"Nick—take Betty *now*. Bets, see you at the altar? Right?"

Mrs. Baxter began to sing "When I survey the wondrous Cross" as she unwrapped the wet child, who at once spread out its wet legs and went thankfully to sleep.

A t last there was a message for Elisabeth Macintosh when she returned to the Old Colony Hotel. She was called over to the reception desk and an official-looking letter was put into her hands. The envelope came from Edward's London Chambers and it chilled her. Her name was typewritten. So, it was all over.

She took it upstairs—the bedroom still untouched, the two beds a mess, but she found a red light flashing by the telephone. Which first? Face the one you fear.

She opened the letter and inside, in Edward's beautiful, clear script, read, *I have wonderful news. Ross will bring you to the Old Repulse Bay Hotel tonight to celebrate it. I have not had a minute—literally, I mean it—to telephone or write. You will soon see why. I love and long for you, Edward.*

She contemplated the message light for a while and then rang down to reception. While they dialled up the message, she sat with the blunt heavy block of the black receiver in her hand. At length, after much clicking, a voice, a recording from somewhere: *This is Mr. Albert Ross, consulting solicitor to Mr. Edward Feathers QC. I am to call for a Miss Elisabeth Macintosh this evening to take her to dinner with Mr. Feathers and his team. The dress code will be formal. Six o'clock.*

Who is this pompous ass? The famous Loss the Demon Dwarf? So, we shall meet. I'm not going to like him. I'm being played with by all of them. I've half a mind . . .

And "dress code formal'! What in hell? I've no money and

nothing clean and Edward must—should—know it. As if he did!

She went to the waste-paper basket and fished out the dress.

No. I couldn't. I can never wear it again. It feels cold and wet. I can hardly bear to touch it. (But she held it to her face.)

I suppose I could get them to press it. Laundry service? But just touching it, looking at it, makes me want to cry. With happiness, private happiness, not with guilt. Once only. It is a sacred dress. And she pressed her face into it and remembered Veneering's hands and skin and hair and sweat as the dress lay like a slop of spinach on the wood floor of the weird tree house. I will never wear it again.

Time? It's still only two o'clock. I've over three hours. Food? Not hungry. Perhaps try. Get room service. Get a saté from a stall.

She turned in her cotton clothes into the poor streets again, stepping through litter and ordure. A man without legs sat, his crutches splayed, opening shellfish, the shells thrown about him. She bought a pork saté from a boy yelling "Saté" insolently in her ear. Then she bought a warm, soft prawn fritter and stood eating it all. It smelled sweet and good. Looking up above the street stalls she saw on a hoarding a huge photograph. It was a young European girl naked to the waist and smelling a rose. It was, undoubtedly, Lizzie.

Well, of course not. How could it be? Lizzie was an intellectual. She'd been at Bletchley Park. And she was, or said she was, a lesbian. One didn't think about it. She was always coming and going to Hong Kong. She told you nothing. There were rumours of her having something to do with the Chief of Police. She had known some terrible people, even at school. But she'd been serious, hard-working. But naked to the waist and a rose! Smelling the rose! Lizzie! Well, she does say she's broke. No, I'm just tired.

I am wonderfully, deeply tired and I want him again. And again. And for ever. And I don't mean Edward.

She wandered the street stalls, licking the prawn juice off her fingers. She peered into fragments of looking-glass, demons and cartoon toys. Wherever she went among the stalls were clusters of children eating where they stood, quietly, prodding their chopsticks into thimble dishes of fish and pork. Oh, how could I ever go West again? I'll stay here. With any-one who wants me. One or the other. With anyone.

She had shocked herself. She had meant it. She'd go with a man who would let her roam in the market. "I'll go down fast," she told the poster. The girl with the rose now did not look like Lizzie at all. It was some American film star. Hedy Lamarr. She wondered how much the girl had been paid.

She was in the Old Col Hotel again. It was half past four in the afternoon. Make-up? Borrow Lizzie's. (God, I look tired.) Dress? Green dress. I forgot to get them to iron it. It smells and I don't care. I'll never, never own such a beautiful dress again. And nobody will ever know. He won't be there. Not at Edward's party with its "wonderful news'—whatever that is.

When she was dressed she looked—after a little hesita-tion—out of her window and saw a white Mercedes parked outside, its windows dark and its number plate so short it looked like royalty.

"I shall certainly not hurry," said the new Elisabeth and sauntered forth, her hair curly again, springy after the shower. I'm walking differently, she thought. They say you can always tell when a virgin is a thing of the past.

The car with the black windows gave no sign of remarking on her non-virginal condition, her walk, or on anything about her. When she stopped beside it nothing happened and she felt snubbed. If there was a driver inside, he was invisible. This was not a car you could tap or try a door handle. It might set off some terrible alarm.

The crowds were surging now from work. They parted around the Mercedes and then came back together again beyond it. Nobody looked at her or noticed her. As Nick had said this morning at the noisy family flat, "You get lonely here, you know. It's not that they dislike you so much as that they aren't interested. They just blot you out. Just occasionally they make it plain. You can be sitting on a bus with the only empty seat the one beside you, and there'll be Chinese standing thick down the middle of the bus all down the centre aisle, and there'll never, ever, be one of them who will sit down beside you. We are invisible."

Elisabeth, standing in her green dress by the car, now felt invisible. She decided to turn back. After all, I'm not just *anyone*. She would go back to the bedroom and wait to be properly taken to Edward's party. I am a grown woman.

And yet, I'm still telling myself stories. I have not had the courage to throw away childish things. You'd never take me for a linguist and a sociologist and an expert in ciphers, and all of it after being in the Camps. There is something missing in me. I'm empty.

Tears began to come. She knew that it was love that was missing. Edward was missing. She had forgotten all about him. Put him ruthlessly into memory.

"Good afternoon," said someone behind her and she looked down to see a very short, thickset troll of a man wearing a brown felt hat. He removed it.

"I am Albert Loss. I cannot say my 'ahs.' I am the instructing solicitor and almost lifetime friend of Mr. Edward Feathers QC. I am instructed to drive you out to Repulse Bay to dine with him."

A white-uniformed driver now stood beside the car's opened doors. She was put behind the driver and Ross next to her on a built-up seat that set them on a level. The air-conditioning after several minutes was cool and silent, and the car slid carefully through the crowds and away.

"You said something—" she turned to Ross. "You said something like 'QC.' Edward is too young to be made a Queen's Counsel."

"He has just been made one. I mentioned it in my telephone message."

"No! *Has* he? I never took it in. Oh, how wonderful! He never told me he'd applied. Oh, I see! *Now* I see. This is to be a celebration."

"Not altogether. He has other things to say. I shall leave the rest to him."

"Oh, and he so deserves it. Oh, I hope he's letting himself be happy about it."

"He will never let on," said Ross, "but he has been frequently smiling." He removed his hat, turned it over, unzipped a small zip inside the crown and removed a pack of cards. He did up the zip again, dropped the hat to the floor and set up a little shelf. He began to deal himself a hand.

"I like cards, too," she said. "But will there be time? I thought we were almost there."

"There is always time for cards and reflection. They are an aide-memoire. I am a compulsive player and I have a magnificent grasp of fact. My memory has been honed into an unbreakable machine. There is half an hour more of this short journey. We have to make a diversion on the way."

"Won't Edward wonder? Worry?"

"He knows you are with me."

"But where are we now?" She looked through the one-way glass window. "You can't be driving a car like this up here."

"It will take little harm. I agree that my London Royce would be more appropriate. And the card tray there is firmer."

"But this is an awful place. Wherever are we going?"

Stretching away were building sites and ravaged landscapes. Squalor and ugliness.

"It is your bread and butter—shall we say *our* bread and

butter? And also our caviar. We are approaching the reservoirs, the sources of legal disputes that will support us all for years to come. Off and on."

"But it's horrible! It's a desecrated forest. It's being chopped down. Miles and miles of it."

"There are miles more. Miles more scrub and trees. They will all, of course, have to go in time, which is sad since so much was brought here by the British. Like English roses in the Indian Raj the trees here grew like weeds. It was once a very good address to have, up here, you know. The dachas of the British. I still have a small one here myself, just to rent out—here we are in the trees again—which I intend to sell. The area is not safe now after dark. The reservoir workers begin to frighten people. They troop through the trees at sundown, like shadows. Here we are. My little investment." And the car stopped in a glade on a mud patch where a dilapidated wooden box of a dwelling seemed to have become stuck up a tree.

"Oh, no!" she said. "Oh, no—oh, no!"

The zigzag notice *Danger of Death* was in place at the foot of the ladder. The driver lifted Ross out of the car and locked the car again behind him and Elisabeth inside watched the little man unlock the gate, shuffle painfully up the ladder stair, unlock the front door and disappear. When he came out again the driver lifted him back to his seat, relocked the car doors.

Ross sat on his perch and said nothing.

"Can we go? Can we *please* go now?" she said. "Please, I don't like it here, it's horrible."

"I let it by the hour," he said. "Night or day. It has been a good investment."

"It's disgusting. Vile. Please can we go to Edward? Tell him to start the car. Does Edward know you own this?"

"Certainly not. When I bought it, it was for myself. A haven of peace in my difficult life, watching the cards. But I have let things slide. I live in so many places. I let it, in a very discreet way. And I am getting rid of it now."

"Yes. Please. Can we go?"

"On one condition," said the dwarf. "That you will never think of it or of any such place again."

"Of course not. Of *course* not. Look, I'm feeling cold—"

"And that you will never leave Edward."

"He knows. I've told him I'll never leave him. I swear it."

"If you leave him," said Ross, "I will break you."

At their destination the driver got out to open her door, and Ross tossed over to her a green silk purse.

"You left your passport behind," he said.

CHAPTER NINE

S he heard laughter. Cheerful shouting. English laughter
and across the terrace saw Eddie's legal team all drinking
Tiger beer. There were six or seven of them in shirts and
shorts, and Edward standing tall among them without a tie,
head back, roaring with laughter. The cotton dress would have
been right.

Edward came striding over to her, stopped before he
reached her, held out a hand and took her round a corner of
the terrace out of sight of the others. He looked young. He
held her tight. He took both her hands and said, "Did you
think I'd forgotten you?"

"Yes."

"Do you know what's happened?"

"Yes. You've got Silk. You're a QC."

"No. Not that. Do you know that the Case has settled?"

"No!"

"It's taken sixteen hours. Sixteen solid hours. But we've settled out of court. Neither side went to bed. But everyone's
happy and we can all go home. Ross is packing the papers. The
other side's off already. Veneering left this morning so the air's
pure again."

"Eddie—you've all lost a fortune. *How* much a day was it?
Thousands?"

"No idea," he said, "and no consequence. I've got the brief
fee. It'll pay for the honeymoon. I've told Ross and the clerks
to get it in, and then that I don't want any more work until I'm

back in London. I've said two months. I've told him to give everything to Fiscal-Smith."

"Whoever's that?"

"Someone who's always hanging about. Takes anything and pays for nothing. The meanest lawyer at the Bar. An old friend."

She sat down on the parapet and looked across the sea. He hadn't asked her one thing about herself. Her own plans. He didn't even know whether she had a job she had to get back to. If she had any money. About when her holiday ended. She tried to remember whether he'd ever asked anything about her at all.

"We might go to India," he said. "D'you want a cup of coffee? You'll have had dinner somewhere, I hope." He and the noisy group of liberated lawyers had dined very early. Final toasts were now going round. Taxis arrived. Farewells. More laughter. Edward and Elisabeth were alone again under the same stars as before. After a time she said, "I'd like to stay in the hotel here tonight, Eddie. I love this place. And no, I haven't had dinner."

"But we have our hotel rooms Kowloon-side. And haven't you the Australian friend? She'll wonder where you are. And I haven't a shirt up here. For tomorrow."

"She's left for Home, tonight, I think. We only met up here. We're old friends. We take it lightly."

She watched him.

"There's the wedding to plan."

"Oh, yes," she said. "I keep forgetting. I suppose that's my job. By the way, I haven't any money at all."

"Oh, I'll deal with that."

"Not until I'm thirty. I'll be quite well-off then."

He smiled at her, not interested.

They hardly spoke on the ferry. At Kowloon the lights of the Peninsular Hotel blazed white across the forecourt. The Old Colony was lit down the side street with its chains of cheap lights and was resounding with wailing music and singing. It was still only nine o'clock.

"It's only nine o'clock," she said. "Goodnight then, since you say so," and at last he seemed to come to himself.

"Yes. Nine. All out of focus. I'm sorry. Come in. Come in to the Pen and I'll give you dinner. We'll both have some champagne. Betty?"

She was staring at him. "No," she said. "I'm going over to some friends in Kai Tak."

"Kai Tak! Isn't that a bit off-piste?"

"Yes. So are they. They're missionaries. Hordes of kids. Normal people. In love with each other. My friends."

"Elisabeth—what's wrong? It is *on*, isn't it?"

Sitting in the taxi she said, after a minute, "Yes. It's on. But I need the taxi fare."

"Shall I come with you?"

"No. I'll be staying the night. Maybe longer," and she was gone.

She saw him standing, watching her taxi disappear, and then the hotel's white Mercedes roll along with all the legal team waving at him, making for the airport and Home. In very good spirits.

He was, in fact, unaware of them, but saying to himself that he'd made some mistake. Had made an absolute bloody bish. I wish Coleridge were here. I'm not good at pleasing this girl.

Betty, bowling along through the alleys round Kai Tak, was thinking: He's shattered. He looked so bewildered. He's so bloody good. Good, good, good.

Well, I'll probably go through with it. I'll be independent when I'm thirty. I'll probably put a lot into it. I'll damn well work, too. For myself. QC's wife or not. And at least I have a past now. No one can take that away.

CHAPTER TEN

S ince the night of celebration at Repulse Bay and the end
of the land reclamation Case and the horrible parting
outside the Peninsular Hotel, Elisabeth had moved in
with Amy at Kai Tak. It was at Amy's command.

"Have you room for me?"

"Yes. There's a camp bed. And don't be grateful, you'll be
very useful. Take the baby—no, not that way. Now, stick the
bottle in her mouth—go on. Right up to the edge. She won't
choke, she'll go to sleep and we can talk before Nick comes in."

The other children were already asleep. Mrs. Baxter must at
some point have been taken up to her barbed-wire fortress.
The Buddhists were practising silence on the floor below.

"Now then," said Amy. "Date of wedding?"

"Edward's arranging everything. The licence. I expect I'll
have to be there at some point for identification. In case he
should turn up with someone different."

"You're being flippant."

"Not that he'd probably notice."

"Now you're being cheap. Seriously, Elisabeth Macintosh—is it on? It is a Sacrament in the Christian Church."

"I'm being told yes from somewhere. Probably only by my
rational self. There's no way I will say no, yet I don't quite
know why. Marriage will be gone in a hundred years in the
Christian Church. There'll be women priests and homo
priests. Pansies and bisexuals."

"You're tired. You live alone. What does Isobel say?"

"She's disappeared. As she always did. She was never any help with people's troubles, was she? She just stared and pronounced—if she could be bothered. She's burdened with her own secrets but she never lets on."

"I suppose she must tell someone. Some wise and ageing woman with a deep, understanding voice. And a beard."

Elisabeth laughed and said, "Can I pull this teat out now? She's asleep."

Nick came in. It was very late. Very hot.

Elisabeth, lying on the camp bed near the kitchen sink, listened to the clamour outside in the sweltering streets, the thundering muted lullaby of the mah-jong players in all the squats around.

"I have no aim," she said. "No certainty. I am a post-war invertebrate. I play mah-jong in my head year after year trying to find something I was born to do. I have settled on exactly what my mother would have wanted: a rich, safe, good husband and a pleasant life. All the things she must have thought in the Camp were gone for ever. Impossible for me, the scrawny child playing in the sand. Hearing screams, gunfire, silences in the night, watching lights searching in the barbed wire. I should be the last woman in the world to recreate the old world of the unswerving English wife. I am trying to please my dead mother. I always am." She slept.

And woke to Mrs. Baxter flopping about with teacups saying, "I tried not to wake you. Are you staying long? Shall we say a prayer together?"

She and Elisabeth were alone, except for the baby, whom Mrs. Baxter ignored. Nick, Amy and the rest were already about the Colony and the nursery school and the clinics. The noise from the streets was less than in the night and the monks below were still silent. The telephone rang and it was Edward.

"Found you at last. Are you safe?"

"Of course. I'm going shopping."

"Shall I come?" He sounded afraid of the answer.

"No. Do I have to come and sign things?"

"Not yet. I'm organising it. I'm planning our trip. Oh—Pastry Willy wants us to dine with them tonight."

"Can't," she said. "Sorry. Next week? I must earn my keep here."

"As to that, are you all right for money?"

"Rolling in it," she said.

"Unexpected expenses—? Wedding dress and presents for . . ."

"You're the one for presents. First, Eddie, to Amy. She needs them. Don't dare to give her money; she'll just put it into a savings account for the children. Look—I'm staying here. They're my family. Until the wedding."

"Willy's wife will be upset."

"No. I want to be married from Kai Tak with the planes all roaring overhead."

"Can you—I mean. Darling"—"Darling!" Progress?—"is there anywhere to wash there? A bathroom. To get ready on the day?"

"No idea. I must get on. I have to clean the kitchen."

"Shall I come over? I think I should."

"It's a free and easy place. Don't come in spats."

"What on earth are spats?"

"Oh, stuff it, Edward."

Mrs. Baxter, pale as a cobweb, had been listening at the kitchen table where she was doing something with needle and thread. "Was that a conversation with your fiancé?"

"I suppose it was, Mrs. Baxter."

She was silent as Elisabeth scoured away at the scum in the rice pot, black outside, silver within. Huge and bulbous. The black and silver raised a sense of longing in Elisabeth, of memory and loss: the outdoor kitchen in Tiensin, the servants' shouting, the stink of drains and cesspits, the clouds of dust, the drab sunlight and her mother appearing at the veranda door. The amah would come and pick up little Elisabeth, wiping her face with a grey cloth. She saw her mother's plump arms open towards her as she stretched her own stubby ones up to her mother. They all laughed. Her mother had been a blonde. She had twirled around with glee, swinging her baby. The servants were scouring the rice pots until their silver linings shone.

"You are not looking happy, Elisabeth."

"But of course I'm happy, Mrs. Baxter."

"I am not a happy woman, either. I believe that you and I are very much alike. I thought so as soon as I saw you. I thought, She is born to tears and wrong decisions and she will need the consolation of Jesus Christ."

"You've got me wrong, Mrs. Baxter. I was thinking of my mother who never stopped laughing. I was a baby. She was beautiful, loving and hardly ever went to church."

"Died in the Camps, I hear? Well, I shall pray for you," and she took out her handkerchief.

"Mrs. Baxter. I am about to be married. I intend to be very happy. I'll discover no doubt if I need Jesus Christ. And in what form. If it is in the form of sex and married love, then Jesus is for me. But I haven't much hope."

Mrs. Baxter sat thoughtfully. Later in the day when the family were all home again, she still sat thoughtfully. When Amy said that it was time for her to be taken home she said, "I was a bride once."

"And I bet you looked lovely."

"Yes, Amy, I did. I had a very good dress, and it has survived. Elisabeth could wear it."

"Thank you, but I . . ."

"Yet I feel that I should like to buy her a new one. I know a dressmaker and his wife who can complete it in three days including covered buttons down the back. I shall see to it all if you will draw me a pattern. I still have my wreath of orange blossom that went round my head, but it is rather flat and discoloured."

"Oh—I'll get one made for her," said Amy. "It can be my present. And I'll get the shoes. Those green ones she has are the shoes of a whore."

"What I *do* possess," said Mrs. Baxter, "and it will be in perfect condition in a tin trunk against weevils, is a veil of Indian lace. It is patterned with birds and flowers. St. Anne's lace—a little pun—my name is Anne—made by the nuns in Dacca in what was then Bengal. You shall wear it—no, you shall *have* it. What use is it to me but as a shroud?"

"Betty—you could keep it for the baby," said Amy, and the baby hiccuped on yet another bottle, and the other children put rice in their hair.

"My wedding day," said Mrs. Baxter, "was on a green lawn at the High Commission in Dacca and there were English roses." She wept.

"Accept," said Amy. "Quick. For God's sake."

"Thank you very much indeed," said Elisabeth. "I believe your veil will bring me happiness."

"Oh, I shouldn't count on that," said Mrs. Baxter.

PART TWO

Happiness

CHAPTER ELEVEN

When he was very old and had retired to the Dorset countryside in England, and Betty dead, Old Filth, as he was always called now, reverentially and kindly, would walk most afternoons about the lanes carrying his walking stick with the Airedale's head, pausing at intervals to examine the blossom or the bluebell woods or the berries or the holly bushes according to the season. The pauses were in part rests, but to a passer-by they looked like a man lost in wonder or meditation. A dear, ram-rod straight man of elegiac appearance. As he grew really old, the English countryside was sometimes on these walks shot through for an instant by a random, almost metallic flash of unsought revelation.

One November day of black trees, brown streams blocked with sludge and dead leaves, skies grey as ashes, he found himself in his room at the Peninsular Hotel again, and it was his wedding day.

It was early and he was looking down at the old harbourfront YMCA building, everything ablaze with white sunlight. The flash of memory, like an early picture show, was all in black and white. The carpet of his hotel room was black, like velvet, the curtains white silk, the armchairs white, the telephones white. In the bathroom the walls and ceiling were painted black, the towels and flowers were white. There lay on a black glass table near the door of the suite a white gardenia and he, Edward Feathers himself only just taken silk (QC), at all of eight a.m., ready dressed in European "morning dress" and a shirt so white that it mocked its surroundings by looking blue.

All these years later, he saw himself. He had been standing gravely at the window wondering whether or not to telephone her.

Breakfast?

He had not ordered a cooked breakfast. It would seem hearty. Others no doubt would be sitting down in their suites to bacon and eggs on the round black glass table, napkin startlingly white. But for Edward—well. Perhaps a cup of coffee?

Should he ring his wife-to-be? Amy's number? His—his Elisabeth? But then the telephone shouted all over his room.

"Hello?"

"It's me," said Elisabeth.

"I was going to telephone you."

"It's supposed to be bad luck," she said.

"No, it's bad luck for me to *see* you before the church. I was thinking of—er—saying, well—well, how to get there—well, don't get the time wrong. Will those missionaries get you there? Willy could fetch you."

"I'll be there, Edward."

"All set, then?"

"All set, Edward. Edward, are you O.K.? Are you happy?"

"Don't forget your passport. Tell them to throw your suitcase in the back. Oh, and don't forget . . ."

"What?"

A long silence and he watched the seabirds leaning this way and that over the harbour.

"Don't forget . . . Elisabeth. Dear Betty. Even now—are you sure?"

There was the longest pause perhaps in the whole of Edward Feathers's professional life.

And then he heard her voice in mid-sentence, saying, "It could be cold in the evenings. Have you packed a jersey?"

"My breakfast hasn't arrived yet. Then I have to pay the bill here. Are you dressed? I mean in all your finery?"

"No. I've a baby on my knee and Amy and everyone are shouting. But, Eddie, if you like we can still forget it."

"I'll be there," he said. Silence again for an aeon. "I love you, Betty. Don't leave me."

"Well, mind you turn up," she said briskly. Too brightly. And put down the phone.

He had no recollection in the Donhead lanes after Betty's death of any of this except his own immaculate figure standing at the window.

"I am not going," said Bets, hand still on the phone. "It's off."

Amy planted a glass of brandy beside the bride's cornflakes. "Come on. Get dressed. I've done the children. What's the matter?"

"What in *hell* am I doing?"

"The best thing you ever did in your life. Looking ahead at last. Here, I'll do your hair."

Edward's luggage had already gone ahead to the airport. He paid his bill at the desk, the management far from effusive, since they'd expected him there for another two months. But they knew he would be back, and he tipped everyone correctly and shook hands all round. They walked with him to the glass doors and bowed and smiled, nobody saying a thing about his stiff collar and tailcoat so early in the morning. "You don't need a car, sir? For the airport?" "No, no. I'm going across to church first." "Ah—church. Ah." The gardenia in his buttonhole could have been laminated plastic.

He set out to his wedding alone.

Briefly he thought of Albert Ross. Ross had vanished. Eddie had no best man.

Oh, well, you can marry without a best man. No one else he'd want. It was a glorious morning. He remembered his prep-school headmaster, Sir, reading Dickens aloud, and the effete Lord Verisoft walking sadly to his death in a duel on Wimbledon Common with all the birds singing and the sunlight in the trees.

"I am alone, too," he said in his mind to Sir. "I haven't even a Second to chat to on the way."

He thought of the old friends missing. War. Distance. Amnesia. Family demands. "I have married a wife and therefore I cannot come." Oxford friends. Army friends. Pupils in his Chambers. Not one. Not one. Oh my *God*!

Walking towards the exquisite figure of Edward Feathers—well, not so much walking as shambling—was Fiscal-Smith.

From Paper Buildings, London EC4!

They both stopped walking.

Then Fiscal-Smith came rambling up, talking while still out of earshot. "Good heavens! Old Filth! This hour in the morning! Gardenia! Haven't you been to bed? I'm just off the plane. Great Scot—what a surprise! Where are you going?"

"Just going to church."

"Case settled, I hear. Bad luck. I'm here for the Reclamation North-east Mining Co. It hasn't a hope. Oh, well, excellent! Thought you'd be on the way Home."

"No, not—not just at once."

"*Church* you said? I'd no idea it was Sunday. Jet lag. I'll walk there with you."

"No, that's all right, Fiscal-Smith."

"Glad to. Nothing to do. Need to walk after the plane. Should really have shaved and changed. I always travel now in these new T-shirt things. Feathers, you do look particularly smart."

"Oh, I don't know . . ."

"Ah. Oh, yes. Of course. You've just got Silk. All-night party. Well done. You look pretty spry, though."

"Thank you."

"Well, very spry. Good God, Feathers, you look like *The Importance of Being Earnest.* Nine o'clock in the morning. What's going on?"

Eddie stopped and turned his back on St. James's church. At that moment, from the belfry a merry bell began to ring. "Private matter," he said and held out his hand. "Goodbye, old chap. See you again."

"There's a clergyman waving at you," said Fiscal-Smith. "Several people in bright dresses are round the church door. Smart hats. The padré—he's coming over. He looks anxious—"

"*Goodbye*, Fiscal-Smith."

"*Hello!*" cried out the parson. "We were getting worried. Organist's on "Sheep May Safely" third time. You are looking very fine, my dear fellow, if I may say so. Now then—best man? Delighted. At the risk of sounding less than original I have to ask if you have the ring?"

"Ring?"

"Wedding ring? Let me see it. Best man—by the way my name is Yo. Yo Kong. I am to officiate. And you are?"

"Well, I'm called Fiscal-Smith. I've just arrived."

"Well done, well done. Right on time. The ring."

Fiscal-Smith stood in unaccustomed reverence, and Feathers gave one of his nervous roars and took a small box from his pocket.

"Very good. Splendid. Very good indeed. Now if you will accompany me, both of you, to the front pew on the right. The bride should be here in five minutes."

"Bride?" said Fiscal-Smith out of a tight mouth.

"Yes," said Eddie, staring up at the east window.

"Who the hell is she?"

"Betty Macintosh."

"*Who?*"

"Decided to get on with it. Case settled. No time to contact a friend."

"Friend?"

"Best man. Quite in order to go it alone."

"Oh, I don't mind. If you'd told me I'd have shaved. And I dare say you'll be giving me a present. Usual thing."

"Of course. And you won't mind giving presents to the bridesmaids?"

"*What?*"

"I take it they all want the same. A string of pearls," and Eddie was suddenly transported with boyish joy and began to boom with laughter, just as the organ left off safely grazing sheep and thundered out "The Wedding March."

The two men were hustled to their feet and arranged alongside the front pew. Fiscal-Smith was handed the ring box and dropped it, and began to crawl about looking down gratings. Edward's old headmaster, Sir, used to say, "You don't find many things funny, Feathers. The sense of humour in some boys needs nourishment." But this, on the wedding day that he had greeted as if going to his death, Eddie suddenly saw as deliriously dotty. He guffawed.

A rustle and a flurry and a gasp, and the bride stood alongside the groom who looked down with a cheerful face maybe to wink at good old Betty and say, "Hello—so you're here." Instead his face froze in wonder. A girl he had never seen stood beside him in a cloud of lace and smelling of orchids. She carried lilies. She did not turn to look at him. The face, invisible under the veil, was in shadow.

He could sense the delight of the small congregation—must be Amy and her husband, and Mrs. Baxter and some children and, oh yes, of course, Judge Pastry Willy and his wife Dulcie. Willy was "giving Betty away." How they were all singing! Singing their heads off: *From Greenland's icy mountains to India's coral strand.* (A paean to the Empire, he had always thought. Whoever had chosen it?)

Someone had put hymn books into the hands of the bride

and groom and the best man in his coloured T-shirt, who was singing louder than anyone with the book upside down. (You wouldn't have expected Fiscal-Smith to know any hymns by heart.) The bride was trilling away, too, reading the hymn book through the veil.

I don't know this girl, Eddie thought. I suppose it's Betty. It could be anyone. She's singing in tune rather well. I didn't know that Betty could sing. I don't really know anything about her. I wonder if some other men—other man—does? I don't know her tastes. I only know that terrible green dress. I don't know the colour of her eyes. Oh!

The bride had been told to lift her veil to make the promises and there to his relief was Betty in his pearls, and her eyes were bright hazel. And she was standing with her right foot on his left foot, and quite hurting him. They made the tremendous promises to each other, like automata, and he was told that he might now kiss her.

Tears in his eyes, he leaned towards Betty who leaned towards his ear after the small, obligatory kiss. "Who on *earth* is the best man?" just as Fiscal-Smith dropped the now empty ring box for the second time and turned to check how many un-necklaced bridesmaids there were. And, for the first time that day, Fiscal-Smith smiled, on finding that there were none.

CHAPTER TWELVE

Honeymoon Letters

Letter one: A letter from the bride to her friend Isobel Ingoldby, of no fixed address.

Dear Lizzie,

I'm writing with no real idea yet of where to send it. Perhaps to the Old Col, in case you left a forwarding address. Are you east or west? Back in Oz, forward to Notting Hill, or in pursuit of some passion in the Everglades or one of the Poles?

I've done it. Wore ancient veil belonging to old bird. A Missionary Bird once in Dacca all butterflies and flowers to cover my homely face and a new dress that was a present from her too, and shoes from Amy and flowers from Uncle Pastry who walked me down the aisle and handed me over. Antique idea but rather amazing. Eddie gave a sort of hiccup as I drew up alongside. I gleamed at him through the lace and I could see that he was worried that I might be someone else. He likes all evidence to be in the open. When I came to lift the veil—as does God at death—he looked startled, then breathed out thankfully. I'd made an effort with the face and had my hair cut where the grandee expats used to go, one of them looking down at me from a benign photograph on the wall. Must be long dead, but somehow I know her. Could have been part of my childhood. Friend of Ma, I guess. Red nails, shiny lips like a geisha girl with kind eyes. She's going to be my icon. I shall grow old like her, *commanding* people and being a perfick lady, opening bazaars. I'll live in the past and try to improve it. You'll know me by my hat and gloves, and hymn book too, like the mission-ary who got eaten by the cassa-wary in Tim-buk-tu . . . something something hymn book too.

Well, I suppose I got eaten in HK at the church but I'm not unhappy, being digested, just a little shaken. I don't know if Eddie's happy—who does know about him?—but I'd say he isn't shaken at all. The only thing that worried him apart from my heavy disguise under the antique table-cloth was his best man. You'd think Eddie would have been ashamed of Fiscal-Smith but he's loyal to friends. And he has some funny friends, like the Dwarf—who was nowhere to be seen—and now this battered scarecrow. He thinks my friends are funny too, citing the excellent Mrs. Baxter who does nothing but cry.

And if he knew I know you, what then! Don't worry, ducky. I'm not jealous of his memories or that you were in flagrante delicto (more jargon) once upon a time. "Let it be our secret that I know you," as your lesbian pals undoubtedly bleat.

I don't think you and Eddie'd have much to say to each other now, Lizzie, whatever you both got up to in the school hols before the war.

And I find I have everything to say to him morning, noon and night. Old Filth, as he is so charmingly called— I can't care for it—is full of surprises. And I do enjoy the way people *defer* to him. I am but a hole in the air but they run after him, bowing. And why I like this so much, Lizzie, is that he doesn't notice it. And he doesn't think it odd to have friends like Fiscal-Smith and the seven dwarfs. Well, only one dwarf to date but you never know who will turn up next.

And he trusts me utterly, Lizzie. Never suspected a thing about you-know-what. And I've put it out of my mind. It was some sort of hypnosis. Terrifying! No, I never think about it. Of course, Eddie's a bit of an enigma himself and it makes me pleased with our Enigma years at Bletchley Park. You and I know about silence. Not one of us spilled a bean, did we? And the fact that I'll never really crack Eddie in a way gives me a freedom, Lizzie. Oh, not to misbehave again, oh dear me, no, but to have an unassailable privacy within my own life equal to his. This *must* be how to make marriage work. I have been married three full days. I know.

We're in Shangri-La, Lizzie. It's called Bhutan, and way round the back of Everest. He organised it all between the Case settling and marrying me. That's what he was doing the two days he vanished in Hong Kong. First he fixed a plane to Delhi—no, first the wedding breakfast at the Restaurant Le Trou Normand where Amy tried to breastfeed at the table and Eddie and Fiscal-Smith looked up at the ceiling that was all hung with fishing nets with fake starfish trapped in them, like Brittany, and the manager removed her to an annexe.

"Off to Delhi now," says groom to bride and "Delhi? We're not going to *Delhi*. Not *Agra*? Not the Taj Mahal with all the tours?" says bride to groom: "I've not seen the Taj Mahal, as it happens," he says, "but no, it's a stopover. I couldn't get much of a hotel, though."

Nor was it. The tarts paraded the corridors and *used* our room when we were down at dinner (British Restaurant wartime standard) and Edward inspected the bed-covers and roared, and we slept in chairs and next day he refused to pay and confetti fell out of my pockets and the manager smirked. Bad start.

But *then* I experienced the superhuman power of the

Great Man's fury. Heathcliff stand back. Result: somehow comes along an Embassy car and chauffeur to take us to the airport, no Taj Mahal but a silent journey with Eddie like Jove on his cloud. And the cloud gave way to mountains and the mountains were the Himalayas and then the mountains started to change and soften and a pale-green, misty valley country began. Its architecture of wood and stone and bright paint is like a pure and unworldly Vienna. Tall, huge blocks of apartments like palaces. Cotton prayer flags blow in clusters from every hilltop and street corner and everyone—children and grandpas and cripples and monks—give each prayer wheel a little shove as they pass.

And now we have reached a rest-house high above a valley where a green river thunders, foaming along between forests standing in the sky and luminous terraces of rice. At a meeting of waters stands a stupa. Even from up here its whiteness and purity hurt the eyes. High up here we listen to the thunderous waters and then, high above us again, are monasteries hidden in the peaks, and eagles.

We arrived yesterday on a country bus and we passed this stupa far below at the meeting of the rivers. It is like the huge snow-white breast of a giantess lying prone with a tower on top, like a tall white nipple. Reclining by the roadside on a wooden bridge was a human-sized creature examining its fingernails like a courtesan, not interested in us. Bus stops still. Driver cries, "Look, look! It is a langur, the rare animal you see on our postage stamps!" and the langur langur-ously yawns, putting a paw over its mouth—I swear—and vanishes.

> I'd like to be a langur
> Sitting by a stupa
> Eating chips and bang-ur
> Wouldn't it be supa?

Now, in this Bhutanese rest-house, I am completely happy and I hope Eddie is. He spends hours sweeping the view with his binoculars and peace on his face. The walls of the rest-house are made of crimson felt hung inside heavy skins. The red felt flaps and groans in the wind. It is damp to the touch. Monks and monkish people shuffle about. The appearance of the management puts the Savoy Hotel to shame. They wear deep-blue woollen coats, the Scottish kilt, long woollen socks knitted in diamond patterns like the Highland Games and dazzle-white cuffs turned back over blue sleeves. The cuffs are a foot deep. There's a whiff of Bluecoat Boys and of Oliver Cromwell. Puritan? No. There must be a lot of sex about, for the villages team with children and (wait for it) all the government offices are painted with murals several storeys high, with giant *phalluses* (or *phalli*?) on which Eddie sometimes lets his binoculars rest and even faintly smiles.

So, it's all O.K., Lizzie-Izz.

Love you. Love you for not being at the wedding. If Eddie knew I knew you and was writing he'd send his love, but I'd rather he didn't. I must keep hold of his love all to myself at least at first, until I understand it.

Dinner is served. Looks like langur fritters.

Your old school chum
Bets

(Letter stamped by Old Colonial Hotel, Hong Kong "To await arrival" and eventually thrown away.)

Two: A letter from the bride to her friend Amy of Kai Tak.

Amy, my duck, I'm writing from Dacca in East Pakistan but when I write to The Baxter (next one) I'll call it Bengal and I have to say that Bengal suits it better, even sans Lancers. The climate remains the same. Every other change political and historical is on the surface. I can't remember if you and Nick worked here? Actually you can't see much surface for most of it is water. It is hardly "a land" but part of the globe where the sea is shallow and the sinuous silky people are almost fish but with great white smiling teeth. The "lone and level land" stretches far away and the crowds blacken it like dust drifting. Nowhere in the world more different than the last place, i.e. the first call in our Honeymoon Progress which is becoming *global* and all arranged in secret and string-pulling by Eddie.

First, Bhutan. We were dizzy there, not with releasing passions, but with altitude sickness. We were level with the eagles. There was also a bit of food poisoning. I managed not to buy the goat's cheese they sell on the mountainside like dollops of soft cream snowballs set on leaves. "You would last one hour," says my lord. In the rest houses the food came before us on silver dishes and looked ceremoniously beautiful: mounds of rice with little coloured bits of meat and fish and vegetables in it, warmish and wet, and only after a terrible day and night did we realise that anything left over is mixed in with the new stuff next day. Tourists are few. Probably mostly dead. The king hates tourists and you usually have to wait a year. Eddie was at Oxford with him after the war and I was all for dropping in our cards in the hope of getting some Oxford marmalade and Christ Church claret. Eddie said no. Eddie is . . . but later.

First, beloved Amy, thank you from all parts of me for all you did for me and the speed at which you did it. I *hope* you liked Edward? He is monosyllabic in a crowd. He very much liked you and Nick and was full of admiration for you controlling and producing a family among the poor and needy and weak in the head. He never mentioned your children, which is a bit frightening. He doesn't know I want ten—plus a nanny and several nursemaids and a nursery floor at the top of a grand house in Chelsea on the river. I can't help it. I read too many Victorian children's books of Ma's in China. And I miss my Ma. But don't worry. I'll probably be marching against the Bomb, unwashed and hugely pregnant like the rest.

Eddie couldn't believe you have always been my best friend ever. He thought you'd be pony club and debutanting and hot stuff on the marriage market. "She was," I said. Do you find that much-travelled men are the most insular? Like Robinson Crusoe? If he hadn't got stuck on that island, Robinson Crusoe'd have got stuck on another. Of his own making.

I'm writing myself into a mood to say real things to you and maybe I should now quickly write myself out of it. Do you remember that book about marriage (Bowen?) that talks about the glass screen that comes down between a newly wed couple and all their former friends? I'm not going to let this happen but I can see, after that terrifying 1662 marriage service, that it can eat into one. Well, it was you made me go through with it. Said I was at last being practical. I wasn't sure that you still thought so when you met Eddie and I wish he hadn't stared so steadily and so high above your head.

Loyalty. And so I'll only say that we had a ghastly first night in Delhi, propped up in basket chairs because harlots had been using our beds. Then we went in a solid car (called "An Ambassador') up the Himalayas to Darjeeling where we were greeted by old English types and cold mutton and rice pudding and porridge, and our own room looking directly at dawn over the Katmanjunga. The occasional English flag. There was early-morning tea and everything perfect between white, white linen sheets. In the middle of the night Eddie said, "I can't apologise enough," which I thought weird after his spectacular performances. "About the Delhi hotel," he said.

There was some ghastly hang-up in his childhood. I don't want to know about it. I'd guess half the men with his background are the same. Well, he was so happy in the mountains.

Then after Bhutan we came on here to Dacca.

I've seen a chair in a dark shop. It is rose-and-gold, a patterned throne from some old rajah's palace, but all tattered. I longed. I yearned. Eddie said, "But we haven't a home yet." This had not occurred to me. "We could send it to Amy at first." He looked at me and said, "She wouldn't thank you." You and I aren't very good at domiciliary arrangements, Amy. You leave yours to God and I'm still imprisoned by the past, and expect it to come again. It won't, any more than sherbet fountains. It's to be "Utility furniture" now for ever. I said, "Sorry." And he said, "Hold on," and he went into the back of the dark shop and came out saying, "I've bought it. It can go to Chambers."

And this, not the great rope of pearls he gave me, and not the ring and that, not the moment he saw me in the Baxter butterflies, was *the* moment. Well, I suppose when I knew I loved him.

I'll write to the Baxter next and explain about leaving the veil behind. In twenty years I'll come to your little girls' weddings. During the twenty years I'll have been endlessly breastfeeding in the rose-red chair, and anywhere else I choose. Times will have changed. Maybe we'll be having babies on bottles? Or in bottles? Maybe men will be extinct too.

But women will always have each other. You gave me *such* a wedding.

Love to Nick and the babes—by the way has the new one come? Don't let Baxter tears fall on its sweet head but give it a X from
Betty

Three: A picture postcard from the bride to Mrs. Hildegarde Maisie Annie Baxter of Mimosa Cottage, Kai Tak, Hong Kong.

Dear Mrs. Baxter,
This is only a note until I get home when I'll write to thank you properly for the veil. I have left it for the time being with Amy but I think you should see it back in its box. I fear for it among the hordes in Sunset Buildings. It *made* the wedding.
I am sure we'll meet again and I'm so glad you could come to the restaurant though I'm sorry about the bouillabaisse.
With love from Betty *Feathers*

(Card discovered unposted fifty years on in the Donheads down the cushions of a great red chair.)

Four: A letter from the bride to Judge Sir William Pastry of Hong Kong, posted in Valetta, Malta.

Valetta, Malta
Dear Uncle Willy,
We are up at "Mabel's Place" and I don't think I have to explain that it's the medieval palace of the great Mabel Strickland on the hilltop and the blue sea all around. The walls must be six feet thick and inside there are miles of tall and shadowy stone passages, slit windows *for arrers*, no furniture except the occasional dusty carpet woven when Penelope was a girl, massy candelabra standing on

massy oak chests. Our bed could be rented out in London as a dwelling: four posts, painted heraldry, old plumes drooping thick with dust, thick bedlinen like altar cloths. Wow!

But I expect you've been here lots of times. One day you'll make a wonderful governor of Malta and they'd love you as much as they love Mabel in her darned stockings and tweed skirts. If you won't do it then I'd push Edward for governor instead. We'd bring up our ten children here and become passionate about the Maltese, and have picnics on the beach (the Maltese perched on chairs and making lace) and watch the British flag going up and down with the sun. Until it's folded up and put away.

But you won't even think of it. Are you still wanting Thomas Hardy and Dorset? I can't think why. Dorset sounds stuffy—full of people like us—and Malta is cheerful, flashing with the light of the sea. And they still *like* us here and we like them. That will become rare. Quite soon, Edward thinks.

But at present Grand Harbour is alive with British ships hooting and tooting, and the streets are alive with British tars and all the girls roll their black eyes at them on their way to Mass which seems to take place every half-hour. Their mothers, believe it or not, still stride the corkscrew streets in flowing black, their heads draped in black veiling arranged over tea trays. Oh—and flowers everywhere, Uncle W! Such flowers!

It's been terribly bombed, of course, and it's pretty filthy. Sliema Creek is covered by a heavy carpet of scum. The Royal Navy swims in it though the locals tell them not to. It's the main sewer. They wag their heads. There's a rumour of bubonic plague and yesterday a big black rat ran across Mabel's roses not looking at all well.

Of course the food is terrible, as ever it was. It was we

who taught them Mrs. Beeton's mashed potato! There is not much in the way of wine. *But* the wonderful broken architecture from before the Flood stretches everywhere: hundreds of scattered broken villages—Africa-ish—the occasional rose-pink palace decorated like a birthday cake. There are about a hundred thousand churches, bells clanking all day long and half the night. Dust inside them hangs as if in water, incense burns and the roofs (because of the war) are mostly open to the sky.

There is a passion for building here and they're all at it with ropes and pulleys. Restoring and starting anew. It would be wonderful for Eddie's practice: plenty of materials. Malta is one big rock of ages cleft for us. It is full of cracks and overnight the cracks fill with dew and flowers. The smell of the night-scented stocks floats far out to sea.

(Scene: Hong Kong
Willy's Dulcie: You aren't *still* reading Betty's letter!
Willy: She grows verbose. Don't like the sound of it.)

It will remain a mystery that the island never fell to the enemy. It was dive-bombed night and day, the people hiding deep in caves and (I gather) quarrelling incessantly and threatening each other's authority most of the time. There was almost a revolution. Then, in limped the battered British convoys with flour and meat and oil and sugar, and the pipes all playing and the cliffs black with cheering crowds.

(Willy: Now it's military history. She's holding back.
Dulcie: She's going to be a British blimp in middle age if she's not careful. What about the honey moon?
Willy: I think she's coming to that.)

We arrived here by sea from Rome. We flew to Rome from East Pakistan and we arrived in East Pakistan from Bhutan! I think we were the only tourists. The king of Bhutan is pretty insular but he let us in because he was at Christ Church with Eddie. Not that they met. Then or then. He's an insular king—like you and Thomas Hardy. And maybe George VI.

London tomorrow. We'll be in Eddie's old London pad until we can find somewhere else. The Temple's bombed to bits still. I think—but don't spread it—that Eddie wants to come back to live in Hong Kong and so do I, especially if you and Dulcie stay. Don't be lured back to the dreary Donheads.

I'm sorry. I run on with no means of stopping—Oh, God—History!

(Willy: I think she's stopping.
Dulcie: You'll be late for Court.)

I have so much to tell you, my dear godfather I've known since Old Shanghai. This was to have been a simple letter of thanks. Thanks for being such a prop and stay at the wedding, for giving me away, for being so diplomatic at Le Trou Normand about Amy breastfeeding (tell Dulcie sorry about that, I didn't know it would upset her) and especially when Mrs. Baxter was sick. You were wonderful. I'm afraid my Edward kept a seat near the back! He was silent for a long time but as we passed through Sikkim en route for Darjeeling and we saw slender ladies plucking tea leaves with the very tips of their fingers—their saris like poppies in the green, their little heads bound round with colours and I was transported with joy—he said, "I am not enough for you."

Oh dear—I have been carried far away. Please, dear Uncle W, don't show Dulcie this. Well, I expect you will.

In Dacca Eddie bought me a red chair. The old, old man who sold it lived far down the back of his shop in the dark, his eyes gleaming like a Maltese plague rat. The chair is to be sent to the Inns of Court, The Temple, London EC4!

Oh—I don't seem to be able to concentrate on thanking you. If only Ma and Pa were here. "You are my mother and my father," as the Old Raj promised India, or rather they said, "I am."

Isn't it odd how Hong Kong holds us still? Isn't it odd how the "Far East" has somehow faded away with the Bomb? Do you understand? Now the British live out there by grace. I shall call my first daughter Grace.

I promise, dear Uncle Willy, to grow more sage: more worthy of your affection. I shall grow tweedy and stout and hairy, with moles on my chin, and I shall be a magistrate and open bazaars in support of the Barristers' Benevolent Society. You won't be ashamed of me.

Thanks for liking Eddie, with much, much love from
Betty x

(Letter left in Judge Pastry's Will to Her Majesty's Judge Sir Edward Feathers QC, residing in the Donheads, carefully dated and inscribed and packed in a cellophane envelope, and bequeathed to Edward Feathers's Chambers where it may still be mouldering.)

CHAPTER THIRTEEN

Y ou are grinning all over your face, Mrs. Feathers."
"I'm happy, Mr. Feathers. I'm writing to Pastry Willy."
"About a hundred pages, at a guess. Come on. It's a
picnic."

"Picnic?"

"On the cliffs, Elisabeth. With the local talent. Well, the
local English talent. Quick. No 'PS xx.' Envelope, stamp and
off. Silver salver at the portcullis. Take your suncream and I've
got your hat."

"I love you, Edward Feathers. Why are we going off on a
picnic with all these terrible people? We could be eating
tinned pilchards with Mabel."

"It'll be tinned pilchard sandwiches on the cliffs. Come on,
there's a great swarm going. Planned for years. Since the end
of the war. It's all expats with no money, no education and big
ideas. All drunk with sunlight. They drifted to Malta. They
can't go home. Nothing to do."

"Is it the British Council?"

"Certainly not. It's the riff-raff of Europe. The Sixpenny
Settlers. We have to go. It's polite. There's to be wine."

They arrived at the picnic where everyone was lolling about
in the sun on what seemed to be an inland clifftop, though you
could hear the sea far below. There was a long fissure on the
plateau, stuffed full of flowers. There was a trickling sound of
running water.

"I thought there were no streams on Malta," she said.

"There is one. Only one," said a languid man lying about nearby with a bottle of wine.

"We found it a year ago. Nobody knew of it. Yet it's no distance from Valetta," said somebody else.

"Ah,"—the languid man—. "We find that the island gets bigger and bigger."

Some daughters, English schoolgirls in bathing dresses, neat round the thighs, were laughing and jumping over the rift in the rock. And then a shriek.

"What's happening? What's happening, Eddie?"

"I think they're jumping the crack."

Elisabeth ran across and lay on her stomach and looked down into the slit rock and its channel of flowers. It was less then a yard wide. The spot of emerald ocean below seemed distant as the sky above. "Oh, if they slip! If they slip!" Betty yelled out.

But the girls' mothers were sitting smoking and examining their nails, and one of them called, "They won't. Don't worry."

Then one girl did. A leg went down and she had to be hauled out fast. Everyone laughed, except Elisabeth, who again lay face-down. There was the notion that there was no time, nor ever had been, nor ever would be. She said, "Eddie, there's a little beach down there. I can see breakers. I'm going down by the path."

"If there is a path."

"I'll find one. I'll go alone. Don't follow me."

They had not been apart since the wedding.

The languid man lying near with his wine bottle called out, "I say, you're the barrister chap, aren't you? I want to ask you something."

"I'm off. I'll see you down there, Edward. Come for me in one of the cars. Don't hurry."

"You'll miss the picnic."

"Good. Don't drink too much. The road down will be screwy. Might be safer to dive through the crack."

Edward turned grey. He strode over and grabbed her arm above the elbow.

"Let go! Stop it! You're like a tourniquet! *Edward*!"

His eyes were looking at someone she had never met.

Then he let go of her arm, sat down on the stony cliff and put his hands over his face. "Sorry."

"I should think so."

"I went back somewhere. I was about eight."

"Eight?"

"I killed someone—"

"Oh, Eddie, shut up. I'm going . . . No, all right, then. All *right*. I won't. Go and talk to that awful man. I'll sit here by myself."

"Something wrong?" the man called. "Honeymoon over? Something I said?"

"No," said Edward.

"The war," said the man. "POW, were you?"

"No. Were you?"

"God, no. Navy. Shore job. Ulcer. Left me low. Wife left too, thank God. Look." He heaved himself up and came over to Edward. "Can you get me a job? In the Law line? Something like barristers' clerk. No exams. Something easy."

"Barristers' clerks don't have easy lives."

"I'd really like just to stay here. On Malta. Do nothing. Just stay with our own sort."

"I can't stand this," said Elisabeth. "Eddie, come with me down the cliff." She stepped over the man and said, "Oh, drop dead, whoever you are."

CHAPTER FOURTEEN

T he streets around Victoria Station were dark and the taxi crawled along in a fog so dense that kerb-stones were invisible and even double-decker buses were upon you before you knew it. The cab driver stopped and started, and they sat silent until he said at last, "Ebury Street. Yes? Ten pounds." He had brought them all the way from the airport, their luggage piled around them and under a strap on the front and on top on a frame. "Thanks, sir. Good luck, sir."

She had never seen Edward's part of London. She had never seen him in a house at all. Always it had been hotels and restaurants. She had no idea what his maisonette in Pimlico would be like, and still less now they had drawn up outside it in thick fog. She had always been with him in sunlight.

"I should carry you over my doorstep," he said, "but it's going to be a bit cluttered," and he unlocked the front door upon an unpainted, uncarpeted stairwell with the yellow gloaming of the fog seeping in through a back window. There was an untrampled mess of mail about the floorboards and the smell of cats and an old-fashioned bicycle. Uncarpeted stairs went up and round a corner into more shadow.

"Home," said Edward.

"Whose is the bike?"

"Mine."

"*Yours? Can you?* I mean I can't see you riding a bike."

"I ride it every Sunday morning. Piccadilly. Oxford Circus. Not a thing on the road. I'll get you one."

Upstairs there was a kitchen that housed one chipped enamel-topped table and a chair. Under the table were old copies of the *Financial Times* and the *Daily Telegraph* so densely packed that the table legs were rising from the floor. A rusty geyser hung crooked over a Belfast stone sink. Cupboard doors hung open against a wall. On the table, green fish-paste stood in an open glass jar and a teacup from some unspecified time. It had a mahogany-coloured tidemark inside it.

Edward smiled about him. "I have a cleaner but it doesn't look as if she's been in. I've never actually met her. I leave the money by the sink and it disappears—yes, it's gone, so I suppose she's been. I hope the bed's made up. I'm not good at all this. I'm hardly ever here. There's a laundry round the corner and an ABC for bread."

"You *live* here! All the time? Alone? But Eddie, it's so unlike you."

"Oh, I don't know. I've never been fussy."

There was a Victorian clothes airer attached to the ceiling on a pulley with ropes that brought it up and down. Sitting on one of the rails of the airer was a rat.

Over the years this homecoming became one of Elisabeth's famous stories, as she sat in Hong Kong at her rosewood dining table with its orchids and silver and transparent china bowls of soup. Contemporaries discussing post-war London. Elisabeth became glib, inspiring like memories among guests who were all of a certain age. They joked proudly of the drabness of that fifties—even sixties—London; the insanity of the National Health Service ("free *elastoplast!*"), the puritanical government. Elisabeth, always pleasant, never joined in about politics. She revered the British Health Service, and turned the conversation to the London she came to as a bride, to Edward's unworldliness in seedy Pimlico, his hard work, his long hours in Chambers. But when she told the homecoming story, which became more colourful with the years, she could not decide why she somehow could never include the rat.

She had screamed, run from the kitchen, down the stairs and out into the fog, and stood shaking on the pavement, Edward following her and shouting, "Betty—for God's sake, there were rats on Malta. *Plague* rats. And Hong Kong. And what about Bhutan and the snakes coming up the bath pipes?"

"We never saw one."

"What about the Camp in Shanghai?"

"That was different. And we kept the place clean. We've got to leave, Eddie. *Now.*"

"You don't know how hard it is to find anywhere. Even one room. Everywhere is flattened. And Ebury Street is SW1. It's a good address on writing paper."

"That rat wasn't there to write letters!"

Forty or so years on, in Dorset in her Lavendo-polished house and weedless garden, driving her car weekly to the car wash, refusing to keep a dog because of mud on its paws, a blast of memory sometimes overcame her. There sat the rat on the airer. It was her falling point. It was the rat eternal. It had been the sign that she must now take charge.

"Isn't there a hotel? Isn't the Grosvenor around here? At Victoria Station? We'll get the luggage back on the pavement and go there in a cab."

"We'd never get another taxi in this fog," he said, and at once a taxi swam out of the night, its headlamps as comforting as Florence Nightingale.

"I'm not sure if I've any English money left," he said.

"I have," she said. "I bought some at the airport. Slam the front door behind you."

She climbed in, and after a moment he followed.

And at Grosvenor Place they were out, they were in the foyer and the cabman paid off while Edward still stood frowning on the pavement in his linen suit. "This hotel smells. It smells of beer and tobacco and fry. It's probably full up." But she secured a room.

In bed he said, "I always rather liked rats."

That night in the Grosvenor in an unheated bedroom, shunting steam trains clamouring below, yellow fingers of fog painting the window and a mat from the floor on top of the skimpy eiderdown, Edward began to laugh. "I am the *rat*," he said, grabbing her. "I came with you in the taxi."

Scene in HK. Rosewood dining table. In middle age.
Fin de Siècle.

Edward (*to guests*):	End of my freedom, you know. Minute we reached London, she took me over. She and the clerk and, of course, Albert Ross. Needn't have existed outside work.
All:	Well, you *did* work, Filth! How you worked!
Edward:	Yes. Work at last began to come in. Remember, Betty?
Elisabeth:	I do.
Edward:	Don't know what you did with yourself in the evenings, poor child. You looked about sixteen. All alone.
Elisabeth:	Not exactly.

CHAPTER FIFTEEN

By the morning the fog had lifted and Edward was off to Chambers with his laundry and papers by nine o'clock. Across the table of the gloomy breakfast room at the Grosvenor Hotel, he handed Elisabeth the keys of the maisonette.

As soon as he'd gone she picked up the keys, asked for the luggage to be brought down and taken round to the station left-luggage office. She paid the bill and set off on foot, bravely, to Edward's horrible domain.

As she reached the corner of Ebury Street the fog rolled away and she saw that Edward's side of the street was beautiful in morning light. The façade was faded and gentle and seemed like paper, an unfinished film set, almost bending in the wind. The eighteenth-century windows that had withstood the bomb blasts all around were unwashed, yet clear, set in narrow panes. Little shops on to the pavement ran all along, and doors to the houses above had rounded fanlights. Each house had three storeys. There were two tall first-floor windows side by side with pretty iron balconies. The shop at street level beside Edward's front door seemed to be a greengrocer's with boxes and sacks spread about the pavement and a very fat short man in a buff overall was standing, hands in pockets, on the step. "Morning," he said, blowing air out of his cheeks and looking at the sky.

"Are you open yet? Have you—anything?"

"*Anything*? I'd not say *anything*. We have potatoes. Carrots. Celery, if required."

"Have you—apples?"

He looked at her intently and said, "We might have an orange or two."

"Oh! Could I have two pounds?"

"Where you been then, miss? I'll sell you one orange."

She followed him inside the shop where a doom-laden woman was perched high on a stool behind a desk.

"Look at my ankles," she said, sticking one out. It bulged purple over the rim of a man's carpet slipper, unstockinged. "D'you want a guess at the size of it?"

"It looks horribly swollen," said Elisabeth.

"It's sixteen inches round. Sixteen! And all water. That's your National Health Service for you."

"But you must go to the doctor at once."

"And who does the accounts here? You reached home, then?"

"Home?"

"Next door. "Mr. Feathers is home," they said, the electrician's across the road. Mozart Electrics."

"We're—we're just passing through. I'm Mrs. Feathers."

"Well!" She rolled her eyes at her impassive husband, who was again on the step cornering the market. "Married!"

"You can have two," he called over his shoulder. "But don't ask for lemons."

"Sack that cleaner," said his wife. "She stays ten minutes. You'll have to get scrubbing."

"Oh, well. I don't think we're staying. We want to get something nearer the City."

"You'll be lucky," said the woman. "But you are lucky, I can see that. There'd be a thousand after next door the minute you handed in the keys."

"I saw a rat. Last night. We left."

"Oh, rats. They're all over the place, rats. Mr. Feathers used to complain sometimes, though he's a perfect gentleman.

'Have you by any chance got a dog, Mrs.—er?' (He calls every-one Mrs.—er.) 'Does your dog like rats?' We said we didn't know but we took it round and it stands there looking at this rat"—a huge wheezing and shaking soon taken up by the greengrocer on the step, the rolls of fat beneath the buff vibrating—"and it turns and walks out. The dog walks out. It was a big rat."

"Well, I can't live here," said Elisabeth.

"I'll get you the Corporation," said the wife. "You'll be clean and sweet there soon, you'll see. D'you want some kippers?"

Elisabeth turned the key in Edward's lock and then stood back for a while on the pavement, watching the electrical shop across the road opening up. A very arthritic old person stood watching her.

"Go on in," he called. "You'll be all right. 'Ere, I'll come in with you," and like one risen painfully from the dead he slowly crossed the road, cars stopping for him. "Takes me over an hour now to get up in the morning," he said. "Now watch that bike. The stairs is steep but if I take it slow . . . I'se easing. Now then . . ."

In the kitchen the airer was unoccupied and through a beautiful window, its glazing bars as fine as spars, lay a long, green, tangled garden full of flowers. Upstairs and upstairs again were bedrooms with tipping floors and simple marble fireplaces. Edward's narrow bed stood like a monk's pallet in the middle of one room, on a mat. One fine old wardrobe. One upright chair. A decent bathroom led off, and now the higher view showed a row of other gardens on either side. On the other side from the green grass was a small lawn and forest trees blocking out Victoria Station's engine sheds.

"Don't you get too far in with her next door that side," said the electrician. "I don't mean Florrie with the ankles. I mean t'other side. You all a'right now?"

"Yes. Well. I shan't be staying. We saw—well—rats."

"From the river," he said. "They have to go somewhere. There's worse than rats. Now, this is a good house and so it should be. We hear it's two pound a week rent. Mind, it's all coming down for development soon. Miracle is that not a bomb touched it. All the big stuff came down—Eaton Square and so on—not a window broken here. Artisans' dwellings, we are. But panelling original pine. I'll leave you for the moment."

"Thank you," she called down after him. "Very much. Could you tell me why you're called Mozart Electrics?"

"Well, he was here as a boy," said the arthritic, amazed that the whole world did not know. "One day there'll be a statue."

She found her way to the garden and there were fruit bushes and a cucumber frame, and over the fence to the right an old woman with a florid face was watching her.

"Good morning," she said. "I am Da-lilah Dexter. You may have heard of me. I am an actress but equally concerned with gardening. And I hear that you have just married Edward."

"How ever—?"

"News flies through eighteenth-century walls. We heard you arrive last night but then you were gone. I suppose he's off to his Chambers?"

"Yes. We're just back—"

"From a long honeymoon. It will be hard to adjust. I suggest you come in for hot cocoa and to meet Dexter."

"I don't think . . ."

"I will put on the cocoa and leave open the front door."

"This," Delilah said, pointing, "is Dexter."

The house was like the green room of a small theatre, the sitting room apparently immense since the wall opposite the windows (hung with roped-back velvet like proscenium arches) was covered by a gold-framed mirror that reflected an

older, softer light than was real. The mirror had a golden flam-
beau at either side of the frame where fat wax candles had
burned to the last inch. The looking-glass reflected a collapsed
man in a black suit, his legs stretched out before him on a red
velvet chaise longue that lacked a leg. His face was ivory. He
waved an exhausted greeting.

"Dexter," announced his wife, "is also an actor. A fine
actor, but in his later years he only plays butlers."

"How interesting . . ."

"Butlers have been our support for years. Unfortunately the
new drama is uninterested in butlers. It is all tramps and working-class women doing the ironing. But still, here and there,
Dexter finds a part, or rather directors find a part for him. He's
the ultimate butler. He very much favours the Playhouse where
they still tend towards the country-house comedy, and long
runs. At present he is in a play where his part ends with Act
Two and so he gets home for supper. They let him off the final
curtain."

"I hope always to be let off the final curtain," said Dexter.
"And as I always wear black I need spend no time in the dressing room. I can leave this house and be on stage in nine minutes."

"But if you fell over in the street?"

Both actors looked at Elisabeth with disdain.

"We are professionals," said Delilah. "We can dance on a
broken leg. If Dexter *should* get late, he could borrow
Edward's bicycle. I'll top up your cocoa with a little green
chartreuse."

When Elisabeth had opened every window in the house
and propped open the front door with the bicycle, she followed Edward's telephone wire under a cushion and phoned
the Westminster Council about the rat. Then she got busy with
the labour exchange and went across to Mozart Electrics about

a cleaning agency. At the National Provincial Bank on the corner she opened an account and she attacked the gas showrooms to dare them not to replace the geyser. "They'll not show up for a month," said Delilah Dexter, but someone came round in an hour and stayed until hot water crept forth. Elisabeth found a saucepan, cleaned out spiders and ate kippers.

"They were very good," she told the greengrocer's wife.

"Yes, They're from Lowestoft. These are Lowestoft kippers—we've gone there two weeks' holiday for twenty-seven years, even in the war. You'll be all right, they keep. We'll be back there in a few months and I'll get you some more. We don't like change. We're here."

Edward, returning uneasily—and late—that evening to the Grosvenor, found no sign of his wife or his luggage. He walked back dispiritedly to Ebury Street to find every light in the house ablaze, every window open and a smell of kippers noticeable as far away as Victoria Station. His wife on his doorstep, arms akimbo in a borrowed overall, was deep in conversation with the fruit shop, and Mr. Dexter was making his way solemnly down the street dressed as a butler.

"The end of Act Two," said Dexter, raising his bowler hat.

PART THREE

Life

CHAPTER SIXTEEN

W ell, yes. There is money," Edward agreed. "Yes."
(Reluctantly.) "The fees do begin to roll in at last.
But I feel we should not be rash."

"Decorate white throughout," said Betty. "The electric
shop knows a couple of men down the mews. Then the new
place, Peter Jones in Sloane Square, it's reopened. It's the place
for all carpets and curtains. And furniture. Do you think it's
time we had a car?"

"Good God, no!"

"It could stand in the road."

"It would need lights at night."

"We could have a wire through the sitting-room window.
On a battery. They all do."

"It's against the law. It's carrying a cable across the public
highway. One day the whole street will catch fire."

"The fruit shop van stands outside all the time. By the way,
he says he'll deliver free."

"Since he's only next door . . ."

"And Delilah Dexter's going to help me with the interior
decoration."

"Which one is Delilah Dexter?"

"Married to the singing butler. They know you. Leave it all
to me, but I need a bank account of my own. And something
to put in it."

"That," said Filth, "is, I imagine, usual now."

Delilah was very decisive when the bank account was in place. The whole house was to be the very purest white, like Lady Diana Cooper's used to be in the Thirties, though she wasn't, Delilah found, the purest white herself. Nor was England. "And we'll have one sitting-room wall in simulated black marble, surrounding the white marble chimney piece. And crimson and silver brocade striped curtains. The sofa and chairs are good—Edward says they came from Lancashire but can't remember how. They can be loose-covered in pale citron linen. And the carpet should be white. Fitted to the walls. And thick and fluffy."

"I'm not sure that Edward . . ."

"Oh, and silver candlesticks with black candles on the chimney piece with a tall looking-glass behind them. It happens that I have some silver candlesticks somewhere. We used them in the Scottish Play. Now, let me go ahead."

"The Chambers want to give us a wedding present," said Filth three weeks later, standing outside the sitting-room door and wondering whether to remove his shoes. "This white carpet. It's where we *eat*?"

"Oh, we'll eat in the kitchen now. It's beginning to be considered O.K.."

"I'm sorry. I couldn't eat in a kitchen."

"It's not like it used to be. It will be clean."

"The Chambers," he said, in his bony stockinged feet, "want to give us an armchair. I told them we have one coming from the East."

"Dear love," she said. "We'll not see that again."

Filth looked sad.

"What's wrong?"

"I remember your face when I bought it. Ecstasy."

"Oh, I was being childish. Look, tell them we want a *black* chair from Woollands of Knightsbridge. I've seen it in the window. It has cut-out holes in it like Picasso. It sprawls about. It will add a revolutionary touch."

When the chair arrived it still had the price tag attached. Twenty-two pounds!

"Crikey," said Betty. "Your Chambers must like you. We'd better give a party."

"I never give parties," said Filth. "They know me."

"They don't know me," she said. "Come on. I'll make a list. I've done coq-au-vin for dinner, all red gravy. It's in the kitchen."

"Very well," said Filth and, later, politely, "Very good."

"I wasn't sure about leaving the feet in."

Filth's splendid face began slowly to crack into a smile. Regarding her, he began to laugh, a rare and rusty sound.

"Well, I was born in Tiensin," she said.

"Do you know what you are, Elisabeth Feathers?"

"No?"

"You're happy. I am making you happy."

"Yes. I am. You are. Come on. Eat up your feet."

She thought about it as she cleared up the unconscionable amount of washing-up engendered by the coq-au-vin, as Edward sat in the Picasso chair, his papers for the next day fanning out all around him on the white carpet. Getting down to them on his knees for a moment, he got up covered in white fluff, but said nothing.

"You are happy," said Delilah next morning over the garden wall as Betty hung out washing. "What are those queer little tabs? Is it a variety of sanitary towel?"

"No, it's Edward's bands," she said. "Barristers' bands to tie round his neck in Court. They have to be starched every day. He used to have them sent out, which is fine in Hong Kong, but here—he says they are four pence each."

"Aren't you going to get a job? Did you ever have one?"

"Yes. Foreign Service once."

"Oh. Clever, are you?"

"Yes. I am. Very. But I'm having a rest. I can't help it, Delilah, being clever. Oh, God!" The washing line came down in the flower bed.

"But when the baby comes?"

Betty, scrabbling and disentangling Edward's under-garments, froze.

"Well? I'm right, am I not? I can always tell. To an actress it is vital."

Betty sat back on her heels, stared up at the flamboyant trees behind Delilah's head. Said nothing.

"Do I speak out of turn? Most humble apologies."

"No, no, Delilah. Not at all."

At length Betty said, "Yes."

"There's a doctor down the road. He's set up his brass plate except that it is not brass but a piece of cardboard in the window. It is one of these new Indian doctors who are coming over. I believe they're very good, if you don't mind them touching you."

Betty got up and went into the house and stood in thought. She stared at the white carpet.

"That will have to go," she said.

She looked at the long windows open to the floor and the road below, and wondered if the balcony outside was strong. She smiled and addressed the black candles from the Scottish Play and said, "I thought I couldn't be happier and I find that I am," and alone she set off to the doctor.

And that day she walked and dreamed, smiling lovingly at every passer-by, crossing roads when lights were red, touching heads of children. At Buckingham Palace she stood gazing through the railings like a tourist. She crossed to the steps of the monument to Queen Victoria and looked up at the ugly, cross little face. Scores of children! she thought. And madly in love.

In St. James's Park she leaned on the railing of the bridge and watched the ducks circling busily about and every duck became a celestial duck and the bridge was made of silver, and diamonds were scattered about on the muddy path. The willows swung and sighed over the water. She walked up Birdcage Walk and across Horse Guards Parade, shabby and colourless with wartime sandbags still here and there in sagging heaps. She walked past the door of Number 10 Downing Street that needed a coat of paint, and to the river that rolled deep and fast beside her and would do so long after she was dead. And the baby too.

She walked past the end of Northumberland Avenue, past Cleopatra's Needle, the flaking dying Savoy Hotel with its medieval-palace cellars. She walked up to the Strand, crossed over into Aldwych, up to the Temple and to Edward.

"Yes?" said the clerk, sharpish. "What name please? Mr. Feathers is in conference."

"I'm Elisabeth Feathers. Betty Feathers. I've come to thank you for the chair."

A clutch of girls behind massive typewriters all looked up at the same moment and a junior clerk, like Mr. Polly in a stiff collar, dusted a chair and brought it for her.

"We can't disturb him," said the clerk. "I'm so sorry. But he won't be long. Congratulations on joining our Chambers!"

"Well, I'm not a barrister," she said. "Maybe I will be one day. I feel I could do anything. Oh, and we're giving a party." As she spoke and they all sat observing her she knew that she looked beautiful. Happiness makes you beautiful. I am happy and beautiful as an angel . . .

The door into the clerks' room opened and Edward came in and stopped, astounded.

Beside him, reaching not much above Edward's waist, stood Albert Ross.

"It's all right," one of the typists was saying. "Mrs. Feathers? It's all right. You just fainted for a moment. Here. Water. All right? Sit up carefully."

"Jet lag," Edward was saying. "We've been home for weeks but we almost covered the globe on our honeymoon. Elisabeth, you've been working too hard at the bloody house."

"Where is he?"

"Who?"

"Ross, Albert Ross. I thought I saw him standing beside you."

"You did. He's gone. Don't worry, we'll both be seeing more of him soon. There's a big new Case in Hong Kong. Betty, sit quite still until they get us a taxi. I'll come back with you."

"No. Don't fuss. I'm fine. I just couldn't stop walking. I walked all the way from home."

"But it's miles! It must be four or five miles!"

"It was lovely. I just thought I'd call in."

When Mr. and Mrs. Feathers had gone, Charles, the head clerk, went to the pub and the junior clerk for his sandwiches. The typists brought out their packed lunches and thermos flasks and cigarettes. One girl lay back in her chair. "Pregnant," she said. "Well! Good old Filth."

After the miscarriage of her child at four months, Elisabeth was to be in Hong Kong again with Edward and it was universally agreed that it would be excellent for her health. "Look at the colour of you," said Delilah. "Milk-white, pinched and drawn, and staring eyes. Go back to your old friends and sit in the sun."

"I like my new friends," she said. "I've never had friends I like better. I can stand on the doorstep in my dressing gown and watch the world go by. In Hong Kong they open the hotel door for me and I wear gloves and a hat to keep my English skin milk-white. Like my grandmother."

"But you're not recovering. Not like us at your age. Gave thanks when it happened. Better than back streets and penny royal."

"Don't. Please."

"I'm sorry, Elisabeth. Dexter and I had none and we never felt the loss. We had each other. And work."

Elisabeth drifted in her narrow garden. She didn't go out into the beautiful Regency crescents and squares behind Mozart Electrics towards Knightsbridge and Hyde Park, where the war-torn houses were being returned to their natural composure. Old cottages built for nineteenth-century artisans and mews houses and stables for grooms and horses round Chester Square were going freehold for a song. "We should buy one, I suppose," said Edward. "It might be useful." But she refused to go to look.

The streets around Victoria were full of prams. Once she took a bus to Hyde Park ("for the air," said Delilah) and there were wild rabbits in the bushes. The Peter Pan statue was being repaired in Kensington Gardens. Unchanged, the nannies in navy-blue uniform and pudding-basin hats were striding out behind baby carriages, each bearing a spotless baby. The war seemed to have made no difference. Some perambulators had crests painted on their flanks. When Elisabeth sat down on one particular park bench, two nannies approached her and one of them said, "Excuse me, but this seat is only for titled families." She walked the side streets after that but there was nothing that brought her comfort.

At last she said, "Well, I'd better go to Edward."

"You had. But I'll miss you," said Delilah. "Next time you're here you'll be laughing again. I promise. And we'll go to the music hall together and see *Late Joys*."

Without saying goodbye to anyone she picked up a note Delilah had put through her letter box, looked across at the drawn curtains of the electrician who was getting up later and later now, and stepped into the taxi for the airport. She left no message for her new Jamaican cleaner, who had saved her life, because she could not face her. Even to think of her made her cry.

It had been the cleaner's morning.

Elisabeth had, from the start, given her her own key. Singing, the young woman had come tramping up the stairs, flung open Elisabeth's bedroom door, flung in the vacuum cleaner. Then stopped. Betty in bed. Eyes black pools. Sheets to chin.

"I'm losing the baby."

"God a mercy! Where gone the doctor?"

"He came but he went. We've been expecting this. Things

began to go wrong two weeks ago. He's coming back. He didn't think it'd happen yet. Well—I *suppose* he's coming back."

"And sir? Does sir know?"

"I phoned."

"When you phone, ma'am?"

"An hour ago. He's busy. He's finishing a set of papers."

The woman plunged at the bedside telephone. Then she was yelling from the window on the street. Then she was calling from the back window on the gardens where Delilah was regarding her flowers. Then she was boiling water. Then she was propping open the street door with the bicycle so that the ambulance men could run straight through. She had found a chamber pot with roses painted round it and set it by the bed, soothing Betty and telling her it would soon be over now.

"It's coming in waves," said Betty. "It's like labour. Like they told us in the classes. Maybe I'm full-term? Maybe I'm just having a baby?"

"No, ma'am," said the cleaner.

"Hold my hand," said Betty.

"Give me this Chambers number. Right. Now then. Mr. Feathers, this is your cleaner speakin'. You get you skinny arse home. Here. Now."

A scuffle of people at the street door. The cleaner shouting down the stairs. A scream from the bed.

"Don't look, don't look," Betty shouted to the cleaner. "It's all over. It's in the . . ." and she screamed again. "Get the dog out! The bloody dog." It was Delilah's dog. A daily visitor. It sniffed the air. Then fled.

"It's the dog of the rat!" And she fainted. As she fainted she saw the little sliver of life slopped wet in the chamber pot. It had beautiful miniature hands.

Edward was too late to see. And too late to see her, for she had been taken off on a stretcher. Neighbours stood about the open door watching the arrival of the doctor, and the cleaner roaring at him. Edward had walked from the tube station, bringing with him his heavy briefcase to finish his work at home.

At the hospital they wouldn't let him see her.

CHAPTER EIGHTEEN

A decade or so on, in their golden house in the row of judges' houses on the Peak, protected from the world which he was paid to judge and in which Elisabeth worked all the time with her charity work, certain friends would occasionally touch on the Feathers' childlessness. Betty, so fond of children—what a shame—etc. Betty had grown expert in her replies.

"Oh, I don't know. I don't think either of us was very child-minded. We knew nothing of children. We'd never had brothers or sisters ourselves. Poor Filth was a Raj orphan, you know. My parents died very young, too. We were ignorant."

"You've had a wonderful marriage."

"It's not over yet, thank you."

(Ha, ha, ha.)

"You must have been a child yourself, Betty, when you married. So young."

"Yes," Elisabeth always said, "I was."

Hong Kong had embraced her again, wrapping her in its dazzle and warmth and noise: the smells of her childhood, the food of her childhood, the lack of false sentiment of her childhood. They took a furnished apartment on the Mid-levels and women friends came round for drinks and chat at lunchtime, and they went shopping with her in the blinding light of the big stores. She bought embroidered pillowcases and guest towels. She grew languid and lazy, and drifted away from Amy. Someone said that she should take up Bridge.

"Take her out of herself," said a Scottish banker's wife to the wife of an English judge. "Who hasn't had a mis?"

The other woman said that she had to drive up into the New Territories and Betty could come too.

"I'm looking for a rocking horse," she said.

"A *rock*ing horse?"

"The grandchildren want one. We'll get it shipped home. They're twenty-five pounds in Harrods and these are just as good. There's an old chap up there somewhere who makes them. They look a bit oriental but that's part of the fun. He sells them unpainted but then we could stipulate."

"You mean stipple them? I don't think . . ."

"No, no—we could tell him what we want. A bay or a grey. That sort of thing. I'll ask the grandchildren in Richmond Gate what they'd like."

"Is it tactful? Children's toys? If we're taking Betty?"

"Oh, come on. She's got to get over this and have another."

So they set off into the New Territories in a smart little car, Betty smoking Piccadilly cigarettes. The city did not disappear so much as change and become a canyon between concrete cliffs of new housing for city workers. "Further than this?" said the judge's wife looking at the map. "I've never been as far as this. Oh yes, here's that little temple. In those trees. Shall we go in? Have a breather?"

It was midday and very hot. The courtyard of the temple was silent, its surrounding trees unmoving. There was no chatter of birds. On the temple steps a dead-looking dog lay like dried-out leather, one lip lifted as if in disdain. In the courtyard in front of the steps sat two old men at a table. They wore traditional black tunics and trousers, and one had a pigtail and a wisp of beard. They were playing chess under the

trees and all was black and white except for the bold red lacquer of the soaring temple. Occasionally a grey leaf detached
itself from the trees and fell about the chess players like pale
rain.

"Well! You'd have thought they might have stood up," said
the banker's wife, "as we went past. And I don't like the look
of that dog. It's ill."

"It's hot," said Elisabeth. "It's having its siesta like the
whole of Hong Kong. Except us. And the chess players."

"Well, don't go near it. A bite could kill. Oh, look here!
This is monstrous!"

The temple steps were cracked and littered with papers and
Coca-Cola cans, and the portico broken. The figures of the
Buddha inside, arms raised, more than life-sized, were thick
with dust. At a desk to one side, presumably selling things, a
heavy girl lay sprawled asleep, head on arms. Her desk was
thick with dust and dust seemed to emanate from the walls and
ledges high above, resting on all the carvings like snow. The
girl opened her eyes and made a half-hearted move to get up.

"Look here," said the judge's wife. "This won't do. What
sort of impression does this make on the tourists?"

"Well, it's very Chinese, Audrey."

"Not New Territories Chinese. It's all very well sending people to prison for graffiti on the new tower blocks where nobody
goes except the workforce, but what about our own image
here? This temple is in the guidebooks. Everyone comes."

"There don't seem to have been many recently," said Elisabeth.

"I'm not surprised," said Audrey and began to harangue
the girl in execrable Cantonese. The girl drooped again, but
said nothing.

"I think we should report this. I really do. Betty, have a
word with Edward. I'll speak to Ronnie. We'll see they hear
about it in Government House. It isn't fitting."

"But it's their religion," said Elisabeth. "It's nothing to do with us. Perhaps dust doesn't matter to Buddhists."

"Oh, but it's more than dust. It is slovenly."

"And neglected," said the banker's wife.

"It's theirs to neglect, I suppose," said Elisabeth. "If they wish to."

"Hong Kong is still ours to administer," said Audrey, and Elisabeth walked away, handing some dollars to the girl as she passed. The girl was pregnant.

Elisabeth went down the temple steps, stopping to stroke the dog, and her eyes were full of shame and tears as she stood in the glaring courtyard looking across at the chess players.

There was now a third man pondering the board. He was standing facing her, a blond European, dressed in khaki shirt and shorts, and when he looked up and across at her she saw that it was Veneering.

The querulous voices of the women floated out from the temple behind her and she walked forward across the court-yard towards Veneering's beckoning arm. He put his hand on her shoulder and said, "Come with me. There are some seats lower down in the trees," and they dropped down to a wooded track, passing the old men by. The old men did not stir.

There was a red-painted bench and they sat down and Veneering said, "*Whatever* are you doing out here?"

"I'm on the way to buy a rocking horse."

They looked at each other for a minute or more and Veneering said, "I heard that you have been ill."

"Yes. The rocking horse is not for us. It's for one of the others. She's a granny."

"Then she should have had the tact not to bring you."

"She's one for soldiering on. Getting over things. Following the flag."

"She sounds like my son Harry. He's a blimp."

"How is he?"

Veneering smiled and said, "Skiving off cricket. Says he has a limp. I've told him to go running. He'll get to Eton all right. Probably be a scholar."

"Is he happy?"

"Oh, Harry's always happy."

They fell silent and Elisabeth said, "I didn't know you played chess."

"It's just to keep up with Harry in the holidays."

"Does Elsie . . . ?"

He gave her a look.

"Give Harry my love," she said. "Is Elsie . . . ?"

"It's Saturday. She's at the racecourse. Elisabeth, are you going to live here always with Edward?"

"Why?"

"Because if you are I'll have to go. I'm going to apply for a judgeship in Singapore. Hong Kong, the English Bar here—it's too small."

She said nothing for a long time and then they heard the women coming back down the steps of the temple and passing by them through the courtyard above.

"I want to go back to London now," she said. "I was so happy there after the—honeymoon."

"And Edward?"

"Who knows where Edward is happy? He belongs to Asia. He was born here."

"So they tell me. Betty, we can't go on. Both of us living here. You look so ill. So sad."

"We may change."

"Don't be ridiculous."

"And I will never leave Edward. I must go. They're shrieking about, looking for me."

"Give me your London number."

"It's—we're—in the phone book. Don't ring me."

She ran up the track and joined the other women in the car.

"Elisabeth!—Where were you? You look exhausted."

"Just wandering about."

They roared off, erratic and talkative, towards the rocking-horse maker.

E lisabeth began to be elusive. She was not seen at anything. She sat staring out to the harbour below and said
very little. "You're not picking up," Edward said one
evening at the Repulse Bay Hotel where he'd taken her for dinner, the stars and moonlight magnificent. "Betty, they're telling
me you are ill."

"Who?"

"Well, Willy and Dulcie, among others."

"And are you worried?"

"I want you to see a doctor. Have a check-up. You were
told to go back to a hospital in three months."

"Was I?"

"You were. When they let you travel out here with me, you
promised to see someone. They said the medicine here is very
good. Well, we all know it is."

"Oh, I'm just low."

"I know. You are bound to be. It will take time. They told
me you would need—er—cherishing."

"And do you cherish me, Edward?"

"Well, I try. You frighten me these days, Elisabeth. I—well,
I still can't"—the stutter threatened—"quite get over my luck
in having you. All the time."

"Edward, how sweet!"

He looked at her. Watched for a sneer. Betty—sneering!

"Well, as a matter of fact, I'm scared of losing you," he said.

One day, while he was at work, she rang up Amy who said, "Come over."

"Could you come here, Amy? It's not easy for me," and Amy soon—though not as soon as she would have done once—arrived, and without a child in tow. They sat in Elisabeth's smart sitting room with drinks.

Amy said, "You're drinking whisky."

"Yes."

"In the morning."

"Yes. It's for the pain."

"What pain?"

"Well, if you want to know, I'm bleeding. Most of the time."

"You're *what*?! Great heavens, I'm taking you straight to the hospital. Now!"

"Oh, it's all right. I've always had trouble. For years after the Camp. There was nothing for years. Nobody menstruated. Then with me it began to go the other way. Embarrassing. Scarcely stopped. One of the pleasures of pregnancy was the relief from it."

"Does Edward know?"

"Of course not. I don't think he's ever heard of menstruation. We sleep apart now, mostly."

"But someone . . ."

"No. I'd probably have told Delilah. But you know we *don't* talk about it, do we? Look at novels."

"Be damned to novels, you're seeing a consultant."

"Well, let's keep it from Edward."

"Not on your nelly," and she rang Edward to say she had made an appointment with a mainland-Chinese gynaecologist. Edinburgh-trained.

"Ah, Edinburgh-trained. That sounds very good, Edinburgh." (The Scot speaking, though he had never been to Scotland.) "I perhaps should go with her?" he said faintly.

"I don't want him," said Elisabeth.

But the consultant thought otherwise and, after X-rays and examinations, telephoned Edward to tell him that he was to come with his wife to the hospital and bring with him a decent bottle of wine.

He told Edward that Elisabeth needed surgery. There was every sign of trouble. He believed that a complete hysterectomy might be necessary.

"But I'm not even thirty. I'm childless. *No!*"

"You've put your body—no, history has put your body—through hard times. You were half starved in the Internment Camp. And I believe you lost your parents?"

"Yes. It was all jolly rotten." (Who is this speaking through my lips?) "But I'm basically strong as a pit pony. Well, I *look* like a pit pony, don't I?"

Nobody laughed.

"Think about it. I can do the operation here or I can send you to the best people in London. No, no—not Edinburgh. Too far from home. Your friends will be in London."

"But Edward's in the middle of an Arbitration."

"Think about it. But not for long. You should have it done *now.*"

Edward said, clearing his throat in his embarrassed and famous roar, "Are you suggesting this might be cancer?"

"It's possible. I'll leave you to talk it over. Oh, dear—oh, hold on . . ."

Edward was gripping the edge of the doctor's desk and sliding to the floor.

"For heaven's sake!" Betty was holding him up in her arms and glaring at the doctor. "Open the wine," she said. "Have you a corkscrew? Then you shouldn't have told us to bring it. Water, please."

Amy was breastfeeding the newest child when Elisabeth arrived, the previous baby now crawling about and heaving itself up on supporting objects such as Mrs. Baxter's difficult leg. Mrs. Baxter was deep in a missal.

"Don't worry about her," said Amy. "She's not listening. Let me think."

Elisabeth took the child on her lap. "All I need to decide," she said, "is whether to get it done here or in London."

"Oh, London," said Amy. "No question. You'd be O.K. here but they're better with Chinese than European cancers. There are different treatments. Look—go home at once, have it done, and let Edward fly back to see you when the thing adjourns. When is it? Within a month?"

"Yes. He's in a bit of a state. He doesn't speak."

"Well, he'll be in a worse state if you go into hospital here. He'll have to be coming to see you every day from the other side of Kowloon. Maybe for two or three weeks. He'll concentrate better if you're far away."

"D'you think so? Edward can always concentrate."

"Yes, I do think so. And we'll all look after him."

"You mean I just buy myself an air ticket and turn up in the Westminster Hospital all by myself?"

"Certainly. Why ever not? The bloke here will send them your medical records. What would you do if you weren't married? You'd get on with it by yourself."

"Yes, indeed," said Mrs. Baxter, waking up. "You must now be the Bride of Christ."

"I always think that sounds blasphemous. And silly," said Elisabeth.

"Well, Christ would say get on with it. Trust me," said Amy. "Think of the woman with the issue of blood for twelve years. Trust. You'll be rewarded."

"Reward?" said Mrs. Baxter. "Is there any reward? I'm beginning to doubt it."

"Oh, Mrs. Baxter, do shut up."

"*I am lonely and bored,*" intoned Mrs. Baxter. "*Reassure me, Good Lord.*"

"Mrs. Baxter!"

"*And inform me about it. Is there any reward? I'm beginning to doubt it.* Poor child, poor child," she said. "And scarcely left the altar."

Elisabeth and Amy began to laugh. "Wherever did you get that awful verse? This isn't a tragedy."

"Not yet," said Mrs. Baxter.

It was from the moment of laughing that Elisabeth knew that she would recover. The knowledge that she would never have children lay deeper and she did not, presently, disturb it. Taking one thing at a time.

CHAPTER TWENTY

The haemorrhaging that had been heavy but monthly had become fortnightly and then almost continuous so that she travelled to London first class. She spent many of the fourteen hours' flight in the aircraft toilet to the distress of other passengers.

On landing, things let up for a while. The car that Edward had ordered was waiting for her and she was back in the embrace of the little house in Ebury Street within two hours of landing. Flowers had been sent by Edward and arranged on the black table by Delilah, with trailing leaves and swatches of blood-red roses falling like a ballerina's bouquet. There was food in the fridge, a bottle of wine, the bed made up. She rang the hospital, which expected her the day after tomorrow. "You need to settle after the journey," said the Almoner. "And well done."

The phone rang and it was Edward. The familiar lovely voice, the familiar understatements. Case going well. Missing her. Desmond and Tony taking him out to dinner. Very civil of them. Amy had rung. He had forgotten to ask Betty if she had enough money.

"Yes. And I have forgotten to remind you that before long, I shall be thirty and come into my inheritance."

He was not interested and only said several times how much he felt he should be with her. But his voice did not convince.

The haemorrhaging came and went. She had begun to get

used to it. She'd be glad to be rid of the whole beastly business. Blood, blood. Women and blood. The "blood line." Lady Macbeth. The phone rang again and it was Delilah next door. Should she come round? "No. Sleep's what I want," said Elisabeth lying down on the bed.

But sleep is no part of jet lag, and blood and sleep are not good bedfellows. "Oh, dear God," she prayed in the beautiful plain bedroom with its lime-washed walls. "Maybe I'd better ask them if I can go in now." Tears came. "Dear God—oh, it sounds like a letter—dear God, I can't suffer any more. No child will come out of this. I'm suffering more than if it was labour, and nothing at the end of it."

The phone by the bedside rang and it was Veneering, in Hong Kong. "You went Home then. Someone said so. Thank God. Look—Elisabeth, there is a very bad thing."

"What? Edward? Not Edward, oh, God, no. No, we just spoke."

"It's Harry. My son, Harry," and the line fell silent. At last, when it revived, Veneering was in mid-sentence: ". . . operate tonight."

"I missed that. The phone cracked up. What's happening?"

"Harry is very seriously ill. They've just had the X-ray of his leg. His femur. He's been limping . . ." The voice faded again.

"Yes? Terry?"

"The school had him to the local hospital and the X-rays show . . ." Emptiness again. Then "show a hole in the femur the size of a hen's egg. The leg is on a thread. It's about to break. They want to operate tonight."

"Tonight! Tonight? Where?"

"In south-west London. It's not far from you. It's a small hospital and there'll be a bed for you there. In Harry's room. It's the hospital this man likes—he's said to be the best surgeon in the world: but they always say that—it's where he likes to operate. I'll give you the number. The Housemaster's taking

Harry in now and he'll stay until you come. He said he'd stay all the time, but was there somebody closer? I can't get there until tomorrow. I'm taking the first plane out. Will you go? Just be there during the operation?"

"Yes."

"It's a miracle you're back in London. It was just the slightest hope. I had to ring. Yet I was sure you were in Hong Kong."

"Tell me exactly where and when. I'll phone the school now."

"He loves you, Betty."

"And Elsie—?"

"Oh, she's coming over, too. The day after me."

"I'll go at once. I'll try to be there ahead of him."

"I love you, Betty."

Ordering the taxi, scrabbling in her still-packed luggage for night things—medication, sanitary towels, sponge bag—she found that the haemorrhaging had stopped and she no longer felt ill. She thought of the woman in the Gospel whose issue of blood of twelve years had stopped as she touched Christ's garment so that he felt faint with the love she had drained from Him. Christ understood women. He romanticised nothing.

She arrived at the little hospital near Barnes Common ahead of Harry, and was told to wait in the room they were to share until he went down to theatre. Someone came in and asked her to go to see the surgeon who was standing in his consulting room examining X-rays, slotting them up on a wall against lights.

"Ah, come in and look at these, Mrs. Veneering. Good afternoon."

"No, I'm not a relation, just a close friend. I'm sorry. I'm a bit squeamish. I can't look. The father will soon be here. I'm so sorry."

"Don't be squeamish. By tomorrow this X-ray will be far out of date."

He flung down into a pedestal chair that began to revolve, this way and that. The music goes around and around, she thought. But no, it does not. The end is silence.

The surgeon stretched out his legs and rested his heels on a window ledge, the back of his head towards her. They both stared at the sun setting over Barnes Common.

"Mrs. Veneering"—she thought: Oh, let it go—"Mrs. Veneering, we shan't know that this is cancer until I have seen it with my eyes, but when I do, I shall know at once. The cyst seems to have sharp sides to it. Cancer usually has a woolly edge. A turbulent look. I believe that there is just a hope that this is not cancer and if not I shall go on at once to fill the cavity with bone chips which we'll take from another part of Harry's body where we hope they will coagulate. The cavity is very big. The operation to fill it will take most of the night. The longer you wait the more hopeful you can be. If I come to see you quickly it will mean that it is bad news and we shall be stitching him up at once. Then you and I and Mr. Veneering will talk together about the next step."

"You mean there might be an amputation?"

"Oh, we won't talk about that now."

"If it is cancer, how long will Harry live?"

"About eighteen months."

"Does Mr. Veneering know?"

"Yes. We spoke. But you will know the diagnosis before he does, as we are not able to reach him during the flight from Hong Kong. I want you, please, to stay here until he comes."

"Well, yes. Of course."

"You'll be in Harry's room and we'll see that you have supper. Don't drink any alcohol. It does not help."

"Thank you."

They shook hands and she said to him, "How do you manage?" and his glance moved away from her and he began to straighten the pages on his desk.

"How do *you* manage?" he said. "As a parent?"

When she got back to the room with the two beds there was Harry sitting waiting with his Housemaster from school. He was bright-eyed and making jokes, and when she came in he leapt to his feet and flung his arms round her neck.

"If it isn't Mrs. Raincoat! Why ever are you here?"

"Your father sent me my orders."

"He does have a cheek, my dad. I'm glad you're here, though. There's a great do on about my leg."

"He's worried."

"He's crazy. I'm fine. I mean, they're not going to cut it *off*. Goodbye, sir. Thank you for bringing me in. Sorry. I'm fine with Mrs. Raincoat."

"Your old nanny?"

"No," said Elisabeth. "But don't be embarrassed. It's been said before."

"The school will be in touch all the time. You have the number?"

"I'll stay until Harry's father arrives."

"Goodbye then, Veneering. Good luck. We'll be saying our prayers for you in Assembly."

"It must be bad, then," said Harry. "That'll make them sit up. I'll be playing cricket again next season, sir. That'll disappoint them."

"He got out pretty quick, didn't he? Was he glad to see you! Hey, Raincoat, what's it all about?"

"We'll know in the morning. Your father will be here. He's flying over now and I'll be standing by till he arrives."

"Staying *here*? In the hospital? You must all be nuts."

"Yes. I am, anyway. Now, be quiet and say your prayers.

Here are a lot of people and a trolley, and they'll take you down to start things off any minute."

"They're coming to take me away, tra-la," said Harry. "Goodbye. See you tomorrow, Raincoat."

She left him being told to take off his shoes and she walked down the long green corridor towards the glass doors and the canteen and the trivial world. She took some food and coffee and sat down with it and looked at it. Then she got up and walked out of the hospital into the Upper Richmond Road where the people were tramping or driving or walking or biking about, and the grit was blowing in their faces. When she got back to the room it was empty and Harry's bed had only a sheet on it. Hers was turned down neatly for the night. The hospital was quiet and she felt light, without sensation or presence, and sat down on the basket chair that faced the door.

A nurse put her head round it, her face trying to disguise her pity with a smile that showed huge teeth. There was a row of the ugly new biro pens along her starched top pocket.

"There you are, Mrs. Veneering. All right? Harry is in theatre now and I expect you'd like a cup of tea."

"No, thank you," and she sat staring at the closed door asking God for the operation to be the long one. The long, exhausting, difficult, delicate one that would ensure that he would live for more than eighteen months.

"If I come to speak to you within the first hour," he had said, "that will be bad news."

Dear God. Please do not let me hear him coming within the first hour. Please let me wait all night long before I hear the sound of his feet. Tell me then how to bear the waiting. She listened and in minutes heard the sound of his feet.

It was at that moment, very early morning in Kai Tak, that Amy woke up and began thinking about Elisabeth. She should now be safely in London, resting from the journey before going into the hospital on Wednesday.

Should she ring? All of three pounds? And it might upset Bets if she thought that Amy was nervous about her. Amy the strong? Or it might wake her up just as she'd got to sleep after a long flight.

But yes. Amy would ring.

In Ebury Street, opposite Mozart Electrics, the phone rang and rang and was not answered. Well, then, Amy would ring Edward before he left the Peninsular Hotel for the Arbitration and send love, and hope that all was well. Edward said: Yes, all was perfectly well. He had spoken to Betty just after she arrived home and she was going to be resting all day and tomorrow. Perhaps it would be best not to bother her, for she had sounded perfectly normal. Yes—a very good journey. Thank you, Amy!

Hmmh!

Then Isobel Ingoldby rang Amy in Kai Tak. Isobel was in Singapore but she knew all about Elisabeth. She'd been trying to telephone her in London, but no reply. Had Amy any news?

"No. And it's odd she doesn't answer," said Amy who had tried again. "What about the neighbour? Shall I ring her? She's called Da-lilah Dexter, if you can believe. I could get her through International Enquiries."

"I have her number," said Isobel. "If I don't ring you back it means that all's well."

In half an hour Isobel rang Amy back. "The Dexter saw her leaving the house just after she arrived home. She had an overnight bag with her and got into a taxi. She didn't say good-bye to anyone and she left the front door wide open. No, she *isn't* at the Westminster Hospital. I rang it. She's expected there tomorrow. Look, I shouldn't worry. She'll be staying with a friend or something."

"I might just ring Edward again. I could go round to the

Arbitration," said Amy. "Or I could try to speak to the solicitor, the demon dwarf. He knows everything. Albert Ross. He's probably sitting in the Arbitration rooms."

Isobel said, "Well, be careful. He doesn't like Betty. He's bonded to Teddy with hoops of steel. He's frightening."

"To hell with that," said Amy and left a message at the Arbitration for Albert Ross to ring her at lunchtime. Ross did not ring.

She rang again and said that she was unhappy about her friend—her *school*-friend—Mrs. Feathers—who seemed to have disappeared from her London address. Ross did not call back.

At last she lost patience, phoned Nick to come home from work, left all the children except the baby with Mrs. Baxter, and turned up outside the conference room of the hotel where the Arbitration was being held and marched in.

The room was empty.

She sat down for a minute in the cigarette smoke. There were ashtrays and a few scattered pens, and a disquiet in the air. Then she flung off again to the hotel's reception desk.

"They have adjourned," said the concierge. "The Counsel for the contractors has had to fly suddenly to London. Illness. A child."

"Good heavens! Mr. Feathers? But I spoke to him today."

"No, Mr. Feathers is for the architects. This is Mr. Veneering. Would you like to speak to Mr. Feathers's instructing solicitor? He could tell you more. He is somewhere about."

"No. Thank you. It's rather confusing. This is all to do with *Mrs.* Feathers. It's nothing to do with Mr. Ross."

"Ah, but it is," said Ross behind them, and she turned and saw that he was seated in the foyer, his legs stuck out before him showing the soles of his tiny feet, his great head a sort of centrepiece to the mound of orchids and potted palms arranged on the marble floor. His hat lay beside him.

Ross did not look up from his playing cards as she walked across to him, the baby on her hip, and, still without looking at her, he said, "Mrs. Feathers has gone off with Mr. Veneering. Mr. Feathers does not know. I know, but no one else knows. I shall see that the matter is resolved. Mr. Feathers will *never* know, and if you or Miss Isobel Ingoldby ever let him know, I will break you. Is that clear? I will break you both."

CHAPTER TWENTY-ONE

I f I come to speak to you within the first hour of the operation," the surgeon had said, "That will be to bring bad
news. I have to make this clear. You do understand?"
"Yes."

It was hardly half an hour since they had brought her tea
and told her that the operation had begun when she heard the
swing doors slam-bang at the end of the corridor and feet running.

Of course the feet need not be his. Harry could not be the
only patient in this silent little hospital. The feet were running.
It could be anyone. But the feet stopped outside her door. And
at the same moment she realised that the feet had been *running*. Nobody runs to break bad news. The feet had been *running*!

She stood up and a man opened the door clumsily, pushing
it with his shoulder. He had a turban of dark green cloth round
his head and a green apron tied about with tapes. He was holding up his hands and arms at right-angles from the elbow as if
he were a priest at votive offering. Or maybe a janitor. There
was a smell of disinfectant.

The eyes, however, were the surgeon's eyes, very bright. He
said, "Mrs. Veneering, all is well. All will be perfectly well,"
and was gone.

All she could think was: Now he will have to take all that
off and scrub up again before he can go back to do the chips

of bone. And she sat down again and looked at the closed door.

She sat on and on until someone suggested she changed into night things and went to bed. "I shan't sleep," she said, but slept almost at once.

When she woke she was in familiar trouble, gathering her towel and sponge bag and clothes, finding a bathroom. Returning, two solid young nurses were looking down at her sheets with amazement. In shame—she could not say one word to them—she went along to the duty nurse outside, and the duty nurse smiled at her.

It was the toothy nurse. "I can see into theatre from my little room," she said. "The lights were on all night. It must have been *nine hours*! I thought, "Oh, that poor boy, he's still in there. But he's alive. They'll get him back.""

"It's not, after all, cancer, nurse. Did you know?"

"Oh, we all know. Word went round. All round the hospital. We've all been thinking of you."

"Thank you."

"Mr. Veneering's just arrived. They're telling him the good news downstairs."

"Then," said Elisabeth, "I'll go. I'm not Harry's mother, nurse, but I know his father very well. They'll both be all right now. They won't need me."

At the entrance to the hospital she asked the desk to get her a taxi and kindly ring the Westminster Hospital—she gave them the correct extension—to say that she was coming in this morning, at once.

CHAPTER TWENTY-TWO

Her hysterectomy, the nurses told her the next day, had been "very necessary."

'There were pre-cancerous cells," said the surgeon. "They were in one ovary and the womb is gone too, but we have left you with the other ovary so that you won't suffer a premature menopause."

"Thank you."

"We're really delighted that you came to us so quickly. And just in time. You are young and strong, Mrs. Feathers. Is your husband about the hospital today?"

"He's about his work on the other side of the world."

"Brave girl. Brave girl."

(Oh, shut up, she thought. Meet Amy.)

"And he will soon be coming back? You are going to need a lot of care. Have you any children who could help?"

"No. I am not yet thirty."

"Oh, yes. Yes, of course. I'm sorry."

"Not as sorry as I am."

Yesterday when they returned her to the ward after the operation she had partly woken and found that she had changed sex and century. She was a man, a soldier being tipped into some sort of mass grave. She smelled the wet earth of France. When she woke much later there was sunlight all round her body, which was neatly arranged under a thick white sheet. Bouquets and clumps of flowers were all around her. I am on my catafalque. And I have woken up. How embarrassing for them. I will sit up very slowly in the middle of the service as they sing me out. Someone pushed her down against a pillow and, when she woke next, Filth was sitting by the bed, reading *The Times.* He glanced across, saw her open eyes and smiled, stretching to her hands and kissing her fingers and wrists.

"You came," she said.

And he said, "Of course. I'm going back on Monday. Short adjournment."

"You'll kill yourself. Jet lag—" and dropped asleep.

When she next woke he was asleep in the chair and she watched his peaceful face.

"He is open as the day."

"What?" he said. "What?"

"You are as open as the day."

"Why should a day be open? I've often wondered. Some days are sealed off, thanks be. I don't want to open up the day of your operation again."

"I thought of you. Now and then."

"Needless to say, the other side was to have been Veneering, but he bunked off back to London. Left his junior, a useless fellow, and I ran him into the earth in double quick time. I got here for breakfast. Saw two moons rise."

"Shall you see two more rise, going back?"

"I didn't come here to look at moons." He rested his head against their clasped hands on the bed sheet.

She said, "I'm sorry, Edward. No children now," and slept.

She woke again and he said, "D'you know, I never really wanted any children. Only you."

When she woke next he had gone, and when she left the hospital two full weeks later it was with Isobel Ingoldby.

She had found Isobel standing at the foot of the bed, tall as a camel and eating a pear.

"Home," she said. "I'm taking you."

"Oh, Lizzie. Lizzie-Izz."

"Wrap yourself up. It's turning towards autumn. Get this on over your sweater." It was a brown and gold pashmina, warm and light and smelling of spices.

The nurses were kind, full of congratulations about how well she had done. They settled her into a taxi and into the world again.

"But we're not going towards Pimlico! Lizzie, we've missed the roundabout."

"Yes."

"Izz, why aren't we going to Ebury Street?"

"Because we're going to the Temple."

"That's wrong. That's Eddie's Chambers. It's *wrong*. We have this flimsy lovely house in Ebury Street."

"Talk later," said Isobel. "I just do what I'm told. Here's the Embankment and we drive under the gateway and—my goodness! Teddy's certainly made his mark. The Inner Temple! Here's your new apartment. Gor-blimey, first floor looking at the river."

"But where's all our . . . Where's my *house*? Our white carpet? Wedding presents? What's Eddie been up to? The black chair?"

"I've no idea. There seems to be plenty still to unpack. There's a huge *red* chair, none too clean. *Superb* rooms! However did he get them? Rooms in the Temple are like gold. Oh, well, I suppose he is made of gold now. Mr. Midas."

Elisabeth walked to the window and looked across the river at the rising post-war blocks of cement.

She said, "What's happened to them? They'll have got bread and milk in for me, and ordered the papers. They'll worry."

"Hush. Too soon."

"Tell me."

"No. Well, oh, all right. Ebury Street is being pulled down.

The hospital knew but didn't want to tell you. You said it was fragile. All the bombing . . ."

"Pulled down! No! Not in three weeks."

"No. Not yet. But they've started demolition at the Victoria end. They said—your pals—"Don't let her come back." They've mostly been rehoused already."

"What about Mozart Electrics? Across the road?"

"Someone told me—I went round there—that he's gone into a home. Very crippled."

"And Delilah? And the butler? And the greengrocer?"

"The greengrocer's gone to Lowestoft. I found the building firm. Teddy had organised the furniture to come here to the Temple and they gave me a key to have a look around. I collected your post off the floor."

Elisabeth stood watching the river for some silent minutes and said, "Well, he's taken everything from me now."

"Oh," said Isobel. "*No*! Poor Teddy! And working like hell."

"He could have told me."

"He was told not to upset you. The Chambers know. They'll be coming. He arranged everything, except me. He doesn't know we know each other—remember?"

"Yes. But I forget why."

"Don't think too hard. Listen, you're going to have help here—shopping and ironing and so on."

"You are *crowing*!"

"Why? *Crowing*? Me?"

"Because I shouldn't have married him. You said so."

"God's truth!" shouted Isobel. "I traipse round builders, I look up neighbours, I get your post, I fetch you home . . ."

Elisabeth turned back to the river and said, "Had they started the demolition?"

"Yes. The bank on the corner has closed and the little paper shop, and there's scaffolding up. At the back in those gardens . . ."

"Yes?"

"They were chopping down the trees. Listen, get Teddy home and stop crying. You're menopausal."

"I can't. I'm not. I'm rational and sad," she said.

"Then go off with bloody Veneering! I can't do more," and Isobel slammed away.

Elisabeth walked to another window in the new lodgings, to try to see Lizzie cross the Temple yard towards the alley to the Strand and the Law Courts. It was very quiet in the new apartment that was presumably now her home. She saw that there were flowers in cellophane with cards pinned to them, a pile of letters on a desk. She looked in the one small bedroom with two single beds, fitted end to end. A midget kitchen and a bathroom made for giants, with a bath on feet. And silence. Silence from the corridor outside and the scene below, and from the uncaring river.

She thought: I'm on an island in an empty sea. I'm cast away. Her legs felt shaky and she sat down trying to remember that being alone was what most of the world found usual. She thought that in childhood she'd been in crowded Tiensin, a crowd of Chinese servants day and night. In the Shanghai Camp, people and people, a slot in a seething tent; my hand always held by my mother, or riding on my father's back. The crowded ship to England, the crowded London school, the crowds of students at her all-women Oxford college, the return to Hong Kong and the infrastructure of Edward's world. Now this solitude. Double-glazed silence. I suppose I must just wait. It's the anaesthetic still inside me. I have memory so I must still be here. I have nobody, but I have memory. There was a knock on the door.

But the door of the apartment seemed a mile away and she could not move. She stared at the door and willed it to open of its own accord and after a moment it did, and Albert Ross walked in.

"No! Get out! Go away!"

He took off the broad brown hat and sat down on the red chair and looked at her from across the room.

"Go away. I hate you."

He twirled his shoes, regarded them and, without looking at her, said, "I've come to apologise. I dealt you the Five of Clubs. It was a mistake. I seldom make a mistake and I have never apologised for anything before, being of a proud nature."

She watched him.

"The Five of Clubs means 'a prudent marriage not for love.'"

She watched him.

"I am very much attached to your husband. I saw only your faithlessness. It affected the pack. I was wrong."

"You were always wrong. You stole his watch once."

He became purple in the face with rage and said, "Never! He gave it to me when I had nothing. It was all he possessed. He trusted me. It was to save my life."

"You are cruel!"

"Here is a telephone number you must ring. It will be to your advantage."

"I don't need your help."

He sighed and put out a hand to his hat and she thought, He may have a knife. He could kill me. He is a troll from a stinking pit.

But he brought out of the hat only the pack of cards, looked at it, then put it away.

"This is a transition time for you. You still don't see your way. This telephone number is from someone who cares about you. Her name is Dexter," and he put a visiting card on the table and was gone.

A dream, she thought.

She did not move, but slept for a minute or perhaps an

hour, then crossed to the table where there was no visiting card. She searched everywhere, under the table, even along the passage outside the door. Nothing.

Then the telephone rang and a voice said, "Might I have the honour of addressing Mrs. Edward *Feathers*?"

"Delilah!"

"Aha," said the familiar phantom voice. "Seek and ye shall find! I am speaking from the West Country. From Dorsetshire. England."

"Dorset?"

"You will remember that we have our country estate in Dorset? Well, it is, by some, designated 'country cottage.' Now that we have been cast out of our London home we have taken refuge in it."

"But where exactly, Delilah?"

"Well, we are not *exactly* on the estate, but some fifty miles away in the fine city of Bath where mercifully Dexter has been granted God's gift of *The Admirable Crichton*."

"Who—?"

"The *comedy* of that name written in honour of the immortal figure of the English butler. Second only to the incomparable *Jeeves*. Five performances a week plus matinées, good cheap theatrical lodgings thrown in. Alas, however, he is in at the final curtain every night and grows a little wearier each day."

"Oh, Delilah!"

"But we find ourselves affluent, well-housed, awaiting the compensation for our London home. Our country property is deserted. We hear that you are recovering from surgery and our little empty dacha in the woods awaits you, if you would like to stay in it. For ever if you like."

"*Like to!*"

"It is yours to use as long as you like. I am in touch with dear Eddie's clerk. He will make all the arrangements. Why do you weep?"

"With joy and disbelief. Oh, Delilah, it's like a musical!"

"There is, I fear, no music at our dacha," she said, "except the music of the rooks and the morning chorus of a myriad other species of feathered creature; the pizzicato of the rain and the crashing tympani and singing strings of the west wind. There's no electricity, dear, no running water and no abominable telephone."

"Oh, it's *not* abominable! How else could we be talking?

"Milk and bread are delivered daily to the lane—a little climb up from the back of the house. Also the daily papers. You can give them lists of groceries and you will pay in the basket provided before you go home. No one will disturb you. Dexter has a splendid theatrical library, if a trifle damp, and there is the evening softness of lamplight."

"Delilah—I'm a bit potty at the moment. I've had surgery and I'm still full of anaesthetic. I've just had a hallucination. Is this another?"

"Hallucination, dear? No. Hallucination demands vision. Nor am I an aural manifestation. The return fare from Waterloo to Tisbury Junction is modest and you will be met. Contact Eddie's clerk. Bring a wrap for the early mornings so that you can walk in the dew. And an insect repellent. You will be quite alone."

"Are we going to meet there, Delilah—dear, beloved Delilah? I'm so bloody lonely."

"Very good for you, dear. And I hardly think we'll meet. My duties to Dexter are very onerous. He sends his love. We shall possibly meet again one day, of course. These things may happen. I don't suppose"—her voice trailed away to nothing, then came back like a thread on a lute string—"you've heard anything about the gardens? They haven't cut them down, have they? My London forest trees?"

She said, "No, no. I'm sure not," and the line clicked shut.

But the phone number? She couldn't call Delilah back. She must telephone Chambers. She must think of timetables on the Southern Railway. She must make lists of supplies. She must phone Edward. She must think of supper.

In the fridge she found milk and food, and on the table yet another bouquet of flowers from Edward and a note from the Inn with the times of Sunday services at the Temple church. Then the phone began to ring again and again, friends from near and far. The world grew smaller and smaller and so crammed with kind enquiries that she left the receiver off. Kind and rowdy, the city surged up to her from the river and the Embankment and the Strand, rich and glorious. Tomorrow she would be coping with rooks.

Then she saw, in the mail on the desk, a packet from Hong Kong lying beside the cards and she took it across the room and slowly and carefully opened it. Inside was a short double string of pearls with a diamond clasp and a note saying, *He is better. He will live. Return these at your peril. For ever V. PS: Where did you go?*

CHAPTER TWENTY-THREE

It was a train ride of pure celebration. A train ride like
childhood's. Edward's Chambers saw her on to the platform and right into the reserved seat for Tisbury Junction.
The clerks gave her chocolates and told her that there would
be a taxi waiting. At Tisbury she climbed out upon the single-
track platform and sat on a seat in the sun and, like an old film,
a man came along and said in a country voice, "Taxi, ma'am?
Let me take your case."

He drove along the lanes and she saw a tree above a hedge
like a hen on a nest, then a long stone wall, and in a gap in the
wall she looked down upon a dell and a massive stone chimney
pot attached to something unseen. The driver and the bag
went ahead down the slope until they were on a level with the
chimney pot and looking at an almost vertical track below and
a thatched roof.

"I'll never get the case down there. This must be the back.
There must be a front way somewhere."

"What shall we do?"

"I'll have a try."

He trundled and slithered, Elisabeth following, and they
arrived at a paved yard and a back door. She paid him.

"You O.K. here, miss?"

"Yes," she said, liking the "miss." "Thank you," and leaving the luggage in the grass she went looking for the front door
where she had been told there would be a key under a mat. She
could find neither door nor key and the silent valley beyond

watched. In an outhouse which was an earth closet there was a huge black iron key and she thought she would try it in the back door, and set off further round the gentle, sleeping house and came to a front door with a Yale key in it, waiting to be turned. Inside were dark rooms and the smell of damp books. She saw furniture under dust sheets, a paraffin lamp with a cloudy globe, a box of matches alongside and a fresh loaf on the table.

It was not yet dusk and so, after standing a kettle on a black stove that seemed to be warm, she walked outside again into the garden.

It was a glade cut out from woodland. The stretch of grass that led to more faraway trees was not so much lawn as meadow where vanished trees were waiting somewhere to reclaim their home. She felt the stirring of life under the grass and saw spirals of bindweed standing several feet high seeking some remembered support. They swayed as if they were growing under water. There was nothing more, only the dwindling path, the dwindling light, the pearly quiet sky.

She returned to the house, removed the kettle, found a staircase behind a cupboard door, reached a bedroom with wooden walls and smelling of cedar trees. She opened the window and looked at the glimmer of the evening and without even a drink of water, without locking the house or turning a key or taking off her coat, she lay down on the patchwork quilt and listened to the end of the day. Soon all the small sounds stopped, and she slept.

It was an eerie dawn, blowy and cloudy, and she had no idea where she was. When she remembered, she listened for the rooks but they were silent. She was afraid for a while that yesterday's journey belonged to someone else. Then, rolling from the bed, walking to the window, she saw that this was a strange place but in some way she knew it. The window looked at a wall of vegetation so close to the glass that she could stretch and touch if she opened it. She saw the roof of a shed that must be the earth closet. Yet she had remembered golden space.

And then she remembered that she had chosen the tiny back bedroom to sleep in. The other room with its mighty feather bed had seemed too intimately a part of the Dexters' lives to disturb. She went downstairs, dragged the black kettle across the wood-burning stove until it was over the hotplate—still hot. More wood was needed and when she looked, there it was. She found a tin teapot and a tea caddy that said it was a present from Blackpool. A jug of milk stood in a bowl of water on the pantry floor. Across the top, it had a muslin cloth weighted down with little coloured beads. The pantry stones were cool under her bare feet.

She carried her tea with her towards a door—the cottage was shadowy—which she pushed open to reveal the stretch of meadow-lawn cleared from the forest. The trees around were wildly tossing and the grass was wet with dew. A fox stood still in the middle of the space, staring at her with black eyes, interested in an alteration of the scene. A dead bird hung down heavy and soft on either side of the fox's mouth. It turned tiptoe on its black feet and was gone. Then the wind dropped and lemon-coloured light soaked over the garden and the river spread wide to the horizon where above the far trees a triangle of hilltop was crowned with a knot of trees like a garland.

It was warmer now. She sat outside on the shabby wooden balcony and drank the tea. She thought of her new London home that commanded a view of a thousand nameless lives. Here she was alone of her kind. She felt perfectly happy, no more lonely than the fox, or the rabbits she began to see in the bracken, or the strutting pheasant which appeared now at her feet. No telephone would ring, no car stop on the road above, she would hear no human voice.

Amy, in her Kai Tak slum, would say, "Betty, this will not do. You need a cause." Elisabeth thought of the hollow-cheeked crowds in the stinking streets. The old man who sat with no legs, his crutches splayed across his patch of the street, breaking open crustaceans, chanting the prices, cracking the shells. Urine in the pools. "We must forget *ourselves*, Bets. Our Englishness." Amy had not been in the Camps.

She sat on, looking towards the topknot garland of the next-door village and saw to one side of her, higher up than the Dexter trees, a flicker. There must be a building up there, and her heart plunged. No—too dense. An illusion. She looked back down her vista of meadow, and two children were walking hand in hand. They paid her no attention and slipped back into the tall grass. Later, a young man crossed from one side of the garden to the other but further away. He was lean, unkempt, dark-skinned, alert and self-contained. Some sort of Gypsy. He was swinging something like an axe and did not look towards the house. She heard the distant sound of the car bringing her groceries on the road above. The rooks began their civic racket. I must decide what to do with the day, she thought. But not yet.

On the balcony was a long wooden chair with a footrest and padded cushions, and she thought: That will be damp, but lay down and found it warm and sweet-smelling, and she fell asleep again.

All week she stayed alone in the house and garden, collecting groceries from the top of the steep slope, leaving money and details of supplies for the next day. A can of soup, a piece of cheese, three apples. She worried at first about water. Someone had left out two jugs on the slab in the pantry, otherwise there was only a stream. She washed in the stream, boiled some of it, eventually drank it unboiled, catching it in a tin mug as it rushed by. She liked the earth closet. Seated there, the door wide to the view, she commanded territory crossed by Roman cohorts on the march to Salisbury.

On the third day she began to notice things to do in the garden and spent a morning getting out weeds, shouldering them in armloads to what seemed to be a compost heap. She amazed herself. She did not know where her knowledge came from. She marvelled at the rich soil—remembering the scratching in the earth by the skin-and-bone labourers in the lampshade hats of her Chinese childhood. She imagined a continuing supply of vegetables and along an old red wall a sea of European tulips. Then she remembered that this was Delilah's garden.

In the evenings, after a first attempt when black flakes flew to the ceiling and the wick roared like a petrol fire, she mastered the oil lamp and sat reading the books about old theatre productions and biographies of great actors. Sometimes, prising a book out of the damp shelves, she let loose a sheaf of theatre programmes. Some were signed flamboyantly with forgotten names, some smelled of long-dead violets. Once or twice a pressed flower fell out—a gardenia (gone brown) or a rose—and crumpled before her eyes when she tried to pick it up. Some of the books were inscribed, *To my darling Delilah, the ultimate Desdemona*, or, *To my own Mark Antony from his adoring wife* and the date of over half a century ago.

Love, thought Elisabeth. Adoration. Was it all just theatre?

CHAPTER TWENTY-FOUR

One day she woke up and forced herself to think: When am I going home?

In fact she knew the date. Somewhere it was written down, perhaps on her return railway ticket. A taxi was to pick her up that morning, to put her back on the London train. She remembered that.

But when was it? She had no way of knowing the date: no radio, no daily paper. Letters had come for her but she had not opened them and they would not have helped. She would ask the village shop to put tomorrow's newspaper in with her baked beans. They would not keep the *Telegraph* or *The Times* or the *Manchester Guardian*. Perhaps they only had the weekly local paper. She thought she'd try for the *Daily Express*. When she collected it, she found that she had only one day left. This day. The taxi would be here to take her towards London before nine o'clock tomorrow morning.

She could hardly bear it.

Suppose she ran from the house tomorrow and hid in the woods? She could creep back again in the evening? Or on another evening? She could sleep in the woods.

But then, word would go round. The village shop (wherever it was) would come making enquiries. Friends in London—Chambers—even Edward in Hong Kong.

I'm still trapped, she thought. I'll have to go.

She cleared the kitchen of the glorious squalor she had made in it. She dusted. She trimmed the lamp, thinking that there were very few people left in the world who could trim a lamp (and where had she learned? And when?). Fitting back its beautiful globe, she smashed it to pieces and was horrified. The lamplight had been the wonder of her evenings and the carrying up of the heavy lamp, one hand shading the light, to bed at night. Oh, Delilah! Oh, if there were a telephone . . .

Well, no. Thank God. And I don't know the number. I shall leave you, Delilah, a huge sum of money to replace the lamp. I shall scout the London markets for a new one.

She scrubbed the whole house clean. That evening she walked down the garden and looked at the red wall in the fading light. The rooks grumbled their way to bed.

In the morning she gathered her things together around the door and ate some bread. There was a fumbling shadow outside the window and she saw the Gypsy person ambling about outside. He was trying to look in.

"Yes?" she called, not opening the door. "Yes?" He was trailing the thing like an axe. "Who are you?"

He mouthed words at her. She thought: The poor thing's simple. But the axe made her hesitate. He was speaking of a key. He needed a key. The taxi would be coming.

"But the *axe*," she said.

"It's for the w-w-w-wood. Firewood."

She brought him in. "I'm so sorry. I was afraid of you."

Among the things she had been leaving for the Dexters were two bottles of village shop wine and she handed them now to the Gypsy. He looked bewildered so she gave him some money. He took the key and the money and went ahead of her with her case and, when she was through the front door, he locked it behind her and put the key in his pocket. He went ahead, up the steep bank through the slit in the wall, not helping her, and when she had climbed the perilous slope there was her suitcase beside the road, and he was gone.

She sat down then on a stone on the roadside, her back to

the wall. It was not yet a quarter past eight. It was beginning to be cloudy. Cloudy and wettish. England in October, although it was only September. Nobody passed by.

I had to be here for the taxi, she thought, before nine. I hadn't thought of rain. It's only eight twenty.

Out of her bag she dragged the brown and gold pashmina and wrapped it round her. When the rain began she rearranged the coloured silk to cover her head. Bright against the dark bushes she sat on in the rain and when the village shop van passed she waved, but she had paid her bill yesterday and the car went by.

Nobody came. The rain became heavier. It was after half past eight now and the wind blew the rain in surges and began to sound angry and bitter. The rain lashed back.

Elisabeth looked up the road and down it, and wondered how far it was to the village. Below her the cottage was all securely locked up. Maybe she should stumble down the slippery path again and shelter in the earth closet.

No. Ridiculous. The taxi was taking her to catch a particular train. At Waterloo Station a cab had been ordered by Edward's Chambers to take her back to the flat in the Temple. All arranged. Foolproof.

But no taxi.

I'll go and see if there *is* a house up there, she thought, and shuddered. She was frightened of houses in woods.

No. She would walk into Salisbury, carrying her suitcase. Her scar still hurt and still bled a little but she didn't care. She tightened the silk cloth about her, picked up her suitcase and heard the sound of an approaching car. Thank God! Oh, thank God!

She stood holding the suitcase as the car spun into sight and it was not a taxi, but an ordinary private car going by. It was travelling very fast and splashed past her and down the hill, and vanished round the bend in the road and was gone.

So much, she thought, for answers to prayer.

She gripped the handle of her suitcase tighter, turned to face what she hoped would be Salisbury, soaked now to the skin, and heard the same car roaring back again up the hill, so fast that she had to jump into the side of the hedge.

The car stopped, the driver's door flew open and Edward stood in the middle of the road.

Wet to the skin, enclosed in his long arms, Elisabeth began to cry and Edward to set up the curious roaring noises that had overtaken him since his stammering childhood but now only when he was on the point of tears.

She said, "Oh, Eddie! Oh, Filth!" her wet face against his clean, warm shirt.

She thought: I love him.

He said, "I thought you'd left me!"

PART FOUR

Life After Death

CHAPTER TWENTY-FIVE

S cene Hong Kong.
Crackle and swish of limousine bringing the Judge home from court at exactly the appointed hour (insert clock: 7 P.M.).

Interior. Elisabeth waiting for him in living room of Judges' Lodgings, a row of mansions behind a wall and steel gates, guarded. She has an open library book face-down upon her knee. Outside, Edward Feathers's driver rings the front-door bell.

Elisabeth counts silently. A full minute. Longer. Two minutes.

Slip-slop feet of Lily Woo from kitchen across polished hall.

Lily Woo: Good evening, sir.

Slip-slop she goes back.
Edward (Filth) takes off shoes in hall. Clonk, then clonk. Puts on house shoes left him there by Lily. We hear him go to wash in cloakroom. He opens living-room door and sees Elisabeth as ever waiting. (Pretty dress, neat hair, gold chains, perfect fingernails. She is changed.)

Filth: Gin? All well?
Elisabeth: Yes, please. And no. Not all well. Today I've
                had a revelation. I am now officially old.
Filth: Ice? Old?
Elisabeth: Yes, and yes. Today I heard myself telling

someone on the Children's Aid committee that we'd been living in Hong Kong for over twenty years and that it seems no more than about six; and where did all the years go? Saying that, I'm old.

Filth: God knows where they've gone. Into the mist.

Bell rings outside in hall. Tinkle, tinkle. It is a small brass honeymoon bell from India. Slip-slop of girl's feet again as she returns to kitchen. Filth looks into his gin and vermouth and gulps it down.

Elisabeth: You're drinking too fast. Again.

Filth: I need it. Various things. What's this, being old?

Elisabeth: I feel it. Suddenly. I'm melancholy at things changing. So, I'm old.

Filth: They need to change. It's a place of changes. Annexing Hong Kong set the scene for change at the start. It will never settle down. Never be contented. But what did we bring but good? Work. Medicine. The English language. The Christian faith. And the Law. With all its shortcomings they don't want to change the Law.

Goes over to the drinks tray.

Elisabeth: That was the dressing bell. Dinner in twenty minutes.

Filth: Or three-quarters of an hour. She's sloppy.

Elisabeth: Yes. Go on. Go up. Have a shower and change your shirt. You can have a whisky after dinner.

Scene Dining Room.

A quiet dinner. The silver and glasses are reflected in the rose-wood dining table. Lamb chops, peas, new potatoes. (Lily Woo has learned to cook them very well and sometimes it is a pleasant change from chopsticks.) English vicarage tonight.

Filth: It would be good to finish off with cheese now.

Elisabeth: It would be astonishing to finish off with cheese. There's not a speck of it in the Colony. Your mind is going!

After dinner Filth stares at tomorrow's Court papers. He goes to bed early, without the whisky. In the middle of the night Elisabeth wakes to find him in her bed, his head on her breast. She takes him in her arms.

Filth: I condemned a man to death today.

Elisabeth: I know. I saw the evening paper. Was he guilty?

Filth: Guilty as hell. It was a *crime passionel.*

Elisabeth: Then he is probably glad to die.

They lie awake for a long time. The hanging will be at eight o'clock. Elisabeth has set the bedside clock half an hour fast and seen that Lily Woo has done the same to the grandfather striking clock downstairs. They lie awake together.

Filth: Capital punishment must go.

Elisabeth: They'll take years.

Filth: They'll have their own Judiciary by then. Someone spat at the car today when I left Court. They are changing. Lily Woo took five minutes to answer the bell tonight.

Elisabeth:	No, only two. But I know what you mean. Respect is fading. Well, I don't know if it was ever there. In the jewellers', the girls hardly bother to lift their heads when I go in. They just go on threading the jade. They used to get me the best stones. They still get them for Nellie Wee.
Filth:	Oh, well. She's famous.
Elisabeth:	Well, I'm quite famous. I do my best. I try to be like Amy used to be. I *have* got the OBE. And half my girlfriends are Chinese.
Filth:	I used to say that when you were sifting through the jade in the market your eyes changed to slits and you became an Oriental.
Elisabeth:	Slits, with English eyelashes. Filth, we do need to live out here, don't we? We're life-time expats. Aren't we?

Filth (*after a long, long pause*): I don't know.

They took a holiday in a tin bus and bowled along on the Chinese mainland through Canton. For miles the road was lined with rusty factories all dropping to bits. "These were sold to us by the Russians," said their guide. "We were conned." In the shadows of the rusted chimneys lay wide stretches of murky water sometimes with lotuses. White ducks floated among the lotuses on the foul olive-green water. The road was terrible, full of gritty holes, narrow and mean. Tall factories trailed hundred-foot stripes of mould down their sides, like dark green seaweed. All the small windows were boarded up.

The bus stopped for photographs and most people got out and stood in a row looking down on men scratching the surface of fields. The cameras clicked. The men were so thin you could see their bones under their belted cotton blouses. Their hats were the immemorial lampshades, colourless and beautiful. "Make sure you get the hats in," shouted the photographers. The fieldworkers continued to drag their sticks along the soil and never once looked up.

"Do they dream of Hong Kong?" said Elisabeth.

"We don't know what they dream of."

The bus lurched on and the guide beseeched them to look to the right, at the distant and very modern restaurant where they would be stopping for lunch. "On no account look *left*. Do not *look left*."

Everybody looked left to where a ragged column of men in white robes and pointed hats jogged along the side of a field. Several of them carried a bundle tied to a pallet on long poles.

"It's a funeral," said Betty. "To see a funeral means bad luck."

"That's a Chinese funeral," shouted another tourist on the bus. "Or it's the Ku Klux Klan."

The driver rattled on down the winding road and up the track to the restaurant. Someone shouted, "Isn't it bad luck to see a Chinese funeral?"

"I saw no funeral," said the guide. "What funeral?"

A very old English couple held hands, without looking at each other. "We were born here," they said. "We've been away a long time." "I was born in Tiensin," said Betty. "I grew up in Shanghai." They looked at her and nodded acknowledgement. "We are displaced people," said the old woman and Filth said, "I suppose you didn't know Judge Willy?" "What, old Pastry? Of course we did," and they all smiled. "When Pastry Willy was born, you know, there was only one godown in Hong Kong."

The bus reached a town where they all got off and went into a big store where the tourists began to run about excitedly, buying ceramic vases and teapots and enormous electric table lamps with Chinese scenes running round them, half the price of Hong Kong and a tenth of the price of Harrods. Filth asked

Betty if they wanted a new table lamp. "No," she said, "not these," and was astonished to find that an image had appeared among the chinoiserie of a heavy brass oil lamp with a globe and chimney, and a thick white cotton wick. As she looked, the misty globe cleared and a flat blue flame appeared along the wick. It bounced up violet, then yellow, becoming steady and clear. A wisp of blue rising from the chimney. Betty stretched towards it and her hand passed through nothing.

"What are you doing?" asked Filth.

"I don't know. Having a vision or something. Some sort of memory thing. It must be because of those old expats finding their own country. Let's go back to the bus. There's absolutely nothing for us here."

Back in Hong Kong she said, "Filth—have we made up our minds? Will we be retiring here?"

He said, "I don't intend to retire at all. I've masses still to do."

"You'll soon be over seventy."

"I'm a better judge the older I get."

"You all say that."

"I'll get the hint if they want me to retire."

"So you're just going to sit in judgement in a dying colony for the rest of your life?"

"If you must know, I've been asked to take a break and write up the Pollution Laws. It will be internationally important."

"They have actually approached you, then?"

"Yes."

"Oh, well, congratulations. When would I have been told? You know what they'll say?"

"Yes. 'Filth on Filth.' I'm not stupid."

"Sometimes I think there's a wit at work in the Lord Chancellor's Office, unlikely as they look to be. They choose you for your dotty names. Like 'Wright on Walls.'"

He nearly said, "Next will be 'Veneering on Shams,'" but didn't.

"I feel quite honoured, as a matter of fact," he said. "And another thing, I've been chosen to rewrite *Hudson*."

"Who on earth is Hudson?"

"We've been married for a thousand years and you don't know *Hudson*!"

"Only his Bay."

"How very amusing. Ho-ho. *Hudson on Building Contracts*. I dare say I'll get a knighthood."

"How thrilling. But couldn't you do this anywhere?"

"Well, London would be easiest. Or Oxford. The Law Library. Cambridge, maybe, but I'm not from that quarter. But, well, bit of a harsh old-age after here. No servants. No decent weather. Holidays in the Lake District. Cold. Raining. All these groups of singing boys strumming out rubbishy songs. And the food!!"

"Yes," she said. "The food. But there's opera as well as the Beatles, and there's the London theatre and concerts."

"Everyone talks about going to the theatre and concerts but how many of us actually go? And London's not England any more. We'd be just another old couple."

"We could look around. It's twenty years since we went anywhere in England except London. We could go and look up Dulcie and Pastry Willy. Willy must be getting on a bit now. In Dorset."

That same night, at the end of the Long Vacation and the trip to Canton and three months since the execution, Betty heard Filth yelling in his sleep and ran into his room. He woke, moaning, saying that they were going to hang him. After the handover in '97 they would take him and hang him.

The following morning neither of them mentioned the night and he was driven smoothly in to Court as usual, but Elisabeth began to make plans for England and wrote one of her sketchy letters to Willy in the Donheads of Dorset.

Dear Dulcie and dear Willy,

We are coming back to see England again for a while and we would so much like to see you in particular. Time has not passed. We so often think of you. Christmas cards are not enough.

Could you write and say if you will be about around Christmas? Could we spend a night or so with you, or could you find us somewhere? We won't stay long because we'll be exploring. We don't quite know what to do with our future.

With best love, as ever

Betty (once Macintosh of Shanghai)

PS How are your children? Have you grandchildren?

CHAPTER TWENTY-SIX

T wo profiles, one imposed against the other, like images
of royalty upon a medallion struck for a new reign:
Edward Feathers and his wife Elisabeth, motoring into
the sunset on the A33 through Wiltshire on a frosty winter's
afternoon.

They were looking for Pastry Willy and Dulcie, and
wondering if there would be anything to say after so long.

"Didn't they have some children?" Betty said. "A girl. She
must be quite ancient now."

"No. Born very late. Still young. Susan."

"Oh, lawks yes," said Elisabeth. "Sullen Susan."

"Sullen Sue," said Filth. "I'm glad we have no sullen daughter."

She said nothing. They were passing Stonehenge.

"We turn off quite soon. Just past Stonehenge. There's
Stonehenge."

He drove on, not turning his head. She made the sign of the
Cross. Still not turning his head, Filth said, "What on earth are
you doing?"

"Well, it's the usual thing to make the sign of the Cross
passing Stonehenge. There are thousands of accidents. It's the
magnetism of the stones."

He said, after a time, "I sometimes wonder where you hear
these things."

"It's common knowledge."

"There are accidents because drivers all say "There's Stonehenge—look!" and turn their heads. I have a certain amount of sense."

"Well, then, quick! Turn left. Here's the road to Chilmark. You nearly skidded! It's much narrower. And winding. Oh, look at that tree. It's enormous. It's just like a hen!"

"A hen?"

"Like a huge hen nodding on a nest. Up at the top of a tree—we've gone under it now."

"A hen in a *tree*?"

"Yes. And I've seen it before."

"Very unlikely. We've not been here before."

"I came down here alone once. After that operation. It was somewhere here. Somewhere."

"No, that was much further west. I know. I came and found you. It was near Somerset. It was way beyond Bath. Near the theatre and those Dickensian people you liked then."

"I suppose so," she said. "We couldn't find them either. We never saw them again. Did we?"

"Well, didn't they die?"

"I suppose—I can't remember if we heard or not. I did write. I sent them a replacement of something I broke. I can't remember . . ."

A very old man appeared out of the hedge and crossed the road in front of them. He was carrying an axe.

"Elisabeth—what is it now?"

"I don't know. I just have the feeling I've been here before. A shuddering."

"When people say that," said Edward, "nobody ever knows what to reply, like when they tell you their dreams. Here's a notice saying 'The Donheads,' whatever they are. St. Ague is the one we're after. 'Ague'—what a name! Here's the hill marked on the map she sent. It could be quite soon now. What a maze."

"I think it's to the left. No, we've passed it. It was that double driveway, wasn't it, dividing left and right? Down and up."

"No," he said. "We have to pass a church first. It says on the map. Here's a church. Here's Privilege Lane. Oh, yes indeed! Very nice! Trust old Willy! Wrought-iron gates!—oh," and "Hello Willy! What a marvellous place!"

(Mutual exclamations of joy and Willy at once takes Elisabeth up and away from the house to the top of the garden and Edward takes the luggage while Dulcie goes to make one of her soufflés.)

"What a view, what a view, Willy! What a white and golden view! And Uncle Willy, we'll *never* call you Pastry any more. You're brown as a nut. It must be Thomas Hardy."

"Thomas Hardy was always going up to London to the theatre but I never leave the Donheads," and he began to totter back to the house, Elisabeth pretending that she needed his arm when they both knew that he was needing hers. He said, "We have a surprise for you. Two surprises. One is Fiscal-Smith."

"Oh, Willy, no! How *could* you?"

"Motoring through looking for a cheap bed and breakfast, he says. Then, miraculously, remembering us."

"But have you room for us all? You said Eddie and I could stay with you tonight."

"Yes. Of course. Vast great place, this, in spite of the thatch and the button windows. Someone else is staying, too. Our second surprise: Susan. From Massachusetts. She says she's not seen you since she was at school."

"No. She hasn't. Is she alone?"

"Don't ask. Husband trouble in Boston. She's walked out on him and the child. She doesn't say much. We just let her thump around the countryside on a local horse. We're used to it. Always doing it."

"Oh, I'm so sorry, Willy."

"Aha—there's Fiscal-Smith at the front door! The wedding party is complete."

The table in the palatial cottage was laid for a pre-war, middle-class English afternoon tea. There were dozens of postage-stamp sandwiches, brown and white bread and butter (transparent), home-made jams and seed cake. Dulcie sat behind a silver teapot.

Susan, however, was crouched in a corner on a rocking chair near the fire and her baleful eyes surveyed them. She had a mug of tea in one hand and was barefoot. As Betty and Filth came into the room her mouth was wide open ready to receive the slice of cake that was approaching it via her other hand.

"Susan," cried Elisabeth, as was required.

"Oh, hullo."

Filth nodded curtly. He was surprised to find her familiar, and a shadow from his schooldays passed before his eyes. Another girl at someone's house during the war. Isobel Ingoldby. Tall Isobel, with her loping golden beauty, and her dark moods. He had thought that women were less disagreeable now. He watched this one bleakly. Oh, thank God for Betty.

Everyone sat down.

Later came dinner and Susan ate from a private menu. Again, for Filth, the great wave of memory and—well, actually—desire.

The next day Susan was not about at breakfast but passed the window later upon a steaming horse, not turning her head.

Fiscal-Smith left early. He was aiming to drop in on another old colleague, known to have a spare bedroom, who lived near York. "Have you looked around up there, Filth? Decided where to settle? You are coming Home, I hope? It would be good to have you nearby."

But were they coming Home? They had certainly worked at it. Filth had prepared an itinerary as thoroughly as he had done for their expeditions to Java and Japan during Bar vacations. They had borrowed a tiny flat in the Temple as a base, hired a good car, bought maps and guidebooks and set forth anti-clockwise, up the Great North Road (now called the A1 and much faster than it used to be.) They by-passed Cambridge because it was so cold and not Oxford, and proceeded towards East Anglia which seemed colder still, and windy. They stayed a night with a delightful ex-judge who had taken up poetry and market gardening. They met his friends who were all, it seemed, growers of kale. They explored the eastern seaboard but Filth found the sea colourless and threatening, and Betty found the glittering churches too big for flower arrangements.

They drove on, up to York which was impersonal and then up to the Roman Wall where they had Hong Kong friends whose bodies and minds had shrivelled against the climate. Approaching the Border country they surveyed Scotland across the lapping grey waters of the Solway. "If our genes are here," said Filth, "we ought at least to give Scotland a try."

So they stayed at a grand hotel on Loch Lomond and visited another retired lawyer from the Far Eastern circuit, Glasgow-born and seeming ashamed of ever having been away. He was full of a Case to do with some local mountains that had been stacked with warheads in the seventies. They were all there, *oh* yes. He himself was not for Aldermaston. Always good to have defences. Bugger the Russians. They wondered if his mind had been touched, perhaps by radiation.

They stepped back from Scotland like people on the brink of a freezing plunge without towels, and turned south-east towards the Lake District and Grasmere because Betty had liked Wordsworth at school. Pilgrims queued outside Dove Cottage and the lakeside was thick with Japanese. They felt foreigners.

"There must be something wrong with us," she said. "We are jaundiced has-beens," and they stopped off at a roadside pub as pretty as a calendar to think about it. The pub was just outside the delectable little town of Appleby. It was 1.30 P.M.

182 · JANE GARDAM

and they asked for lunch. "*This* time of day?" said the proprietor. "Dinner here's at twelve o'clock! *Sandwiches*? You can't ask him to make sandwiches after one o'clock. He needs his rest."

So back south. They agreed, unspokenly, not to look at Wales where Filth had suffered as a child, nor Lancashire and west Cumberland where at his prep school—though they never talked about it—they both knew he had been unbelievably, almost unbearably, happy. A time sacred and unrepeatable.

Down the M6 they drove, and the air warmed. They spent a night in Oxford but did not look anybody up. (Too cliquey. Too long ago.) They drifted south towards Pastry Willy. And, for Betty, a dream garden that had probably never existed. She didn't explain this. She wore new armour now.

And then the hen in the tree and a man with an axe.

Before they left Privilege Hill Betty said, "I've remembered, the place I stayed when I was convalescing was called Dexters. At least the people were called Dexter. D'you remember them? From Ebury Street? They were actors." But Dulcie and Willy, waving from the wrought-iron gate, said there was nobody they'd heard of called Dexter in the Donheads.

"Goodbye," they all called out to each other. "Thank you. Oh! How we'll miss you," and Willy took Elisabeth's bright sweet face between his hands and kissed it.

Susan went back to Boston the following week and, leaving, said, "Those Feathers—I can't stand them. Never could. So bloody *smug*. And politically *ignorant*. And culturally *dead*! And childless. And selfish. And so bloody, bloody *rich*."

"Elisabeth," said Dulcie, "wanted ten children."

"Oh, they all say that. Posh brides with no brains."

"Elisabeth has brains," said Willy. "She was at Bletchley

Park in the war, decoding ciphers, and Filth passed out top in the Bar Finals. And they're neither of them posh!"

"Dry as sticks," said Susan.

"No," said Willy.

"Wasn't there some sort of scandal about *her*?" Susan's eyes gleamed.

"*No*," said Willy.

"Oh, well," said Susan. "Her memory's not much. There's a house called Dexters here in the village. I passed it out riding. It's down that lane that divides. One up one down. You can't see it from the road."

"Oh, nonsense, we'd know it."

"The Dexter place, all you can see is down its chimney unless you go round to the front entrance, down the hill, towards Donhead St. Anthony. It's been a ruin for years. I asked because it's being all done up."

"Darling, why didn't you *tell* them?"

"Why should *they* live here? I can't."

So the Feathers settled down for a London winter in the Temple, Filth working on his Pollution Bill, excellent Sunday lunches in the Inner Temple Hall after church, theatres, old friends and an occasional weekend in Surrey. They grew dull. Filth went back to Hong Kong for a while, but Betty stayed behind.

Old Willy died in the New Year and Betty asked Dulcie to stay with her in the flat, which was close to the Temple church where the memorial service would be held. Betty had gone to the funeral of course, in the Donheads, and seen Willy lowered into the Dorset soil in his local churchyard. Susan had not come from America but she would be at the memorial service. Betty invited her to stay with her in the Temple, too, but this was left uncertain. Which is to say that Susan did not reply.

Oh, well, thought Elisabeth.

It was a splashy, showery day and the congregation arrived shaking umbrellas and stamping their wet shoes in the porch of the Temple church. Willy had been so contentedly old, they were all telling each other, that this was a celebration of his life, not a lament. There were a few old lawyers from Singapore and Hong Kong and some Benchers from all the Inns of Court who faced each other sanguinely across the chancel, occasionally raising a hand in greeting.

Betty sat wanting Filth there. She felt very sad. Dulcie next to her was perfectly dressed in Harrods black with a glint of Chanel, eyes streaming, and sulky Susan was gulping and snuffling into a big handkerchief. Betty hadn't bothered much with what to wear or whom to greet. She sat thinking of Willy and old Shanghai and nursery rhymes a thousand years ago. I do know love when I see it, she thought. He loved me and I loved him. Nobody much left. And she tried to ignore the hatchet face, directly across from her, of Fiscal-Smith in a black suit worn slippery with funerals.

There was a scuffle and commotion and, across the church, Fiscal-Smith made room ungraciously for a stumbling latecomer who was nodding left and right in apology. The Master of the Temple was already climbing to the pulpit to read from the Holy Bible. The latecomer looked at Betty across the chancel, directly head-on to him, and gave a delighted wave. It was Harry Veneering.

"Come on out to tea," he said afterwards.

They were all gathering outside the church or crammed into the porch and some had begun to walk over the courtyard to the wake in Parliament Chamber. It was not quite raining but damp, and many of them were old. The senior Benchers were filing away from the church through their private door under umbrellas, and Dulcie and Susan were being cared for by the Master of the Temple.

"Come on, don't go that way," said Harry Veneering to Betty. "Come with me round here past these gents on the floor," and he took her elbow and led her away among the circle of Knights Templar on their tombs, swords in place. Chins high.

"Promising juniors who didn't quite make it," said Harry. "I'd have been the same if I'd gone to the Bar. The Army was for me. Mind, the Army didn't seem to do them a lot of good, proud bastards pretending to be like Jesus. Killing everybody. Taxi!"

"Where are we going?"

"The Savoy."

"But it's only a two-minute walk."

"We're not walking. I'm an Officer in the Brigade of Guards."

"And," she said, "we haven't booked."

"Oh, they'll find me a table."

He gave the saluting doorman a wave, and took her through the foyer laughing and smiling around. Yes, of course, sir, a table. No, of course not, sir. Not too near the piano. They sat in an alcove where lamplight and warmth denied the soggy day.

"Yes," he said, "*full* afternoon tea and, *yes*, the glass of champagne. Naturally. And—" he looked at her and took her hand.

"Harry, stop this at once. They'll think you're my—what is it called?—toy boy!"

"Oh, but I *a m*," he said. "Mrs. Waterproof and galoshes!— Hey—look at my right thigh!" He stuck out his leg just in front of the approaching waitress, and there were shrieks and laughter.

"Harry—*will* you sit down. You're no better than when you were nine."

"I wish they served lobsters," he said.

Shriek.

"And I wish I was under the table again, missing my plane back to school. I wish—I wish I'd never grown up."

"Harry, how dare you! How *can* you? All we did!"

"Sorry. Yes. Look at my thigh. It's twice the width of my left one, twice as strong. Whenever I have X-rays it makes them faint. Wonderful operation. Did you read in the papers? I climbed the Eiger."

"Yes, I did."

"Not that I'm the first."

"No, you're not. And how did it get in the papers?"

"I attract attention. Like my father."

Pouring pale-gold tea she said, "And where is your father? And your mother? I thought they'd be here at the service."

"Pa's in Fiji doing an Arbitration. I suppose Ma's at home in HK. I don't hear much from her."

"You hear from your father?"

"Oh, yes. But I'm in his black books at the moment."

"Why?"

"Don't go into it. Extravagance. I think he rather likes to boast about it really. Makes me seem a toff."

"He's been very good to you."

"So have you, Miss Raincoat. You are my true and only love. Someone told me you were with me all night long before I nearly had my leg chopped off."

A waiter came with the champagne.

"It's true," Harry said to him. "She was with me all night long. Out on the Russian steppes. She stopped them amputating my leg. Then things got out of hand and we were attacked by wolves . . ."

"Will that be all, sir?"

"Oh, no!" said Harry. "Lots more to come."

"Harry," she said. "I must go back to the wake and look after Dulcie. She's staying with me."

"Where's Hyperion?" he asked. "Can't he look after her?—Filth, I mean. Sir Edward?"

"He's abroad. He's arbitrating, too. He's retiring soon and then we're going to live in Dorset, near Dulcie."

But he was staring at the clock across the room. "Good God in heaven," he said. "Good *God*!—The time! I have to go," and he began to pat his pockets. "I'm dreadfully late. I—my wallet!"

"It's all right," she said. "I'm taking you out to tea. Next time you can give me dinner. At the Ritz."

"I will! I'd love to. Mrs. Burberry, my angel of light," and he was gone, flitting through the room and out of the foyer through the glass doors into the Strand.

She followed after paying the huge bill and walked back into the Temple and into the sombre celebration for her dear old friend. As she came into the room she seemed to see him somewhere in the crowd watching her and lovingly shaking his head.

"I haven't a son," she told the ghost. ("Oh, *hello*, Tony! Hello, Desmond!") "I haven't a child. I've no one else to be unwise with. I so love him."

CHAPTER TWENTY-SEVEN

Dexters was an immediate success. There was very little of the old cowman's cottage left. All had been enlarged and the garden opened widely to the view. The entrance was no longer the breakneck business of Elisabeth's first haunted visit and there was electricity, an Aga, a telephone, a splendid kitchen, two bathrooms, a dining room for the rosewood table and a hall wide enough for the red chair. And a terrace, facing the sunset for gin on summer evenings. The great stone chimney remained. Dexters was private and quiet but not so isolated that the two of them would one day become a threat to the social services when they became seriously old. There was a shop half a mile away, the paper and the groceries were delivered, as of yore, and the church stood up unchanging near Dulcie on Privilege Hill. There was a room for Filth to work in surrounded by his shelves of Law Reports, and a hidden garage for one modest car. The almost virgin—if there is such a thing—garden beckoned, and deliveries began of Betty's plants. A gardener was found and a cleaner who also did laundry. There was the smell of leaves and dew when you opened the windows and the smell of the new wood floors within, and the wood-burning stove. Betty gathered lavender and scattered it in chests of drawers.

And so they settled. The curtains of lights and fireworks and the clamour and glamour and luxury and squalor of Hong Kong were over for them. The sun rose and set less hectically, less noticeably, but more birds sang. The rookery was still there, the nests, now huge and askew, weighing heavily in the branches, the birds—probably, said Filth, the same ones—still disputing and objecting and arbitrating and condemning, passing judgement and gathering further and better particulars. Filth said that so long as they were there he'd never miss his profession.

Memory changed for both Edward and Elisabeth. There were fewer people now to keep it alive. Christmas cards dwindled. Instead, Betty began in October to write letters to the best of those left. Not many. Amy and Isobel and a couple of dotty cousins of Edward. Just as she had rearranged herself into a copy of her dead mother on her marriage, now she began to work on being the wife of a distinguished old man. She took over the church—the vicar was nowhere—and set up committees. She joined a Book Club and found DVDs of glorious old films of their youth. She took up French again and had her finger- and toenails done in Salisbury, her hair quite often in London where she became a member of the University Women's Club. She knew she still looked sexy. She still had disturbing erotic dreams.

She quite enjoyed the new role, and bought very expensive county clothes, and she wore Veneering's pearls (Edward's were in a safe) more and more boldly and with less and less guilt.

As ever, she kept Veneering's diamond clasp round the back of her neck in the daytime and only risked it round the front at dinner parties where sometimes it was exclaimed over. Filth never seemed to notice.

One day Filth said, "Do you remember that I once took part in an Arbitration at The Hague?"

"The International Court of Justice? Of course I do. I didn't see you for months. You said it was dreary."

"That fellow was on the other side."

"Veneering," she said. "Yes."

"We kept our distance. You didn't come out."

"I did, actually. Just for a night or two. I met a school-friend in a park. I don't remember much. It was after we—we married."

"Well," he said, looking through his glass of red wine and tipping it about. "I've been asked there again."

"What! It's been years . . ."

"It's an engineering dispute about a dam in Syria. I've done a few dams in my time. The two sides have been rabbiting on, squandering millions. They want to bring in a couple of new arbitrators to sit above the present ones."

"*Could* you? Do you want to? Aren't you rusty?"

"I could. I'd like to. I don't think so. Come too. The Hague's a lovely place and there's so much around it. There's Delft and Leyden and Amsterdam and Bruges. Wonderful museums. Paintings. Oh, and good, clean food. Good, clean people. Good for you!"

"I'll think. But you should do it."

"Yes. I think so. I think so."

"The International Court of Justice! At your age."

"Yes."

"But," he said a week later, "it's out of the question. Guess whom they want as the third replacement arbitrator?"

She licked her fingers. She was making marmalade.

"Easy," she said. "Sir Terence Veneering QC, Learned in the Law."

"Yes."

"Does it matter? Isn't it about time . . . ?"

"Well, I suppose so!" said Filth. "And he's the only other one who knows as much as I do about dams. It would be a fair fight. I needn't speak to him out of Court."

"Is he 'Dams'?"

"Yes. He got the Aswan Dam once. I'd have liked that one. However, I got the dam in Iran. D'you remember? It wouldn't fill up. Very interesting. They'd moved half the population of the country out and drowned all their villages. I won that. I had death threats there, you know."

"You always thought so. Will this dam be interesting?"

"*All* dams are interesting," he said, shocked.

Later, eating the new marmalade at breakfast, she said, "But I don't think I'll come with you, Filth, my darling. If you don't mind."

"Why not?"

"Oh, well. It's Easter. I'm needed at church. And so on."

"Dulcie could do all that."

"Well. No, I'm happy here, Eddie. I'm used to you being away, for goodness sake. It's not like in East Pakistan with only three telephone lines."

"Well, I'll go. Actually"—he gave his crazy embarrassed roar—"I have actually accepted the job so I'll go and I'll come back at weekends. I can be back here every Friday night you know, until the Sunday night. And—you never know—you might change your mind and come out to me for a weekend? We could stay somewhere outside The Hague."

So she was alone in the Donheads through the early spring. It was a bitter Lent, cold and lonely. When Eddie's car dropped him off at Dexters each Friday night and she had dinner ready for him and news of village matters, he seemed far away and unconcerned.

"Are you enjoying the International Court of Justice?"

"Well, 'enjoying?' The creature is still poisonous. Still hates me. But I'm glad to be there. Betty, come out and join me. We can stay away from The Hague and all that. It's such a chance for you. Buy bulbs."

"Oh," she said.

"You can order a million tulips there," he said.

"Tulips," she said.

"Well, think about it."

"I love you, Filth. Oh, yes, well, yes. I'll come!"

CHAPTER TWENTY-EIGHT

S o she went. They stayed in an hotel near Delft and Edward was driven from there to The Hague and back each day, so she saw nothing of the Court.

And the tulip fields were in their glory and she booked for all the tours to see them, sometimes staying overnight, and each time ordering quantities of bulbs for Dorset, to be delivered in October. She talked ceaselessly to other gardeners on the coach tours and on the canal boats, and forgot all else.

She shopped. She bought a broadsword from an antique shop because it reminded her of Rembrandt's warrior. She bought a blue and white Delft knife with a black blade and broken handle because it might once have cut up fruit in Vermeer's kitchen. She bought three seventeenth-century tiles for Dulcie—a boy flying a kite, a fat windmill, a boat with square sails gliding through fields—and, for Amy, a heavy copper pot, trying not to think of the postage. She bought a print of a triptych for Mrs. Baxter. She walked for miles—the presents were always delivered back to the hotel—down cobbled streets between tall houses and a central canal. From windows, faces looked out and nodded. These must be homes for the elderly, she thought. What shining, broad faces. They wore round white caps with flaps. She expected Frans Hals at any moment to come flaunting down the street. All just out of sight.

On the fourth Saturday morning, the day Filth usually flew home for the weekend, he had to take documents back to the Arbitration room.

He brought his locked briefcase to the breakfast table and set it at his feet and she said, "Edward, aren't you rather over-doing it? We could just drop the papers off on the way to the airport."

"No, I may have to talk to the other two. They'll be there."

He was wearing his dark Court suit of striped trousers and black jacket, a sober tie, a starched shirt and Victorian silk handkerchief.

"I'm sure the others won't go dressed like that," she said.

"I dare say not, but it's correct. I'm carrying papers." Filth and Betty agreed to meet back at the hotel after lunch.

She took a taxi to a gallery she hadn't been to before where there were some seventeenth-century flower paintings, and walked round and round the sunlit rooms, empty because it was not yet the Easter holidays and there were no tourists. She felt embarrassed at the clatter of her feet in the silence and tried to tiptoe from one room to the next, the sun throwing gold stripes across the polished floors. Doors stood open between the galleries, the sun illuminating other distances, withdrawing itself from foregrounds, changing direction, splashing across a distant window or open door. Inside the building, everywhere was silent and, outside, the canal was black and still. She looked for a chair and found one standing by itself and sat down. But the gallery was disappointing. She sat looking at paintings of dead hares with congealed blood on their mouths, swags of grapes, pomegranates, feathered game collapsed sightless on slate slabs. In a corner of the room was a wooden carving, the head and shoulders of a man on a plinth, the wood so black it must have lain untouched for centuries in some bog, the cracked wood perfect for the seamed and ancient face, heavy with all the miseries of the world.

But it was the hat that informed the man. It was clearly the hat that had inspired the carving. It had a tight round crown and a cartwheel of an oak brim, biscuit-thin, spread out much wider than the stooped shoulders. The hat of a religious? A pilgrim? A wandering poet? Had it all been carved from one piece of wood? Was the hat separate? Did it lift off? She became hypnotised by the hat. She had to touch it.

She heard footsteps and a gallery attendant stood in the doorway, then passed on, his careful, slow feet squeaking.

Then she heard in an adjoining gallery two voices.

"Well, what about me? What am I to do?"

"Go back to lunch at the hotel. Or a restaurant. Go and rest. We'll be off at four o'clock."

"I want to go to Beirut for the weekend."

"*Beirut*! It's across the world! And it's nightclubs and narcotics. Whatever . . . ?"

"I want to go for a massage. Get my hair cut."

"*Beirut*!"

"Yes. I'm bored. It's the place now. I'm going to Beirut."

An overweight figure passed sloppily across an open doorway into a further gallery and it was Elsie Veneering. Another shadow followed and Elisabeth heard their voices on a staircase. "But what shall I *do* all the *afternoon*? Where shall I go? I can't sit having lunch alone." Elisabeth heard a taxi drive away. She closed her eyes and listened, and very soon heard him coming back up the stairs.

He said from a distance, "I saw you as we came in. She's gone," and she opened her eyes on a small seedy man without much hair, feeling in his pockets for a cigarette.

She said, "You can't smoke in here," and he said, "No, I suppose not."

He was wearing blue jeans and a brown shirt. He didn't look much.

She was wearing a new long tight-fitting coat with a round fur collar and a trimming of the same fur down the front, disguising the buttons, and then circling the hem. It gave her a young waist and legs. Her hair had been cut in Amsterdam. He said, "You are much more beautiful now. But I loved your looks then, too."

They sat in silence, he across the room on the only other chair. They looked at one another, and his smile and his eyes were as they had always been.

He said, "This bugger in the hat, he's like that dwarf who, history relates, nicked Filth's watch when they were kids and sold it," and he got up and whispered in the man's oak ear, "Albertross—I gotcher!" and lifted the wide oak brim and shouted out, "Eureka! It's a separate entity!"

And dropped it. She screamed.

He said, picking it up, "It's O.K. It's bog oak. Seventeenth century, harder than iron. Oh, and the bloke's name is Geoffrey. It says so in the label: *Bought at Harrods.*" He crammed the hat back on the head and the attendant came back and stared as Veneering bent to the oak ear, disarranging the hat, and said, "Hush, be still." He crossed to the attendant and shook hands with him. "It's my grandfather. He was a hatter. Rather a mad one. Nothing's broken," and the man went quickly away.

"No, I'm not laughing. I'm not," she said, "I'm not. I'm not."

And he took her hands and said, "When did you last laugh like this, Elisabeth? Never—that's right, isn't it? We've messed our lives. Elisabeth, come away with me. You're bored out of your head. You know it. I know it. And I'm in hell. It's our last chance. I'll leave her. It was always only a matter of time."

But she got up and walked out and down the circular staircase, the water from the canal flashing across the yellow walls. He leaned over the rail above, watching her, and when she was nearly down she stopped and stood still, not looking up.

"You're not wearing the pearls."

She said, "Goodbye, Terry. I'll never leave him. I told you."

"But I'm still with you. I'll never leave you. We'll never forget each other."

On the last step of the staircase she said, "Yes. I know."

CHAPTER TWENTY-NINE

All that summer Elisabeth gave herself to the garden. Dexters as a house was now perfect. Its terrace had been built to sit out and eat on in warm weather. The warmth of autumn and winter was beginning to be talked about, and the fact that there was no need now to escape to winters abroad. Filth sat for hours watching Elisabeth toil.

"I sit here and bask," he said, "I am shameless. But she won't let me anywhere near, you know. If I pull out a weed she screams and says she'd been keeping it for the Chelsea Flower Show. All I do is wash up and pour out drinks. Oh, and I can occasionally hold a hosepipe."

Filth's last Case, the dam at The Hague, had groaned its way to a close. The judging was over and done, and the terrace was now his stage. He worked at *Hudson on Building Contracts*, sat reading long and hard, mostly biographies of heroes of empire, and bird books. He kept binoculars at his elbow though he seldom picked them up. Each morning he read the *Daily Telegraph* wondering which political party he belonged to and hating them all. He wished Betty would discuss it with him. Or anything with him. In the evenings she sat yawning over seed catalogues and he often had to wake her up to go to bed. On Fridays they drove in to Salisbury to the supermarket and ate a modest lunch at the hotel. Every second month a crate of wine was delivered to Dexters by Berry Brothers of St. James's. On Sundays at half past ten was church. They never missed and never discussed why. "We are hedonists," he told friends. "The last of our kind. No chores. We are rich, idle, boring expatriates and fewer and fewer people come to see us. Have a glass of Chablis."

The year passed. The Handover took place in Hong Kong and they watched every minute of it on television. They discussed the Governor and his three beautiful daughters as if they were their own family, and when the daughters were seen to weep, Betty and Filth wept too. They watched the Union Jack come down for the last time.

"We're getting a bit senile," he said and she went out to the garden and began to turn the compost with a fork.

She stayed outside for hours and Filth had a try at preparing supper and broke one of the Delft dishes. They had a wakeful night in their separate bedrooms and were only just asleep when the rooks started up at dawn.

"I'm going up to London next week," he said. "There is a Bench Table at the Inn. I can stay overnight with someone or other." (They had long since given up the flat.) "Or we could go together. Stay at an hotel. See a show."

"Oh, I don't think so . . ."

"You're getting stuck, Betty."

"No, I'm making a garden. We'll open for Charity next year."

"I don't know what you think about hour after hour. Day after day. Gardening."

"I think about gardening," she said.

"Well," he told Dulcie in the lane, "I suppose this is being old. "All passion spent"—Shakespeare, isn't it?" and Dulcie pouted her pink lips and said, "Maybe."

After Filth had set off to London, Dulcie went round and found Betty, brown as a Gypsy, busy with the first pruning of the new apple trees.

"Does that gardener do *nothing*?"

"He does all the rough."

They sat over mugs of coffee on the terrace, staring down the wandering lawn towards the new orchard and out to the horizon and Whin Green. Dulcie said, "Are you sure you're well, Betty?"

"Fine, except for blood pressure and I've always had that."

"You don't say much, any more. You seem far away."

"Yes, I'm a bit obsessive. I'll be going on gardening outings in coaches before long with all the other village bores. Look, I must get on. I'm working ahead of frost."

"Who are those people in the garden?"

"What people?"

"I saw some children. A boy and a girl. And a man."

"Oh, yes. It's a garden full of surprises."

One day, deep beyond the meadow grass, beyond the orchard and the apple hedges, on her knees and planting broad beans, she saw two feet standing near her hands. They were Harry Veneering's.

"Harry!"

He was delighted when she shrieked.

"I've found you, Mrs. Waterproof! I heard Filth was up in London. Thought you might be lonely."

They had lunch at the kitchen table and he drank a whole bottle of wine (Filth would wonder!) and made her laugh at nothing. As ever. He mentioned his father.

"Does he know you're here?"

"No. I'm a grown-up. I'm going bald. Anyway, we're not getting on too well, the old showman and I."

"Oh? That's new."

"No. It isn't. He thinks I'm rubbish. He's thought so for years." He took a flower from a jar on the table and began to pull it to bits. He kicked out at a stool.

"Harry! You may be losing your oriental hair but you're still eight. What's wrong?"

"I'm supposed to be a gambler."

"And are you?"

"Well, yes, in my own small way. He's always bailed me out. Now he says he won't. Not any more."

"How much?" she asked.

"Never mind. I didn't come for that."

"Of course not," she said, watching him. Now he was picking at a pink daisy.

"Stop that!"

"Oh, sorry. Well, I'd better be going."

"How much do you want?"

"Betty, I have not asked. I'd never ask."

"How much do you owe?"

He slammed away from the table and looked down the garden. "Ten thousand pounds."

Then he pushed past her out of the back door and disappeared.

In time she went and found him smoking in the dark alley where she had first arrived at the house, leaning against the great chimney breast. He was in tears.

"Here's a cheque," she said.

"Of *course* I couldn't!"

"I have a lot of my own money. It's not Filth's. I spend most of it on the garden. If I'd had children it would all have been for them. I've not had a child to give it to."

He hugged and hugged her. "Oh, how I love you, Mrs. Raincoat. How I love you."

"Come. You must go home now. You're a long way from London and it's a nasty road. I'll walk with you to the car."

"No, it's all right. Oh, thank you, so very, very much! Oh, how I . . ."

"I'll just get a coat."

"Don't. I'm fine."

But she insisted and they walked together down the drive and up the hill towards the church.

"I'm just round this corner," he said, "and I'm going to hug you again and say goodbye. I'll write, of course. At once."

"I'd like to wave you off."

Very hesitantly he walked beside her round the side of the churchyard to where his car was parked. It was a Porsche.

"You don't get a thing for one of these second-hand," he said.

CHAPTER THIRTY

W hen the Porsche was gone she turned for the house, stopping quite often and staring at the familiar things in the lane. Loitering gravely, she nodded at the old Traveller in the hedge, busy with his flail. (He must be a hundred years old.) He stopped hacking at the sharp branches and watched her pass and go towards the front door.

Inside it on the mat lay a letter which must have been wrongly delivered somewhere else first because it was grubby and someone—the Traveller?—had scrawled *Sorry* across the envelope. It had come from Singapore to her, care of Edward's Chambers. Though she had scarcely seen his handwriting— once on the card with the pearls so many years ago—she knew that it was from Veneering.

There was a half-sheet of old-fashioned flimsy airmail paper inside signed *THV* and the words: *If Harry comes to see you do not give him money. I'm finished with him.* She threw it into the wood-burning stove. Then she went into the garden and began clearing round the new fruit trees, toiling and bashing until it was dark.

"Hello?" Filth stood on the terrace.
"You're back! Already. There's not much for supper."
"Doesn't matter. London's all eating. Come in. You can't do much more in the dark."

"I've made a vow today," he said. "I'll never work in London again. I can do *Hudson* just as well at home, with a bit of planning of references. I am tired of London which means, they tell me, that I am tired of life."

"Possibly."

"Which makes me think that you and I ought to be making our Wills. I'll dig them out and revise them and then we'll make a last trip to London, to Bantry Street, and do the signing."

"All right."

"Could we go up and back on the same day, d'you think? Too much for you?"

"No, I don't think so."

And he began to make meticulous revisions to his Will and appendices of wishes. Did she want to read it? Or should he look over hers?

"No, mine's all straightforward. Most of it to you and Amy. If you die first it will all go to Amy's children."

"Really? Good gracious! Right, we'll get on with it then. Take three weeks—getting the appointment and so on, I'd think. We want everything foolproof."

So the appointment was made for 3.30 P.M., on a November afternoon, which was rather late in the day for the two-hour journeys, one up and one down. The new young woman at the firm was excellent and therefore very busy. Never mind.

But getting ready on the day took longer now, even though shoes were polished and all their London clothes laid out the night before. Betty had seen to it that their debit cards and banknotes, rail cards, miniature bottle of brandy (for her dizziness) and the tiny crucifix left to her by Mrs. Baxter were all in her handbag, along with the pills for both of them (in separate dosset boxes) in case for any reason they should need to stay overnight.

Filth was still upstairs, fighting with cufflinks, Betty, ready in the hall, sitting in the red chair, and the hall table beside her was piled up with tulip bulbs in green nets. They had smothered the telephone and Filth's bowler hat. There'd be a roar about that in a minute. ("Where the hell—?") She fingered the tulip bulbs through their netting, thinking how sexy they felt, when the telephone began to ring. She burrowed about under the bulbs to find the receiver and said, "Yes? Betty here," knowing it would be from a nervy sort of woman at her Reading Group that afternoon. Betty had of course sent apologies weeks ago.

"Yes? Chloë?"

"Betty?" It was a man.

"Yes?"

"I'm in Orange Tree Road. Where are you?"

"Well, here."

"*Exactly* where?"

"Sitting in the hall by the phone. On the satin throne."

"What are you wearing?"

"Wearing?"

"I need to see you."

"But you're in Hong Kong."

"No. Singapore. I need to see your face. I've lost it. I have to be able to see you. In the red chair."

"Well, I'm—we're just setting off for London. Filth's putting on his black shoes upstairs. He'll be down in a minute, I'm dressed for London."

"Are you wearing the pearls?"

"Yes."

"Touch them. Are they warm? Are they mine? Or his? Would he know?"

"Yours. No, he wouldn't notice. Are you drunk? It must be after dinner."

"No. Well, yes. Maybe. Did you get my note?"

"Yes."

"I didn't tell you in it that Harry was given a medal. Twice mentioned in despatches last year. 'Exceptional bravery.' Northern Ireland."

"No!"

"Hush-hush stuff. Secret service. Underground sort of stuff."

"Should you be telling me this?"

"No. He never told us at the time. Very, very brave. I want to make it absolutely clear."

"I believe it. I hated your letter. I saw him about a month ago and he was miserable. He said you thought he was rubbish. He didn't ask me for money. Terry? Terry, where've you gone?"

A silence.

"Nowhere. Nowhere to go. Betty, Harry's dead. My boy."

Filth came down the stairs, looking for his bowler hat.

In the London train Filth thought: She's looking old. An old woman. The first time. Poor old Betty, old.

"You all right, Betty?"

"Yes."

Her eyes seemed huge. Strange and swimmy. He thought, She must watch that blood-pressure.

He saw how she looked affectionately at the young Tamil ticket inspector who was intent on moving them to a cleaner carriage in the first class. She was thanking the boy very sweetly. "Perfectly all right here," said Filth, but Betty was off down the aisle and into the next carriage. Silly woman. Could be her grandson. Still attractive. You could see the bloke liked her.

At Waterloo they parted, Filth to lunch in his Inn at the Temple, Betty he wasn't sure where. The University Women's Club right across towards Hyde Park? Whoever with? And why was she making off towards Waterloo Bridge? The solicitor's office was in Holborn. He watched her almost running

206 · JANE GARDAM

down the flight of steps, under the arches and over the maze of roads towards the National Theatre. Still has good legs, bless her. He stepped into a taxi.

Betty, at the National Theatre, made a pretence of eating lunch, pushing a tray along in a queue of people excited to have tickets for *Electra* in an hour's time. She headed for the foyer (Harry is dead) and got the lift up to the open-air terrace where there were fire-eaters and mummers and people being statues and loud canned music played. (My boy Harry.) Beside her on the seat two young lovers sat mute, chewing on long bread rolls with flaps of ham and salad hanging out. When they had finished eating they wiped their hands on squares of paper and threw the paper down. Then in one simple movement they turned to face each other and merged into each other's arms.

She decided to go at once to Bantry Street. If she walked all the way she would arrive just about on time. On Waterloo Bridge, once she had climbed the steep concrete stairs the crowds came down on her like the Battle itself. She kept near the bridge's side, sometimes going almost hand over hand. People in London move so fast! (Harry is dead.) Some of them looked her over quickly as they passed, noticed her pearls, her matching coat and skirt. The silk blouse. The gloves. I'm antique. They think I'm out of Agatha Christie. (Is dead!) My hair is tidy and well cut, like the woman . . . the woman in . . . the woman like my mother in the hairdresser in Hong Kong. The day the crowds of shadows were to pass me in the night towards the house in the trees. *He is dead.*

At the Aldwych she felt dizzy and found a pill in her handbag and swallowed it, looking round to see if by any chance Filth was anywhere about. He'd be in a fury if he couldn't find a taxi. He'd never get a bus. He wouldn't much care to walk. No sign.

Oh, but why worry? He always could find taxis. He was so tall. Taller still when he brandished the rolled umbrella. He'd forgotten the bowler hat, thank goodness. It was still under the tulips. The last bowler hat in London and my boy is dead.

Here was Bantry Street and there, thank God, was Filth getting out of a taxi and smiling. The driver had got out and was holding open the door for him. Filth looked somebody. His delightful smile!

But it was the last smile of the day. On the next train back to Tisbury they sat opposite one another across a table in a determinedly second-class carriage. Betty was pale and Filth sat purple in choleric silence.

The solicitor had not been there! She had children ill at home and either had not remembered or the firm had forgotten to cancel the appointment. And at the reception desk—and the place looked like an hotel now, with palms in pots—they had not even seemed apologetic.

"*Salisbury*," he said, after an hour. "We'll take the damn things into Salisbury to sign. Perfectly good solicitors there and half the price."

"I always said so." Betty closed her eyes. (Harry.)

"It is a positive outrage. I shall write to the Law Society."

(My boy, Harry.)

"We are, after all, no longer young."

"No."

"Nor are we exactly nobodies. They've been our solicitors for forty years, that firm."

"Yes."

She opened her eyes and watched Wiltshire going by. On the way out she had thought that she'd seen a hoopoe in a hedge. Filth would have been enchanted but she had not told him. *Very brave.* Despatches. Northern Ireland. Harry. No, no. He is not dead. My Harry.

208 · JANE GARDAM

And, seeing the first of the chalk in the rippling hills she knew that she would leave Filth. She had to go to Veneering.

Filth now closed his eyes and, opposite him, she examined his face. He looked like a fine portrait of himself, each line of his face magnificently drawn. Oh, such conceit! Such self-centredness! Such silliness and triviality! I'll tell him when we get home. And a wonderful lightness of heart flooded over her, a squirm of ancient sexual pleasure.

It will probably kill him, she thought. But I shall go. I may tell him at once. Now.

The train had begun to slow down for Tisbury Station. It usually stopped just outside for several minutes, for the platform was short and they had to wait to let the fast London-to-Plymouth train through. Betty looked out of the window and on the tapering end of the platform, way beyond the signal and just as they were sliding to a halt, she saw Albert Ross. He was looking directly at her.

Filth was standing up, ready to get out. He came round to her and shook her shoulder. "Betty. Come along. We're here. Whatever's wrong now?"

"Nothing," she said.

In the car that they had parked outside the station that morning but a thousand years ago, she said, "I saw Albert Ross. Standing on the platform. Waiting for the train from Plymouth to go through."

Filth was negotiating Berrywood Lane—a tractor and two four-by-fours, two proud girls on horseback—and said, "You fell asleep."

"No. He looked straight at me."

There, on the hall table, lay the tulip bulbs.

I'll wait till I've planted them, she decided. I can't leave them to shrivel and rot, and she took off her shoes and climbed the stairs to bed. I'll tell him tomorrow after lunch.

She was up early, not long after dawn, and ready in her gardening clothes. She would change later, after she had packed. It was a damp, warm day, perfect for planting and she arranged the bulbs in groups of twenty-five for lozenge-shaped designs each in a different colour along the foot of the red wall. The planting round the apple trees was finished already. With her favourite long dibble, she began to make a hole for each bulb. She liked to plant at least six inches down. Then you could put wallflowers on top of them to flower first, but this year she had left it a bit late for that. She humped herself about on the planting mat, put a little sharp sand in the bottom of each hole, laid a bulb ready beside each. How stiff and cumbersome her body was now. How ugly her old hands, in the enormous green gloves. A hectic sunlight washed across the garden and she went into the house for a mug of coffee. Edward was in the kitchen, silent in his own world.

"Bulbs finished yet?"

"Not quite."

She went back to the garden and he followed her, carrying his stick and binoculars on to the terrace. She stood with her coffee, and all at once the rooks started a wild tumult in the ash trees: some dreadful disagreement, some palace revolution, some premonition of change. They began to swoop about above the branches and their ramshackle great nests, all over the sky, like smuts flying from a burning chimney. She was down the garden on her knees again now and saw that Veneering's pearls were lying in the flower bed beside her. For the first time in her life she had forgotten to take off a necklace when she went to bed. Nor had she noticed them when she washed and dressed this morning. They must have slipped from her neck. She was eye to eye with them now, on her haunches, head down. She picked them off the soil and let them pour into one of the holes for the tulips.

My guilty pearls, she thought. I hope the sharp sand won't hurt them.

She had rather seized up now. She was in a difficult position on hands and knees. If I can get on my elbows . . . she thought. Goodness—! Here we go. Well, I never was exactly John Travolta. That's better. Now the bottom half.

She rested, and from her lowly place noticed out on the lawn how the bindweed was piercing the turf, rising in green spirals, pirouetting quite high, seeking something on which to cling. The wild, returning to the garden.

She could see Filth, too, sitting on the terrace with his coffee, staring up at the rooks through his binoculars. Then he put down the binoculars and picked up his Airedale-headed walking stick and, quite oblivious of her, like a child, pointed it up at the rookery and shouted, "Bang, bang, bang." Then he swung the stick about for a left and a right. "Bang, bang, bang."

He's quite potty, she thought. It's too late. I can't leave him now.

But then she did.

Filth, letting his binoculars swoop away from the rookery and down across the garden a minute later, saw her lying in the flower bed, particulary still.

PART FIVE

Peace

CHAPTER THIRTY-ONE

T hree years later—the years Edward Feathers saw as his torture and suffering and the village called his fortitude—came the extraordinary news that the house next door to Dexters, the monstrous hidden house above him, had been sold.

One winter's day, a single van arrived and was quickly away again. Who had bought the upper house nobody knew. After a time Edward Feathers, on his morning constitutional to the lane end to collect his *Daily Telegraph* from the length of drainpipe attached to the rough handrail at the foot of the slope, saw that a second bit of drainpipe had been fastened to the handrail of his new neighbour across the lane. The paper was not the *Daily Telegraph*. It was thicker and stubbier and from what he could see it was the *Guardian*.

How insolent! To copy his invention for a rainproof newspaper without his permission! He marched off on his emu legs, chin forward, plunging his walking stick into the road. He met his neighbour Dulcie, bright and smiling as usual. When he had slashed his way by she said to her dog, "So—what's the matter with *him* today?"

She did not know what was to come.

About a month after the newcomer's arrival a new telephone was installed (the Donheads move slowly) and the newcomer used it to telephone the village shop in a more distant Donhead. He thanked them for the delivery of his daily paper and would the shop kindly put up a postcard in their window advertising for daily help? What was the going rate? Excellent. Double it. And stipulate laundry. The newcomer had lived in the Far East and was ashamed to say that he was totally incapable of looking after himself.

"Oh, dear me," they said. "And no wife, sir?"

"My wife is dead. She was Chinese. I'm afraid she had no idea how to do laundry either. We had servants."

"We'll do our best," said the shop. "You sound just like your neighbour. He was from Singapore-way. He's a lawyer."

"Oh."

"What name shall I put on the card, sir? Perhaps you are a lawyer, too?"

"Yes, I am, as it happens."

"Well, fancy that. You may be friends."

"My name is Veneering."

"Your neighbour is Sir Edward Feathers."

There was a terrible silence. The telephone was put down. "Funny one we've got now," said the shop to Eddie Feathers's daily who was in buying marmalade for him. "Not a bundle of fun."

"Makes two of them," said Kate, and half an hour later, letting herself into the Feathers domain, "What about this, then? Next door it's another lawyer and he's from Singapore-way, too. His name's Veneering. That's a queer name if ever. Is it Jewish? He's wanting a domestic, and don't you worry, I've said I'm not available. There's enough to do here. I'll find him someone but—Sir Edward, what's wrong? You've turned greenish. Sit down and I'll get you your cup of tea."

Feathers sat silent, stunned out of thought. At last he said, "Thank God that Betty is dead."

Over the way Veneering sat on by the telephone for a long

while and said at last, "I must move. Thank God that Betty is dead."

After a time looking at his fire, burning brightly in the great chimney, Feathers also said, "I must move."

A bombshell coincidence?

Yet it was really not so very unlikely that Veneering had lighted on this particular house. The Donheads are thick with retired international lawyers, and house agents' blurbs do not always mention English county boundaries. Dorset is large and, anyway, Veneering had no idea of the Featherses' address. He was not the detective his son had been. No, the only really curious thing was that after their mutual discovery they never met. Filth, far too proud to change the route of his afternoon walk, kept to the same paths as before, went to church as before, drove to the same small supermarket as before, kept the same friends. It was Veneering who kept himself out of sight. He was, quite simply, never about. Cases of wine were delivered at quite frequent intervals and the village shop would drop off meagre groceries on his porch up the hill. His cleaner came when she felt like it and reported that he was obviously someone "in reduced circumstances" and his garden was left to go wild. Sometimes a hired car would come out from the station to take him to the London train and drop him at home again after dark. Later, it was reported that the circumstances could not have been that much reduced for the hired car began to transport him all the way. When people called at the house with envelopes for Save the Children or Breast Cancer, they were ignored. The postman said he delivered very little up there. There was seldom a light.

Once, when a much younger Hong Kong lawyer called on Filth and Filth walked him back to his car at the end of the lane, the lawyer said, "Didn't Terry Veneering retire down this way?" before remembering the myth of the clash of the Titans. But surely over now?

"Lives next door," said Filth.

"Next door! Then you are friends."

"Friends?" said Filth. "Never seen him. Certainly don't want to. That's his personal bit of drainpipe he's put up. He copied mine. He never had an original idea."

"Good God! I've a mind to go and see him myself. He went through it, you know. This is ridiculous."

"Go if you like," said Filth, "but you needn't bother to come and see me again if you do."

Filth walked that day further than usual and returned home after dark. It was getting towards Christmas, and Kate and the gardener had hung fairy lights around his length of lead piping. There was a holly wreath on his door and a spangle of coloured lights shone from his windows. He could see the light of his coal fire in the sitting room, a table light on in the hall showing Christmas cards standing about. As ever, the right-hand bend of the lane and the house above were in total darkness.

Don't expect he's there, thought Filth. Playboy! Probably lives half the time in his London club. Or with a whore. Or with several whores. Or in Las Vegas or somewhere vulgar for Christmas. Disneyland.

After the hellish years without Betty, Filth was, however, beginning to learn how to live again. The remorse. The loss of the sense of comfort she brought, her integration with the seasons of the year, her surety about a life of the spirit—never actually discussed. Often, when he was alone in the house and she seemed to be just at his shoulder, he would say aloud to her shadow, "I left you too often. My work was too important to me." He did not address the first days of their engagement though. Never. Never.

Christmases alone he liked. Positively liked. With Betty

unavailable there was nobody he wanted to be with. He and Betty had gone in the last years to the hotel in Salisbury together for Christmas lunch. No fuss. No paper hats. No streamers to get caught up in all her necklaces. Now he went alone to the same hotel, the same table. Taken there and returned by taxi. Then a good read, a whisky or two before bed. This year, his fourth without her, was to be exactly as usual.

Except that it was snowing. And it had been snowing very hard since he got up. The snowflakes fell so fast and thick he could not say whether they were going up or down. He could not even see the barrier of trees that shielded him from his neighbour.

And this year—no sign of the taxi. It was already half an hour late. Filth decided to ring it up but found that his phone was dead. Ha!

He padded about—getting very late indeed now—and was relieved to hear a loud bang and slither outside in the drive. But nothing further.

Taxi's crashed against the wall in the snow, he thought, and went out of the front door one step only and still in his slippers and without his coat. But there was no taxi, only a great heap of snow that had slid from his roof into the drive. And the snow was falling faster than ever.

And behind him he heard his front door click shut on its fine Chubb lock.

And at the same moment, up behind the trees, Veneering was humped in bed, wearing a much-used fleece and his pyjamas, and thick woollen socks, under two duvets. He had examined Christmas Day with one eye, then the bedside clock with the other, groaned as he flexed his wrists and ankles, seen that his bedroom, with the old drugget on the floor and the navy-blue cotton curtains he had inherited from the farming family, was damp and dreary as usual but that round the black edges of the curtains was a suffusing, imperial dazzle. Hobbling from the bed, pulling back a curtain, he saw the snow.

The sky must be somewhere out there, too, the treetops below him, Whin Green. But all he saw was dancing snow so thick he couldn't tell if it was going up or coming down. *Coming up*, he thought, afraid. Was he still drunk from last night? *Or am I standing on my head?* He concentrated and, looking down, made out a patch of shadow, a certain darkness around—what? Yes. It must be old Filth's chimney stack, the flashing round its base on the roof. Yes. The chimney was there and a great sloppy patch of snow had melted round it and— wha-hey! As Veneering watched he saw the shadow moving and the whole slope of wetter warmer snow (he'd have his central heating on full tilt of course) slipped away to the ground and he heard the thunderous slap as it landed.

Kill him if he happens to be under it, thought Veneering. But I shouldn't think he is. He'll be at some ghastly party with "all the trimmings." He thought of Betty long, long ago sitting up very straight and perky with the paper streamers tangled up in her necklaces. Maybe sometimes his pearls . . . He was making for his bed again when the front-door bell rang.

Veneering pulled on some trousers and another fleece over the first and something in the way of shoes and the bell rang again. Who the hell . . . ?

Looking out of his sitting-room window he saw Filth standing in his porch in a cashmere cardigan and slippers, and soaked to the skin. Very doleful face, too. Well, well. This'll kill him. Ha! The old fool's locked himself out. Went out to investigate the bang. Ha!

He answered the next peal on the bell and they confronted each other. Filth's magnificent face dropped open at the jaw like a cartoon and Veneering remembered that he hadn't shaved. Not yesterday either. Feathers, expecting Achilles, saw a little old man with a couple of strands of yellow-grey hair across his pate, bent over with arthritis. Veneering, expecting the glory of Agamemnon, saw a lanky skeleton that might just have been dragged dripping from the sea full fathom five and those were certainly not pearls that were his eyes.

"Oh, good morning, Filth," said Veneering.

"Just called to say Happy Christmas," said Edward Feathers, crossing Veneering's un-hollied threshold.

"Good of you to call," said Veneering. "I'll get you a towel. Better take off the pullover. I've a duffel here. And maybe the slippers? There's a fire in here."

Together they entered Veneering's bleak sitting room where he switched on a brown electric heater where soon a wire-worm of an element began to glow into life. "We can put the second bar on if you wish," said Veneering. He did so. They looked at it. "*O, come let us be merry,*" said Veneering, "Don't want to get mean, like Fiscal-Smith."

A faint smile hovered round Filth's blue lips.

"Whisky?" said Veneering.

They each drank a gigantic, neat whisky. On a table lay an immense jigsaw only half finished. They regarded it, sipping. "Too much damn sky," said Veneering. "Sit down."

In a glass case on legs Filth saw a pair of chandelier earrings. He remembered them. On the mantelpiece was a photograph of an enchanting young Guards officer. The fire, the whisky, the earrings, the steady falling snow, made Filth want to weep.

"Another?" asked Veneering.

"I should really be going."

"I was sorry to hear about Betty," said Veneering, looking away.

"I was sorry to hear about Elsie," said Filth, remembering her name, her beauty, her yellow silk dress at the Hong Kong

Jockey Club. Her unhappiness. "Tell me, what news of your son?"

"Dead," said Veneering. "Killed. Soldier."

"I am so terribly sorry. So most dreadfully sorry. I hear nothing. Oh, I am so very sorry."

"I sometimes think we all hear too much. It is too hard—the suffering for each other. I think we had too many Hearings all those years."

"I must go home."

Filth was looking troubled and Veneering thought: In a minute he'll have to tell me that he's locked himself out. Let's see how he'll get round that.

"It was good of you to come, Filth."

Filth said nothing for a while. Then, "I really came to ask you if I could use your phone. Mine's out of order. Expecting a taxi."

(Well done, thought Veneering. Good opening move.)

"Mine will be out of order if yours is, I expect. But by all means try."

The phone was dead.

(And the village is three miles away and the only spare key will be with his cleaner and it's Christmas and she won't be back until the New Year. And I've got him.)

"As a matter of fact," Veneering said, "I've meant to come and see you several times."

Filth looked into his whisky glass. He felt ashamed. He himself had never dreamed of doing any such thing.

"Only trouble was I couldn't think of an excuse. Bloody hot-tempered type I was, once upon a time."

"Bloody good judge, though," said Filth, remembering that this was true.

"You were a bloody good Advocate. Come on. One more.

"The only excuse I could think of," Veneering said in a minute, "was that there's an old key of yours hanging up here in an outhouse. Has your address on it. Must have been here for years. Probably the last people here had been given one for emergencies. Maybe you have one of mine?"

"No, I don't think so," said Filth.

"Shall I get it? Or some other time?"

"I may as well take it now."

On Veneering's doorstep, the snow now thinning, wearing Veneering's unpleasant overcoat, he heard himself say, "I have a ham shank at home. Tin of crabmeat. A good bottle. If you care to come over for Boxing Day?"

"Delighted," said Veneering.

Down the slippery slope went Filth, holding very tightly to Veneering's yews. He put the old Dexter key in the lock. Would it turn?

It did.

CHAPTER THIRTY-TWO

That spring Veneering began to play chess at Dexters once a week. Then twice a week, on Thursdays and Sundays. Each time, before he arrived, Filth moved Betty's pink umbrella from the umbrella stand in the hall to the cupboard under the stairs. Later he would bring it out again. He also moved, right out of sight, the rather magisterial photograph on the chimney piece of Betty holding up the OBE for her good works and replaced it with one of himself and Betty laughing together in Bhutan on their honeymoon. Veneering appeared to notice nothing in the Feathers' house except the chessboard.

As the year warmed they began to meet occasionally to walk in the lanes, and Veneering grew less yellow and arthritic. He tended to stop for every passer-by for conversation and cross-examination. His charm revived and he began again to take pleasure in everybody he met, especially if they were female. Females were always "girls." He used the old upper-class lingo, thought Filth. Must have learned it at embassy parties. Certainly not in Middlesbrough where he was born. Filth's snobbery was now appalling.

The "girl" Veneering liked best was pretty Dulcie, and on meeting they would stand bobbing about in the lane together while Filth inspected the sky or sometimes pretended his walking stick was a golf club and tried out a couple of swings. They sniff round each other like dogs, he thought. Come on, Veneering, you'll catch cold.

"I begin," said Filth to Betty's shadow, "to wish I'd left the bloody key where it was. I'm stuck with him now."

But he was not. On one chess Thursday, Veneering said, as he took Filth's queen, "Oh, by the way, I'm going on a cruise."

Filth took his time. He rather interestingly shifted a knight and took Veneering's bishop. "Oh, well done!" said Veneering. "Yes, I'm off to the Mediterranean. Sailing to Malta. Getting some warmth into my joints."

"I'm told it can be bitterly cold in Malta in March."

"Oh, I'm hoping to stay with the Governor. I've met him once or twice. Nice wife."

"You sound like Fiscal-Smith. You're not going on a cruise with him, are you?"

"Good God, no. I'm striking out."

Filth waited to see if he'd suggest that Filth himself might accompany him. He did not.

"Betty and I found that the few expats left on Malta were pretty ropy. She called them 'the riff-raff of Europe.'"

"Did she? Oh, well, we're all riff-raff now. I wouldn't suggest Malta was the best place for you, Edward. Sea can be unpleasant and you're too old to fly. Insurance would be tricky."

"I know the sea, and you are hardly younger than I am. What about *your* insurance?"

"Not bothering. I've pots of money if I catch the Maltese flu and have to go to hospital. I dare say the Governor would see me right anyway."

Filth thought that using a phrase like "see me right" was what he had always detested about Veneering.

The evening before he left for his cruise Veneering called on Filth with a supermarket bag full of leftovers of food that he thought Filth might like to make use of, and details of his cruise line. Filth took the leftovers into the kitchen and put them in the rubbish bin. He returned and said, "Why?"

"Well, then someone could let me know if there was a crisis."

"You mean you'd want to know if I should kick the bucket?"

"Well, yes, of course."

"In order to return for my funeral?"

"Certainly not. I'd probably send the odd flower. I'd come later for your memorial service. It wouldn't be for several months, so I would be able to finish my philanderings. But yes, I'd want to know."

Then he realised what he'd said. "Not, of course, that I've ever been a philanderer. Never. I was always serious, which was why my life has always been so exhausting—whatever it looked like. I do know how to love a woman."

But he was getting in deeper.

Filth sat mute. This time Veneering had gone too far. His restored health had also restored his outrageous conceit. He was still the same—*bounder*—as before.

"I'll walk home with you."

"Oh." Veneering hadn't planned to leave just yet. He could smell Filth's supper cooking.

"Must get my walk in before dusk," said Filth. "Come on," and he took his stick from the umbrella stand where (damn) he had forgotten to remove Betty's pink umbrella. And (double damn) as, holding open the door for Veneering, he saw Veneering look at it, Bloody Hell—*touch* it!

Filth gave his queer roar. He led the way out, not to the lane end, but down his garden, past the tulip beds, the still-leafless orchard, past Betty's still-wonderful kitchen garden, her pond, her spinney, and somehow they were back at the house again but now facing the steep track that led up a bank from an alley behind a shed.

"That's the old earth closet," said Filth. "Come on, I'll show you a quick way home," and he began to spring up the slippery bank like a boy.

Veneering followed on all fours.

"Good God, where are we going?"

"To the road," said Filth. "You'd better take my hand. When we were just a cottage there used to be an opening on the lane up here. You had to climb through—ah, come on."

Veneering hesitated, but eventually they stood together on the upper road in the coming dark.

"I found Betty standing here once," said Filth. "Long ago. She'd been very ill. Somehow she found this place. To convalesce. The station taxi brought her to this opening on the road and she stayed here all by herself. I forget for how long. It seemed very long to me. I couldn't phone. She didn't answer my letters. I was in the middle of the Reservoir Case. You'll remember it."

"Well, you couldn't just abandon it."

"No? Well—I wonder . . . She disappeared. Was she with you, Veneering? Not down here at all?"

"I swear to you, no. I was on the Reservoir Case, too, remember?"

"What do I remember? Didn't you leave your junior? One fantasises. I came looking for her. Found her in the end, standing here in the road in a browny-gold silk thing, soaked to the skin, her suitcase beside her. I'd been round and round, through all the bloody Donheads. Thought I'd never see her again. When I did find her, her wet face became—well, delirious with happiness. As if she saw me for the first time. And I knew I need never worry about you ever again."

Veneering said, "I'll get back to my packing."

"*But*," said Edward Feathers QC (Learned in the Law) "—and I'll walk up with you—*but* she never knew the truth about me. For two nights after Betty and I became engaged to be married in Hong Kong I was with the girl who'd fascinated and obsessed me ever since I was sixteen. She happened to be passing through Hong Kong. I didn't know she knew Betty. I didn't connect her with the girl Betty was just then travelling with. I didn't even know that she and Amy and Betty were at the same school. Not until after Betty died. Then I found out that Betty and Isobel had been together at Bletchley Park, too. Betty had always called her Lizzie.

"But when I found Isobel again, there in Hong Kong, just after I'd made Betty promise never to leave me, I forgot Betty completely. For two nights I was with Isobel in my room at the Peninsular Hotel. There can't be anything more disgusting, more perfidious than that. Veneering? The only equally disgusting thing would be if some other man had that night been with Betty. Would it not?"

"It happens. This sort of thing, Filth."

"Oh, it *happens*—but only if you are an absolute swine. Don't you think? Wouldn't you say? If you examine your meagre self? Veneering?"

"Look—it's over half a century ago. We were young men."

"Yes. But I did something worse to Betty. I knew she wanted children. Ten, she'd said. I suspected that I was infertile. Something to do with—perhaps mumps at school. Apparently I talked to Ross—when I had fever in Africa. I can't remember any of it. Nobody knew any of it, except perhaps Isobel.

"So you see I'm not a saint, Veneering. She was worth ten of me. Yet, from the moment I found her standing here in the road I knew she would never leave me now. You were nowhere. Goodbye, old man." And Filth walked back down the slope.

Below, beside the earth closet, Filth shouted up, "Look, Veneering, it doesn't matter which of us was father of the child."

"*Child*!"

"The child she lost. Before she had the hysterectomy. Yours or mine, it was not to be. What matters is to face something quite different. Betty didn't love either of us very much. The one she loved was your son. Harry."

"Yes," he said, his pale old face peering down. "Yes. I believe she did love Harry."

"Why else would she have given him ten thousand pounds?"

"That is a lie! It is a *lie*! She told me herself that Harry never asked her for money."

Filth, despite himself, softened. "I don't expect he did. Betty was always ready to give, whether any of us asked or not."

So that's fixed him, thought Filth. I've won. That night he went slowly up his stairs to bed, pausing a little breathlessly on the landing. "Checkmate," he said.

But then, later, lying in bed, every button done up on his striped pyjamas, clean handkerchief in his pyjama pocket, he wondered why he did not feel triumphant. There was no relish. No relish.

Well, he thought. That's the last I'll hear from him.

Veneering did not return from Malta. He broke one of his arthritic ankles on a stony slope where there was a deep slash in the rock masked by the night-scented stocks that grow wild all over the island and make it such heaven in the spring. A thrombosis followed and then Veneering died.

When the news was broken to Sir Edward Feathers he said, "Ah, well. He was a great age. He hadn't looked after himself very well. I shall miss the chess."

About two weeks later, the Maltese postal service being so slow, a picture postcard arrived for Filth at Donhead St. Ague. It said,

We are bathed in glorious sunlight here [Oh, so he got to heaven then, did he?] and I'm having a wonderfully revitalising holiday. A pity that it would have been too much for you. Today I'm going to see the one fresh-water spring on the island (life like an ever-rolling stream, etc.) with a man who says he once met you and you offered him a job as your clerk. Seems very unlikely. But memory tells all of us lies. Looking forward to our next encounter. Kind regards. T.H.V.

Filth did not attend Veneering's memorial service. He thought it would be theatrical to do so. The Great Rapprochement. Dulcie would tell him all about it. Kate the cleaner was a bit tight-lipped with him, saying that he could have shared a car with someone, but he said, "I have things to see to. I am planning a journey of my own."

"Well, I hope it's not a cruise."

"No, no. Not a cruise. I'm thinking of going back to my birthplace for a last look round. Malaya—they call it Malaysia now, like a headache. I shall be going by air."

She gasped and shrieked and ran to tell the gardener and Filth saw the pair of them deep in conversation as he plodded on with *Hudson* in his study. He was negotiating about who would continue with *Hudson* when he was dead. Veneering would have been the obvious choice. Ah well.

He was beginning to miss Veneering more than he would admit. When the *For Sale* notice went up again so vulgarly in the lane it gave him a jolt. When lights of the ugly house again appeared through the trees, he was drowsing with his curtains undrawn and he woke with a start of pleasure that turned to pain as he remembered that Veneering would not be there.

"You can have anything you want of mine if I don't come back," he had said.

Filth had said, "Oh, nothing, thanks. Maybe the chessmen."

One afternoon during a St. Martin's summer, his bony knees under a tartan rug, Filth was snoozing in the garden when he became aware of a movement in one of the fruit trees and a new next-door child dropped out of it eating an apple. The child began to wander nonchalantly over the lawn as if he owned it. Filth had been reading minutes of the latest Bench Table of his Inn. He felt like throwing the child back over the hedge.

"Sorry," the child said.

"I suppose you're wanting a ball back."

"I haven't got a ball."

"Well, what's that in your hand? And I don't mean my apple."

"Just some old beads I found in that flower bed." And he vanished.

They're so bloody self-confident, thought Filth. My prep-school Headmaster would have settled him. Then: What am I saying? Sir'd have set about teaching him something about apples.

"Keep the beads," he called. "They're yours."

The night before he was to leave for his voyage home to Malaya, Filth felt such a surge of longing for Betty that he had to sit down and close his eyes. The longing had included guilt. Why guilt? Because he was beginning to forget her. Forget his long desire. "Memory and desire," he said aloud, "I must keep track of them or the game's up." Then he thought: Or maybe let them go?

There was a ring at his doorbell and a family stood grimly on his doorstep, father, mother, son and daughter.

"Might we come in? We are from next door," said the father (a gent, though long-haired). "We need to speak to you on a serious matter."

"Come in."

They filed into the hall. "Sebastian," said the father and the boy held out Betty's pearl necklace.

"He says you gave it him. We want to know the truth. He says he found it in a flower bed."

"Yes. I did. He did. Perfectly right." (The look in the parents' eyes. Think I'm a paedophile?)

"You see—sir," said the father. "We believe these pearls to be valuable."

"Yes. I expect they are. They were my wife's. Given her by some old boyfriend. She threw them away. Silly woman. She had much better ones from me. Mine have been inherited by some cousin, I think. These—well, I'll be glad to see the last of them. Her "guilty pearls", I called them."

"Well, really—we couldn't . . ."

"I'm just off on a trip. Look, if you want to repay me could you just keep an eye on the house while I'm away? I have a spare key here. For emergencies." He handed them the key that knew its way about their house. "I hear that you are what is called 'Green.' And aren't you intellectuals?"

"I'm not," said the little girl.

"Dad is," said the boy. "He's a poet."

"Good, good—"

"And I'm going to do bed and breakfast," said the wife. "I hope you don't mind if I put up a sign on our lane?"

CHAPTER THIRTY-THREE

When he stepped off the still-vibrating plane and smelled the East again, the hot airport, the hot jungle, the heavy scents of spices and humans and tropical trees and tropical food, Filth forgot everything else and knew that memory was now unnecessary and all desire fulfilled. Betty at his shoulder, he fell into the everlasting arms. The mystery and darkness and warmth of the womb returned him to the beginning of everything and to the end of all need.

His memorial service, several months later at the other side of the world, was distinguished but rather small. It was so very long since Sir Edward Feathers had been in practice. His years alone with *Hudson* had been solitary and long, and his age was so great that few lawyers could remember him as a person.

Nevertheless quite a good scattering turned up. In the Benchers' pews the Lord Chief Justice sat, for Feathers had been a great name in his time—when the Lord Chief was probably still at school. The Master of the Temple preached on Feathers' integrity and advocacy ("in a style no doubt we would now find a little dated!"), his bravery in World War Two, his long, quiet, happy marriage. His charm. He had kept clear of politics, given himself entirely to the importance of the tenets of English Law. We shall not see his like again . . . etc.

"Who's that creature?" asked one of Amy's children. Amy's grandchildren and children made quite a mob in the public pews. "Just below the pulpit. He looks like a pickled walnut."

Albert Ross had, in fact, been asked by an usher to move from the seats reserved permanently for Masters of the Temple but had taken no notice. Across from him in an equally regal seat in the Middle Temple Benchers' pews, a legitimate lawyer who looked preserved in aspic was glaring across at him. It was Fiscal-Smith accompanying dear old Dulcie. He had a cheap-day return railway ticket sticking out of his pocket.

In the body of the church, across from Amy's family but a modest pew or so behind them, sat the family of Sir Edward Feathers's neighbours, the mother wearing a double string of remarkable pearls. Several pews around had filled up quite nicely with members of the Bar of the Construction Industry, particularly those from the Chambers that Sir Edward and the pickled walnut had founded. There was a clutch of clerks, one of whom had been in his pram when Sir Edward was sitting disconsolate in a draughty corridor without any work one winter's afternoon.

Then a tall and beautiful and very old woman came in and slid in beside Amy, looking at nobody. She wore a pale silk coat and her face was an enigma.

"Who's that? She's like the collarbone of a hare," said the poet. "I bet it was his mistress."

They sang the usual hymns, "I vow to thee my country" being the most inappropriate. Filth's country had never been England.

Outside afterwards, they all gathered to hear the bell toll once for every year of Filth's life and it seemed as if it would go on for ever. It was autumn and gold dry leaves scratched under their feet.

The dwarf, the pickled walnut, was being helped into his Rolls-Royce. He handed his large felt hat to the Chief Clerk. "I've done with it," he said. "Keep it in the Chambers. It is your foundation stone."

"Aren't you coming in to the wake, Mr. Ross?"

"No. Plane to catch. I am en route to Kabul. Goodbye."
Waving a hero's wave he was spirited away.

"Is it all a pantomime?" asked one of the children and the
poet said, "Something of the sort."

Inside the Parliament Chamber of the Inner Temple Hall
the wine was flowing now and the famous hat went from hand
to hand. Someone said, "He's supposed to have kept his playing cards in that hat."

"Well, there's a zip across the inside of it."

So they unzipped it and found the playing cards fastened in
a pouch.

"What's that other thing in there?" asked the next-door
boy.

It was a small oilskin packet tied with very old string, and
inside it was a watch.

ACKNOWLEDGEMENTS

My thanks to kind friends Charles and Caroline
Worth, who have tried to check the topography
of Hong Kong in the 1950s—an almost impossible task, and to Richard Wallington, who has
answered a number of questions about the
English Bar in Hong Kong. Thanks to William
Mayne, for information about East Pakistan.

And gratitude to Richard Ingrams who,
almost ten years ago now, asked for a Christmas
story in the *Oldie* and released from somewhere
in my sub-conscious Sir Edward Feathers QC,
who has dominated three books and a large part
of my life ever since. Particular thanks to my
editor Penelope Hoare who has been, as ever,
indispensable. Any remaining mistakes are my
own.

Most of all, thanks to my husband David
Gardam, especially for memories of our travels
to places where the English Law continues to be
heard.

Jane Gardam
Sandwich, Kent
2009

ABOUT THE AUTHOR

Jane Gardam is the only writer to have been twice awarded the Whitbread Prize for Best Novel of the Year (for *The Queen of the Tambourine* and *The Hollow Land*). She also holds a Heywood Hill Literary Prize for a lifetime's contribution to the enjoyment of literature.

She has published four volumes of acclaimed stories: *Black Faces, White Faces* (David Higham Prize and the Royal Society for Literature's Winifred Holtby Prize); *The Pangs of Love* (Katherine Mansfield Prize); *Going into a Dark House* (Silver Pen Award from PEN); and most recently, *Missing the Midnight*.

Her novels include *God on the Rocks* (shortlisted for the Booker Prize), *Faith Fox, The Flight of the Maidens* and most recently *Old Filth*, a *New York Times* Notable Book of the Year.

Jane Gardam lives with her husband in England.

Carmine Abate
Between Two Seas
"Abate populates this magical novel with a cast of captivating, emotionally complex characters."—*Publishers Weekly*
224 pp • $14.95 • ISBN: 978-1-933372-40-2

Muriel Barbery
The Elegance of the Hedgehog
"Among the most exhilarating and extraordinary novels in recent years."
—*Elle* (Italy)
336 pp • $15.00 • ISBN: 978-1-933372-60-0

Stefano Benni
Margherita Dolce Vita
"A modern fable...hilarious social commentary."—*People*
240 pp • $14.95 • ISBN: 978-1-933372-20-4

Timeskipper
"Thanks to Benni we have a renewed appreciation
of the imagination's ability to free us from our increasingly mundane
surroundings."—*The New York Times*
400 pp • $16.95 • ISBN: 978-1-933372-44-0

Massimo Carlotto
The Goodbye Kiss
"A masterpiece of Italian noir."—*Globe and Mail*
160 pp • $14.95 • ISBN: 978-1-933372-05-1

Death's Dark Abyss
"A remarkable study of corruption and redemption
in a world where revenge is best served ice-cold."
—*Kirkus* (starred review)
160 pp • $14.95 • ISBN: 978-1-933372-18-1

The Fugitive
"The reigning king of Mediterranean noir."
—*The Boston Phoenix*
176 pp • $14.95 • ISBN: 978-1-933372-25-9

Steve Erickson
Zeroville
"A funny, disturbing, daring and demanding novel—Erickson's best."
—*The New York Times*
352 pp • $14.95 • ISBN: 978-1-933372-39-6

Elena Ferrante
The Days of Abandonment
"The raging, torrential voice of [this] author
is something rare."—*The New York Times*
192 pp • $14.95 • ISBN: 978-1-933372-00-6

Troubling Love
"Ferrante's polished language belies the rawness of her imagery, which
conveys perversity, violence, and bodily functions in ripe detail."
—*The New Yorker*
144 pp • $14.95 • ISBN: 978-1-933372-16-7

The Lost Daughter
"A resounding success…Delicate yet daring, precise
yet evanescent: it hurts like a cut, and cures like balm."
—*La Repubblica*
144 pp • $14.95 • ISBN: 978-1-933372-42-6

Jane Gardam
Old Filth
"Gardam's novel is an anthology of such bittersweet scenes,
rendered by a novelist at the very top of her form."
—*The New York Times*
304 pp • $14.95 • ISBN: 978-1-933372-13-6

The Queen of the Tambourine
"This is a truly superb and moving novel."
—*The Boston Globe*
272 pp • $14.95 • ISBN: 978-1-933372-36-5

The People on Privilege Hill
"Artful, perfectly judged shifts of mood fill *The People on Privilege Hill*
with an abiding sense of joy."—*The Guardian*
208 pp • $15.95 • ISBN: 978-1-933372-56-3

Alicia Giménez-Bartlett
Dog Day
"Delicado and Garzón prove to be one of the more engaging sleuth teams
to debut in a long time."—*The Washington Post*
320 pp • $14.95 • ISBN: 978-1-933372-14-3

Prime Time Suspect
"A gripping police procedural."—*The Washington Post*
320 pp • $14.95 • ISBN: 978-1-933372-31-0

Death Rites
304 pp • $16.95 • ISBN: 978-1-933372-54-9

Katharina Hacker
The Have-Nots
"Hacker's prose, aided by Atkins's pristine translation, soars [as] she admirably explores modern urban life from the unsettled haves to the desperate have-nots."—*Publishers Weekly*
352 pp • $14.95 • ISBN: 978-1-933372-41-9

Patrick Hamilton
Hangover Square
"Hamilton is a sort of urban Thomas Hardy: always a pleasure to read, and as social historian he is unparalleled."
—Nick Hornby
336 pp • $14.95 • ISBN: 978-1-933372-06-8

James Hamilton-Paterson
Cooking with Fernet Branca
"Irresistable!"—*The Washington Post*
288 pp • $14.95 • ISBN: 978-1-933372-01-3

Amazing Disgrace
"It's loads of fun, light and dazzling as a peacock feather."
—*New York Magazine*
352 pp • $14.95 • ISBN: 978-1-933372-19-8

Alfred Hayes
The Girl on the Via Flaminia
"Immensely readable."—*The New York Times*
160 pp • $14.95 • ISBN: 978-1-933372-24-2

Jean-Claude Izzo
Total Chaos
"Izzo's Marseilles is ravishing. Every street, cafe and house has its own character."—*Globe and Mail*
256 pp • $14.95 • ISBN: 978-1-933372-04-4

by the same author

Fiction
A Long Way From Verona
The Summer After the Funeral
Bilgewater
Black Faces, White Faces
God on the Rocks
The Sidmouth Letters
The Pangs of Love and Other Stories
Crusoe's Daughter
Showing the Flag
The Queen of the Tambourine
Going Into a Dark House
Faith Fox
Missing the Midnight
The Flight of the Maidens
The Man in the Wooden Hat

For children
Bridget and William
The Hollow Land
A Few Fair Days

Non-fiction
The Iron Coast

Illustrated
The Green Man

OLD FILTH

Jane Gardam

OLD FILTH

Europa
editions

Europa Editions
214 West 29th Street
New York, N.Y. 10001
www.europaeditions.com
info@europaeditions.com

Library of Congress Cataloging in Publication Data is available
ISBN 978-1-933372-13-6

Gardam, Jane
Old Filth

Book design by Emanuele Ragnisco
www.mekkanografici.com

Printed in the USA

CONTENTS

*Lawyers, I suppose, were
children once*

(Inscription upon the statue of a child
in the Inner Temple Garden in London)

To Raj Orphans
and their parents

PART ONE

SCENE: INNER TEMPLE

The Benchers' luncheon-room of the Inner Temple. Light pours through the long windows upon polished table, silver, glass. A number of Judges and Benchers finishing lunch. One chair has recently been vacated and the Benchers are looking at it.

The Queen's Remembrancer: I suppose we all know who that was?

Junior judge: I've no idea.

Senior judge: It seemed to be a famous face.

The Common Sergeant: It was Old Filth.

JJ: *What!* But he must have died years ago. Contemporary of F. E. Smith.

CS: No. It was Old Filth. Great advocate, judge and—bit of a wit. Said to have invented FILTH—Failed In London Try Hong Kong. He tried Hong Kong. Modest, nice chap.

SJ: Hard worker. Well—the Pollution Law. Feathers on Pollution.

CS: Filth on Filth.

SJ: An old joke. He must be a hundred.

CS: Nowhere near. He's not been retired all that long. Looks a great age, though.

QR: Transparent. You could see the light through him.

CS: Magnificent looks, though. And still sharp.

QR: He's up here doing things to his Will. He's got Betty

with him. She's still alive too. They've had a soft life. Far Eastern Bar. And made a packet. Looked after themselves.

CS: Never put a foot wrong, Old Filth. Very popular.

QR: Except with Veneering.

SJ: Yes, that was odd. Out of character.

QR: For such a benevolent old bugger. D'you think there are mysteries?

SJ: Old Filth mysterious?

QR: It's a wonder he's not just a bore.

CS: Yes. But he's not. Child of the Raj, public school, Oxford, the Bar—but he's not a bore. Women went mad for him.

QR: Coffee? You going through?

CS: Yes. Ten minutes. My Clerk's packing in the next case. He'll be ranting at me. Tapping his watch.

QR: Yes. This isn't Hong Kong. Coffee? But it was good to see the old coelacanth.

CS: Yes. Yes, indeed it was. Tell our grandchildren.

THE DONHEADS

He was spectacularly clean. You might say ostentatiously clean. His ancient fingernails were rimmed with purest white. The few still-gold hairs below his knuckles looked always freshly shampooed, as did his curly still-bronze hair. His shoes shone like conkers. His clothes were always freshly pressed. He had the elegance of the 1920s, for his garments, whatever they looked like off, always became him. Always a Victorian silk handkerchief in the breast pocket. Always yellow cotton or silk socks from Harrods; and some still perfect from his old days in the East. His skin was clear and, in a poor light, young.

His colleagues at the Bar called him Filth, but not out of irony. It was because he was considered to be the source of the old joke, Failed In London Try Hong Kong. It was said that he had fled the London Bar, very young, very poor, on a sudden whim just after the War, and had done magnificently well in Hong Kong from the start. Being a modest man, they said, he had called himself a parvenu, a fraud, a carefree spirit.

Filth in fact was no great maker of jokes, was not at all modest about his work and seldom, except in great extremity, went in for whims. He was loved, however, admired, laughed at kindly and still much discussed many years after retirement.

Now, nearing eighty, he lived alone in Dorset. His wife Betty was dead but he often prattled on to her around the house. Astonishingly in one so old, his curly hair was not yet grey. His eyes and mind alert, he was a delightful man. He had always been thought so. A man whose distinguished life had run steadily and happily. There was no smell of old age about his house. He was rich and took for granted that it (and he) would be kept clean, fed and laundered by servants as it had always been. He knew how to treat servants and they stayed for years.

Betty had been successful with servants, too. Both she and Old Filth had been born in what Americans called the Orient and the British Raj had called the Far East. They knew who they were, but they were unselfconscious and popular.

After Betty's death the self-mockery dwindled in Old Filth. His life exploded. He became more ponderous. He began, at first slowly, to flick open shutters on the past that he had, as a sensible man with sensible and learned friends (he was a QC and had been a judge), kept clamped down.

His success as an advocate in Hong Kong had been phenomenal for he had had ease, grasp, diligence and flair. His career had taken off the minute he had begun to be briefed by the Straits-Chinese. It was not just that scraps of eastern languages began to re-emerge from his childhood in Malaya, but a feeling of nearness to the Oriental mind. When Old Filth spoke Malay or (less ably) Mandarin, you heard an unsuspected voice. Chinese, Malay and Bengali lawyers—though often trained at Oxford and the Inns of Court—were thought to be not straightforward but Filth, now Old Filth and after his retirement often Dear Old Filth, had found them perfectly straightforward, and to his taste.

All his life he kept a regard for Chinese values: the courtesy, the sudden thrust, the holiness of hospitality, the pleasure in money, the decorum, the importance of food, the discretion, the cleverness. He had married a Scotswoman but she had been born in Peking. She was dumpy and tweedy with broad Lanarkshire shoulders and square hands, but she spoke Mandarin perfectly and was much more at home with Chinese ways and idiom than she ever felt on her very rare visits to Scotland. Her passion for jewellery was Chinese and her strong Scottish fingers rattled the trays of jade in the street markets of Kowloon, stirring the stones like pebbles on a beach. "When you do that," Old Filth would say—when they were young and he was still aware of her all the time—"your eyes are almond-shaped." "Poor Old Betty," he would say to her ghost across in another armchair in the house in Dorset to which they had retired and in which she had died.

And why ever Dorset? Nobody knew. Some family tradition somewhere perhaps. Filth said it was because he disliked everywhere else in England, Betty because she felt the cold in Scotland. They both had a dismissive attitude towards Wales.

But if any old pair had been born to become retired ex-pats in Hong Kong, members of the Cricket Club, the Jockey Club, stalwarts of the English Lending Library, props of St. Andrew's Church and St. John's Cathedral, they were Filth and Betty. People who would always be able to keep servants (Filth was very rich), who would live in a house on The Peak, be forever welcoming hosts to every friend of a friend's friend visiting the Colony. When you thought of Betty, you saw her at her round rosewood dining table, looking quickly about her to see if plates were empty, tinkling her little bell to summon the snakey smiling girls in their household livery of identical cheongsams. Old Filth and Betty were perfectly international people, beloved ornaments at every one of the Memorial Services to old friends, English or Chinese, in the Cathedral. In the last years these deaths had been falling thick and fast upon them.

Was it perhaps "The Pound" that drew them to Dorset? The thought of having to survive one day in Hong Kong on a pension? But the part of Dorset they had chosen was far from cheap. Betty was known to "have her own money" and Filth had always said merrily that he had put off making judge for as long as possible so that he hadn't to live on a salary.

And they had no children. No responsibilities. No one to come back to England for.

Or was it—the most likely thing—the end of Empire? The drawing-near of 1997? Was it the unbearableness of the thought of the arrival of the barbarians? The now unknown, but certainly changed, Mainland-Chinese whose grandparents had fed the baby Miss Betty on soft, cloudy jellies and told her frightening fairy tales?

Neither Filth nor Betty cared for the unknown and already, five years before they left, English was not being heard so much in Hong Kong shops and hotels and, when it was heard, it was being spoken less well. Many familiar English and Chinese had disappeared to London or Seattle or Toronto, and many children had vanished to foreign boarding schools. The finest of the big houses on The Peak were in darkness behind steel grilles, and at Betty's favourite jeweller the little girls behind the counter, who sat all day threading beads and who still seemed to look under sixteen although she had known them twenty years, glanced up more slowly now when she rang the bell on the armour-plated door. They kept their fixed smiles but somehow found fewer good stones for her. Chinese women she knew had not the same difficulty.

So suddenly Filth and Betty were gone, gone for ever from the sky-high curtains of glittering lights, unflickering gold, soft-green and rose, from the busy waters of the finest harbour in the world and the perpetual drama of every sort of boat: the junks and oil tankers and the private yachts like swans, and the comforting, bottle-green bulk of the little Star Ferries that chugged back and forth to Kowloon all day and most of the night. *This deck accommodates 319 passengers.* Filth had loved the certainty of the *19*.

So they were gone, far from friends and over seventy, to a house deep in the Donheads on the Dorset-Wiltshire border, an old low stone house that could not be seen from its gate. A rough, narrow drive climbed up to it, curving towards it and out of sight. The house sat on a small plateau looking down over forests of every sort and colour of English tree, and far across the horizon was a long scalpel line of milky, chalky downland, dappled with shadows drawn across it by the clouds. No place in the world is less like Hong Kong or the Far East.

Yet it was not so remote that a doctor might start suggesting in a few years' time that it might be kinder to the Social Services if they were to move nearer to civilisation. There was a village half a mile up the hilly road that passed their gate, and half a mile in the other direction, also up a hill for their drive ran down into a dip, were a church and a shop. There were other houses among the trees. There was even a house next door, its gateway alongside theirs, its drive curving upwards as did their own, though branching away. It disappeared, as did their own. So they were secluded but not cut off.

And it worked. They made it work. Betty was the sort of woman who had plotted that the end of her life would work, and Filth, having Betty, had no fears of failure. They changed of course. They discarded much. They went out and about very little. Betty wrote a great many letters. They put their hearts into becoming content, safe in their successful lives. Filth had always said—of his Cases—"I am trained to forget." "Otherwise," he said, "how could I function?" Facts, memories, the pain of life—of lives in chaos—have to be forgotten. Filth had condemned men to death. Had seen innocent men convicted. As a Silk he reckoned that fifty per cent of his Cases had gone wrong. In Hong Kong the judges lived in an enclave of palaces but behind steel gates guarded night and day.

In The Donheads they felt safe behind the lock of their old-fashioned farmhouse door that could never accidentally be left on the latch. Betty gardened, Filth read thrillers and biographies, worked now and then in his tool shed. He kept his judge's wig in its oval black-and-gold tin box on the hearth, like a grey cat in a basket. Then in time, as there was nobody but Betty to be amused, he moved it to his wardrobe to lie with his black silk stockings and buckled shoes. He had not brought the Black Cap home.

Betty sat sewing. She often stared for hours at the trees. They went to the supermarket in Shaftesbury once a week in their modest car. A gardener came to do the heavy digging and a woman from a nearby village came in four times a week to clean, cook and do the laundry. Betty said that Hong Kong's legacy was to make foreigners unable to do their own washing. After Betty died, the gardener and the woman continued to work for Filth. Filth's lifetime of disciplined charm survived well.

Or so it seemed. Looking back, Filth knew that beneath his apparent serenity the years after Betty's departure had been a time of mental breakdown and that mental breakdown in someone conditioned to an actor's life (which is the Bar) can be invisible both to the sufferer and everyone else.

And this—the event he came to see as the beginning of enlightenment—occurred one Christmas, two years on. The cleaning lady started it.

Letting herself in with her door-key, talking as usual before she was over the threshold, "*Well,*" she said. "What about this then, Sir Edward? You never hear a thing down this way till it's happened. Next door must have moved. Your next door. There's removal vans all up and down the drive and loads of new stuff being carried in. They say it's another lawyer from Singapore like you."

"Hong Kong," corrected Filth, as he always did.

"Hong Kong then. They'll be wanting a domestic I dare say, but they're out of luck. I'm well-suited here, you're not to worry. I'll find them someone if they ask. I've enough to do."

A few days later Filth was told, courtesy of the village shop, the new neighbour's name. It was, as the cleaning lady had said, indeed that of another Hong Kong lawyer and it was the name of the only man in his professional life, or come to that his private life, that Old Filth had ever detested. The extraordinary effect this man had had upon him over many years, and it had been much remarked upon and the usually buttoned-up Filth had not cared, was like venom sprayed from the mouths of Chinese dragons.

And the same had gone for Terry Veneering's opinion of Old Filth.

Betty had never spoken of it. Kept herself apart. Became silent, remote. Filth's Clerk, other lawyers, found the enmity almost a chemical, physical thing. In Hong Kong, the Bar watched. Old Filth, delightful wise Old Filth and swashbuckling Veneering, did not "have words" in Court, they spat poisons. They did not cross swords, they set about each other with scimitars. Old Filth believed that Terry Veneering was all that was wrong with the British masters of this divine Colony—jumped-up, arrogant, blustering, loud, cynical and common. And far too good at games. Without such as Veneering—who knows? Veneering treated the Chinese as if they were invisible, flung himself into pompous rites of Empire, strutted at ceremonies in his black and gold, cringed with sycophancy before the Governor, drank too much. In Court he treated his opponent to personal abuse. Once, when they were both still Counsel in an interminable case about a housing estate built over a Chinese graveyard (the housing estate mysteriously refused to prosper), Veneering spent days sneering at primitive beliefs. Or so Old Filth said in, and out of, Court. What Veneering said about Old Filth he never enquired but there was a mutual, seething dislike. Betty became haggard with the subject.

For Veneering got away with everything, snarled Filth. He bestrode the Colony on his thick legs like a colossus, booming on at parties about his own excellence. During a state visit by royalty he boasted about his boy at Eton. Later it was all "my boy at Cambridge," then "my boy in the Guards." "Insufferable," cried Filth. Betty said, "Oh, hush, hush."

Filth's first thought—now—was: Well, thank God Betty's gone. His second thought was that he would have to move.

However, the next-door house was as invisible as Filth's, its garden secret behind the long band of firs that curved between their joint drives. These trees grew broader, taller, all the time, and even when the leaves of other trees fell and it became winter, there was neither sight nor sound of the new neighbour.

"He's a widower, living alone," said the cleaning lady. "His wife used to be a Chinese."

Old Filth remembered then that Veneering had married a Chinese woman. Strange to have forgotten. Why did it stir up in him such a mixture of hatred and smugness—almost of relief? He remembered the wife now, her downward-looking eyes, the curious chandelier earrings she wore. He remembered her at the racecourse in a bright yellow silk dress, Veneering alongside—great coarse golden fellow, six foot two; his strangled voice trying to sound English public school.

Old Filth dozed off then with this picture before him, wondering at the clarity of an image thirty years old when what happened yesterday had receded into darkness. He was nearly eighty now. Veneering was a bit younger. Well, they could each keep their own corner. They need never meet.

Nor did they. The year went by and the next one. A friend from Hong Kong—young chap of sixty—called and said, "I believe old Terry Veneering lives somewhere down here, too. Do you ever come across him?"

"He's next door. No. Never."

"Next *door*? My dear fellow—!"

"I'd have been wise to move away."

"But you mean you've never—?"

"No."

"And he's made no . . . gesture?"

"Christopher, your memory is short."

"Well, I knew of course you were . . . You were both irra-tional in that direction, but . . ."

Old Filth walked his friend down to the gate. Beside it stood Veneering's gate, overhung by ragged yews. A short length of drainpipe, to take a morning newspaper, was attached to Veneering's gate. It was identical to the one that had lain by Old Filth's gate for many years. "He copied my drainpipe," said Old Filth. "He never had an original notion."

"I've half a mind to call," said Christopher.

"Well, you needn't come and see me again if you do," said courteous Old Filth.

Seated in his car in the road the friend considered the mys-tery of what convictions survive into dotage and how wise he had been to stay on in Hong Kong.

"You don't feel like a visit, Eddie?" he asked out of the car window. "Why not come out for Christmas? It's not so much changed that there'll ever be anywhere in the world like it."

But Filth said he never stirred at Christmas. Just a taxi to the White Hart at Salisbury, for luncheon. Good place. No paper hats. No streamers.

"I remember Betty with streamers tangled up in her hair and her pearls and gold chains. In Hong Kong."

But Filth thanked him and declined and waved him off.

On Christmas morning, Filth thought again of Christopher, as he was waiting for the taxi to the White Hart, watching from a window whose panes were almost blocked with snow, snow that had been falling when he'd opened his bedroom curtains five hours ago at seven o'clock. Big, fast, determined flakes. They fell and fell. They danced. They mesmerised. After a few moments you couldn't tell if they were going up or down. Thinking of the road at the end of his drive, the deep hollow there, he wondered if the taxi would make it. At twelve-fifteen he thought he might ring and ask, but waited until twelve-thirty as it seemed tetchy to fuss. He discovered the telephone was dead.

"Ah," he said. "Ha."

There were mince pies and a ham shank. A good bottle somewhere. He'd be all right. A pity though. Break with tradition.

He stood staring at the Christmas cards. Fewer again this year. As for presents, nothing except one from his cousin Claire. Always the same. Two handkerchiefs. More than he ever sent her, but she had had the pearls. He must send her some flowers. He picked up one large glossy card and read *A Merry Christmas from The Ideal Tailor, Century Arcade, Star Building, Hong Kong to an old and esteemed client*. Every year. Never failed. Still had his suits. Twenty years old. He wore them sometimes in summer. Snowflakes danced around a Chinese house on stilts. Red Chinese characters. A rosy Father Christmas waving from a corner. Stilts. Houses on stilts.

Suddenly he missed Betty. Longed for her. Felt that if he turned round now, quickly, there she would be.

But she was not.

Outside there was a strange sound, a long, sliding noise and a thump. A heavy thump. It might well be the taxi skidding on the drive and hitting the side of the house. Filth opened the front door but saw nothing but snow. He stepped quickly out upon his doorstep to look down the drive, and behind him the front door swung to, fastening with a solid, pre-War click.

He was in his bedroom slippers. Otherwise he was dressed in trousers, a singlet—which he always wore, being a gentleman, thank God—shirt and tie and the thin cashmere cardigan Betty had bought him years ago. Already it was sopped through.

Filth walked delicately along the side of the house in his slippers, bent forward, screwing his old eyes against the snow, to see if by any chance . . . but he knew that the back door was locked, and the French windows. He turned off towards the tool shed over the invisible slippery grass. Locked. He thought of the car in the garage. He hadn't driven now for some time, not since the days of terror. Mrs. Thing did the shopping now. It was scarcely used. But perhaps the garage—?

The garage was locked.

Nothing for it but to get down the drive somehow and wait for the taxi under Veneering's yews.

In his tiptoe way he passed the heap of snow that had fallen off the roof and had sounded like a slithering car. "I'm a bloody old fool," he said.

From the gate he looked out upon the road. It was a gleaming sheet of snow in both directions. Nothing had disturbed it for many hours. All was silent, as death. Filth turned and looked up Veneering's drive.

That too was pristine silk, unmarked by birds, unpocked by fallen berries. Snow and snow. Falling and falling. Thick, wet, ice cold. His thinning hair ice cold. Snow had gathered inside his collar, his cardigan, his slippers. All ice cold. His knobbly hands were freezing as he grasped first one yew branch and then the next. Hand over hand he made his way up Veneering's drive.

He'll be with the son, thought Old Filth. That or there'll be some ghastly house party going on. Golfers. Old cobwebs from the Temple. Smart solicitors. Gin.

But the house when it came in view was dark and seemed empty. Abandoned for years.

Old Filth rang the bell and stood on the porch. The bell tinkled somewhere far away inside, like Betty's at the rosewood dining-table in the Mid Levels.

And what the hell do I do now? He's probably gone to that oaf Christopher and they are carousing in the Peninsular Hotel. It'll be—what? Late night now. They'll have reached the brandy and cigars—the cigars presented in a huge shallow box, the maître d' bowing like a priest before the sacrament. The vulgarity. Probably kill the pair of them. Hullo?

A light had been switched on inside the house and a face peered from behind a curtain in a side window. Then the front door was opened slightly by a bent old man with a strand or two of blond hair.

"Filth? Come in."

"Thank you."

"No coat?"

"I just stepped across. I was looking out for my taxi. For the White Hart. Christmas luncheon. Just hanging about. I thought I'd call and . . ."

"Merry Christmas. Good of you."

They stood in the drear, unhollied hall.

"I'll get you a towel. Better take off your cardigan. I'll find you another. Whiskey?"

In the brown and freezing sitting-room a jigsaw puzzle only one-eighth completed was laid out over a huge table. Table and jigsaw were both white with dust. The venture looked hopeless.

"Too much damned sky," said Veneering as they stood contemplating it. "I'll put another bar on. I don't often sit in here. You must be cold. Maybe we'll hear your car from here, but I doubt it. I'd guess it won't get through."

"I wonder if I might use your phone? Mine seemed to be defunct."

"Mine too, I'd guess, if yours is," said Veneering. "By all means try."

The phone was dead.

They sat before two small, red wire-worms stretched across

the front of an electric fire. Some sort of antique, thought Filth. Haven't seen one like that in sixty years. Chambers in the years of the Great Fog.

In a display case on the chimney-piece he saw a pair of exotic chandelier earrings. The fire, the earrings, the whiskey, the jigsaw, the silence, the eerily-falling snow made him all at once want to weep.

"I was sorry to hear about Betty," said Veneering.

"I was sorry about Elsie," said Filth, remembering her name and her still and beautiful—and unhappy—Chinese face. "Your son—?"

"Dead," said Veneering. "Killed. Army."

"I am most terribly sorry. So dreadfully sorry. I hadn't heard."

"We don't hear much these days," said Veneering. "Maybe we don't want to. We had too many Hearings."

Filth watched the arthritic stooped old figure shamble across the room to the decanter.

"Not good for the bones, this climate," said Veneering, shambling back.

"Did you think of staying on?"

"Good God, no."

"It suited you so well." Then Filth said something very odd. "Better than us, I always thought. Better than me, anyway. And Betty never talked about it. She was very Scotch, you know."

"Plenty of Scots in Hong Kong," said Veneering. "You two seemed absolutely welded, melded, into the place. Betty and her Chinese jewellery."

"Oh, she tried," said Filth sadly. "She was very faithful."

"Another?"

"I should be getting home."

It dawned on Old Filth that he would have to ask a favour of Veneering. He had already lost a good point to him by call-

ing round wet to the skin. Veneering was still no fool. He'd
spotted the telephone business. It would be difficult to regain
his position. Maybe make something out of being the first to
break the silence? Maturity. Magnanimity. Water under the
bridge. Christmas Day. Hint at a larger spirit?

He wouldn't mention locking himself out.

But how was he to get home? Mrs. Thing's key was three
miles off and she wasn't coming in again until New Year's Day.
He could hardly stay here—Good God! With Veneering!

"I've thought of coming to see you," said Veneering.
"Several times as a matter of fact, this past year. Getting on,
both of us."

Old Filth was silent. He himself had not thought of doing
anything of the sort, and could not pretend.

"Couldn't think of a good excuse," said Veneering. "Bit
afraid of the reception. Bloody hot-tempered type, I used to
be. We weren't exactly similar."

"I've forgotten what type I was," said Filth, again surprising
himself. "Not much of anything, I expect."

"Bloody good advocate," said Veneering.

"You made a damn good judge," said Filth, remembering
that this was true. "Better than I was."

"Only excuse I could think of was a feeble one," said
Veneering. "There's a key of yours here hanging in my pantry.
Front door. Chubb. Your address is on the label. Must have
been here for years. Neighbours being neighbourly long ago, I
expect. Maybe you have one of mine?"

"No," said Filth. "No, I've not seen one."

"Could have let myself in, any time," said Veneering.
"Murdered you in your bed." There was a flash of the old black
mischief. "Must you go? I don't think there's going to be a taxi.
It would never make the hill. I'll get that key—unless you want
me to hold on to it. For an emergency?" (Another hard look.)

"No," said Filth with Court decorum. "No, I'll take it and see if it works."

On Veneering's porch, wearing Veneering's (ghastly) overcoat, Filth paused. The snow was easing. He heard himself say, "Boxing Day tomorrow. If you're on your own, I've a ham shank and some decent claret."

"Pleasure," said Veneering.

On his own doorstep Filth thought: Will it turn?
It did.

The house was beautifully warm but he made up the fire. The water would be hot, thank God. Get out of these clothes. Hello? What?

He thought he heard something in the kitchen. Hello? Yes?

He went through and found it empty. The snow had stopped at last and the windows were squares of black light. He thought, peering forward into the gloaming: Someone is looking in. But he could see no signs of footprints anywhere, and drew the curtains. He peeped into cupboards to make sure of things for tomorrow. Didn't want to look a fool. There was a can of shark's fin soup. Tin of crab-meat. Good rice. Package of parmesan. Avocado. Fine. Fine.

Behind him in the hall he heard something like a chuckle.

"Who the hell is that? Hello?" (Had the fellow had two keys? *Murdered you in your bed*.)

"Edward, Edward, stop these fantasies! You are too old. You are no longer seven." A man's voice. Good God, I'm going senile. "Yes, Sir," he said. "Kettle. Hot water bottle. Bath. I'm old."

The phone rang.

"You back safely?" asked Veneering's voice. "I thought I'd try the phone. We're in touch again."

"Oh. Thanks, Veneering. One o'clock tomorrow?"

"Yes. Would you like me to bring my chessmen?"

"Got some. Maybe next time."

"Next time."

So it wasn't Veneering, he ruminated in the bath, idly watching his old greying pubic hair floating like fern on the delicious hot water. Steam filled the bathroom. He almost slept.

Better get out. Somehow. Or it'll be all over.

He turned his lanky frame so that he was on all fours, facing the porcelain floor of the bath, balanced on his spread hands and his sharp knees (one of them none too excellent), and slithered his feet about to get some sort of purchase near the taps. Slowly the long length of him arose, feet squeaking a little. He pulled the plug out and watched the soapy water begin to drain, bubbling round his now rosy feet. He thought of another river. Black and brown babies splashing. A girl all warmth and laughter, his head against her thighs. The water gurgled away.

Getting more difficult. Must get a shower. Won't have one of those bloody mats with suction pads, though. Won't have what they call the Social Services. Veneering doesn't, you can see. Mind, Veneering doesn't look as if he has baths at all. Poor old bugger.

Wrapped in a white bath towel he padded about. Slippers, bath robe. Perfectly well. Take a little something to bed? No—eat it over the telly? Anchovy toast. Tea—enough whiskey. Ha!—blaze up, fire. Mustn't drop off.

"Don't drop off," said a woman's voice. "Don't drop off the perch! Not yet."

"Hey, hello, what? Betty?"

But again, nobody there.

Hope I'm not feverish.

"And I'm not being a fool," he shouted to the door of Betty's old bedroom and shut his own bedroom door behind him.

Perfectly in charge.

The bed was warm, and his own. Extraordinary really, the idea of sharing a bed. Bourgeois. Something Betty and I never talked about.

"This is not the time of frenzy," he heard himself say out loud as the images of the day merged into dreams. He was clinging to someone on a boat-deck and the sea a silver skin. There was screaming but it was somewhere else and hardly woke him. "We dealt with all that," he said, "in what they call my long, untroubled and uneventful life."

"Sleep, Filth," said a voice. "Nobody knew you like I did."

Which of them said that? he wondered.

"Yes, yes, yes," said Auntie May of the Baptist Mission, striding up the gangplank. "Now then, here we are. Excellent."

The motor launch, now and then trying its engine to see whether it would be safe to let it die, stirred the black water around it, rocked and snorted. All across the wide river, small waves slapped and tipped. Heat seemed to drip from the trees like oil. It was summer, the monsoon coming, and when it did the river traffic would die. This was why they were getting the baby home at only one week old. Otherwise he would have been stranded in the Port where he had gone to be born. Here they were, safely home, but it had been a near thing. A two-day journey and Auntie May, after she had seen him safely to his father's house, would have to make it back again herself, alone and at once.

On the journey out to the Port not much more than a week ago the baby not yet born had travelled the river in a native boat with his mother and the Malay woman who was now climbing the grass ladder to the landing stage, sorrowful and frightened, behind Auntie May. She had carried her own baby for she was the wet nurse who had been taken to Mrs. Feathers's confinement in case of an emergency should Mrs. Feathers have been unable to feed the child herself.

Nobody had expected Mrs. Feathers to die. The Clinic at the Port was good, the Baptist Mission efficient and known to her already for she had been a nurse before marriage to Feathers, the District Officer of Kotakinakulu province. She was a tough, lean Scot, like her husband, solid as a rock. She had nursed him through his war wounds of 1914, quieted his shell-shock, coped with his damaged ankle, borne his mad rages, loved him. She had been born in the East herself, loved the climate, the river, the people, and had never ailed for a day of this her first and straightforward pregnancy. She had brought to the Clinic only the wet-nurse and her prayer book, knowing that she would be back within the month. As she left she had been helped a little into the open boat but had not looked back. The landing stage stood on its high crooked stilts with only one person watching the boat disappear round the bend of the river—a girl of twelve called Ada, the wet-nurse's eldest child. As stick-thin as the landing stage itself, the girl wound her arms about the rough branches and stayed long after the boat had disappeared.

Comfortable in the long low boat, Mrs. Feathers in her loose cotton dress—never a sarong—she was the District Officer's wife—had scarcely looked pregnant. The baby had dropped low in the womb and become very quiet, which its mother knew meant the birth was imminent. In the Long House where they had rested that night, she had not worried that the child might be born early. With the peaceful happiness that often predicts labour, she had smiled and knitted a tiny lace jacket, fondly taking a strand of wool at a time and loosening it, holding it high. She had knitted most of the night, listening to the baboon on the roof clacking like a typewriter in short, unaccountable snatches of baboon monologue.

The wet-nurse, her own baby beside her, lay on the floor, terrified at being a day's journey down river from home. She whimpered.

"Now, now," said Mrs. Feathers, patting her. "Hush, don't be afraid. Tomorrow we'll be at the Port and the next day the new baby will be here. I know. Then soon we shall all go home." And she held up the jacket and looked at the pattern by the light of the kerosene lamp on the floor. She knew that the baby would be a girl and was finishing off the little garment with pink lacy scallops.

She finished the last scallop the following night in the Clinic but gave birth to a long, rangy, red-headed, eight-pound boy. She was delighted with him (Edward) and passed the jacket to the wet-nurse's silky brown baby, who never wore it, and the next day puerperal fever began its cruel course and three days later Mrs. Feathers died.

Ten days after that, the Welsh missionary Auntie May was plodding firmly on board the river steamer which might be the last to run before the onset of the monsoon, one big hand on the rail of the gangplank, the other arm tight round the swaddled child. Behind came the weeping and now indispensable wet-nurse with her baby. She had wept for two days. Auntie May never wept.

She had, however, felt a great plunge of spirits as the river boat rounded the bend of the river before the District Officer's landing, for there was nobody there except for the same young girl sitting at the ladder's top with her arms tight round her knees. The boat lay in the water, silent, waiting for people to appear. Nobody. Auntie May knew that though there was neither telephone nor mail direct to the District Officer's quarters, and their attempt to send a cable had failed, the news of his wife's death would certainly have seeped through to Alistair Feathers. She had half expected him to turn up at the Port to bring his son home himself. News flies fast through the jungle. Attendance at his wife's funeral would of course have been impossible, for the body had to be buried immediately, then, in Kotakinakulu province.

"Not here," Auntie May allowed herself to say.

The wet-nurse was not surprised, however. Mr. Feathers had not come down to the landing stage to see his wife leave. Their goodbye—for them, a very affectionate goodbye—a kiss on the cheek (however had this child been conceived?)—had taken place inside the verandah of the house. A quick embrace, then out and down the verandah steps, Captain Feathers calling to the others to be ready. The wet-nurse was being well-paid and had been groomed for her possible job of nursing the baby with quantities of good food, and watched over against the betel nut and alcohol. Her elder daughter had come down to the landing stage, helped Mrs. Feathers to the gangplank—Mrs. Feathers had suddenly turned and given the girl a kiss—and watched the boat sidle towards the current and then pass from sight.

Here the girl was now, against Captain Feathers's orders, and she had watched for two days, her legs pressed against the banana-leaf barrier, desperately watching. At the Port these choppy waves had been nowhere to be seen and the river had run oily and thick, seemed hardly to move. Here though, up river, there were no glow-worm lights on the great invisible nets, no sounds of fishermen calling from boat to boat. No ghostly cartwheels of weed, flying like skaters on the surface of the running river, almost outstripping it. No crocodile snout at the Port. No plop or scream of waterbird dropping on prey. Here on the landing stage, up river, fat metallic lizards moved about, long jaws angled for grubs in the leaves. They moved silently around her feet. She kicked them away. They were harmless things.

And here was the river boat. Would Mrs. Feathers be there? If she was indeed dead her strong, young body, her bright happy face would be already decaying in the wet earth of the Port's Christian cemetery.

The boat's engine reawakened with a roar and the boat approached the landing stage. Ada, the brown girl, twisted her arms tighter among the banana leaves. Here came lights. Men—not the District Officer—appeared to catch ropes.

The boat anchored, the engine stopped, the boat rocked and shuddered and Ada's mother and her baby sister and big Auntie May from the Mission began to disembark. Auntie May carried a light bundle.

When she had both feet on the rickety platform, Auntie May looked at the girl and asked if she were the wet-nurse's big daughter. Ada said yes, and looked at the bundle, and Auntie May put it in her arms. Ada's mother went by, head-down over her own baby, afraid of seeing the District Officer somewhere in the shadows.

But there was no District Officer. Alistair Feathers was at his desk working, tonight not even drinking.

When Auntie May was admitted, he shook hands with her and sent for a servant to see her to her room, show her the bathhouse, make sure that food was taken to her.

"I can stay for several days," she said. "I'll risk the monsoon. To see that all is as well as can be for him."

"F-f-for him?"

"For your son. He is Edward. He's a fine boy."

"Good. Good."

He did not ask to see the baby who, by the time Auntie May left a week later, was the amazement of the village. A child with bright-blue eyes and white, white skin and curly chestnut hair. After Auntie May had left with a donation of ten pounds to the Mission, he gave orders for Ada to take charge of the child. Auntie May had already given orders (and the ten pounds) that Ada should sit each evening with the baby on the steps of his father's verandah. This she did for many months, but Alistair Feathers never came near.

During the monsoon Ada and the baby moved up the steps and on to the verandah and sat there listening to the deluge, the crashing steaming torrent of the rain, and at last the girl was told by the District Officer's servant to go away and take the child to live with her and his wet-nurse in their family hut. And so the baby's first years were in the Long House among brown skins, brown eyes, scraps of coloured clothes, the Malay language; often sleeping, sometimes making musical singing, dreamily passing the time against the roar of the river and the rain. At night the lamps swung from the rafters and the baby watched the flames with their haloes of moths, heard the baboons with pleasure, saw the silver lizards without fear— their questing, swinging heads—and the geckos hooked into the mesh of the walls puffing out their lurid throats. He listened to the racket of the rats in the thatch, once watched with rapture as a fat snake came sliding up from a post-hole. Observed it being killed. He was satisfied by the nourishment of the wetnurse but passionate in his love for the girl.

Soon he stretched to pat her face, suck her chin, her ear. One day, at two months, gazing at her he gave a crow of laughter like a boy of two. Because of the memory of the child's kind mother, the Long House respected him and accepted him, an ivory child in their warm dun dust, and he was passed about, rocked to sleep, talked to and sung to and understood only Malay. By the time he was one he rolled and tottered and waddled in the village compound with the other children. There were a number of pale-skinned half-caste children from the Raj's peccadilloes. Sometimes this child's father crossed the compound but seemed not to see him, not to notice his wife's chestnut curls.

The village observed the District Officer. Captain Feathers was a strong just governor, but nobody liked him. His child was given extra attention and, from Ada, intense, unswerving, obsessive adoration.

When the child was four and a half, Auntie May came back. Big and strong, off the boat and over the landing stage to the compound, she looked about her, at once spotting Edward with his orange hair, naked and sucking a mango, his feet and hands as pale with the mud of the compound as the other children's. She made no move towards him—the women were watching from the dark openings of the huts—but nodded and smiled in his direction, to his surprise, for his mouth fell open—and went on to climb the steps of the verandah.

She was expected: there had been correspondence for some time. But Captain Feathers had not been at the landing stage.

She had not seen him for four and a half years but rumour had it that he was unchanged in his attitude to his son, that his shattered ankle was worse and that he was drinking heavily. It was said he had become eccentrically pedantically absorbed in his work and the management of his District. He was celibate.

No girls were brought to him by their mothers as "extra servants," though he was handsome still, his eyes bright with malaria. He turned away from the women's beauty to the beauty of the whiskey in the glass. It did not seem to harm him. He had the Scottish immunity. He drank alone, for he had no friends. "Oh, Miss Neal. Auntie May. G-g-good evening."

He looks tired, she thought.

She had come to take the child down to the Port, to be taught English for six months before the journey Home, where he would live with a Welsh family until he was eight. After that, he would go to his father's old Prep school and then his father's old Public school. Auntie May knew of the Welsh family with whom he was to be fostered. They were used to Raj Orphans. There would be home-cooked food, and it would be cheap (Alistair Feathers was a Scot). And there were two aunts about, his sisters, in Lancashire which was not really far away from North Wales.

"And of course," said Auntie May at dinner, watching the lowering of the whiskey in the glass at the other end of the lamp-lit table, "you will have to take him to Wales. In six months' time. And you will by then have paid for him in advance."

Alistair Feathers's eyes stared. Outside, the madhouse noises of the jungle. Inside, the servant padding about, taking plates, setting down others, offering fruit.

"He seems well and happy," he said. "I have never seen the need for him to go Home. It's not the law."

"You know perfectly well that it is the custom. Because of the risk of childhood illnesses out here. You went Home yourself."

"I did," said Alistair. "So help me God."

Auntie May on the whole agreed with him. She'd seen great damage. Some children forgot their parents, clung to their adoptive families who later often forgot them. There were bad tales. Others grew to say they'd had a much better time in England away from their parents, whom they did not care for. There were children who worked hard at growing stolid and boring, and made marriages only in order to have roots of their own at last. They never told anything. And Auntie May had never been sure about the ferocity of Eastern childhood diseases. But in this case there was no mother.

"You've had no leave in ten years, Alistair. It isn't safe. Nobody knows better than you what happens out here to District Officers who work too hard. They drink and go native."

Alistair fastidiously poured another whiskey and said, "At least I still change for dinner."

He was in dinner jacket and black tie that would have been acceptable at the Ritz. Not a bead of sweat. Auntie May in sarong and sandals, her chin a little more whiskery, her arms resting almost to her elbows on the table a little more muscular, had put on weight and felt hot. She looked at Alistair and had to admire. She wanted to take his hand. Her hardest task now as she grew older in the Ministry was to deal with her longing to be touched—hugged, stroked by anyone, any human being—a friend, a lover, a child or even (and here she scented danger) a servant. Of either sex. She prayed about it, asking that God's encircling arms would bring comfort. They did not.

"Alistair, you have no choice. You have a son who has no mother. At Home there will be your sisters, both unmarried. They will love a little nephew. They don't answer any of my letters but you say you've been making arrangements, telling them? You have to take leave and accompany the boy home. It's what his mother would have done."

Alistair rose and limped about, his crooked shadow everywhere. Outside in the steaming night there was an upsurge of voices across the compound and the crowing of a cock. A drum began to beat.

"It's the festival. They're sacrificing a cockerel."

"You don't need to tell me, Auntie May."

"Your son is watching. Do you think this is the right way of life for a Christian child?"

"He isn't a Christian child."

"Yes, he is. I saw to that. He was baptised at birth. His mother held him. It's not the Baptist way but she asked for it. In case he didn't survive the river boat. He is baptised in the name of the Father, Son and Holy Spirit who have nothing to do with the slitting of a cock's gullet at the full moon."

"They are calling on their god," said Alistair. "There is no God but God. I'm nearer to their gods than yours ever was to me in 1914. Can the child not go on as he is?"

"No," she said and left it at that.

The next day she went looking for Edward and found him in the river shallows where Ada on the bank was rubbing at coloured cloths, the pair of them calling and laughing. Other children stood in the water sending showers of it over each other and Edward and Ada, with their round dark hands. Edward began to do the same and kicked more of it about with his long white feet. Ada, pretending to be furious, dropped her cloths and ran in amongst them, splashing back. All the heads bobbed away into the rocks like black floats. Edward splashed forward and took Ada round the waist and buried his face against her thighs. "You are my leopard," cried Edward Feathers in the Malay of the compound. "My beautiful leopard and I want to *eat* you alive."

This, thought Auntie May, will not do.

That night at dinner she said so.

"He goes Home, Alistair. If you won't take him, I will. I'm due some leave, too. There will be other English children on board. There always are. I'm told there may be two of his cousins joining a ship Home from Ceylon. We may pick them up. We shall be able to go the short way through Suez next year. Your sisters must organise warm clothes for Liverpool."

"They wouldn't know how," said Alistair. "They're independent spinsters. Play a lot of golf."

"Very well. I'll contact the Baptists. In Lancashire and in Wales. And I shall also—" she looked hard at him "—inform the Foreign Office. How well do you know your son, I wonder?"

"I see him."

"I've sent for him to come here now. Tonight." She clapped her hands and shouted for the servant in the Raj voice of thunder.

The servant looked at his master, but the master continued to open and shut a little silver box that had been his wife's pin-box and now held his tooth-picks. Then he took up his glass and looked into its golden depths.

"Yes. Very well."

Edward was brought in from just outside the door where he had been watching and holding Ada's hand. He blinked in the glare of light, stared at the tall man's queer clothes—the starched shirt, the gold watch chain—and the gleam of the table-silver and glass he had never seen before.

"Now then, Edward," said Auntie May. "Greet your father, please."

The child looked mystified.

"Your father. Go on."

She gave him a push. "Bow, child. Hold out your hand."

The child bowed but scarcely took his eyes from Alistair's pinched yellow face and sandy square moustache.

Alistair suddenly threw himself back in his chair, dropped the silver box on the table and looked straight at Edward for the first time. His wife's genial blue eyes looked back at him.

"Hullo," he said, "Hullo—Edward. And so you are going away?" Like Auntie May, he spoke in Edward's own Malay.

Edward wriggled and turned his attention to the silver box. "Did you know that you will be going away?"

"They say so," said Edward.

"You are going first with Auntie May to the Port. For half a year. To learn to speak English, like all British boys have to do."

Edward fiddled with the box.

"You hear English spoken sometimes, don't you? You understand what it is?"

"Sometimes. Why do I have to? I can talk here."

"Because you will one day have to go to England. It is called Home. They don't speak Malay there."

"Why can't I stay here?"

"Because white children often die here."

"I shall like to die here."

"We want you not to die but to grow up big and strong."

"Will Ada come?"

"We'll see."

"Can I go back to Ada now?"

"Here," the father called as the child made off to the verandah where Ada stood in the shadows. "Here. Come back. Take this. It was your mother's," and he held out the silver box.

"Does Ada say I can?"

"I say you can. I am your father."

"You can't be," said Edward.

Silence fell and Auntie May's hands began to shake.

The servants were listening.

"And why not?"

"Because you've been here all the time without me."

Auntie May left with Edward next morning. She felt sick and low.

I'm lugubrious, unattractive, bossy and a failure, she told God. I shan't come here ever again. That man can rot.

Alistair, however, had been on the landing stage, leaning only a little on his stick, spick and span in his khaki shorts and sola topi. He had shaken hands with Auntie May, acknowledged Ada. Had shaken hands with the little boy, and asked if he had the box safe. Then he had given the order for the boat to be cast off, and had limped away.

"Wave," said Auntie May, but Edward did not.

Nor did Alistair turn to look at his son's second—and last—journey down the black river.

As the trees on either winding bank blotted out the landing stage, Edward, who had been struck dumb by the sight of Ada left alone on the tottering platform, began to scream "Ada, Ada, Ada!" and to point back up river. Auntie May held him tight, but he screamed louder, and writhed in her arms. She spoke sharply in Malay and he bit her shoulder, wriggled free and seemed about to jump overboard. A sailor caught him by the belt of the shorts that Auntie May had brought and that had astonished him. The sailor lifted him high. Water poured down the sailor's silky arms. "Hai, hai, hai," he laughed and Edward lashed out at him, sobbing. He was a tall, strong boy for four and a half but the boatman lifted him into the air like a swathe of flowers. Something of the boatman's smell and his happy eyes reminded the child of Ada, and the sobbing lessened and he went limp.

"Why does she stay? Why is she not here?"

"If she came with you, you would never learn English. You and she would talk Malay, as we are doing now."

"I will talk Malay with you always."

"Not after we get to the Port. You will learn something new. Ada will follow."

"Follow?"

"She will follow to the Port when you have to go Home."

Edward gave a shuddering, hopeless sob. He had just left Home. What would Ada do without him at Home? He was placed in Auntie May's lap and looked at her with eyes nearly mad and shouted "Ada! Ada!" He tried to hit Auntie May, and swim for it, but she grabbed him in her muscular arms and tried to rock him. He became limp again. The sobs that shook his body began to become farther apart. He hiccupped and tried to speak, but it came out jerky and odd: "Ek, ek, ek—" like the baboon on the roof. A cupfull of drink appeared from a bottle in Auntie May's bag. (Auntie May had negotiated these hateful kidnappings before.) The drink was dark and sweet and he gulped it in the middle of a last shuddering sob. She passed the empty cup to the boatman and rocked the child, allowing herself the pleasure of a child in her arms, knowing that this stringy, red-headed boy would never tempt her into lullabies or spoiling comforts. But he was warm against her broad chest, and now he slept. She seethed against the father, the system, the Empire which she had begun to think was not God's ordinance after all, and how had she ever thought it could be? Duty to these people was what mattered now. Well, to all people. Love and duty.

Six months later the two of them took ship to England alone.

There was no sign of the District Officer, no sign of Ada, and they travelled steerage—Alistair had been vague to Auntie May about how much more money he had to spare, and she was nervous lest the child became over-excited by uniforms and orchestras. There was also the question of table manners for someone who had not sat at tables until six months ago at the Port. At first Edward had tried to eat beneath the table. The Mission had done better with his English than with his social graces. All that Auntie May had heard from Captain Feathers since they parted was a letter saying that all financial arrangements had been made for the boy and that he would come into his own money in time. His father's sisters had been written to and had the address of the Public school where he would go when he was fourteen. Money had been sent to the foster parents in Wales.

Auntie May wrote back, making sure the father had the boy's Welsh address correctly, and told him that a letter would be written by Edward every week as soon as he could write. She made clear that Edward was not himself at present. That, at the Port, while he had absorbed English easily—he would be a linguist she was sure—he had become passive and listless and glum and when he talked now it seemed to be with some difficulty, as if he had a constriction in the throat like an old clock trying to gear itself up to strike. "A-a-a-a-ack." You longed to say the word for him. You sometimes almost wanted to shake him for he seemed to be doing it on purpose. When the words were eventually freed from the clockwork in the gul- let, or the mind, out they poured far too fast, and when he paused for breath it was "ack-ack-ack, ek-ek-ek" again. At the Mission, other children had called him "the monkey" and he had in fact become rather like one of the bony, pale-orange baboons with their hot red eyes.

He never asked for Ada again.

At Colombo the ship took on more passengers and Auntie May suspected that two of the many white children with their ayahs and mothers might be Edward's cousins travelling (of course) first-class. There had been rumours of this but she had made no enquiries. The two cousins were girls, one a little older than Edward, the other even younger. They would be spending the next four years together, all three, in Wales, with the Didds family. Edward might be taunted for his father's apparent poverty if these cousins knew he was on the lower deck. There might be jealousy.

In this Auntie May was wrong. Whatever web the children were to make between themselves, it would always be too tight-knit for jealousy or taunts. But Auntie May kept her counsel, did her best with the stammering Edward as they crossed the molten-silver disc of the Indian Ocean beneath a beating sky. It was very hot in steerage but both were used to heat. From the upper deck in the first-class, dance music floated down to them.

Stately Old Filth—Eddie Feathers—was nodding after lunch for a moment in the smoking-room of the Inner Temple before taking a taxi to his family solicitor to make his Will.

It was autumn but very hot. The flowers in the Inner Temple garden blazed. The River Thames glittered, and, coming out of his post-prandial nap he was a gawky boy, crossing the equator again, watching mad capers by the grown-ups. Neptune in a green wig. Auntie May had been lying down and so he had wandered towards the upper deck and seen faces and elegance he'd never known. He stood and gawped. People were drinking coloured liquid out of vases on stalks, puffing smoke from their lips. Ladies with hard, sad eyes wore long tight glitter and laughed a lot. A man in black and white held a woman in gold, their bodies fused as they moved languidly about to the wailing, meaningless music. A wave of great desolation had swept across Eddie. He was never, ever after, to understand it. He knew that before long he'd be back on this ocean, maybe for eternity. He had no words for all this then, and not even now in the armchair in the Inner Temple, coffee cup alongside.

As he came round from the day-dream he heard two of his peers—old judges he'd known for years—coming along the passage to the smoking-room talking about him. He had been sitting next to them at luncheon.

"Remarkably well preserved."

"Well, he's from Commercial Chambers. Rich as Croesus. But he's a great man."

"Pretty easy life. Nothing ever seems to have happened to him."

Nothing.

WALES

The whitewashed stone farmhouse stood high, with fields all around it and a view of rick-rack stone walls laid out towards cliffs above the sea. In front of the house was a farmyard of beaten earth and a midden with a headless chicken lying on it and a cockerel crowing near. The door of the farmhouse stood open. On the yard in front of it, spaced out well away from each other, were three children, Eddie the only boy and the tallest.

He was eight now, looked ten, and startlingly white, though this may have been the pallor of a red-head. He was standing almost to attention, as if awaiting execution or about to declaim a speech. The other two figures were also looking theatrical, set in their positions on stage. Waiting for something. Babs and Claire. Claire sat on the corner of the wall. Babs leaned darkly against an outhouse. Chickens ran about. The children were not speaking to each other.

Inside the house was Auntie May again, packing up. She was softer now, less bristly, about to marry another missionary and off to the Belgian Congo very soon. But first she was finishing her job with Edward Feathers. "I never desert," said Auntie May. "Especially after such a tragedy as this."

The tragedy was apparent, she thought, as soon as she'd seen Edward's closed face, his frightening dignity. He had stood there in shorts long-grown-out-of—could they have been those she'd found for him three-and-a-half years ago?—his hair cropped to near-baldness, his white face empty.

"Auntie May," she'd said, "You remember Auntie May?" He seemed not to know her. She looked at the two girls, whom she was to take away and look after until their parents—or some relatives somewhere—would come to claim them.

The children had been excused the funeral. People in the village had taken them in.

Babs, dark and unsmiling, stood picking at her fingernails, stage left. Pink little Claire sat on the wall, wagging her feet, down stage right. When Auntie May had arrived and said, "I am Auntie May," Claire had smiled and raised her arms to her for an embrace.

Babs had jerked away from Auntie May, as if expecting a blow.

Edward, whom Auntie May had cared for, did not go near her. He had looked at her once, then walked away through the gate in the stone wall, off-stage right, and now stood alone, gazing at the sea.

You would expect them to draw together, Auntie May thought.

"I'll see if all's ready," she had said. "I'll lock up the house."

After Auntie May had gone into the house the children did not stir but began to observe a small motor car working its way towards them from the cliff road. It turned into the maze of stone walls. A car was rare. This car was fat and business-like with a cloth roof and rounded, tinny back and a high, rubber running-board down each side. Mudguards flowed like breaking waves over the solid wheels and the windows were made of orange celluloid, rather cracked. A short man jumped out and came jollily to the foot of the garden steps. He was talking.

"—I dare say," he said. "Eddie Feathers, I dare say? Excellent to meet you. I am your new Headmaster and my name is *Sir*. Always *Sir*. Understood? The school is small. There are only twenty boys. They call each other by their surnames. I have one assistant, Mr. Smith. He is always called Mr. Smith, my assistant, whatever his real name. Different ones come and go. This Mr. Smith is something of a trial but very good at cricket, which I am not. And so, good morning, Eddie, and these are your sisters, I dare say?"

"C-cou-cousins," came out of Edward's mouth. He liked this man.

"I know nothing of girls," said Sir. "I know everything about boys. I am a very good teacher, Feathers, as your father may remember. By the time you leave my Outfit there is not a bird, butterfly or flower, not a fish or insect of the British Isles you will not recognise. You will also read Latin like a Roman and understand Euclid like a Greek."

"Will he still have to do Welsh?" asked blonde Claire.

"Welsh! I should hope not."

"What if you get a *stupid* boy?" asked Babs from the shadows (and thought: I do not like this man; he'll change Eddie).

"Eddie isn't stupid," said Claire and, suddenly aware—for here came Auntie May with luggage—that Eddie was going away, she jumped from her plinth and hugged him as she had never done in all the terrible years since they met at Liverpool Docks. She began to cry.

"Sh-shut up, Claire." Eddie turned to the man accusingly and said, "Claire never cries." He looked down at Claire's top-knot, felt her arms round him, did not know what to do about it and carefully removed himself.

"Auntie May," said Auntie May to Sir. "I am Auntie May."

"Ah, the redoubtable Auntie May. You are seeing to the girls, I hear? This would be quite outside my territory. I teach only boys. My establishment is very expensive and very well-known. I am unmarried, as is Mr. Smith, but let me say, for all things good should be noised abroad, that there is absolutely nothing unpleasant going on in my school. We are perfectly clean. There is nothing like that."

"Well, that will be a change for him," said Auntie May. "There's been nothing pleasant here."

"So I understand. Or rather I do not understand for such events are beyond comprehension in a well-run Outfit. There is no corporal punishment in my school. And there is no emotional hysteria. One can only suppose that these things are the result of the mixture of the sexes. I never teach girls."

"What happened here was not to do with a school. These children went to the village school."

"Which accounts for the pink child's regional accent. Come, boy, say your goodbyes. At my school nobody leaves with an accent."

"Goodbye," said Eddie, looking only at Sir's face. He remembered to shake hands with Auntie May and say, "Th-th-tha-thank you." Ignoring the girls, for the three of them would all their lives be beyond formalities, he picked up some of his belongings, Auntie May some more and Sir none at all and they processed to the car, where Sir unfastened broad leather straps and the back was lifted, like the lid of a bread-bin.

"It's marvellous. Your car."

"Marvellous, *Sir*."

"Marvellous, Sir."

Sir stood back and watched the luggage being put inside the bread-bin. Then he nodded at Auntie May, pointed to the dickie seat and watched Eddie climb in, Babs and Claire looking on nonchalantly from above.

"You have the address?" said Sir to Auntie May. "And Feathers has yours? Not too many letters, please; we have work to do. He should write regularly to his father only. No letters from the girls or from this village. I think that was the understanding? Why does the boy stammer?"

"It began years ago."

"Nothing in the least to worry about now," said Sir, cranking an iron handle in front of the bonnet, then flinging it over the car into the dickie, just missing Eddie's head, and leaping behind the wheel to keep the engine alive. Without a toot or a wave or a word of farewell he reversed on the springy grass and flung the car back into the stony lane and went bounding between the low walls and out of sight; leaving a considerable silence.

It was Babs who burst into tears.

"Now then, this stammer," said Sir, an hour or so later, "I suppose it's never mentioned. That's the current policy."

"It—it—it was. At the sch-school."

"Ah, well they were Welsh. The Welsh have an easy flow and cadence. They can't understand those of us who haven't. I, for example, am not musical. Are you?"

"I d-don't know."

"Chapel? Chapel?"

"I d-didn't sing. If I did they all turned and l-l-looked. Babs sang. B-b-b *can* sing."

"The dark one?"

"She sang clear and sh-sh-sharp. Not at all sweet. Not Welsh singing. They d-didn't like it. So she went on."

"A prima donna. Girls are very difficult. Hush. Stop a minute. I see swifts."

He stopped the car in the middle of a leafy lane with trees. Swooping about in high pleasure were some dart-shaped birds cutting the air high and low and gathering invisible flies. "Listen!" said Sir. "Hear that?"

"It's rather like b-bells."

"Good, good. You will never forget swifts now. There are birds, you know, who actually do sound like bells. They're bell birds and they call to each other across the rainforests of Eastern Australia. Don't let them tell you there are no rain-forests in Australia. I have been there. Is that understood? I dare say?"

"Y-yes, Sir."

"Good. And it is writhing with dragons."

"D-d-, Sir?"

"They are a form of armadillo, enlarged wood-lice. (The common prawn is related to the wood-louse.) Fat low beasts and over-confident. Rather disgustingly beautiful."

"Like the lizards in Kotakinakulu?" said Eddie, amazing himself by the memory of the platinum lizards with crocodiles' merciless eyes, steel slit of a long mouth, not seen since . . .

"Seen some, have you? Interested Darwin. You'll have to tell the others, stammer or no stammer. Claudius had a stammer. Have you come across Claudius?"

"Claudius who?"

"Who, *Sir.* Claudius the Emperor of Rome. Splendid fellow. The Prince of Wales has a stammer. He's having lessons for it."

"Did he get it in Wales?"

"I shouldn't wonder. Pity they didn't send him to me."

On sped the car. When they reached main roads conversation ceased. Sir's long scarf kept flapping behind him into Eddie's face. A precarious mirror hooked to the car at the height of Sir's ear but in front of him showed Sir with concentrated gravity clenching his teeth on a curly pipe, unlit. Now and then he squeezed a grey rubber bulb attached to a small trumpet and a high bleat sounded off.

The rubber thing reminded Eddie of something vile. Old Mr. Didds's constipation. Eddie's face disappeared from Sir's mirror, and Sir drew to the side of the road and stopped. "Just letting her cool down somewhat. Where are you? On the floor, I dare say?"

Eddie was squashed down on the floor of the dickie, knees to chin and pale green.

"Feeling sick? Not unnatural. Breathe slowly. It may be the car. Others have felt the same."

After a while Eddie scrambled up.

"You could come and sit beside me but I never allow it. You are in my care. Do you know much about cars?"

"It's the f-f-first—"

"First time in a car? Excellent. You can write the experience down. Did they teach you to write?"

"Yes. In a w-ay."

"You mean they struck you with rulers? Beat you about the head?"

"Y-yes."

"This does not happen in my Outfit. If you do not work—do not *try*—then Mr. Smith takes you for a run. All weathers. Along the shores of the lake."

"D-do we wear labels?"

"Labels?"

"We carried labels on our backs."

"Did this happen to you?"

"To all of us, it d-did. Babs had UGLY. I had MONKEY."

"And the pink girl?"

"Oh, she never got c-caught. Well, they l-liked her."

"Nothing can be further from my Outfit," said Sir, closing his eyes for a moment. "What do you think of my mirror?"

"M-m-m?"

"On the car. It is very much the fashionable touch, invented I am surprised to say by a lady. The first driving mirrors were adapted from the powder-case in a lady's handbag. They were hand-held. So that you could see if anything was coming along behind. One day, they'll be compulsory for both sexes I dare say. I see you are unaware of powder-cases? Perhaps you know no ladies? Have you a mother?"

"She died when I was b-b-b—"

"Several boys in my Outfit have suffered similarly. We are almost all of the Raj. I try not to see any of the mothers."

The car was re-cranked and off they went again. In the dickie it grew very cold about the ears. Eddie crouched down a bit but was afraid to take himself out of range of the mysterious powder-case mirror. Sir stopped in a wooded valley and passed Eddie a bottle of lemonade, taking a swig himself from a flask with a silver top and wrapped in basket work. Eddie smelled something powerful and sweet. It reminded him of the silver box which his father had given him and which he had given to Ada.

"Not long, now," said Sir. "We are on the borders of what is known as the English Lake District. It is the Old Kingdom of Cumbria and where I chose to set up my Outfit. I dare say you have not heard of our purple mountains and silver rivers?"

"I c-can't remember. Sir."

"Never fell to the Romans. Home of the poet Wordsworth who had a happy education."

"Y-yes, Sir."

"You know all this, I dare say?"

"I did—didn't—"

"Can you read, Feathers?" Sir asked casually.

"N-n-not yet m-much."

"Never mind. Won't take two ticks. Great times ahead. Now, here we are."

A high and very ugly brown stone castle towered out of a mountain forest beside a black lake, and as they turned and began to climb up a drive edged with blue hydrangeas a bell rang ahead of them and various boys began to emerge from the undergrowth looking eager and wild. Sir gave a salvo on the bulb and the boys began to jog up the drive, beside the car, some of them cheering.

"Supper time," said Sir. "Sausages, with any luck. We've a good cook. You like sausages, I dare say?"

An elfin child burst out of the front door and flung himself in front of the car, arms spread.

"One day I'll turn you into a single dimension. A pancake. A pulp for a pie," said Sir.

"Can I put the car in the garage for you, Sir?" said the alert-looking boy.

"Of course, of course. Rub it down, will you, and give it a drink?"

The boy took the driver's seat and, though his head was not far above the instruments panel, steered slowly and carefully into the garage where it fitted like a toy in a box.

"Very accurate boy," said Sir. "Name of Ingoldby. He's in charge of you for your first half-term. Very well done, Ingoldby. A garage to contend with."

"It's not so much a garage," said Ingoldby, "as a kennel for a medium-sized dog. Hullo."

"Ingoldby—Feathers," introduced Sir, shaping the future.

THE DONHEADS

Seventy years on in Dorset, an extraordinarily warm November, Teddy Feathers, Sir Edward, Old Filth was fussing about which tie to wear for a trip to London. He and Betty were going to the solicitors to make their Wills.

Downstairs in the hall Betty, perfectly ready, sat waiting on a sort of throne of gilded wood and faded, shredding silk which had been scarlet when they bought it in Bangladesh. She had found it in a cavernous incense-smelling shop in the backstreets of Dacca's Old Town. Stroking the pale rose satin now with her fingertips, she tried to remember what it was that had made her buy this chair. A bit of showing off, she thought. Well, some people brought back stuffed animals. She had asked if she might try sitting in it. It had been right at the back of the shop and she had looked out from it down the blackness to the dazzle of the doorway and the passing show of the street, the tangle of the rickshaws, the dignified old gentlemen in turbans, the women like briskly floating butterflies, the clusters of black heads in all the high windows. A procession of princelings had gone by, each carrying a silver dish piled with steaming plum pudding. Well of course she knew that it was only tin-foil and cow dung. But they were jolly and grave at the same time, like the Magi.

"Yes, I'll take it. I'll take the chair."

And here it was now, standing on the Dorset parquet beside the teak chest, and her fingernails, rosy as the silk, were stroking it.

On the teak chest were net bags full of tulip bulbs waiting to be planted. Today would have been the perfect day for it. Tomorrow might be cold or wet and she would be feeling a bit done-in after this jaunt today. Why Filth still had to have a London solicitor she did not know. Twice the price and half the efficiency, in her experience. The very thought of London made her dizzy. No point in telling Filth. No arguing with Filth.

And the bulbs should have been in two weeks ago for she wasn't the walking talking calendar she used to be. She didn't like dropping to her knees very much, at any time. She'd even stopped in church, though it felt louche, just squatting. The Queen Mother still knelt in church. Well, probably. Filth said that Queen Mary had knelt until the very end.

Filth still kept to a timetable. He'd booked this appointment weeks ago. 3.30 P.M. Bantry Street, W.C.1. The Wills would now be ready for signing. He'd been urgent about it lately and she wondered if he'd been having the dizzies again. His slight heart attack was several years ago. She stroked the satin.

Then her fingers strayed to the bulbs in their bags and she touched them—like a priestess giving a blessing. The fat globes inside the nets made her think of the crops of shot game-birds laid out on a slab—somewhere in her childhood's China, maybe? And, as a matter of fact, thought Betty, stroking, these fat potential globes under their skins were very like a man's balls, when you came to think about it.

Not that I have, for years.

She heard Filth above stairs drop a shoe and swear.

But if I *seriously* think about it, as an artist might, or a doctor, or a lover dreaming . . .

She closed her eyes and under the pile of bulb bags the telephone began to ring. She felt about until she reached the receiver, pulled it free and said, "Yes? Betty." She said again, "Yes? Hello? Betty," knowing that it would be someone from her reading group, which was meeting in the village that afternoon, and which she had notified yesterday that she would be away. The writer they were studying (studying!) was driving all the way from Islington to interpret her novel for them. Betty thought that she ought to have better things to do. It must be like discussing your marriage with strangers. "Hello? Is that you, Chloe?"

"Betty?" (A man.)

"Yes?"

"I'm in Orange Tree Road. Where are you?"

"Well, here."

"Exactly where?"

"Sitting in the hall. By the phone. On the satin throne."

"What are you wearing?"

"Wearing?"

"I need to see you."

"But you're in Hong Kong."

"I need to see you. To see your face. I've lost it. I have to be able to see you in the chair."

"Well, I'm—we're about to go up to London. Filth's putting his shoes on upstairs. He'll be down in a minute. I'm dressed for London."

"Are you wearing the amethysts?"

"Don't be ridiculous. It's nine o'clock in the morning."

"Pearls."

"Oh, well, yes."

"Touch them. Are they warm? Are they mine? Or his? Would he know?"

"Yours. No, he wouldn't notice. Are you drunk? It must be after dinner."

"No. Well, yes. Maybe."

"Is—are you alone?"

"Elsie's lying down. Betty, Harry's dead. My boy."

The line died as Filth came bounding down the stairs in a London suit and black shoes. He swirled himself into his overcoat and looked about for the bowler hat which he had resurrected. It lay among the tulips. He reflected upon it and then let it lie. Mustn't be antique. The taxi was here.

"Phone-call?"

"Nothing—cut off."

They travelled first-class, though unintentionally as they both thought first-class was vulgar and only for expense-account people.

The ticket-collector, weighing up their age and clothes, had thought differently, seeing Teddy's rolled umbrella and Betty's glorious pearls and the rubbish on the floor around their polished shoes.

"You can upgrade, sir, if you like." (The wife looks very pale.) "Just the next compartment and four pounds extra if you're seniors."

"Perfectly well here, thank you," said Filth, but Betty smiled at the man's black Tamil face, gathered up her bag and gloves and set off on her jaunty heels down the coach, tottering through the swaying connecting doors towards the firsts, away from what she still called "the thirds."

They paddled through the water spilling out from under the doors of the W.C.s and settled in a blue velvet six-seater compartment. Four of the seats were slashed down the back with the stuffing coming out. Graffiti covered the ceiling but the floor was cleaner. Filth thought of the train to Kuala Lumpur, the mahogany and the hot food handed in, and sat facing his wife in the two unslashed seats on the window side. The fields, woods, hedges, uplands of Wiltshire, white chalk shining through the grass, flickered by.

Betty suddenly saw a hoopoe in a hedge. She looked at Filth to see if he had noticed it, but he was abstracted. The lines between his nose and mouth were sharp today, cruel as the slashes down the seats. Whatever had he to be bitter about?

His boy is dead. His boy, Harry.

The Tamil drew the door open.

"Better, sir?"

"Very nice," said Betty.

"Four pounds? Is that *each*?" asked Filth.

"Don't bother with it, sir. When you look at the seats . . . But it's cleaner. Take my advice and get straight into first-class on the way home. You'll be Day Returns?"

"Oh, yes. We don't stay in London longer than we can help." The man wondered why the lady's eyes were so bright. Like it was tears. Real old. Could be his grandma. And yet— she was smiling at him.

"We're going to London to sign our Wills."

"Ma'am, I'm sure there's plenty of time."

Filth blew his nose on a starched handkerchief and drew down his eyebrows as if in Court. "In your profession, I wouldn't count on that."

"Too right," said the man. "Takes our lives in our hands, we do on the railways. Safer flying. But that's how I like it. When you gotta go, you gotta go? Right?"

"Right," said Betty.

"Quite right," said Filth. He was noticing Betty, her face tired through the make-up. He looked at her again as the train swayed insolently through Clapham junction. She must get her eyes seen to. They looked moist and strange. Old, he thought. She's never looked old before.

"Lunch?" he asked.

"What?"

"Where are you having lunch? Shall we go somewhere together? Simpson's?"

"But you're going to the Inner Temple."

"I can change it. Nobody's expecting me. Don't know a soul there now."

She was silent.

"Then we could get a taxi to the place—the solicitor together. Not arrive separately. Hanging about on pavements." "No," she said. "I've made arrangements at the Club."

"You don't have to go. There's never anybody else there."

"That's why I go. To keep it going. I'm meeting somebody this time."

"You didn't tell me."

She thought: You didn't ask.

At Waterloo she stood with him for his taxi, the driver coming round to help him in. The door was slammed and he tapped his window and called "Betty—where did you say you were going?" but she was gone. He saw her as he was taken down the slope, fast as a girl on her still not uninteresting legs, nipping through the traffic towards the National Theatre side. Must be walking all the way to the Club, he thought with pride. Crossing the bridge, down the Strand, Trafalgar Square, the Mall, St. James's, Dover Street. Remarkable woman for over seventy. She loved walking. Strange the hold that University Women's Club had over her. Never been there himself. Betty, of course, had never been to a university. She'd vanished now.

He had not seen her take a right down the steps towards the Film Theatre and the Queen Elizabeth Hall. In the National Theatre she took a tray and shoved it along in the queue of the audience for the matinee for *Elektra*.

She had no idea what she ate. She took the lift to the high level of the theatre and sat outside alone in the cold air. She was meeting nobody. There were buskers everywhere: acrobats, musicians, living statues, contortionists and a sudden deluge of sound from a Pavarotti in a loin cloth. The waves of the canned music made the pigeons fly. Two people sat down on the seat beside her, the girl with her hair in two wings of crinkled gold. Heavy, sullen, resentful, the boy slumped beside her, his mouth slack. The music and the voice blazed away.

His boy Harry is dead.

The girl lit a cigarette, her fingers and thumbs chunky with rings.

Rings on her fingers and bells on her toes—and goodness knows where else, thought Betty. She shall have music wherever she goes. Oh, I do hope so.

The girl was staring at her.

"I like your hair," said Betty.

The girl turned away, haughtily. "Nothing lasts long," said Betty, and the boy said, "We could go for a Chinese."

They thought about it.

Then the two of them turned to each other on the seat and in one fluid movement entwined themselves in each other's arms.

His boy is dead, thought Betty and got up.

She wandered away down steep, spiral stairs and at the riverbank watched the water streaming by, the crowds, the silver wheel high in the air dotted with silver bullets. Beautiful. It jerked awake. Jerk, stop, fly. Round and round.

Terry's boy is dead.

And I'm not, she thought. Filth and I are going to live for ever. Pointlessly. Keeping the old flag flying for a country I no longer recognise or love.

When she saw the state of the traffic down the Strand she wondered if Filth would make it to the solicitor's in time. He liked ten minutes zizz after lunch in the smoking-room of the Inn. Hopeless without it. She thought of him, tense and angry, traffic-blocked in his taxi. A few years ago he'd have sprung out and walked. He had been a familiar sight, gown and papers flapping, prancing to the Law Courts. "Look, isn't it Old Filth?"

When he'd been very young and not a penny, not a Brief, before she knew him, he'd always, he said, had a bowler hat for going home. "Why?" she had asked.

"To have something to raise to a judge."
You never knew when Filth was being sardonic or serious.

He was not being sardonic today. With the help of the rolled umbrella he was signalling to taxis outside his Inn on the Embankment. He moved his feet rather cautiously and looked ancient, but still handsome, beautifully dressed, alert after his ten-minute nap, someone you'd notice. But the traffic streamed by him. Nothing stopped. He'd never get there. Too old for this now. He'd be late for Court. He began to be frightened as he used to be. His throat felt tight.

I'll walk to Bantry Street, thought Betty; his taxi might over-take me. And she struck out into the crowd. In her Agatha-Christie country clothes and pearls and polished shoes, she strode among an elbowing, slovenly riff-raff who looked at her as if she was someone out of a play. Pain and dislike, bewil-derment and fear, she thought, in every face. Nobody at peace except the corpses in the doorways, the bundles with rags and bottles; and you can't call that peace. She dropped money into hats and boxes as she would never have done in Dacca or Shanghai, and would have been prosecuted for doing in Singapore. Beggars again in the streets of London, she thought. My world's over. Like Terry's.

Her heart was beating much too fast and she slowed down at Bantry Street and felt in her handbag for a pill. But all was well. Here was Filth, grave and tall, being helped out of a taxi.

"Well, good timing," he called. "Excellent. Nice lunch? Anybody there?"

"No one I knew."

"Same here. Only old has-beens."

The Outfit

"Ingoldby—Feathers," Sir had said outside the Prep school in the Lake District mountains.

Ingoldby that day became not only Eddie Feathers's first friend but a part of him. They sat down that evening side by side for the sausage supper. From the next morning they shared one of the ten double desks, with tip-up seats and a single inkwell. Listening to Pat Ingoldby's endless talk, Eddie, at first painfully and hesitantly, began to talk, too. Ingoldby waited patiently when the clock had trouble ticking, never breaking in. Over four years the stammer healed.

Despite Sir's strictness about no best friends and daily cold showers, nothing could be done about the oneness of Ingoldby and Feathers. They read the same tattered books from the library—Henty, Ballantyne and Kipling; picked each other for teams. They discussed the same heroes. Ingoldby was dark and slight, Eddie Feathers four inches taller and chestnut-haired, but they began to walk with the same gait. A funny pair. And they made a funny pair in the school skiff on the lake but almost always won. Ingoldby's wit and logic expunged the nightmares of Eddie's past. They were balm and blessing to Eddie who had met none previously. He never once mentioned the years before he arrived at Sir's Outfit and Pat never enquired about them or volunteered information about himself. The past, unless very pleasant, is not much discussed among children.

On Sports Day, Colonel Ingoldby arrived and Feathers was introduced to him and soon Feathers was visiting the

Ingoldbys in the school holidays. Sir wrote to Malaya describing the excellence of the Ingoldbys and saying that they would like to have Eddie with them for every holiday. A handsome cheque came from Kotakinakulu to Mrs. Ingoldby and was graciously received (though there had been no accompanying letter).

At fourteen both boys were to move on to the same Public school in the Midlands and Mrs. Ingoldby asked Eddie how he felt about continuing the arrangements. Would his aunts—whom he had only once seen—be jealous? Insulted? "We've become so used to you, Eddie. Jack is so much older than Pat. They're too far apart to be close as brothers. I think Pat is lonely, to tell you the truth. Would you be very bored to become part of the family? Now, do say so if you would."

"Of course I'd love to be."

"I'll write to your father."

From Malaya, there was silence, except for another cheque. Nor was anything heard from the aunts. Mrs. Ingoldby said nothing about the money except, "How very kind and how quite unnecessary," and Eddie was absorbed into the Ingoldbys' life in their large house on a Lancashire hilltop where the Colonel kept bees and Mrs. Ingoldby wandered vaguely and happily about, smiling at people. When Pat won an award to their next school, Colonel Ingoldby opened a bottle of Valpolicella which he remembered having drunk ("Did we dear?") on their honeymoon in Italy before the Great War. The following year Eddie won one, too, and there was the same ritual.

Mrs. Ingoldby was Eddie's first English love. He had not known such an uncomplicated woman could exist. Calm and dreamy, often carrying somebody a cup of tea for no reason but love; entirely at the whim of a choleric husband, of whom she made no complaints. She was unfailingly delighted by the surprise of each new day.

The house was High House and stood at the end of a straight steep drive with an avenue of trees. Old and spare metal fences separated the avenue from the fields which in the Easter holidays of the wet Lancashire spring were the same dizzy green as the rice-paddies of South-East Asia. Far below the avenue to the West you could look down the chimneys of the family business which was a factory set in a deli. It was famous for making a particular kind of carpet, and was called The Goit, and through it, among the buildings of the purring carpet factory, ran a wide stream full of washed stones and little transparent fishes. "I am told our water is particularly pure," said Mrs. Ingoldby to Eddie Feathers ("Such an interesting name").

"I suppose it has to be, for washing the carpets," said Eddie. "But what about all the dyes?"

"Oh, I've simply no idea."

"Teddy" they called him, or "My dear chap" (the Colonel). Pat called him "Fevvers," as at school, but otherwise often ignored him. He was different at home and went off on his own. He sometimes sulked.

"He has these wretched black moods," said Mrs. Ingoldby, shelling peas under a beech tree. "Does it happen at school?"

"Yes. Sometimes. It does, actually."

"D'you know what causes them? He was such a sunny little boy. Of course he is so clever, it's such a pity. The rest of us are nothing much. I keep thinking it's my fault. One's mother becomes disappointing in puberty, don't you think? I suppose he'll just have to bear it."

Eddie wondered what puberty was.

"I suppose it's just this tiresome sex business coming on. Not, thank goodness, *homo*-sex for either of you."

"No," said Eddie. "We get too much about it from Sir."

"Ah, Sir. And poor Mr. Smith."

"Yes," said Eddie. "And the Mr. Smiths are always changing and Sir broken-hearted and we have to take him up Striding Edge and get his spirits re-started." Eddie had come some distance since the motor ride from North Wales.

"Your mother must feel so far from you, across the world."

"Oh no, she's dead. She died having me. I never knew her."

"And your poor father, all alone still?"

"I suppose so."

"I'm sure he loves you."

Eddie said nothing. The idea was novel. Bumble bees drowsed in the lavender bushes.

"*My* parents didn't love me at all," said Mrs. Ingoldby. "They were Indian Army. My mother couldn't wait to get rid of me to England. She'd lost several of us. Such pitiful rows of little graves in the Punjab and rows of mothers, too. But she really wanted just to ship me off. I'm very grateful. I went to a marvellous woman and there was a group of us. We completely forgot our parents. My mother ran off with someone—they did, you know. Or took to drink. Not enough to do. They used to give orders to the Indian servants like soldiers—very unbecoming. Utterly loyal to England of course. Then my father lost all his money. He was rather pathetic, I suppose."

"D-d-did he come to see you? In England?"

"Oh, I suppose so. Yes. I went to live with his sister, my Aunt Rose, when I grew up. It was very dull but I had nice clothes and she was very rich. I was never allowed to be ill. She was what is known as a Christian Scientist. Influenza in 1919 was tiresome. Everyone was dying. When my father turned up one day, a *footman* answered the morning-room door if you please (Aunt Rose had never opened a door in her life), and she just said, 'Oh, there you are, Gaspard. You must be tired. Here is your little girl.' D'you know, he burst into tears and fled. I can't think why. Oh, how lucky I was to meet the Colonel."

Walking across the fields with Pat, Eddie made about the only comment on anyone's life he had ever made.

"Your mother seems to feel the same about everybody. Why is she always happy?"

"God—I don't know."

"She's not bitter at all. Nobody liked her. Her parents sound awful if you don't mind my saying so."

"You've had Aunt Rose and the footman? They were all barmy, if you ask me. Raj loonies."

"She seems to feel—well, to like everybody, though."

"Oh, no, she doesn't. They were brought up like that. Most of them learned never to like anyone, ever, their whole lives. But they didn't moan because they had this safety net. The Empire. Wherever you went you wore the Crown, and wherever you went you could find your own kind. A club. There are still thousands round the world thinking they own it. It's vaguely mixed up with Christian duty. Even now. Even here, at Home. Every house of our sort you go into, Liverpool to the Isle of Wight—there's big game on the wall and tiger skins on the floor and tables made of Benares brass trays and a photograph of the Great Durbar. Nowadays you can even fake it, with plenty of servants. It wasn't like that in my grandfather's generation. They were better people. Better educated, Bible-readers, not showy. Got on with the job. There was a job for everyone and they did it and often died in it."

"I think my father will die in his. He thinks of nothing else. Sweats and slogs. Sick with malaria. And lost his family."

Pat, who was unconcerned about individuals, slashed at the flower-heads. "I'll be an historian. That's what I'm going to do. It's the only hope—learning how we got to be what we are. Primates, I mean. Surges of aggression. Today'll be history tomorrow. The empire is on the wane. Draining away. There will be chaos when it's gone and we'll be none the better people.

When empires end, there's often a dazzling finale—then—? Germany's looming again, Goths versus Visigoths."

"But you'd fight for the Empire, wouldn't you? I mean you'd fight for all this?" Eddie nodded over the green land.

"For the carpet factory? Yes, I would. I will."

"You *will*. Fight then?"

"Yes."

"So will I," said Eddie.

Wandering about that last peacetime summer with the Ingoldbys, Pat now seventeen, Eddie sixteen, the days were like weeks, endless as summers in childhood. They walked for miles—and at the end of each day of sun and smouldering cloud and shining Lancashire rain—stopped at the avenue. In the soft valley, more certain than sunset, the factory workers set off for home after the five o'clock hooter, moving in strings up The Goit and through the woods on paved paths worn into saucers and polished by generations of clogs. Sometimes on the high avenue, with the wind right, you could hear the horse-shoe metal of the clogs on the sandstone clinking like castanets.

Wandering on, the two of them would watch the Colonel in a black veil puffing smoke from a funnel stuffed with hay, and swearing at his bees. "If he'd only be quieter with them," said Pat. "Want any help, Pa?"

"No. Get away, you'll be killed. They're on the rampage."

"Oh—tea," said Mrs. Ingoldby. "You're just in time. I'll get them to make you some more of the little tongue sandwiches. Did you have a good walk?"

"Wonderful, thanks. Any news?"

"Yes. Hitler's invaded Poland. Don't tell your father yet, Pat. He can do nothing about it and there's his favourite supper. Oxtail stew."

"It's not all an act, you know," said Pat, the thought-reader, Mrs. Ingoldby having gone up to change for dinner. "It's a *modus vivendi*. Old-fashioned manners."

"I like it."

"Not upsetting the guests, yes. But she keeps anything horrid inside, for her own safety. My mother's not the fool she makes herself out to be. She's frightened. Any minute now, and farewell the carpet factory and security. It's going to be turned over to munitions. Ploughshares into swords. It's been our safe and respected source of income for two generations. This house'll go. Jack's going into the Air Force, and I intend to."

"You?"

"Yes. I suppose so. After I've got in to Cambridge. If they'll have me. Get my foot in for later."

He didn't ask about Eddie's plans.

"As I've been through the OTC," said Eddie. "I suppose I'll go for a soldier. My father was in something called the Royal Gloucesters—I don't know why. He might get me in there."

"By the way," said Pat, like his mother avoiding rocks in the river. "All that about footmen and Ma—it's balls, you know. Too many Georgette Heyers."

"But your mother's so—" (he was going to say innocent but it didn't seem polite) "—truthful."

"She's self-protective," said Pat. "Can you wonder? She was through the Great War, too."

That evening after dinner they listened to the wireless with the long windows open on to the lawn. A larch swung down black arms to touch the grass. A cat came out from under the arms and limped across the garden and out of sight. It was shaking its paws crossly.

The news was dire. After the Colonel had switched it off, you could hear the clipped BBC tones continuing through the open windows of the servants' sitting-room. Shadows had suddenly swallowed the drawing-room, and it was cold.

Mrs. Ingoldby draped a rug about her knees and said, "Pat, we need the light on." The heart-breaking smell of the stocks in the nearest flower bed engulfed the room like a sweet gas.

Pat lit up a cigarette and the cat walked back over the grass, a shadow now. Two green lamps of eyes blinked briefly. Pat put the light on.

"Whatever's the matter with the cat?"

"Don't talk to me about the cat," said the Colonel. "I threw it out of the bedroom window."

"Pa!"

"It had done a wee on my eiderdown. I threw the eiderdown after it. I'd have shot it if the gun had been handy. I'm keeping it loaded now for the Invasion. That cat knows exactly what it's doing."

"Do be careful, dear. It's not a Nazi."

"Cats and bees and the world, all gone mad. I tell you, there'll be no honey this year. Everything's a failure. I'm thinking of buying a cow."

"A cow, dear?"

"There'll be no butter by Christmas. Powdered milk. No cream."

"Why ever not?"

"It'll be rationed. Forces first. Are you a fool?"

At bedtime Eddie leaned out of his bedroom window—the bedroom now seemed altogether his own—and looked at the dark and light rows of the vegetable garden, the Colonel's obedient regiment standing to attention under a paring of moon. Silence until six o'clock tomorrow, and the factory hooter. Then the chorus of clicking feet trudging down The Goit as if nothing could ever change. Along the landing he heard the trumpet-call of the Colonel, "Rosie—do *not* shut the window.

And don't bring in that eiderdown. It stays there all night. I dare say it *will* rain. Let it rain."

Eddie could make out the square shape of desecrated satin lying up against the house like a forlorn white flag.

TULIPS

The morning after the ghastly day in London—the solicitor had muddled her diary or had had to stay at home with sick children or her mobile phone was out of order or a mixture of the three, which had meant their trip to Bantry Street had been for nothing—Filth was seated in the sun-lounge, very fierce and composing a Letter of Wishes to add to his Will. He wondered if he was quite well. A wet square of eiderdown kept floating into sight. Tiredness. He was half-dreaming. Wouldn't say anything to Betty.

The November sun blazed. It was almost warm enough to sit out of doors but Filth liked a desk before him when he was thinking. He liked a pen, or at least one of the expensive type of Biro—several because they gave out—and a block of A5 of the kind on which he had written his careful Opinions. Diligent, accurate, lucid, no jargon, all thanks to Sir, his Opinions used to be shown to juniors as models of the form. Then they had left him for the Clerk's rooms, where they were typed. First by a single typist—Mrs. Jones, who in between whiles did her knitting, often in her sealskin fur coat for there was no central heating. Later there were five typists, later still twenty. Over the years Filth had scarcely noticed the changes, from the clatter of the old black Remingtons and all the girls chain-smoking, to the hum and click of electronics, to the glare of a screen in every Barrister's room, the first fax machines, the e-mails and the mysterious Web. He was relieved not to have had to cope with all this as a junior or a Silk, and that by the time he made judge and lived in Hong Kong he had stepped into a world so advanced in electronics that he could hand everything over to machines but keep his pen too. His hand-writing—thanks again to Sir—was much admired. He had been in Commercial Chambers. The construction industry. Bridges and dams.

And what a great stack of money I made at the Bar, he thought. It was a noble act becoming a judge on a salary. *Letters of Wishes ... Bequests to Friends ...* I've left it too long. The best friends are all dead.

And no children to leave it to. He looked across from the sun-lounge to Betty planting the tulips. She seldom spoke of children. Never to children when there were any around. She seemed—had always seemed—to have no views on their bar-renness.

As it happened, had he known it, she was thinking of chil-dren now. She was wondering about yesterday, when she and Filth had made an abortive attempt to give what they had by dying. The death of Terry's child. The solicitor forgetting her job because of her children's measles. This dazzle of a morn-ing, thirty years beyond her child-bearing years. The trees across Wiltshire were bright orange, yellow, an occasional ver-milion maple—what a slow leaf fall—spreading away from the hillside garden, the sun rich and strong, the house behind her benign and English and safe, as well-loved now as her apart-ments and houses in the East. There would have been grand-children by now, she thought and heard their voices. Would we have been any good with them? She could not see Filth look-ing at a grandchild with love.

She had never been sure about Filth and love. Something blocked him. Oh, *faithful*—oh, yes. Unswerving unto death. "Never been anyone for Filth but Betty." And so on.

All this time in the tulip bed, she had been on her knees and she tried now to get up. It is becoming ridiculous, this getting up. Ungainly. Not that I was ever *gainly*, but I wasn't lumberous. She lay down on her side, grinning, on the wet grass. And saw that her pearls had come off and lay in the tulip bed. They were yesterday's pearls, and for the first time in her life she had not taken them off at bedtime nor when she bathed in the morning. "I am becoming a slut," she told them. Her face was close against them. She said to them, "You are not my *famous* pearls, though he never notices. You are my *guilty* pearls. What shall I do with you? Who shall have you when I am gone?"

"No one," she said, and let them slither out of sight into one of the holes made ready for the tulips. With her fingers, she filled the hole with earth and smoothed it over.

Then she brought her firm old legs round in front of her so that they lay across the flower-beds. She noticed that each hole had a sprinkle of sharp sand in the bottom, and hoped the sand would not hurt the pearls.

Still not out of the wood, she thought. Hope Filth doesn't look up, he'd worry.

She rested, then twisted herself, heaved and crawled. The legs obeyed her at last and came round back again and she was on all fours. She leaned on her elbows, her hands huge in green and yellow gloves, and slowly brought her bottom into the air, swayed, and creakily, gleefully stood up. "Well, I was never John Travolta," she said. "And it is November. Almost first frost."

Amazed, as she never ceased to be, about how such a multitude of ideas and images exist alongside one another and how the brain can cope with them, layered like filo pastry in the mind, invisible as data behind the screen, Betty was again in Orange Tree Road, standing with Mrs. Cleary and Mrs. Hong and old friends in the warm rain, and all around the leaves falling like painted raindrops. The smell of the earth round the building-works of the new blocks of flats, the jacarandas, the polish on the banana leaves, children laughing, swimming in the private pools. The sense of being part of elastic life, unhurried, timeless, controlled. And in love. The poor little girl selling parking tickets in her white mittens against the sun. Betty's eyes filled with tears, misting her glasses. Time gone. Terry's boy gone.

Trowel in hand, a bit tottery, she turned to look up the garden at Filth.

Since yesterday he had been impossible. All night catafalque-rigid, sipping water, at breakfast senatorial and remote. The Judge's dais. He had frowned about him for toast. When she had made more toast and set the toast-rack (silver) before him he had examined it and said, "The toast-rack needs cleaning."

"So do the salt-cellars," she'd said. "I'll get you the Silvo. You've nothing else to do today."

He had glared at her, and she wondered whether his mind, too, was layered with images. Breakfast on The Peak for eleven years at seven o'clock, misty, damp and grey, she in her silk dressing-gown making lists for the day, Filth—oh so clean, clean Filth—in his light-weight dark suit and shirt so white it seemed almost blue, his Christ Church tie, his crocodile briefcase. Outside the silently-sliding Merc, with driver waiting in dark-green uniform, the guard on the gate ready to press the button on the steel doors that would rise without creak or hesitation. And the warm, warm heavy air.

"Bye, dear."

"Bye, Filth. Home sixish?"

"Home sixish."

Every minute pleasantly filled. Work, play and no chores.

And the sunset always on the dot, like Filth's homecoming. The dark falling over the harbour that was never dark, the lights in their multitude, every sky-scraper with a thousand eyes. The sky-high curtains of unwinking lights, red, yellow, white, pale green, coloured rain falling through the dark. The huge noise of Hong Kong rising, the little ferries plying, the sense of a place to be proud of. We made it. We saw how to do it. A place to have been responsible for. British.

"I'll do the silver later," said Filth. "I shall be busy this morning with my Letter of Wishes. I shall see to my own Will."

"I suppose I should do a Letter too," she said. "I'd thought the Will would be enough. But after yesterday—"

"The less said about yesterday the better. London solicitors!" and he rose from the toast-rack, still a fascinatingly tall and taking man, she thought. If it wasn't for the neck and the moles he'd look no more than sixty. People still look up and wonder who he is. Always a tie. And his shoes like glass.

"I'm going to plant tulips."

"I'll clear up the breakfast."

"Do you mind? It's not Mrs. T's day."

"I want to get on with the Will whilst I'm still in ferment."

"Ferment?"

"About that woman. Solicitor. You know exactly. Lack of seriousness. Duty. Messy. The distance we travelled! Messy diary. I expect her diary's on a screen."

"Watch your blood-pressure, Filth. You've gone purple."

He flung about the house looking for the right pen.

"You could do it on the computer. You can make changes much quicker."

(They both played the game that they could work the computer if they tried.)

"I shan't be making many changes."

"The point is," she said, "be quick. Get everything witnessed. Locally—why not? So much cheaper. We might die at any time."

"So you said all the way home in the train. Solicitors!"

"So you have often said."

He glared at her, then softened as he watched her healthy, outdoor face and her eyes that had never caught her out.

"I hate making Wills," she said. "I've made dozens," and looked away, not wanting to touch on inheritances since there was nobody to inherit. She didn't want to see that Filth didn't mind.

"I think," said Filth, astonishingly, "one day I'll write you a Letter of my Wishes. My personal wishes."

"Have you so many left then?"

"Not many. Peace at the last, perhaps."

And that you will never leave me, he thought.

And now, standing with the trowel, head racing a bit with the effort of being John Travolta, she closed her eyes against dizziness. She opened them again, shaded them with her hand and saw him seated above her in the sun-lounge. He had some sort of wrap over his bony, parted knees. The drape of it and the long narrow face staring into the sun made him look like a Christ in Majesty over a cathedral gate. All that was needed was the raised hand in blessing. His eyes were closed. How long is he going to last? she thought. How he hates death. However, Christ in Majesty opened his eyes and raised a hand not in blessing but holding an enormous gin.

"Gin," he called down. "Felt like gin."

I won't get any nearer to him now, she thought, turning to pick up the bulb-basket, taking off her gloves. Too late now. The holes look good, but I'll do the planting tomorrow. There might be a frost. I won't risk them out all night on the grass.

THE FERMENT

After her funeral, Filth, now old as time, was at his desk again. Garbutt, the odd job man, trundled a wheelbarrow stacked up with ivy between the sun-lounge and the tulip bed. Garbutt's jaw was thrust forward. He was lusting after a bonfire. The woman, Mrs. Thing, arrived at Filth's shoulder with a cup of coffee, then with a Ewbank sweeper.

"Lift your feet a minute and let me get under them and then I'll leave you in peace," she said. "Here's more letters. Shall I come back with your ironing tonight? I could make you a salad. The way he goes at that ivy!"

"Thank you, no. Perfectly capable," said Filth. "I must keep at desk."

"I liked the ivy," she said. "Not that my opinion . . ."

"It's done now," said Filth.

"I'm sorry. Well, there's plenty in the fridge and you've only to phone up . . ."

"Letters," he said. "Letters. Many, many letters," and he picked one up and waved it about to get rid of her. There were no black-bordered ones now, thank God. They had disappeared with the Empire. This one was in a pale green envelope and came from Paris. As the woman, Mrs.-er, slammed the front door and Garbutt stamped past again with the empty barrow, Filth had the sensation of a command not to open this letter and looking across the garden saw Betty standing on the lawn watching him with an expression of deep annoyance.

"Ha!" he said, and stared her out. "Leave me be," he shouted. He picked up the ivory paper knife to slit the envelope and saw the name: *Ingoldby*. He stared, looked back at the now empty lawn, looked down again.

Not the Colonel or Mrs. Ingoldby, long ago gone. Not Jack or Pat. No issue there. *I. Ingoldby*, it said on the envelope and so it must be Isobel. Ye gods.

Well, I'd better face it.

The year that Eddie left Sir's Outfit for his Public school, he was to spend the summer as usual at High House. Pat Ingoldby, a year older, had left Sir the year before but had written a weekly letter from the new school to Eddie and Eddie had written back. Other boys did the same with absent brothers. Sir had insisted from the start on weekly letters to parents and, although Eddie had had none back from his father, the habit had continued until Pat moved on. Then Eddie had struck, and asked to write to Mrs. Ingoldby instead of his father and, as Eddie's stammer was threatening again after Pat's departure, Sir agreed, and Mrs. Ingoldby did write back occasionally, in a hand like a very small spider meandering across the thick writing paper and passing out and dying off in the faintest of signatures. Years later, in a different life, Eddie found that his father had kept all his letters from Sir's Outfit, numbered carefully and filed in a steel safe against the termites. Eddie's letters to Mrs. Ingoldby and to Pat did not survive.

Sir had also insisted on letters being written to Auntie May, who occasionally sent a postcard; Uncle Albert, her missionary husband, once sent the school a coconut for Christmas.

Pat's short, succinct, witty letters from the new school were a great pleasure to Eddie. He absorbed everything offered for his information: accommodation, lessons, boys, games (which were more important than church), menus, lack of humour among staff. Both boys missed each other but never referred to the fact, nor to the fact that the fraternal arrangements of the holidays would of course continue. Eddie wrote to his aunts, one of about three letters in his five years with Sir, asking if he could have some of the money his father had put aside for him, to give Sir a present, and Aunt Muriel sent a ten shilling note.

"I don't accept presents," said Sir, looking briefly at *Three Men in a Boat*. "This is a clean school. No nonsense. But yes, I'll have this one. Send your sons here when you've got some. Present us with a silver cup for something when you're a filthy rich lawyer, I dare say? Yes. You'll be a lawyer. Magnificent memory. Sense of logic, no imagination and no brains. My favourite chap, Teddy Feathers, as a matter of fact. I dare say."

"Thank you, Sir. I'll always keep in touch."

"Don't go near Wales. And keep off girls for a while. Soon as girls arrive exam results go down. Passion leads to a Lower Second. Goodbye, old Feathers. On with the dance."

High House—it was now 1936—where Eddie now brought all his (few) possessions, was reassuringly the same and here was Pat on the railway platform, taller and spotty, with a deep voice but still talking. Talking and talking. There was to be a girl staying, he said, but not to worry as almost at once she was going off on holiday to the Lake District with his mother.

"She's here already. She's a cousin. Pa's niece. She's causing trouble."

But up at the House there was no sign of this cousin and nobody mentioned her and she didn't show up all day.

The next day at breakfast Eddie asked the Colonel about her.

"How's your niece, Sir?"

"Done very badly in her Higher School Certificate. And she's too old to try again. I tell her nobody will ever ask her what she did and she'll forget it herself in six months. She'll find a husband. Poor fellow."

"One can't be sure," said Mrs. Ingoldby. "She's rather *secretive*. I've a feeling that a husband isn't on the cards. And very stubborn, I'm afraid. I've sent her breakfast up as she has a headache. *And* she's upset."

The next day there was a sighting of Isobel Ingoldby pacing about the garden, up and down, up and down in the rain with a haversack on her back.

"Is she going somewhere?" asked Pat.

"She talks of Spain. She has an urge to help the rebels. I thought I might telegraph her parents."

"Let her be," said Pat. "She'll be in for dinner."

"But did she have *breakfast*?"

"Well, it was all laid up for her on the sideboard."

"I wouldn't want her going home and saying we'd given her nothing to eat. And oh dear, look! Maybe she *didn't* have breakfast."

Isobel could be seen writhing about in her haversack and then disembowelling it on the grass. She took from it a hunk of bread, stood up, tilted back her head and began to devour it. Her eyes seemed closed. Praying perhaps.

"I think she may be a little peculiar," said Colonel Ingoldby. "There is some of that in the Ingoldbys. Not Pat, of course, dear, and certainly not Jack."

Elder brother Jack, the beloved, now passed through High House only very occasionally. Sir and the family's traditional public school had seen him to Cambridge and he was there or abroad most of the time, swooping through his old home, once or twice a summer, bringing rare and various companions, playing wonderful tennis, clean and groomed, at one with his parents' world. Mrs. Ingoldby, like a dog which awaits its master, seemed to know by instinct when he was on the way. "Just a mo. Isn't that Jack?" They would listen, then continue life, and a few minutes later would come the splutter and roar of Jack's car, its silver body tied up with a classy leather strap.

Eddie had an instinct about Jack, too; that Isobel was being kept away from him and that was why she and Mrs. Ingoldby were off to the Lake District. That was why Isobel was peculiar. Seeing Isobel in the garden he could tell that the Lake District and her godmother would not be sufficient for her.

"Oh, do bring her in," said Mrs. Ingoldby, "or at any rate someone go and talk to her . . . You, Eddie. Would you go? You'll be new to her—she finds us boring. You could talk to her about the Spanish Civil War. I don't want any stories about our neglecting her going back to Gerard's Cross."

So Eddie had walked rather awkwardly across the lawn and into the trees, on his fourteen-year-old lengthening legs and oval knees. His curly hair; his hands in his pockets like some of the more blasé of the Mr. Smiths' had been. His feet in scruffy sand-shoes very huge; his height endearing. His voice, breaking, was surprising him all the time by sudden booms and squeaks. Yet there was grace about him. He hadn't taken in a thing about the Spanish Civil War.

The girl was standing with her back to him. The rain had stopped and it was becoming a warm and honeyed July morning and in the hills below stood the factory chimneys rising brown and mighty like Hindu temples.

"Oh, hullo," he said.

The girl stopped munching and turned. She stared.

"I'm Edward Feathers. Pat's friend. I've been told to ask if you—well, if you might be coming in for lunch?"

The girl was gigantic; bony, golden and vast; as tall as Eddie and certainly pretty old. She could be twenty. Her face was like a lioness's—flat nose, narrow brow, wide cheekbones, long green eyes. Supreme self-command. Wow!

Her legs were bare and very long, like his own, and her sandals had little leather thongs separating the toes.

Eddie felt something happening to his anatomy and though he had no idea what it was he began to blush.

She looked him up and down and began to laugh.

"I don't go in for eating round a polished table," she said. "I need to be out of doors. They know that."

"They didn't seem to. Oh, well, OK, then. I'll tell them." And he fled.

"She says she doesn't like eating round a polished table."

"Oh, God," said Pat.

"That's her mother," said the Colonel.

"I'm afraid I'm going to have a difficult time with her in the Wastwater Hotel," said Mrs. Ingoldby.

"Maybe the table won't be polished," said Pat. "Anyway, why take her? Jack's abroad."

His mother gave him what in any other woman would have been a searching look. "I *am* her godmother," she said, "and her mother *has* gone off with a Moroccan drummer."

"I don't blame her," said Pat. "Fevvers' mother went off, and he doesn't go eating in the trees."

"Oh, Teddy! I didn't know! I thought your mother only *died*."

"She did only die," said Eddie. "She died when I was two days old."

"She must have caught sight of you," said Pat.

"That will do," said his mother, and "Damn bad luck," said his father, "don't suppose there were many Moroccans in Malaya."

"There were a lot of drummers," said Eddie and began to squeal and cackle. The Colonel and his wife looked baffled and embarrassed.

Pat had given Eddie some sort of sudden freedom. Eddie's ideal mother, whom he had always thought of as an Auntie

May sort of person, became a houri, off to bed and that with a Moroccan drummer! Pat had given him confidence. Right from the very start. And crikey, he needed it, now, after that thing that had happened to him in the trees. He wondered whether to mention it to Pat; then knew that it was the first thing ever that he couldn't discuss with him.

Pat was watching him.

"Shall we go out on bikes?"

"Yes, great. Yes, please."

"OK, Ma?"

"Yes. But what are we to do about Isobel?"

"It's out of our hands to do anything about Isobel."

And the leopardish girl went prowling past the windows, haversack in place and reading a map.

"She's a fine looker, I'll say that," said the Colonel.

"Jack thinks so, too," said Pat.

The two of them trudged up a hill, pushing their bikes, wishing for modern three-speeds and not these childhood toys with baskets. "And you—hein?"

Eddie said nothing.

At supper Isobel appeared and sat down at the Colonel's right hand. She leaned back in her chair and glittered her eyes. "What a pretty dress," said her godmother. "Were you thinking of taking it to Spain? I'm sure it has to be dry-cleaned. It will be difficult at the frontier."

Isobel messed with her food.

"Oh, dear. I'm afraid you've stopped liking fish-pie. You used to love . . ."

"It's fine," said Isobel, scraping it about with the tips of the prongs of her fork. She had picked out all the prawns and now leaned her sun-burnt shoulders towards Eddie and began to pick prawns off his plate.

"Yummie," she said, and Eddie found himself in trouble again beneath the tablecloth. He blushed purple and Pat exploded in his glass of water.

"I think she's after you," Pat said after dinner, playing tennis with Eddie in the dark. "Go easy. She's a cannibal. It's going to rain. We'll have to go in. Get the net down. She'll be out there somewhere, gleaming in the bushes. Aren't you going to laugh?"

But Eddie, busy catching up tennis balls, winding up the net, said nothing. On the way back to the house he slashed at vegetation for all he was worth.

"Sorry I spoke," said Pat. "Only joking."

"Oh, shut up," said Eddie. "I can't stand your cousin. OK? Sorry."

But they stopped at the bench for the view from the hill. "Can't see much, but we could maybe hear the nightingale. Then we could send a card to Sir," said Pat.

"It's too late for the nightingale. And too far north."

"D'you want a weed?" Pat lit up a cigarette.

"No fear."

"It turns on the girls. Not that you seem to feel the need."

"It's disgusting. It's all disgusting," Eddie yelled out and pushed Pat off the seat and sat on him. Pat flailed about and then began to sing:

> "My friend Billy
> Had a ten-foot. . ."

"Stop it!"

> "He showed it to the boy next door.
> Who thought it was a snake
> And hit it with a rake
> And now it's only . . ."

And they rolled about, fighting as they had done for years, stopping the clocks for a minute longer.

But there was a change somewhere. He and Pat were moving on. Glaciers would soon come grinding them apart, memories would be forgotten or adapted or faked.

Eddie followed Pat heavily into the house that evening and even Pat looked thoughtful. In the drawing-room the Ingoldbys were talking their pointless evening birdsong. No sound of Isobel anywhere.

As Eddie lay in his adored High House bed the rain began to patter down again outside and he jumped out to shut the window where the moon soon disappeared behind the rain clouds. He climbed back into bed.

All the following years, the memory or dream of what happened next never quite left him. His bedroom door opened and closed again, and the goddess—lioness—girl was at the end of his bed. Standing and watching, brooding on his inability to take his eyes off her.

She then walked to the window and looked out. He knew that something was expected of him but had no idea what it was. Not long ago, he would have shouted out, "Help! Burglars!" In time, in only a few years, he supposed, from books he'd read in the back of bookshops near Sir's, he and the girl would have merged their flesh together in some sort of way in the bed. But he didn't know what happened next. And didn't want to know.

She's old and she's evil and she only wants to hurt, he thought.

"Eddie?" the shadow whispered from the window. "I wonder what you think of me?"

She walked back across the room and he found that he could sit up straight under the blankets and confront her, brave as brave as—*Cumberledge*. There! He'd said the word. Cumberledge. Wherever he was now. Silent Cumberledge whose spirit had never been completely broken.

Eddie would finish her, as once already in his life he had finished a woman. "I think you're bad. A bad woman," he said. "Get out."

And she was gone.

The weird dream (or whatever it was) was never quite obliterated. He had not so much kept it to himself as denied it. In a way he never understood, it both shamed and saddened him.

Why ever? Nothing had happened. He had won. He had silenced the sirens. If there had been sailors on board, they would not have had to tie this Ulysses to the mast. So sucks to sexy Isobel, the cradle-snatcher.

Yet, all his life—regret.

Isobel and Mrs. Ingoldby were gone first thing next morning. And when Eddie next met Isobel it was in another world and a great many people were dead.

The Donheads

A nd so it was Isobel. The green letter was from Isobel. A letter of condolence for the loss of his wife.

Dear Teddy (if I still may, Sir Edward), I have just seen in the *New York Times* here in Paris the very sad news of Betty's death and I am writing to say how very much I feel for you, and for all of us, come to that, who knew her and will miss her.

(*Miss* her? *Knew* her?)

I wonder just how much you remember? I wonder how much you remember of anything before you met Betty and became the icon of the jolly old Hong Kong Bar? Before you *really* met me? We never mentioned High House, did we? Again?

It hardly outlasted the War, you know. You and Pat were so very much together there. You and Pat were the spirit of the place, and I was a hole in the air. Did you ever know, I wonder, after you met Betty, that she and I were at school together? I went to High House after the Higher School Certificate disaster. She left St. Paul's Girls in triumph. But they had me later in the War at Bletchley Park and there we met again. Bletchley Park was full of innocent, nice girls (not me) who had a very particular aptitude (crosswords) for solving cyphers and things, as you will be hearing in a year or two when ALL IS TOLD (the fifty-year revelation). That is how we won the War. How we stopped the U-Boats. So we were told. We were schoolgirls, Teddy. I was still a schoolgirl when you met me. Do you remember my teenage sulks? I was a schoolgirl five years on—no. Not five years on. Not in Peel Street. Oh, my beloved Teddy.

I was so pleased when you married Betty. I would have destroyed you, my sweet, beloved Teddy. But because of—well, I expect you have forgotten—but because of the day your great big feet came left, right, stamp, stamp down Peel Street and I was waiting for you and then—. Well, because of this I think I am allowed to write to you now. Oh, look—forget Peel Street. Kensington. Peripheral. I loved you from the moment you came walking (embarrassingly!) up to the trees at High House. I loved you and I love you.

Betty and I always exchanged Christmas cards. I expect you didn't know. You probably never noticed mine. Betty was a very untouchable woman. Nobody knew her—though I always suspected that there was a great well—*comprehension*—with someone, somewhere. She wasn't very pretty. She always sent me a Christmas card.

I was so very sorry to see in the *NY Times*—my word, she was a surpriser! You and I, Teddy, won't make the *NYT*—I was so very sorry to see in the obituary that there were "no children of the marriage." It is—in every language—a bleak little phrase. It means that you and B had a sadness, for when I last saw Betty forty years ago, she told me how much she longed for a child. We were in a park at the Hague. You were at the Court of International justice, against Veneering. Betty and Veneering—what a saint you were, Eddie!

I have no children either, come to that. And no partner (Christ! Christ!—"*partner*"). I can no longer bear a partner, but I most desperately regret not having had a child. You guessed, Eddie. I think. There wasn't the word "gay" then and it was something you didn't care to think about. But I believe you guessed.

I hope you still have friends about you in the south of England (NOT your place, I'd have thought?). Dear Teddy, everyone always loved you in your extraordinary never-revealed or unravelled private world. I am one of those who know that you were not really cold.

Sincerely yours, Isobel.

Filth picked up this letter and then its envelope and dropped both in the waste-paper basket. His face had taken upon it the iron ridges of a stage or television version of a prosecuting Counsel before he rises to the attack.

He found air-mail stationery of antique design. He addressed the envelope and attached three expensive stamps to be sure of covering the French postage. He drew the old-fashioned flimsy paper towards him, pushed aside the cheap Biros and took up his Collins gold pen (a retirement present from the lawyers of his Inn). He filled the pen from the ink bottle. Quink. Black. He wrote:

> Sir Edward Feathers thanks Miss Isobel
> Ingoldby for her kind letter of condolence.

He dated it, muffled himself into a coat, tweed hat and woollen gloves, took his walking stick and the letter, and set off down the drive and up the village hill to the post office.

He dropped the letter into the red box that still said, *V.R.* and strode inexorably home again. One or two people on the hill noticed him, and stopped what they were doing as he passed, glad to see that the old boy was going out again, ready to speak to him if he noticed them.

But he went by, the lanky, old-fashioned figure of long ago, walking painfully between the over-hanging trees of his drive. He passed Garbutt without a glance.

Isobel Ingoldby.

He sat again to his desk and wrote three more letters, replying to the formal, kind messages of condolence. Several times the telephone rang and he heard the drone and click of the answerphone and paid no attention. Lunchtime came and went. He wrote more replies to letters including one (good heavens!!) from Cumberledge in Cambridge. Billy Cumberledge. What is this? What's this? I need Betty.

Mid-afternoon, and he walked into the kitchen and looked hard and long at the fridge and did not open it. He boiled up water but, when the kettle clicked off, did nothing about it. He stood at the kitchen window idly swirling water from the hot tap around in the little green teapot to warm its inside, standing until the steam began to scald his fingers. Then he poured himself a glass of milk and walked to the study where the newspaper lay ready for him by his armchair. He sat, and regarded his rows of law books, his grand old wig-box now laid out again upon the hearth. Eventually he dozed and awoke with the sun gone down behind the hills, and the room cold.

He wondered wherever the glass of milk had come from. He had not drunk milk since Ma Didds in Wales. She must be here. He heard the hated voice. "You don't leave this cupboard until you've drunk this glass of good milk and you'd better not stir your feet because there's a hole in there beside you deep as a well and you'd never be heard of more." The long day, and not let out till bedtime, and six years old.

He walked over to the wastepaper basket and re-read the letter. It existed. It had not been a dream. She had waited over forty years. The letter of a cruel spirit. "Loves me"—how abhorrent. She is a lesbian. "Not cold"—enough! Betty wanting a child . . . How dare she! This Ingoldby, the last traitor of all the traitorous Ingoldbys.

Oh, I am too old for any of this.

He took the milk back to the kitchen and poured it down the sink, opened a cake-tin and cut himself a slice of Betty's birthday cake and ate it rather guiltily because it wasn't yet stale. Then he poured himself a whiskey and soda, walked into the sun-lounge and held the letter up towards the tulip-bed.

"Betty?"

Emptiness. Silence. And silence within the house, too. Outside a most unnatural silence. Not a car in the lane, or a plane in the sky, not a human voice calling a dog. Not the church clock on the quarters, not a breath of wind, not a bird on a bough. All darkness as usual from the empty invisible house next door. Then a fox walked tiptoe over the December grass, its brush trailing but its ears pricked. At the steps that led up to the sun-lounge it turned its head towards Filth and smiled.

He remembered the Ingoldbys' delinquent cat angrily shaking its paws at the time of the breaking of nations. 1939. The roar of the Colonel that had shattered the family's self-deception and serenity. Then that earlier shadow, three years before, of the girl. Her shadow detaching itself from the blacker shadow of the yews. The term before he went to Public school.

SCHOOL

Eddie found himself very much the junior to Pat at Chilham School when he followed him there in 1936. At first they were in different Houses. Eddie, after Sir's Outfit, was able to cope easily with the new place's idiosyncrasies. He was good at getting up in the morning and untroubled by Morning Prep at 6.30 A.M. The work was easy. He was good at games. He liked the slabs of bread and jam halfway through the morning. Whenever he caught sight of Pat he sent him a salute and Pat, untroubled that he was senior to Eddie, saluted back or did his Herr Hitler imitation. They naturally continued to keep together whenever possible. After matches—they were both in good teams—they would walk unselfconsciously round and round the playing fields, talking. They were soon a famous oddity, and were spoken to about it.

"It is not as if you were brothers," said the Headmaster when the case was at length referred to him, the highest court.

"We've been brought up as brothers," said Pat. "Sir."

"But even brothers here do not go about together all the time."

"What do you say, Feathers?"

"I can't think of anything, Sir."

"Do you, we wonder" (this was a trap) "wish you were in Ingoldby's House?"

"No, not specially. I've never thought about it. I'm with the Ingoldbys all the holidays."

"How very unusual."

"My father knew his father in the Great War," said Pat, astonishing Eddie who hadn't known of it. "We're a sort of subfamily."

It was a mystery.

"There seems no *physicality* about it," said the Headmaster to their Housemasters. "They're both very bright. And very unusual, but then all boys are unusual. Put Feathers in Ingoldby's House might be the best thing. Treat them like other brothers here."

Pat, most ridiculously young, went up to Cambridge for several days for the university entrance exam. The phoney war was over and the Battle of Britain had begun. The journey would not be unexciting. Pat made much of taking his gas mask.

Without him that week the school felt dull and empty and for the first time Eddie realised that he had made no friends. He felt an outsider as he lay in his bed in the dormitory.

"Is Ingoldby some relation?" came a shout in the dark.

"Not of mine," said Eddie.

"You don't look like him," came another shout. "Not like his brother Jack did."

"I'm not his brother. How d'you know what his brother Jack looks like?"

"In the team-photographs. Holding cups and shields. Head boy in a *gown*. Hamlet in *Hamlet*. Just a taller Ingoldby. Good looking, not carroty."

"I come from Malaya."

"Do they all have red hair there?"

"Yes. Every one of them."

"Doesn't Ingoldby's brother mind?" someone shouted far down the row of beds, made brave by the black-out curtains.

"Mind what? I'm his brother's friend, too."

"Mind your being so important to him?"

A searchlight began to scale the walls, to pierce the black windows. It was joined by another and they danced together for a while, searching for German bombers on the way to Liverpool.

"Why ever should he? Jack's in the Air Force. He's got more important things to think about. I dare say," Eddie added, like Sir.

"What do Ingoldby's parents think?"

"I've never asked them. They've always wanted me there." (And, he thought, they're mine. Blood of my blood and bone of my bone.)

"Where's your own family then, Feathers?" shouted an up-and-coming man. "Where's your own family?" (They were braver with Ingoldby away.)

"My father's in Malaya."

"Was he in the Great War? Smashed up?"

"Yes."

"Why doesn't he come and see you?"

Pat returned from Cambridge with an assured place to read physics, having decided that history was all out of date—oh joke!

"After this War," they had said, "you have your foot in the door by being accepted by the college now. You can be deferred if you wish. Volunteer and wait to be called. They'll give you the first year. Excellent papers."

But on the way home from Cambridge, overnight at High House, he had managed to volunteer for the RAF at the end of the summer term.

"If I'm spared," he said to Eddie, in a Methuselah voice. "Bloody raids, here every night. Why didn't they evacuate us? We're going to be clobbered."

"They think slowly here," said Eddie. "Sir moved his Outfit the minute Chamberlain wagged the white paper."

"Chamberlain saved us," said Pat. "Gave us a year to make more broomsticks to look like rifles. Even the carpet factory's making tents now. I don't know where they'll be using them. Africa?"

"Sir's gone to America."

This made them unhappy.

They were lying between damp grey blankets, among rows of other boys in the school's underground shelters, water running in rills down the walls. Far away a never-ending thunder meant that somewhere was being flattened again. York? Liverpool? Even as far away as Coventry.

The same week, on a night when there had been no air-raid siren, a drenching cold and moonless night and the boys asleep in their dormitories, every alarm bell in the school had begun to ring, followed by hooters, whistles and military cries. The dormitory doors were flung open and every boy ordered to dress immediately and gather by his House front door.

"And uniform, please, if you are in the Corps."

"What—puttees, sir?"

"Puttees, Ingoldby."

"They take a good five minutes, sir."

"Then die, Ingoldby. Or get moving."

Out from all the seven Houses of the school streamed boys of several ages in various attire. Each one was handed a rifle, Officers' Training Corps or not, and five rounds of ammunition.

"Invasion. Get on there. It's the Invasion. Go!" and five hundred boys, some trailing khaki bandages on their legs, some in their pyjamas and without their dressing-gowns ("*dressing*-gowns"), were quickly lost in the midnight fields and ditches of the North Midlands. Somebody cried "Hark!" and some of them heard the death knell: the cry of the bells from all the muffled steeples. This was later denied.

"Oh," said Pat, still purring from the Cambridge grown-up claret, "INVASION. Five rounds. Bang, bang, bang, bang, finish. Farewell the red, white and blue."

Those who knew how, loaded their rifles. Those who didn't, dropped their cartridges in the mud. There was occasional unfortunate friendly fire (though the phrase had not then been invented and the one used was balls-up) and a few disagreeable misfortunes with bayonets. There was the occasional, but not serious, scream.

Then, the silence. Darkness and rain settled over the North's infant infantry who did not trouble the landscape or the night, which passed with very few prayers and still fewer orgasms or unexpected desire. Little poetry was engendered. After several hours some word of command must have been passed and the great old school found itself staggering from the ditches, crossing the sodden ugly fields, falling into bed again at 4 A.M.

But at 6.15 A.M. it was pre-breakfast Prep, as usual.

It had been a false alarm.

"We're going to lose this war," said Eddie. "Am I right, Pat?"

"Can't speak," said Ingoldby. His hair looked like black lacquer which someone had painted on his head. His face was carmine. Under the bedclothes in the dormitory he was wearing last night's Army uniform sopped through and caked with mud. At the end of his bed, purple feet stuck out. Above them, his semi-putteed legs.

"You know the whole bloody issue was nothing?" someone was saying. "A barrage-balloon come loose over the Vale of York, for God's sake. Trailed its cable over the electric pylon and blacked out the North. Invasion, my foot!"

"Invasion, my feet," shuddered Ingoldby, looking with interest down his body under the blankets at them. "Sometimes there are two of them, s-s-sometimes—oh God! S-s-sometimes four."

He was found to have pneumonia and put in the school San. There, he was scooped from all friends, and therefore of course from Eddie, and absorbed into the antiseptic of the nut-cracker-faced Matron in charge. Days passed.

On one of them, in a free-period, Eddie on his ostrich legs went walking to the San and found this woman seated just inside the door knitting an immense scarf in khaki wool that curled inwards down the sides like a tube.

"May I go and see Ingoldby, Matron?"

"Certainly not. You know the rules."

"How is he?"

"That's my business."

"Would you give him a message?"

"You know that's not allowed, neither."

"I'll ask Oils, then."

"Ask away."

Eddie knocked on Mr. Oilseed's door and found Oils, his Housemaster, late of Ypres, France, sitting one-eyed and holding a little glass weight at the end of a silver chain, swinging the chain gently over a desk covered with mountains of unmarked essays.

"Matron says I can ask to visit Ingoldby, sir."

"Now—where is Ingoldby? I forget."

"He's in the San, sir. As a result of The Fiasco. The other night."

"Fiasco? Oh, I don't think we should assume that. It was a valuable exercise."

"It's said that Ingoldby has pneumonia."

"'It is said,'" said Oils, "is not a phrase I ever recommend. It does not commend itself. Ingoldby's parents are coming later today."

"But, sir . . . I'm pretty well part of that family, you know. Since I was eight."

Oils let the fine chain ripple and fall into a heap upon the green baize of the desk. (What *was* he doing? Sexing a child?) He continued to stare at it.

"Feathers," he said, "the times are moving on, but very slowly."

"Yes, sir?"

"There is something today that is a wonder in the school. This *Victorian* and bourgeois school. This is that the unnatural closeness between you and Ingoldby has not been terminated. There are certain explanatory circumstances but, as we who were in the trenches know, emotions have to be contained. This, like your Prep school, is a school in which we endure."

"I loved our Prep school, sir."

"I suggest that you go back to your study and read Kipling."

"Kipling's childhood was very like mine and he *was* queer. I should like to appeal."

"I beg your pardon?"

"I have the right of appeal here."

"To whom, may I ask?"

"To the Headmaster first, sir. Then to the Board of Governors. Finally in the correspondence columns of the *Times*."

"On what grounds?"

"Slander, sir. And antediluvianism."

He left Oils' study and made for the Headmaster's House where no foot trod unbidden except those of the old spider himself and his paddly housekeeper. Eddie stood outside, and turned the great iron ring on the tall gate. The flagstones were slimy, the windows glimpsed through tangled plants.

"Come round the side," said a threadbare voice from behind a pane. "Kitchen."

"Ah, yes," said the Head after blinking at the daylight Eddie brought in with him, "Tussock, isn't it?"

"*Tussock*, sir? I'm Feathers."

"Ah, Feathers, Feathers. 'The life of man is plumed with

death.' It's part of a plea of mercy by a seaman to Queen Elizabeth the First."

"I know, sir."

"Do you? We aren't told whether it was successful. I knew your father, Feathers. He was a boy here when I was. How is he?"

"I never see him. He's in South-East Asia. I think he's gone to Singapore now."

"Yes. Of course. And that's what we must talk about. I've been pondering the matter all week, Tussock. But first—what?"

"I want to visit my friend, Ingoldby, in the San, sir. I am told by Mr. Oilseed that it is an unholy desire."

"Yes, yes. You would be."

"It's obscene of him, sir, to say a thing like that."

"Yes. But it's an old obscenity. Very primitive. Age gives these flabby ideas weight. Oh yes—and *parents*. No, the reason for isolation of patients in the San is the possibility of infection."

"But, it's pneumonia. Caught in the performance—"

"—ah, yes. The invasion by barrage-balloon. I slept through it."

"All I want is to wish him well. Put my head round the door. You'd allow me if he were my brother. Wouldn't you, Headmaster?"

"Yes. Yes, I would. And you are a prefect. And, I understand, fairly sane. Yes." The Head had shrunk in his chair. "Particularly today, I would." He pointed to a second armchair across the fireplace. "Stick another log on the fire as you go by, would you? Will you have a cup of tea? We ought to be talking about your future. We have a bit of a worry with you—oh, nothing to do with this David and Jonathan business. We all grow out of every loyalty in the end."

"It's called friendship, sir."

"Yes. Yes. And you won't be seeing much more of Ingoldby. Your father has written to us to say that he wants you to leave school after Christmas. He wants you to go to Malaysia. Or Singapore. We have been giving it a lot of thought."

"He—what?"

"He thinks you should be evacuated from England. To get away from the bombing. Place of safety. He was—I needn't tell you—through the last one. And he's been out of touch with British politics. We're trying to persuade him to let you take the Oxford entrance exam first."

"But it's children who are evacuated. And women. I'm going on eighteen."

"Until you are eighteen, your father has the say."

"But I've his sisters. My guardians. What do they say?"

"We have written to the Misses Feathers and they replied in a very—sanguine—manner. Busy women. War work, one supposes."

"I don't know. I've hardly seen them. Am I to leave school after *Christmas*?"

"And here is tea. Let us hope for crumpets though it will be only marge."

"May I go now? I want to think."

"If you feel it wise. One can of course think too much. Your father tended to think too much."

As Eddie opened the door of the study, there came padding towards it an old lady in slippers pushing a tea-trolley. The teapot was muffled in a knitted crinoline of rose and orange frills and had an art-nouveau lady's head on top, a black painted curl against each porcelain cheek. Whenever afterwards Filth beheld such an object—at a church fête, perhaps, at the end of his life and long after the precise reason for it had been lost—he found himself near tears.

The old woman handed Eddie a silver dish full of crumpets and indicated a brass crumpet-stand on the hearth.

"Oh, good. Jam," said the Headmaster. "This is Ingoldby's friend, Mrs. P."

"Ingoldby's a nice boy," said the housekeeper, "and so was his brother, God rest him." She left the room.

"What's this?" cried Eddie.

"Sit down a minute, Feathers. I was coming to it. I'm sorry. But tomorrow I shall have to give the news out in prayers. I'm glad you came over. Jack Ingoldby's plane has been reported missing over the Channel. His brother doesn't know. We're waiting until he is better. He is being taken home tomorrow. Keep it to yourself."

Eddie ran from the penumbrous house to the nearest public phone box, on the corner of the playing fields, and dialled Trunks for a long-distance call. He asked for the High House number and was told by the operator to expect a long wait. "Will you be ready when a line comes free? Maybe twenty or thirty minutes, dear, and you must have the right money. One shilling and a sixpence and two pennies."

"I haven't got thirty minutes."

"Try later, dear. And it's cheaper." She cut him off.

He ran back to his House and began a letter to Mrs. Ingoldby, but the words were senseless. I can't write formalities, I can't. I'm the family. She'll want to hear my voice. She'll be expecting to hear it. They'll have been trying to get me and nobody's told me. He sat, thinking, then wrote:

> Dear Mrs. Ingoldby,
> I am thinking of you all the time,
> your loving Eddie.

Have I the right to be their loving Eddie?

The voids of his ignorance opened before him. I'm still the foreigner. To them. And to myself, here. I've no background. I've been peeled off my background. I've been attached to another background like a cut-out. I'm only someone they've been kind to for eight years because Pat was a loner till I came along. I'm socially a bit dubious, because they know my father went barmy. And because of living in the heart of darkness and something funny going on in Wales. And the stammer.

He signed himself

Sincerely yours, E. J. Feathers

He stuck a penny-ha'penny stamp on the letter and took it to the postbox as the evening Prep bell rang. It was his night to invigilate the little boys in the House but he doubled back to the San.

The windy restless afternoon was done and clouds covered the moon. It was damp but not viciously raining now. At the top of the San's staircase he looked into Matron's room where her coal fire blazed and the ghastly scarf lay abandoned. There was the smell of her meaty supper and a clink from her kitchen. Coals crashed, then blazed up in the grate. He walked on along the corridor expecting the San to be rows of beds, blanket-rolls, empty lockers with open doors, the smell of Detto! But there was Pat in a small lone room with a blanket over his head.

"Hey—Pat?"

Pat sat up. His head rose out of the blanket, its folds draped around his shoulders.

"Where are you, Fevvers? Put the light on."

"How are you? They wouldn't let me in."

"Fine. I'm going home tomorrow. I'm ravenous. But, listen—"

Noises as of torn cats on a roof top issued from Pat's chest.

"Good God!"

"It's the Banshee. They're giving me some new weird drug. It's going to cost Pa something. I can make it sound like distant machine guns, listen."

"They'll fix it," said Eddie, considerably frightened. "I've just written to your mother."

"Well, keep it cool. There's a scare on. Jack's missing."

"I—don't know anything—"

"Yes, you do. If I've heard in here, you'll have heard it out there. If he's. . ."

Silence.

". . . if he's gone, well then, he's gone. It's what he believed in."

A poker was being rattled about in the grate next door.

"You'd better go, Fevvers. She'll have an orgasm if she finds you. 'This is a CLEAN school.'" He began wheezing.

I'll . . . Shouldn't I ring High House?"

Pat's black eyes became blacker. A certain hauteur. "Nope. Leave them alone. I'll be home tomorrow. There's nothing you can do. It's family stuff."

Eddie turned for the door, amazed at how cold he felt.

"Oh, and hey—Ed?"

"Yes?"

"Don't join the RAF. You couldn't handle it. And don't join the Navy—you've done the sea."

"I can't see myself in the Army, not any more. I couldn't kill someone I was looking at. I mean, at his face. The point is, you can't join the RAF. Not now. I mean, God—for your parents' sake."

"Oh yes I can," said Ingoldby. "They'll survive even if I don't. My parents. I've told you—they don't really feel much. Bye—see you sometime, Fevvers."

A couple of days later and after no luck with the High House telephone though Eddie tried several times, a letter came to him from Pat in dithering writing.

Dear Ed,
    I'm fine now but staying home.
    I'll not be coming back, lad,
    When all the trees are green,
    I have to join the pack, lad,
    And drink my Ovaltine.

Take the lead soldiers we had at Sir's. Melt them down for plough-shares or a sixth bullet, whatever. Will you gather up my stuff?—Pa forgot it and so did Matron-La-Booze. Hang on to it till—when? The clothes-brush you always fancied, my godfather's, it's from Bond Street (he used eau-de-cologne and had a mistress in Clarges Street) you can have but it will cost you a penny.

Regards PI

A few days after the news that Jack Ingoldby was missing came the news that he was certainly killed. It was the sort of notice the Head was giving out repeatedly at assembly that term. Hundreds, maybe thousands, of people in East Kent saw the planes from the dogfights of the Battle of Britain come spinning and flickering down to sizzle in the Channel or burst into flames in the orchards. Parachutes blossoming out would raise a cheer; but most pilots were invisible and people went on with what they were doing, like harvesters in medieval France during the Hundred Years War. Nevertheless, a certain and recorded and undeniable filmed death was a shock.

There was no further card from Pat nor response to a second letter from Eddie to High House. Half-term was coming but there was no sign that he would go as usual to the Ingoldbys. He was, it seemed, to go at last to his guardians, for a jokey invitation had been received by the Headmaster from the Bolton aunts. But still he hung about the school until the very last minute in case a call should come from Pat.

As the cab to take him to the train for Bolton was arriving, he tried once more with a thumping heart to telephone High House.

"Hullo?"

"Who's that?"

"Is that—the Ingoldbys?"

"It's Isobel."

"Oh. Hullo. It's Eddie. Teddy Feathers."

"Oh, hullo."

"I just rang to see . . . To hear . . ."

"Yes?"

"It's half-term. Should I come over?"

"Oh no. I shouldn't do that. Pat's not here. He's gone off somewhere to volunteer again."

"How is—Mrs. Ingoldby?"

"Oh, she's fine. Very patriotic, you know."

"I'd love to see her."

"I'll tell her."

"Actually, would you tell her that I won't be in England much longer?"

"Joining up?"

"Not exactly. I'm too young. My father's sent for me."

"Whatever for?"

"Could you tell them? The Ingoldbys?"

"What?"

"Well, say goodbye. And s-s-so many many thanks. I'll be on the other side of the world."

"So will a lot of people."

"Say I'll write. I'll *always* write. Thank them for . . ."

"OK. Bye."

"I'd love to hear . . . ."

But she was gone.

So Eddie picked up Pat's belongings and shook hands with Oils, and stepped into the taxi for Bolton where, even with Pat's extras, there was not enough luggage to justify a taxi from the station, so he walked to the house, surprised that he remembered how to get there after a single visit long ago; the half-term holiday after the Didds' business in Wales. His father had come to England for the first and only time and had taken the eight-year-old Eddie to see his sisters.

It was a sleek, boastful, purple-brick house like a giant plum standing back from the road behind a semi-circle of lawn with shaven edges and Victorian (purple) edging tiles. In a round bed stood the winter sticks of roses.

Aunt Hilda appeared, flinging wide an inner vestibule door of rich cream paint and crimson and blue glass panes, and cried out, "Muriel! He's here. It's the boy. Come in, come in. We should have written. You've arrived—well done! We've sorted everything out. Your passport should be here by Christmas. Excellent. *Muriel.*"

They were in the hall now and Aunt Muriel was coming down the stairs in tweeds and a hat. "Dear old chap—how like Alistair."

"There's a pretty important golf today," said Hilda, "and we're just off. Not a tournament nowadays of course, the links are so restricted. But still quite a highspot. So we'll go on ahead. You settle in, then you can join us for lunch or tea? No distance. Take the bike from the garage. We must fly. Duties on the course—so few men now. The lunch won't be at all bad. You're very thin."

They departed, their car's rear window nearly covered by patriotic slogans. *Careless talk costs lives*, he read. He wandered through the house.

There were brass urns full of ferns and an ironwood table topped with a brass disc engraved with dancing Orientals. In a sitting-room were crowds of family photographs. Odd, he thought. He was family but they had shown no interest in him since he was eight. He wondered if photographs were substitutes for hospitality. Looking around, he saw no photographs at all of children. And nobody who could possibly have been his mother. He had no idea what she had looked like. Most of the photographs were of people a generation older than his aunts, bearded or braided, sepia, stern and sad. Beside them, were other photographs and more fern in brass containers. On a table by themselves were golfing trophies and a silver cup engraved *Hole in One, Hilda Feathers*. There was a magnificent fireplace of wood and tiles, with a shiny clock with icicle pointers let into the chimneypiece. Instead of coals there was a pleated fan of paper, and in the hearth a miracle of barbola work covered in thonged parchment and filled with newspaper spills to save matches.

Then he saw, on the mantelpiece, a photograph of a dazzling young man in open-necked khaki shirt and shorts, arms crossed and a cigarette burning nonchalantly in one hand, and, on the other wrist, a big, beautiful, seductive gold watch. On his head, an army beret without a badge, like a Frenchman, and eyes dark, wise, amused and most beautiful. On the silver frame was engraved Alistair, 1914, and there was a little jug of flowers arranged beside it, as if the photograph was of a dead man, or like a funeral bunch upon a grave. Flowers for the dead. But this was his father. No doubt of it. Eddie knew.

And his father was alive enough to have sent for him, to get him out of another set-piece of butchery like the one that had all but extinguished him and his country in 1914.

Eddie picked up the photograph and felt pride. He wanted it. He'd nick it. It was his. He wished Pat could see it, or the vile Isobel. Had Colonel Ingoldby really known his father? Why hadn't he ever said anything about him? His father's wonderful face, a poet's face, he thought, and with an exciting hint in it of his own. It occurred to him that he must write again, after years, to his father.

And now. Write now.

He turned to the writing desk—brasses galore (*The Snake and His Boy*, a row of ugly monkeys)—and searched around for writing paper, found his own fountain pen, stared at the laurels outside the window, the bald lawn, the grey street. The gate flung open. *No Hawkers or Circulars* nailed to it on a plaque.

Dear Father

I am at Aunt Muriel's having left school this morning for half-term or, for all I know, for good. I only heard this week that I'm to leave school and come out to you. I *wish* you could have written to *me* about it. The Head says they've been discussing it with you for some time, and Aunt Hilda says my passport will be ready by Christmas. I'm seventeen and shall soon be eighteen. It is ten years since you saw me and I've had nothing from you of any kind except I suppose all my expenses have been paid and I'm told there is a bank-book for me sometime soon. So thank you for that.

But our last meeting was so horrible and unhappy and I wish you could have written, even once, years ago, to put that right.

Nobody had told me that you have a stammer and nobody had probably told you that I had one then (Sir cured mine) and I think [the pen began to take on a most uncharacteristic volition of its own] that I tried just to forget you. The Ingoldbys were so kind. Just now I've seen a photograph of you on the mantelpiece here at the aunts—first time I've seen them since you were here when I was eight—taken in 1914, and you don't look all that much older than I am now. It made me very regretful. I felt you might be a father I could have talked to.

However, no go. So would you very kindly read the following points that will state briefly my reasons for not wanting to come and live with you in Malaya or Java or S'pore or wherever?

(1) I should at Christmas be going to Oxford for an interview at Christ Church for a place after the War.

(2) I want, after that, to volunteer for the Army.

(3) For me to be "evacuated" out of danger now, at my age, is absolutely unheard of in England at the moment. I should have to travel with children aged between seven and twelve. Whatever would the ship's company think of me?

(4) I would lose my English friends for life. It would be a continuing stigma. I am six-foot-two and look older than my years. I am *very fit*.

and (5) and sorry to sound gung-ho, but I believe that I should be fighting for my country. I *can't* run away. You haven't heard

Churchill. Even people like you, the bitter ones of '14/18, listen to him. I have lived in this country since you sent me here as almost a baby. Had there been [the pen was beginning to race and Eddie's face wasp red with a rage he had had no knowledge of] any friendship, any contact, between us, if you had *once* written to me not just handed me that pin-box, it might be different.

I shall argue these points with my aunts—though they seem to be very indifferent listeners. I've tried to argue with the school. All they say is that until I am eighteen you can do more or less what you like with me.

Do you *want* me with you on these autocratic and loveless terms?

Sincerely, E. J. Feathers

He read the letter through, and by the end of it was seeing not the god-like young soldier of the photograph but the father who had turned up at Sir's Outfit soon after the Ma Didds' affair, the affair that was—and still was—his closed, locked box. He saw a lank and trembling figure sitting in Sir's study, the mountain trees of the Lake District tossing blackly about in the wind through the window behind him. The figure had sat cracking his finger joints.

Sir had kindly left the two of them together ("just out here if you need me, Feathers's") and father and son, neither clear which of them Sir was referring to, had stared long and hard at the pattern on the carpet.

Eddie remembered the hands. How his father had clasped and unclasped them. How the knuckles had cracked like pistols. He remembered the thin shanks of his father's legs in the old-fashioned European suit; the bald head; the lashless eyes that looked almost blind. How the man shifted in his chair, said nothing, looked at a wristwatch far too big for the wrist. The watch that must have come through the Great War with him. The watch in the photo. Maybe it had been an amulet?

Eddie had been far too frightened to speak and reveal his stammer, especially after he heard a long staccato rattle begin in his father's throat and realised—who better?—that his father stammered, too. He became inexorably mute. His father was asking a question. If he tried to answer it, his father might think his son was mocking him.

Tears came. Eddie did not look again at his father's face. The patterns on Sir's carpet swelled and ran together into chaos and oblivion.

When Sir returned, father and son both jumped up and Sir said to Eddie, "Away you go then," and Eddie fled back to the classroom, to Pat Ingoldby and the lead soldiers under the desklid, and nobody ever mentioned this interview with his father again.

Once, only once, had Eddie met the aunts. Yet he knew that these aunts no longer talked about their brother. Not a breath in them confessed to the twitching, half-mad widower with the yellow face and strange eyes. (Once at Ma Didds's one of his cousins, probably Babs, had said, "Your pa has malaria," and the other had said, "No, he doesn't. My mother says it's opium.") Nor did these Bolton aunts, out on the numbing golf course, any longer ever say a word about the young, quizzical, handsome, alert spirit that had been their brother and with whom they had grown up.

Eddie went through the address book on the desk until he found his father's name. After Kotakinakulu, there were many crossings out. The current address seemed to be Singapore. It did not sound very grand. A back-street address. An instinct, some gentle gene in Eddie, made him write a P.S. before he licked the air-mail envelope:

> P.S: I should like to say, though, Father, you've been very generous to someone you clearly found it impossible to like. Now that I've really thought about it, your wanting me to come to you in order to survive the War seems [he was going to write "very civil"] a miracle of unexpected kindness.
>
> Eddie

And so, he thought, I spoil my case.

He did not go to the golf-course lunch, but found his way below stairs to a kitchen where a diminutive old woman was folding paper spills for the grate. She looked depressed and paid him no attention, so then he lay on his bed in a room with eiderdowns and heavy flowered curtains and huge lampshades and wondered if this was all.

He stayed on, apparently invisible, for a week. And then for several weeks, while he waited to hear from school about the Oxford interview. There was no reply to his letter to his father and, though he often wondered if today there might be a cable, none came. He spent the days mugging up for the possible Oxford interview—there was a good public library in the town—and thinking unhopefully about life. From his bedroom window, steamed with delicious heat from a Victorian iron radiator, his dreams merged into other bedroom windows. One, that mystified him on the edge of sleep, was an unglazed slit with the black knives of banana plants against a black sapphire sky. This dream always woke him.

His Bolton bedroom now was rich in Lancashire splendour, the carpet pure olive-green wool overflung with white roses. The heavy curtains, interlined for the black-out, were damask within and without. The eiderdown was of fat rose-pink blisters and beside the bed was a lamp with pink silk and bead fringes. The wallpaper could have stood by itself, thickly embossed with gold, and the blankets were snowy wool, and satin-bound. "You are in the best spare," said Muriel. "The wardrobe may be a Gillow." "Now put the fire on if you need it," said Hilda. "Both bars. We have to go out now."

Going out was their refrain. Eddie's life was beyond their interest. They dwelt like Siamese twins in each other's concerns and in the present moment. Every morning they came down to the breakfast-room talking before they saw you but telling you their plans. Their eyes were always blanks. They were always in one of a number of uniforms but always the same as each other. There was the Red Cross officer with stripes and a cockade; the WVS plum and dark green; a scarlet and grey ensemble reminiscent of the North-West Frontier; and a white and navy serge with wings on the head indicative of some variety of military nurse. They left the house every day by eight-thirty and were never home till supper. On Sundays they were up betimes for the eight o'clock Communion, and later sat knitting gloves and listening to *Forces Favourites*. There was a nice medium sherry before a heavy supper each evening. The midget maid crept about doing wonders with the chores and a muscular woman came in for the rough and a man for swilling down the yard. Each day Eddie ate his lunch alone at one end of the mahogany dining table, also a suspected Gillow, laid up with lace mats and shining silver. He received no mail and the phone never rang for him.

"Now, don't you overwork," they shouted. "You'll get in. It's your father's old college. There's a nice flick on at the Odeon," and they clashed shut the vestibule door not interested in his answer.

The winter gathered. Once or twice he grew desperate to telephone the Ingoldbys but dared not because of Pat's bombshell: *It's family stuff.*

The air-raids in the North-West had for the moment stopped but the dogfights went on in the South-East and Eddie wondered whether Pat had his pilot's wings yet. "They're sending them up after twelve hours' instruction," said an old soldier at the golf club. "They're running out. Slaughter of the innocents." "I heard after *six* hours," said someone else. "Six hours' flying instruction and they're in their own Spitfire."

According to the six o'clock news on the wireless each evening huge numbers of the Boche were being shot down, twice as many casualties as our own. But the bulletin always ended with "a number of our own aircraft are missing."

At last he set off for the Oxford entrance exam in a blizzard and a series of unheated trains, each one packed down every corridor with troops, all smoking, drinking, sleeping, hawking, balanced against each other or jack-knifed on their knees on the floor. Coughs, oaths, laughter, glum silence, sudden waves of idiotic singing (*Roll out the Barrel, Tipperary*) from the War before. The final train groaned out of a station to stop as if for ever outside Stratford-on-Avon in the dark. Planes droned above. ("Dorniers?" "No, Messerschmitts.") More soldiers sank upon their haunches, heads into their spread knees, asleep. The crumpling sound of bombs, the W.C.s surrounded by the desperate, jigging up and down. When you did get inside, heel holding the door to behind you, the lock broken, the floor awash, the smell was rank, no water in the taps. No lavatory paper. "*Roll me over in the clover,*" sang the soldiers who mostly had never seen clover. "*Roll me over, lay me down and do it again.*"

Eddie burst from the train at Oxford station and looked for someone on the gate to take his ticket and tell him how far his college was. There was no one and no taxi. No one at all. It was bitter midnight and in his head he could still hear the horrible singing.

Then, stepping out down a dark road something changed. Out from clouds sprang a great white moon and showed pavements and roads of snow, sleeping buildings, spires and domes all stroked by dappling snow. There was not a soul, not a light and not a cry.

Over some bridge he went in such dazzling moonlight he wondered there were not crowds turned out everywhere to see it. He walked exalted, his feet light and the moon came and went, and then soft flakes began to fall. He looked back and saw his footprints already softened by the snow, the snow ahead of him waiting to be imprinted. He had strayed into medieval Oxford like a ghost.

And nobody to direct him and he was growing cold. A great silent street widened. A church stood in the middle of it, its windows boarded, its glass taken into safety. He wondered whether its door might be open and then saw opposite a large building that might be a hotel where he might try to get them to answer a bell and tell him where to go. Then, behind him, he heard a sound from the black church and all at once there was a figure beside him, a muffled-up giant who was graciously inclining his head towards him, the head bound about by some sort of scarf. The man was wearing a flowing macintosh like the robe of someone in the absent stained-glass.

"May I help you? Did I frighten you? I was in the church." The young man swung a key. He was very young indeed to be a clergyman. He, too, must be a ghost.

"I'm looking for a college called Christ Church."

"You are going in absolutely the wrong direction. Follow me," and the soft and boneless giant went padding away with Eddie following.

"There," he said, in time. "Straight ahead."

"My train was late."

"Bang hard for the night-porter. Are you all right now?"

The snow had stopped and the moonshine gleamed out again.

"Excuse me, are you—someone in the church?"

"No. I do fire-watching there. And praying. I'm a student." Eddie felt his kindliness and confidence and cheerfulness.

"Goodnight," said the young huge fledgling. "Good luck. I suppose you're up for the entrance exam?"

"Yes. Tomorrow."

"I'm leaving tomorrow. I'm joining up."

Eddie felt ridiculous regret. And then confusion. Somehow, he knew this man.

"Thanks," he said. "It was a mercy I met you."

They went their different ways, but when Eddie stopped and looked back, he found that the muffled giant was doing the same thing, looking back at him.

"Feel sure I know you," Eddie called. "Very odd."

Then the man waved and padded out of sight down a side street and Eddie was trying to rouse his college.

As he fell asleep in a monkish bed in a mullioned room he thought: How can I possibly leave all this for Malaya?

A few days later, "I suggest," said the man who might in time become his tutor after the War, if that time ever came, "I suggest that you come up as soon as possible."

"Does that mean I'm accepted, sir?"

"Of course. Goes without saying. You wrote excellent papers yesterday. Well taught. Were you at Sir's? I thought so. And your public school is very clever with closed scholarships, though I hear you are rich enough not to need one."

(Am I? thought Eddie. I've ten shillings a week.)

"Now, I suggest you volunteer for the Navy. It takes them a year to process you, so you can get your Prelims done with here, before you go, and you'll have a toe in the door for when you're demobilised. You'll be reading history?"

"I'm not quite sure, sir, what . . ."

"Your father was here. How is he? Still about, I hope?"

"He lives in Malaya. Well, I think he may be in Singapore now. I hardly know him."

"I'm sorry. I heard shell-shock? Poor chap. But he'll be proud of you now."

Eddie swam with guilt. Ought he to say? His father had ordered him out of the country. His father had no notion or memory of Oxford. His father had—shell-shocked or not—organised a passport and visa and made his sisters get Eddie his jabs. He was to be "an evacuee." Well, he would not do it. No. He would come to Oxford where he was welcome and admired and befriended and a familiar ghost had directed him to a safe haven after midnight. He would say nothing.

"May I come up next term, sir?"

"Ah, not quite so fast. But leave it to me. We'll find you a room in Meadow Buildings, where your father was."

As he fell asleep in the beautiful ice-cold room with his coat and the hearth-rug over the blankets, and watched the moon light the snowy rooftops, he briefly wondered about money. Will my father pay my fees if I refuse to go out to him? Will my scholarship be enough? I might be poor. I've never been really poor. Well, hell, so what? And he watched the moon bowling along, lighting the sky for the bombers.

I could live and die here, he thought. They'll never destroy this. I'll stay and fight for it.

And with these noble thoughts he slept.

By morning the snow had gone as if it had been dreams and it was raining hard and the pavements soiled and splashy. From the mullioned window could be seen people hurrying, bent forward, miserable and mean along the streets, and it was not the fairy city any more. The bedroom door opened and a lugubrious man called a Scout came carrying hot water in a jug across to a washbowl and asked if he would be taking breakfast early so that his room might be cleaned? For some panic-stricken reason Eddie said, No, he would be leaving before breakfast. "Very good, sir," said the Scout, eyebrows raised, and Eddie wondered whether to leave him a tip and, if he didn't, whether it would be remembered next term and held against him. In the end he left a shilling on the dressing-table, took his bag and went head forward into the slushy street. As he butted along against the wet and the umbrellas, bicycles wetting his trousers as they passed him, melancholy struck. Was this place after all a delusion? It was criminally cold. Nobody had said goodbye to him. Hot water in a jug and the W.C. three flights down. Not a word about the date of his return. And he was bloody hungry. He turned into a tea-shop because the steam on its windows promised warmth, but once inside it was cold and crowded and dark, with people sitting in buttoned-up clothes. A long and silent queue stood by the counter, each one holding a ration book in a gloved hand and hoping for an extra cake.

But yet there was a sort of warmth there in the fug and Eddie edged further in to the shop where there were tables and chairs. They were all smoking and reading newspapers or warming their hands on their coffee cups. He sat down at a table where a girl was leaning back in her chair, smoking through a cigarette holder and watching him. Her legs were crossed and one high-heeled shoe was swinging up and down from her big toe.

"Is it all right to sit here?"

He sat, and looked around him to see what was on offer in the way of breakfast.

"I've not had breakfast," he said. "I'm up here for my entrance exams. I suddenly wanted to go home, so I skipped breakfast. Now I'm hungry."

"Which college?"

"Christ Church."

"You'd have been given a good free breakfast there. Even in the vacation. Quails' eggs and flagons of porter I shouldn't wonder. Small talk about the Christ Church Beagles. It won't survive the War, you know, Christ Church. Thank God. You don't look *exactly* Christ Church. I'll say that for you."

"I don't know a thing about it. I was told to apply. It could have been St. Karl Marx's College for all I know about it."

"I'll bet your father was there."

"Yes, he was. Actually. I can't help that."

She leaned forward to the ashtray, looking at him carefully, and he looked back into bright hazel eyes which were somehow familiar. He remembered the giant who had also been familiar.

I'm over-tired, he thought. Over-excited. "I've not seen my father in ten years," he told the girl. "He's a very hard-working civil servant. Out East."

"I've not seen mine for years, either," she said. "He's still bashing away in India. And I know you, you're Teddy Feathers."

The eyes became at once the ten-year-old eyes of his cousin Babs—eyes that he had last seen pouring out tears by the fuchsia bushes in Ma Didds's garden. The long, tapping finger over the ashtray became little Babs's fierce claw which could pick out any tune without thought on the chapel harmonium. Just out of sight somewhere was the watchful pink and gold of their six-year-old cousin, Claire.

"Babs?"

"Teddy."

Eddie ordered them both some milky bottled coffee and a Marie biscuit and Babs lit another cigarette.

"So. You live in Oxford? I'd no idea, Babs."

"No. I'm up. At Somerville. I'm packing it in, though. It's no time to be here. I'm volunteering for the Navy. I'll be gone by next week."

"Where's Claire?"

"Oh, I don't know. She's married. Straight from school. Didn't you hear? She's in East Anglia somewhere among all the airfields. As far away from us as possible. Well, she would be, wouldn't she?"

"I don't see why."

"She was very passive always. And they made sure we were

never to meet up again—or they tried to. Wanted us to drop each other dead. So—what's been happening to you, old Teddy-bear?"

"*Did* they? Try to stop us?"

"Well, you had some sort of crack-up, so I heard. Began to chatter like a monkey. A Welsh monkey."

"I never cracked up. Do I stammer now?"

"No. You talk proper. You'll do for Christ Church." When she smiled, she dazzled. There were smoker's lines already etched on her face but sunlight was still behind them.

"I've got myself into one hell of a bigger mess now," Eddie said. "I've nobody to tell me the answers. I find I don't know how to—proceed."

"*Proceed*," she said, and leaning forward stroked his wrist. "I always loved your words. I suppose it was books. Your father sent you so many books at Didds's."

"Did he? Nobody told me. What? Were the books from him?"

"You weren't wanting to hear anything good about your father then. *Proceed*," she said. "Maybe you'll be a lawyer? A Barrister, but it'd be a pity to cover that hair. *Proceed*—look, you proceed by yourself now. You don't need Claire or me or Auntie May. Get on with life! You can take decisions," she said, "if anyone can."

They both looked down at the insides of their coffee cups.

"You were bloody wonderful," she said, "that day. Braver than any of us and eight years old."

"I've not made a decision since," he said. "That must have been my one decisive moment."

"Where did you go in the holidays all these years? You can't have been alone?" she asked him.

"School friend. Sort of second family to me."

"Can't they help now? And what about your pa's sensible sisters?"

"They are psychologically deaf," said he.

"They're just reacting against your pa," she said. "Don't forget they were all Raj Orphans themselves. They say it suits some. They come out fizzing and yelling, 'I didn't need parents,' and waving the red, white and blue. Snooty for life. But we're all touched, one way or another."

"I don't think it suited my father," said Eddie. "He's gone entirely barmy."

"Yep. I heard. You know, my lot and Claire's are still in India, and I never give them a thought. Not after ten years."

Eddie realised that since the Ma Didds' horror he had never given a thought to either Babs or Claire. Not a thought.

"Have you a girlfriend, Eddie?"

"I never meet any girls. I just work. And play games. And read."

"Come home with me now," said Babs. "To my digs. There's no one there." She put out her cigarette. "We'll go to bed. We have before."

Eddie, scarlet, was aware of a drop in the background conversation at the nearby tables. Babs's voice was beautiful and old-fashioned, a penetrating voice like Royalty, clear and high and unconcerned, and he stumbled out of his chair, withdrawing his hand from beneath hers. "Sorry. Can't. Getting a train. Might miss it."

And she leaned back, laughing, and called across the steamy shop—the still-immobile cake-queue—"We'll never forget each other, Teddy-bear. Never." He fumbled at the door. "You and I and Claire. And Cumberledge. Whatever happens to us. Never."

He was on the train, sopped through with Oxford's rain. He watched the tangled hedges threaded with the dead spirals of last year's weeds. This was an empty, slow, uncertain train that trundled insolently through anonymous stations, their names painted out with coarse black brush-strokes to confuse the

Germans when they eventually arrived. Station waiting-rooms stood barred; cigarette- and chocolate-machines stood empty with their metal drawers hanging out. It was not until he had changed trains in Manchester (I could still be in her bed) that he remembered that he had left Babs to pay for the coffee.

He was sitting now in another railway carriage looking, above the man sitting opposite, at a pre-War watercolour reproduction of a happy artless English family on a sunny English beach. The other picture frames below the rack held patriotic slogans and he wondered if the sand-castle country scene had been deliberately preserved. The clean-cut daddy; the Marcel-waved mummy; the innocent little one; the happy dog, Towser. Presumably in some people's memory? He closed his eyes to keep them from tears. He dozed and found himself in a richer place, a sleep-laden, dripping dell with drops on every great leaf, the clattering of banana leaves, black children dancing in foetid puddles on the earth—earth beaten hard as concrete with dancing feet but which could become in moments under the warm rain a living mud. Laughter. The smell of sweet hot skin. He was being tossed up high in some-one's arms and he was looking down again upon a brown face, white teeth, gloriously loving eyes. The eyes of the man across the carriage were staring at him as Eddie woke.

"You all right, lad?"

"Yes. Sorry. Was I snoring?"

"No. You were moaning. Want to see a paper?"

"No, no. I was . . . I think I must talk in my sleep."

"Here. I'm reading the *Deaths*," said the man, "and I've dis-covered something quite important. See what you think. Just see what you think—no prejudice. Just look down the list of places and you can tell which deaths are from enemy action. You can tell from the *Times* exactly where the raids were, dates given. Nobody's thought of it here, I'll bet. I'm writing to the authorities. I'll bet the enemy has noticed."

Eddie, scrambling from the tropical dream, said, "Careless talk costs lives."

"D'you want to see, though? Just you see what I mean. It's a bloody check-list for the enemy," and he passed across the outer pages of the *Times*. Eddie arranged them as a barrier between himself and the man and began, automatically, as his eyes refocused, to read in alphabetical order. He immediately read: *Ingoldby, Patrick, aged eighteen years, RAF*, a date of one week before, and *For King and Country*.

THE TIME OF FRENZY

When Betty died suddenly, planting the tulips the day after their day in London attempting to sign their Wills, Filth's astonishment lifted his soul outside his body and he stood looking down not only at the slumped body but at his own, gazing and emptied of all its meaning now.

"It has happened," "It has occurred," "Keep your head," said the spirit to the body. Stiffly he knelt beside her, watching himself kneel, take her hand, kiss her hand and put it to his face. There was no doubt in either soul or body that she was dead. Dead. Gone. Happened. Lost. Over.

Throughout the funeral service he silently repeated the words: Dead. Lost. Happened. Gone. A small funeral, for neither of them had much in the way of relations and Babs and Claire did not take—or so he assumed—the *Telegraph* or the *Times*. Filth, the ever-meticulous, had lapsed. He forgot (or pretended to forget) that you should telephone people. His old friends were all in Hong Kong or with their Maker. A small funeral.

Touchingly, some members of his former Chambers turned up and his magnificent old Clerk, once the Junior Clerk who had been a schoolboy with pimples, was there in the church, magisterial now in a long Harrods overcoat.

"So sorry, sir."

"How very good of you to come, Charlie. Very kind."

"Mr. Wemyss is here, and Sir Andrew Bysshe."

"Very kind. Very long way for you all to come."

The dark, serious, pallid London figures in the second pew. The rest of the mourners were locals, mostly church ladies, for Betty had been on the flower rota. She had been very forceful with the flowers, banging their stalks down hard in the bottom of the green bucket, commandeering the Frobisher Window from the moment of her arrival, a position not usually offered until you'd been in the parish for several years.

Betty stood no nonsense from flowers. In Hong Kong she had once done the cathedral, and the Hong Kong iris, the Cuban bast flower, the American worm seed and the Maud's *Michellia* had all known their place there. She harangued flowers. She wanted of all things, she often said, to have a flower named after her. "The Elizabeth Feathers. Long-leaved Greenbriar?" Filth had thought sometimes of organising such a thing for her; he'd heard that it was not really expensive. It was a birthday present always forgotten. Filth was not taken with flowers. He found them unresponsive, sometimes even hostile. It was tulips, he thought, that had got her in the end.

As he stood beside the grave and thought of his long life with Betty and his achievement in presenting to the world the full man, the completed and successful being, his hands in their lined kid gloves folded over the top of his walking stick, he was aware of something, somewhere. He looked up at the sky. Nothing, yet he was being informed, no doubt about it, that there was something in him unresolved. He was inadequate and weak. If they knew, they would all find him unlikable. Despicable. Face it.

Yet he felt nothing. Nothing at all.

They had put on a do for Betty afterwards in the church hall. Tea and anchovy sandwiches and fruit cake and the ubiquitous pale green Anglican crockery, known from the Donheads to Hong Kong to Jamaica. He took nothing, but moved among the guests magnificently, like a knight of old. He talked of the weather. Of their kind journeys to the Donheads. A nice woman, when they had all gone, offered him whiskey and he must have drunk it for he found himself looking down into an empty glass when she suggested seeing him safely home.

"Are you going to be alone here tonight, Edward?"

"Oh, I shall be perfectly all right. Perfectly."

Outside, the tulip bed had been tactfully raked over and Filth and the woman (Chloe) stood looking carefully beyond it from the sun-lounge and over the hills. The woman smelled nostalgically of some old scent—not Betty's, he thought. It was the scent, he supposed, but suddenly (and the nice woman had long lost her waistline and her hair was grey) Filth experienced an astonishment as great as the sight of Betty dead—her untenanted body, her empty face. Filth experienced a huge, full-blown, adolescent lust.

At once, he walked away from the woman, and sat down in the sitting-room alone.

"I could sit with you for a while."

"No thank you, Chloe, I think as a matter of fact I'd like to be by myself now."

When she had gone he sat for a time. (Lost. Over. Gone. Finished. Happened.) She was not here. She was dead. Not here. But, he felt, elsewhere. They had both detested the macabre Chinese funeral rites and the Oriental notions of an afterlife. They were (of course) Anglicans and liked the idea of Heaven, but whether the spirit survived the ridiculous body they had never discussed. They certainly had never considered the idea that they might meet again in another world. The notion is rubbish, now thought Filth.

"Don't you think?" he asked Betty directly for the first time, speaking to a point above the curtain rail.

There was no reply.

Yet he slept well. The lust had retreated and the next morning early, properly dressed with a purplish tie, he telephoned his two cousins.

From the first, Claire in Essex somewhere, there was no reply, not even from an answerphone. It rang on and on. The second was Babs, who lived now for no known reason somewhere on Teesside called Herringfleet. She was alone in the world and, Betty had thought, a little odd now. Babs had known Betty at school (everyone, he thought, seems to have known Betty at school). Betty and Babs had been at St. Paul's Girls School and had the Paulina voice.

So that it was Betty who answered the phone. "Hello?" she said, "Yes? Teddy?"

(Betty must be staying up there with Babs, he thought, caught his breath and plunged into hell.)

"It is Babs?"

"Yes. I suppose so. Barbara."

"Edward. Betty's husband."

"I know."

"I'm afraid I have bad news."

"I know. I saw it in the paper. Poor old thing."

"Well, I'm not exactly—"

"I mean Betty. Poor old thing."

It was Betty talking. He longed for more.

"I thought you would want to know . . ."

"Yes, what?"

"The funeral's over, Babs. I thought you'd be glad to know that she died instantly. She can't have known a thing about it. Wonderful for her, really."

"Yes. That's what they say."

Silence.

"Babs?"

Now a long silence. Then a crashing waterfall of musical

notes on a piano. Filth remembered that Babs had something to do with music. Even in Herringfleet presumably. "Babs, is that a piano?"

The scales ceased. Then Schubert began. On and on.

"Babs?"

Eventually, he put down the telephone and tried the other cousin again. Again, no answer. He thought of Chloe yesterday and then there was a shadow of someone watching him somewhere from a wood.

Again, the astounding lust. Lust. He put his face in his hands and tried to be calm. What is all this? He found himself praying as he had never prayed at all during the funeral. And very seldom during Betty's life.

"Oh Lord, we beseech thee . . . direct our hearts and minds in the knowledge and love of God."

He had not shared a bed with Betty for over thirty years. Double beds were for the bourgeoisie. Sex had never been a great success. They had never discussed it. They had disliked visiting friends who had not two spare bedrooms. Betty had joked for years that the marriage would never have survived had Filth not had his own dressing-room. She had meant bedroom.

Had he ever *desired* Betty? Well, yes. He had. He remembered. He had desired everything about her. Her past, her present, her future with him. Her sweet, alert, intelligent face, her famously alive eyes. He had wanted to possess every part of her for she had fitted so perfectly into his life's plan. She had made him safe and confident. She had eased old childhood nightmares.

But—this. Not ever this. Where did this lust come from? Were she alive, could he have told her about it? She who had never done a passionate act. She would have sent him to a doctor.

But yet—so very close they had been. Sometimes at night in Hong Kong, hot and restless in the swirling mists of the Peak, the case of the previous day, or worse, a judgement lingering, he had gone to her room and lain beside her and she had stretched out a hand.

"What's this?"

"Nothing."

"Bad day?"

"I condemned a man to death."

Silence.

She would never have taken him in her arms from pity. Never presented her body to him as a distraction. Never indicated: Here is balm. Take me. Forget it. Your job. You knew there would be this to face here. You could have stayed in England.

Instead . . .

"Was he guilty?"

"As hell."

They lay quiet, listening to the night sounds on the Peak.

"*Crime passionel*," he said.

"Then probably he will be glad to die."

He said, "You still shock me. If you had been the judge . . ."

". . . I would have done as you did. There is not an alternative. But I would have suffered less."

(But I would have wanted you to suffer more. I want you to make me resign because I disgust myself. I feel, truly, filth.)

"I should have stayed in Chambers at home in the Temple. Famous Feathers of the Construction Industry. Sewers and drains."

But Betty had already fallen asleep again, peacefully against his shoulder, unconcerned, proud of him, a very nice woman. An excellent wife for a judge. And two miles off, in a sink across the spangled city, the condemned man, like a small grey bird, his mean little head on its scant Oriental neck soon to be crushed bone, lay alone.

I got out just in time, he thought when they retired and came home to the Donheads. Couldn't take much more emotion alongside the drudgery. Still can't manage emotion. All under control. I am a professional. But why this lust? This longing?

"Babs?"

It was the following morning and he was telephoning her again, "Babs, I want to come and see you."

Betty's voice answered—he remembered that it had been Veneering he'd once overheard saying that Betty's voice was like Desdemona's.

"Babs?"

"Just a minute."

A full tempest of Wagner was stilled somewhere. "Yes? Teddy again? What?"

"Babs—may I come and see you?"

"Yes. I suppose so. All right. When?"

"Any time. This week? Next week?"

"Yes. All right."

He heard a sob, which surprised him.

"Babs, don't cry. She died so easily. A ful-ful-ful-filled, a splendid life."

"I'm not crying for Betty," she said, "or for you, you old fool," and she crashed down the phone.

He didn't telephone again; he wrote. He would visit her the following Friday and perhaps stay the night?

There was no reply.

However, in the new, footloose and irrational way that his body was behaving, Filth made his preparations, taking the car to be checked over in Salisbury, looking out for something good of Betty's as a present for Babs.

He would have liked it so much more if he had been going to Claire. He wished she would answer the phone. He searched for the address to write to in Hainault where her

Christmas cards came from, but the only card he could find was very old and blurred with no postcode. Nevertheless he wrote to say that he might perhaps be passing near her next Saturday. He told her about Betty.

No reply.

As Mrs.-er set down his morning cup of coffee on his desk, Filth gave the mighty roaring garrumph that had often preceded his pleadings in Court. (There was a rumour that it was the remains of some speech impediment though this seemed unlikely in such an articulate man.)

"Ah-argh. Aha! Mrs.-er, I meant to tell you I'm going away. Taking a short trip. Leaving on Friday. Doing a round of the family. What?"

"I didn't say anything."

"Travelling by car," he said.

"Then I *will* say something. You're out of your mind, Sir Edward. Wherever do you think you're going?"

"Oh, it's up in the north somewhere."

"You haven't driven further than Tisbury station in years. That car's welded to the garage."

"Not at all. I've had it checked over."

"Sir Edward, it's the motorways. You've never driven on a motorway."

"It's an excellent car. And it's a chance for you to have a break, too. You've been very—very good these past days. Take a holiday."

"If you insist on going, I'll not take a holiday. I'll steep them grey nets in your bathroom window."

"You could, actually," he said, not looking at her, "perhaps do something about Lady Feathers's room. Get rid of her—er—the c-c-c-clothes. I believe it's usual."

"Sir Edward." She came round the table and leaned against the window ledge looking at him, arms folded. "I've something to say."

"Oh. Sorry. Yes, Mrs.-er. Mrs. T."

"Look, it's too soon. You're doing it all too soon. You started in on the letters before the funeral. You ought to let them settle. I know, because of Mother. And it's too soon to go round handing out presents, you'll muddle them. I'm sorry, but you're not yourself."

"Mrs.-er, if you don't want to do Lady Feathers's room I'm sure that Chloe—the one from the church—would do it."

"I'm sure she would, too. Let's forget all that though, I'm only interested in stopping you driving. Now then."

His face, with the light from behind her full on it, she saw must have been wonderful once. Appealing, as he gazed at her.

She carried a mug of coffee out to Garbutt who was waiting near the house wall that stood raw and naked without its ivy.

"He's off in the car. Visiting."

"On his own?"

"Yes. On the motorways. I've told him he's not rational yet. She'd have never let him. He doesn't know what he's doing. He's answering every letter return of post and ticking them off on a list, every one hand-done and different and she's scarcely cold. There was a green one—"

"Green what?"

"Letter. From Paris. He threw it in the bin. It upset him. He wrote out an answer and they say he was up the street with it in his hand before the postman was hardly gone."

They both regarded the wall.

Garbutt knew she had read the letter in the waste-paper basket. He would not have read it.

"You know, he's never once called me by my name. She did, of course."

Garbutt finished his coffee, upturned the mug and shook the dregs out on the grass. "Well, I can't see we can do much about it. He's the Law. The law unto himself."

"I tell you, we'll both be out of a job by Monday and who else is he going to kill on the road? That's what I care about."

"He might make it," he said, handing her back the mug. "There's quite a bit to him yet."

Nevertheless, on the Thursday afternoon Filth found the gardener hanging about the garage doors.

"I've had her looked at," said Filth, "I seem to be having to tell everybody. She's a Mercedes. I'm a good driver. Why have you removed all the ivy?"

"It was her instructions. Not a fortnight since. Sir Edward, you're barmy. It's too soon. You're pushing eighty. She'd say it was too soon. You haven't a notion of that A1."

"Is it the A1 now? I must look at the map. Good God, I've known the Great North Road for years. I was at school up there."

"Well, you'll not know it now. That's all I'll say. Goodbye then, sir."

Filth looked up the seaside town of Herringfleet where Babs hung out and was surprised. He'd thought it might be somewhere around Lincolnshire, but it was nearer to Scotland. Odd, he thought, how I could still find my way round the back streets of Hong Kong and the New Territories with my eyes shut and England now is a blur.

Whatever was Babs doing up there? Where would he stay if she couldn't put him up? There seemed to be no hostelry in Herringfleet that the travel guides felt very happy about.

But he went on with his plans, polishing his shoes, looking out shirts. He loved packing. He packed his ivory hair brushes, his Queen Mary cufflinks from the War and, rather surprising himself, *Betty's Book of Common Prayer*. Maybe he'd give it to Babs. Or Claire, if he ever found her. He folded two of Betty's lovely Jacqumar scarves, packaged up some recipe books and then, in a sudden fit of panache, swept a great swag of her jewellery from the dressing-table drawer and poured it into a jiffy bag. He put the scarves and recipe books into another jiffy bag and sealed both of them up.

On Friday morning early, Mrs.-er standing on the front doorstep with a face of doom and Garbutt up his ladder at work on ivy roots and not even turning his head, he made off down the drive and headed for the future.

His eyesight was good. He had spent time on the map. The day was fair and he felt very well. He had decided that he would proceed across England from left to right, and somewhere around Birmingham take a route from South-West to North-East. Very little trouble. His visual memory of the map was excellent and he plunged out into the mêlée of Spaghetti Junction without a tremor, scarcely registering the walls of traffic that wailed and shrieked and overtook him. He admitted to a sense of tension whenever he swerved into the fast lane, but enjoyed the stimulation. Several very large vehicles passed him with a dying scream, one or two even overtaking him on the driver's side although he was in the fast lane. One of these seemed to bounce a little against the central reservation.

Filth was intrigued by the central reservation. It was a phenomenon new to him. He wondered who had thought of it. Was it the same man who had invented cat's-eyes and made millions and hadn't known what to do with them? He remembered that man. He had had three television sets all quacking on together. Poor wretched fellow. Death by cat's-eye. Well, that must be some time ago.

Lorries in strings, like moving blocks of flats, were now hurtling along. Sometimes his old Mercedes seemed to hang between them, hardly touching the road. Seemed to be a great many foreign buggers driving the lorries, steering-wheels left-hand side where they couldn't see a thing. Matter of time no doubt when they'd be in the majority. Then everyone would be driving on the right. Vile government. Probably got all the plans drawn up already. Drive on the right, vote on the left. The so-called left, said Filth. Not Mr. Attlee's left. Not Aneurin Bevan's left. All of them in suits now. Singapore still drives on the left, though they've never heard of left. Singapore's over, like Hong Kong. Empire now like Rome. Not even in the history books. Lost. Over. Finished. Dead. Happened.

Two dragons, Machiavellis, each carrying a dozen or so motor-cars on its back, like obscene, louse-laden animals, hemmed him in on either side of the middle lane. Surely the one in the fast lane was breaking the law? Both seemed impatient with him, though he was doing a steady sixty-five, quite within limits.

He could feel their hatred. One slip and I'm gone, he thought with again the stir of excitement, almost of sexual excitement, "One toot and yer oot," as the bishop said to the old girl with the ear-trumpet. Wherever did that come from? Too much litter in old brains.

Ah! Suddenly he was free. The lorries were gone. He had turned expertly eastwards—with some style, I may say—and into Nottinghamshire.

He found himself now on narrower two-way roads broken by enormous, complicated country roundabouts. Signs declared unlikely names. Fields began, the colour of ox-blood. (Why is ox-blood darker than cow's-blood?) Clumps of black-green trees' stood on the tops of low hills. Streaming towards him, opening out before him, passing him by, were old mining towns all forlorn. Then a medieval castle on a knoll. Then came an artificial hill with a pipe sticking out of its side like a patient with nasty things within. Black stuff trickled. The last coal mine.

Black stuff wavered in the wind. Never been down a coal mine, thought Filth. There's always something new. (But no.

Over. Finished. Gone. Dead.) Better stop soon. Seeing double. Need to pee. Done well. One of these cafés.

But now there were no cafés. They had all disappeared. "Worksop," said Filth. "Now, there's a nasty name. Betty would be furious—*Worksop!*" She hated the North except for Harrogate. "Why ever go to ghastly Babs? You're mad. She's mad. I met her after you did." (Oh, finish, finish, finish.)

He came upon pale and graceful stone gates leading to some lost great estate with the National Trust's acorn on a road sign. He turned in and drove two miles down an avenue of limes. Families shrieked about. He found a Gents and then returned stiffly to the Mercedes in the car-park. People ran about taking plants from a garden shop to their cars to plant on their patios. If I had ever loved England, he thought, I would now weep for her. Sherwood Forest watched him from every side, dense and black.

On again, and into the ruthless thunder of the traffic on the A1; but he was in charge again. Bloody good car, strong as a tank, fine as a good horse. Always liked driving. Aha! Help! Spotting a café he turned across the path of a conveyor of metal pipes from the Ruhr.

A near thing. The driver's face was purple and his mouth held wide in a black roar.

Shaken a little, Filth ate toasted tea-cake at a plastic table and drank a large potful of tea. The waitress looked at his suit and tie with dislike. The man at the next table was wearing denim trousers, with his knees protruding, and a vest. Brassy rings were clipped into all visible orifices. Filth went back to the car for a quick nap but the rhythmic blast of the passing traffic caused the Mercedes to rock at three-second intervals.

"On, on," said Filth. "Be dark soon."

And, two hours later, it was indeed pretty dark and he must have reached Teesside. There was no indication, however, of any towns. Only roads. Roads and roads. The traffic went swimming over them, presumably knowing where it was going. Endless, head-on, blazing head-lights. It is only an airport now, he thought. My spacious lovely North. We are living on a transporter. Up and down we go. *We shall chase you up and down.* That swine Veneering liked *Midsummer Night's Dream.* Silly stuff, but you can't help quoting it. Forest of Arden. Forest of Sherwood. Gone, gone. Finished. Dead. Like Garbutt's ivy. Betty would have been in a fury. "You could have been in *Madeira* by now, in a nice, elderly hotel. And you go to Babs on Teesside. And here's a place called *Yarm.* What a name! *Yarm.*"

"You wouldn't think so if we were in Malaysia."

"Don't be silly, Filth."

"Or the dialects. Malay lacks consonants."

"*Yarm* seems to lack everything."

"Oh, I don't know. Rather a fine-looking town. Splendidly wide main street. Shows up the Cotswolds."

"Well, don't stop, Filth. Not now, for goodness sake. You've only half an hour to go. *Get* there."

Just outside Yarm he saw a signpost which amazingly, for he had not been here before, he recognised. Standing back on a grim champaign behind the swishing traffic stood the Old Judges' Lodging, now a hotel. Once the Circuit judges would have lived there throughout the Quarter Sessions. No wives allowed. Too much port. Boring each other silly. Comforting each others' isolation with talk. Every evening, like cricket commentators between matches, discussing their profession. Finished. Gone. Dead. Hotel now, eh?

"Ha?"

Sign for Herringfleet.

Babs.

What a dire town. And not small. How to find 25 The Lindens? Here was the sea. A cemented edge of promenade. A line of glimmer that must be white sandy beach. Long, long waves curving round a great bay, and behind their swirling frills, spread into the total dark, was the heaving black skin and muscle of the ocean. Sea. How they had hated the sea in Wales. The cruel dividing sea. How could Babs ever choose this?

He had stopped the car on the promenade where, looking blank-eyed at the sea, were tall once-elegant lodging houses now near-slums, bed-and-breakfast places for the Nationally Assisted, i.e., the poor. No lights. The rain fell.

"The Lindens? What?" shouted a man on an old bike. He got off and came across and stuck his head through the window. The smell was chip fat and beer and no work. "The Lindens, mate? (Grand car.) Just over to your right there. You'll not miss it, pal."

It was a terrace of genteel and secretive houses on either side of a short street bordered by trees. The trees were bulging with round gangliae from which next year new sprouts would shoot like hairs from a mole. Revolting treatment. What would Sir say? Number 25.

At the top of steep stone steps there was a dim light above a front room and another light in a window beside it. A gate hung on one hinge. There was a sense of retreat and defeat. He remembered laughing, streetwise, positive Babs in the Oxford tea-shop. *We'll go to bed. We have before.* Laughing, wagging her cracked high-heeled shoe from her toe.

It was so quiet that Filth could hear the beat of the sea two roads away, rhythmic, unstoppable. "Too soon," it said. "They were right. This is histrionic nonsense. You've arrived too soon. You're in shock. You'll make a fool of yourself. There's nothing here."

Suddenly, at the top of the steps, the front door was wrenched open and a boy ran out. He came tearing down, missing several steps, belted along the path towards Filth at the gate. One hand held a music-case and with the other he pushed Filth hard in the stomach so that he fell back into the hedge. The boy, who was wearing old-fashioned school uniform, vanished towards the sea.

Badly winded, Filth struggled out of the hedge, dusted down his clothes, picked up the fallen parcel of presents, looked right and left and gave his furious roar. The quiet of the road then re-asserted itself. The child might never have been.

But the front door stood wide and he walked uneasily up the steps and into the passage beyond, where, as if he had stood on a switch, a torrent of Chopin was let loose in the room to his right.

"Hello?"

He stood outside its open door.

"Hello there? Babs?"

He knocked on the door, peered round it. "It's Teddy."

The music stopped. The room appeared to be empty.

Then he saw her by the back window, staring into the dark. She was wearing some sort of shawl and her hair was long and white. She seemed to be pressing something—a handkerchief?—into her face. Without turning towards him further, her voice came out from behind her hands, clear and controlled. And Betty's.

In one of her very occasional cynical or bitter moods which Filth had never understood, and which usually ended in her going to London for a few days (or over to Macao from Hong Kong), Betty had said, "Look, leave me alone, Filth. I'm in the dark. Just need a break."

"I'm in the dark, Teddy-bear," now said Betty's voice inside this crazed old creature. "You shouldn't have come. I should have stopped you. I couldn't find the number."

"Oh, dear me, Babs. You're ill."

"Ill. Do you mean sick? I'm sick all right. D'you want tea? I make it on my gas-ring. There's some milk somewhere. In a cupboard. But we don't take milk, do we? Not from our classy background. I'm finished, Teddy. Broken-hearted. Like Betty. You'd better go."

(Like Betty? What rubbish—never.)

"I can't stay more than a few minutes," said Filth, realising that this was absolutely so, for the room was not only ice-cold and dark, but there was an aroma about. Setting down his parcels on a chair piled with newspapers, he touched something unspeakable on a plate.

"Babs, I had no idea . . ."

"You thought I was well-off, did you? Sky television and modems? Well, I am well-off, but because I am still a teacher of music. I live alone. Betty always warned me against living alone. Said I'd get funny. But I prefer to live alone. Ever since well, you know. Wales. I had mother of course until last year. Upstairs. I still hear her stick thumping on the floor for the commode. Sometimes I start heating up her milk. But I'm glad she's gone. In a way."

"Then," said Filth, prickling all over with disgust, making stabs at various shadows to find perhaps somewhere to lean against or sit. "Then it can't *all* have been bad." He had begun to lower himself into what might have been a chair when something in it rustled and streaked for the door.

"Ah," he said, easing his shirt-collar. "And you have a dog."

"What dog? I have no dog."

"I'm sorry."

"I'm not sorry. Even with a dog I would be utterly alone. And I am going mad."

"*Well*"—he had sprung up from the chair and was standing to attention—"Well" (half-heartedly). "Well, I'm here now, Babs. We must sort something out. Get something going. Betty wouldn't want . . ."

Babs had left the window and was fumbling about. A light came on and an electric jug was revealed. A half-empty milk bottle was withdrawn from an antique gramophone. Cups and saucers were wrested from their natural home upon the hearth.

"You see, I'm quite independent. No trouble to anyone. Sugar? No, that's not *us*, either, Teddy, is it?"

"Babs, let me take you out somewhere for a meal."

She flung her long hair about. "I never go out. I watch and wait. First Flush? Do you remember?"

For a dreadful moment Filth thought that Babs was referring to the menopause, though that, surely, must be now in the past?

"First Flush?"

(Or maybe it was something to do with Bridge? Or the domestic plumbing?)

"*Tea*, Teddy. First Flush is *tea*. From Darjeeling." (She pronounced it correctly. Datcherling.) "Don't you remember?" She seemed to be holding up a very tattered packet marked *Fortnum and Mason, Piccadilly*. "He gave it to me always for years. Every Christmas. In memory of our childhood. You, me, him, Claire, Betty."

"But we weren't in India, Betty and I. I hadn't met Betty. You and I and Claire were in—Wales."

She looked frightened.

"But he sent me tea from India. They took him back there after . . . Year after year from India he sent me tea."

"Who?"

"Billy Cumberledge."

"Babs?"

"My lover."

"Oh, I'm so sorry, Babs. And he died, too?"

"I'm not sure. I used to see him in Oxford. He was a lovely man. She could never touch his soul, never break him utterly. He and I—no, you and I, Teddy. We got into one bed that night to be near together while Claire went to get help."

"I'd forgotten." (A wave of relief. So that's what she'd meant in the tea-shop.)

"Yes, he was my lover. But not my last lover. My present lover you may have seen just now as he went scampering down the steps."

"But that was a schoolboy . . ."

"Yes, but a genius. I don't do examination work now, except for this one. He is a genius."

"Yes. I see."

They drank the First Flush which was not noticeably refreshing.

"This is of course a First Flush of some time ago."

"Yes," he said. "Some time ago."

The lights in the street came on and revealed a Broadwood piano by the front window and a piano stool lying on its side. He remembered the terrified boy.

"Edward," she said, abandoning the tea to the grate, "oh, Edward, we were so close. I have to tell someone. I am in love again."

"Oh—Oh dear—"

"He is fourteen. You know how old I am. Way over seventy. It makes no difference."

Something out in the passage fell with a crash to the floor and there was the sound of running water.

"It's that dog," she said, weeping. "Everyone's against me. I need God, not a dog."

All that Filth, now deeply shaken, could say was, "But you haven't got a dog."

"Haven't I? Of course I have. I need some protection, don't I?" (And, sharply, in Betty's voice.) "Come on now, Filth. Work it out."

A cat ran down the hall as Filth stepped out into it, and water was still dripping from a vase of amazingly perfect lupins.

"Let me help." Filth stood, unbending.

"It's all right. They're artificial. I always put them in water though, it seems kinder. I arrange them for *him*. The boy. My boy. I don't somehow think he'll be coming back."

"He won't?"

"No." She clutched the shawl around her and bent forward as if butting at a storm.

"You see—I showed my hand."

"Your hand?" (Again, he thought hysterically of Bridge.)

"I showed my hand. I showed my heart. I showed my . . . Oh, Eddie! I fell to my knees. I told my love."

Filth was now on the top step. Very fast, he was on the bottom step. "So sorry, Babs. Time to go. Sorry to leave you so . . ."

"Don't worry about the flowers," she said. "It wasn't your fault."

She was now on her knees crawling about in the water.

"So sorry, Babs. Not much help. Terribly sorry. God, I wish Betty . . . I'll try and think what's to be done."

He could not remember getting back into the car nor the road he took next, but in time found that he was hurtling back in the dark and then into the blinding lights of traffic coming towards Yarm. The Judges' Hotel was before him, agreeably behind its lawns like a flower in a gravel pit. He drove through its gateway with care for he was beginning to shake, and at its great studded doors he stopped. A cheerful young man, in a livery that would not have disgraced Claridges, but eating a sandwich, bounded forward and opened the driver's door.

"Good evening, sir, staying the night? Out you get, leave the key, I'll park it. Any luggage? Nasty weather!"

Filth stepped in to a black-and-white marble hall with a grand staircase and portraits of judges in dubious bright oils hanging all the way down it. How very odd to be here. Yes, there was one room left. Yes, there was dinner. Yes, there was a bar.

Filth removed his coat in the bedroom and regarded the two single beds, both populous with teddy bears. A foot-massager of green plastic lay by the bedside and a globe of goldfish with instructions for feeding them ("Guests are asked to confine themselves to one pinch"—was it hemp?). There were no towels in the bathroom but a great many plastic ducks. The noble height of the room that had in the past seen scores of judicial heads on the pillow seemed another frightening joke. I suppose I don't know much about hotels now, he thought and had a flashback of the black towels and white telephones and linen sheets of Hong Kong.

For the first time in many years he did not change his shirt for dinner but stepped quickly back into the hall where the eyes of the old buggers on the staircase, in their wigs and scarlet, gave him a sense of his secure past. Glad I got out of the country though. No Circuits in Hong Kong. No getting stuck in luxury here for weeks on end with the likes of Fiscal-Smith. He wondered where the name had come from. Hadn't thought of the dear old bore for years.

Good heavens.

Fiscal-Smith was still here. He was sitting in the bar in a vast leather armchair and as usual he was without a glass in his hand, waiting for someone to buy him a drink.

"Evening, Filth," said Fiscal-Smith. (Ye gods, thought Filth, there's something funny going on here.) "No idea you'd be here. Thought you'd retire in Hong Kong. How's Betty?"

"We retired and came Home years ago," said Filth, sitting down carefully in a second leather throne.

"Oh, so did I, so did I," said Fiscal-Smith. "I retired up here though."

"Really."

"Got myself a little estate. Nobody wants them now—it's the fumes. It was very cheap."

"I see."

"Or they *assume* there are fumes. Actually I am out on the moors. Shooting rights. Everything."

"How is . . . ?" Filth could not remember whether Fiscal-Smith had ever had a wife. It seemed unlikely. " . . . the Bar up here these days?"

Fiscal-Smith was looking meaningfully over at the Claridges lad, who was hovering about and responded with a matey wave.

"Have a drink," said Filth, giving in, signalling to the boy and ordering whiskeys.

"Don't be too long, sir," said the boy. "Dining-room closes in half an hour."

"Yes. Yes. I must have dinner. Long drive today." He was beginning to feel better though. Warmth, whiskey, familiar jargon. "Are you staying the night here?" he asked Fiscal-Smith.

"I don't usually. I go home. Always a chance that someone might turn up from the old days. Very good of you. Thank you. I'd enjoy dinner."

They munched. Conversation waned

"Fancy sort of food nowadays," said the ancient judge. "Seem to paint the sauces on the plates with a brush."

The waitress patted his shoulder and shouted with laughter. "You're meant to lick 'em up. Shall I keep you some tiramisu?"

"What on earth is that?"

"No idea," said Filth, his eyelids drooping.

"Trifle," said the waitress. "You're nothing now, if you haven't tried tiramisu."

"Is this usual?" asked Filth, reviving a little with coffee.

"What—trifle? Yes, it's on all the time."

"No. I mean the—familiarity. They're very matey. I never worked the Northern Circuit."

"It's not mateyness."

"Well, it's not exactly respect." Filth's mind presented him with Betty ringing for the invisible and silent maids. He suddenly yearned for that sycophantic time in his life, like a boy thinking of his birthday parties. "They're very insensitive. And I can't understand the teddy bears. I always detested teddy bears."

"What teddy bears?"

"The beds are covered with them. Is it a local custom?"

"I'm afraid you are ahead of me, somewhere. But of course, yes, it's different up here. Very nice people."

"But you're not local, Fiscal-Smith. Is there anybody to talk to? On your estate?"

Fiscal-Smith took a second huge slice of cheese. "No. Not really. Sit there alone. I like it here though." (Old Filth's grown stuffy. Home Counties. How does Betty put up with him?) "They're rude to your face but they boast about knowing you. House of Lords, and all that. It's a compliment, but you have to understand it. Good friends at The Judges to an old bachelor."

All but one of the lights were now switched off in the dining-room, where they were the only diners left. The waitress looked out from a peephole.

"Yes, we've finished, Dolly. I think I'll stay the night. Too much wine for driving. 'Ex-Judge drunk at wheel.' Wouldn't do."

"Yes. Keep it within closed doors," said Dolly. "But I don't think there's a room ready. The housekeeper's gone off."

"Twin beds in your room, Filth?"

"Well, I'm afraid . . .

"Room One?" said the waitress. "Yes. Twin beds."

"No," said Filth in the final and first, utterly immovable decision of the day. "No. Sorry. I—snore."

"Oh, then, we'll find you somewhere, Lord Fiscal-Smith. Come along. The trouble will be bath-towels. I think she hides them."

"Shan't have a bath." He tottered away on her arm. "Borrow your *razor* in the morning, Filth."

"We can do a razor," she said. "Did you say he was called Filth?"

She handed Fiscal-Smith over to the Claridges boy who was drinking a glass of milk in the hall.

When Filth lay down on one of his beds the room rocked gently round and round. "Pushing myself," he said. "Heart attack. I dare say. Sir? Good. Hope it's the finish. And I'm certainly not lending him my razor."

Then, it was morning.

The goldfish were looking at his face on the pillow with inquisitive distaste. On the floor a heap of bears gave the impression of decadence. The bedside clock glared out 9.30 A.M. which filled him with shame, and he reached breakfast just in time.

"So sorry," he said.

"That's all right, dear. You need your sleep at your age."

Far across the bright conservatory, where breakfast was served, bacon and eggs were being carried to Fiscal-Smith whose back was turned firmly away from all comers as he perused the *Daily Telegraph*. Filth changed his chair so that his back was also turned away from Fiscal-Smith. Outside, across the grey Teesside grass, stood magnificent oaks and, above them, a deep blue autumn sky and a hint of moorland, air and light. The *Telegraph* was beside Filth's plate. He must have ordered it. Couldn't read it. Not yet. Rice-Krispies.

"Oh dear no, thank you. Nothing cooked."

"Oh, come on. Do you good."

She brought bacon and eggs.

Why *should* I? thought Filth, petulant, and clattered down his knife and fork.

"I'm disappointed," said the waitress, bringing coffee.

He drank it and looked at the oak trees and the light beyond.

Must get out of this wasteland. Not my sort of place at all. What was Babs doing here? What was I doing, coming to visit her? Rather frightening, what grief can uncover in you.

Don't you think so, Betty? Just as well I wasn't in the middle of a case when you went. But you'd have dealt with it. Got me through.

Remembering, then, that the cause of the grief was that she could no longer get him through anything, he gulped, shuddered, watched the oaks, as his eyes at last filled up with tears.

A hand came down on his shoulder but he did not turn. The hand was removed.

"So very sorry, old chap. So very sorry," and Fiscal-Smith was gone.

It was some time later—breakfast still uneaten, Filth's back the only sign of anyone in the room, silence from the kitchen—that the oaks began to return to their natural steadiness. Filth, his face wet, blew his nose, mopped with his napkin, took up the newspaper, opened it, shook it about. He found himself looking straight into Betty's face.

Obituary.

Good gracious. Betty. No idea there'd be an obituary. And half a column. Second on the page. Good God: Red Cross; Barristers' Benevolent Association; Bletchley Park. Dominant personality. Wife of—yes, it was Betty, all right. Fiscal-Smith must have been reading it. Good God—*Betty*! They'll never give me half a column. I've never done anything but work. Great traveller. Ambassadress. Chinese-speaking. Married and the dates. No children of the marriage.

He sat on. On and on. They cleared the table. They did not hurry him. On and on he sat. They changed the cloth. They said not a word.

At some point he began properly to weep. He wept silently behind his hands, sitting in this unknown place, uncared about, ignorant, bewildered, past it.

Much later they brought him, unasked, a tray of tea. When at last he had packed his case and paid his bill at the desk in the marble hall and was standing bleakly on the porch as the boy brought his car, he remembered that he had invited Fiscal-Smith to join him for last night's dinner, and that this had not been on the bill.

"Don't you worry, sir," said the receptionist. "He's paid it himself."

She said no more, but both understood that this was a first. And that it was touching. It lifted Filth's desolate heart.

He drove for an hour before addressing Betty again. "You never know where help's coming from, do you? Yes. You're right. I'm ten years older than yesterday and I look it." ("*Fool*," he yelled at a nervous little Volkswagen. "Do you want to be *killed*, woman?") No more gadding about for a while.

"But stop worrying. I'll get home. I'm a bloody good driver." The car gave a wobble.

He thought of the hotel which loomed now much larger in his consciousness than the Babs business (Babs had always been potty) and he understood the goldfish, the bears, the box of Scrabble in the wardrobe, the tape deck and the vast television set in the room. They were an attempt to dispel the sombre judicial atmosphere of the place's past. The seams of the Judges' Lodging had exuded crime, wickedness, evil, folly and pain. All had been tossed about in conversation each night over far too much port. Jocose, over-confident judges.

Well, they have to be. Judges live with shadows behind them.

There are very good men among them. Mind you, I'd never have put Fiscal-Smith among those, the horrible old hang-erand-flogger.

"Seems we were wrong, Betty," he said, turning the car unthinkingly Eastward in the direction of the Humber bridge.

And on it sped for three hours, when he had to stop for petrol and saw signs for Cambridge.

Cambridge?

Why Cambridge? He was making for the Midlands and home in the South-West. He must have missed his turning. He seemed to be on the way to London. This road was called the M11 and it was taking its pitiless way between the wide green fields of—where? Huntingdonshire? Rutland?—don't know anything about any of them. Claire lives somewhere about down here. Hainault. Never been. Must have the address somewhere. Hadn't intended to come. Hadn't consciously intended to come. Had quite enough. Saffron Walden? Nice name. Why are you going to see Claire? You haven't seen her since—well, since Ma Didds.

Betty knew her. Betty saw her. Why must I? Wasn't Babs enough?

He drew out in front of a Hungarian demon. Its hoot died slowly away, as at length it passed him, spitting wrath as he swayed into the slow lane. Mile after mile. Mile after mile. Fear no bigger than a child's hand squeezed at his ribcage. "If it's a heart attack, get on with it," commanded Filth.

But he drew off the motorway and dawdled into a lane. There were old red-brick walls and silent mansions and a church. A by-passed village, like a by-passed heart. Not a café. Not a shop. He'd perhaps go and sit in the church for a while. Here it stood.

The church appeared to be very well-kept. He pushed open an inner red-baize door. The church within echoed with insistent silence. There was the smell of incense and very highly-varnished pews. A strange church. The sense of many centuries with a brash, almost aggressive overlay. You'd be kept on your toes here. Never had much idea of these things, thought Filth. Lists pinned up everywhere. All kinds of services. Meditations.

The lamp is lit over the Blessed Sacrament. Vigils. *Quiet is requested.* An enormous Cross with an agonised Christ. That always upset Filth.

This terrible silence.

He sat in the south aisle and closed his eyes and when he opened them saw that winter sunshine had lit up a marble memorial to some great local family. It was immense, a giant wedding cake in black and pink and sepia. Like an old photograph. Like a sad cry.

Filth got up and peered closer. He touched some of the figures. They were babies. Dozens of babies. Well, cherubs, he supposed, carved among garlands of buds and flowers, nuts, leaves, insects, fat fruits. More marble babies caught at more garlands at the foot of the pyramid, all naked, and male of course. They were weeping. One piped its eye, whatever piping was. Their fat lips pouted with sorrow. They stood, however, on very sturdy legs with creases across the backs of their knees, and their bottoms shone. There was a notice saying that the memorial had three stars and was thought to have been designed by Gibbons.

Well, I don't know about that, thought Filth. What would Gibbons be doing here? And he gave one of the bottoms a slap.

The air of the church came alive for a moment as the baize door opened and shut, and a curly boy came springing down the aisle. He wore a clerical collar and jeans. "Good afternoon," he cried. "So sorry I'm rather late. You're wanting me to hear your confession."

"Confession?"

"Saturday afternoons. Confessions. St. Trebizond's. Half a mo while I put my cassock on."

He ran past the weeping pile and disappeared into a vestry, emerging at once struggling into a cassock. He hurried into something like a varnished sedan chair which stood beside the rood screen, and clicked shut its door. The silence resumed.

Filth at once turned and made to walk out of the church, clearing his throat with the judicial roar.

He looked back. The sedan chair watched him. There was a grille of little holes at waist level and he imagined the boy priest resting his head near it on the inside.

It would be rather discourteous just to leave the church.

Filth might go over and say, "Very low-church, I'm afraid. Not used to this particular practice though my wife was interested . . ."

He walked back to the sedan chair, leaned down and said, "Hullo? Vicar?"

A crackling noise. Like eating potato crisps.

"Vicar? I beg your pardon?"

No reply. All was hermetically sealed within except for the grille. Really quite dangerous.

He creaked down to his knees to a hassock and put his face to the grille. Nothing happened. The boy must have fallen asleep.

"Excuse me, Vicar. I'm afraid I don't go in for this. I have nothing to confess."

"A very rash statement," snarled a horrendous voice—there must be some amplifier.

Filth jumped as if he'd put his ear to an electric fence.

"How long, my son, since your last confession?"

"I've—" (his son!) "—I've never made a confession in my life. I've heard plenty. I'm a Q.C."

There was a snuffling sound.

"But you are in some trouble?"

Filth bowed his head.

"Begin. Go on. 'Father I have sinned.' Don't be afraid."

Filth's ragged old logical mind was not used to commands.

"I'm afraid I don't at the moment feel sinful at all. I am more sinned against than sinning. I am able to think only of my dear dead wife. She was in the *Telegraph* this morning. Her obituary." Then he thought: I am not telling the truth. "And I am unable to understand the strange games my loss of her play with my behaviour."

Why tell this baby? Can't be much over thirty. Well, same age as Christ, I suppose. If Christ were inside this box . . . A great and astounding longing fell upon Filth, the longing of a poet, the deep perfect adoring longing of a lover of Christ. How did he come on to this? This medieval, well of course, very primitive, love of Christ you read about? Not my sort of thing at all.

"My son, were there any children of the marriage?"

"No. We didn't seem to need any."

"That's never the full answer. I have to say that I saw you touching the anatomy of the cherubs on the Tytchley tomb."

"You *what*?"

"Reveal all to me, my son. I can understand and help you."

"Young man," roared Filth through the grille. "Go home. Look to your calling. I am one of Her Majesty's Counsellors and was once a Judge."

"There is only one judge in the end," said the voice, but Filth was in the car again and belting on past Saffron Walden.

He drove very fast indeed now, as the roads grew less equipped for him. I am a coelacanth. Yes. I dare say. I have lived too long. Certainly, I cannot cope—cope with a mind such as I have. The bloody little twerp. Wouldn't have him in my Chambers. *I can* drive, though. That's one thing I can do. My reactions are perfect, and here is a motorway again.

And hullo—what's this? Lights? Sirens? Police? "Good afternoon. Yes?"

"You have been behaving oddly on the road, sir. It has been reported."

"I have been stopping sometimes. Resting. Once in a church. In my view, essential. No, no need for a breath test. Oh well, very well."

"You see. Perfectly clear," said Filth.

"Could we help you in any way?"

"No. I don't think so."

"Your licence is in order?"

"Yes, of course. I am a lawyer."

"It doesn't follow, sir. I see that you are eighty-one?"

"With no convictions," said Filth.

"No, sir. Well, goodbye, sir."

"There is one thing," said Filth, strapping himself back in his seat with some languor. "I do seem to be rather lost."

"Ah."

"I don't suppose you know this address. Hainault?"

"We do, sir. But it's not Hainault. That is in Essex. It's High Light. Not High Note. A house called *High Light*. And we know who it belongs to. We know her. It's five miles away. Shall we go ahead of you?"

"She is my cousin. She can never have had any Christmas cards. Thank you. And thank you for your courtesy and proper behaviour. A great surprise."

"You oughtn't to believe the television, sir."

"Who the hell was he?" one policeman asked the other. "He's like out of some Channel Four play."

A Light House

Claire in her house all alone sat in her shadowless kitchen and down came her beautiful little hands slap-bang across the *Daily Telegraph*. She closed her eyes and sat for a full minute, "No," she said. "Of course it's not Betty. Someone would have told me."

She opened her eyes, removed her hands and stared down at Betty Feathers' eyes which looked back at her with sharp but pleasant intelligence. "Well," she said, "an obituary for Betty." She smoothed the paper, read Elizabeth Feathers, MBE, and then the whole thing.

The phone rang. She folded the paper and turned it on its back. She walked to the phone.

"Hullo?"

"Beware. The Ice Man Cometh."

Claire sat down quickly. The quiet life she had diligently followed over years was the rent she paid to a weak heart. Her control, balance, yoga, good sense, none of it natural to her, had been necessary if she was to see her husband out. She had told the doctor that it was essential she outlive him, and the doctor had thought her wonderful and her husband a weak old bore. Now, as a widow, Claire found that creeping about and being careful was a habit she could not drop. She would have liked a lover, but the heart battering about inside her made the practice impossible. Today, it was beating like an angry butter-fly under a jam jar.

"Claire? Claire? Are you there? It's Babs."

"Oh yes," she said. "Babs. Yes, of course. You always did sound like Betty."

"Can't help it. I suppose you were at the funeral. In at the kill."

"I've just this minute seen the *Telegraph*. An utter shock."

"Well, it would be the hush-hush Bletchley Park thing. She wasn't there for long. I never thought she was very clever. She's had a pretty good life with him. You might have told me about the funeral. She had some wonderful rocks."

"Rocks?"

"Jewellery."

"Oh. Had she? I didn't know she was dead until now."

Claire had been wild about Filth since she was four, but as inscrutable then as now she sat prettily in her pink dressing-gown with her hand firmly against the butterfly.

"He turned up here yesterday. He only stayed ten minutes. He brought me some recipe books but I can't find them. He'll be en-route to you now. At a guess."

"He would have telephoned. Though I suppose I do tend to switch it off."

"He's not himself, I warn you. He never told me when he was arriving. Then ten minutes later he was gone. Actually I wasn't very well. I'm not a very well woman."

"But why did he come? We haven't seen either of them in years. All that way! Dorset! She can't have died more than . . ." She glanced at the folded paper. She would look properly later.

"Just over a fortnight. He was bringing us keepsakes. I'd rather hoped she'd made a Will. I think he thought better of giving me the recipe books. I expect he'll offer them to you."

"But I'm diabetic."

"Yes, well, I don't suppose he remembers that. Just at the moment."

"No," said Claire.

"He was very strange. He fled the house. I seemed to horrify him. I can't think why. My ways are not everybody's ways, of course, but knowing what we three have been through together . . ."

"Your ways were not everybody's ways then."

"Neither were yours."

"Why not?"

"All that *perfection*, Claire. *Nauseating* perfection. From the start."

Silence.

"Claire?"

"Yes?"

"Sorry. I only meant that it's a bit chilling."

"It seems," said Claire, "that Betty's death removes barriers. It's bringing corpses to the surface. I can honestly say I never had anything to hide."

"Oh, no?"

Claire was watching through the huge window an immaculate Mercedes nosing about in the lane. It paused, considered, started off again and cruised out of sight.

"You'd better ring me if he turns up," said Babs. "He looked to me as if he was in need of special care, like they used to say of drawn-thread work on laundry lists. Get him to see someone."

Elgar's *Enigma Variations* began to boom in Babs's background.

"Laundry lists? Hello? I can't hear you."

Claire put down the phone.

The car must have turned somewhere down the road, for here it was nosing slowly back again. "He won't come here," she said aloud. "He doesn't need me. He never did and we won't be able to look each other in the eye. 'It was Betty who made him,' Isobel Ingoldby used to say. I never believed her. He's made himself. Made his impeccable, astringent self."

The phone rang again.

"Well, all I can say, Claire, he was shaking all over and grey in the face and terrified of my poor animals under his feet. Gob-*smacked*, outraged by my little lover with his little music-case."

"What are you talking about, Babs? I wish you wouldn't say 'gob-smacked.' It doesn't become you. You're not a teenager."

"Yes, I am. At heart I am fourteen."

The car had now stopped at Claire's gate and Filth's stony face, with the Plantagenet cheek-bones and thick ungreying curly hair, could be observed, peering out.

"When old women say that," said Claire, "'I'm just a girl inside,' I . . ." The butterfly was hammering now on iron wings. Filth's long right leg, like the leg of a flamingo but in Harris tweed, was feeling for the pavement. "I," said Claire, "cease to find them interesting."

"I may not be interesting, but it was me he turned to at Ma Didds, when you went running down the village."

Claire let her fingers stray about over the glass table-top, feeling for her butterfly-subduing pills. And here came the old flamingo, the old crane, lean as a cowboy still. What? Six-foot-three, and still melting my heart.

Well, he seemed to be carrying the parcel of recipe books.

"I must go now, Babs. The laundry man's here. And Babs, you're drinking too much. Goodbye."

"Have you any luggage? I hope you'll be staying the night?" she asked at once.

Filth jack-knifed himself into a small, gold-sprayed Lloyd-loom chair and his knees were nearly up to his chin. Light fell upon him like a greeting as in fact it always did upon every-body inside the rambling bungalow which Claire had moved into a few years ago for that very reason, and because it was sensible for someone with A Heart. The building followed an easy circuit. Sitting-room led into kitchen, kitchen led into bathroom, bathroom led into Claire's bedroom and out to the hallway again. Off the hall was a second bedroom and bathroom, the bedroom narrower and full of hat boxes and tissue paper and old letters and Christmas lists spread permanently over the bed. In each room she kept a supply of pills and on the bathroom mirror she had stuck a list, written in her beautiful calligraphy, of all the pills she took, and when. "You make poetry of every word you write," the Vicar had said, but Claire had passed the compliment by.

"I have a spare room, Teddy."

"I could take you out to dinner," he said, without enthusiasm.

"I don't go out for meals. I hardly go out at all. I watch the Boy Scouts doing my gardening outside my windows. That is my fresh air."

"You have a beautiful complexion, nevertheless," he said. "And you have the figure of a—of an angel."

He saw Betty's jolly old rump above the tulip bed. Her weather-beaten face. "A hundred in and a hundred more to go," she had called. "I don't want a gin. Could we miss lunch?" Then over she fell.

He looked now long and piercingly—but unseeingly—at Claire's open and beautiful face. She'd been a sunlit, lovely child who'd grown plain (or so Betty had told him). A stodgy bride in horn-rims. Then pretty again, and now beautiful. He remembered being told that she had ruled her children by a mysterious silence, her adoration of them never expressed. Betty said the children had felt guilty about it, knowing they could never deserve her; they had become conventional, monosyllabic members of society. Her nice husband, Betty said, had taken to drink. Claire (Betty said) believed that marriage and motherhood meant pain. Betty had agreed with her about children, and thought that Claire lived for the moment when they fled the nest and she was peacefully widowed. And here she sat now, gentle, shoulderless as a courtesan on her linen-covered sofa, smiling. (Filth turned to Betty on his interior telephone to ask what she thought about it, but Betty had left the phone off the hook.)

"Of course!" he said. "I remember. You have diabetes. You can't come out to dinner. Let me . . ." he had never gone shopping in his life. "Let me go and forage for us."

"So you *will* stay?"

"I'd be—delighted."

"Teddy, there's no need to forage. The girl gets me what I want. There's a freezer. And there's whiskey."

"Whiskey?"

"Oh, just for anyone who drifts in. The police—very nice people, out of hours. They come here when I fall over. The Vicar. The woman down the road with one eye. The window-cleaner. I'm fond of the window-cleaner. I have him once a week, though 'have' alas is not any longer the word. I 'have' a weak heart."

Filth's eyes were startled as a dog's. This silvery, powdery woman.

"Oh, Teddy," she said. "So easily shocked."

"Well, Claire, really. We are way over . . . seventy."

"Yes. And I have a weak heart."

She poured him an immense whiskey and sat on, smiling beyond him out through the gleaming clean window.

Soon Filth eased himself down in the chair, tilted his head back on the curved rim and looked up at the ceiling which was studded with dozens of trendy spotlights, like an office. He took another deep swig of whiskey and sighed.

"Our mutual cousin, or whatever she is, Babs, exists in perpetual darkness and you in perpetual light."

"Yes," she said. "It's odd. I can't get enough of it. Maybe my eyesight's going. I'd love a cataract operation, wouldn't you?"

"I'm lucky there," said Filth. "I brought you a present, by the way. Betty wanted you to have them."

"Oh, yes?" She looked canny. She examined his face for lies.

"Nothing much. Family stuff mostly. Some from way back. She wanted you to have them. She was insistent. If she departed first—only you."

"What about Babs?"

"She'd put something else aside for Babs. As a matter of fact we were in the m-m-m-middle of our, what's called 'Letters of Wishes.'"

"I see. She had other friends?"

"Yes. Don't know how well she kept them, though. Not exactly friends. At the funeral . . ."

"Ah yes. The funeral."

"Didn't bother you with the funeral. Sorry now. Thought I'd spare you. Never get this sort of thing right. And a big journey. Our time of life, it's a funeral a week in the winter. They don't do anyone any good."

"I hope mine will be private. On the Ganges on a pyre."

"I never read obituaries. No idea Betty was getting one."

"Did nobody turn up at the funeral, Teddy?"

"No idea."

"Teddy—?"

"Didn't look around. Eyes front. Usual hymns. Discipline and all that."

"Of course," said Claire. (Oh, where was the boy, the blazing young friend in Wales?) "Of course. You were with the Glorious Gloucesters in the War."

He gave her a look.

"I believe there was a pack of church ladies," he said. "From the flower committee. Coffee rota. One of them walked me home and made herself rather too friendly. I'm told you have to watch this."

"Was there a wake?"

"Bun-fight in the church hall."

"Nobody from Chambers?"

"Oh, yes. Yes. My Clerk. Retired now. Very civil of him."

"Well, you made him a packet."

Again the look.

"And there were a few from the Inn. Hardly knew them. Can't think why they came, trains being what they are."

"But, Teddy, they may have wanted to come. They were fond of Betty. Maybe it helped them to wear a dark suit, make an effort on your behalf. Respecting you. Helping you."

"Helping me?" He looked at his glass. "Nonsense, Claire. Whenever did I need help?" He seemed outraged. "We all come to an end."

"Teddy, you must grieve for her. You will soon. It hasn't hit you yet, but listen, there may be a very bad time coming. You were married nearly half a century and you never—I'd guess strayed?"

"Strayed?"

"You were never unfaithful to Betty with another woman?"

"Good God, no."

Yet his eyes were dazzling, hungry eyes. Claire thought how Betty had underestimated him. And fooled him.

"Then, Teddy, you are in trouble. You are in shock." ("She should have seen you on the motorway," said Betty to Filth on her mobile.) "Why else would you have come charging round the country after Babs and me?"

"How did you know about Babs?"

"She rang."

"Was she drunk? She was drunk yesterday. On tea from Fortnum's, or worse. Very squalid."

"You can be a cruel man, Teddy. More whiskey? Hello, who's this?"

Outside in the road a motor-bike came clattering up to the gate and a young man in a medieval black helmet with belligerent lip got off and stood looking at the Merc.

"Oh, Lord, it's the Vicar. I'll get rid of him. Unless of course . . ."

"No thanks," said Filth as the Vicar removed his disguise and emerged as the cherub of the sedan chair. "I'll find your spare bedroom and lie down," and he seized his bag from the hall and made off.

"Ah, I see you are not ready for each other at the moment," called Claire.

The young man in the road, having walked round the car and examined the number plate, climbed back on his bike and roared away.

"He saw I had a visitor," said Claire, and went to the kitchen to look in the freezer. Fish fingers. Oven chips, but she kept these for Oliver so she and Teddy mustn't eat them all. A square of mild cheddar in plastic. Flora margarine and frozen peas. Splendid. Though Teddy never noticed what he ate.

"Or anything else," she said, sadly, and mistakenly.

Parents' weekend, thought Claire's younger son, Oliver, in Wandsworth on Friday, flinging a few crumpled things into a sports bag. Wonder if I need petrol. Trip to the bank machine. No need for condoms, anyway, all by myself. Might step out and buy some real flowers for Ma, not petrol-station ones. Saturday morning.

He was happy to be going to see his mother and trying not to face the fact that he was happier because he was going alone. Vanessa, at present snarling and snapping incisively into the sitting-room phone, was off in a moment to her own parents in Bournemouth. They arranged these filial visits every other month, Oliver ringing his mother every week to check up on her diabetes, Vanessa ringing hers, who was hale and hearty, every three. When Vanessa was not about, Oliver sometimes rang Claire in between times from station platforms, airports, or the forecourt of the Wandsworth supermarket. He had premonitions about his vague and undemonstrative mother and found it hard to look at the advertisements in the papers showing resigned old women with bells round their necks like Swiss cattle lying waiting for rescue, or for the end. He knew that, should his mother fall over, she would never ring for help, but would lie there, thinking. Thus she would be avenged for his believing her immortal. Another part of him said that his mother was a cynic, even a torturer. Then he thought: And I am a swine, and don't believe in selflessness. He adored her.

Vanessa was brisker. The three-weekly call to Bournemouth was always made at 6 P.M. sharp on a Friday, and she set aside half an hour. She was a Barrister in Shipping Chambers, a prestigious area and rare for a woman. She had had to swim enjoyably hard to keep up with the tide. She was respected in the Chambers and held in awe in Bournemouth where her parents knew nothing of the Bar except what they saw on television. She regaled them, third Fridays, with accounts of her daily round—from the 7 A.M. orange juice in the super-nova kitchen, to her reading Briefs last thing at night. ("A case you'll be seeing in the papers.") Her Opinions were not usually complete before midnight.

"Well, I'm sure I don't know how you fit it all in," her mother said. "How do you do your housework and shopping and cooking? And laundry?" (And where are the children?)

Vanessa ignored her. Work first. No philosophising.

"Whenever do you see your *friends*?" asked her mother. (Or us?)

"Oliver and I have it all under control. We eat out. Friends at weekends. We probably see more friends than you do."

"I miss your friends, Vanessa," said her mother. "Every weekend we saw your friends, all through school and Cambridge, they used to come. I miss your friends." (And I miss you, too. I don't know this sharp-faced, black-suited, almost bald-headed, lap-top sprite.)

"I ring you every three weeks."

"Yes."

"Last time I couldn't get through. You were engaged."

"Yes. We do occasionally have another phone-call."

"And what about *this*?" Vanessa said now, marching into the hall as Oliver picked up his sports bag en-route for a workout. "They're not going to be there."

"What? Your parents?"

"My consistent and saintly parents say they'd no idea I was coming down this weekend. They're going to a Fortieth Wedding Anniversary on the Isle of Wight. They said they told me. They're going senile. Parents of some of my *primary-school* friends I've not seen for twenty years. They said why don't I go, too, for goodness sake!"

"Well, why don't you?" Oliver saw, and his spirits fell, the way things would now develop. "Better come with me and visit my Ma," he said, not looking at her.

"Half-way to Scotland? On a Saturday morning? And there's only a single bed. No thanks."

"We could go to a hotel. Stay in Cambridge if you like."

She wavered while he kept his balance. He loved her. They would have a nice time. It was just that alone, with his mother, he could slop about with his shoes and socks off. Read the tabloids. Pick his nose.

"And what do I do there to pass the time?"

"In Cambridge?"

"No, fool. In your mother's house looking out at nothing and nothing looking in. All that silence as she sits and smiles."

"At least she never asks when we're getting married."

"Well, neither does mine."

"Your father does."

"Oh—does he? I'm surprised."

"Because he doesn't like me? You're right. He asks in order to smirk when I say not yet. You're too close to your aged P, dear, it's unhealthy."

She frowned and began to bustle about. He thought her tiny waist and neck miraculously beautiful. He'd have liked her in a silk kimono and little silk shoes. They'd been together six years and she was thirty-two and as rich as he was. She could stop work tomorrow and . . .

"Come on," she said. "We're at it again. I'm sorry. It's just the bloody *Isle of Wight*. They could have said: I'll come with you."

"And it's all right," she said, "I'll behave. I won't sulk. I won't go and lie down with a headache. I won't say 'Thanks, I'm fine' when she offers me another fish finger."

"I'll ring and tell her," said Oliver. "And I'll book a hotel for tomorrow night. Or you could go in the spare bed and I could have the sofa? OK, OK, I didn't mean it."

"Fine," he said ten minutes later. "I've booked the George at Stamford and I've told Ma. Turns out we couldn't have stayed with her anyway. She's got an old chum there."

"Oh no! She's going the same way as mine."

"No, he's all right. Sort of cousin. She fancies him. Family solicitor or something down in the West Country. Nice."

"Solicitor? Oh well then, we can't go. He'll be all over me. Oliver, let's get the Eurostar to Paris."

But he had had enough. "If you don't want to come, stay here. That's it. I shan't come back here if you won't come with me now."

She looked hard at him, thinking things over. He was big. And good. He was clever. He was loyal. He could be as ruthless as his mother. I don't like his mother, but I do like him.

"Coming then?" he asked on Saturday morning—he had slept on the sofa bed in the study. "Coming for a spin to see the Mater in the motor?"

"OK," she said. "Agreed. Can't wait to meet the family solicitor."

A LIGHT HOUSE

F ilth lay in the light, pale bedroom after a very long night's sleep, and opened his eyes upon the hat-boxes stacked now on top of a 1930s wardrobe with varnished panels of marquetry fruit and flowers and an Arts and Crafts iron latch. One hat-box, labelled *Marshal and Snelgrove*, and another, *Peter Robinson*, engaged him. He had known them somewhere else. A child's voice inside him cried out for someone to come and help him in some way. To come and love him. Explain some fear. Only she could help.

The name would not come. He tried to scream, but the scream wouldn't come. Terror took hold. He could not move. They were the wrong hat-boxes. The right hat-boxes had been battered and mouldy. He could hear the sea, the vile sea. He could hear Ma Didds coming. After breakfast she would beat him because he'd wet the bed. They all wet their beds.

There was a gentle tapping at the dqor and Filth felt about himself and he was dry. Oh, salvation, thank you God. Wonderful relief. Let her come. Let her come and look. She'd get him for something else today, but not for that. As she got Cumberledge almost every morning. Boiling the sheets in the copper, putting them on the line for all to see.

"Eight years old," she'd say.

"She's a bit afraid of me though," said eight-year-old Teddy Feathers. "Because I can pierce her with my gimlet eyes. One day I shall blind her," and he practised the look on the bedroom door. Claire came through it in her rose-pink dressing-gown.

She was carrying a huge cup and saucer painted with brown flowers and a primrose-coloured inside. In the other hand she carried a tipping silver sugar-basin with some silver sugar tongs sticking out.

"I can't do trays," she said. "And I can't remember about sugar. I do remember no milk."

She put the cup down on the bedside table. "Are you awake, Teddy? You look glazed." She moved some old dress-boxes from a chair and sat down. "I'm glad I insisted on a house with decent-sized bedrooms."

"A danger, I'd have thought," he said, relaxing, drinking the hot tea. "Open invitation. People arriving and demanding beds. Thinking you're a boarding-house. We keep—I keep—our spare bedrooms quiet."

"Oh? Why? I like company. I like open doors."

"Well, watch out for the window-cleaner." He was pleased to find yesterday's conversation totally in place, like yesterday's Court-hearing used to be.

"And the Vicar," he added.

"Oh, the Vicar is perfectly safe. He's slightly charismatic, or working at it, but he's sound on the *Gospels*. And I love women priests, too, don't you?"

"Not altogether," said Filth, "but there they are."

"No. I keep the spare bedroom at the ready, dear Teddy, not for the window-cleaner, despite his lovely hairy chest, nor for the fifty-thousand to one chance that the beloved of my childhood should turn up after twenty years in need of a bit of peace. No—I keep it for Oliver. And of course I have to have somewhere to do up my Christmas presents."

"Oliver?"

"Not that I send many now. Only about three apart from your handkerchiefs. But I like to be able to spread the wrapping paper out. And then there is the ironing . . ."

"Who is Oliver?"

She paused to regard with pity someone who did not know Oliver. When it comes to people's children, she thought, Teddy looks at emptiness.

"Oliver is my younger son. Your second cousin twice removed, or something of the sort. He has your eyes, and your height but he's beginning to run to fat. He's almost as clever and as handsome as you were." (And I hope you've left him some money, she thought.)

"Oh," said Filth, unconvincingly. "Yes, yes. Of course. A nice little chap. I remember."

"You haven't ever met him. He's nearly forty."

"Oh. Yes. I see. Betty and I were hopeless at all that."

"All what?"

"Genealogy."

"Yes. You were ahead of your time. Genealogy's over. It's a wise child now all right that knows its own father. You know, Teddy, the withering of the family tree is one of the saddest things ever. Who else can you turn to when you're old and sick without having to feel grateful?"

Filth, lying like a knight on a slab, holding his cup to his chest, swivelled his eyes at her.

"They don't marry any more," she said. "Surely you've noticed? It's over. Their children are unbaptised so there'll be no baptismal record. Our times will become dark as Romano-Britain."

"Genes not genealogy?"

"Exactly. I know you don't care for children . . ."

He drank the tea and waved the empty cup for her to take, sat up in bed and looked uneasily at the hat-boxes.

"The hat-boxes were your mother's," said Claire. "I've no idea how they got here."

"Anyway," she then said. "You will have to meet a thirty-six-year-old child today. Oliver's coming for the weekend with Vanessa."

"Vanessa?" (Which one was this?)

"Yes, Vanessa. She's his partner. She's at the Bar."

"Is Oliver at the Bar?"

"No, he's an accountant. *Vanessa*'s at the Bar. His partner."

Filth was about to say that at the Bar there are no partners, but lost confidence.

"They live together, Eddie dear. They 'co-habit.' They have 'co-habited' in Wandsworth for six years."

"In Wandsworth! They're not doing too well, then?"

"Wandsworth, dear Eddie, is now the crème-de-la of the Euro-chics."

"Rubbish. It's where all the taxi-drivers live."

"Not now. It's full of rich thirty-year-olds who owe thousands on their credit cards and go to Tuscany for their holidays but have never heard of Raphael."

"They sound particularly unattractive."

"Yes, they are. But they seem to have a very good time."

"And two of them are coming here? Look here, Claire, I'll be off. Can't have your boy arriving with nowhere to sleep."

"He's staying with Vanessa at the George at Stamford, so don't fuss. I've told them you will be here. They'd be mortified if they thought they'd pushed you out."

"I very much wonder if they would?"

"Don't wonder, Teddy, *learn*. You'll like Vanessa. You'll have so much to talk about. She's Inner Temple, like you. And nobody—" she said, taking the empty cup towards the door, looking kindly back at him, speaking of the only area in which she had been blinded for life, "—nobody, if I dare say so, could possibly dislike Oliver.

"And what they do all have nowadays—this isn't the sixties (I must give all these old things in the dress-boxes to Vanessa)—what they do have now, Eddie, when they come here, is perfect manners."

And so they bloody should, thought Eddie.

And it was afternoon and Filth was drinking tea again and Vanessa sat near his hammock on the wide, shaven lawn in front of the house, adding more hot water to the teapot from a silver thermos jug. There were small sandwiches. It was a warm late November and Claire's dahlias glowed and dripped with sunlight. The exposed garden, on a corner—High Light was an end-of-terrace site on a rise, like a Roman villa built over a hill fort—looked down and across at a shiny shallow lake where boats were moving about and children shouted. Beyond, straggled the town and, beyond that, droned the invisible motorway like bees in the warm afternoon.

Oliver had taken his mother out in his car for tea in Saffron Walden, a suggestion she had greeted with the luminous silence which was always followed by refusal.

"I've not been into the town for—"

"Oh, come on. You'll be fine."

(The black butterfly opened its wings.)

"It's no distance and we'll have the top down. It's a lovely day."

"*Not* on the motorway, Oliver."

"Of course not."

"I can't take the motorway. Not until I'm dead."

"What are you talking about?"

"The crem is on the motorway. I really don't care for it."

"Ma, would I take you to the crem?"

"Though I dare say you can get a cup of tea there," she said. "Darling, what if the doctor saw me as we pass the surgery?"

"We won't pass the surgery."

"I think we have to."

"Then we'll disguise ourselves."

"Oh, Oliver—what as?"

"Barristers. We'll borrow Vanessa's and old funny-face's wigs."

"I don't think they travel with their wigs."

"Well, get a big hat out of the spare room, and some dark glasses."

"I haven't enjoyed anything like this for years."

"Hold on to your hat."

"I will. I wore it at poor Babs's wedding. It must be thirty years old."

"Is Babs still alive?"

"What? Can't hear. Are you *sure* this isn't the motorway? *Oliver*! How dare you! This is Cambridge. It *was* the motorway."

They sat by the Cam and the low sun shone through the straps of the willows. Students called to each other and splashed about, or glided along. King's College Chapel reared up like a white cruise-liner on a grassy sea. "I've organised tea for us," he said. "Come on. It's not far."

She walked lightly beside him on the tow-path and over a bridge. Fat common people in tight clothes licked ice creams and ate oozing buns and shouted. Some, despite the season, had bare midriffs. Some looked at Claire's hat. She was enchanted.

"It's a shame so many young people are bald now," she said. "I wonder why? Is it Aids or this awful chemotherapy? I'm sure we never had either."

"It's the fashion, Ma."

"Oh, it can't be. That's dreadlocks."

"No, they're out. Or at any rate localised."

"Do they go over their pates every day like their chins? Will you be doing it, Oliver?"

"Ma, I'm nearly forty and I'm a chartered accountant."

"Yes, and you have lovely hair, Oliver. What is Vanessa's hair like—I mean, when she lets it grow?"

But they had reached Oliver's old, undistinguished college;

a door and a staircase of someone of distinction; a huge, gentle old man. Claire did not catch his name. He was expecting Oliver and was pleased to see them and he nodded at Claire and looked affectionately at her hat. They sat in a room with a tall window that seemed to let in little light and where mountains of books and furniture were deep in dust. They ate cinnamon scones. Other crumby plates lay about the room among the books and balled-up garments that suggested socks and what Claire thought of as woollies. What a peaceful quiet place. What a nice man. How nice for him to know Oliver.

"We thought we'd make for Evensong at King's," said Oliver. "Have we missed it, d'you think?"

"Oh, no. Still the same programme," and the old man began to talk about politics. "I am very fond of Oliver," he said as he stumbled along with them to the door of the chapel. They all said goodbye.

"Tired?" asked Oliver as they sat down in the choir stalls.

"Not in the least. Did he put on that performance just for us? I didn't know there were any left."

"Any what?"

"Eccentrics. Had you told him we were coming?"

"Yes, I rang him up. At the petrol station."

"From a call box?"

"From my handset."

"You keep his number?"

"No. I dialled directory enquiries."

"You are wonderful, Oliver."

"I am."

"The world is full of miracles," she said, "but I think you set it all up. There were computers and internets and e-mails hidden in all those books, and he was an actor who does E. M. Forster parts. I really loved him. Who was he?"

"Who's E. M. Forster? Anyway, he liked your hat. He was the Dean." Delighted with the day, the music, the chapel, he said, "You're a cynic, Ma. Go on—he fancied you. Have him over."

They stood for the *Nunc Dimittis*, and Oliver wondered what havoc Vanessa was wreaking on poor old Uncle Eddie.

"Have you always practised in Dorset?" asked Vanessa from her canvas chair.

"No, no. I returned there. Travelled a lot."

"That was rather good luck."

"Very good luck."

"You found some ex-pat clients? Over the years?"

"Not exactly ex-pats," he said. "The locals."

"I often think," she said (Vanessa was magnanimous to people who were no threat), "that to be a family solicitor, in any country, is to be the most useful person in the world. You have to be so subtle. And cleverer than any Barrister. Anyone can be a Barrister. The Bar finals are a joke, you know. Solicitors' finals," she said, "are a marathon by comparison."

"I believe so. So they always said. But it is so long ago."

She thought: He is quite unaware of me. He is Methuselah. Why do I care? He is so mysterious. I hadn't expected to be drawn to someone as old as this. Sad silence. He's so old he's almost gone, yet he's sharp—sharper than Oliver. I like his eyes. I wish he'd open them again.

The striped canvas hammock had come from Harrods—a present from Oliver to his mother, last birthday, like the huge, navy-blue sun-umbrella worked by rope pulleys, as for a yacht, supposed to be supported by a dollop of concrete that the window-cleaner and the gardener and the Vicar together had not been able to budge from where the van-man had dropped it by the gate. Claire had begun to grow trailing plants over this base and the umbrella, unwrapped but in cobwebs, was still propped in a corner of the car-less garage. Today Oliver had made an effort and had fixed up the hammock, just before lunch. It hung inside an outer wooden cradle, rather like a horse-jump at a gymkhana. There were no trees in Claire's garden and the hammock stood out in high display. Passers by along the avenue looked curiously at the old long person stretched out in it, fine nose pointed at the winter sky.

A rope hung beside the hammock ending in a baroque blue tassel.

"I could swing you if you like," Vanessa suggested, wondering at herself. She had refused Filth's offer of the hammock for herself as firmly as she always refused a seat from a man on the Underground. She often offered her own seat on the Underground to an older woman. Sometimes these older women refused, too, not feeling older. Great games are played on the Underground, she thought, the premier sport being that everyone avoids everyone else's eyes. Oh, how happy I am to have enough to think about. Work to do. How pleased I am to have mastered the pleasure—never acknowledged—when scanned, leaned against, breathed upon in the Underground by a man. I've got rid of that.

"Do you mind being stuck up here in the hammock in full view of Saffron Walden, Eddie?"

They had called him Eddie. And sometimes Teddy. They had not properly introduced him. They behaved as if she must know him. "Shall I give you a swing with the rope?"

"You sound like Mr. Pierrepoint," he said, without opening his eyes. "I don't feel exposed. No, not at all, thank you. No, I don't need to be rocked."

"Who is Mr. Pierrepoint?"

"I'm glad you can't remember. He was the hangman. His last hanging was of a woman, Ruth Ellis, who shot her unfaithful lover a few weeks after losing his baby and whilst her mind was disturbed."

"Oh yes, well, of course, I know about that. They buried her in quick-lime at Wormwood Scrubs prison, didn't they?"

"They did. Before you were born, but not long before, I think."

"I think," she said, pouring tea through Claire's Edwardian tea-strainer, "we have to forgive history a very great deal."

"I think," he said, "that we should forgive history almost nothing.

"I met the government hangman of Hong Kong," he said soon, a breeze over the dahlias, a breeze over the lake, the hammock gently moving. Hot, hot November. "Had a long talk with him. An Englishman. Not a bad man. Not at all sadistic. Just unimaginative and conformist. Common, ugly English man. A good husband, I believe."

"Hadn't two wives left Pierrepoint though?"

"Yes. Yes, there was that. I am glad of that."

"And he resigned after Ruth Ellis didn't he?"

"Yes. That was interesting."

"You've had a varied practice then, down in Dorset?"

"I told you, young woman, I *retired* to Dorset long ago. Away from the cut and thrust. The heat and dust."

At heat and dust something flickered in Vanessa's head. A novel? A film? Something to do with lawyers abroad? "Have you Oriental blood?" Filth asked.

"Certainly not, I come from Bournemouth."

"You remind me of someone with kind hands. You are very beautiful. How old are you?"

"I'm thirty-two."

"Did you have children? When you were young? You *must* have Oriental blood. Your age is not obvious."

"Well thanks, I'm sure. You'll be saying 'younger than she are married mothers made' next."

"Oh, I'm not interested in your past life."

"Well, I'm glad of that. You're not like my parents."

"What about Oliver?"

"Oh, he doesn't think about it. Never has. Marriage, kids. Good God, no!"

"Then he'll leave you," said Filth, closing his eyes.

"Let him. He'd miss me."

Filth said nothing.

"It's the way of the world now," she said. "It must be incomprehensible to your generation."

"Not entirely."

"It won't change back, you know. We meet, we part. Life is pretty long nowadays to be satisfied by a single sexual partner."

"And my lot will soon all be dead?" said Filth.

"Oh, of course I don't mean that—that your generation is without influence. No. *Personally*, I respect your generation. I respect your attachment to duty and the Law, your lifetime dedication. But we live so long now that there's time for three or four professions and partnerships. And we all have aides—"

"Yes, you have Aids," said Filth. "I don't know much of the technicalities of 'Aids' with small or upper case 'A.'"

"You see us, though—don't you—as negative?" she said. "Selfish? Everyone under, say, forty?"

"At the moment I feel it about everyone under a century but I dare say this will pass. My wife would have no patience with me."

"I'm sorry you've lost your wife. Was it long ago? I'd have enjoyed meeting her," said Vanessa kindly to the imagined Betty: the marmalade-maker, Bridge-player, no doubt church-flower arranger, and the grandchildren in the holidays. "Did you have many children?"

"We had no children."

Should she say she was sorry? Then she knew she was sorry. Sorry for him. The wife was probably—

"Sorry," she said.

"It was deliberate. Think carefully before you bring children into the world. Betty and I were what is called 'Empire orphans.' We were handed over to foster parents at four or five and didn't see our parents for at least four years. We had bad luck. Betty's foster parents didn't like her and mine—my father hadn't taken advice—were chosen because they were cheap. If you've not been loved as a child, you don't know how to love a child. You need prior knowledge. You can inflict pain through ignorance. I was not loved after the age of four and a half. Think of being a parent like that."

"Yes. I suppose."

"A parent like you, for instance, young woman. What child would want a parent like you?"

She was furious. "*I* was loved," she said. "I'm still loved by my parents, thank you very much. And I love them. We have difficulties, but it's normal family life."

"Then I made a mistake," he said, still not looking at her. "Maybe it's your hair. It is so thin. I'm sorry."

"My hair is a Sassoon cut and it cost one hundred pounds." She flung about with the cups and tea-tray and made to go off into the house.

"I have my career," she said. "I know it's what all women say, but it's true. It matters to me and to Oliver and to the economy of the country. I make a lot of money. I can have a child when I'm fifty."

"See if you do," he said. "I hope you don't. Children are cruel. They are wreckers of the soul. I hate children. I am a paedophobe. Betty knew we must not have a child because of the child I was myself. I would have damaged a child. I don't mean physically, of course."

(The old thing's deranged, she thought in the brightness of Claire's kitchen, washing up the lunch and the tea-cups. Whoever is he? Some sort of hypnotist? Thinks he's the Oracle. Why is he attractive? He scares me. And I damn well will have some children. When it suits me. *And* with Oliver. Or someone.)

She wrung out the dishcloth (no washing-up machine) and hung up the tea-towel. God, I'm behaving like a daughter-in-law. Oh Lord, here's Oliver and his Ma and Claire will say, Thank you dear, you shouldn't.

"Thank you dear, you shouldn't," said Claire thinking how fierce and snappish Vanessa looked. She's like a little black fox, she thought. What has Eddie been saying to her?

"Has it been very dull?" she asked.

"Not at all. I think he's asleep."

"Now we must think about supper. We have eight beautiful eggs."

Oliver saw Vanessa's face.

"No, Ma. Thanks a lot but Vanessa and I have booked a table at the George. You've enough on your hands with Eddie and, anyway, I want to put some flowers on Dad's grave on the way. OK? We'll be back after breakfast. I'll bring us all some lunch."

"Are you sure?" (Relief!)

"It's been quite a day for you."

"I suppose it has."

"OK, then. Off, Vanessa. Say goodbye to the Great Man for us, Ma, and don't let him keep you up half the night with sophistry."

"All he does is sleep," said Claire. "And I'm glad. It means he feels he knows us well. He just turned up," she told Vanessa. "After hundreds of years. His wife was a friend from way back. She died less than three weeks ago."

"Oh, *no*! Not three weeks!"

"Such a shock. She seemed set to live for ever."

"Oh, Oliver!"

"What?"

"You should have told me. I've been chatting on about—about marriage and how interminable it must seem!"

At the churchyard she was still angry. They walked up the path together, Oliver carrying flowers, Vanessa her laptop.

"Makes me look so *gauche*," she said. "So *insensitive*. You
are the strangest family. You tell people *nothing*. No, I'm not
helping to put flowers on your father's grave, I never met him."

"Go on into the church then. There's the famous marble
Gibbons."

"The what? I hate Culture."

"Three stars in all the guide-books. Known locally as The
Four Brass Monkeys."

"What is it?"

"Memorial to some great family, can't remember who.
Nobody can. Sort of marble pyramid of fruits and flowers and
cherubs weeping. Mum knew it when she was a child, too."

"How ghastly. Why monkeys?"

"Gibbons, sweetie. Surname of Grinling. They think he did
the drawings for it. Worth seeing. You can't help stroking it.
Bite the peaches. Pat the bottoms. It's never been vandalised.
It was our job to wash it when we were kids. Get in the cracks.
Took hours. Saturday mornings."

"You had a sensational childhood."

She pranced into the church through the self-sealing door
and Oliver fished about for a green tin vase with a spike that
his subconscious remembered would be behind the dead-
flower bin near the tap. He pushed the spike into the grass
above his father's head, arranged the flowers, stood up and
leaned against the headstone and took note of his father's name
and the space left for Claire's. He thought how much he'd like
to have a talk with his father. On the other hand he knew every
word of it.

"How d'you think your mother's looking?"

"Very well, Pa. You mustn't worry."

"Can't say I think she's looking well. I led her a dance, you
know."

"I know."

"Not coming home till dawn. She was always out looking for

me. As far as Stamford. Found me once hiding behind some dustbins. I thought she was the police. Old Contemptibles' Dinner, or something. Not the behaviour for a bank-manager. Marvellous woman."

"I'll bet she never cross-questioned?"

"No. Never."

"Mine grumbles. Cross-questions. Very cross questions!"

"What, this new one?"

"Well—we've been together six years. She's not new."

"Grumbles all the time, does she?"

"Well, criticises mostly. It's her job. Analysis of motives, then development and execution."

"Sounds like Eddie, dry old stick."

"Yes. A lawyer. And a 'new woman.'"

"Ah, your mother couldn't be labelled. Result of that childhood."

"Ma's pretty much all right," he said. "You *can* bury your childhood. Not that I want to."

God, but I miss him, he thought, and watched Vanessa marching forward from the church, hopping the graves, laptop tightly clutched.

"There's a boy in there dressed up as a Vicar and he came up and asked if I wanted him to hear my confession. And I swear—I swear—he looked me over to see if I was pregnant."

At the George they went straight in to dinner, Vanessa first twirling off her shirt to reveal a black silk camisole beneath, the size of a handkerchief. Her sloping white shoulders and tiny white neck against the panelling turned heads. Claret. Roast beef carved from the silver dome. Vanessa shone and talked, oblivious. The waiters admired. She nattered on about the Vicar and the marble babies crying and holding shields against their private parts. It hadn't seemed a Christian monument to her, three stars or not.

"Did you say so?"

"Yes, I did. And I told him I had nothing to confess and he

said, "My child, then you are in a bad way." I nearly socked him. What are these people *doing* in the church now, Oliver?"

"He sounds a bit of a throw back to me. You don't see them now in the church at all. It's a rare sighting, a clergyman in a church, out of hours."

"I think he hides in there all day, and then he pounces. He sees guilt all the time. He's a monster."

"He's a friend of Ma. She likes him."

"Oh no! Then that's it."

"That's what?"

"She'll want him to marry us."

"What did you say?" They were in their grand bedroom after the coffee and the crème brûlée, both of them happy with wine. "Marry us?"

But she was somewhere else now. "Oliver, what room is this? It's the bridal suite. Look at the hangings, and the drapes. It's obscene. And whatever is it costing us?"

"A hundred and fifty pounds—so what? It was all they had left."

"But we could have gone to a B&B. We're supposed to be going to Thailand."

"We can afford it."

"Well, you might have asked me first. Oh, well. Never mind," and she took off her handkerchief top and cast off the rest of her clothes. She lifted her legs high in the air. "Haven't I wonderful feet?" she said.

(God, Oliver remembered, I forgot to bring any condoms.)

"OK," she said. "Pass my purse."

"Why?"

"I'll give you my half of the hundred and fifty pounds."

"No. Let me do this one," he said. "I let you in for it. Only young once."

Remembering the old fossil who'd thought she was past the

age of childbearing, she said, "Why are you still in your clothes?"

When they went back to Oliver's mother the following morning Vanessa was surprised to find how disappointed she was that the old chap was no longer there. The hammock, which had stood out all night in the dew, now hung empty and Claire, still in her dressing-gown, was standing looking at it.

"Yes," she said. "He's gone. I couldn't keep him, although it's Sunday and he'll have a terrible journey. He asked me to say goodbye to you. Now I do hope" (untruthfully) "that you'll stay for lunch?"

"Yes, we've brought it," said Oliver, smiling about. "Supermarket."

"We'll have to stay, anyway," said Vanessa, "until Oliver's taken the hammock down. And what about that umbrella business in the garage? I said it was too big when he bought it. Shall we get it changed for you?"

Claire blinked. "How very kind of you. As a matter of fact the church could do with it. For fêtes."

(Oh, Ma—oh, Ma! Don't push her.) Oliver started to fling things out of bags and into the microwave. (Keep it cool. Keep off the Vicar!)

"I met your Vicar yesterday," said Vanessa.

"I'm afraid he's all over the place," said Claire.

They eyed each other.

"Oh, and by the way," said Claire, when they began to go. "Would you take this parcel with you? I think it's only recipe books. Eddie wanted me to have them. His wife's. She never used them. I don't want them. They were meant for someone else. Betty was a dreadful cook, so they won't be thrilling, but they'd be her mother's. Quite historic. Old Raj puddings from Shanghai. Tapioca."

"Ma, I'll put them in the bin."

"No," said Vanessa, "I'd like them. Thanks."

And back again in Wandsworth where it was dark and the velvet curtains shrouded the windows with Interior Designer bobbles—I'm not sure I like Victorian stuff any more, thought Oliver—rain had begun to fall. "I think we're getting stuck in the nineties," he called through to the kitchen where Vanessa was scuffling about. "You know, we could get a manor house in Yorkshire for this. Commute from York. What's happening?"

"The recipe books," she called back. "But it's not recipe books, it's a box. It has gold clasps on it, and a drawer in it and—oh, good God."

Out of the box showered jewels. Gold chains, brooches, earrings. They glimmered on the kitchen table.

"Look!" she said. "Look at the jade! Look at these blue things. Look—look at this!" Out of a plush bag fell a magnificent rope of pearls. "Oliver! These aren't recipe books. Here's a note."

> Dear Claire [it said], I've given the recipe books to Babs. Betty wanted you to have the trinkets. They'll need cleaning and restringing and so on. Some of them she hadn't worn for years. But they're very much the real thing. The pearls were given to me long ago. Eddie.

"But I can't have these. I can't possibly keep them. There's thousands of pounds here. Thousands! Look—Aspreys 1940! Look at this jade ring—it's like an egg! Oliver!"

"I'll ring mother."

"She's delighted," he came back saying, "and you're to keep them."

"Did she say singular or plural 'you'?"

"Shall I ask her?"

"Not yet. Let me think. No—I don't have to think. I won't have them. They'll think that's why I married you."

"Come on," he said. "It's not going to be in the papers. Nobody's to know we've got them but me."

"I never wear jewellery." She stroked the gold adoringly, the jade ring.

"You could change."

"I *never* change. Was that old Eddie out in the East a lot, Ollie? Oh—Ollie!" She had seen the signature on the note and the letter-heading, for frugal Filth was still using up his old Chambers writing paper. "It says here, *Sir Edward Feathers*."

"Yes. That's him. Cousin Ed. Ridiculous name."

"But Oliver, Edward Feathers is Old Filth."

"I hope not."

"Oliver, *Old Filth* is a legend. At the Bar. I thought he'd died years ago. He was a *wonderful* advocate. He had a stammer."

"A stammer? Yes, well, Eddie does sometimes make odd noises."

"Oliver—it was *Old Filth*. Of Hong Kong. And he became a wonderful judge," and she began to moan.

"What's so dreadful?"

"I told him all about the Bar. And how easy it was to pass the Bar exams. And I asked him if he'd always practised in Dorset. Oh, Oliver!"

"Vannie, I have never seen you so discomposed."

"I want to die."

"Will you marry me?"

"Yes, of course. But, oh, *Oliver*!"

Filth was invited to the wedding six months later but could not remember Vanessa and could not think whom he knew in Bournemouth. The groom's name rang no bell. Some relative? Was he Claire's? But he refused the invitation. Claire, true to form (and because she had not been told of Betty's funeral), did not get in touch. She attended the wedding, the Vicar driving her. He did not officiate but enjoyed the fun and talked about sin to Vanessa's mother. Babs turned up with her hair short and blood-red. She and the Vicar got on famously and danced the night away.

And Claire waved the pair off to Thailand, hoping the baby wouldn't be born there, though they can do wonders with premature babies now.

Vanessa gave Claire the rope of pearls she'd worn to the altar to look after until she returned.

Claire took care of her heart to be sure of seeing the grandchild.

She wrote to tell Filth of the birth three months later. Edward, they were calling him. Edward George.

Thus is the world peopled.

PART TWO

SCENE: INNER TEMPLE

The smoking-room of the Inner Temple, almost deserted.
It is much re-furbished: easy chairs stand about.
Portraits of distinguished former Benchers on the walls,
the one of Mr. Attlee gaunt and glazed—seeming to be wring-
ing his hands. One wing chair has its back to the rest and Mr.
Attlee seems to be looking down at it. Filth is in the chair half-
asleep. Post-prandial. No one can see him. Enter the Queen's
Remembrancer and the Purveyor of Seals and Ordinances.

The Queen's Remembrancer: He must have gone.
The Purveyor of Seals and Ordinances: To get his hair cut?
QR: Possibly. Very great surprise to see him again.
PS&O: Looks well. Amazing physique still. Nothing ever been
        wrong with him.
QR: Nothing ever did go wrong for him.
PS&O: Nothing much ever happened to him. Except success.
QR: There's talk of a rather mysterious War, you know.
        Didn't fight.
PS&O: A conchie?
QR: Good God, no. Some crack-up. He had a stammer.
PS&O: Pretty brave to go on to the Bar then.
QR: Remarkable. He joined a good regiment. It's in *Who's*
        Who. The Gloucesters. He had something to do with
        the Royal family.
PS&O: *Had* he indeed!
QR: And there was something else. Someone gave him a

push upstairs somewhere. Or out East. There's always something a bit dicey about that circuit. A lot of people you can't really know socially but you have to pretend to.

PS&O: Betty was very O.K. though. Don't you think? Don't you think? There was of course Veneering. Veneering and Betty. Aha!

QR: What do the likes of us know, creeping round the Woolsack at Home and round the Inns of Court?

PS&O: "What should they know of England
Who only England know."

QR: Kipling. You know Kipling had a start like Filth? Torn from his family at five. Raj Orphan.

PS&O: Kipling didn't do too badly either.

QR: Kipling had a crack-up.

PS&O: Did he stammer?

QR: He went blind. Half blind at seven. Hated the Empire, you know. Psychological blindness.

PS&O: Are you having coffee?

QR: No. I just came in looking for Filth. Just missed him.

PS&O: Did we imagine him?

QR: I expect he was having his last look round.

Exeunt. Room apparently empty.

Filth rises from the chair and takes a long last look at Mr. Attlee.

Filth: Have I the courage to write my Memoirs?

Attlee: Churchill had. But on the whole, better not. Keep your secrets.

The Watch

In that train of 1941, after the Oxford interview, Eddie had pushed the *Times* back into the hands of the man opposite, left the compartment and walked down the corridor where he stood holding tight the brass rail along the middle of the window. The train stopped very often, filled up. The corridor became crammed with people mostly silently enduring, shoulder to shoulder. Even so it was cold. Water from somewhere trickled about his feet. Troops started to climb in—maybe around Birmingham. These troops were morose and quiet. Still and silent. Everyone squashed up tighter. It grew dark. Only the blue pin-lights on all the death-mask faces.

And Eddie stood on.

At some point he left the train and waited for another one that would take him to the nearest station to High House, and there he jumped down upon an empty, late-night platform. After an unknown space of time he found that he was travelling in a newspaper-van that must have stopped to give him a lift. It dropped him outside the gates of the avenue which were closed and guarded by two sentries with rifles. He walked off down the lane, then doubled back through a hedge, then across in the darkness to the graceful iron railings of what he felt to be his home.

The house stood there with lightless, blindless windows and the dark glass flashed black. The place was empty. But there were army vehicles everywhere in the drive and a complex of army huts where the land began to drop away above the chimneys of the old carpet factory. Eddie walked round the resting, deserted house and met nobody. He began to try the familiar door handles: the side door from the passage into the garden with its dimpled brass knob; the door to the stables; the kitchens. All were locked. He grew bolder and stood beneath a bedroom window and called, "Mrs. Ingoldby? Is anyone there? It's Eddie." He rattled the door of the bothy where the gardener had lived. Nothing. No dog barked. In the garage, there was no old car, the car in which you had to put up an umbrella in the back seat when it rained. The Colonel's vegetables stood scant and scruffy, Brussels sprouts like Passchendaele. The beehives had disappeared.

He set off on foot back to the railway station; slept the rest of the night on a bench along the wall of the waiting room with its empty grate; reached his aunts' warm house by the following lunchtime.

There was no car outside it and so "Les Girls," as they liked to be known, were not at home, but Eddie had his key and planted his bag and his icy feet on the rug in the hall. He stood.

He heard Alice, the midget maid, creeping up from the kitchen. She gave a chirp of surprise, touching her fingers to her lips, and Eddie remembered he'd slept in his clothes, wet through since Oxford, and was unshaven. He found—with the old terror—that he couldn't speak.

"Mr. Eddie. Come, come, come," she said and led him down to her kitchen and gave him tea and porridge which he could not eat. "Oh dear, oh dear, oh dear," she said. "Have you failed your exams?" She had been sitting beneath her calendar of the King and Queen and the photograph of Mr. Churchill in his siren-suit, making more paper spills for the upstairs fireplace. Vegetables were prepared on the draining-board, the kitchen clean, alive and shining. "Oh dear, oh dear. I expect you have heard the news."

"Yes. I read it in the paper."

She seemed puzzled, and he remembered that nobody in this house cared a fig about the Ingoldbys.

"I'm meaning their news, Mr. Eddie. Miss Hilda's and Miss Muriel's. I don't know what's to become of us all now. Or this house. Or you and me, Mr. Eddie. Mind, I'd seen it coming. There's been talk for years. They think I'm deaf. They never told me a thing, never warned me. I've been here nearly twenty years. It was little to expect."

"They've never sacked you, Alice?"

"In a sense, yes, Mr. Eddie."

The slam of the front door above. The clash of the vestibule glass. The shriek of Hilda spotting the bag in the hall. "He's back. See? Now for it—Eddie? Where are you?"

"Yes. I'm back." His head rose up from Alice's cellar rabbit-hole, and he saw that the eyes of the girls were particularly wild. He thought: They must have won a cup. "Have you been on the course?" Then he saw they were wearing Air Force blue with several stripes. Not golf.

"We have some news for you," said Muriel. "Better get it over and tell you right off. We're getting married."

For a dizzy moment Eddie thought they were marrying each other.

"You'll easily guess who," said Hilda, and mentioned two names from among the red faces at the golf club.

"Married!"

He thought: Whatever for? Old women. Over forty. And this great house full of their stuff. And Alice.

"Go and wash, Eddie dear. Then come and have some champagne. It's been on the cards for years but of course we couldn't split up and leave you until we'd got you off our hands."

He looked at their untouchable hands.

"But you mean you'll be living apart now?"

"Oh, quite near each other. And near Royal St. Andrews. In Scotland. All four of us."

"Does my father know?"

"We've written. He's known for several years that we—well, we put off our plans. For you. That's why he's been so generous to us while you've been living here all these years."

"Living here?"

"Yes. Ever since you were a tiny."

When he came downstairs again Alice was anxiously laying up the dining-table. The silver and glasses shone. When she saw him she scuttled out of sight.

"What about Alice?"

"Oh, she's much too old to move in with either of us. Someone else will probably take her. She's got her Girls' Friendly Society. And she's over seventy and pretty well" (Hilda whispered like a whistle) "*past it*. She *ought* to retire. So it all fits in."

"*Fits in*?"

"Alice retiring. You going out to Alistair as an evacuee. And this tragedy of the Ingoldbys."

"Yes," he said. "I know. I saw it in the *Times*. I'm surprised you did. Or that you even remembered—their name." (Tears, tears, stop. And, bugger it, my voice is going.)

"Of course we remembered. They used to have you over there. Very kind to help us out. Anyway, someone rang up."

"Someone? Who? Please, *who*?"

"I'm afraid I didn't ask. It was a girl. Quite a young voice. Yes, Isobel. Isobel Ingoldby. That would be a sister? Rather snooty we thought. La-di-da."

"Did she leave a number?"

"No, no. Very quick she was. Now dear, no brooding. Let's talk about you. And Singapore."

"It's Singapore you're going to," said Hilda. "Alistair'll meet you there. Safest place in the world."

"Did you pass your exams?" asked Muriel.

"Yes."

"Jolly good. Something to look forward to after the War. Your tickets are all fixed up and you leave next week."

"And bottoms up," said Muriel, with the champagne. "Here's to all of us."

"And we have a present for you," said Hilda. "He said you were to have it when you left school. We've kept it for you. It's your father's watch."

To Colombo

After a torrid and joyless Christmas with the brides- and grooms-to-be—gravy and turkey from somewhere and gin galore—Eddie was ready for the voyage to his father. He'd given ten pounds to Alice and promised her a postcard. He would have given wedding presents to Les Girls, but would have had to ask them for the money. He had only the money for the journey to Londonderry to pick up his ship; that and his Post Office Book with fifteen shillings in it and a new cheque book he didn't know how to use.

The day dawned. The vestibule door slammed behind him and his luggage was in the car, the watch on his wrist.

Both brides had *genuinely* (they said) intended to see him off from Liverpool—the journey from Bolton was short—and had dressed for it in excellent pre-War mufti of tweed and diamond-pin brooches, uniforms set aside; but at the last minute Hilda was called away by her beau to discuss some marital arrangement, and Muriel drove Eddie to the dock alone. There they got out of the car, she landed him a smacking kiss, said how she envied him a wonderful voyage into the sunshine and out of the War—

"Aunt Muriel—?"

—and how they would *miss* him, and how she was looking forward to seeing him in Oxford after the War—

"Aunt Muriel, I'm sorry—"

"Yes?"

"It's just that I have no money."

"Dear boy, you're going to have plenty of money. You'll have all that we are having to give up, now that you're gone. Your allowance."

"Yes. But I mean for now. I've only about a pound."

"You won't need money on board ship."

"Something might go wrong. We might be stuck half-way."

"Oh, Eddie—what a fusspot. Alistair's meeting you."

"I'm not sure how long—"

"Well, *I* don't know. I don't know that I've much with me. Would five pounds—?"

"I think I shall need perhaps a bit more."

She scratched in her purse and came up with seven pounds, twelve shillings and sixpence.

"There," she said, "you've cleaned me out."

Then she was gone, dropping from his life unlamented and unloved. He felt shaken and depressed, as if another boy, a sunny, golfing chap, would have done better.

She tooted her horn at the harbour barrier. The clashing and hooting, the crowd at the ferry. He saw her big amiable face as she turned the corner.

The ferry was no trouble. The sea, hatefully grey, was thank God calm. He stood at the rail watching the submarines of the English Navy busy in the Irish Sea practising the sinking of U-Boats. The West coast of England dwindled behind him.

There were tickets in code on his suitcase, and someone beside him watching the U-Boat exercises said, "You'll find plenty of them things if you's away over the water. Stiff with U-Boats."

On the train towards Londonderry—blank scenery—the idea occurred to him that he should have roused himself to take an interest in what lay ahead. He did not even know the length of the journey. Then it all slid away. He wondered languidly if he'd even find his ship.

But somehow here he was at the dock of a huge bay and some sort of official had his name on a list.

"Travelling alone? No group? Don't think we'll tie a label on you" (Eddie towered over him). "All plain sailing up to now?"

"Yes thanks."

"But no more plain sailing for a while. The convoy's not ready. She'll be in harbour at least three weeks."

"Three *weeks*?"

"Yes. Here's your billet address. Don't worry, we won't forget you. Can you get there by yourself or do you want a school bus?"

"I'll find it. I've left school."

The man looked at him curiously as he turned away.

"What's the bus fare?" he called, but the man was gone.

He found the bus, and the journey was not very expensive and he got out in green mild country to the West of the city and saw that he was to be on a farm where a maidservant greeted him and brought him a glass of buttermilk. He was at present the only lodger.

"Evacuees comes and goes," she said. "Poor little souls, crying and that, and hung with tickets. See *me* letting a bairn go where there's none it knows. Who's sending yous off, then? You's old for an evacuee. Or is yous home abroad then? Or is yous not for fighting?"

He hated her.

He walked in the fields, helped on the farm. The empty days followed each other. Time stood still. When the servant girl—she smelled of earth and corn and her eyes were aching and knowing—passed behind his chair at dinner with the tatey stew and the heavy suet puddings she leaned very close over him. Sometimes she ran her warm hands through his hair. One night she came to his room and tried to get into his bed, but he was terrified and threw her out.

Then, after a week and still no ship, he found himself looking for her and when she came over the fields with the buttermilk his heart began to beat so loud he blushed.

"Is there no letters you should be writing? Is there nobody should know?"

He felt her kindness and that night wrote, on scented paper she gave him from her bedroom drawer, to his school. He told them about Oxford and that his aunts had despatched him to Singapore. He thanked old Oils who'd taught him history and asked him to tell Oxford how he'd been powerless to stay and would be back as soon as ever he could. He could not write to Oxford himself. He was too wretched. He felt weak, guilty, a schoolboy, a pathetic child again. And he couldn't tell Oxford where to reply.

Then he wrote to Sir, but could find nothing to say that mattered. In neither of his letters did he mention Pat Ingoldby. His weakness and self-loathing numbed him. He began to stammer again, and so stopped talking. When he woke one night in his white clean bed, the room full of moonlight, the old closet, the bare floor, the ewer and wash-basin and soap dish on the marble washstand, the pure whiteness of his towel for morning, he turned to the girl and let her do what she wanted.

Which he found was what he wanted. And she made it easy. The next night he was waiting for her and took control. "You's wonderful," she said and he said, "Well, I'm good at games," and she laughed into the pillow. He had a feeling that the farmer and his wife knew. The next night she didn't come. He was desolate. Desperate. "Where were you?" he said next day, but she stared and went out to do the dairy. She was in his room that night again but he did not enjoy it. As she washed in the soft soapy water in his bowl she said, "How much money is yous going to give me?" and when he said he only had a few pounds she didn't believe him. "All right then—you can give us yous watch."

He said, "Never. It was my father's."

At breakfast there was a message brought by a farm boy that his ship was near to sailing. He packed and was at the bus stop without breakfast, leaving a shilling on his bedroom mantelpiece. The leaving of the shilling pleased him. A man who knows the rules. A Christ Church man. A man of the world. The buttermilk girl had disappeared.

And when he reached the dock this time, he felt jaunty and no longer worried that he'd be herded into a group of small children and weeping parents. He presented his papers to an office on the quay. A whole fleet now lay at anchor. A mammoth fish tank of troop-ships, battle-cruisers, destroyers, freighters, cargo boats, awaiting release.

An old-time tar spat over the rail of his own ship.

"Is this the *Breath o'Dunoon*?"

"It is, so. Step aboard."

"Am I the only one?—the only evacuee?"

"Not at all, there's one other. He's below."

Eddie clambered with his case down three metal ladders into smelly darkness and walked along a narrow passage that dipped towards the middle. It was way below the water line. Les Girls had not been interested in classes of cabin on the *Breath o'Dunoon*.

Nobody was to be seen. The sound of the sea slopped about. There was a dry, clicking noise coming from behind a cabin door.

He opened the door and found two bunks at right angles to each other, so narrow that they looked like shelves, each covered with a grey blanket. On the better bunk, seated cross-legged, was a boy, busy with a pack of cards. One of his very small hands he held high in the air above his head, the other cupped in his lap, and between the two, arrested in mid-air, hung an arc of coloured playing cards, held beautifully in space. As Eddie watched, the arc collapsed with lovely precision and became a solid pack again in the cupped hand.

"OK, how's that?" said the boy. "Find the lady."

He was an Oriental and appeared to be about ten-years old. His body, however, seemed to have been borrowed to fit the cabin and was that of a child of six. The crossed legs looked very short, the feet dainty. The features, when you looked carefully, were interesting for they were not Chinese though the eyes were narrow and tilted. He was not Indian and certainly not Malay. After thirteen years, Eddie still knew a Malay. The boy's skin was not ivory or the so-called "yellow" but robust and ruddy red.

"OK then," said the boy, "don't find the lady. Just pick a card. Any card. OK?"

"I have to settle in."

"You'll have months for that. We're in this rat hole for twelve weeks."

"*What*! I hope not. I'm only going to Singapore."

"Me too. Via Sierra Leone. Didn't you know? We change ship at Freetown, if one turns up. Choose a card."

Eddie sat on the other end of the bunk.

"Go on. Pick a card. No, don't show me. Very good. Nine of diamonds. Right?"

It was the nine of diamonds.

"Are you some sort of professional?"

"Professional what?"

"Card-sharp."

"Yes," said the boy. "You could look at it that way. I'm Albert Loss. I'd be Albert Ross—I have Scottish blood—but I can't say my Rs, being also Hakka Chinese. Right?"

"Why can't *other* people call you Albert Ross?"

"You can, if you want. They did at school. And they called me Coleridge. 'Albat Ross.' Right? *Ancient Mariner*. They like having me on board ships, sailors. Albatrosses bring them luck."

"Are you a professional sailor, too?"

"I've been around," said Loss. "D'you play Crib?"

"No."

"I'll teach you Crib."

"Are there going to be some more of us on the ship?"

"More what?"

"Well—" (with shame) "—evacuees."

"No idea. I think it's just the pair of us. OK? Pick another card."

"I'm going back on deck," said Eddie.

"OK. I'll come with you. Watch them loading. It's corned beef. We unload at Freetown and she'll sail full of bananas."

"Bananas? To the Far East?"

"Don't be stupid. We change ship at Freetown, hang about. The *bananas* get taken Home by the *Breath o'Dunoon* for the Black Market and the Commandos."

"I've not seen any bananas in three years."

"Well, you're not in the know. You can eat plenty in Freetown. Flat on your back. Nothing moves in Freetown. There's RAF there, and they've all gone mad. Talking to monkeys. Mating with monkeys."

"How do you know all this?"

"Common knowledge. I've done this trip before. Often."

"How old are you?"

The boy looked outraged. Eddie saw the long eyes go cold. Then soft and sad. "That's a question I don't often answer, but I'll tell you. I'm fourteen," and he took from his pocket a black cigarette with a gold tip, and lit it.

Thirty-six hours later there were signs that the huge herd of ships might be thinking of sailing. Eddie asked again if they were the only passengers.

"Four months. Just you and I."

"I suppose so." Loss spat black shag at the seagulls. "Shag

to shags," he said. "I am also rather witty. I'm a master of languages as well. I could teach you Malay."

"I speak Malay," said Eddie. "I was born there."

"Mandarin, then? Hindi. All one. Nice watch."

"It was my father's."

Days, it seemed, later they saw the last of Ireland sink into the sea. The prow of the ship seemed to be seeking the sunset, such as it was, rainy and pale. Great grey sea-coloured ships like lead pencils stood about the ocean and smaller brisker ships nosed about them. The *Breath o'Dunoon* looked like a tramp at a ball. The Atlantic lay still beneath its skin.

"We're in a convoy."

"Well, of course, we're in a convoy," said Loss. "We can't go sailing off to Africa alone. We're not a fishing boat. It's a widespread War.

"Mind you," he added, "we'd probably get there faster if we were a fishing boat. The convoy always goes the speed of the slowest ship. And we're headed out to the West for days on end, to get clear of the U-Boats. Nearly to America, zig-zagging all the way.

"Am I right?" he condescendingly enquired of the Captain at whose none too clean table they were dining. The Captain ignored him and spooned up treacle pudding.

"Is that all we're going to do all the time? I've brought no books. I thought it would be just a few days."

"You can do the cooking if you like," said the Engineer Officer. "You couldn't do worse than this duff. It's made of lead shot. Can you cook, Mr. Feathers?"

"No, not at all."

"I can cook," said Loss, "but only French cuisine."

"You can both peel spuds," said the Captain, "but remember to take that watch off, Feathers."

"And keep it away from *him*," said the Engineer Officer, pointing at Loss. "Ask me, he's escaped from a reformatory school for delinquents."

"It was Eton," said Loss. "I was about to go to Eton. Do you play Crib?"

"Not now," said the Sparks, "but I'll thrash you when I do."

They left the rickety *Breath o'Dunoon* at Freetown for a blazing beach where the air throbbed like petrol fumes. The jungle hung black. Black people were immobile under palm trees. Nobody seemed to know what should happen next. After a shabby attempt at examination by the customs, where interest was taken in the watch, the two of them stood about, waiting for instructions. There were none. The crew of the *Breath o'Dunoon* were taking their ease before the unloading of the cans of meat, and the Captain had disappeared. There was a suggestion that they should give up their passports which they ignored.

Heat such as Eddie had never known blasted land and sea. The smell of Africa was like chloroform. Inland from the port were dancing-hot tin sheds, one with a red cross on it, asphalt, some apologies for shops, and RAF personnel in vests and shorts. More black people stood about in the shadows beneath the trees.

Beyond the white strip of beach the mango forests began and Albert Loss sat down neatly under a palm tree and ate one, first peeling off the skin with a little knife from his pocket, then sucking. He took out a notebook and began to make calculations. Eddie ate bananas and thought about the buttermilk girl, with some satisfaction.

He watched the rollers of the Atlantic. "I think I'll bathe," he said. "Get rid of the banana juice." He licked his fingers and ran down to the sea and was immediately flung back on the beach. He tried again and was again spat out. He lay with a ricked back and a badly grazed knee as the waves slopped over him with contempt.

"The sun's dangerous," Loss announced from the edge of the jungle.

But Eddie, exalted to be free, warm, deflowered and full of bananas, lay on in the sand. The dangerous part of the journey was over. They had seen no U-Boats, and there would be none on the next ship for they were out of range now. They were taking the Long Route down Africa to the Cape, and out to Colombo to refuel. Then Singapore and safety. And the next ship might be better. Even comfortable. A Sunderland flying boat suddenly roared from beyond the mangoes and came towards him along the sea, bouncing like a loose parcel chucked from hand to hand. It blundered to an uncertain lopsided stop some way out. Bloody planes, thought Eddie. I want to sleep. He was sated, different—happy.

"How many bananas have you eaten?" asked Loss.

"Thirty-six."

"You are intemperate. I wouldn't have thought it."

"They're miniature bananas. They're nothing."

"They're very over-ripe. Where did you get them?"

"Off a heap. Under a tree. Any objection?"

Loss watched him.

"No. I am glad you have some powers of enjoyment. D'you want a game of Patience?"

"It's about a hundred and five degrees. I want a beer."

Eddie stumbled up the beach, to a stall under the trees where a massive lady in orange appeared to be in a trance but took his English money into her pink palm.

"You've left your watch lying on the sand," called Loss.

"Look after it," Eddie shouted. "D'you want a beer?"

"Certainly not. Not that stuff. And don't touch the bottled water. I've been here before."

Eddie lay back in the sand and went to sleep.

Waking he felt about him, sat up and began to swig from a dark bottle. His head began to swim deliciously. He lifted his legs in the air. Loss observed him.

"You are behaving quite out of character," he said. "I have known you six weeks, but I know this to be out of character."

"I like this character."

"I am amazed. You have a rational mind."

"I've slept with a woman," said Eddie. "Yippee."

Loss chose not to comment.

After a pause for thought Eddie said, "Have you been here before?"

"Somewhere like it. Down the coast."

"Oh, I've been somewhere *like* it. Plenty of this. Worse."

"When?"

"When I was five. When I came over to England with a missionary. Auntie May, she was called. To live in England on my own."

"On your own?"

"No. With a woman called Ma Didds. Professional foster mother. Me and two vague cousins I'd never heard of. It wasn't safe for Raj brats to stay in Malaya. We died off after five. And before five in hundreds. I felt pretty well in the East but I hadn't a say in the matter. 'Terrible for the parents,' everyone says but I hadn't a mother and my father lived in a world of his own. Anyway, all Raj Orphans forgot their parents. Some of them attached themselves to the foster parents for life."

"Not you?"

"No."

"Where did you go?"

"Wales. It was Wales or Norfolk. Wales was cheaper."

Suddenly he knew that it must have been his aunts who had chosen it. "What about you, Loss?"

"Something of a mystery, my parents. They didn't send me

to England until I was ten. And they didn't call it 'Home.' They weren't Raj."

"What did you do in the holidays?"

"Oh, I always went to Singapore."

"You couldn't have done. There wasn't time."

Loss continued to play Patience with a cloth over his head.

"Well," he said vaguely. "I got humped about. I am a natural traveller. We are of Hakkar stock."

"So you keep telling me. Were there many Hakkars going to Eton?"

"I beseech you, Feathers. You may have found your tongue at last and it is all very interesting, but do not drink any more of the beer. And leave off the bananas."

"Why?"

"I shall have to look after you. I can see the fruit moving. It will be a humiliation."

"For me or for you?" shouted Eddie, tight as a tick, flat on his back, feet in the air, peeling a thirty-seventh banana.

"Both of us," said Loss. "Here. Cover yourself. Here is your shirt. You are calling attention to us."

"Not true," yelled Eddie. "They're all drunk here. Look at the beer cans everywhere. Or they're drugged—look at them all just standing staring. All des-o-late. All the best ones dead. We're going to lose this War so we may as well drink and die."

Another flying boat split the air with sound. "Bundle of spare parts," shouted Eddie. "Won't make it back. Torpedo boats bang bang—down. England won't last six months against Germany. Churchill's a buffoon. Ham actor. Country's finished. Europe's finished. Thank God I'm going away."

Someone from the Red Cross hut came down the beach and took him off, Loss walking thoughtfully behind.

Eddie, put to bed, raved for three days. Loss moved into the Missions to Seamen and watched a scorpion hanging from a rafter, ate mangoes and played cards with anyone who would give him a game.

The Missions to Seamen medical man was troubled by Eddie. "How old is he?" he asked Loss. "Your friend. The other evacuee—a schoolfriend?"

"I am not an evacuee," said Loss. "I am travelling home to pursue my life. Feathers is a young friend of mine, no; for I only met him on the *Breath o'Dunoon*. He is an unwilling evacuee. His father sent for him to return to Malaya. He wanted to stay and Do His Bit."

"Did he? Well, now he's yelling and ranting about dead pilots and the Battle of Britain."

"That's over," said Loss. "I expect he's lost best friends. There are those with best friends. I avoid such. He'll be OK. He needed to blow up."

The doctor looked dubious.

But by the time the Portuguese freighter arrived a fortnight later to carry them on, a gaunt, monosyllabic (but not stammering) Feathers was allowed to continue his journey.

"He's strong," said the Purser. "There's those get malaria soon as they get to Freetown. He's not had that. There's blackwater fever if you so much as look at the swamp. He's not had that. Just the guts. The guts and the brains. He'll recover."

"He drank palm-beer from a bad bottle," said Loss, tightlipped as a Methodist.

"Maybe, lad, it saved his life." The Purser was the only Englishman on the new ship, and spoke Portuguese. He had avoided the call-up, he said, because of flat feet. "I dare say the bugger'll live," he said. "He's walking."

But as they sailed—their neutral flag flying or rather hanging limp on the mast—down the bulge of Africa and at last out upon the hot-plate of the Indian Ocean, day after day, day after day, Eddie lay prone in the sick bay, hardly eating, drinking only lime juice, not talking but muttering and yelling in his sleep. Loss, three flights down in the noisome, sweaty bilges, sat on his bunk and wrote up his log book. He also sat with Eddie several hours a day thinking his Hakkar thoughts. In the night he went on deck and sat about learning Portuguese from the crew. He watched each morning the raising of the neutral flag to ensure that the sea and the sky and the sea-birds (there were few now) and the enemy submarines (there were none) knew that this was a craft on peaceful business.

In time, Eddie got up and began to wander on deck, sit against the davits, lean over the rails. He felt so alien and remote from anything that had happened to him before that tears of weakness filled his eyes and reflected the tremendous starlight. He was hollow, a shell on a beach—but safe at last. I could be OK now, he thought, if I could stay here for my life on the circle of the sea.

Loss watched him and considered the ranting he'd heard in the sick bay and risked saying, once, when they were sitting on the creaking deck under the moon, "Tell me about Ma Didds. Go on. You'll have to tell somebody, some day."

But Eddie froze to stone.

Breezily on another occasion, the crew eating fish stew, Eddie crumbling bread, Loss said, "I suppose you know that there are those who believe that endurance of cruelty as a child can feed genius?"

"I have no genius," said Eddie, "and never would have had."

"Bad luck," said Loss. "It is perhaps a pity that *I* wasn't sent to Ma Didds."

"She would have broken even you."

But this conversation was a turning point, and Eddie

seemed to relax. As the heat grew ever stronger, the sea a shimmering disc wherever you looked, and the two boys shrunk into any patch of shadow under the life-boats; and as the engines chuntered on, and the wake behind them curdled the water, and the sea beneath held its mysteries, and as time ceased, Eddie began to sleep again at night and exist, and often sleep peacefully again in the day. Once or twice his old self broke through. He wondered about his father and whatever the two of them would do in Kotakinakulu—or Singapore or Penang, or wherever his father was now—but soon he dismissed all thoughts of the future and the past, and lazily watched Loss dealing out the cards.

"Do you smell something?" asked Loss. "Do you smell land?" Eddie sniffed.

"We're still too far out."

"Lanka," said Loss, "was said by the poet to be the Scented Isle, the Aromatic Eden, the last outpost of civilisation. We've half a day's sailing ahead. We should be sensing it now."

"What—flowers? Wafted over the sea?"

"Yes. You can always smell them. It gives a lift to the heart."

After a time Eddie said, "I do smell something. Not flowers. Something rather vile. I was wondering if there was engine trouble."

"I have noted it, too," said Loss, and went to the rail and stared hard into the Eastern dazzle on the sea.

"It's smeary," said Eddie, joining him. "The sky's smeary."

In half an hour the smears had turned to clouds black as oil and soot, lying all along and high above the curved horizon. The ship's engines were slowing down.

Then they stopped and fell silent, the wake hushed, and the crew called to each other, gathered along the rail to stare.

Then a torrent of excited Portuguese splattered out from the tannoy on the bridge.

"I'll find the Purser," said Loss. "But I know what it is." He listened. "There's been a signal. There has been a signal from Colombo. Singapore has fallen to the Japanese!"

"The *Japanese*? What have they to do with us?"

"We have seen no newspapers. We have heard no news since Christmas. We have been nearly four months aboard."

"Singapore is impregnable."

"It seems not."

After dark, very slowly, the ship began to move on towards Colombo, though whether, said the Purser, they would get their refuelling slot was uncertain. Black smoke covered all the hills. The rubber plantations were all on fire. The dawn seemed never to come as they sailed nearer and nearer the murk.

And they were all at once one of a great fleet of battered craft, most of them limping towards harbour, a macabre regatta, their decks packed with the bandaged and the lame.

"They're wearing red flowers in their hats," said Eddie. "Most of them."

"It's blood," said Loss.

Some of the bandaged waved weakly and uncertainly put up their thumbs and, as the boats reached harbour, there came feeble cheering and scraps of patriotic songs. "They're singing," said Eddie. But *There'll always be an England* trailed away when the refugees on board were near enough to see the whole port of Colombo crammed with other English trying to get away.

"They look numb," said Loss.

"They look withered," said Eddie. "Like they've been days in water. Shrivelled. Hey—you don't think Singapore can really have gone?"

Loss said nothing.

Then, "Look ashore," he said, and pointed at the thousand fluttering Japanese flags that were flaming on every harbour-side roof and window.

"I don't think that they will be any safer here," said Eddie.

"Nor will any of us," said Loss.

All at once, high above the Fragrant Isle and to the South, there was a startling scatter of light. Several groups of tiny daylight stars, triangles of silver and scarlet that the sun caught for a moment before they were lost in the smoke. Aeroplanes.

"Like pen nibs," said Eddie. "Dipped in red ink."

"Japs," said Loss.

The British Army was everywhere on the quays, top brass striding, the Governor with his little cane, the refugees being welcomed but too dazed to understand. A procession of stretchers. Eddie saw one old woman on a crutch asking courteously if anyone had seen her sister, Vera; then collapsing. Crowds hung over the rails of the Customs and Excise who were unhurriedly examining credentials even of the stretcher cases.

"What will happen to us?" said Eddie. "We'll vanish in all that. The bombing here will start any time."

"We're to refuel and turn round," said Loss—he had found the Chief Engineer. "It'll be quite a time before we're refuelled though, and we'll be taking on refugees."

"Turn *back*?" said Eddie. "To Sierra Leone again?"

"No. Back to England. All the way. Probably via Cadiz."

"I must get a message to my father."

"If you send a message, it will have to be in Japanese."

The ship somehow sidled into the madhouse harbour, the engines shuddered loudly, then stopped, and they were tied up and the first gangplank let down. Loss and Eddie stood above it, side by side, like lamp-post and bollard. Loss, now that Eddie looked down, had with him his suitcase and haversack.

"Feathers, I'm staying."

"You're *what*?"

"I'm staying here. D'you want to come with me?"

"You can't stay. You've no money. You'll be on your own."

"I've a bit of money and I won't be alone. I've a couple of uncles. Attorneys. Everyone's an attorney in Colombo. I shall be an attorney one day. So will you, I can tell. I'll be safe from the Japanese. I'm not British. Not white. Come with me. My relatives are resourceful."

"What about the customs?"

"Oh, I am adept at slithering through."

"Loss, you'll disappear. The Japs'll be here in a week. After they've bombed Colombo into the sea. If you don't get killed by a bomb, they'll dispose of you and no one will know."

"I tell you, Feathers, I am lucky. I am The Albat Ross. I'll give you my pack of cards. An Albat Ross feather. A feather to Feathers. Here you are. Oh, could you give me your watch? For emergencies?"

"It's my father's."

"I may need it."

The masked face. The humourless, cunning, dwarf's eyes . . .

"Yes, of course." Eddie took it off and put it in Loss's out-stretched hand.

"See," said Loss. "You'll be safe. Just look—," and he pointed up behind Eddie at the mast-head "—an albatross. You don't often get them this far South."

Eddie looked and saw nothing. He turned back and Loss had gone.

THE DONHEADS

Cracks like shots and a roar followed by heavy black smoke emerged from the region of the bonfire, just off-stage from Filth's sun-lounge, and Garbutt, looking older now, went rebelliously by with yet another load of leaves.

I don't know what's the matter with the man. He knows how I feel. It's too soon to burn. The stuff hasn't died down. He's not normal.

Garbutt came back, past him again, a fork over the barrow for the next load. Each time he passed his jaw was thrust out further, his eyes more determinedly set full ahead.

He's a pyro—pyro. Pyro-technic? Pyrocanthus? Pyrowhatever (words keep leaving me). He's destructive as old Queen Mary. Pyro—pyro? How can I get on here?

And to whom could he complain now old Veneering was gone?

He was amazed at his regret for Veneering. It was genuine grief. Veneering the arch-enemy had become the familiar and close friend. The twice-a-week chess had become the comforting note in an empty diary. There had been visits to the White Hart for lunch, once even for dinner, in Salisbury. Once they had taken a car to Wilton to look at the Vari Dycks. Veneering turned out to be keen on painting and music and Old Filth, trying to hide his total ignorance of both, had accompanied him. Veneering read books. Filth had not been a reader. Veneering had introduced him to various writers. "Only of the higher journalism," he'd said. "We won't tax our addled brains.

Patrick O'Brian. You were a sea-faring man, Filth, weren't you? In the War?"

"I hate the sea," said Filth, putting down O'Brian.

"I'd quite like a cruise," said Veneering, but saw Filth look aghast. "I'd not have even thought of a cruise once," said Veneering. "I was beyond cruising before you came round that Christmas Day."

"Yes," said Filth with some pride. "You were in dry dock."

Muffled up, the two of them walked sometimes round the lanes, Filth instructing Veneering in ornithology.

"You are full of surprises," said Veneering.

"My prep school Headmaster," said Filth. "He went off to America in the War and I suppose he died there. He didn't keep up with any of us. He'd done his duty by us."

"Very wise."

"I tried to find him when I came back from my abortive attempt at being an evacuee. We had to turn for Home, you know. Took three months. Four months, going out. Singapore fell before we got there. My father was there. He died in Changi."

"I'd heard something of the sort."

"I used to make a joke of it. Dinner parties. All the way to Singapore, and about turn, back again."

"It can't have been a great joke."

"No. The journey home was worse than going out. We were stacked with casualties. They kept dying. There was none of the Prayer Book and committal to the deep and *Abide with Me* and so forth. They were just shovelled over. I hung on. I kept imagining Sir—my Headmaster—would be waiting for me at Cadiz. Or my Auntie May."

"I had not thought you the type for an Auntie May."

"Missionary. Wonderful woman. There was another missionary on the boat. A Miss Robertson. She died of gangrene and they shovelled her off, too."

"Have you written about all this?"

"Certainly not. Old Barrister's memoirs are all deadly. Don't you think?"

"Yes. But maybe you'd have surprised us."

"I've grown my image, Veneering. Took some doing. I'm not going to upset it now."

"You mean upset *yourself*?"

"Yes. Probably. Have some more hock."

But Veneering gone—ridiculous to have taken a cruise at his age—Filth's loneliness for the old enemy was extraordinary, his mourning for him entirely different and sharper than his mourning for Betty. He'd told Veneering more than he'd ever told Betty—though never about Ma Didds. He'd even told Veneering about the buttermilk girl. Veneering had cackled. He'd told him about Loss. "Did you tell me about that before?" asked Veneering. "It rings a bell. Did I know him?"

"You're wandering," said Filth. They were playing chess.

"Not far," said Veneering, taking his queen.

I suppose Memoirs might be in the order of things, he thought, with Veneering dead and his house next door torn apart, windows flung wide, a family with children shouting, crying, laughing, breaking through his hedge; the parents growing vegetables and offering him lettuces. Once a child from Veneering's house had landed at his feet like a football as he sat in the garden reading the Minutes of a new Temple Benchtable. He wanted to throw the child back over the hedge. "Sorry," the child said.

"I suppose you want your ball back."

"I haven't got a ball."

"Well, what's that in your hand?"

"Just some old beads."

Giggles from the bushes.

"I found them in that flower-bed."

He vanished.

Bloody self-confident, thought Filth. I don't understand children now. Sir would have flayed him. Then: What am I talking about? Acting the Blimp. Sir wouldn't have flayed him. He'd have lectured him on birds.

But, too late for that, he thought.

He sat to his desk and attempted a Memoir, but found it impossible. Opinions, judgements had made him famous, but how to write without opinion or judgement? Statement of facts—easy. But how to decide which were the facts? He shrank from the tremendous, essential burden of seeing himself through other people's eyes. Only God could do it. It seemed blasphemous even to try. Such a multitude of impressions, such a magnitude of emotion. Where was truth to be found?

"Why did you become an advocate, Filth?" Veneering used to ask. "Don't tell me you wanted to promote the truth."

"Justice. It interested me."

"And we know that justice is not the truth."

"Certainly not."

"But it's some sort of step towards it?"

"Not even that. Do you agree?"

"I agree," Veneering had said, busy with his ghastly jigsaw. "The Law is nevertheless an instinct. A good instinct. A framework for behaviour. And a safeguard (good—bit of the church roof) in time of trouble. *Parlement of Foules—Chaucer.*"

"Rooks have a parliament," said Filth, keeping his end up.

But though his Memoirs went on endlessly, and rather impressively as he thought them through in the small hours of the night, sometimes to the accompaniment of his beating heart and too much whiskey, when it came to getting them upon paper they would not come. They made him feel so fool-ish. He felt Betty looking over his shoulder and saying kindly, "jolly good." He sat in the sun-lounge each morning, defeated, and Garbutt went tramping by. Oh, how could one concen-trate? And, oh great heaven! Here came that Chloe in lacy mauve and a perm, round the back of the house and waving a cake. To think he had once . . .

He deliberately arose, holding his tartan blanket round him and shuffled to the other side of the table to sit with his back to her, facing the door to the sitting-room which immediately opened and in came the cleaning lady, Mrs.-er, with a cup of tea.

Decisions came fast to Filth, all decisions except what to include in his Memoirs. Mrs.-er put down the cup and saucer, talking the while, saying that that Chloe from the church was wanting to give him another sponge.

"Mrs.-er," he said, "I've been meaning to tell you. I am going away."

"Away? Oh, yes?"

"Yes. I am going to Malmesbury."

"*Malmesbury*? Down Gloucester?"

"Yes. I was there in the Army during the War. Just for a look round."

"If it's hotels, be careful. There'll be steps and stairs you don't know. Remember poor Judge Veneering."

"It is not a ship. I'll leave my address."

"I'll pack for you."

"Thank you, I'm sure I can manage. And I'll be hiring a car."

Two minutes later he saw her outside, furiously conferring with Garbutt, the mauve woman having disappeared. Their excitement maddened him.

The next day, she came in to tell him that if it was a hotel he ought to have new pyjamas.

He said, "Oh, and Mrs.-er, when I come back I intend to manage here alone."

"*Alone?*"

"I think I am becoming too dependent on you all. I'm going to employ the Social Services. The Meals on Wheels. I'm sorry, Mrs.-er."

"After all these years you still don't know my name," she said. "That's it, then. I'll go now. Get yourself to Malmesbury."

He saw her clacking at Garbutt on the lawn and marching away, and felt gleefully cruel. He opened the glass doors and waited till Garbutt went by.

"I know what you're going to say," said Garbutt. "I'll just see the fire's out, then I'm off. You know where to find me if you change your mind. Her name's Katey, by the way. You've gutted her."

In the hotel at Malmesbury, journey safely accomplished, splendid room looking across at the Abbey, smell of a good dinner floating up, his unrepentant euphoria remained. Their blank faces, ha! Their disbelief. They'd see he was his own master yet. And here in Malmesbury not a soul knew him. He stumbled on the stairs and limped into the dining-room, rather wishing he'd brought his walking-stick for his explorations tomorrow.

The ankle next morning was the size of a small balloon and he telephoned the Desk for assistance. They suggested bringing him breakfast in bed which outraged him. Staggering down a steep flight of stairs between two waiters, he somehow made the breakfast-room. Outside it was pouring with rain and people went by behind umbrellas at a forty-five degree angle against the wind. Unable to walk from the table, he enquired whether there was a doctor who could come and see him and was told the way to a surgery. It was not far, they said, but Old Filth couldn't even reach the hotel's front door and sank upon an oak bench. People passed by. A whole coachload of tourists streamed past, chattering about the disappointing weather. He asked if the Desk would ring for a doctor to call to examine him.

"You'd have to go to the hospital for that. For an X-ray."

"I only need a GP's opinion."

The Desk stared. "You'd have to go round to the surgery. They don't do home visits now unless it's serious."

He asked the Desk to call a taxi.

The paving stones between the taxi and surgery door shone slippery and menacing. He hesitated. The umbrellas continued to go by. At last he was helped in, and found a room crowded and silent like a church and one girl at a screen with her back to the audience.

"I need to see a doctor."

"Yes." She handed him a disc saying "21."

"Do I wait here?"

She looked surprised. "Where else?"

"This means that there are twenty people ahead of me?"

"Yes."

"What sort of wait will that be?"

"A long one."

"An hour?"

"Oh, nearer two."

He rang the Desk and asked for his luggage to be collected and brought down to the hotel foyer. And would they kindly ring the car-hire company to come and take him from the surgery, then back to the hotel and then home to the Donheads.

"It wasn't even Malmesbury I really wanted to go to, it was Badminton. Just down the road," he told this driver.

"It is. Just as it ever was. Down the road and down the hill."

"I was there in the War. Wanted to have another look. I was in the Army." (His ankle was hell.)

"There's a good hotel near there where you could keep your foot up. They might get you a doctor. Were you there with the Royals? They'll be pleased to see you if you were. Still the same sort of place."

(Anything better than creeping home to shame and emptiness.)

"I might give it a try. Thank you."

They swooped from the hill to the plain. Through the rain he saw the great house again, the broad quiet streets of the village, the stretch of woodland, the wide fields.

"Terrible weather for sight-seeing," said the taxi man. "I'll take you right home when the time comes, if you like. I'll just look in here and see if there's a room. It'll cost you, mind."

Exhausted, he sat in the foyer of the new hotel which was calm and gracious. Someone brought him a stool for his foot. Someone else said they were going to get a doctor. The rain eased and Filth was brought lunch on a tray alone in the lounge. He was tired, humiliated and—something else—what? Good God! frightened. I have been frightened! He sank into himself, dozed, was helped to a big ground-floor bedroom with a view across the parkland, and very cautiously, a snip at a time, allowed himself the past.

"Would you very kindly put my name and address in your address book, young man?" said the ragged skeleton beside him on the boat-deck as they left Cadiz. "I fully intend to reach Home, but, if not, I would like to be sure that Vera knows what happened to me. That's to say, of course, if she gets Home herself, which I doubt. She was always rather feeble without me to get her anywhere. I am Miss Robertson. Miss Meg. She is Miss Vera. We're daughters of the late Colonel Robertson. Teachers. This is our only address in England now. It belongs to some old chums from school who've always paid us a little rent. I hope we'll get on together now that I shall have to live with them. Well, school's a long time ago, you know."

Her skin was pale and glazed with fever and her eyes far too bright. Her wooden crutches lay beside her and she tried all the time to clutch their handles. "Have you a pen, young man? Turn to 'R' in your address book." Eddie lay immobile. Someone crept up to Miss Robertson and wiped her face with a cloth. Other people muttered together that she should have been detained at Cadiz. She had been formidably against it, even in fever. She had to get Home.

"If *any* of us gets Home," she had said. "I hear that there's one ship a day being sunk just now in the Channel."

As it grew dark, one night, he heard Miss Robertson whisper, "Look in my little bag. There's some trinkets. Take them, young man, and give them to your sweetheart." The little bag lay pushed up under the life-boat blocks and the crutches near it. There was a cold clean breeze. When daylight came, where Miss Robertson had been there was a stain.

The smell beneath the life-boat where she had lain had gone too.

She had been complaining of the rotting smell on the ship. Eddie had not cared about it, hardly noticed. "Gangrene," he heard someone say. "The stink was from herself. The boy don't look much better. He's filth all through."

A crewman went away for a bucket of water and scrubbing brush, and Eddie, eyes closed, stretched to touch Miss Robertson's walking aids and found his hand on the bag. He took it and pushed it beneath him, later found a corner for it in his own suitcase with his father's photograph and Pat Ingoldby's clothes-brush. Through his headache and fever, and through the now endless vomiting, he found himself thinking that he was becoming like Loss. A scavenger. Survival. Take anything. Old lady. Couldn't see her own doom. Her isolation. Talking about address books.

The ship sailed on like some faery invisible barge. The sea shone, still and blue. No planes. No U-Boats. Other craft nowhere near. Way out, towards the West, fishing boats. A wonderful calmness.

A kind of whisper went round at last among the humped and now many fewer passengers; a sibilant, urgent word. "Yes. Yes, it is. It's land. Yes. Yes. It is."

And cold now. Eddie was unwrapped first from his life-jacket then put inside a tarpaulin. Someone washed his face as he vomited. Cleaned him when he shat his clothes. "Here's another going, if you ask me."

Now he was left alone.

The odd thing, said the speck of the rational in Eddie within him—he guarded it like his life—the odd thing is that I did once have an address book. Alice gave it to me. In the kitchen. Leather. Small. Red. Someone had given it to her, but, she said, "I don't need it. I never had any addresses to write to." One day, at the billet in Londonderry, Eddie had written in it, for comfort, all the addresses he knew. School. Oxford, the Ingoldbys (hopelessly), Sir, Auntie May, one or two schoolfriends even though he'd never write to them. Not Les Girls. Not the buttermilk girl. As his temperature soared now he began to wonder if he'd ever again find the addresses of his cousins. If the old address in Kotakinakulu would ever find his father. He had had no address for Loss. By now there was probably no Loss to write to.

Then he remembered that he had not seen his address book for a very long time. He felt about in his bag and it was not there and he knew, without any question, that Loss had stolen it. God knows why, except he was a natural crook. A delinquent. The bastard. Vanished, and with my watch. And no Loss. No loss. But such a monstrous act! Cutting Eddie off from every hope of contact.

Loss's defection was the metaphor for Eddie's life. It was Eddie's fate always to be left. Always to be left and forgotten. Everyone gone, now. Out of his reach. For the first time, Eddie was utterly on his own.

He had his passport—yes, he felt that in the bag. He had Pat's brush. He had Miss Robertson's pouch. He felt fat beads inside it and pulled them out. A great string of pearls. Thank goodness Loss wasn't there. They'd be gone in five minutes. Lightness almost mirth filled Eddie as the ship, charmed, blessed, unhindered, sailed slowly, slowly, up the Irish Sea and such as could gathered at the rail and gazed unbelieving at the peaceful green Welsh hills. Over the Styx, thought Eddie. Crossing the bar.

Aeons passed and Eddie, wrapped in blankets, shaking with fever but ice-cold, a structure of bones, was dumped on a stretcher and carried through customs unhindered, and ashore. At the ambulance station in his fever he looked for a car like a bread-bin but found instead a man playing with a yo-yo. He was familiar. He was old Oils, his Housemaster. Standing alongside him was Isobel Ingoldby.

Diagonally falling drops alighting on the windowpanes of Gloucestershire, and Old Filth awoke in the new, ever-silent hotel to see a girl smiling down at him, holding a tray of tea. He thought: Oh God—the buttermilk girl! Then, seeing the sweet open smile, thought: No.

And I am an old man, he thought.

"I am an old man," he said.

"I've brought you a cup of tea. Is it true you were a soldier here, sir?"

It took him some time to remember where he was. Near Badminton.

"I was stationed at Badminton," he said. "In the War."

"My gran was at Badminton then. In the War. Queen Mary was here but we all kept it quiet. They said nobody would want to kidnap her but my gran said—she was parlour maid at the house—that she had three bags ready packed to take her to America. In the attics."

"That was probably true. Though she might not have gone herself."

"One was full of jewels."

"Oh, I'm sure that was true. That would have gone into safety."

"Did you know her, sir?"

"Yes, I did."

"Is it true she was always cutting down trees?"

"Yes, it is."

"Especially ivy. She hated ivy. She had half a platoon chopping down ivy. They say the first year she didn't realise it would grow back again.

"I expect it was the way she'd been brought up," said the girl. "My gran says she was kept in a band-box as a girl. Never opened her mouth—well, her mother never stopped talking— and what a bottom! Her mother's, that is. Lovely woman. Real old England, her mother. Queen Mary was brought up in Teck, which is German, and she didn't like Germans. My gran said she'd been brought up to gravel paths and never seen a field of hay. And my gran says it was all psychological, the ivy."

"Your gran sounds a very perceptive woman."

"She is. My mother sang for Queen Mary, you know."

"Sang?"

"In the village school. Queen Mary used to turn up there unexpected and sit at the back. She had a turned-up nose."

"Oh. I never noticed that."

"Yes. Look at the stamps. She was embarrassed by it, my gran thinks. She had never been thought a beauty. But she was a beauty, my gran says. And all that about being a kleptomaniac was wicked lies. And she never forgot a birthday."

"That's true."

"And she fancied some of the subalterns. She liked them with a stammer, did you know that? My uncle had a stammer. He was one of her four motorbike bodyguards and she chose him for his stammer. She said, 'I have a son like you.' She meant the King."

"D'you know, I never knew that," said Filth. "I didn't make the connection."

"Won't you go out now and sit in the sun? I'll help you. My gran has a terrible leg. I wouldn't be surprised if it was gangrene. What's the matter? Have I upset you? Now then, you know the doctor said yours is but a bad sprain. You'll be fit in a week. Shall I ask my gran to come up here? She'd love a talk."

"Do you want to talk with my gran?" the girl asked the next day, bringing him a breakfast tray and no refusals. "It'd be a breath of life to her. Maybe she'd remember you."

"I hardly remember myself."

"She said there was one always reading. Law books. She got them for him, Queen Mary. And chocolate. He used to hold her wool for her. He'd been through it, she said. Very good-looking. Oh yes, and he had a stammer, She found him—now what was it?—very *personable*. That's what we heard her tell her lady-in-waiting. 'The Captain's very personable, isn't he?' She took up very close to him after her son got killed, the Duke of Kent. He was nearest to her, that one, they said. She never cried though. She and this soldier—he was a junior Platoon Commander—I asked gran when I got home last night—this soldier used to sit with her by the hour. She even used to pass through the library when he was reading in there, not looking up. Deep in his books. He was invited to stay in the house you know. Dine with them all. The Duke and Duchess—and my, there were some sparks flying there—them being kicked upstairs in their own home and all the best rooms taken over by Queen Mary *and* her fifty servants."

"This all sounds very credible."

"He refused though, the young Captain. He said he had to be with his men in the billets in the stables and Queen Mary couldn't but say he was right. I believe now and then she was poking about the stables too, searching out ivy. And maybe—" she had his tie straight now and his socks on and his polished shoes ready for him. "He was very good-looking, my gran said." She thoughtfully looked Filth over. "And very young and nice."

"I was young but far from nice," said Filth. "I don't think I'd better meet your gran."

"I'd like a look round the stables, though," he said, the next day. "When I'm walking again."

"I can get you a wheelchair."

"No. No thanks."

"Queen Mary used to go round in a horse and cart to save petrol. No side to her. They used to put a couple of basket chairs in the cart and hoist her and the lady's maid up into it and one of the bike boys shouted up, 'You look as if you're in a tumbril, Ma'am,' and she said, 'Well, it might come to that.' So she can't have been *altogether* no fun."

"I think she wasn't *much* fun. She hadn't had *much* fun," said Filth.

"Oh that terrible King!" said the girl. "All those pheasants. All he ever thought about, my gran said. Where the children came from, we'll never know, my gran said."

"Yes, that's often a puzzle," said Filth.

He was in a private room. It might be a cabin of some sort. Outside the window there were trees but trees do not grow in the sea and the sea still moved beneath him, up and down, up and down, lift and drop. Seven months at sea. But the clouds above the window sailed along without the elf-light from the sea beneath them. And these tree tops? A woman ran by him and her hat was a plume of white starch. Her dress was navy blue but she, too, had nothing to do with ships. She had a face of wrath and across her broad front hung a watch and chain. She did not speak. He floated away.

Later he opened his eyes on a member of the Ku Klux Klan seated at the end of his bed playing cat's cradle with some bed-tape.

"Hello?" Eddie said and the dreadful figure looked up with surprise. It was Oils again.

"Hello, sir."

"Hello, Feathers. Well done. Awake?"

"What for, sir? Why well done?"

"Getting home."

"Not in my hands, sir."

Adrift again. He was remembering the image at the end of the bed when it was suddenly present again.

"Hello, sir. Why are you in those clothes?"

"They're antiseptic, Feathers. You're infectious."

"What have I got?"

"A variety of things."

"Will I recover?"

"Yes. Of course. In time. Then you can come back to school until it's time to go to Oxford."

Away he floated. Nurses came and went and put needles in different parts of him, and tubes. Did unspeakable things to him. They wore masks. An unpleasant one told him he'd no right to be there. "You should be in the Hospital for Tropical Diseases," she said, "but it's too far off. They're doing tests on you there. We're not equipped here. We've had to ask for volunteers."

"What for?"

"To nurse you."

"Thanks."

Here was the Ku Klux Klan again, now back with the yo-yo. "The Headmaster sends his good wishes. He says you must convalesce at school."

"Thanks. You mean in the San?"

"I suppose so, Feathers, but we've not planned anything yet."

"I won't go in the San."

"The Headmaster has offered you a room in his house."

Remembering the tea-cosy, Eddie flinched.

"My aunts have gone to Scotland somewhere," he said. "I don't know where. If you find out, don't tell them. But I'd like to know about my father. If you can find out somehow."

"I have to go now," said Oils. "Ten minutes at a time."

A nurse came in one day with mail which lay by the bed for several days.

"Shall I read it?" asked another nurse. "Well, this is nice, it's from your aunts. It says: '*Bad luck, Eddie dear, what a hoot.*'"

"The police found them," said Oils on his next visit, embarrassed. "Your aunts."

"Can they be lost again?"

"I'd think so," said Oils.

"This visiting card's been stuck to your locker since the first day you came in here," said the Red Cross hospital librarian, pushing round her trolley. She always stopped by his bed though he read nothing. Masks had been abandoned now. "You're not ready to read yet, are you?"

"I don't think so."

"I don't blame you. These are all awful old trashy paperbacks. They have to be burnt in case they get into the general library and spread infection. They can't get librarians for this ward. I wipe all the books in Dettol—not a nice job. Shall I read you this visiting card, it says *Isobel Ingoldby*, that will be the girl that brought you in, her and the schoolmaster—he's a funny one."

"Has she been back?"

"Yes. Several times. When you were not with us."

"Where does she live?"

"The card has her address. It's in London."

"However did she find me here?"

"How did you find me, Mr. Oilseed? I'm glad you're out of your overalls, sir."

"You're not infectious any more. You're to sit up at the window tomorrow."

"But how did you know I'd be on that particular ship?"

"There were signals sent of some sort. From Colombo. To me and to Ingoldby's sister and maybe to others but we haven't heard. The Admiralty tracked the ship. Ingoldby's sister has some underground job there somewhere. Something to do with the Admiralty."

"*Underground* in the Admiralty? Was it signed? What was it—a telegram?"

"It was a cable. Unsigned. I gather it came by way of a place called Bletchley Park. Where Isobel Ingoldby was."

"Could it have been from my father?"

"No," said Oils. "No. Sorry. I don't think so. Singapore isn't in touch. Some prisoners have got letters out, somehow . . . but no . . ."

"D'you think someone in Colombo got a message to him?"

"I'd not think so. Not unless someone knew every single one of our addresses."

They moved him by ambulance to the South of England and Oils said goodbye, with some relief, Eddie thought. "By the way, we've informed Christ Church. You are not forgotten. As soon as you're released."

"Thanks. Thank the Headmaster for me, sir."

"Yes. Of course. And well done again. You're fit now."

"But I'm going to another isolation ward. The Plymouth Naval Hospital. Whatever for?"

"The ways of medical men are very strange."

"Sir—thanks for being so brave."

"Nothing brave about me," said Oils. "Matter of fact you've cheered me up. Glad you're better."

In Plymouth, in the isolation wing, he kept apart from the rest who were thoroughly dispirited, most of them gnarled old salts who swore considerably and talked of past delights. One of them had been at Gallipoli, and he talked on through the night of the horrors of the deep. "There was one sailor," he said, "looked ninety. Homeless. Living miracle. He was so riddled with corruption—look, one day on deck he coughed up something with legs and a backbone.

"A backbone," he said. "I've never forgotten it. What's the matter with the lad? Squeamish?"

Slowly they let Eddie walk about outside along the old stone terraces. It was autumn. The air was sweet.

Then one afternoon came Isobel, striding along.

"They wouldn't let me in before," she said. "They didn't tell me what you'd caught, either. Whatever have you been doing? You never left the ship, did you?"

"I a-a-ate bananas in Freetown."

"Your stammer's come back."

"Only i-i-in-intermittently."

"You're keeping something to yourself."

"I suppose so but I don't quite know what."

She leant towards him and stroked his arm. "You look like a grub," she said. "One of those things you can see through."

He was in tears. "Sorry. I'll be OK in a minute. Don't go."

"I have to get the train back. I've come two hundred miles."

"Isobel."

"You've got my card and number."

"Come next leave."

"My next leave maybe I'll go to Scotland to flay your aunts."

"*Don't,*" he said. "I'm nothing to do with them now. Just get me near to you. Somehow. For ever."

"Child," she said, and was gone.

And—six full months later—"You are passed and fit, Feathers," said the Surgeon Commander, RN, with a facial tic and a foghorn voice who ran the hospital like a cruiser, each patient to attention each at the end of his bed. "I suppose you will now depart to Oxford?"

"No, sir. I've decided not."

"Yes?"

"I'm going to join up, sir."

"We've just got you shipshape. You may prove we've been wasting our time. A very expensive case. Expensive and unsavoury. But good show."

"I'm sorry, sir."

"You will want to join the Navy, I suppose? Return to the source of the trouble?"

"No, sir. The Army. My father was in the Army. I'd like to join his old regiment."

"No accounting for taste," said the Commander. "Foolish of you. The sea is pretty well ours now. The going is easier. The Army's just about to move to the thick of the last long shove. It will be slow and bloody, and you don't look like a soldier."

"I think I might be, sir. Given the chance."

He felt naked on the hospital forecourt. He travelled to

Gloucestershire alone. It was as terrifying as the journey to a first school, as horrible as his first walk with Babs and Claire to the Welsh baby school when he was five. He'd been feeling ill with the Welsh winter then. There had been a pain in his chest—but every time he had turned to look back at the farm-house, Ma Didds, as usual clutching her stomach, holding her little stick, had waved him furiously on.

He missed the safety of the hospital.

Now it was a ride in a train again into a different world, the West Country, Eastward from Plymolith, across a beautiful river, soil the red of sunset, a change of trains; and into Gloucestershire. Someone had given him a bed-and-breakfast address and a warm soft-voiced old couple saw that he had a hot water bottle. There was a boiled egg for breakfast. An egg! "Joining up?" they said. "Make the most of the egg, now." He borrowed a bike and turned up at the recruiting office, in Gloucester; where he was expected.

There were three of them behind the desk and they looked at him with considerable interest. They spoke of his health. He had been cleared one-hundred-per-cent fit and he was brown from the air and sea off Plymouth and he looked every bit of his nearly nineteen years. His hair was curly again and auburn. His weight was now normal. His eyes were alive.

"Your father's regiment?" they said. "The Gloucesters?"

"Yes, sir."

"I know your father."

"I'm afraid I hardly do, sir. I was on my way—"

"So we understand. There is, I suppose, no news from Changi?"

"No, sir."

"I hope very much that we'll hear something and that he will hear of you. Well do what we can."

The middle one nodded at the other two who got up and went out.

"We have a proposal to make to you, Feathers. You were a member of your school's OTC, I understand, and have done some basic training—can march and so forth?"

"Well, I could, sir."

"It doesn't leave you. We have decided to send you to the platoon that is guarding Queen Mary."

Eddie stared. "But she's well guarded, sir. And she's in the Pacific Ocean or somewhere."

"Not the ship. The Queen. The mother of our Monarch. She is down here in the West Country. We have one hundred and fifty men in her defence and four particular bodyguards. What's the matter?"

"It is not s-s-soldiering, sir."

Instead of darkening with rage, the Colonel's blue eyes shut and opened again quickly.

"Only a run-in, Feathers. Not for the rest of the War. It is to finish your restoration. I notice you have a stammer and I have heard that it can be chronic. You would find it hard to give orders. The stammer must be removed."

"It is only i-in-int-int-ermittent, sir. It re-t-urns when it is comm-comm-ented on."

"You will report to Badminton barracks tomorrow at four-teen hundred hours. Understood?"

"Yes, sir."

"But there is one more thing. Your health."

"I'm a hundred per cent, sir."

"I wonder if you know what has been the matter with you, Feathers?"

"Fever, sir. A bug from Sierra Leone. Pretty lethal, I sup-pose. They never told me."

"You have been infected, Feathers, with three different types of parasitic worm. And certainly from Sierra Leone."

"Sir?"

"But that has not troubled us. The worms are gone. We

know how to treat these things. But the other thing was more serious. You have been suffering from a venereal disease."

"What is that, sir?"

The Colonel looked at him warily.

"You have been in close contact with a woman."

"She died of gangrene, sir, on the ship after Cadiz. I only did what I could. Miss Robertson. She was over seventy—"

"I doubt that she was the source of the infection. What I am saying, Feathers, is that you have acquired sexual knowledge through a most unpalatable source. Isn't this true?"

A long and thoughtful silence.

"It was dark, sir. I never really looked at her. I never thought of her as palatable or unpalatable. She just climbed in. I'd no idea how to do it, and she had. She gave me buttermilk, sir. It was in Northern Ireland, sir."

The Colonel paced hurriedly across to the window and stood looking out intently.

"Were you taught *nothing* at school, Feathers?"

"I have won a scholarship to Oxford, sir."

A sort of sob from the window. A pause for recovery.

"Feathers, I have decided that this disreputable episode should not be passed on to Badminton. Primarily because of Queen Mary. I hope I am not being unwise."

"Thank you. Yes, sir. I can't think that Queen Mary would be in any danger from me."

"Go! Enough!" roared the Colonel. "You're dismissed, Feathers. Go."

Afterwards the Colonel wondered if he'd been made fun of. Beaten in argument. Run rings round.

Feathers wasn't certain, either.

And so, this October, Filth was in a wheelchair being pushed round the Badminton meadows around Badminton House by the nice girl and her grandmother, their feet crunching on the crystalline grass. They stood at a distance from the great house.

"The cedar's gone," said Filth. "Well, well."

"Oh, the cedar's gone," said the grandmother. "Not so very long after Queen Mary. The sixties. She'd be pleased. It was what might be called a running sore, that tree. 'Have it down,' she told the Duchess (and her hardly moved in!). 'It's in the wrong place. It blocks the light.' 'Lord Raglan used to climb in it,' says her Grace. 'It's not to be touched.' '*Over my dead body,*' the Duchess said. I heard the very words."

"The tree was still the issue when I arrived," said Filth.

He had not seen Queen Mary his first month at Badminton, after a three-week OCTU course in another camp. Once he saw a silvery pillar above him on a terrace. Once again he seemed to see something moving slowly inside a long glass gallery. Then one day, reading in the vegetable garden—he had begun to order Law books from London—there she was, watching him from over the hedge. It was a hot day but she was dressed in full rig—a long coat and skirt, pearls and brooches, and a rucked hat like a turban with a sweep to it. He stood up at once and she gave a strange half-bow and turned away. There was an attendant nearby who was knitting on four-peg needles. Knitting steadily, she turned about and followed the Queen. The next week he was invited to the house to tea.

It was served in the large salon where new acquaintances were tried out. If they made the grade there would be a future invitation to Her Majesty's private sitting-room upstairs. Big test. The Queen sat doing needlework, her lady-in-waiting sat picking over some scraps of cloth, and a fat noisy woman was shouting.

"*Over my dead body,*" she was saying, "will you cut down my tree. Cut down my spinneys, my ivy, my woodlands, my bramble bushes. Cut down my *house*, but not the tree."

Queen Mary continued with her blanket stitch. The lady-in-waiting looked exhausted and the fat woman came up along-side Eddie Feathers as the twelve-foot high doors to the salon were being held open by footmen in scarlet.

"She's impossible. I'm the Duchess of Beaufort. I know I look like somebody's cook, but that's who I am, and this is my house. She's only an evacuee," she spat as she blew past, the doors being silently closed behind her.

Queen Mary looked across at Eddie and smiled.

After the tray had been put down (margarine on the bread, pineapple jam but really made from turnips, a terrible seed cake and some oatcakes) Queen Mary passed him an almost transparent cup half-full of pale water.

"Cream?" she asked.

"No, thank you."

She nodded. There was no cream, anyway, and the milk looked blue.

The lady-in-waiting brought out a box of pills and dropped one in the Queen's cup and one in her own. "Saccharine?" she said.

"Oh, no, thank you."

"It is quite true. What my niece says is perfectly true. I am only an evacuee. A very unwilling evacuee."

Eddie wondered what to say. "I was once an evacuee," he said. "And very unwilling. And far too old."

"I am far too old," said the Queen. "How old were you?"

"Eighteen."

"Good gracious. How humiliating for you."

"Yes. It was. My father sent for me to Malaya, to escape the War."

"How disgraceful of him."

"He had had a very bad time in 1914."

"Yes. I see. But you escaped? To tell you the truth I don't altogether feel ashamed to have escaped. It was the Government's decision I should come here. They told me I would be much more trouble in London. In case of kidnap. Personally I think that a plane might come and bundle me off more easily from here. That of course is why you're all here. A hundred and fifty of you. Quite ridiculous."

"Yes, your Maj—"

"Call me Ma'am."

"You must miss being at the heart of things—Ma'am?"

"I don't, now. I'll tell you more another time."

She looked pointedly at the lady-in-waiting who gathered up a skein of mud-coloured wool and passed it to Eddie who was having trouble with the turnip jam. "Hold Her Majesty's wool, please."

Eddie held out his hands and the wool was arranged upon them in a figure of eight. The lady-in-waiting began to roll it up into a ball. He felt a ninny.

"Do you think you will enjoy soldiering?" asked the Queen, looking hard at him.

He blushed and began to stammer.

"Ah yes. I see. You'll get over it. I know a boy like you."

He walked in the park with her through the next hard winter. The ground was black, the trees sticks of opaline ice.

"We shall just walk up and down," said Queen Mary. "For an hour or so. We must get exercise at all costs. D'you see how the wretched ivy is coming back?"

"Did you walk like this, Ma'am, before you came here?"

"I've always tried to walk a great deal. You see my family runs to fat. They eat too much. My dear mother would eat half a bird and then a great sirloin for dinner, and she loved cream. And the Duchess—I used to walk in Teck but only round and round the box-beds. Sandringham was the place to walk, but somehow one didn't. One went about in little carts to watch them shooting. And one didn't walk in London of course. I luckily have magnificent Guelph health."

"I have never been to London."

She stood still with amazement. "You have never been to London? Everybody has been to London."

"Most of Badminton village has never been to London."

"Oh, I don't mean the village. I mean that a gentleman, surely, has always been to London?"

"No, Ma'am. I've been in Wales and in the North—"

"You haven't seen the galleries? The museums? The theatre?"

"No, Ma'am."

"That is a personable young man," she said that evening, hard at work arranging family photographs in an album before getting down to the red despatch boxes the King sent her daily. She read them in private, and nobody was quite sure how many, but probably all.

"Very good-looking indeed," said Mary Beaufort. "He'll be useful at dinner parties."

"We don't give dinner parties," said the Queen. "It would be out of kilter with the War effort. But we could ask a few of the Subalterns."

"We could."

"In fact it seems quite ridiculous that a boy like that should be billeted down in the stables. Why can't he come and live in the house, Mary? Do you know, he has never been to London?"

Eddie refused to live in Badminton House. He said he must stay with his platoon. He began to find the tea parties rather trying. The mud-coloured wool had been overtaken by a cloud of unravelled powder-blue which clung to his uniform in tufts. He let it be known that he had to work hard, and he settled to his Law in the stables.

But the tall shadow would fall across his book and he would have to find a garden chair and she would sit with him among the dying dahlias in the remains of the cutting garden—every foot of land, she had instructed, to be used for vegetables. The Duchess fumed, and one day came thumping down to look for Eddie and complain.

"She brought fifty-five servants," she said. "She's stopped them wearing livery because of the War and Churchill in that awful siren-suit. Six of them are leaving. They've worn scarlet since they were under-footmen and they're old and say they can't change. Can you do nothing with her?"

"What—me? No, your Grace. Couldn't; c-c-couldn't."

"Well, you'll have to think of something. Distract her."

"I've stopped the tree. Well, I hope s-s-so."

"Oh, good boy. But listen, she's determined to take you to London. Her chauffeur, old Humphries, is half-blind and not safe. Once he lost Her Majesty for over an hour in Ashdown Forest. She won't sack him. And she makes him stop and pick up any member of the forces walking on the road. Once she picked up a couple who were walking the other way and once it was an onion seller. She'll be murdered, and then we'll all be blamed."

"Eddie," said the Queen, a little later. "I am determined to get you to London. When I first came here I went back every week, you know, on the train. Then it became painful because of the bombing. The Guildhall. The City churches. All gone. And of course the antique shops are all closed or gone to Bath (you and I might perhaps go to Bath one day). But I have a great desire to see London again. It might not be patriotic to insist that the Royal coach be put back on the train, but I have plenty of my petrol ration untouched, and you could do the driving, on the main roads, Eddie, if it is too much for Humphries. We shall of course need two outriders."

"I'm sorry, but I can't drive, Ma'am."

The expedition was put off until Eddie had learned to drive, instruction being given in a tank on the estate.

"I can only drive a tank, Ma'am," he said when a London visit was again suggested.

"The principle must be the same," said the Queen.

"We must clear it with Security."

She looked imperious. The ex-Empress of India. "Well, we'll go out wooding, Eddie. Get my bodyguards and my axe. No, I'll keep my hat on. I'm determined to take you to London."

It was fixed at last that Queen Mary should make the journey to London by the train, the Royal coach still being rested in a siding near Gloucester. Some of the Badminton staff were sent to wash it down and the stationmaster of Badminton railway station had to look out for the white gloves he had worn to haul the Queen aboard the 6.15 A.M. in 1939 at the beginning of her evacuee life.

"Good luck, Ma'am."

The lady-in-waiting followed her in, and Eddie and a couple of Other Ranks with rifles took up their posts.

"Hope you don't meet Jerry, Ma'am," said the stationmaster. "Everyone stand back from the lawns."

"Oh, the bombing is totally over," said Queen Mary. "I shall go to the Palace and have a look at the ruins of Marlborough House. And there is a little shopping—"

He blew the whistle and waved the flag. The Queen's progress had cheered him up. She'd be back on the 5.15 from Paddington. She wasn't dead yet.

"She's got some spirit," he told the empty platform. Even at Badminton there were no porters. "We're better off than Poland. Or Stalingrad."

Just before Paddington, Eddie in a different side-carriage alone, the Queen sent for him and handed him a slip of paper.

"Here are the things you ought to see. I haven't given you too many. It is not only a first visit but you will find it confusing without signposts, and all the bomb-damage. You ought to have time for the Abbey and take a glance at St. James's Park and No.10. And Big Ben. Here we are. It's a pity you don't know anyone who could show you about. Have a splendid time. Now, lunch—I really don't know what to suggest."

"I'll miss lunch, Ma'am. It's going to be a tight schedule."

She stepped from the train. There was a bit of rather old red carpet down for her and she stood in silver grey with doves' feathers in her toque, grey kid gloves, ebony stick. A whisper began—"It's Queen Mary. Hey look—Queen Mary"—and a crowd gathered up like blown leaves. There were feeble hurrahs and some clapping, growing stronger, and the little crowd closed round Her Majesty and the lady-in-waiting. The two bodyguards melted away.

Eddie, all alone, made at once for the taxi-rank and the bed-sit in Kensington of Isobel Ingoldby.

"I'm not sure how far it is," he told the taxi-driver, after waiting in a long queue, tapping his leg with his military stick. His uniform helped him not at all for everyone seemed to be in uniform. "It's Kensington. Off Church Street."

"Twenty minutes," he said, "unless we're unlucky."

"You mean an air raid?" Eddie was looking round the Paddington streets disappointedly. This was London: sandbags, shuffling people, greyness, walls hanging in space.

"Nah—air raids ain't a trouble now. We've licked all that. We have him on the run, unless he starts with his secret weapon, he talks about. Not that we believe he's got one."

(They really do talk like the films, Eddie thought.)

"You're here. D'you want to borrer a tin 'at?"

He was set down at the end of a narrow curving street of shabby cottages with gardens. There was no paint anywhere and grime everywhere. Nobody much about, and most windows boarded up. Isobel Ingoldby's number must almost certainly be a mistake for it had Walt Disney lattice windows, and a shaggy evergreen plant trailing over it which would have sent Queen Mary into action before she'd even knocked at the front door. There was a squirrel made of plaster on the doorstep and a tin case full of empty milk bottles with a note saying *None today. Do not ring.*

It's somebody's who's out. This couldn't be hers, he thought, at the gate, as the door opened and she was standing there.

His first thought was a blankness.

She was ordinary.

She was big and ordinary and bored.

She had a cigarette in her hand and leaned back against the door saying, "Come on in then," as if he had come to read a gas meter.

Her hair was untidy and too long. Her feet were bare and she wore a shapeless sort of dressing-gown.

"Ciao," she said, closing the door behind him. He saw how tired she was, and sad.

And maybe disillusioned? Was she disillusioned about him, too? She'd last seen him in hospital, pale and almost dying, the centre of attention. But she had made no effort of any kind though she'd known he'd be coming. He'd written a fortnight ago. She looked as if she'd just turned out of bed. She was even yawning.

"You're tired?" he said.

"No. Well, yes. I'm always tired. Ghastly job."

"I thought you were some sort of egghead hush-hush type?"

"I am. Of a cryptic variety."

"What d'you mean?"

"Secret. D'you want—?"

She vaguely gestured towards the kitchen.

"Tea or something? A wee?"

"No. I thought of taking you out to lunch. To the Savoy, or somewhere?" He'd heard of the Savoy. He looked anxiously at her night clothes.

"I was there yesterday."

"Isobel—what is it?"

"What's what?"

"What have I done? Have I changed or something? You said to come."

She put out the cigarette on the hall table ashtray, caught sight of herself in the mirror and said, "Oh my God! I forgot to comb my hair." She turned to him and grinned and it was as if the sun had come out. The sloped cat's eyes were alive again. Her long arms went up behind her head to gather up her hair into a bundle and she pinned it there. A piece of it fell down, a lion-coloured tress. Slowly, she pinned it back again, her fingers long, and lovely, and her fingernails painted the most unflinching vermilion. The dressing-gown fell open when she dropped her hands and stretched them out to him.

"Oh Eddie. You are golden brown like a field of corn."

Her fingertips were at his collar. When he took off his British warm, then his officer's jacket, he saw that she had loosened and then removed his tie. She draped it over a wall-light and then was in his arms.

On the kitchen floor, naked, he thought the taxi must still be outside. He had got out of it only a minute ago. Then he forgot all that; where he had come from, where in the world he had landed, which was upon a kitchen floor, the filthy lino torn and stuck up with some sort of thick paper tape. There was an old fridge on tall legs. It was gas. Lying on the floor beside her, then above her, he could see the fridge's blue flame. It must be the oldest fridge in the world—oh, my God, Isobel. Isobel.

Later, oh much, much later, they rolled apart.

"I don't like this lino," he said. "It's disgusting."

"You're spoiled. Living in palaces."

"I was not living in palaces when you last saw me."

"You were hardly living at all."

They had moved on to a tiny sitting-room which was in darkness. It smelled of booze and dust. They felt their way to a divan that stank of nicotine.

"Why is there no light?"

"Do we need it?"

"Oh, Isobel."

"It's blacked-out. Permanently. Convenient. We've never taken down the shutters since the Blitz."

"*We?*"

"The other girl and I."

"Is she likely to come in?" His head was on her stomach. His tongue licked her skin. She was warm and alive and smelled of sweat and spice and he went mad for her again.

Later, "Who is she?"

"No one you know. She's Bletchley Park. Like me."

"It's a man, isn't it?"

"No. No, certainly not. Shall we go upstairs?"

The bedroom was lighter. It had a sloping ceiling and the windows looked country as if there had once been fields outside. It had the feel of a country place; a cottage. So here's London.

"It is a cottage," she said. "London's full of cottages. And of villages. This bed is a country bed. We found it here."

The bed was high and made of loops of metal. Its springs creaked and groaned beneath them.

"Please never get rid of it. Keep it forever."

The hours passed. Wrapped, coiled, melded together they slept. They woke. Eddie laughed, stretched out to her again.

"You are like a jungle creature," he said. "In an undiscovered country."

"Eddie," she said at last, winding herself into the sheets, "I have something very important to say. How much time have we got? When's your train?"

"Five-fifteen."

"It's nearly five o'clock already."

He fled the bed, he ran for the stairs, he limped and hopped into scattered garments, he yelled with terror.

She laughed and laughed.

He found one shoe, but the other was gone.

"This will finish me," he said. "This will be the end of the Army for me."

She howled with laughter from the bedroom; came laughing down the stairs wrapped in the sheet, lighting a new cigarette.

"Don't laugh at me."

"I am in love with you, Eddie."

"I have a bad reputation already. With my Colonel. And I am in charge of Queen Mary. Oh God—there's my shoe!" He was in his jacket, in his British warm, had found his cap as she wrapped herself around him.

"Eddie, Eddie. You look still the boy in the trees at High House."

"What time is it? Oh God. I've fifteen minutes. There won't be a taxi."

But there was a taxi. God has sent me a taxi, he thought. It was standing outside the door. "Paddington," he said. "In ten minutes. I'll give you ten pounds." He did not look back to see whether she was watching.

"Ten pounds, sir."

"Thank you. Thank you very much." (It's only what I'd have spent at the Savoy. God but I'm hungry.)

"Yes. Platform one. Where's the bit of carpet? Is it gone?"

It was there. And word had gone round. Somehow a crowd had gathered beside the Royal coach and the top of the toque with its doves' feathers could be seen passing between the clapping avenue of loyal subjects. The lady-in-waiting was invisible, a small woman to begin with, and no doubt weighted down now with more wool. The bodyguards were already on the train. Eddie gave a brief nod to the guard and jumped into his private cabin, slammed the door and fell on the banquette. I'll go along in a minute. Just get my breath.

The train began to steam slowly, powerfully, inexorably away from London.

Go along in a minute, he thought and fell asleep.

He woke to a crash and shriek of brakes. The whole train jolted, shuddered and stopped. Outside it was now dark and he jumped from his long blue velvet couch and made for the corridor, to meet one of the bodyguards coming to find him.

"Emergency, sir. Probably unexploded bomb on the line. Queen Mary's sent for you."

The lady-in-waiting was trembling. From outside came a series of shouts. The train began to shunt backwards, squealing and complaining.

"It's the Invasion," said the lady-in-waiting.

"Don't be ridiculous, Margaret," said the Queen. "Eddie, take her along to your compartment and find her an aspirin. She needs a rest. Then come back again and we can talk. I want to hear every single thing you've done today."

"So *tiresome*," she said an hour later. "The carriage so dark. These blue spot-lights are very clever but they're just not bright enough to read by." She fell silent. "But it's nice to look out at the moonlight."

"Yes, Ma'am." (And he realised she was afraid. He'd heard that though she never showed it by a tremor she was terrified of kidnap.)

"And you did no more than that, Captain Feathers?" (Captain Feathers? What's this?) "No more than go about in taxis? You didn't even go to the Savoy for luncheon as you'd so wished?"

"I'm afraid not. I found London—overwhelming. Kensington seemed quite like an unknown vil-vill-vill-village."

"A *village*? How very odd. I was born there. In Kensington Palace. I never felt it a village."

"I—couldn't find Kensington Palace."

"Oh dear," she said.

The train at last jerked forward, stopped, jerked again and then began to steam sweetly along towards the West.

"That is a pity," said Her Majesty. "By the way" (looking out at the moonlight) "whatever has become of your tie?"

On the way home from their walk about the meadows around Badminton House, Old Filth asked the girl and her grandmother if they would stop the wheelchair at the post office for him to buy postcards. "No, no," he said. "Let me get out and walk. Do me good," and he hopped into the shop and back again, carrying three postcards of the village, all ready and stamped. He was able to hop around the car, and hold open the door for the grandmother as the girl put the folding chair back in the boot.

"So extremely kind of you," he said. "A splendid afternoon." Sitting by the reception desk he thought he would write the postcards at once though it was too late for the post, for a cloud no bigger than a man's hand had gathered around the recollection of his departure from home. He would write to Mrs.-er—to *Kate*—and to Garbutt. Perhaps he would write to lacy Chloe, too, and make her day.

Then he found that he had never had Mrs.-er's (Kate's) address. It was somewhere in the next village. It would be offensive to send it c/o Garbutt, for she had preceded Garbutt in his employment by years. He addressed one card to Garbutt at the house down the hill from his own, well known to him. Peep o'Day. Easy to remember. So was Chloe's: The Manor House, Privilege Lane. On Garbutt's card he wrote, "Please say I'm sorry to Kate."

He had one card left over now and wrote it to Claire, mentioning that he had sprained something but was otherwise having a very good holiday by himself in Gloucestershire at this beautiful hotel. He was exalted. His optimistic self, he felt, was just around the corner.

But in the early hours of the next morning he woke with a chilling certainty that all was not well. He switched on his bedside lamp, hopped from the bed, opened a window upon the night. He shivered, and then flushed and sweated. He went for a pee, then drank a glass of water, hopped back, hot and cold by turns, clambered between the sheets. He knew that he was ill.

He knew that he was very ill. He had no idea what it was, but he knew that he was not in control. He lay and waited.

He stretched his hand out to the bedside table drawer and felt about for the never-failing *Gideon's Bible* that had seen him through many a sleepless hotel night during his legal life. In skyscrapers in Hong Kong, in the Shangri-la in Singapore, the dear old Intercon in Dacca. Lonely places, until he'd been married and able to take Betty along with him. He thought he needed a *Gospel* tonight, and turned up one of Christ's dingdongs with the lawyers.

He wondered, the pages shaking as he turned them, why Christ had so hated lawyers when He'd have been such a brilliant one Himself. Christ, when you considered it, was simply putting a Case. He may well have been enjoying the lawyers' examinations of him. Pilate's was his most respectable interrogation. Pilate had not been a lawyer, but another excellent lawyer manqué. Pilate and Christ had understood each other.

"We still use a little Roman Law, here," he told Christ tonight. "The Law can always do with a going-over as you pointed out then. Execution should be entirely out. Execution leads only to victory for the corpse. You proved that," he informed the Holy Ghost.

He dreamed for a little, drifted, read the Sermon on the Mount, remembered hearing that no child nowadays has heard of the Sermon on the Mount and most guess it is a book or a film. He thought benevolently how he should like to be upon another Bench listening to Christ going for the defence in a Case to do with, say, a land-reclamation.

A fist grabbed him in the chest and pain shot through him. He could not breathe. He stretched for the bell and kept his right hand on it as the pain sank down, then surged up again. It's the Hand of God, he thought. And nobody but God knows where the hell I am.

Garbutt's house was empty when the phone began to ring the next morning. He had gone to Privilege Road to help the tedious Chloe with her asparagus bed and they were both down in the garden when her phone began to ring, too.

"I'll leave it," she said. "It won't be anything."

But it rang on.

She caught it as the other end was about to put it down.

"I'm very sorry to hear it," she said. "Yes. He's a neighbour but not a *close* friend. No—I don't think there are any relations. Well, he's over eighty. He's never had anything wrong with him in his life. The time comes. He's not very popular here in the village, I'm afraid. He treats his servants badly. Very difficult for you. I think there are some cousins in Essex. Oh, I see, you've tried them. Well, I can't help you. Goodbye."

"Sir Edward's had a heart attack," she said, returning to the asparagus bed. "I said last week it was blood-pressure, the way he was behaving."

"What? Where?" said Garbutt.

"Well, around his heart."

"Where was the call from?"

"I didn't ask."

Garbutt blundered her out of the way, ran through her French doors and across her pastel Chinese carpet, dialled 1471, then pressed three.

"He's in hospital," said the hotel. "The ambulance came very quickly. We were surprised. He'd been so much better. He'd been out in the afternoon and eaten an excellent dinner."

"Had he been ill already, then?"

"Yes, he arrived with a sprained ankle. Do you want the name of the hospital? I hope you will excuse us asking but will there be funds to pay his account?"

"Funds have never been a trouble to him."

"Thank you. We were beginning to grow very fond of him."

"People do," said Garbutt, and phoned Kate, and then his wife.

Garbutt found Filth, looped up to drips and scans, trying to shut out the quack of the television sets and the clatter of the public ward where male and female lay alongside each other in various stages of ill health. Like Pompeii.

It was an old hospital. The windows were too high to see anything except the wires and concrete of unexciting buildings and the sky. The light was not the pearly light of yesterday in the meadows of Badminton, which Filth was trying to remember and decide when and where it had been and whom he had been with. Memory, he thought. Memory. My memory has always been so reliable. Perhaps too reliable. It has never spared me. *Memory and desire*, he thought. Who said that? *Without memory and desire life is pointless*? I long ago lost any sort of desire. Now memory.

Suddenly he knew that this was what had been the matter with him for years. He had lost desire. Not sexual desire, that had been a poor part of his nature always. He had been furtive about the poverty of his sexual past. Dear Betty—she had been very undemanding. He had never told her about the buttermilk business and had skimmed over Isobel Ingoldby. Whatever would the young make of him today? It seemed they were all like rabbits and started haphazardly as soon as they reached double figures. He found them repellent.

And homosexuals repellent, if he were honest. And divorce repellent. Blacks—here he was disturbed by a cluster of different coloured people surrounding his bed. These are not the black people of the Empire, he thought, and then realised that that was exactly what most of them were. "Any of you chaps Malays?" he asked. "Malaya's my country. *Malaysia* now, of course. And Ceylon's Sri Lanka, Lanka's what my friend Loss called it, and he should know. It was full of his uncles. That's what he said before he went down the trough. Bombed by the bloody Japanese, I expect. Oh, sorry." The lead figure in the performance around his bed was Japanese. "Didn't realise. It's your West Country accent."

"OK, grandpa," said the Japanese. "Take it easy."

Filth's days passed. Various bits of equipment were detached from him. Once he thought that Garbutt was sitting at the end of the bed and gave a feeble wave. "Very sorry about this. How's Mrs.-er? Very sorry to have upset Mrs.-er. Feeling better. I'd like to see a priest, though." Then he slept, and woke in the night trying to ring a bell for a priest.

"It's not Sunday," said a nurse. "Or are you a Catholic? You're getting better. Talk to them in the morning. Go to sleep, old gramps. Think positive."

Times have been worse than this, he thought. Much worse.

It's just there's no chance of many more of them, of times of any sort, now. That's absolutely rationally true, a serious, even beautiful equation. Life ends. You're tired of it anyway.

No memory. No desire. Yet you don't want it to be over. Not quite yet.

Bloody memory.

"I was very happy round here, you know, in the War," he said to a passing Sikh. "I was a friend of Queen Mary. She remembered my birthday. She sent me chocolate."

"Who's Queen Mary?" asked the Sikh in an Estuary accent. "The Queen Mum?"

"While I lived here in Gloucestershire," said drowsing Filth, "I rather buried my head."

"Bury it now," said the Sikh, "and get to sleep."

"Before I go," said Filth, "I really do want to see a priest."

But when they found him a priest next day, he was feeling much better, was loosed from his bonds, was sent to a terrible place to wash, was given cornflakes and a type of meat which smelled of onions and was laced with a fluid called "brown sauce," and was told that he would later on be going home.

Moreover, the priest, when he arrived, was wearing jeans and a T-shirt and Filth did not believe in him. He would have preferred a female to this one, and that was saying something. His confession would have to be postponed. He sat and read the *Daily Telegraph* in a small, contained cubicle, his carrier bag at his feet. He sat there all morning, and at some point dozed off, thinking of other occasions in his life of total reversion, of failure.

After six months he had been posted away from Badminton. The War had changed. We were now on the winning side and there was a new jauntiness. Queen Mary's staff unpacked her three suitcases in the attics and he was sent to the War Office on the mistaken premise that he was a linguist and well-connected. He experienced the Mall on VE Day and was released to Oxford much more quickly than his War record deserved.

He took a First in Law after only two years and was called to the Bar and set about the much harder matter of finding a seat in somebody's Chambers.

It was the winter still talked of, half a century on: 1947.

Memory and desire, he thought.

CHAMBERS

The January rain of 1947 slopped down upon dilapidated Lincoln's Inn Fields, puckering the stagnant surfaces of the static-water tanks implanted in its grass. Eddie Feathers observed it from the passage in a small set of undistinguished Chambers in New Square. He kept the door open between the passage and the Senior Barrister's empty room on the front of the building, otherwise he had no view except the dustbins at the back. On days like this and on days of smog which were getting more frequent though coal was rationed to a bag a week, he could look through the door to what he might look forward to if the old fellow stopped coming in altogether. A good old room with magnificent carved Elizabethan fireplace and a large portrait of the Silk's unhappy-looking wife: the sort of wartime bridal face that wished it had waited.

In an adjoining, equally historic, equally dusty room but lacking an uxorial photograph sat the only other member of Chambers, usually asleep. These rooms had been built as legal Chambers hundreds of years ago and had housed a multitude of lawyers from before the Commonwealth. Wigs in these rooms had been worn naturally, like hats. Then even hats around Chambers had gone—bowler hats had also just about disappeared by 1947, though Eddie Feathers had bought one for five excessive pounds, and it hung, laughably, on a hook inside the Chambers' street door.

The passage was bitterly cold. There were no carpets, no curtaining, a small spluttering heater. He sat before a splintered table where transcripts of a dispute stood two feet high, almost indecipherable blueprints concerning the installation of new water-closets throughout a bombed government building, his annotation of which went down at about a sixteenth of an inch per hour. Sir, his school, his college, Queen Mary, all pointed stern fingers at Eddie. Habit dictated. There had been black hours before. Diligence gets you through. Keep going. Oh God why?

Gloucestershire and Oxford kept breaking in on him. Christ Church meadow, the bells stumbling and tumbling, calling down the High. The wallflowers—the smell of the velvet wallflowers outside his set of rooms. The emptiness of his Quad, returning home at night. Hardly a soul about. Music from the open windows. And the spring there, and the politics and the friends. Too much work. Too much work to go to parties, even to attend the Union, meet any girls, too many men just up from school drinking themselves silly, schoolchildren who had missed the War. Leaving Oxford had surprised him by its finality.

The rain fell. In the far room with the door shut he heard the comatose, under-employed Head of Chambers fart and yawn. The fart was an elderly fart—lengthy, unmusical and resigned.

Eddie found that he was crying, and mopped his face. He thought he might as well go home for the day.

But, no. Better not. Another quarter-inch of notes. No point in going out in the rain. It was a longish walk to the Aldwych tube station and he had no macintosh. There were a couple of changes on his tube (everyone wheezing and smelling of no soap) to get back to his bed-sit in sleazy Notting Hill. Then out again for something to eat at an ABC café: sausage and mash, stewed apple and custard, keep within a shilling. There was still no sign of his inheritance. He'd been told it might take years to prove the death, let alone the Will. He was still unable to put his mind to the imagining of his father's end. No friend of his father, no official notification from the Foreign Office. Eddie pushed down the guilt that he had made no enquiries.

There had been no communication from the aunts. "I shall learn one day," was all he allowed himself.

He must get a bike. Save the fares. He was earning a hundred pounds a year devilling for the absent Silk with the difficult wife. Three hundred a year in all, with the very odd Brief. He had one good suit, kept his shoes soled and heeled, washed his new-fangled nylon shirt every evening and hung it round the geyser in the communal bathroom at his lodgings, to dry for the morning. To keep up appearances before solicitors and clients. Not that there were any clients. Not for him. Not for years yet. Maybe never. Nobody knew him. Along the passage the old Silk farted again.

It had been nearly a year ago that Eddie, walking round the once-beautiful London squares one evening—without money there was nothing else to do, he was putting the hours in until bedtime—had thought of the building and engineering aspect of the Law. The War was over. One day—look at Germany—rebuilding of the ruins must surely occur in this country. Building disputes, he thought. There'll be hundreds of them. Enquiring about, he had found a set of engineering Chambers that had been bombed and moved into this backwater of Lincoln's Inn.

There was not even space for a Clerk's room. This had had to be rented across a yard. The Senior Clerk, who looked like an unsuccessful butler and spent much time in rumination, left early after lunch for South Wimbledon. The clever Junior Clerk, Tom, hideously unemployed, worked like mad around the pubs at lunchtime among the Clerks of other Chambers, trying to get leads on coming Cases and plotting where he would move to next. He liked Eddie and was sorry for him. "I should pack it in, sir," he said one day. "You're worth better than this—First from Oxford. I can't sell you here. Go to New Zealand."

I might, thought Eddie today, looking through the door to the grander room and then beyond it out of the old, absent

Silk's window to the rain falling. Between the building and the Inn garden where stood a great tree which had survived other wars, a white Rolls-Royce was parked. He could see the chauffeur inside it in a green uniform. Not usual. Eddie sighed, and lifted the next pages of transcript off the pile.

The street door of the Chambers now banged open against the wall and feet came running towards Eddie's alley. The Junior Clerk, macintosh flapping—he'd been waiting to go home—flung open his door and shouted, "Come on, sir. Quick. Quick, sir! Get up. Leave those papers. Get into that front room. Behind the desk. You've got a client."

"Client?"

"New solicitor. Get the dust off those sets of papers. Smarten your clothing. Where's that classy clothes-brush of yours? Here. I'll put his wife's photo out of sight. Wrong image. You're young and free to travel. I think you're on the move."

"Move?"

"I've got you a Brief. It's a big one. Four hundred on the Brief and forty a day. Likely to last two weeks."

"Whoever—?"

"Don't ask me. It's Hong Kong. It's a Chinese dwarf."

"You've gone insane, Tom. It's a hoax."

"Turned up in that Rolls. I've had him sitting in the Clerk's room twenty minutes. I'll bring him over."

"WAIT!"

"Wait? Wait? Look, it's a pipeline failure in Hong Kong. You're on your way."

"A *Chinese dwarf*?"

"Come back. Where you going, sir? I bring him over here to you, you don't go running after him."

"Where is he now?" Eddie shouted from the courtyard.

"He's still in the Clerks' room. I told him I was coming to see *if* you were free. I bring him to you. *Gravitas, sir.*"

But Eddie was gone, over the courtyard, under the lime tree, running in the rain. The chauffeur in the Rolls turned to look, raising an eyebrow.

Eddie ran into the Clerks' room, where Albert Loss was seated on the sagging purple sofa playing Patience.

"*Coleridge!*"

"Spot the lady. Kill the ace of spades."

"*Coleridge*! God in heaven, Coleridge. But you're dead. The Japanese killed you."

"Colombo didn't fall. You are an amnesiac. There were initial raids. And then they left us alone. You should have stayed. I found my uncle. Several of them. All attorneys. And so I became one too."

"This is the most wonderful . . . How ever did you find me?"

"Law Lists, my dear old chum. Top of the Law Lists. Thanks to me. I directed you, you will remember, towards the Law. And now I am Briefing you. My practice is largely in Hong Kong. I hope you have no serious family ties?"

"Not a tie. Not a thread. Not a cobweb—*Coleridge!*"

"Good. Then you can fly to Hong Kong next week? First class, of course. We must not lose face before the clients. We'll put you up in the Peninsular."

"I'll have to read the papers."

"Nonsense, Fevvers. You'll do it all in your head. On the plane. Open-and-shut Case, and I taught you Poker. You can think. I'm flying back myself tomorrow."

"This is a dream. You're exactly the same. You haven't aged. By the way, what happened to my watch?"

"Ah, that had to be sacrificed in the avuncular search. But you have aged, Fevvers. You have been aged by your Wartime experiences, no doubt?"

"You could say that. Coleridge, come on! Let's go out. Where are you staying?"

"The Dorchester, of course. But there is no time for social

punishment. I fly tomorrow and I must see my builders. I'm buying a house in the Nash Terraces of Regent's Park. All in ruins. Practically free at present. If you want it to rent, after the pipeline, it's yours. By the way, were you met?"

"Met?"

"At Liverpool? Off the old Portuguese tub?"

"Yes. Yes, I was—"

"I was forced to borrow your address book. I'm afraid it has fallen by the way. My uncles were very close to the Corps of Signals. And of course I have a phenomenal memory."

"You should be a spy."

"Thank you, but I am in gainful employment. It's very good to see you, Feathers. Very nice clothes-brush. Do you want it?"

"Yes. *Coleridge!*"

"And by the way," Albert Loss said at the car, the chauffeur towering above him, holding a brolly, "while I'm away in Hong Kong, do make use of the Royce."

LAST RITES

"Indigestion," said the hotel to Claire over the tele-phone. "A very bad case of indigestion."

"He said on the postcard a sprained ankle."

"The indigestion followed. It was the prawns. Looked iden-tical to a heart attack. He's been in hospital. He's back here again now recovering from the hospital. Can we get him for you? He's out in the sun, well wrapped up. Who shall we say?"

"Will you say Claire? And that I had his postcard."

"We were very glad of those postcards."

"Hello," said Filth, tottering in. "I was wondering if some-one could find me a priest."

The bar listened. The nice girl came and sat him in a chair. Dialling the number for him, handing him the phone, she said, "Sir Edward, the priest business was last week."

"What? Hello? Claire? There are things I want to get off my chest. This episode was rather alarming. Some unfinished busi-ness. You know what I'm talking about."

"I have no idea."

"You and I and Babs."

"What about us?"

"And Cumberledge?"

There was silence.

"Oh, long, long ago," she said.

"But I need to tell someone, even so. What happened to your priest? The one in the church with all the marble babies?"

"Do you mean Father Tansy? I thought he was anathema to you."

"Well, yes. He was. But I keep remembering him. Can you find him for me?"

"But you're in Gloucestershire. And I hear you can't walk and have had a suspected heart attack."

"False alarm. Got over-excited reading the Gospels."

"Say goodbye to her now, Sir Edward. We'll bring you your lunch in the lounge. You still have to take care."

"Goodbye, Claire. Thank you for ringing. I'll ring again."

The day wore on. He sat in remote reveries. They brought him tea.

Bloody good of them to have me back here, he thought. All thanks to Loss I can pay for it. Set me on my path. But I've worked for it myself, too. I've worked for my millions. Survived them too. Loss didn't.

He began to doze and was woken by the nice girl and her grandmother with a bunch of asters. "You should keep off prawns," said the grandmother. "After seventy you should keep off prawns. You never saw Queen Mary even look at a prawn."

"It may have been the banana split," said her granddaughter.

"I don't eat bananas," said Filth.

Next day came a letter from Claire in her trailing bright blue handwriting.

Dear Teddy,
It so happens that Father Tansy is coming to your part of the world to visit his Boys' Club in Falmouth. Babs will be with him. It all seems prophetic. I have told them where you are.
As to the matter of our rotten childhood, old cousin, you should forget it. I have never let what we did trouble me, even in dreams. I had no difficulty with it at the time and I've never felt the need to speak about it since. Oliver, for instance, does not know, and

neither did my late-lamented husband. What would now be called "The Authorities" spirited us all away so fast after the death that it didn't get much into the papers. Now, it would have dominated the telly for a month.

D'you know that I met Cumberledge again? It was only a few years ago. As a matter of fact, it was the day you were staying with us, when Oliver took me to Cambridge for tea with some grandee from his old college, a Dean who's still in residence. Someone who was kind to Oliver when he was up. Well, all the time we were in the old boy's rooms I felt puzzled, as if I knew him. He seemed quite unaware of me. My surname has changed and it was three-quarters of a century on and Oliver had never mentioned that I'd been a Raj Orphan. Oliver told me his name on the way home and after you'd all gone I sat down here in High Light and wrote him a letter, hoping I wasn't stirring up something best forgotten. We struck up a thoroughly boring correspondence.

I'm not sure whether I'm pleased or not that he never referred to the murder. Well yes, of course I'm sure. I was not pleased. I should have liked to hear what he thought we'd all been at. I often think, when I'm reading in the papers about a murder, that the murderer is the last person to be aware of the crime. Sometimes he is not aware of it for years, I'd guess. Well, you'll know all about that. Murderers are the possessed.

I'm not saying there's no such thing as guilt. And wickedness.

I'm saying there is confusion and derangement in the mature murderer. What is so interesting about our murder is that there was neither. No confusion. No derangement. We three—not Cumberledge—were absorbed in the process of handing over responsibility to the powers of darkness whom we had met as children, and who had met us. We were thoroughly engaged, us three. Still untamed. We were of the jungle.

Poor Babs—she's probably the best of us—went mad. She's maddish most of the time. But she's still Babs. Ma Didds was cruellest of all to her. Stopped her singing. Gagged her mouth. Babs became castrated. Ugly in mind, body and estate. Grows uglier now. And yet I remember her dazzling for a while when she was in the War.

You, dear Teddy, Ma Didds feared because of your height and strength and prodigious good looks. Oh, how unfair are our looks! Didds knew she could never make you ugly. She worked on your stammer. She was afraid of your silences. You were not like a child then. You are more of a child now. Betty came and stripped the years away from you in what looked like the perfect marriage. She never asked for more than you could give. Others gave her passion. You were a saint about Veneering. You were a wall of alabaster. You saved each other. You and Betty. I'd guess, neither of you ever spoke of it.

But nobody ever loved you like I did, Teddy.

Yet I was the coldest of us. I was the harshest. I was the actress. I was the little pretty one who never did wrong. I was the one who suggested the murder.

Cumberledge never made a decision in his quiet life (I don't know how he got so high up in the Army before he was wafted into Cambridge). He was utterly passive—all his weeping and screaming as she approached him with the whip (I am writing down what I have never before even been able to think about). But something deep in him remained untouched by her. I bet he became amiable and soppy. A man always falling in love.

You, Teddy, were horribly touched by her. You became no good at love. I don't think you ever had many friends at school. I'm the same, if I'm honest. I can't love. I'm all charm. Babs needs love. Needs it as her daily bread. Will try for it anywhere. But she repels, the poor old thing. Doesn't wash now—that's a bad sign. It won't help her with Father Tansy. She says she once had an *affaire* with Cumberledge. All fantasy.

D'you know, the one who needed love most was Ma Didds. All the hatred was love gone wrong. What did she ever get from old Pa Didds and all that chapel?

Not that as children we could have been expected to know, but I had an inkling when she took me on her smelly old lap and crooned over me and gave me buttered bread. I knew already where my bread was buttered. I'd been sent away younger than any of you, and my parents were faceless; but I was, and am, the toughest. I'm very glad I thought of the murder. I thoroughly enjoyed it. So don't fret. It was you who struck the blow, dear Teddy, but they can't hang you now. Love from Claire

He tore the letter up.

I am old at last, he thought. I should be cold too. But I am casting off the coldness of youth and putting on the maudlin armour of dotage. I am not a religious man. Claire does not shock me, as she would most people. *Why* do I want a priest?

Rites? Ceremonies? I despise myself. It's all superstition. Yet I know that I must tell someone that when I was eight years old I killed a woman in cold blood.

The West wind of the equinox bashed suddenly against the conservatory glass of the hotel lounge where Filth sat, now alone. Then the wind stopped and he slept. In his sleep he heard the steady beating of a drum, and started awake, thinking that it was his heart. They helped him back to his bedroom where the grandmother's asters shone on the window-sill.

"I am so undeservedly lucky," he said to the chambermaid later, beginning the repair of his damaged image. (Claire's terrifying letter.) He smiled his lovely smile.

"Lucky in material things anyway," he said when he was alone again, curtains closed, lying in the sweet dark. "Their kindness is only because they've found out that I'm rich. There'll be no trouble with the bill." Considering other people's pragmatism, he found that Claire's beastly letter receded.

But, dropping into sleep, a great face flooded across his dream landscape, filled the screen of his sleeping consciousness, loomed at him—disappeared. "Go away, Veneering," Filth shouted after it. "I'm not ready to talk. Not yet."

A few days later, Father Tansy turned up at the delectable hotel, with a woman in a wavy nylon skirt and grey nun's headgear who turned out to be Babs.

Filth was in bed again. He had been advised to stay there for a day or two and not trouble himself with visitors, and his curtains were pulled across the daylight when the manager of the hotel knocked and eventually put his head around his door, and switched on the light, and Babs and the priest beheld the catafalque figure of Filth under the sheet, his ivory nose pointed upwards, the nose of a very old man.

"Perhaps not long?" said the manager. "Don't stay too long." Babs said she would go out now and take her dog for a walk.

Then Father Tansy shut the door behind him, opened the curtains and switched off the light. He picked up the bedside phone and ordered room-service luncheon in an hour's time. Then he ran round the bedroom removing drooping asters and opening all the windows. He found Filth's dressing-gown and manoeuvred him into it, heaved the old bones off the bed, slid the ivory fans of Filth's feet into his Harrods leather bedroomslippers, sat Filth on an upright chair and set a table in front of him.

"Have I shaved?" asked Filth. "Oh dear, I do hope so."

"Never mind that," said Tansy. "Wake up. You have sent for me at last. I have been waiting patiently."

"You have a great idea of your own importance," said Filth. "I remember you, awash in that great marble church."

"Not my own importance," said Tansy. "I follow Another's importance. I try to follow the personality of Christ, and am directed by it."

"I don't believe in all that," said Filth. "But there's something, somewhere, that's urging me to talk to a—well, I suppose, to a priest. You are the only priest I know. How you got here, I don't know. What I'm doing here, I don't know. I've been dreaming lately. About Queen Mary."

"Queen Mary?"

"Yes. And my father. And a—murder. And other loose ends."

Father Tansy waited with bright eyes, like a squirrel. "Carry on."

"I suppose it's going to be a confession," said Filth. "I'm glad you're not hidden in one of those boxes. I'm not up to that."

"I know."

"I can't start until Babs comes back. She's part of it. And I've been seriously ill."

"Sir Edward, you can begin by telling me what's the matter with you. And I don't want to hear about prawns and strained ligaments."

After a time Filth said, "All my life, Tansy, from my early childhood, I have been left, or dumped, or separated by death, from everyone I loved or who cared for me. I want to know why."

"You are a hero in your profession, Sir Edward."

"That's an utterly different matter. And in fact I don't believe you. Nobody remembers me now at the Bar. My work is quite forgotten. I was once famous for some Pollution Law. All out-of-date now. I want to tell you something. When my Chambers were moved to a newly built office block, like a government department, costing millions which by then we could all afford—there were thirty-six members of Chambers when I decided to go permanently to Hong Kong—the old Clerk, who was retiring, took me down into the basement under the Elizabethan building where I began, and there was a sea of Briefs there, three feet deep, bundled up with pink tape. 'We don't know what to do with it,' he said. 'We've decided to get a firm in to throw it on a dump.' That was years of my life. Years and years."

"It's not often," said the priest, "made as clear to us as that. I see it in my empty pews."

"It has all been void. I am old, forgotten and dying alone. My last friend, Veneering, has died. I miss him but I never quite trusted him. My most valuable friend was a card-sharp and my wife hated him though he made our fortunes at the Far Eastern Bar. He was killed on 9/11. A passenger in one of the planes. Still playing cards, I imagine. Hadn't heard from him for years."

Babs came back in and made the dog lie down. It immediately climbed on Filth's bed and lay looking across at him as if he'd seen him somewhere before.

"The point is," said Filth, seated at his table, recovering a little of his former authority when addressing the Court, "the point is, I have begun to wonder whether my life of loneliness—always basically I have felt quite alone—is because of what I did when I was eight years old, living with Babs and Claire in Wales, fostered by a woman called Mrs. Didds."

Babs scratched her leg in its thick grey stocking and looked out of the window. "Go on then, Teddy," she said. "Spit it out."

Father Tansy, no trace now of the prancing comic of his parish church, his Office completely dominating him, sat still, and nodded once.

When Filth was obviously unable to begin, Babs said, "Oh, I'll do it, then."

There was a silence.

"She hurt us," Babs said. "She had that sort of smiling face, plump and round, that when you look closer is cruel. Nobody had noticed. Probably, when she first fostered children she was different. Pa Didds was a nice old man but he just sat about. Then he died. They'd had no children of their own. By the time the three of us arrived, she'd begun to hate children, but she had to keep on fostering because there was nothing else. They went on sending her children. From all over the Empire. When the children complained . . . Most never did, they thought she was normal. Anyway the children couldn't complain until they'd got away, somewhere else. And there wasn't anywhere else. We were all sent to her for four or five years. You know, longer than we'd been *alive*. The complaining ones were thought to be cowards. We had to copy the Spartans in those days. You should have seen the illustrations in children's books of the Raj then. Pictures of children beating *each other* with canes at school. The prefectorial system. Now it would be thought porn. It was Cumberledge, of course, she hated most."

"He was there when we arrived," said Filth. "In bed. Not speaking. He was pale and fat and sobbing and he didn't come down to tea. 'What's the matter with the other boy?' Babs asked. 'He's wet his bed again,' Ma Didds said, and she laid one of her long whips over the table. 'And he'll have to wash his own sheets.'"

"I shared a room with him," said Filth, eventually. "He smelled and I hated him. He slept on the floor to save the sheets, but then he'd wet his pyjamas. He used to take them off and lie on the boards, but then she'd beat him a second time for removing his pyjamas. We had to watch."

"How long did it last?"

"Years," said Babs. "They merged, the years. It seemed our whole lives. We forgot there had been anything different. Anything before."

"Not altogether," said Filth. "Claire—by the way, she never hurt Claire—Claire was younger and very pretty and she used to sit her on her knee and comb her hair. Before Pa Didds went off into hospital and died, he used to be nice to me and Babs. There were several good moments."

"He liked you," said Babs. "Took you for walks. He never took me for walks. I used to sing hymns very, very loud. She hated my singing. She bandaged my mouth."

"And the end of the story?" asked the priest.

"Claire decided on the end of the story one day while we were gathering the hens' eggs in the hen-house. It was our job. We liked it—all the fluster and the commotion and the rooster crowing. It was a day when Cumberledge had been flogged and flung back to his bed and was crying again. It was almost as if Ma Didds loved Cumberledge in some horrible cruel way, especially after Pa Didds died. As if she hated herself. She used to sit rocking herself and holding her stomach after we'd all gone to bed. We peeped over the stairs and saw her. As if she had a baby inside her."

"She shut me in cupboards," said Filth. "I began to stammer even worse than I did already. Then she would shout at me to answer her politely, and when I couldn't get any words out she'd bang my face against the wall or box my ears, and shout at me again to answer her."

"She fed us well," said Babs. "Great plates of food. Big

stews and home-made bread. 'You should see the food they eat,' she told them at the chapel. 'Fat as pigs.' She stuffed us. Except for Claire. Claire left half of hers and smiled at Ma Didds like an angel. She never punished Claire."

"Claire is the cleverest of us," said Babs.

"And so—?" said Tansy.

"And so, this evening in the hen-house, Cumberledge indoors, inarticulate as ever, Claire, she was only six, said, 'I think we should kill her.'"

"We all three knew how to do it. We'd had ayahs. And Eddie had his amah."

"I used to watch her and the whole village in the compound," said Filth. "They would kill a cockerel as a sacrifice and then they'd beat a drum. The incantations went on for hours. They burnt things that belonged to the one they wanted dead. Hair. A button. And feathers from the cockerel. Then the person died."

"You believed it?"

"Oh yes. It was true. It happened. Always."

"I knew how to kill a cockerel," said Filth. "Ada could do it. I used to watch. But when I tried to catch Ma Didds's rooster, it was too strong for me, so I caught a hen and killed it instead. It's very easy. Ada used to tie the legs together and then break the neck by twirling it hard, upside down, round and round, in the dry mud. I did it on the floor of the hen-house. Ma Didds was at chapel. We were always alone on Sunday nights. I cut off its head with the bread knife and took it inside. Claire had taken some of Ma Didds's hair out of her comb. We took the matches and lit the hair and the hen's head in the hearth, and Babs sang."

"I sang *There's a friend for little children*," said Babs, "*Above the bright blue sky*, and Eddie banged saucepan lids together. We hadn't expected the hen's head to smell so bad or to be so difficult to burn. Then we heard her coming and we all ran upstairs."

"We'd forgotten to shut the hen-house door," said Filth, "and that was the first thing she saw, and one or two hens roosting on the roof. She came thundering in and took up a cane and then she smelt the feathers. She shouted, 'Cumberledge!' and started up the stairs. When she went upstairs, she always had to hold her stomach up. It hung down. It was repulsive. So she came up the stairs holding her stomach in one hand, and her other arm raised holding the cane. 'This time I'll *break* you, Cumberledge!'"

"But at the top," said Babs, when Filth could not continue, "Eddie stepped forward from the room he shared with Cumberledge. Claire and I had come out of our room and were standing near. Cumberledge did not move from under his bed. He didn't see it. But we saw. We saw Eddie catch hold of her wrist, the wrist holding the cane high. He was above her on the stairs and taller than her already. And he just stood there, holding her wrist above her head. And she said, 'Let go my wrist. I am going to see to Cumberledge.' And she had to clutch her stomach with her other hand."

"And so," said Filth, "I let go of her very suddenly so that she fell backwards down the stairs. And lay still at the bottom of them. Before she lay still, there was a—crack. Like a snapped tree."

"I ran to clear up the burnt head," said Babs, "and Eddie went to look after Cumberledge. Claire put on her coat and went down to the village to get help. But she was a very long time because it was a dark night and she got lost. She's always hated the dark. So Teddy and I got into bed together to be close. We couldn't make Cumberledge get in with us. In the end Teddy and I went to sleep and we only woke up when they were clearing Ma Didds away. She wasn't dead, as it turned out, but she died the next day. They had to do an emergency operation on her for cancer of the stomach. That's what she died of, they said. She'd have died in a few days, anyway."

"*What?*" said Filth. "Nobody ever told me that."

"And the other boy? Cumberledge?"

"Cumberledge's so-called guardians took him away at once. There was a scandal about his condition and he vanished from us. We were kept down in the village until Auntie May could come, and Eddie's Sir."

"Were questions asked?"

"So far as I know, none. There had been rumours for a long time. But Welsh villages stick together against foreigners, and we were all very foreign children there. Wales was more secretive in those days and the language defeated us. But nobody suggested anything criminal about us."

"Nobody," said Babs. "Claire even got some presents. Everyone always loves Claire."

In this expensive and benign hotel in the English late autumn light, they sat, all three, in silence.

"You have come to me asking for absolution?" asked Father Tansy. "You repent?"

Eddie Feathers, Old Filth, the judge, Fevvers, a Master of the Inner Temple, Teddy—pillar of justice, arbitrator of truth said nothing.

"No," he said at last. "I don't. I can't."

"No, I don't either," said Babs. "And I know Claire doesn't."

"Did Cumberledge survive? Is he sane?"

"Very much so," said Filth. "I next met him in the dark in Oxford. During the War when I was lost in the snow. I didn't realise who it was. Between eight and eighteen we all change utterly. Yet years later I somehow realised. He was coming out of a blacked-out church. He had a calmness and a kindness. He was Army. He wrote when Betty died. His essence was unharmed."

"He became a grandee," said Babs. "He's retired to Cambridge. A grandee."

"There are those who are given Grace," said Tansy. "But you yourself wanted to make some sort of confession, Sir Edward?"

"I wanted to express my pity," said Filth. "My pity for her. For Ma Didds. I've tried hundreds of Cases, many more wicked than anything here. Some I still cannot bear to think about. I don't mean I cannot bear to think about my judgements—you have to be thick-skinned about that—I cannot bear to think about the cruelty at the core of this foul world. Or the vengeance dormant even in children. All there, ready, waiting for use. Without love. Cumberledge was given Grace. That's all I can say. We were not."

They still sat on.

The dog stretched on the bed and yawned and jumped down, bent over and rested its head on Babs's knobbly knee.

"We'll say the General Confession," said Tansy. "Together."

They did, Filth remembering it being hammered into him by Sir.

Tansy then said, "Let us pray. Remember these Thy children, oh merciful Lord. Heal them and keep them in Thine everlasting arms."

THE REVELATION

His house was clean and polished, his garden neat. A note on the kitchen table said, *Butter, cheese, milk in fridge. Eggs. Bread in crock. Bacon, etc. Welcome home. Kate.* Through the windows, looking towards the Downs, he saw movement in his apple tree and a next-door child dropped out of it, eating fruit, and wandered nonchalantly over the lawn as if he owned it. The hedge must have a hole in it, he thought. It might as well stay. His mail had been neatly stacked on his desk, the fire laid ready to light. She'd stuck some shop flowers in a vase.

It had been a good drive home. Most enjoyable. Christmas coming.

Very pleasant seeing poor Babs again. And the parson chap. Holiday full of events. And tomorrow he must see the doctor.

His ankle was very much better, and he had no trace of trouble with his heart—or digestion. All that was the matter with him now was the onset of winter aches and pains. His arthritis was remarkably mild for his age, they always said, especially considering the age of his damp old house.

"I am about to make another journey," he said the next day after his visit to the surgery in Shaftesbury. "Good morning, Mrs. Kate. How very good to see you. Thank you for the provisions. The house looks very well. I've brought you a keepsake from Gloucester. Where's Garbutt?"

*

"Garbutt," he said. "Good morning. Did I imagine it? Yes, of course I did. You didn't by any chance visit me in wherever it was I've been? I had some sort of dream. There were some very odd doctors. They thought I'd had a heart attack. Perfect nonsense."

"Thanks for the postcard," said Garbutt.

"Now then, you haven't got rid of me yet, either of you. I've made a decision. I'm flying to the East for the New Year."

"You'd never get the Insurance," said Kate.

"You've not flown in years. It's knees on your nose now," said Garbutt.

"I shall be flying First. I always did. I always shall. I can afford it. Judge Veneering left me his set of Law Reports and I shall sell them for six thousand pounds."

"You won't get Insurance."

"You can't go alone."

The two of them were closing on him like assassins.

"I have never felt so well. My little holiday has set me right. The doctor says that there is no need for the more lethal injections against diseases now. And I have the right clothes already in my wardrobe. No shopping."

They muttered off, to confer.

"Flying's not safe any more," said Kate. "Not since the Twin Towers. New Year's just the time for the next attack. And you'll be flying to a Muslim country, like as not."

He paid no attention but asked Garbutt if he would go up in the roof and look for the suitcase he and Lady Feathers had brought back from Bangladesh on their last trip.

Kate said, "Madeira's nice. Why not settle for nearer?"

"No. Bangladesh. I must see Bangladesh—or maybe Lanka again. And I might just continue. On into Malaysia, then up to Borneo. Kotakinakulu. Where I was born."

"Then I despair," said Garbutt.

"Bangladesh is where the brasses come from."

He had given Kate the beaten copper bowls of his heyday, after Betty died, to stop her from cleaning them twice a week at his expense.

She said, "If I understand the nine-o'clock news, Bangladesh is the place half the time under water and no good for arthritis. I'm sorry, but that doctor's notorious. He's never been beyond the golf course. He's never even been to Grand Canary where we go—nice and near and no chance of Economy-class thrombosis."

"He's told you. He's not going Economy-class," said Garbutt. "He says it's full of children joining their families out East for the school holidays. Makes him angry. Says in his day it took six weeks and you went once in five years. Says they're all spoilt now, and playing music in their ears."

"It's the luggage that really bothers me," said Garbutt.

The suitcase was immense. He got it out of the roof like a difficult birth. Its label called it a Revelation.

"Revelation was once the very best luggage," said Filth. "They were 'revelations' because they expanded."

"They were them heavy things that went out with porters," said Kate. "Can't we get you one borrowed? From that Chloe?"

"Absolutely not," said Filth.

"No way," said Garbutt.

"Get something on wheels with a handle, then," she said; and "What's this, there's something written on it in brass studs?"

"ISLAM," Filth said.

"Well that settles it. You can't carry that. You'll be thought a terrorist."

"Islam was the name of a distinguished lawyer in Brunei. A friend. He gave me the suitcase to bring back our presents. We bought a great many—they have so little there. It was the least we could do. Buy and buy."

"Let's get it open then," said Garbutt.

Inside were lurid hessian table mats, cross-stitched sacking table cloths, wilting saris and some indestructible straw matting. There was also a heavy little bundle of amethysts. He had sometimes suspected Betty of light-hearted smuggling. He sent all the other stuff to a church sale and asked Garbutt to scrub the case and polish it. It came up a treat.

"You can tell Class, I'll say that," said Kate. "But I wish you'd reconsider, Sir Edward. We're hardly over your last."

He stared her out.

And so into the Revelation went Filth's impeccable underwear; his singlets and what he still called his knickers; his yellow cotton socks from Harrods, twenty years old; some silk pyjamas; two light-weight suits and a dinner jacket (because one can never be quite sure where one will be invited). He added two sponge (antique phrase) bags, one for shaving things and bars of coal-tar soap, the other for his pills. Separate pills for use on the journey would go into his passport case. There was ample room in the Revelation for more.

"You could get all your things in here, too," he called out to Betty over his shoulder—then felt a pang in the upper chest. He was doing it again. Talking to her. And as if she would ever have dreamed of sharing his suitcase! So strange that, since his extraordinary peregrination to the West Country, Betty was back in his life again. Brief pains, real pains of longing for her now. Guilty pains. He had been neglecting her memory. *Memory and desire*—I must keep track of them. Mustn't lose hold.

On Christmas Day he attended church at ten. He preferred the eight o'clock in a silent church, heady with greenery and winter-scented flowers, but eight was getting early for him now. The ten o'clock was restless with children and everyone shaking hands with each other and the Vicar was called Lucy.

Never mind. He prayed for Father Tansy, and for Babs and Claire. He prayed for the souls of Ma Didds and Sir and Oils and Miss Robertson and Auntie May. This set up other candidates. He prayed for Loss, of course, as he often did, and for Jack and for Pat Ingoldby as he did every day, and for poor old Isobel who'd turned out to be a lesbian all the time. So stupid of him. And most unpleasant. He should have guessed he could never be everything to her.

He prayed—*what, will the line ne'er be done?*—for the nice girl and her grandmother, and for the aunts' little maid Alice, and for Garbutt and Kate. He prayed for the souls of his father and mother. And then he prayed for Ada, the shadow who leaned to him over water which he now was not sure was a memory or the memory of a memory. He prayed for podgy Cumberledge who had come out strong as a lion. How unaccountable it all is. How various and wonderful. He kept on and on praying through the rest of the service. For Veneering, for that unattractive Barrister girl who'd had a baby she'd called after him, for . . . He struggled hard against praying for Chloe and the souls of his aunts—but in the end, he managed it. He didn't pray for Betty. He knew she didn't need it.

He had his usual Christmas dinner at the White Hart in Salisbury and over the next few days put his desk in order, adding a codicil to his Will that left Mrs.-er—Kate (her name was Toms, Katherine Toms) the amethysts. He left Garbutt a cheque, then tore it up and left him a much larger one. He topped up his bequests to the National Trust and the Barristers' Benevolent. And so the last dead days of December passed.

On the thirty-first, he was waiting for the car in the hall, seated upon Betty's rose-and-gold throne, alone, since Kate had her family to think about at New Year, and the car drove him without incident in pouring rain the hundred miles to Heathrow.

The airport was almost empty. There had been "an alert." How ridiculous, he thought. We are letting these people win.

Security was meticulous. He was made to step three times under the scaffold before anyone realised that the alarm signal he gave off came from his old-world eyeglass. The suitcase with its emblazoned studs and Muslim appearance was passed through without a glance. ISLAM. There was a little hesitation about the X-ray picture of Pat Ingoldby's clothes-brush which looked like a gun.

And, then, the plane.

How stewardesses do smile these days, thought Filth. How cold their eyes.

He wondered what it would be like to be hi-jacked? He wondered once again, an hour or so later, when the plane plunged like a stone for a thousand feet over the Alps.

"Just a bit of turbulence." The pilot came strolling through, presumably to give confidence, and Filth was pleased with himself for continuing to drink his soup.

"Are you comfortable, sir?"

He was pleased that the fellow was English. Pilots nowadays tended not to be.

"What route are we taking, Captain? Round the edges?"

"Oh, sure. Well to the South. Not a missile in sight. It'll be dark over Afghanistan. Singapore for a cup of tea and then up to Dacca."

Filth said, "When I first used to come out here, it was Vietnam we had to avoid. Had to refuel twice then. The Gulf. Then Bombay. Bombay's called something else now, I gather. There used to be half a marble staircase on Bombay airport. Gold and cream. Lovely thing. It stopped in mid-air. Symbolic."

"Time marches on."

"Not so sure it marches anywhere in particular though."

He slept. Once, jerking awake from a dream, he yelled out, thinking he was being put into a body-bag. An air stewardess with tendril arms was tucking a blanket around him.

The black night shuddered all around the plane. When he next woke there was a pencilled line of gold drawn round each oval blind.

Dawn already.

"We are in tomorrow," said the girl. "It's the sunrise. A happy New Year."

(You'd think I'd never flown before.)

He watched the dawn.

Later he looked down upon a fat carpet of clouds and saw something he had never seen in his life before. Two suns stood side by side in the sky. A parhelion. A formidable and ancient omen of something or other, he forgot what. He looked about the cabin, but the other two or three First-class passengers were asleep under their blankets and the stewards out of sight.

The whiteness outside the plane became terrible. The plane was a glass splinter, a pin. It was being flipped into eternity, into dissolution. They were beyond speed now, and in infinity—travelling towards what he understood astronomers call "The Singularity."

But they were bringing the orange juice and hot cloths.

And soon it was evening again.

At Singapore a wheelchair had been provided for him. (Very old gentleman with limp.) It stood waiting at the mouth of the wrinkled tube that joined the aeroplane to the earth (and that certainly had not been there in the seventies; they had had to climb down steep stepladders). He disregarded the chair and walked stiffly along the bouncing tunnel and into the air-cooled glitter of the shops, and eventually to the shadowy First-class lounge. Two hours, and a long sleep, later—and he walked easily all the way back.

The seat next to his was now occupied by a young man in an open-necked collarless white shirt and jeans who was already at work upon a laptop. Filth read across a white laminated folder "Instructions to Counsel."

Filth felt garrulous.

"You a lawyer? So was I. I used to work on the flight out, too. All the way out, all the way back. Don't know how I did it now. Straight into Chambers from the airport. We all got used to working through the night, even in London. Mind you, I never went straight from a plane into Court. Never did that. Too dangerous."

"We do now," said the boy. "No time to hang about."

"Dangerous for the client. Dangerous for Counsel. Going into Court not feeling tip-top."

"I always feel tip-top. I say—you're not by any chance . . .?

"Yes. Old Filth. Long forgotten."

"Well, you're still remembered out here."

"Yes. Well, I dare say. I hope so. Ha. Did you ever come across a chap called Loss?"

"No. I don't think so."

"Or Islam?"

"They're all called Islam."

"He's probably dead. Certainly retired. I've got one of his suitcases. Called a Revelation."

A new stewardess, a Malay, browner, silkier, gentler, with more rounded arms and in a sari, came along with potted prawns. "Shall we pull down the blinds for you, sir?"

"No thanks," said the young Silk. "Less than two hours left. Let's watch the stars."

"You married?" asked Filth after a long rumination looking at but not eating the prawns.

"Sure."

"I used to take mine along," said Filth. "Always."

"Mine's in banking. And I don't think she actually would describe herself as 'mine.' We're landing. Good. And we weren't hi-jacked."

As he made to leave the plane, a black misery suddenly came upon Filth like the eye bandage slapped around the face before it is presented to a firing squad. Then he wondered if, in fact, on this journey, he had really hoped only for death . . . Had wanted the knife slipped out of the shoe. The gun in the sleeve. The "Nobody move!" The spatter of bullets and blood. One blessed, releasing explosion. Lived long enough. Get the thing over.

He had been waiting.

For what was there left for him in the Donheads?

Stuck in that wet woodland place with Garbutt and Mrs.-er, and lacy Chloe?

Well, there was still hope for obliteration on the return journey. Might achieve it.

And if I don't—what? I'll move. I'll take a flat in The Temple. Don't know anyone now. Ghastly lot of new Judges. Still, they are one's own.

Bleak, uncertain, nodding thanks to the pretty girl, Filth made gingerly for the door.

From the top of the gangway, the East hit him full in the face. The thick, glorious heat washed on to him and around him, lapped his swollen old hands and his tired feet, bathed his old skull and sinewy neck, soaked into his every pore and fibre. Life stirred. The resting plane was vibrating with heat, the air around it vibrating, the airport vibrating and dancing in the soft dark. High glares and electrics together shone along the low parapet where people were waiting to meet the plane, clustered like dark flies, like frenzied butterflies.

The tremendous chatter of talk, the excitement. The toots and hoots and wails and the drumming. The prayers and the prostrated prayers and the prayer mats. The old, old beloved smell.

Betty seemed to be beside him, grinning away, waving back at all the people. Just at his shoulder.

"Watch it, sir. Let me help you. Is something wrong?"

"Nothing is wrong," said Filth. The kind arms stretched. "Nothing at all is wrong."

For he was Home.

SCENE: THE INNER TEMPLE GARDEN

Scene: The Inner Temple Garden.

Two judges standing beside the monument that is inscribed, *Lawyers, I suppose, were children once.* The bell of the Temple Church is tolling on and on, as it does, once for every year of a dead Bencher's life.

The Queen's Remembrancer: That'll be for Filth.

A Lord of Appeal: There'll be ninety of them then.

QR: Not quite. Nearly. Did you read the obituaries?

L of A: Yes. Short. So difficult to say exactly what he'd done. When it came to it. Not a *great* lawyer. Never changed anything. Very old-fashioned delivery. Laughable, I expect, now. Good judge, of course.

QR: He'd just got off a plane. Did you know? Going back to his roots.

L of A: Game of him. About the most imaginative thing he ever did, I suspect. In his long and uneventful life. Was he travelling alone, d'you know?

QR: Oh, yes. Travelling alone. Quite alone.

ACKNOWLEDGEMENTS

As will be obvious, I am very much indebted to Rudyard Kipling's Autobiography and to his story "Baa Baa Black Sheep." Also to Christopher Hudson's fine novel, "Colombo Heat," about the last days of the Raj in Ceylon (Sri Lanka); I have even taken the liberty of borrowing one of his characters and giving her a walk-on part with a crutch. Sir was suggested by Geoffrey Grigson's autobiography, The Crest on the Silver.

I am also very grateful to friends, dead and alive, who were once Raj Orphans, and to Peter Leyland, K. S. Chung and my husband, David Gardam, all of whom set off in Wartime convoys to the East and two of whom returned.

I am very grateful to the late Michael Underhill, QC, who was for a few months junior Platoon Commander in the Royal Gloucestershire regiment which guarded Queen Mary at Badminton House. He talked to me about it, as did his wife, Rosalie Beaumont, who showed me a charming, innocent correspondence between her husband and Queen Mary. Thanks also to Mrs. Nettles, one-time housekeeper at Badminton, and her sister. I drew on Queen Mary by James Pope-Hennessy (1959) and HRH Princess Adelaide, Duchess of Teck

(1900), a mighty work by C. Kinloch Cooke, Barrister-at-Law. John Saumarez Smith of the Heywood Hill bookshop in Curzon Street kindly introduced me to Osbert Sitwell's hilarious Queen Mary and Others (1974).

To the Benchers of the Inner Temple, the Clerks and members of Atkin Chambers I am particularly grateful for many things over fifty years; especially to Stewart Goldsmith who often got me to foreign parts and home again.

Those who believe that they recognise any of my characters are mistaken, for they are all from my imagination except for Queen Mary; her lady-in-waiting; the Duchess of Beaufort; the stationmaster of Badminton (who, it appears, really did wear white gloves and call the platforms "lawns"); and my husband who in only one instance resembles Filth: he ate thirty-seven bananas on Freetown beach. (There were no ill effects.) His friend at Oundle School, "the best I ever had," was called Pat Ingoldby; he was lost at sea in 1942 and I have made use of his name in his memory.

Any historical mistakes are my own.

Jane Gardam,
Sandwich,
Kent
2004

ABOUT THE AUTHOR

Jane Gardam's first book, *Black Faces, White Faces* (1975), a collection of short stories, won both the David Higham Prize for Fiction and the Winifred Holtby Memorial Prize. Subsequent collections of short stories include *The Pangs of Love and Other Stories*, winner of the Kathcrine Mansfield Award, and *Going into a Dark House*, which was awarded the PEN Macmillan Silver Pen Award in 1995. Gardam's first novel, *God on the Rocks* was adapted for television in 1992. It won the Prix Baudelaire (France) in 1989 and was short-listed for the Booker Prize. She is the only author to have twice been awarded the Whitbread Prize for the Best Novel of the Year (for the *Queen of the Tambourine*, in 1991, and for *The Hollow Land*, 1981). She is also the author of *The Flight of the Maiden*, which was adapted for BBC Radio's Woman's Hour. In 1999, Jane Gardam was awarded the Heywood Hill Literary Prize in recognition of a distinguished literary career. She lives with her husband in England.

Carmine Abate
Between Two Seas
"A moving portrayal of generational continuity."
—*Kirkus*
224 pp • $14.95 • 978-1-933372-40-2

Salwa Al Neimi
The Proof of the Honey
"Al Neimi announces the end of a taboo in the Arab world:
that of sex!"
—*Reuters*
144 pp • $15.00 • 978-1-933372-68-6

Alberto Angela
A Day in the Life of Ancient Rome
"Fascinating and accessible."
—*Il Giornale*
392 pp • $16.00 • 978-1-933372-71-6

Muriel Barbery
The Elegance of the Hedgehog
"Gently satirical, exceptionally winning and inevitably bittersweet."
—Michael Dirda, *The Washington Post*
336 pp • $15.00 • 978-1-933372-60-0

Gourmet Rhapsody
"In the pages of this book, Barbery shows off her finest gift: lightness."
—*La Repubblica*
176 pp • $15.00 • 978-1-933372-95-2

Stefano Benni
Margherita Dolce Vita
"A modern fable...hilarious social commentary."—*People*
240 pp • $14.95 • 978-1-933372-20-4

Timeskipper
"Benni again unveils his Italian brand of magical realism."
—*Library Journal*
400 pp • $16.95 • 978-1-933372-44-0

Romano Bilenchi
The Chill
120 pp • $15.00 • 978-1-933372-90-7

Massimo Carlotto
The Goodbye Kiss
"A masterpiece of Italian noir."
—*Globe and Mail*
160 pp • $14.95 • 978-1-933372-05-1

Death's Dark Abyss
"A remarkable study of corruption and redemption."
—*Kirkus* (starred review)
160 pp • $14.95 • 978-1-933372-18-1

The Fugitive
"[Carlotto is] the reigning king of Mediterranean noir."
—*The Boston Phoenix*
176 pp • $14.95 • 978-1-933372-25-9

(with Marco Videtta)
Poisonville
"The business world as described by Carlotto and Videtta
in Poisonville is frightening as hell."
—*La Repubblica*
224 pp • $15.00 • 978-1-933372-91-4

Francisco Coloane
Tierra del Fuego
"Coloane is the Jack London of our times."—*Alvaro Mutis*
192 pp • $14.95 • 978-1-933372-63-1

Giancarlo De Cataldo
The Father and the Foreigner
"A slim but touching noir novel from one of Italy's best writers
in the genre."—*Quaderni Noir*
144 pp • $15.00 • 978-1-933372-72-3

Shashi Deshpande
The Dark Holds No Terrors
"[Deshpande is] an extremely talented storyteller."—*Hindustan Times*
272 pp • $15.00 • 978-1-933372-67-9

Helmut Dubiel
Deep In the Brain: Living with Parkinson's Disease
"A book that begs reflection."—*Die Zeit*
144 pp • $15.00 • 978-1-933372-70-9

Steve Erickson
Zeroville
"A funny, disturbing, daring and demanding novel—Erickson's best."
—*The New York Times Book Review*
352 pp • $14.95 • 978-1-933372-39-6

Elena Ferrante
The Days of Abandonment
"The raging, torrential voice of [this] author is something rare."
—*The New York Times*
192 pp • $14.95 • 978-1-933372-00-6

Troubling Love
"Ferrante's polished language belies the rawness of her imagery."
—*The New Yorker*
144 pp • $14.95 • 978-1-933372-16-7

The Lost Daughter
"So refined, almost translucent."—*The Boston Globe*
144 pp • $14.95 • 978-1-933372-42-6

Jane Gardam
Old Filth
"Old Filth belongs in the Dickensian pantheon of memorable characters."
—*The New York Times Book Review*
304 pp • $14.95 • 978-1-933372-13-6

The Queen of the Tambourine
"A truly superb and moving novel."—*The Boston Globe*
272 pp • $14.95 • 978-1-933372-36-5

The People on Privilege Hill
"Engrossing stories of hilarity and heartbreak."—*Seattle Times*
208 pp • $15.95 • 978-1-933372-56-3

The Man in the Wooden Hat
"Here is a writer who delivers the world we live in...with memorable and moving skill."—*The Boston Globe*
240 pp • $15.00 • 978-1-933372-89-1

Alicia Giménez-Bartlett
Dog Day
"Delicado and Garzón prove to be one of the more engaging sleuth teams to debut in a long time."—*The Washington Post*
320 pp • $14.95 • 978-1-933372-14-3

Prime Time Suspect
"A gripping police procedural."—*The Washington Post*
320 pp • $14.95 • 978-1-933372-31-0

Death Rites
"Petra is developing into a good cop, and her earnest efforts to assert her authority...are worth cheering."—*The New York Times*
304 pp • $16.95 • 978-1-933372-54-9

Katharina Hacker
The Have-Nots
"Hacker's prose soars."—*Publishers Weekly*
352 pp • $14.95 • 978-1-933372-41-9

Patrick Hamilton
Hangover Square
"Patrick Hamilton's novels are dark tunnels of misery, loneliness, deceit, and sexual obsession."—*New York Review of Books*
336 pp • $14.95 • 978-1-933372-06-

James Hamilton-Paterson
Cooking with Fernet Branca
"Irresistible!"—*The Washington Post*
288 pp • $14.95 • 978-1-933372-01-3

Amazing Disgrace
"It's loads of fun, light and dazzling as a peacock feather."
—*New York Magazine*
352 pp • $14.95 • 978-1-933372-19-8

Rancid Pansies
"Campy comic saga about hack writer and self-styled 'culinary genius' Gerald Samper."—*Seattle Times*
288 pp • $15.95 • 978-1-933372-62-4

Seven-Tenths: The Sea and Its Thresholds
"The kind of book that, were he alive now, Shelley might have written."
—Charles Spawson
416 pp • $16.00 • 978-1-933372-69-3

Alfred Hayes
The Girl on the Via Flaminia
"Immensely readable."—*The New York Times*
164 pp • $14.95 • 978-1-933372-24-2

Jean-Claude Izzo
Total Chaos
"Izzo's Marseilles is ravishing."—*Globe and Mail*
256 pp • $14.95 • 978-1-933372-04-4

Chourmo
"A bitter, sad and tender salute to a place equally impossible to love
or leave."—*Kirkus* (starred review)
256 pp • $14.95 • 978-1-933372-17-4

Solea
"[Izzo is] a talented writer who draws from the deep, dark well of noir."
—*The Washington Post*
208 pp • $14.95 • 978-1-933372-30-3

The Lost Sailors
"Izzo digs deep into what makes men weep."—*Time Out New York*
272 pp • $14.95 • 978-1-933372-35-8

A Sun for the Dying
"Beautiful, like a black sun, tragic and desperate."—*Le Point*
224 pp • $15.00 • 978-1-933372-59-4

Gail Jones
Sorry
"Jones's gift for conjuring place and mood rarely falters."
—*Times Literary Supplement*
240 pp • $15.95 • 978-1-933372-55-6

Matthew F. Jones
Boot Tracks
"A gritty action tale."—*The Philadelphia Inquirer*
208 pp • $14.95 • 978-1-933372-11-2

Ioanna Karystiani
The Jasmine Isle
"A modern Greek tragedy about love foredoomed and family life."
—*Kirkus*
288 pp • $14.95 • 978-1-933372-10-5

Swell
"Karystiani movingly pays homage to the sea and those who live from it."
—*La Repubblica*
256 pp • $15.00 • 978-1-933372-98-3

Gene Kerrigan
The Midnight Choir
"The lethal precision of his closing punches leave quite a lasting mark."
—*Entertainment Weekly*
368 pp • $14.95 • 978-1-933372-26-6

Little Criminals
"A great story…relentless and brilliant."—*Roddy Doyle*
352 pp • $16.95 • 978-1-933372-43-3

Peter Kocan
Fresh Fields
"A stark, harrowing, yet deeply courageous work of immense power and magnitude."—*Quadrant*
304 pp • $14.95 • 978-1-933372-29-7

The Treatment and the Cure
"Kocan tells this story with grace and humor."—*Publishers Weekly*
256 pp • $15.95 • 978-1-933372-45-7

Helmut Krausser
Eros
"Helmut Krausser has succeeded in writing a great German
epochal novel."—*Focus*
352 pp • $16.95 • 978-1-933372-58-7

Amara Lakhous
Clash of Civilizations Over an Elevator in Piazza Vittorio
"Do we have an Italian Camus on our hands? Just possibly."
—*The Philadelphia Inquirer*
144 pp • $14.95 • 978-1-933372-61-7

Lia Levi
The Jewish Husband
"An exemplary tale of small lives engulfed in the vortex of history."
—*Il Messaggero*
224 pp • $15.00 • 978-1-933372-93-8

Carlo Lucarelli
Carte Blanche
"Lucarelli proves that the dark and sinister are better evoked when one
opts for unadulterated grit and grime."—*The San Diego Union-Tribune*
128 pp • $14.95 • 978-1-933372-15-0

The Damned Season
"De Luca…is a man both pursuing and pursued. And that makes him one
of the more interesting figures in crime fiction."
—*The Philadelphia Inquirer*
128 pp • $14.95 • 978-1-933372-27-3

Via delle Oche
"Delivers a resolution true to the series' moral relativism."—*Publishers Weekly*
160 pp • $14.95 • 978-1-933372-53-2

Edna Mazya
Love Burns
"Combines the suspense of a murder mystery with
the absurdity of a Woody Allen movie."—*Kirkus*
224 pp • $14.95 • 978-1-933372-08-2

Sélim Nassib
I Loved You for Your Voice
"Nassib spins a rhapsodic narrative out of the indissoluble
connection between two creative souls."—*Kirkus*
272 pp • $14.95 • 978-1-933372-07-5

The Palestinian Lover
"A delicate, passionate novel in which history and life
are inextricably entwined."
—*RAI Books*
192 pp • $14.95 • 978-1-933372-23-5

Amélie Nothomb
Tokyo Fiancée
"Intimate and honest...depicts perfectly a nontraditional romance."
—*Publishers Weekly*
160 pp • $15.00 • 978-1-933372-64-8

Valeria Parrella
For Grace Received
"A voice that is new, original, and decidedly unique."—*Rolling Stone* (Italy)
144 pp • $15.00 • 978-1-933372-94-5

Alessandro Piperno
The Worst Intentions
"A coruscating mixture of satire, family epic, Proustian meditation, and erotomaniacal farce."—*The New Yorker*
320 pp • $14.95 • 978-1-933372-33-4

Boualem Sansal
The German Mujahid
"Terror, doubt, revolt, guilt, and despair—a surprising range of emotions is admirably and convincingly depicted in this incredible novel."
—*L'Express* (France)
240 pp • $15.00 • 978-1-933372-92-1

Eric-Emmanuel Schmitt
The Most Beautiful Book in the World
"Eight novellas, parables on the idea of a future, filled with redeeming optimism."—*Lire Magazine*
192 pp • $15.00 • 978-1-933372-74-7

Domenico Starnone
First Execution
"Starnone's books are small theatres of action, both physical and psychological."—*L'Espresso* (Italy)
176 pp • $15.00 • 978-1-933372-66-2

Joel Stone
The Jerusalem File
"Joel Stone is a major new talent."—*Cleveland Plain Dealer*
160 pp • $15.00 • 978-1-933372-65-5